The Complete Mindfuck Series
Books 1-5

C.M. Owens writing as
S.T. Abby

Copyright 2019 S.T. Abby
This series was originally published in 2016
No part of this book may be reproduced, or stored in a retrieval system or transmitted in any form or by any means, electronic, mechanical, photocopying, recording, or otherwise without express written permission of the author. This eBook is licensed for your enjoyment only. It may not be re-sold or given away to other people.

The story in this book is the property of the author, in all media both physical and digital. No one, except the owner of this property, may reproduce, copy or publish in any medium any individual story or part of this novel without the expressed permission of the author of this work.

Table of Contents

The Risk.......pg 1
Sidetracked.......pg 123
Scarlet Angel.......pg 235
All the Lies.......pg 371
Paint It All Red.......pg 509

The Risk

Book 1

~~Tim Hoover~~

~~Chuck Cosby~~

~~Nathan Malone~~

~~Jeremy Hoyt~~

So many names left to go…

Einstein said, "*The weak revenge. The strong forgive. The intelligent ignore.*"

Fuck that. Einstein wasn't always right.

Revenge is a dish best served cold… Now that I agree with. It means they forget you're coming for them, and their screams sound so much prettier when the time finally comes.

Chapter 1

I love humanity but I hate humans.
—Albert Einstein

Lana

"You look like you've been stood up," a guy says as I peer up from my phone, discreetly clicking the lock screen into place so he can't see what I'm watching.

I arch an eyebrow as I study him. Good looking, mid-twenties, arrogant smile, dominant posture... He's definitely barking up the wrong tree though.

"Actually, I enjoy eating alone," I tell him with a fuck-off, sweet smile.

He doesn't take the hint, because his eyes narrow with determination. Alphas prefer a challenge. I should have known better.

"I'm Craig. You're..." He lets his words trail off as he rakes his eyes over me, but I say nothing before sipping my coffee. "If you don't give me your name, I'll just call you Beauty."

How original.

His attempt at flattery is overtly untrained and certainly underdeveloped. He's obviously used to getting his way without much of a fuss, which means he never puts forth any effort after catching his prize either. Considering his expensive suit and visible appeal, I'm not surprised.

Plenty of women will overlook his arrogance, confusing it for cockiness, possibly even find it charming.

But I'm the wrong girl.

"How about calling me Not Interested? Because that's the most apt depiction of me at the moment," I tell him, leaning back in my chair, relaxed and fully in control.

"Apparently you haven't gotten a good look," he proceeds, leaning back and pretty much posing in a stance that gives me nothing more to look at than an arrogant ass.

"I've seen more than enough. Still not interested."

His look darkens as he takes a step back.

"Fine. Fuck it. I don't need frostbite on my dick anyway," he says before turning and walking toward a table where another guy is sitting.

The sun is not bright today, considering the overcast. We're just a few of the people who opted for the patio instead of the inside of the coffee house, because it looks like it's going to rain. Even though they're several tables away, I can still see his friend laughing and shaking his head as Mr. Arrogant plops down to his seat, surly and dejected.

I resume watching the footage on my phone, until I feel eyes on me. Mr. Arrogant's friend doesn't look away when I look up and catch him studying me. He's not leering or even acting interested. I'd say he's trying to read me, just the way I do people.

He's also nice looking, but his suit is not as expensive as the other guy's. My observation would lead me to believe they're work mates, but why is one dressed better than the other if they do the same job? He doesn't seem submissive or weighted, the way he would if he was working for Mr. Arrogant. Which means they're equals, but not paid the same? Or maybe Mr. Arrogant comes from money, and this guy doesn't?

Unconcerned, I return my eyes to my phone, pretending I don't notice his intense scrutiny. After finishing my coffee and my D-day screening, I ask the waitress for the bill.

The Risk

"It's already been paid," she says with a soft smile and bright eyes. "And you've already left a tip as well," she adds, winking. "A nice one."

My eyebrows go up, and she motions back with her head as Mr. Arrogant's friend walks off the patio. Mr. Arrogant is nowhere to be found.

"He said to thank you for the entertainment," she proceeds to tell me while fanning herself and watching him walk toward a dark SUV.

"Thanks," I tell her, standing up and heading toward the exit as well.

No flirting, no leering looks of longing, and no waiting around to see if I would come to him after he paid for my food. I don't like it when people are nice for no reason. Saying I was his entertainment isn't enough.

My eyes trail after the silent guy, watching him as he lingers by the SUV, speaking over the phone too quietly for me to hear his words from this distance. I also spot Mr. Arrogant, who is chatting up a pretty girl near the store down the sidewalk. She seems far more interested than I was.

Deciding to appease my curiosity, I head over to the silent guy just as he ends his call. His eyes snap up to mine as I approach, and his eyebrows raise as I pull out a twenty.

"I don't let strange men pay for my food. My mother taught me better," I tell him, waving the twenty in front of him to take.

A slow grin crawls across his full lips, completely transforming his face. His dark blonde hair is tousled just enough to be sexy without being bedhead messy. His strong, chiseled jaw is a stark contrast to his soft, blue eyes. He looks fierce and gentle in the same breath, confusing me all the more. I really can't get a read on him.

"I couldn't get a more entertaining show for so cheap. Trust me, it was worth the small bill," he says with a shrug, pocketing his hands and phone, making a stance that he won't take my money, without using the actual words.

But I'm persistent, and I wave the twenty again. "I still have my rules. Thanks, but no thanks."

His grin only grows. "You always so defensive?" he muses. "Are you constantly worried about the intentions of others? Or is it an extreme feminist position that keeps you on edge about a man doing something as mediocre as paying for your coffee and muffin?"

He *is* reading me. I knew it.

The cheap suit suddenly makes sense, along with the dark SUV. "You're FBI," I note, taking in the fact Quantico isn't too far away.

His grin broadens. "What makes you think that?"

"You're profiling me, for one, which would likely put you to be somewhere in that field, given the ride and attire. Your friend has an expensive suit that he wears to impress, but yours is less flashy. Your posture around him and good-natured ribbing towards him leads me to believe you're equals, despite the financial difference. So I'm assuming he comes from money, and you've earned your own way. The SUV isn't a standardized version. The blacked out windows are too dark to be legally tinted, but I know the FBI are given certain leniencies due to security risks. So am I right?"

I really hate the way he continues to smile, as though he's only more intrigued instead of freaked out. I wanted to freak him out.

"You're not a paid profiler, not FBI, and not affiliated with any military unit," he says, confusing me. "Your outfit is bohemian chic, meaning you're less worried about your outward appearance and more concerned with comfort. You sit alone by choice, and dismiss any attention sent your way. At first glance, you're too feminist for your own good. At second glance, you're someone who is hard to get close to because trust isn't something you share too often. It keeps you from being hurt by people, but it also keeps you from having anyone in your life. At night, when you close your eyes and allow yourself to be vulnerable…that's the only time you dare to wonder what it'd be like to be with someone."

I swallow down the knot in my throat. He's too dead-on. I

The Risk

shouldn't be so easily readable. I've trained against it for years.

"No pets, given the fact there's not any pet hair on you, unless you have those who won't shed. However, I don't see you allowing yourself to become attached to an animal, when you know you'll most likely outlive it and have to deal with the heartbreak of losing said animal. You're detached by necessity, most likely a painful past that pushed you into this direction. A loss, perhaps. Maybe more than one loss. Maybe pushed into solitude by life and staying there by choice?"

When my heart thumps in my chest and I take a shaky step back, his eyes soften even more.

"Sorry. I went too far. I apologize," he tells me just as Mr. Arrogant returns.

"Haven't lost my edge. That chick was just—"

His words die when he sees me in an eye-lock with Mr. Profiler. I feel exposed, vulnerable, and out of my element. I'm not used to that. I've worked so freaking hard to be a fortress of impossible reads.

He just unraveled my confidence with one pull on the right thread.

"Grab a few bottles of water. Long ride," he tells Mr. Arrogant without looking away from me.

I don't know if he leaves or not, because I'm too busy staring right into those gentle blue eyes that really do seem remorseful.

"Life sucks," he says randomly. "Then you die. Might as well live while you're still alive," he adds, sounding completely less insightful than earlier.

It's enough to break the tension, and an unexpected smile slips free from me. He winks as he leans over. "If you ever want help feeling alive, call me. I could use some life as well."

When he draws back, I feel something in my hand, though I never felt him placing anything there. He walks around to the other side of the SUV, and I watch with rapt attention as he gets in.

My eyes finally fall down to the card in my hand as Mr. Arrogant returns to take the passenger side.

Logan Bennett...

His number is attached to his name, and sure enough, he's FBI. When my gaze comes up again, he's leaning on the steering wheel, watching me. Mr. Arrogant's window is down, and he looks annoyed.

"Call me," Logan says, grinning before pulling away from the curb.

Reality is merely an illusion, albeit a persistent one. Albert Einstein said that. My father always quoted Einstein as a way of explaining life when we struggled to understand it. I remember him quoting me that when our lives fell apart. He was hurting the worst, and trying his best to soothe me.

Einstein isn't helping me understand how easily I was just read. Or how vulnerable and exposed I feel in this moment.

My phone buzzes in my hand, and I look down, seeing the alert I set.

I have to be cold. I *need* to be cold. Anything less could fracture the shell in place that I need to execute the plan I've worked too hard on for too long.

Shaking off the residual weakness, I blow out a harsh breath and walk to my car. I drive fifteen miles, find the house I'm looking for, and drive on by. I wait until I'm parked in an abandoned barn before I put on my gloves, suit, and heavy men's boots. I also strap on the backpacks weighted down with rocks... One on my back and one on my front.

Stealthily, I walk toward the house, slip open the door, and silently remove the backpacks, putting them down with careful ease to a chair.

My purse has everything I need in it, so I keep it on me. The heavy shoes come off next, and I silently place them on top of my backpack.

The Risk

Movement upstairs draws my attention, and I slowly make my way to the staircase, careful to keep my steps light and silent. I've examined the floors for a month, finding every spot that creaks or groans.

I know his routine better than my own. Just like I know in five seconds, the water will come on.

Sure enough, the old pipes in the house clank as water shoots through them, and that's when I make my way up the stairs, ignoring the way they creak, because he can't hear a thing with that loud shower.

When I reach his room, my eyes dart to the bed. I know he's single, but I always worry about stumbling across an unplanned woman. I watched the cameras from my phone, and they showed no woman here, but it's still a thought that always plagues the back of my mind.

I breathe out in relief when I see no signs of an overnight guest. Just Ben and his usual messy home.

The shower cuts off, and I'm already in position, ready and waiting. Life would be simpler if I could use a Taser or sedatives. It really would.

Just as he walks through with a towel around his waist, my knife comes down, slicing hard against the Achilles heel. Screams pierce my ears, and I realize that moment of weakness with Mr. Profiler earlier doesn't affect how pretty the screams sound.

I've worked too long, too hard, and too endlessly for this. I should have known one man couldn't take away my edge.

Ben falls to the floor, crying out in agony, while clutching his foot. The towel flops off, exposing every naked inch of him to my eyes.

It makes my stomach roil.

But the terror in his eyes? That gets me high.

"What the fuck? Take whatever you want!" he shouts, sobbing as I approach, watching me with those wide, terrified eyes.

I get off on the terror. I want him to cry for much, much longer.

"What I want is for you to know my name," I say quietly, eerily.

His eyes grow even wider, and he pales when I hold the bloody knife up and run my finger along the backside of it.

"Please don't," he begs, trying and failing to stand up.

He'll hit me if he gets the chance. I'm not stupid enough to get that close just yet.

I pull the wire from my back pocket, and I watch him as he watches me.

"Don't recognize me, Ben?" I ask mockingly, cocking my head. Ten surgeries ago, he might have recognized me immediately.

"No. No," he cries. "I don't know you. You have the wrong person!"

I squat down, noticing the way his gaze shifts. He's preparing to attack me now that I'm in this position. He finds it a vulnerable mistake on my part.

If he only knew…

"I was a sixteen-year-old little girl the last time you saw me," I say with a dark smile. "I'm all grown up now. *Want to play?*"

The last three words are what triggers recognition. I see it in the way his pupils dilate, his nostrils flare, and a sense of understanding washes over his features.

"You," he whispers. "No. No. You look nothing like her. She died," he adds in the same hushed tone.

"I survived," I say back, watching as his fear slowly starts to fade, just as I knew it would.

Right now, he's remembering just how weak I was as that horrified, terrified, sobbing little girl. He's remembering how easily he overpowered me. His mind is playing tricks on him that he's still the one in control, despite the precariously deadly situation.

"You took three turns," I go on, staying poised and ready, but outwardly displaying a weakness I don't truly have, allowing his

The Risk

mind to continue to revert back to that night ten years ago.

"That means three pounds of flesh over the next three days," I go on.

I see it happening before he launches himself at me, screaming in pain as he tries to tackle me to the floor. My knife slams into his shoulder, and another bloodcurdling scream erupts through the air as I spin on my knees, sliding in behind him as his face plants into the floor.

My hand is still holding the knife, and I rip it away in less than a blink, almost simultaneously tossing the wire around his neck, winding it tightly. Then I choke him, reveling in the pained sounds, until he grows limp and unconscious, riding the line of life and death. With the blood loss, he's too weak to fight back. It'd be so easy to kill him right now.

But death won't come too soon.

I don't believe in mercy.

Three pounds of flesh will be extracted while he's awake.

He'll beg and plead.

He'll pray to pass out.

But he will feel it all.

Just like we did.

Chapter 2

As a human being, one has been endowed with just enough intelligence to be able to see clearly how utterly inadequate that intelligence is when confronted with what exists.
-Albert Einstein.

Logan

I finish off my croissant while staring at the gory crime scene photos.

Blood is smeared across the walls with a paintbrush, just like the other four cases we've managed to link together. It's one of the few things that remains consistent. The unsub always paints a wall red with the victim's blood.

"How can you eat while seeing that?" Elise asks while wrinkling her nose and sitting down on the edge of my desk.

Ignoring her question, I ask, "What did they find out about Ben Harris?"

"The M.E. estimated that he was tortured for at least three days. He has parts of him that have been cut off, just like the others. Including the penis," she sighs.

That has me cringing, just like any man would. One of these images is supposed to be a dismembered penis?

"His fingers were all cut off," she goes on, pointing at one picture that was snapped of ten severed fingers lying on the ground. "His chest was slowly pulled off piece by piece. The unsub stopped the bleeding each time by using a barbaric method of cauterization. He wanted the victim alive for those three days specifically. His

The Risk

penis seems to be the last thing to have gone. Ligature marks were found again, and chains were hanging from his basement rafters. We think the unsub stayed true to his profile, leaving the victim strung up in their own home. So far, all the men have had isolated homes too far away for any neighbors to overhear or see anything."

And he's not devolving either. His strikes are controlled, well planned out, and meticulous in detail, even if we don't understand the details.

"The unsub should be a female, considering the groin mutilation in all the kills," Craig says, shuddering as he walks up on our conversation. "Only a woman could handle cutting off a man's junk."

"Women serial killers statistically don't torture. They're actually far more efficient and harder to track down because of that," Elise says dismissively.

"Well, he has to be impotent. Most serial killers are," Alan chimes in, joining us.

There's a reason he and Craig are not profilers.

"I think he's more of a sexual sadist," Elise explains. "Impotence likely plays a part, but just calling them impotent isn't a profile."

"So an impotent sexual sadist?" Craig asks, confused.

"Sexual sadists are often impotent, and they seek out their sexual release through the torture. No signs of rape were found, but it's likely the unsub hasn't evolved and grown the confidence to rape the men yet."

"So a gay sexual sadist?" Craig goes on, still lost.

"Yes," Elise says, nodding.

"All of the male victims were straight, according to witnesses. If they were gay, that theory would make more sense," I add. "All five men were from the same town, yet no one can think of any man who might want to kill all five. However, I know we're missing something."

"Footprints are a size twelve man's shoe made in the dirt on the way to the house. The footprint is solid from heel to toe. Our field expert says that the unsub weighs between two-ten and two-fifteen," Elise announces.

"He'd have to be physically fit to be able to overpower these men the way the unsub has. And very built, most likely. The unsub is overpowering them with sheer brute force. Originally he was only killing alphas, which led to the profile being an alpha serial. But Ben, although physically fit and strong, was very submissive in his line of work. It was why he was so successful, because he liked being in the background instead of in charge."

"Sexual sadism is far more likely, since the last kill. There may be a sexually frustrated trigger, which should narrow down our search. We should also adjust the profile. What else do we know about the victims?"

"These guys were tops of their classes in college, but they were all different ages—from twenty-three to twenty-eight. Victimology only links them through the town and through their isolated homes. They haven't kept in contact, even though they were all friendly when they still lived in town. It's possible the unsub hates the whole town, but why? Is it part vengeance?"

"Possibly," I say more to myself than to Elise.

One kill in Boston. One kill in Denver. One kill in Long Island. One kill in Maine. And now one kill in our own backyard in Virginia. This guy is all over the map, shitting all over a normal hunting ground pattern.

It would seem random if we hadn't made the connection to the same home town. But not the same school. Three of them went to a private school two towns over. So obviously this isn't an old grudge dated back to school ages, especially given the age gap in the victims that would put them in different grades too.

"No kills have been reported in town," I groan. "If it was just two, I'd call it a coincidence. But it's five from that town, yet no deaths within the town limits. What do we know about the town?"

The Risk

"Small. Very small. Five hundred is the population. In the past three years, nothing of any real interest has made the news, other than a wolf that attacked a man in his cow pasture. Very religious town."

"Small, religious towns are notorious for making it hard on gay males. Especially small farm towns. You and Leonard head out there and see what you can find out. Ask about a physically fit male over six feet tall, age twenty to thirty-five, who might have been gay or showed interest in men. Given the religious aspect, it's doubtful he came out. Ask if anyone seemed to struggle or demonstrate a nervous tic frequently after having any sort of contact with an attractive male. All the males killed so far have been physically fit, single, attractive, and very promiscuous with women. It's possible the unsub had feelings for them at some point in time, and retaliated for them not returning the same affections."

I purse my lips, wondering what we're missing. The profile appears solid, and the evidence lines up to support it, but something just feels off. We should have made the connection sooner, but with all the kills so spread out over state lines, we just got wind of this two weeks ago, which was two weeks after the fourth victim.

"Anything else I need to note to the profile before we deliver it to the town's PD?"

"Yeah," I say, sitting up as I study the photos. "The unsub managed to enter each home without it looking broken into. Either the victims know the unsub and trust him enough to let him in, or they didn't lock their doors. Tell them this unsub would have had to be social with them in order to establish that rapport. Also, have we found out what trophy is being taken? The unsub has a personal attachment to these men, and has a sadistic fantasy he's playing out with each kill, though rape doesn't seem to be a part of the fantasy just yet. Obviously he's getting off on the torture alone for now, but given the long gap between kills, he'd need something to hold him over. He'd definitely be taking a trophy."

One month between each kill. The time frame hasn't been changed, and it doesn't look like the unsub is falling apart any time soon, if ever. I was hoping for a rapid devolution that would cause him to start slipping up by now.

"We've checked the bodies over. All the flesh is left behind, and the hair is intact. Also, none of the males were missing jewelry or other personal items, but we can't know for sure, since they all lived alone and had no one to account for their belongings."

We're missing something, damn it. And it's driving me crazy.

"Go home and get some rest. You've been here all night," Elise goes on, placing her hand on my shoulder. "A mind works better after some rest."

"Dig deeper into the town's past. Something has happened there that we don't know about, and—"

"Rest," she interrupts. "I know how to do my job. You're useless if you don't sleep."

Cursing, I stand up and close the file, packing it up as Elise leaves with Leonard to head up north to Delaney Grove. It's an odd town name, and I know I'll have to see it for myself to get any real answers.

Just as I reach the door, Craig catches up to me.

"Did frostbite girl ever give you a call?" he asks, sounding bored. But I know it still pisses him off that she blew him off and chased me down. Even though he viewed the facts out of context and refused to take in the real process of those events.

Again, that's why he sucks at profiling, but he's good at public relations—his place on our team.

I open my mouth to tell him *no*, knowing it will make him feel vindicated and delighted, but my phone rings. My brow furrows when I see the unknown number, and I answer.

"Bennett here," I answer.

"You use your last name when answering a phone, as though the person on the other line might not know whom they've just dialed. It's a very impersonal greeting, which makes me wonder if

The Risk

you also struggle with detachment issues, Agent Bennett," a familiar, feminine voice drawls.

My smile immediately forms, and I wink at Craig as he watches me, waiting for me to put him out of his nosy misery.

"So you really waited the standard three days to give me a call back?"

"Technically, I waited a nonconventional four days."

Right. I haven't been to sleep since we found the latest victim yesterday morning. I'm running on caffeine and sugar.

"Sorry. I've been up all night. It's not another day until I've slept, so I'm still on day three. Will I have to wait four days in between all your calls? Or am I allowed to use this number when I want to?" I ask her, watching as Craig groans and huffs, pouting as he moves out of my way.

"Why have you been up all night?" she asks, diverting the question I asked her.

It's a typical reaction from someone with detachment issues.

"My job. I miss a lot of sleep, and spend a lot of time on the road. I guess I need to say that now before asking you out on a date I may or may not have to cancel because of said job."

I decide to toss everything out there right away, knowing she's already skittish and leery of trusting. The second I read her, she went from cold to haunted in a blink, and those haunted green eyes have been seared into my memory.

With her defenses down, she was lost, almost worried about being hurt just from speaking to me. Call it a hero complex, but I found myself drawn to her right then.

"Good to know. I miss a lot of things too, and I keep weird hours."

My smile only grows, since she's opening up.

"What do you do?" I ask her.

She laughs lightly, and it's a damn good laugh to hear. It doesn't fit her. And it's an easy, free laugh, as though she's not even the same girl I spoke to a few days ago.

"I have an online buy, sell, and trade store. I take a cut from each sell or trade made, and I have to vet some of them if the deal looks too good to be true. For instance, I might have to take a spontaneous trip in the middle of the night if someone in Florida is trying to trade a million dollar yacht for ten thousand dollar car. I can't approve a trade like that until I physically inspect the merchandise and see the proper paperwork. For sales, I can just hold the money paid until the property gets transferred. Trades, however, have to be done by the customers. I'm just a third party arranger who occasionally inspects."

Listening to her talk with such ease is a little confusing to the way I had her depicted... I profiled her as detached and defensive, not easy-natured. Maybe I'm off my game because I'm tired and hearing ease when it's really strain.

"Sounds like fun though," I say lamely. Again, I blame sleep deprivation.

"Not always. Once I had to go inspect one of those 'real' dolls. You know? The sex dolls that are realistically made, unlike the blowup dolls. They're worth like five grand and the guy was trading it for a small pony... Don't even get me started with the concern there."

A laugh escapes me before I can stop it, and I feel her smile.

"Is that the weirdest thing you've ever inspected?"

"While examining the vagina of a synthetic woman made complete with suction in *all* holes wasn't the highlight of my career, it surprisingly wasn't the weirdest."

Again, I laugh, wondering why her switch has flipped from defensive to charming over the course of four days.

"So what was the weirdest?" I ask her.

"Tit for tat. What's the weirdest case you've ever worked?"

The Risk

I think about that as I get in my car. Most of the cases I work are serious, violent, and sadistic. But when I first started…

"I got recruited while I was in college after taking a test I didn't realize was for the FBI. They decided I needed to come work for them, and I didn't see any reason to argue. Anyway, my first case was a small one in Indiana. It was a perv who was collecting panties. At first glance, the guy was a sexual deviant who would eventually escalate to harder crimes than panty thieving. It's why they called us in, because all these women were terrified of a stalker breaking into their homes and stealing their underwear. But the deeper I delved, the more I realized it was actually a juvenile kid. I still thought he was having sexual fantasies. It wasn't until later we discovered he wasn't stealing the panties for him. He was stealing them for his mother, because she always griped about her 'cheap underwear riding up into the crack of her ass.' You don't even want to know how horrified the mother was when we finally found the kid. He hadn't given her the underwear yet. He was putting them all in a box to give her for Christmas."

She gasps then laughs, and I relax in my seat while driving out of Quantico, heading toward my house.

"Sounds awkward. But at least the kid wasn't a sexual deviant." There's a tense note to her tone, but then she clears her throat while I yawn. "You really do sound tired. I'll let you go."

"I'm driving home. I have thirty minutes of free time. Keep me company."

"Hmm, I guess you still want me to be your entertainment."

My smile spreads. "I'd ask for more than just an amusing phone conversation, but I have to head back in as soon as I get some sleep. We had something new turn up in one of our cases, which means the workload is fresh again."

"Hmmm, what would you ask for if you were able to ask for it?" she asks, sounding like she's flirting now, which negates the defensive stance she held just days ago.

"I'd ask for dinner. Maybe even a movie if dinner went well and you didn't have any deal-breaking faults."

She snickers softly. "What faults would those be? Inquiring minds and all that."

"The usual. Eating boogers. Drinking urine… Strap-on fetish where you'd be the one fucking me. I'm not into any of that."

She starts laughing harder this time, and I listen, soaking it in. I don't know why it feels like I've accomplished something by making her laugh. Then again, something tells me she probably doesn't do it too often.

"Well, I never adopted a booger-eating habit. Drinking urine doesn't appeal to me. I'll just have a beer if I'm in the mood to drink something akin to piss. And I'll hide my strap-on until you're a little more comfortable with your sexuality to give it a go."

"Taking a jab at my sexuality. Nice," I state dryly, listening to her laugh some more as I continue to smile.

"So how do you profile people?" I muse when her laughter tapers off.

"How do I do it? Or why do I do it?" she counters.

"Both."

"Well, I do it mostly based on body language in person, and micro-expressions, of course. I pay attention to the wording when it's in writing. I listen to tone and wording over the phone. I do it because I run that online site, and you have to know the bull-shitters from the legitimate users."

"You run the store alone?" I ask, hedging for more personal info.

"I have a business partner. He handles all the tech work, and developed a program to flag potential fake accounts. It cuts out a lot of hands-on work, even though we still sift through the accounts personally."

"And this male partner is just a friend?" I ask, prying farther.

She hesitates, but then she sounds amused. "If you're asking if

The Risk

I'm single, the answer is yes. Have been for a while. I wouldn't have called you and flirted if I was with someone else."

"Well, it sucks that I can't take you out tonight before you get tired of waiting on me to have a free second. I'll be working overtime in search of new leads. But if you're up for coffee, I can meet you in the same place we met on my way back into the office in a few hours. Say five or so?"

"I prefer coffee in the mornings, but you can buy me a muffin. They have excellent muffins."

"Coffee in the mornings," I echo, my grin growing. "Duly noted."

"Are you flirting with me, Agent Bennett?"

"Maybe a little. Are you ever going to tell me your name?"

"Oh, that's right. You don't know my name. It's dangerous to talk to strangers, you know."

"I'm aware. I profile serials for a living."

She's a somewhat tiny thing with haunted eyes, yet joking I should be wary of her. I'm sure the fact she knows I have a badge puts her at ease; she assumes all law officials are good souls with clean intentions. That tells me she's never been in trouble with the law or had any issues with them at all.

"Serials?" she asks, her voice hitching a little, reminding me what I've said.

"Serial offenders. I graduated from serial panty robbers to serial killers. Hope that's not an issue. I've had problems in the past keeping a relationship because of that."

She clears her throat. "Um, no problem. But shouldn't you keep things like that quiet from strangers?"

"It's not classified. I've been on the news a time or two speaking. And besides, I'd rather we weren't strangers. So what's your name?"

She pauses for longer than I'd like. I've gotten her wrong and right, but I'm not sure to what degrees on either front. So I don't even bother guessing why she's quiet.

"It's Lana. Lana Myers. Feel free to investigate me, Mr. Profiler."

The light tone is back, and I cut down the final road to lead me home.

"I'd rather you surprise me, Lana Myers. I only run a non-invasive background check to make sure you're not a felon or fugitive. That could be an issue, given my job," I say, laughing lightly.

She laughs as well, then sighs. "Coffee later?" I ask her.

"Muffin, remember?"

"Right. Sorry. Sleep deprived."

"I'll see you later, Agent Bennett."

"Definitely," I tell her around a yawn as I pull into my house.

She hangs up, and I immediately type in her name in a text to Hadley.

HADLEY: What am I looking for?

ME: A criminal record only.

HADLEY: Done and done. She's clean.

ME: That was fast.

HADLEY: That's what she said.

Chuckling, I put my phone away, and I walk inside. My mind is tired, but I'm still running facts of the case over in my head, thinking of anything we might be missing.

The unsub tortures his victims for days, but not for the same amount of days. Three days this last time. Two days apiece on the first two victims. Four days on the third and fourth victims. The lack of consistency doesn't make sense, neither does the targeted skin that is removed. It's always different, except for the damn dick removal. Sometimes all the fingers are cut off. Sometimes they're not.

The Risk

My house is empty, quiet, and somewhat eerie, considering the case I'm working on. All the victims are a reflection of myself. Single. Alone. Physically fit. Living in a secluded area. Workaholics.

My closest neighbor is a mile down the road.

No one notices the victims missing for days on end. They all call into work. It's a taped recording of a man's voice, from what we can surmise, considering the words are exactly the same. None of the businesses record those calls, obviously, so we're having to trust the person who received the call.

The last body was only found because one of his work colleagues came to find out why he didn't come to work on the fourth day and never called in for that day.

It's depressing to know that no one outside of work notices them missing. The same would hold true for myself.

My eyes scan my house out of habit, looking for anything out of place. Once I feel confident nothing has been disturbed, I take off my gun, set my alarm, and then I drop to the bed.

My eyes close, and I expect to see the images of dead bodies like I always do.

Instead, I'm lost in a set of haunted green eyes I'll be seeing later.

Chapter 3

When you are courting a nice girl, an hour seems like a second. When you sit on a red-hot cinder, a second seems like an hour. That's relativity.
-Albert Einstein

Lana

It's after five when I start looking at my watch, wondering if I really am being stood up this time. I'm not sure what compelled me to call him, flirt with him, then agree to a date. Maybe it's because I need to feel less like a cold monster and more like a woman.

I lived. Others died.

I lived, yet I feel dead.

Maybe I want to feel alive, considering my time may be limited. I should treasure every moment…when I'm not collecting on an overdue debt. It's not exactly romantic to think of a guy while you're slicing another one to pieces, but Logan was definitely on my mind during the three days I spent reaping the debt from Ben.

Not in the dark recesses of my mind that are reserved for revenge either. No. Logan was in the good parts that I thought no longer existed. He awakened a long-gone light as though not all the good inside me had been destroyed.

Just as I'm about to text him and find out if he's okay, there's suddenly a body sliding into the seat in front of me, and my eyes pop up to meet a set of soft blues. I could stare at those eyes all day. The rest of him measures up to those perfect eyes too.

The Risk

He's sin and pleasure wrapped in a package I'm tempted to peek at.

"So sorry," he groans, motioning a waitress over. "There was a traffic jam. I actually had to abuse my power and hit the lights just to get through."

My smile surprises me every time he makes me use it. "It's fine. I was just worried," I lie, well, sort of. I was worried about him, and I was worried I'd been stood up.

His grin is genuine and instant when he sees I'm not pissed, and the waitress shows up, ending the moment of two idiots grinning at each other.

I honestly can't remember a time when my stomach was fluttering around. I was just a teenager when my life was shattered and the illusion of normality forever stayed out of my grasp.

This is the most human I've felt in so long. And it's just a coffee drive-by on his way to work.

We both order, and the waitress walks away after giving him a quick once over and winking at me as though she approves. Not that I need her approval.

"So, what made you agree to meet me?" he asks, apparently skipping small talk. I guess that's wise, since our time will be limited. Not to mention he interrogates for a living, so it's only natural to start a date out that way with him.

I decide against telling him that he makes me feel like a woman instead of the monster I've had to become, since he'd sort of lock me up and throw away the key.

"What made you want to ask me out?" I ask him instead.

His grin spreads wider. "You're deflecting, but I'll bite. You've been in my head. Your turn," he says, leaning up on the table with his elbows.

"You've been in my head too."

"Ah, see, that's cheating. You can't just parrot my words to keep

23

from disclosing too much. That's a commonly used tool in a detached personality."

"Stop profiling me," I say with a teasing smile, but secretly hoping he really does stop.

What if he sees too much? What the hell am I thinking? This is the stupidest date I could possibly go on.

I finally meet a guy I want to see, perhaps even date, and it has to be the one guy who could see right through me?

He's studying me too intensely, but I keep my smile in place, hoping it doesn't seem strained.

"Occupational hazard. I can't turn it off. I wish I could, but I can't."

Great.

He continues to await my reaction, and I try to think of how to properly react. How do normal women react? Do they gush and goo over his badge and skills? Do they get offended by his admission of constant profiling, feeling like he won't let them have that privacy? I have no idea.

"How much has that affected your dating life?" I ask, deciding not to react at all and keep my expressions masked.

He groans while shaking his head and leaning back. "More than I care to admit. Women prefer to tell me how they feel, as opposed to me pointing it out. I've tried to stop, but can't. Consider it a weird personality quirk. I was hopeful with you; you seem to do the same thing."

His eyes find mine, and he really does seem hopeful. He's right. I do the same thing. But for completely different reasons.

He serves justice the best he can.

I serve revenge in the way it needs to be.

"What's your dating life like?" he asks, probing once again.

Like a cobweb with a bunch of dead bugs in it... Again, not the most

The Risk

appropriate answer.

As the waitress comes and drops off our small order, I try to think of the best answer, waiting until she leaves to respond.

"A little dry at the moment."

"Ouch," he says, but he grins.

"Well, not at this exact moment," I say, feeling that stupid, uncontrollable smile spread again.

"So tell me about you." He gestures toward me with one hand while using his other to bring the coffee to his lips.

"Twenty-six. New to the area. Constantly moving. And I have an odd fixation with socks. You?"

He frowns, as though something doesn't sit well with him.

"You move a lot?" he asks, not answering my question.

We do that to each other, I guess. Avoid answering questions to ask our own.

"Yeah. I've lived in almost thirty states. Growing up was sort of boring. We lived in one town. It was small, and everyone knew everything about everyone. After my parents died, it just got worse. Anyway, I've moved all over, trying to find what feels like home."

"Any luck here?" he asks, clearing his throat.

"Maybe," I say with a shrug.

I barely know him, so telling him he's the first thing that's piqued my interest this much would definitely be coming on too strong.

"So your parents..." He lets the words trail off, seeming reluctant to fully ask what he wants to know.

"Car accident," I partially lie, forcing a tight smile.

"Sorry," he says, blowing out a breath.

"It was years ago. Now, about you?" I muse, desperately ready for a subject shift.

He flashes me a smile, but it doesn't reach his eyes. "Twenty-nine. I own a house on a quiet piece of land. It was my stepdad's, but he left it to me before he died. My mother is living with her newest husband in Miami. So it's just me."

"What about your birth dad?" I realize too late that I shouldn't be prying that deep, when I don't want him prying too.

Neither of us gets the chance to pry.

His phone chirps, drawing his attention to it, and he sighs in a way that probably means our short and sweet talk is over.

"Fuck," he says under his breath, causing my lips to twitch.

It's just a word, but I was starting to worry that he was a total choir boy.

His eyes pop back up to meet mine. "I hate to leave this early, but—"

"It's fine," I interrupt, ignoring the small pang of disappointment.

He tosses down a twenty, which is more than enough to cover the possible ten dollar bill.

"I really am sorry," he says, cursing under his breath as he stands.

I stand and make things awkward, because I don't know if I should hug him, touch him at all, or wave like an idiot.

I wave like an idiot.

Sheesh.

He smirks, arching an eyebrow at me. "I'll call you later?" he asks, his smirk turning into a smile.

I'm busy feeling like an ass, so I just nod. I really don't trust my mouth to be any less stupid than this incredibly awkward wave that I'm still doing. It's like my hand has lost touch with my brain, and the damn thing is still waving.

His phone rings this time, and he turns and walks away before

The Risk

answering. I drop back down to my seat, wondering how planning out a brutal murder is easier than dating.

The world is entirely too fucked up.

Chapter 4

Force always attracts men of low morality.
—Albert Einstein

Lana

LOGAN: Steak. I'll be taking you out for steak. Maybe even lobster too. You like red meat and shellfish?

I grin when I see the random text from Logan. Yesterday I was awkward, but then he called and made me forget how unversed I am with all this, because he didn't seem to mind. If anything, he seemed more intrigued.

ME: Yes and yes. I like wine too. Just FYI.

LOGAN: Wine, got it. What are you doing today? Any chance you'll be in town for more coffee? Or a muffin, rather?

I finish concealing the final camera over the entry of the doorway. Getting inside wasn't easy, considering Tyler or his wife locks the doors immediately when they get home or leave. But I finally managed to slip in and leave a window unlocked for later.

No security system. There's only one of my targets planned who has a security system. That'll be on Jake to handle. Jake is a true best friend. How many people do you walk up to, tell them you want revenge, tell them your plan, and then they start helping you keep from getting caught?

I grab my phone and text Logan back, finding it oddly calming to have a normal conversation while plotting.

Maybe I really am psychotic.

The Risk

ME: Not today. I'm on a trade review. I won't be back in until tomorrow.

That's not entirely a lie. I did do a trade review... It just happened to be in the same town.

Tyler's wife is out of town on a conference for work, which gives me plenty of time to check out his home.

The flooring is new, just like the rest of the home. No creaks is a damn good thing. My phone buzzes in my pocket as I make my way through the hallways, checking for anything and everything that might pose a problem.

LOGAN: Tomorrow I'll be a few towns over. Juggling a few cases right now. People just can't seem to stop killing other people.

Gotta love irony.
We're so terribly mismatched that it's not even funny.
If he'd seen the evil I've seen, he'd understand why some people deserve to die.

ME: Have you ever had to kill someone?

Pretty sure that's not the best question to ask a guy you've only had one coffee house date with — if you can call that a date.

LOGAN: Many times. Not all cases end with the perp in jail, unfortunately.

Well, he's killed numerous people the same way with the same methodology and reasoning...so technically he's a serial killer too. It's logically truthful. Other than wearing a badge to find it legally justifiable, we're the same. Well, I torture my victims first, but that's just nitpicking at facts.

LOGAN: Does that bother you?

I'm laughing before I can stop myself, and I groan while shaking my head, happy that there's no one here to hear me. Morbid humor is probably not going to get me far in this relationship.

ME: Not at all. I'm sure you had to do it, or you wouldn't have done it at all.

Sometimes people don't find justice. Sometimes they have to take it.

"Want to play, Victoria? You know you do." Ben's breath feels like acid against my forehead, and I manage to slam a knee up, connecting with his side.

He curses and turns his head.

"Hold her down!" he yells at Tyler. "Or I'll make sure she nails you a few times too."

A scream pierces the night, but it's not mine. I refuse to let them hear me scream.

"You scream pretty," I hear Kyle saying, laughing from somewhere behind us, but I can't see him or what he's doing.

And I don't want to see.

I don't even want to see what they're doing to me.

The memories used to leave me curled in a ball and crying for hours. Now they fuel me. Feed my mission. Drive me forward.

Make me a little murderous.

Shaking my head, I move through the house quicker, hiding the last camera in the stuffed bear on Tyler's bed. Apparently his wife likes stuffed animals. Or at least I hope it's his wife who likes stuffed animals. I'd hate to know I've trembled in fear over a guy who carries around a stuffed bear.

As I enter the last bedroom, I notice it's soundproofed with

The Risk

large amounts of studio padding meant for musicians. This will be the perfect room, since he doesn't have a basement. No windows are in here.

No cameras will be added in this room.

There are a few guitars lined up, all of them nice and shiny.

His whole life is nice and shiny. Just like all of them.

I can't wait to paint it red.

Chapter 5

The only real valuable thing is intuition.
—Albert Einstein

Logan

"Who's the girl?" Elise asks, clearing her throat as she sits down on the edge of my desk.

I'm grinning when I put my phone down, but I mask my expression.

"No clue what you're talking about," I lie, controlling all my micro-expressions.

"You can lie all you want to, but you give yourself away when you look at your phone. There are two reasons a guy smiles at his phone like that. Porn or a girl."

Chuckling, I look away, studying some new evidence on the "Boogeyman" case. I hate it when the media gives the unsubs a name. It only feeds into their delusions and gives them the attention they crave. Fortunately they haven't gotten wind of our mutilated, tortured victims' case yet. I'd hate to know the name they'd conjure up for that one.

"We're sending a team to Boston to follow up the new leads for the kills there. We've isolated the comfort zone and have narrowed down the suspect pool. You good with going? I'm staying current on the mutilate and kill case," I say instead of responding to her other comment.

She blows out a long breath. "Sure. I'll go to Boston. Stop staring at all those pictures though. They're going to give you nightmares," she says, motioning to the shots scattered across my desk. I always have board copies made for my desk. Seeing things from various angles helps you catch what you might otherwise overlook.

"I need to find the true motive behind these kills." I motion to the latest dead and castrated victim.

"Sometimes there is no motive. We profiled the unsub to be sexually frustrated, most likely because he's gay and can't accept that. As a result, he's on his way to becoming a sexual sadist once he does accept it. More than likely he was mocked, taunted, or rejected by these men. The local PD are being slow with getting back to us. I don't think they're taking this guy as seriously as they should. I talked to several townies, but they acted like no one there would ever be gay. As though it's blasphemy to even consider. I wanted to flash pictures of my brother and his husband to them just for shock value at one point."

My lips twitch.

"The smaller the town, the more resistant to outsiders they are. They don't like us meddling in their town, and they sure as hell won't want us there uncovering any dirt that might tarnish their reputation. But eventually we'll have to set up there. The unsub *will* return for his endgame," I say on a heavy breath.

She nods as she stands, and she grabs her keys off my desk before staring down at me as I stay seated.

"Just a friendly reminder…we're all workaholics. It's how we made this team. There're always three or more cases going on at once, despite the lovely way TV depicts us as having just one case at a time and free time in between. Dating… Well, it's not so easy. There's a reason we're all single, divorced, or both. Unless you're sneaking around with someone who works here, you never get to see the person waiting at home for you."

She turns and walks away, casting a look over her shoulder. I shrug it off. We do have some free time. It's not much, but it's enough. I hope. I'd hate to know my life was only spent chasing the psychotic until I die alone.

> ME: **We really need to see each other again. Texting sucks.**

> LANA: **I agree. My fingers are getting cramps.**

> ME: **Anything going on in two days? I have no breakfast plans.**

> LANA: **Two days from now I'll be in West Virginia. What about tomorrow?**

> ME: **Can't. I have to fly up to Boston for a quick briefing. I'll be back tomorrow night, but I have too much work to finish up with. It'll be well after midnight before I leave. IF I leave.**

> LANA: **So, texting is fun, huh?**

I laugh and groan, relaxing in my seat as Craig walks into my office.

"So the County Sherriff from that one-horse town finally called back. Just got off the phone with him. He actually lives there, and apparently thinks he runs all the police departments in the county. Anyway, he said there're 'no gays' living in his towns. 'Those are for city folk who forgot how to be men and women.'" Craig rolls his eyes, and I curse.

"Repression is a breeding ground for serial killers. Him denying anyone could be something other than who he wants them to be isn't going to help us find this unsub before he strikes again."

"I said almost the exact same thing. But he didn't budge from his stance. He thinks it's a coincidence those 'poor boys' got killed. He blames it on moving away from home, because the rest of the world is full of evil. Pretty sure he's working with a cult mentality, and I wouldn't be surprised if all the small towns he's sheriff over drink that water."

"We're going to have to profile the whole town if someone

The Risk

doesn't talk," I grumble.

"You think the unsub is still a resident there?" he asks as he takes a seat in front of my desk.

"I think it's unlikely but possible. We don't have enough information to use for a more specific profile."

He steeples his hands in front of his mouth, his eyes vacantly staring at the top of my desk.

"The media will spin all sorts of theories if they get ahold of this story before we're ready to deliver a concrete profile," he says absently.

"Well aware. At least we know the sheriff isn't going to be spreading the story before we're ready."

He nods, still staring at nothing in particular.

"I don't get how you do it," he says, moving his eyes away from one of the photographs. "How do you get inside someone's head that is this sick and sadistic?"

"How do you handle a thousand and one questions from the media?" I ask with a shrug. "We all have our strengths. I don't get inside their heads. I crawl into their psyche. It's the only way to understand their delusional mentality, because you can't think like a rational person would. A convoluted mind is one that forms its own reality. That's why I need to know more about these kills. He's not leaving behind enough clues to piece together the puzzle."

Chapter 6

I admit that thoughts influence the body.
—Albert Einstein

Lana

My life has started revolving around the chime of a phone. Well, for the past five months, it's been like that, but a different phone. Usually it's the cloned phone that has me leaping and rushing around to grab it. Not my actual phone. Not until Agent Logan Bennett a couple of weeks ago.

    LOGAN: Craig just asked if you were gay.

    ME: Who's Craig?

    LOGAN: You have no idea how much I enjoy that answer. In fact, I just drew a few curious looks about why I'm laughing.

    I have no clue why he finds that so funny.

    ME: Seriously, who's Craig?

    LOGAN: I really want to see you again.

    ME: Well, let's just both quit our jobs so we can finally have a date.

    LOGAN: With the dead ends I'm finding on all my cases, I'm starting to wonder if it isn't time for a career change.

The Risk

ME: If it makes you feel any better, I contemplated a career change too. Met a guy yesterday who was trading all his wife's dildos for a pressure washer. -.- The wife was furious when I showed up to inspect the quality of her "toys."

At least that's true. I hate the times I have to lie to him.

LOGAN: I just spat coffee all over my desk.

ME: How coincidental. She was apparently a spitter too. The husband informed me of that as if I wanted to know. #overshare

LOGAN: Stop. Please stop. Everyone here thinks I'm insane for laughing this hard.

ME: It wasn't the most awkward encounter I've had, but it certainly won't make any of my highlight reels either.

LOGAN: So the dildos didn't get traded for the pressure washer?

ME: Nope. And I learned that she'll need them more than ever, since he won't be touching her for a while, according to her. He wasn't happy when I left. Apparently it was my fault for showing up an hour early, because she would have been gone otherwise.

LOGAN: Okay. You win. I can't compete with that.

ME: #LifeGoals

LOGAN: Do you always go to the coffee shop where I met you?

ME: Umm...that's an abrupt shift in convo, but yes, I do. I moved here a little over a month ago, and that was the first decent cup I found.

LOGAN: Then I wish I had stopped there sooner than that day. I had some downtime two weeks earlier. We could have been doing this in person then.

ME: You don't always go there?

LOGAN: That was my first time. Craig and I went to address some of the higher-ups about some security measures. We only stopped in that day because our regular spot was closed for renovations.

ME: Oh THAT's Craig!

LOGAN: You seriously didn't remember his name?

ME: I only retain the names of people I like or want to kill.

I cringe when I read that back, realizing that's not a good joke — even though it's true — to make to a FBI agent.

LOGAN: Hope I'm on the right list.

I blow out a breath, then smile at the morbid joke, now that I know he's not taking it seriously.

ME: You are. Currently, you're at the top of the right list. It's been a while since I smiled like I do when we talk.

LOGAN: I should have kissed you.

My heart thumps in my chest as I read that back. Then I read it again. And again. And again.

Each time it causes my stomach to flutter, and I try to process all the weird reactions I have to him. He makes me feel and act like the person I never thought I could be again, and I barely know him. I've only seen him twice.

Yet, we don't miss a day speaking. And it's the highlight of my day.

Every day.

Every time.

Every single word.

ME: Yes. You should have. Then I could have been spared the awkward wave I gave.

LOGAN: But the REALLY awkward wave was cute.

ME: Ha. Funny guy. I see how it is. It's been a while since I tried the dating scene.

Actually, it's only been about seven months, but as always, the interest level died after about a month, because all the feelings I wanted to feel never emerged. There'd be a fraction of the spark I feel with Logan, and I'd try to force it, desperate to feel anything other than anger, hatred, rage…brokenness.

I thought I'd lost that ability. I thought they'd taken it somehow.

Then along came exactly what I had been searching for since before I started the kill list. The problem is the fact he's sort of my opposite in the not so good way. Meaning, I kill people and he catches killers. And I can't stop. I wish I hadn't met him so early on in my list.

There are still many more names on my list. I still have to right so many wrongs. My phone chimes, and I look down, smiling before I can help myself.

LOGAN: Then I definitely should have kissed you.

Chapter 7

Imagination is more important than knowledge. Knowledge is limited. Imagination encircles the world.
-Albert Einstein

Logan

"We know from the previous five killings and the mutilations that sexual frustration and possible rejection were the main motives." Even though I feel like there's a shit-ton more to it. "Maybe the unsub feels inadequate, possibly from rejection or something even larger that has happened in the past. We need to find a link, and it starts in that town. Leonard and Elise have returned to Delaney Grove, searching for anyone who might speak. For now, the rest of us will remain here where the last killing happened. It's the freshest crime scene," I tell the group.

They grab their folders and files, and I head to my office, feeling too tired to think straight. For the past two weeks, I've either crashed in my office or driven home for a few hours of sleep.

Unlike most serial killers, this one isn't escalating in time scale or risk factor. He's not getting bolder, which means he's staying smarter. Which sucks for us, because he's not making any mistakes.

The trail is going to go cold. One more week, and there could be another body at our feet.

My phone dings, and I look down at the text, smiling when I see who it is. I have no idea why she bothers speaking to me, since all we've done is text or talk over the phone since the day I had to bail on her at the coffee shop.

The Risk

LANA: You know, I always mocked the Netflix and Chill notion, but now I see the appeal.

ME: I don't even own a TV.

LANA: What???? How????

ME: I keep meaning to buy one...

LANA: Agent Bennett, I'm sorry. This has to end now.

ME: At least call me by my first name if you're ending things.

LANA: Agent Bennett sounds sexier.

That has me smirking.

ME: Oh? Handcuffs turn you on?

LANA: Restraint is a hell no. Not my thing. But I wouldn't be opposed to using them on you... If we ever make it to that level, that is.

My cock stirs in my pants, and I mentally count the months since the last time I even had time to think about sex. By month five, I stop counting, because it's just depressing. I'll need a few dates with my hand before I try taking on Lana and embarrassing myself.

ME: Dinner tomorrow?

LANA: You can do dinner?

ME: No leads right now on my case, so I have some free time. It won't be much free time, but it has to be better than texting all the time.

LANA: I'm not sure about the protocol in this situation.

My brow furrows as I read her last text.

ME: What protocol?

LANA: Am I allowed to say yes to a last minute dinner invite? Or is it frowned upon to seem readily available on such short notice? ;)

That has me smiling and laughing to myself as I sit back and look at the clock. It's after nine, but I really want to see her right now.

ME: It'll be a lot of short notices from me, so I hope you're the kind of girl who can be readily available... Hopefully that sounds better aloud.

LANA: It sounds... Yeah, no. It doesn't sound good, but I get what you mean. Yes to dinner. :) I hope to leave with more than an awkward wave this time.

I fist pump the air, then look up to see a few curious eyes on me through my open office door. Feeling like a fourteen-year-old jackass, I message her again.

ME: I won't walk away with just a wave this time. Who knows when I'll see you again, or if you'll continue to deal with my shitty schedule.

LANA: My schedule is pretty shitty too.

ME: Is it wrong that I'm tempted to ask where you live so I can subtly swing by tonight with the excuse I was in the neighborhood and thought I saw someone too close to your house?

LANA: Is it wrong that I hope you'll break some rules, find my address, and do just that?

The Risk

Groaning, I glance at the time, then at my computer screen. Deciding to totally abuse my privileges, I do look up her address. But that's all I research. Grabbing my phone, I pull up my GPS, grab my 'go bag' from the office, and jog down to my car.

Since it's wishful thinking and incredibly presumptuous to bring a bag, I toss it in the back, hoping she doesn't notice it and realize I'm expecting a lot more than I should be. Obviously I'll leave as soon as I get there if she wants me to, but I'm really hoping she doesn't want me to leave.

Because Lana Myers has been in my head since the day I met her, and it'd be nice if someone noticed I was missing.

Chapter 8

To know the secrets of life, we must first become aware of their existence.
—Albert Einstein

Lana

I stare at my last text and the empty space below it, because he never messages back. Seriously, I suck at flirting.

Groaning, I get up, flicking a gaze over at the monitor on the wall. Tyler walks around in front of the camera in just his boxers, smirking as he texts someone. My secondary phone dings right on cue, and I look down and read the messages he's sending to a girl named Denise.

TYLER: What're you wearing? I'm thinking of you.

I roll my eyes, hoping Denise tells him to fuck himself. But she doesn't.

It's hard to watch them live their lives for a month. I have to watch them loving the freedom they stole from me. The freedom they stole from *us*.

Tyler is the first one who is married, and apparently having an affair. I've been saving him for closer to last, but right now, I can't afford to go *home* and sprint through so many. And sprint is an accurate depiction of how that time will go, considering it'll be too easy to get caught if I try to space it out as I do now.

Jake assured me the feds are investigating our hometown. It

The Risk

was only a matter of time before they linked the kills and made the connection. I'd hoped to have more time before they got on my trail, hence the reason I started the kills outside of town.

It's not like they'll link any of it to me, of course. Lana Myers doesn't exist in that town. Never has.

Victoria Evans died ten years ago. I look nothing like her anymore. They made sure of that. My eyes flick to the small mirror on the wall beside me. Without any makeup, you can see a few faint scars.

I spent a lot of money to help make sure there were as few scars as possible. Victoria Evans was a poor girl from Delaney Grove, but Kennedy Carlyle was an heiress who died in a car accident the same night my death certificate was signed. She was so mangled and unrecognizable that Jake had no problem shifting the info around in the computers.

Kennedy might have died that night, but the stranger I never met saved my life.

I went in as Victoria, left as Kennedy, took on her rich, orphan life, and 'legally' changed her name to Lana Myers to avoid anyone from her past finding me out.

It was the easiest way to build a fund to support us and to change my identity. Jake didn't get good at more inventive forms of identity changes until the past couple of years.

It took a while to see my scars on my face as marks of survival instead of brutal reminders of that night. The scars on other parts of my body didn't heal as cleanly. But the scars on my soul took the longest to deal with.

They say everyone has their own healing process.

The first year of mine was spent mourning for my family and suffering from all the trauma. I cried until there was nothing but sand left to fall from my eyes. I curled into a ball and showered three times a day, never feeling clean.

The second year was spent being angry and seeking outlets. I took on kickboxing first. By the third year, I'd moved on to various other forms of mixed martial arts. Several black belts are mine now.

I never want to be anyone else's victim.

The fourth year was spent getting stronger, dealing with all my fears, and learning to stand on my own without all the sleepless nights.

The fifth year was the first time I could withstand any physical contact. I learned to grow. I learned not to flinch away when someone barely touched me. I learned to be as normal as I could be.

The sixth year was when I could finally handle intimacy without wanting to kill the person touching me. It was the year I decided I was no longer their victim. It was the year I took back control over my life and embraced my future before it was destroyed completely.

The seventh year was when I decided to get revenge. The planning began.

The eighth year was when I started locating them all. I learned all there was to know about them.

The ninth year was spent hacking the case files from my father's trial, learning all the police had, searching for the truth instead of the lies.

The tenth year… The tenth year is when I decided to start killing one a month.

Jake convinced me to be cautious. I'd hate to be caught before I can finish.

My life will happen in between kills. I can have both. Because I doubt I'll make it out of this alive.

Denise decides to text Tyler back, breaking me out of my reverie, and it's a picture of her in a lace nightie. Unreal. If this is how you're supposed to date, then I really am out of my depth. I'm not spending thirty minutes slipping into something like that just for a picture.

The Risk

My phone buzzes as Tyler and Denise send dirty texts to each other. Those dirty texts will find their way to his wife if needed. She sure as hell can't be home when I collect his debt.

My actual phone rings, and I reach over and grab it absently, still reading the latest sick text from Tyler. How does Denise find this sexy?

"Hello?"

"Hey, it's me," Jake says, clicking away in the background. He's always at the computer, lining everything up for me. Best partner ever.

"What're you doing?" I ask, curious.

"Just finished writing Olivia her check, and now I'm working on our website."

"Are you reading this?" I ask him, wrinkling my nose when Denise describes a blowjob in detail for him.

"Unfortunately. What are you doing tonight? I was thinking we'd grab a bite and watch surveillance together. I've already gotten his entry code. You're getting better angles with the cameras with each install."

Idly, I lift my gaze to the monitor, watching as Tyler starts lowering his boxers. Yeah, no. I don't need to see that.

Cutting my eyes away, I answer, "I learn more with each one. His wife is gone a lot on business. There's a conference two days before the planned kill day. She'll be gone all weekend. I can strike then. He's a two and done deal."

"Don't get cocky and strike too soon. When you lose your caution, mistakes happen, and you'll get arrested."

"True. There's a conference the weekend after. I can always prolong the date as well."

"That's better than moving it up, but it's best to stick to a consistent schedule if possible. That way you don't lose focus."

Snorting derisively, I roll my eyes. "No worries on that. My focus can't be derailed."

Their taunts no longer haunt me at night. Now I dream peacefully to the sounds of their screams.

Which I realize is probably psychotic, but I wasn't born this way. They turned me into this. Karma wasn't finding them. Neither was justice. Destiny seemed content with leaving them on their perfect little paths of love, peace, and blissfulness.

Only one person wanted them to suffer. Well, two. Jake wanted them to hurt as much as they hurt me. As much as they hurt—

"You say that, but you seem to lose more of your anger with each kill. You almost seem…a little too peppy these days. For the past few weeks, you've giggled and acted high every time I've talked to you. You getting tired of this? It's not too late to back out."

That has nothing to do with the kills. It has everything to do with Agent Bennett. Not that I'll tell Jake that. He'd flip his lid if he knew I was… Well, I'm not really sure what I'm doing with Logan to be honest, besides smiling like a loon every time my phone goes off with a new message from him.

If I told Jake I'm interested in an FBI agent who happens to investigate serial killers, and is possibly investigating my case, he'd probably flip the hell out.

Because it's stupid.

And I should end it.

But I can't.

When you go so long feeling cold and detached, then a complete stranger ignites the dormant feelings you thought were forever gone…you can't help but be addicted to it. You can't help but revel in the smiles you forgot how to use, or the laughter that sounds unnatural coming from the lips that haven't laughed in years.

Whoa. I need to slow down. I'm one fantasy away from tattooing his name on my ass.

I can't help but wonder how things might have been if my past

The Risk

hadn't been derailed and cluster-fucked to hell and back. I think he would have really liked the old me. I was clever, funny, quick-witted, and slightly dramatic. I also cried if I accidentally killed a bug.

Now... Now I'm a 5'4 package of vengeance that no one sees coming.

"I'm peppy because it feels good. Maybe it's a high from the adrenaline or something," I lie.

"Really?" he asks, sounding confused.

I know Jake supports what I'm doing. He was there. He helped me pick up all the pieces and glue them back together the best he could, even though I could barely stand to be around anyone.

But he doesn't want the grim details, and I doubt he feels comfortable with me telling him it makes me feel like a goofy grinner—even though it isn't the kills making me a goofy grinner. But I can't give him the true facts. Because...World War III and all that. I don't want him to talk me out of Logan, when I've almost done it to myself too many times.

"Really," I lie again.

I really hope I flirted right with Logan. I thought I was following his lead. He often gets called away during the middle of our texting sessions, which means it could be hours before he texts back, so I try not to overthink it.

My eyes flick back to where Tyler is already cleaning up. He's just as quick as I remember.

One more week until kill day.

"I still think you should have nixed the castration. If they dig too deep into the town's history, they could eventually unravel it all too soon," Jake says, reminding me he's still on the phone.

"You remember what they did, right? I want them to feel the worst pain imaginable. I want to remove that last ounce of power... That last shred of dignity."

Blowing out a long breath, I listen to him grow silent on the other end.

When he continues to hold his tongue, I try to put his mind at ease.

"Even if they did figure out a ghost rose from the dead, I take plenty of forensic counter measures. The feds suspect some big, strong guy. I strangle them to render them unconscious, instead of using anything to aide in incapacitating them, the way a woman would normally do. And I do it while they're on the ground so as not to betray my height. I've trained for this for years. Stop worrying."

He sighs harshly. "I hate you leaving the bodies there for them to find. I'd prefer it if you took them to an isolated, controlled location, then dumped the bodies somewhere they'd never be found."

"I wanted them found. I wanted them linked together. I just didn't want it to happen this soon. I want them scared when I start dropping lower on the list. By the time I reach Kyle, I want him to be crying in fear. That's why I'm saving him for last."

"And what happens if he goes to the cops when he figures out the pattern? Eventually this will hit the media, you know?"

I'm surprised it hasn't already.

"I knew the risks going in, and Kyle speaking to the feds about a ghost girl killing people who brutalized her ten years ago isn't one of them. He'd have to explain *why* someone was picking these guys off. You know none of them will ever do that."

A secret like they've kept would eat anyone alive…if they had a conscience. Only they feel they were justified in hurting innocent people.

They strived, succeeded, and went on with life like it never happened. Like they didn't leave us there to die.

One person did die because of that night.

They think it was two.

The Risk

Jake continues to yak in my ear about all the 'what ifs' in the universe. I continue to shift my thoughts away from it all, because Logan keeps creeping to the forefront of my mind.

I'll finally get to see him tomorrow.

Tyler lies down for the night, and I flip the monitor over to regular television. Bedtime seems to be ten consistently so far. In fact, everything he does seems to be scheduled, including his shit breaks.

"I'm getting off here, Jake."

"Fine. Fine. Call me back later."

Hanging up, I start taking inventory. My knives are in a row, lined up inside my homemade multi-sheath. They're clean and wiped free of fingerprints, as always.

I move to the fridge and pour myself a glass of straight vodka. Smiling, I turn on the music, an old vinyl my father used to love. He and my mother danced to this song a lot at night, back before life was derailed in a metaphorical train crash.

As I sway with the music, dancing like they used to, I almost miss the sound of heavy pounding against my door.

My body jolts when I register the sound, and my heart slams into my throat. No one comes here. Ever. It's a creepy driveway with gargoyles at the end just to make it a little creepier. Then there are several signs warning against trespassing.

Not even my mailman dares to venture the half mile driveway to my house. My packages get left at the end of the driveway.

My eyes dart out the window, but I don't see a vehicle in plain view. After flicking off the record player, I push the knives into the drawer closest to me as the knocking persists. I pick up my gun, carrying it as I silently cross the floor to the door.

When I peek through the peephole, my eyes widen and my breath rushes out in disbelief.

"Shit!" I hiss, scrambling to toss the gun into the drawer

attached the table beside the door.

"Come on, pretty girl. Don't tell me you're not home after I broke rules and privacy laws to find you," Logan drawls from the other side of the door.

My stomach flutters as that goofy grin starts to spread, and I swing open the door to a smiling FBI agent. His grin broadens as his eyes rake over me, and he looks back up as an eyebrow arches.

"Best. Greeting. Ever."

I'm confused for a second, so I glance down my body to see that, yep; I'm not wearing pants. I rarely do when I'm at home.

I look back up and shrug, ignoring the way a twinge of heat spreads up my neck. I'm embarrassed? Really? I didn't know I could be embarrassed until this moment.

"Can I come in before anyone sees you? I'd hate to have to show my jealous side so early on," he deadpans, but he winks as I slowly step back, trying not to say or do anything stupid.

Should I run and put on pants? Or will I look like an idiot who forgot to put on pants? Confident girls walk around in a T-shirt and panties all the time, right?

Fucking eh.

"My driveway is sort of creepy, and with all the vegetation growth, no one can see me here," I ramble, then zip my lips.

As soon as he gets the door shut, he turns and his gaze shifts. Something subtle changes, and the amused glint there melts away for something far more enticing.

I start to speak, to explain why I stupidly answered the door without pants, when he's suddenly on me. His hands go to my hair, tilting my head back roughly, and his mouth crashes against mine.

I go from surprised to melting within seconds, opening my lips so his tongue can sweep in and steal what small fraction of sanity I have left.

I moan into his mouth as one of his hands slides down my body, gripping my waist just enough to pull me to him. Both my hands come up and grab onto his shoulders so that I don't sag to the ground.

It feels good. Not awkward or wrong or uncomfortable. It feels so *good*.

The kiss is hungry, almost as though we've both been starved for too long. I realize we're moving too quickly, but I don't give a damn. I give less of a damn when he lifts me and places me on top of the table beside the door, pushing himself between my legs as he devours me.

His hands move up and down my sides, back into my hair, then back down again. It's like he can't touch me everywhere at once, even though he wants to. But he's also sticking to safe zones instead of groping me, despite my state of undress.

It makes me want him even more.

I tug at the front of his shirt and wind his tie around my other hand, pulling him as close as possible. He makes some strained sound before grinding into the vee of my thighs, driving me that much crazier.

"We should slow down," he says against my lips.

"We really should," I agree, still kissing him and pulling him impossibly closer.

"Where's your room?" he asks, trying and failing to break the kiss.

"Down the hall and to the right."

He lifts me and starts walking, bypassing the stairs to the part of the house he definitely can't see. My legs stay wrapped around him as I try not to think of how dangerous this could be.

I never expected him to just show up without warning, and there's an entire murder room upstairs just waiting to be discovered.

Mentally, I do a quick worry list over the things he might find in the bedroom, and realize most everything has already been put away. As long as he doesn't accidentally turn on the monitoring system in my living room, we should be good.

My back crashes against the wall when he stumbles, and my thoughts flee as the kiss grows more aggressive. Too many times I've tried to feel this passion and never felt an ounce of the fire as what's burning between us.

My fingers skate down the front of his shirt until I rip it open, fully opening it and pushing it out of the way as a few buttons skitter across the floor, running with their newfound freedom. Firm skin finds my fingertips, and I moan against his lips when he shudders against me like he feels all the flames I do.

We'll burn good together.

His tongue demands more attention from mine, and I kiss with abandon like I never have before. My hands slide up and tangle in his hair, angling his head so I can devour him properly.

He grunts and pushes away from the wall, walking quickly again.

"Your other right," I say when he starts walking into my guest room on the left where Jake stays when he comes to visit.

He changes course and continues to move quickly. I hear the fan humming in my room as we walk in, and anticipation buds in my core, ready to be released.

He drops me to the bed in a flurry of motion that surprises me, and I prop up on my elbows, taking in the sight of him as he finishes stripping his ruined shirt off. All tan, lean muscle and smooth skin.

A twinge of dread unfurls within me. The scars on my body aren't all hidden. My face was easier to fix than the rest of me.

"Too fast?" he asks, apparently misreading the reason for my hesitation to join him in the getting-naked routine.

"No," I say, forcing my thoughts to blank.

The past can't continue to rule me, and I'm supposed to be beyond the worry of what people will think when they see the scars.

The Risk

He looks hesitant now.

"Lana, I shouldn't have barged in and came at you like a savage. But…" His eyes dip to where my thighs are spread wide, nothing but the thin panties hiding the goods from him. He swallows audibly before meeting my gaze again. "We can slow down. I promise this isn't why I showed up."

A slow smile curves my lips. He's pretty amazing when he's trying to be a good guy.

Climbing up to my knees, I crawl toward him, and his pupils dilate. He's turned on, which doesn't take profiling skills to figure out.

Slowly, I move toward him, and he remains completely still. When I reach him, I lean forward and flick my tongue against the firm flesh on his abs. A quiet sound escapes him, and that seems to snap that small thread of control.

His hand goes to my hair, and with a hard tug, he forces my head back as he lowers his face and finds my lips again. It's rough and hungry, and completely different from anything I thought I'd ever want.

I've been controlling sex since I found it in me to be intimate again. This is the first time I've ever felt comfortable letting a guy lead.

"Where the hell have you been?" he says against my lips, causing me to grin against him as he pushes me down, coming down on top of me.

I'm not sure what that means, but I love the awe in his tone.

My smile dies as I wait for the inevitable panic attack of being pinned down, but it doesn't come. More emotions bud inside of me, and I put all the confusing questions into the back of my mind, deciding to analyze this all later.

For now, I just want to *feel*.

And I do.

I feel his movements against me as he pushes his pants away.

I feel him shift as he slides his hand up my leg, eliciting small shivers from me because of how overloaded my sensory nerves are.

I feel when he touches parts of me that shouldn't be so erotic — the bend of my knee, the back of my calf, the top of my foot.

I feel *everything*, and it all feels perfect.

He starts pushing my shirt up, and I force myself to allow it. He sucks in a breath when he realizes I'm also not wearing a bra. It's escaped his attention since he's avoided any groping.

"Damn," he says under his breath, though it sounds like praise.

He leans back as though he's going to take it all in. Which gives me a second to fully appreciate him, since he's down to his black boxers that are straining to keep certain parts of his body restrained.

I'm confident, until his gaze shifts and zeroes in on what I was worried about.

"What happened?" he asks, not sounding overly concerned or nosy, just curious.

He runs his fingers over two of the scars, and I catch his wrist, stopping him. I can't stand them being touched.

He meets my eyes again, and the concern that was lacking begins to form. He's too perceptive, so it'd be stupid to give too much away with my expressions.

"Car accident," I tell him weakly.

It's a lie, but I'm damn good at lying.

"The same as your parents?" he asks.

If he ever looked into it and found the name I stole, then he'd know that girl was not in the same accident as her parents.

"No. Can we not talk about this right now though?" I ask, my voice teasing now as I slide his hand up to cover my breast.

The heat in his eyes is instantly back, the concern washing away when he sees I'm okay. With slow prowess, he slides down on top

The Risk

of me, and his lips claim mine again.

Nothing else matters in this moment.

We kiss until we're both grinding against each other, desperate for more. I need zero help getting ready, because I've never been so turned on in all my life.

He groans against me before finally lifting away from me again.

"Tell me to stop and I will," he says softly, brushing his lips against mine again.

Just that bit of comfort means more than he knows, because I believe it coming from his lips.

When you read people like I do, you learn who's honest and who isn't. You learn to smell intentions.

"I don't want to stop," I say quietly, refusing to break the spell.

He leans over, grabbing his discarded jeans, and I grin when I hear the familiar rattling sound of a wrapper.

"Just so you know, I've had this thing in my wallet for a while. I really didn't come with expectations—with *hopes*, yes, but not expectations," he says, grinning when he sees my smile.

I arch an eyebrow playfully, and he kisses me again, getting readjusted on top of me. His hands move between us as he lifts his hips, and I resist the urge to look down and watch.

It's sad to say that seeing him roll on a condom would probably send me spiraling into a premature orgasm. It's surreal. I love this feeling. I want to bottle it and save it for rainy days.

When he leans up, I'm forced to watch, and I squirm as that ache grows more pronounced, more insistent. Fairly sure that ache is named desire.

He's definitely not a small guy, but he's also not freakishly endowed. Perfect.

I'm licking my lips before I can stop myself as he starts tugging my panties down. His eyes fall on the bare skin when he removes them completely and he leans down.

The second I feel his breath hit me, my hips jerk up, and I tug his hair, forcing him up my body.

"If you do that, I'll be ruined. I need more," I say just as my lips find his again.

I could seriously kiss him all day, as long as we're also doing more.

Without any further begging, he pushes inside me in one swift thrust that has me breaking my lips away to gasp for air. He rocks his hips, and I realize there's more there than I initially thought, because he goes deeper, filling me fuller.

He stares down at me, lust and longing oozing from his eyes as he keeps eye contact. No words are exchanged as he rocks his hips again, finding a spot inside me that I thought had died.

Sensory overload is a legit thing.

Everything on me is strung tight, just waiting to break. The more he moves over me, the tighter the strings get. My nails dig into his shoulders as he continues to watch the myriad of expressions I must be giving him as he unravels me thrust by thrust.

Then it hits. It hits hard.

Those strings break, and euphoria crackles across my body like a bomb that detonates in my core and explodes outward. It rolls across me, curling my toes, flashing behind my eyelids that shut at some point, and licks across my skin like hot, incredible flames.

When I cry out and thrash beneath him wildly, his rhythm changes, becoming more urgent. I hold on as he drags out my orgasm in a way I didn't know was possible, and then he grunts, his hips jerking against me as he finds his own little version of heaven. At least I hope he feels this good.

Boneless and spent, my arms fall away from him as he drops to my body and kisses a trail down my neck. Definitely moving too fast, but I don't care. We're doomed anyway.

The Risk

The monster never gets the prince. It's always the sweet and innocent princess who wins.

My hands come up, and my fingers twist in his hair, enjoying this feeling while it lasts.

"I plan on a round two, but I'm not Superman. Just give me a few minutes, and I'll make sure you want to do this a lot more," he says against my neck, still nipping and kissing the flesh.

A smile curves my lips, and I sigh happily under him.

"I want to do this all the time."

He chuckles against me, and I find myself hugging him, even though I don't know when it started. He holds me to him, hugging me back.

"Good," he says against me. "Because that was fucking perfect."

It is perfect. Which is why I need to kill the monitoring channel in the living room so that it doesn't work, lock my murder room, and make sure all my weapons stay in there from now on.

Chapter 9

I never came upon any of my discoveries through the process of rational thinking.
—Albert Einstein

Logan

"You got laid," Craig says as I walk in, holding my coffee that I barely managed to get in time this morning.

I forgot what it was like to lose myself in a girl. And I know I've never lost myself in someone so much as I did last night and this morning. Lana is the most unexpected surprise of my life.

I keep waiting to find a flaw, but can't seem to find one. No one can be that perfect. Not that I want to jinx it. I also don't want to find out she's married or something. So I'm close to doing the unthinkable, because she has my head all kinds of fucked up.

"Maybe," I tell him, smirking when he groans.

"The Ice Princess took you but not me?" he asks as I drop to my desk chair and pull up the databases I need.

"It drives you that crazy she didn't eat up your *charm*," I drawl.

"There's a reason I'm the face of this department, and it isn't because I'm the best looking—though we both know I am. The point is, girls eat me up. Women, mothers, daughters, aunts, sisters, nieces... We fuck up, and I explain it away with a charming smile and an 'aww shucks' sort of attitude while throwing in a deep sense of remorse. Anything and everything will be forgiven if you have the right face. It's the truth. Humans are shallow—all of us. Pardon

The Risk

me for finding it a little suspect that she literally had zero interest in me, yet turns around and fucks you."

"I think Logan is way hotter than you," Hadley chimes in, coming to prop up beside me as Craig scowls at her. "And despite what you think, not all women are that shallow. Most of us find someone attractive if they have the right qualities."

"Bullshit," Craig scoffs. "I've done plenty of research on the matter. I'm not just talking out my ass."

I roll my eyes as they continue to bicker, and I start my search. No marriage certificate. No divorce. No children—not that I'd mind, but I'd still like to know. No…living relatives… Shit.

No one? She has no one at all? I already know she doesn't have any personal social media. Just her business profiles, even though there's no mention of her partner on any of them.

I don't dig any deeper than that. I feel like I've invaded her privacy enough. Everything else needs to be things she tells me when she's ready—like the car accident that scarred her.

It must have been a bad wreck, considering one scar travels from her left hip to her right breast. Another one is on her right side, jagged and large. They're old. I could tell from looking at them.

I should have shown her my scars, but I was too busy exploring her body the rest of the night to give her time to explore mine. Every time she tried, I lost control, feeling her hands on me seemed to turn me into a horny teenager all over again.

"You have serious trust issues," Hadley says, drawing me out of my own head.

I notice Craig is gone, but Hadley is reading the latest search over my shoulder. I close out of it and shrug.

"You had me research her background for priors, and now you're checking her facts?"

She cocks an eyebrow at me.

"Ever met someone too good to be true? I was almost late for

61

work this morning because I couldn't seem to pry myself away from her. She literally has no flaws. She's beautiful, smart, sassy, whimsical, and onboard with my hectic schedule, even though most girls immediately have an issue with it. She hasn't once gotten annoyed with me having to cancel things. I showed up at her place unannounced, and she was twice as perfect as I thought possible. So yeah...I can't help but be worried, because a guy can fall fast for a girl like that."

She rolls her eyes and mocks a gag, so I flip her off and start pulling up the latest case files.

"Everyone has flaws. You're just in the honeymoon phase. Eventually she will get annoyed with cancellations and unavailability. Just like you'll eventually start noticing things she does that irritate you. Right now is the shiny happy part that everyone *loves*. It's why so many people get married after barely knowing each other. It's also why they get divorced when they do know each other."

She laughs, and I lean back, mulling that over. I don't remember the 'honeymoon' phase being this damn good in the past.

"I'm overanalyzing this," I say on a sigh.

"It's your nature. It's what makes you good at this job. But I'm telling you, right now the girl could fart out toxic waste that had you pulling on a mask, and you'd think it was cute. It's part of the phase."

She claps me on the shoulder as she laughs and walks away, and I look down as I get a text.

LANA: Your boxers are comfortable.

ME: You're wearing them? Didn't know I left them behind.

LANA: I figured you did it on purpose. So you'd have a reason to come back.

ME: Already got a reason to come back.

The Risk

LANA: Now you have two...

There's a picture attached to the last message of her from the waist down, definitely wearing my boxers. I run a hand through my hair, hating the fact I don't want to be at work for the first time ever. I've always loved the job, yet a girl I barely know has me tempted to take my first ever sick day.

ME: Keep them on. I'll be back tonight, and I want to see them in person.

LANA: Lucky for you I have no plans. And I'll just be wearing these when you get here.

Groaning in frustration, I put my phone away, and I hurry through some of the slim new leads. The hotline tips get more ridiculous every day. The Boogeyman case is getting about as cold as my murder/mutilation case.

Several other cases are on the backburner, since no new murders have popped out. The ones that kill once or twice a year are twice as hard to find. Our only hot case is a murder/robbery serial.

I work, looking through some of the leads, examining the same photos as always. After two hours, I'm at the murder board, still trying to piece together what makes these women the targets.

None of them are overtly rich. They all have different family backgrounds. Different ethnicities. Different hair colors.

Though they were all attractive, there was no rape as incentive. Impotence is a possible in our profile, but...there's something else that is driving him. There's a reason why he selects and stalks these particular women.

My eyes look to their eyes, then their noses, then their mouths... Something clicks, and my heartbeat picks up.

Just as Hadley walks by, I grab her wrist, stopping her as my eyes narrow on one piece of evidence we haven't been able to figure out.

"The lab analyzed that clay you found in the apartment, right?" I ask, lost in thought.

She nods. "Yeah. Nothing special about it. You could buy it at any arts and crafts store. And no one knows why it was there. It wasn't found on the victim or anywhere else in the apartment. They think the unsub brought it in on his shoes or clothes."

"And the faces had all been thoroughly cleaned then bleached. The hair had also been shaven off and the head was cleaned then bleached," I state, still doing the math.

"Yes... Why?"

I look past her to where Donny is.

"Donny, look up art galleries in the area of the robberies/murders."

He looks perplexed, but starts typing.

"Hadley, I need you to get on all the art sites you can find and see if anyone is selling bronze sculptures of faces. Narrow them down to the ones who started in the past four months, when the killings started," I go on, walking toward Donny's desk.

I turn to see her still standing there, confused.

"Now!" I urge her, and she scrambles to her desk.

Donny is typing furiously when I come up behind him. "Four in the area. None are selling bronze sculptures of faces," he says, frowning. "Or was I supposed to be looking for something different than Hadley?"

"Call each one and ask if anyone tried to sell them the bronze sculptures. It'll be faces only."

He picks up his phone to do as I ask, and I go back to my computer, pulling up the program I need. I place all the victims' pictures in the spots, and after a few keystrokes, my suspicions are confirmed.

The Risk

"Symmetry," I say on a long breath.

"What?" Craig asks, coming to look over my shoulder.

"He's choosing them because of the symmetry of their faces. Perfect symmetry, which is supposed to be very rare, if not impossible. He's choosing them because they have it, and he's using their faces to mold art. He's probably trying to sell it, and he's fixated on anyone who has a symmetrical face. Women in particular. He may have a da Vinci fixation as well."

My eyes scan the room, and I spot Lisa clipping her fingernails.

"Lisa, look at anyone in the comfort zone who might have ordered a lot of Leonardo da Vinci prints, or books on da Vinci. Focus primarily on anything revolving around the Vitruvian Man. The unsub would most likely be obsessed with that work."

"And you think this because?" Craig asks, confused.

"Call it a gut feeling. We've solved a lot of cases with my gut."

"Yeah, that's why you keep getting promoted. But how the hell do you fit da Vinci in with clay, robberies, and shaved heads with bleach poured on them?"

"The bleach is a forensic countermeasure, just as shaving and removing all the hair then bleaching the head. He's removing all traces of the clay from the body. The hair is probably being saved for the sculpture too. Not all artists can paint or draw."

"I'm lost," Craig goes on.

"Da Vinci wasn't just famous for his intellect or paintings. There were large sculptures he created that have historians buzzing too. He drew it first, then he molded it from clay or beeswax—depends on which version of the story you hear. From there, he cast it in bronze to create another masterpiece. A man who is fixated on him and symmetry, but can't draw or create art from nothing? That's who we're looking for."

"Nothing," Hadley says, looking frustrated. "Several molds are made from numerous things, but no bronze. Does it have to be bronze?" she asks.

65

"Yes," I say, convinced this is the right lead to chase. "It explains the robberies. He'd sell the valuables he stole to buy the amount of bronze he needs. It's not cheap."

"We've scoured pawn shops and internet sites looking for anyone selling that stuff though," Donny interjects.

"The right shady pawn dealer wouldn't give a damn if we were asking about it, and would lie to keep from turning it over and losing that profit. If this guy is using forensic counter measures, then he's done his homework on where to sell."

Donny resumes his phone calls, and I do something that probably won't help. I pull up the buy, sell, and trade site that Lana runs. She mentioned last night that she leaves things up for a month after they sell with a SOLD sign on it to keep people from asking what happened to it.

I scroll through the jewelry section, since that's what was mostly stolen. But nothing is on there. Maybe I was just looking for an excuse to speak to her. Because I've got it bad and it's pathetic.

"Got something!" Donny says, drawing all of our attention as he returns to the conversation he's having on the phone. "Yes. Did he leave a number or an address to reach him?"

He scribbles something down as we all stand. I put my jacket on and holster my gun. Looks like I'm going to need my go-bag again. Fortunately it has several pairs of clothes.

He hangs up and holds up the paper.

"They've got a guy who has come into two of the four places trying to sell them a 'growing' set of bronze heads."

"Looks like we're flying to New York," Craig says, eyeing me like I'm a weird fucking unicorn. "And I guess we're getting the damn chopper since the department jet is already out on call. Why can't we get our own private jet like they have in the movies and stuff?"

Hadely snorts, and they all talk amongst themselves as I pull out my phone and make a call that actually sucks.

The Risk

"Yes, I'm still wearing the boxers. And eating ice cream," Lana says, sounding bright and fucking giddy.

I hate my timing now. Usually I'm a hell of a lot more excited about a break in a case than this.

"I wish I could be there to see it," I say on a long breath as I grab my vest and other necessities, shoving them into my bag.

"You have to cancel," she says simply, her voice devoid of any emotion for me to read.

"I'm sorry." I have a feeling I'll get used to saying those two words if she sticks around long enough to hear them time after time. "We got a break in the case today. At least I hope so. I'm on my way out of town right now."

"Don't be sorry, Logan. You have a job—an important one. I admire you and what you do. You put monsters away, and I believe you're actually looking for the right man instead of just another merit on your resume."

That's a weird thing to say.

"I definitely look for the right man. What do you mean by that?"

"It's just that…I studied a lot of old cases when I went to college. I took criminology classes. It seemed like a lot of arrests were rushed just to close a case and add another gold star to a stellar reputation. If the killings would stop, people would assume the killers were locked up. If the killings reoccurred, they'd call it a copycat instead of owning the possibility they closed the case with the wrong suspect behind bars."

I'm not sure what cases she studied. They don't tarnish the reputation of the FBI in those classes. If anything, they sing praises to our guys.

"So you took criminology? But you didn't join law enforcement?"

"Decided I didn't have the stomach for it," she says dryly. "Blood and guts churn it."

I definitely don't picture her as someone who could handle the shit I've seen if she has a weak stomach.

"Will you be able to text or call when you're gone?" she asks hopefully.

"Definitely. I'll probably text you from the chopper to apologize again."

"Seriously, don't apologize. Ever. You make a difference. I'd have to be a selfish bitch to expect you to be at my side when someone needs saving. Go be awesome and text when you can."

I stop and lean against the wall of the stairwell, smiling at nothing.

"Have I told you lately that you're perfect?"

She laughs then coughs to smother the laugh. "Trust me when I say I'm on the opposite end of the spectrum from perfection."

"Oh? Will I see these flaws of yours one day?"

She grows quiet for so long that I check to make sure the line hasn't gone dead. Finally, she answers.

"I pray that day never comes," she says quietly. "Now go catch a bad guy. Is it safe to tell me the town so I can watch the news for you? I know you said you were sometimes on the news. If it's against the rules, then don't tell me, because I'd never ask you—"

"I'll be in New York. I'm sure it'll be on all the major channels if this pans out. It's rare to get a break this big, but it could all be wrong. I'm going on a profile that I built myself just a few moments ago. For the record, I'm not supposed to tell anyone."

"Then why did you tell me?" she scolds.

"Because I want you to be *someone* one day."

I don't tell her that I've thoroughly checked her out to make sure she wasn't any type of lawbreaking heathen or anything. Best if this trust thing starts now.

"Well, someday, I hope I am someone. Until then, don't tell me

The Risk

things you're not supposed to."

"Why?" I ask, amused that she's so angry about this.

"Because I respect you. And I never want you to think I expect more than I should. This is about us. Not your job. Please. Promise me you won't ever tell me things you're not supposed to."

Yeah… Told you she's fucking perfect.

"Deal, pretty girl. Keep my boxers warm. I'll text you or call you later."

"Logan?"

"Yeah?"

"Come back in one piece no matter what you have to do in order to make that happen. That's the only thing I'll ever expect. Survive."

A slow smile tugs at the corners of my mouth. "That I can promise."

Chapter 10

Truth is what stands the test of experience.
— Albert Einstein

Lana

"You're dating a fucking FBI agent?" Jake blares over the phone, and I groan, pulling it away from my ear as I park at the restaurant across the street from where Tyler is.

I'm starving, and we can't get a visual inside this office, so I'll stalk from here, since this is where he has reservations.

Right now, this blonde wig is itching the crap out of me, and this red lipstick is definitely causing me to stick out. Add both in with the dark sunglasses and skin tight dress that I'm wearing, and I look nothing like Lana Myers, just in case.

"I already explained how it happened," I tell Jake, wishing I had just kept the confession out of it.

"And you're in New York, where *he* also happens to be."

"Tyler is here, which is why I'm here. He took an unscheduled trip up here, so I got worried he was coming to see one of the others, since Lawrence is the next target and he's also here. He has lunch reservations for two, Jake."

He blows out a heavy breath. "New York is a long way from West Virginia. What's he doing there?"

"I don't know. He went into the same office where Lawrence works."

"The media hasn't gotten ahold of the story."

The Risk

"Yeah, but that doesn't mean they haven't heard several of their friends died recently."

He grows quiet, and I stare out at the restaurant. Tyler has reservations for two here at lunch. That much I found out from the cloned phone. But he hasn't been texting Lawrence. I'm not sure who he's texting.

"Jake? You still there?"

"No," he says, sounding muffled. "I'm right beside you."

I look out my window to find a guy with a goatee, dark glasses, and a stick... I'm not sure what it's called, but it looks suspiciously like the stick the seeing impaired would use to feel their way around. His hair has also been bleached blonde.

I guess we're both incognito.

I climb out of the car, arching an eyebrow at him. "Cowabunga?"

He snorts, but then his lips thin.

"So you decided to come to New York City without telling me?" I ask, crossing my arms over my chest.

He shrugs carelessly. "Same thing you essentially did. I have the same phone you do, remember? I knew you'd be heading out."

He points a finger at me.

"Don't think you're off the hook over this FBI boyfriend thing. That conversation is paused — not over."

I groan, and he smirks as he holds his arm out for me to take.

He looks all classy in his suit. With the way I'm dressed, I look like his high-paid hooker.

"You look good, by the way," he whispers as he guides me down the sidewalk.

"High praise coming from a man who's supposed to be blind," I say with a sweet smile.

He restrains a smile as we walk inside. "Reservation for

Demarco," I tell the hostess. "We requested the terrace, since it's so beautiful outside today."

Just like Tyler requested.

She beams at me, treating me like I don't resemble a call girl with her John. "Of course. Right this way," she says, refraining from calling me Mrs. Demarco in case it's the name of my *date*.

So I guess they're used to this sort of thing.

"You're making me look like a hooker," I hiss under my breath.

Jake covers a laugh with a forced cough, and I stop myself from kicking him with my stiletto heel.

"Pretty sure you did that all by yourself. Trying to stand out?"

"Trying to look the opposite of me," I whisper.

"Good job."

"Ha," I grumble as the sweet hostess seats us.

She flashes all of her beautifully white teeth at us in the best genuine smile I've seen. Maybe she's just a friendly little perky thing.

"Your waiter will be with you momentarily. Enjoy your lunch," she says, still not using names.

As she glides away, I turn my attention on Jake. His glasses have tinted sides that cover his eyes completely, allowing him to look wherever he wants without people noticing where his eyes are directed from the side.

"Clever," I note in a mock, deep southern drawl, and he grins.

"Thought you'd appreciate it," he says, adjusting his glasses for emphasis.

Our table is private enough to speak without anyone overhearing, but I look around for any cameras that might overhear.

"Two above us," Jake says, not having to guess about why I'm looking around. "I can hear those birds like I can hear an alarm going off."

The Risk

So talk in code or type a text. Got it.

They must have audio if he's hinting for me to be silent.

"You're right. Two birds are up there. I'll never understand how you do that," I tell him, keeping with the southern accent I've accidentally committed to.

"I still love your accent," he tells me, grinning.

Asshole.

I look over just as Tyler walks in, and my stomach hits my toes when I see Lawrence with him. They get seated two tables over, and Jake hands me something under the table. I feel it and know exactly what it is.

With subtlety, I pretend as though my earring is loose, and lift my hand to pretend to fix it under the long mane of blonde hair that hides my ears perfectly. Instead of touching the earring, I put in the small ear piece that Jake just gave me.

I pet Jake's hand like an affectionate little hooker, and pretend to devote all my attention to him. "I assume you'll tell me all about your day after we eat?" he asks, sticking with code-speak.

"You know it, darlin'."

He barely stops himself from laughing, but my smile falls away when I hear Tyler and Lawrence speaking quietly to each other.

The earpiece amplifies their words as long as it's facing what I want to hear, so I keep my head angled toward Jake like I'm staring at him affectionately.

"It has to be Dev, man. There's no one else who'd want to do something to us for that night," Tyler is saying.

So they *are* meeting about me. I guess the cat's out of the bag.

"There's no way," Lawrence scoffs dismissively.

"He had a breakdown two nights later and said we took it too far. He fucking cried, dude. Cried like a little bitch. Said we were sick for what we did to them. It's him. That fucker has finally cracked and now he's doing this. He thinks he's innocent since he didn't get his dick dirty that night, and now he's picking us off one by one."

From the corner of my eye, I notice Lawrence shaking his head. I run my hand up and down Jake's arm, pretending to be lost in thought as I read the menu aloud to him, but really all my attention is caught up in the conversation across from us.

"No. It's not him. I talked to his sister, and she said he's been in Mexico for the past two months on a church mission thing."

Dev is the only one I'm not sure what to do with, to be honest. He's the only one who showed remorse, and they did essentially force him to be there that night. He wasn't a victim, by any means. He could have spoken up and said something…anything.

Currently, he's not on my kill list. But he is in the ten fingers column.

Jake gets tired of not hearing, so he discreetly lifts his hand and places another sound amplifier in his ear. It's small enough to not be seen as long as no one stares directly into his ear. Even then, they might assume it's a hearing aid instead of a listening device.

"I'm telling you it's not him. Trust me. I doubt he's even heard anything about this, and Melissa sent me pictures of him from the church mission he's on. He's been texting her daily with updates and such," Lawrence argues.

"Think Melissa is just covering for him? She is his fucking sister."

"She's had a crush on me since we were kids. Trust me, she'd be over that crush if she had any idea what we did, unless she's into that sort of thing. In which case she'd be outing her brother to us if it was him. Either way, she's not covering for him."

"I think it's him. There's no one else it could be."

Lawrence looks around, letting his gaze linger on our table for a fleeting second, and then his gaze moves on, taking in the few people out on the terrace before settling his attention back on Tyler.

The Risk

"It's not him. The night he freaked out, who do you think got him back in line?"

Tyler looks confused.

Our waitress has dropped off some bread, and Jake is ordering for us, so it's harder to hear with so many people so close speaking at once. I strain, making sure I don't miss anything as I force myself to chew on a piece of bread, finding my appetite to be sorely lacking.

"What'd you do?" I hear Tyler ask.

"I told him the same thing that happened to Victoria would happen to Melissa if he ever said a word. After that, they left town, and he started preaching the gospel. That's how he sought penance. He's not out killing people, for fuck's sake," Lawrence hisses.

He may have just saved Dev ten fingers.

And a tongue. His tongue was going to be gone too. It was a special column I was going to draw up just for him.

"Then who else is there?"

"I think that's pretty obvious, don't you?"

"No."

Lawrence slaps his head like he's exasperated. They're acting like this is normal terrace conversation for a late lunch. I assume it's why they picked a restaurant that doesn't have a lot of terrace traffic.

Lawrence has a roommate. Tyler has a wife. I get why they didn't meet up at their homes to discuss this, but why not do it over the phone?

"The entire town hated them after what their father did. Think of the one person who didn't hate them. Here's a hint: his father was their father's lawyer."

Tyler shakes his head immediately.

"No. I saw Jacob two years ago. Ran into him at a company thing, and he fist bumped me. Even told me to call and hang out some time. If he'd known, he would have at least taken a swing. I'm sure they both died before he ever heard the truth. And he left town after that, so it's not like he was around for the rumors."

Lawrence sits back, now looking confused. Jake squeezes my hand a little too hard.

I remember that run-in. Jake does freelance computer work, and Tyler was working closer to where Jake lives now at that time. It was all Jake could do not to kill him, but he knew we had a plan, and he knew this revenge was mine. He knew he had a part to play, but his part was to be the brains. My part was to be their worst nightmare.

"Besides," Tyler goes on, "he's in a wheelchair these days. Some motorcycle wreck put him in the chair a few years ago."

Jake nudges my foot with his, a calculated grin on his lips. We've thought of everything.

"Then I don't know anyone else who would be enraged over a rapist's whore daughter and fag son," Lawrence says coldly.

My stomach churns hearing the way he refers to my brother. My good, honest, strong, loving, incredible brother who never deserved to be mutilated and… So much happened that he never deserved.

Because of them, I was left without anyone. Because of them, the best man who has ever walked the face of the earth died before he could light the world with his smile.

And they think it's okay because he was gay. They think it's okay because I'd had sex with two guys before that night.

They think it makes it alright to punish us so brutally for loving our father…

Jake clears his throat, and I realize that it's my grip that is too tight now. My nails are cutting into his hand.

Loosening my grip, I continue to listen, wondering how much more I can take before I slice both of their throats right now.

Lawrence may die sooner than I planned. I may tie him up with Tyler and let them cry to each other while I cut them both to pieces.

The Risk

"Maybe it's not even related," Lawrence says with a shrug. "Just don't let anyone in your house for a while, and tell your wife to do the same. I'm getting a security system installed in my apartment. You should too. Not that it matters. According to Dad, they're being let in, because there's no sign of a break in."

"Fuck," Tyler hisses. "Fine. I'll get something installed."

Keyless entry locks are my best friends. It's easy to catch the code being punched in on camera. It's also easy to grab a set of keys and have a copy made if they use traditional locks. It just looks like I'm being invited in.

One more thing to keep them off a dead girl's trail.

He grabs a bite of his bread, and I find myself dizzy. It's the first time I haven't heard them begging for forgiveness when this subject gets brought up. Usually it's not brought up until I have a knife pressed to their skin.

They don't have the balls to say this kind of shit when I'm the one making them cry for mercy, beg for forgiveness, and plead for their lives. I've never been more eager to get to the fun part.

Their conversation shifts to the best security systems to get, and I try to calm myself down before I slit both their throats and dicks in the middle of a restaurant.

"I think we should probably consider getting two birds for the new house. What do you think?" Jake asks, apparently thinking the same damn thing I am.

"Think we could do it on such short notice?" I ask him, smiling sweetly even though the taste of vengeance is potent on my tongue.

"I think so. Maybe an extra week at most. Could probably find a better place for them too, just to be safe."

There's a storm shelter behind Tyler's old house that is still up for sale. I could put them both in there, and Jake could do something to keep any realtors from walking in on me while I'm busy killing two boys at once.

"I'm not as hungry as I thought I was, dearest," Jake tells me when the waitress drops off our food.

"Me neither," I say, stabbing my steak much harder than necessary.

Tyler and Lawrence never say anything else worth hearing again. Mostly I hear a few people around them taking bets on if I'm really a hooker or not.

Just as Tyler starts to leave, Lawrence stops him.

"Get a burner phone like I did. Anything else comes up, call me from that phone. No more personal phone calls. Got it?"

So he got a burner phone? How'd we miss that?

Tyler nods, and Jake and I exchange a look.

"If we find out who it is, we don't need anything linking it back to us when we take matters into our own hands. Understood?" Lawrence asks.

"I'd love to see them fucking try," Jake whispers.

My lips twitch. I've never been this excited to kill someone.

We let Tyler be gone for a while before we stand. As we walk past Lawrence's table, his hand shoots up, grabbing my wrist. My stomach roils and my heart hammers in my chest as I fight all my instincts not to rip his throat out here and now.

I look down, glaring at him.

The bastard winks up at me and hands me a card that I take, trying to get away from him.

"Call me sometime, sweetheart. A girl who looks like you needs someone to appreciate all those sights."

I give him a dazzling smile, wink at him, and start walking again, gently brushing his hand away. Oh, I'll give him something to look at. I'll paint the walls with his and Tyler's blood, and I'll let them bleed out as they watch.

It'll be so pretty.

Just as we reach the sidewalk, I stumble over my own feet,

The Risk

watching in disbelief as a SUV rolls up to the curb. Hissing out a breath, I step closer to Jake, practically crawling against his side as Logan hops out.

New York City is way too freaking big for this to be happening.

There's a food truck on the curb, and he and the Mr. Arrogant guy get out to go over there, both smiling like it's a great day. They're in street clothes—jeans and t-shirts. Not their typical suits or anything else. Did I miss something?

"What?" Jake whispers, looking at them then me.

"Boyfriend," I whisper back.

He wheezes out a breath before cursing, and he tugs me along to my car (which is not registered in my name or anything) that is parked way too close to them. It's one of my many 'burner' cars.

The universe is trying to send me mixed signals. First it saves Dev's fingers and tongue. Then it condemns two men to a more brutal death after I discover more than I thought possible from one late lunch. Now it's tossing me directly in front of the man of my dreams?

"You're going to end up running the FBI. That was absolutely amazing," Mr. Arrogant says, genuine awe in his tone as he speaks to Logan.

"That's not what I'm after. I'm just glad we provoked a damn confession. Makes getting home happen that much quicker."

Mr. Arrogant groans while Jake continues to try and draw me toward the car. My ear piece is still in, making their conversation very easy to follow despite the noises on the street. Well, as long as I keep it directed solely at them, which has me walking with my head cocked.

"Back home to the Ice Queen?" the guy says, a touch of snark in his tone.

I bet that's Carter. Or was it Chris? Craig? I can't remember.

Logan's smile is so damn beautiful. "Yeah. Don't be jealous."

79

C-Name guy rolls his eyes, and I watch like a swooning girl on the sidewalk as I drag my feet in my stilettos. My heart was ripped out moments ago, but just seeing Logan is soothing the burn.

"When are you going back?" C-Name guy asks.

"As soon as we know for sure the evidence has followed proper chains of command and is being sealed tight. I don't want this one to ever get away."

"Fucking da Vinci. The shit in your head is scary."

I have no idea what that means.

"You haven't seen half the shit in my head, Craig. I need to call my girl, so order me a burger."

Shit!

I push my phone to silent, hating that I have to let it go to voicemail as Jake opens the door to my car. I get in, remove the earpiece, and let my heart sink when Logan calls. Sighing, I toss my phone aside as I stare up at Jake, who is glaring down at me.

"We'll talk about this later. My place as soon as you can make it."

Nodding, I let him shut my door, and I crank my car. I have two kills to plan, a boyfriend to see, and a best friend to un-piss off. And not in that order.

I'm just the typical American woman.

Or is it the typical American Psycho?

Chapter 11

The only reason for time is so that everything doesn't happen at once.
—Albert Einstein

Logan

"So your girl is like totally loaded," Hadley says, plopping down beside me.

"You're looking into her financials?" I ask incredulously. "That's an invasion of privacy!"

"Meh, I just peeked. She's not a suspect or anything, so I'm not breaking any big rules."

"Just the law," I state dryly.

She grins. "I was recruited for my mad skills with computers and shutting down websites that shouldn't be open. I was placed up here for my forensics expertise. Never once was I wanted for my pristine moral compass. And it was just a little peek. Honestly. But seriously, she's like majorly rich. What's her house like?"

Groaning, I shake my head. Hadley definitely isn't FBI because she's a saint with a badge. She's FBI because it was prison or work with us.

"Don't tell anyone else you did this," I mumble, finishing up the last of the case file that is now ready for the DA.

"Duh," she says, smirking. "So what's her house like? I really want to know."

"Nothing flashy. It's a two story white home that looks nice enough. She hasn't lived there long, so there's no art or anything on the walls. Floors are hardwood throughout, but no marble statues or gold banisters, if that's what you're asking. And her driveway looks like something out of Sleepy Hollow that doesn't at all match the sweet house at the end."

She frowns like she's disappointed. "I wanted mansions and swans in a lake. Damn. Why have all that money if you don't have a nice home?"

"Some people are humble, Hadley. I wouldn't have even known she was rich."

Talking about Lana gets me thinking about her again after I've just stopped. I'm worried I'm demonstrating obsessive behaviors. Which I don't know if I like or not.

She hasn't answered my calls all day, and my texts haven't been responded to either. So I'm surprised when I finally get an answer.

LANA: SORRY!!! My work got in the way this time. Been crazy busy and only had my business phone with me. Just got back into town a few minutes ago.

I didn't know she had a business phone or that she went on a business meeting. But I'm relieved to know I haven't been blown off.

"Is that her?" Hadley asks, reminding me she's still lurking.

"Go away, Hadley. She doesn't have swans in a lake."

She mutters something about a waste before sulking and walking off.

I start to text her, but decide I'd rather hear her voice instead, so I call as I head out to my car.

"Hey!" she answers, sounding a little out of breath. "Again, I'm sorry. I was really busy earlier, and like I said, I didn't have my phone, and—"

The Risk

"Don't apologize. Just wondering when I can see you again. I'm back home. A case is closed, so I'll have a couple of days off as a reward. Why do you sound out of breath?"

"Just finished a necessary workout. And I happen to have exactly two days off as well. My business partner is reworking some things so that we can squeeze in a little extra business this month."

She never talks about her business, and now Hadley has put it into my mind. If she's so wealthy, why does she do so much legwork herself? Why not hire people?

"So we have two days with each other?" I muse, putting a few of the unsolved files in my bag.

"Yes. And I still have your boxers. In fact, as soon as I finish showering, I'm going to put them on."

"Any chance I can come over?"

"That was me inviting you over," she says dryly. "I really suck at this subtlety thing, huh?"

Grinning, I get in my car and start backing out, ready to have some time to unwind. I'd like to get some fresh clothes from my house, but that would take longer.

"Wait! I just thought of something. What if I come to your house? You've seen mine. Show me yours."

Well, that solves that problem.

"It's nothing special, but I'd love for you to see my bedroom."

She laughs under her breath. "I might leave my panties behind as a reason to return."

"I'm not wearing them and eating ice cream," I say, loving the way that makes her laugh.

"Good to know. If you'll give me the address, I'll shower and meet you there. Are you home now?"

"I'm just leaving the office."

"Okay. Then I'll hurry and get ready. Send me the address,

Agent Bennett.

"Back to Agent Bennett?"

"I'll call you Logan later on tonight," she quips, causing an immediate reaction from the wayward appendage that has forgotten I'm closer to thirty than eighteen.

"See you soon."

I hang up and shoot her a text with the address. I probably need a shower too, so at least I'll have time. I also decide to stop and pick up something to cook so that we don't have to leave to go anywhere. We have two solid days, and all I want to do is spend every second getting this addiction under control.

I hurry through the motions of buying groceries, load down my back hatch, and rush home. My phone is ringing as soon as I step through the door of my house. I groan when I see it's Craig.

"Please don't tell me we already have to come back in."

"Well, hello to you, SSA Logan Bennett. I guess that pussy is golden if the company man himself doesn't want to come back to work."

"Craig, if you want to remain pretty in front of the cameras, I'd suggest refraining from speaking about Lana's pussy anymore."

"Right. Got it. Anyway, you told me to call if any new leads came in. Hadley finally figured out the type of knife used by the Boogeyman in his kills. I'm forwarding you a picture."

"Thanks," I grumble, not feeling as appreciative as I should.

"No worries, Logan. No one expects you to come back in tonight or even tomorrow. You closed a major case and just in time to save a girl's life. And hell, you pretty much did it on your own today. No one else would have fucking pieced together a da Vinci fixation from finding clay."

"There were other factors," I point out.

"Yes. Symmetry," he says flatly.

The Risk

"And more."

"I'll let you get back to your two days of peace."

He hangs up just as a text comes through from Lana.

LANA: My GPS says I should be there in thirty minutes. I'm going to see if I can shave a few minutes off that.

A smile spreads as I text her back.

ME: No texting while driving.

LANA: Threatening to arrest me?

Laughing, I put my phone away. Lana is not the girl I first pegged as detached. Lonely, perhaps. But not detached. I've come to realize she's just like me. Solitary but not devoid of possibilities.

After putting all my groceries where they belong, I start removing my shirt, then grimace when I smell the exhaust fumes from the chopper all over me. How did I not realize how bad I reek?

I start to head to the shower, but my phone chimes with a message. Craig has delivered the picture he promised, and the knife is nothing special. But at least we know the model and type to tell the police to search for if the time ever comes.

Not if. *When*. I will catch this bastard.

Studying the photo of the supposed murder weapon has me restudying the case for so long that I don't even realize how much time has passed until there's a knock on my door.

Fuck me.

It's already been thirty minutes, and I've been staring at a case instead of showering off the day's stench.

I jog to the door, internally cursing myself the whole time. When I swing open the door, a flurry of dark hair is all I glimpse before Lana is on me, her lips crashing against mine.

I sure as hell don't protest as I drink her in, tasting her, smelling how incredible... Ah hell.

Reluctantly, I break the kiss, and she steps back, grinning at me. I love that smile and how freely she gives it.

"I smell like shit."

She laughs while shaking her head. "You smell like... I don't know what that smell is to be honest."

"Helicopter. I'll run through the shower, and we will pick this back up where we left off. Make yourself comfortable. I won't take long."

"I don't mind the smell," she says, biting that damn lower lip that has my cock protesting my hygienic needs.

"Five minutes. That's all I'll take."

She bats those long lashes, her grin spreading as she looks around my house, taking in all the sights. My gun is on top of the living room table, and she sidesteps it like it makes her uncomfortable.

"Safety is on," I tell her, winking before I jog to my bathroom and hurry through the motions of showering.

I toss on a pair of boxers after I finish drying off, and I head back out to find Lana at the kitchen island, looking over the Boogeyman case.

"This is brutal," she says, looking up at me with a frown. "Is this the guy you caught?"

"That's my fault. I shouldn't have left that out. You're not supposed to see that."

She frowns.

"Closed case files aren't as classified. Or at least that's what I've read."

"Old closed cases aren't classified. Recent ones are. But this isn't even a closed case. It's an active investigation that I should handle

The Risk

with more care than just leaving haphazardly lying around."

Her lips tense as she takes a long step away.

"I'm sorry. I didn't know. I just saw it and…I shouldn't have just started reading it. Sorry."

I shrug, pulling her to me by the waist, just needing to touch her. I had no idea how much I needed to touch her until she got here.

"Like I said, that's my fault. *But* since you've seen it, how about giving me your opinion."

Her eyebrows go up.

"*My* opinion? My opinion is that guy is sick. Women being raped and left to bleed out slowly by multiple stab wounds is vicious and… Anyway. That's my opinion."

"I meant your opinion about the type of suspect we might be looking for."

She purses her lips.

"I barely glimpsed it."

I pull her over to the file, and I spread out the sheets, including the new picture on my phone that I show her.

"You noted that he let them bleed out instead of saying he stabbed them to death. That's actually important to the profile. Now tell me your opinion."

"I don't want to get you into trouble, Logan. Don't show me things you're not supposed to, and stop telling me things you shouldn't."

She eyes me, scowling a little.

"Right now, there's not a lot they'd do to me if they found out I was sharing details with my girl. I'm a badass. Just read it and give me your thoughts."

A smile spreads over her lips for some reason, but she tucks her hair behind her ear and ducks her head before she begins reading over the files.

"That excites you?" I muse, remembering she said this stuff makes her stomach churn.

"You called me your girl," she says quietly.

My grin spreads as I lean over, brushing a kiss over her bare shoulder since she's wearing a camisole.

"As far as I'm concerned, you are."

She clears her throat, and I lean back, enjoying the hell out of the way she blushes.

Her face turns serious as she studies the file, taking in the details, and reading over it pretty damn quickly.

"At first glance, it looks like overkill because of all the stab wounds. But they're all shallow and not lethal on their own. He most likely does it while he rapes them, pushing the tip of the blade in just enough to draw blood. They get deeper as he goes, because it's part of the high he gets. Rape is usually about power."

"It's almost always about power," I amend. "Contrary to popular belief, there are very few sexual assault cases that have anything to do with sexual desires."

She nods absently, but I notice a distant look in her eyes. "He's a sadist. Relative to the case, he's most likely unable to orgasm without the life threatening pain he inflicts. Impotence was probably a factor in his psychotic break. Maybe he stumbled upon this feeling of euphoria by mistake, and he's escalated now to actually killing women. He gets high on the power, and gets off on the pain."

She blows out a breath as her hands tremble, and I start to apologize. She really can't handle seeing this shit, and it was stupid of me to even involve a civilian who hasn't been desensitized to the point of seeing them as dead bodies and facts instead of people and merciless assaults.

But she speaks before I can.

"He'd be unnoticeable to the world. Probably a blue-collared worker who doesn't draw any outward attention. He'd likely be

The Risk

unsocial, given the struggle he's had with impotence. It would have left him withdrawn because he'd have felt like he was lacking, emasculated even. Now he enjoys the shadows where he's dwelled because it allows him to hunt without being noticed."

Damn, she's good.

She flips another page. "In the beginning, there was a lot of rage—again, that stems from the impotence. Now there's a controlled method to his psychosis. He'll develop an immortal complex where he feels as though he's untouchable. I'd say a white male between the ages of twenty-five and forty. He's right handed, and he has the ability to blend in with the unremarkable. Possibly in the custodial field."

My eyebrows pinch together.

"You were dead on until the custodial field. We guessed someone in law enforcement or security, due to the fact he has been able to gain access to homes with no effort, and the cameras to the apartment buildings have been disabled each time."

She shakes her head. "He may have an understanding of security measures, but most custodial workers do. They come in after hours, spend long amounts of time talking with night shift guards or behind the scenes issues that no one else sees."

I narrow my eyes at her, studying her features as she looks up to meet my gaze.

"What makes you so sure you're right?"

She smirks before sliding a page in front of me. "How he cleaned up after himself. He shined the murder rooms up."

"Forensic countermeasure," I point out. "Most seasoned killers always clean up after themselves."

She nods. "I said *how* he cleaned up after himself. He didn't just clean. The room was spotless, and each surface was cleaned with an appropriate cleaner."

She points to a line. "Window cleaner for windows. No streaks left behind either, whereas it's noted the rest of the windows were dingy." She points to another line. "Hardwood floors were cleaned with hardwood cleaner. No streaks." She points to another line. "The tables were all shined with wood-safe cleanser. No streaks…"

As my head wraps around the facts I should have already caught, she goes on.

"My father was…um…friends with a janitor when I was younger. It's a habit, almost a compulsion, to use the appropriate cleaners for surfaces after so many years of training the mind to use those. If I were you, I'd look for custodial services in the area and check to see if these apartment buildings ever outsourced to individual cleaning companies."

I slide the paper closer, my eyes moving over all the facts. "We interviewed all employees and did background checks," I say absently. "And we considered the cleaning so thoroughly bit to be a case of OCD but ruled it out based on the fact there were different amounts of stab wounds, and they didn't clean anything other than the kill room."

"A lot of custodial services pay cash under the table because it's hard to keep workers. Some of them have a 'don't ask, don't tell' policy because they have to hire whatever walks in needing a job. The company keeps the majority of the money. Workers make crumbs in comparison. So cash under the table that isn't taxed is a big way to draw in more workers, and also keep from having to supply benefits to said employees. It's likely they never mentioned them because they didn't want to have to tell you that."

"You're a fucking genius," I groan.

I grab her face in both my hands and kiss her hard, even though I also want to throttle her at the same time.

"But now I have a call to make," I grumble, feeling her smile against my lips.

"Make your call. Catch a bad guy. Maybe the lead is solid and you can catch him before he kills again."

Reluctantly, I pull up my phone, and dial Hadley. She's going to fucking kill me.

The Risk

Chapter 12

We have to do the best we can. This is our sacred human responsibility.
—Albert Einstein

Lana

I won't lie and say it's not hypocritical to hope he catches the sicko who raped and killed all these women. It's hypocritical because I'm also hoping he never catches me for torturing and killing a string of men.

But it also feels good to listen to him animatedly tell someone this amazing new lead. I'm worried and shocked when he tells Hadley it's me who inspired this new lead. He shouldn't tell them he let his *girl* give him that info on a case I was never supposed to see.

Maybe the fact he called me *his* anything has the butterflies stirring. It's definitely something. The fact he sounds proud of me also makes me feel…*good*. That word again.

My phone rings as he continues to talk to someone else, and I head outside to answer it when I see it's Jake. My eyes stay on the window, keeping up with Logan.

"Hey. Any luck?"

"Lots of luck. I hate rushing this date the way we're going to, but I'm going to help you on these."

My eyebrows go up in surprise.

"Like in person? You're going to do this too?"

The Risk

"Just this once, and only for the securing part."

"No. You can't. You threw up when I tried to give you details, Jake."

"You have no idea how much I wish I had your ability to kill without hesitance," he says quietly, an edge to his tone.

"But you don't," I remind him, still watching to make sure Logan can't overhear me.

"Doesn't matter. I can't risk you taking on something like this alone."

"I can't talk about this right now," I say on almost a whisper when I see Logan hanging up his phone and running a hand through his hair.

"Shit. You're with him? That's still a discussion we need to have."

"I moved my murder room in that secret room you built me years ago."

"You think that's enough to keep a profiler from figuring out you're slowly killing off a list of people?" he asks dryly.

I heave out a heavy breath as I continue to watch Logan through the window. He looks around, then moves to grab a glass.

"You know how it's easy for me to do what I do?"

"Because of what they did to you two," he says, his voice barely above a broken whisper.

"No, Jake. It's because there's nothing but hatred inside of me that's been driving me since I was able to do something other than curl in a corner in fear of them finding me again. I never thought anything else would drive me. I thought after this was over…I had nothing to look forward to after I killed them all. Now… Now there's hope. I never realized the power of hope until he suddenly appeared in my life as though the universe was giving me a gift at the wrong time."

He exhales harshly, and I sag backwards a little.

"I'm glad to hear you have hope, Lana. Really. I am. Just... Just couldn't you have found it with someone who couldn't toss your ass in prison?"

His tone ends on a joking note, but the seriousness of the situation is still present.

"We'll cross that bridge when we have to. Trust me to be cautious."

"If anything ever feels off... If he *ever* asks you questions... Just listen to the questions he asks you. You know what to look for. Promise me you'll get the hell out of there if that ever happens."

"Promise," I tell him, grinning.

"You're going to make me go bald with worry," he groans, as I start walking back inside.

"I'll call you later."

As I hang up and make it back to where Logan is in just a pair of boxers and working diligently on making some type of drink in the blender, I lean against the island, soaking in the sight of him.

He turns and catches me ogling him, and he waggles his eyebrows.

"Do you have to leave?" I ask him, desperately trying to keep any neediness out of my tone.

"Not tonight. Possibly tomorrow, but not tonight."

I smile, even though it's masking a certain level of disappointment. I wanted at least two days, but I'll take what I can get, since it's more than I thought this cruel life would ever allow me to have.

"You're incredible, you know?" he asks, coming closer.

The blender gets forgotten as he reaches me, and I tilt my head back, giving him access just as he bends forward and kisses me long and hard and deep and... There aren't enough words to explain how each kiss gets closer to touching my soul.

The Risk

I almost think it can knock away some of the blackness there, maybe even spread around some light.

His arms come around me, pinning me to him as he lifts me, giving him a better angle on my mouth instead of having to bend over so far.

The guy is just too tall and I'm just too short.

I grin against his lips as my legs come up to wrap around his waist. The only reason I break the kiss is to absorb some of the normalcy of the situation, revel in each second of it.

"So we've made it to the level where you just walk around in your boxers in front of me?"

He winks while sliding me onto a countertop, and I frown as I release him with my legs as he backs away. When he turns around to put his back to me, I take notice of some scars I never noticed the last time I had him naked.

"What are these?" I ask before I think about it.

My fingers immediately dart out to touch one semi-circular scar near his shoulder, and I grimace. I hate for people to touch my scars, and here I am touching his.

He doesn't flinch away the way I do as my finger skims over the marred surface.

"Bullet did that two years ago. Just barely missed the damn vest. Half an inch over, and I'd have had a bruise instead of having a bullet removed. A rookie cleared the scene and missed a guy who had a gun, hiding in a closet. He shot through the door, and I was one of the ones hit."

Another scar is jagged and long, moving from his other shoulder blade to his spine. When my fingers skate across it, he backs into my touch. I wish I could let him touch mine. Maybe he could pull away the painful memories laced inside the scar tissue.

"That one is from a knife." That answer has me swallowing down a painful knot. "It was when I was fresh in the field and the guy I was arresting had a friend that came out of nowhere. He caught me off guard."

"They only get you when you can't see them coming," I say quietly, feeling a twinge of pride. "Because you're too strong for them."

He chuckles while turning back around. My breath hitches when he grabs my hips and jerks me against him, standing firmly between my legs as all our best parts line up.

"I like that you think that way," he says, grinning as he toys with the hem of my shorts.

I run my hands over the muscles in his arms. He flexes on purpose, and I roll my eyes playfully while looking back into his eyes. "You are strong. You're intimidating. People don't see you as weak, so they strike when you're most vulnerable."

"The guy shooting from the closet was shooting blindly," he points out.

"So you're not big and strong?" I ask, then burst out laughing when he lifts me up and starts walking with me.

"Strong enough to handle you," he quips, then slaps my ass with one hand.

"I bet I could take you," I say jokingly, but wondering if I really could or not.

"I'll let you show me your fighting skills later," he says before kissing me again and moving toward a room.

I decide I don't want to know if I can take him or not. I just want to pretend like I'm a normal girl with a normal guy in our normal relationship for one normal night.

***

The sun is creeping up, and I've laughed so much my sides hurt. Neither of us has slept. We've eaten a couple of times, had a lot of sex, and laughed more than I've ever laughed, but sleep hasn't been high on the list of priorities.

I think we're both afraid to close our eyes and lose this fleeting

The Risk

moment of perfection.

Now I'm sprawled across the couch as he tells me about his very happy childhood that isn't filled with dark memories.

My eyes flit around the room, taking in all the pictures of this alleged family he only speaks about in the past tense.

"So what happened? Or is that none of my business?" I ask him, lifting my head up to peer at him.

His smile slowly falls, and I hate myself for asking.

"Never mind. I shouldn't have—"

"It's okay, Lana. Stop apologizing for trying to get to know me," he says, grinning again. He brushes my hair away from my face before resting his hand on my shoulder. "I like you wanting to know more about me than my condom preference."

I snort. Actually *snort*. Kill me now.

It just makes him laugh again.

Shaking my head, I shrug. "I know I can't seem to tell you much about my past, so it's not fair for me to ask about yours," I say on a sad sigh, killing the light moment again.

His face grows serious, and his hand starts running up and down my back as I lay my head down on his chest.

"Tell me what you want to when you're ready," he finally says, kissing the top of my head. "I get that not all pasts are as easy as mine was. As for my parents… My mom got a little wild in her mid-thirties, and she divorced a good man in pursuit of wild sex and rich men. Things were fine until then. I never actually knew my real dad, other than knowing he was in the military. He sent a few pictures to me with letters, as though I wanted to see his face. My stepdad was always my true father, in my opinion. He came into the picture when I was two and raised me like his own."

I run my fingers along his chest.

"Any exes I should be worried about?"

He strangles on air before laughing. "No. Not at all. All the relationships have ended on really bad terms. I sort of suck at being a boyfriend since I'm married to my job."

He groans while running his hand through my hair, and I lift my head, staring into his eyes.

"Just don't let me fuck this up, because I kinda like you," he says, smirking at me.

Gah. All I do is grin like an idiot no matter what he says. "I kinda like you too."

He thumbs my lower lip, settling in more comfortably while pulling me over on top of him completely. Despite the firm body, he's surprisingly comfortable.

"What about you? Any exes I should worry about?" he asks, studying my face.

He studies all my expressions. Fortunately I've trained against them. But this is one question I can answer honestly.

"I've only ever had one truly serious relationship, and I would rather set him on fire than speak to him ever again. Other than that, nothing serious since then, and that was over ten years ago. The rest have been…experiments?"

Okay, I need to shut my mouth because I'm talking too much.

"Experiments?" he asks, reminding me to learn when to stop.

"Wrong word. Um… Hopeless and pointless attempts at having something, then learning no spark was there."

Good recovery, Lana.

"There's a spark here," he says reverently, still running his hands over my bare back.

Smiling, I nod. "There's definitely a spark."

He pulls me forward, running his lips along mine. Just as I decide to deepen the kiss, he gets a call.

Cursing, he snatches his phone from the floor. It's stayed in

The Risk

whatever room we've been in all night.

"Bennett here."

The phone is so loud that I hear the woman on the other end.

"Hey, we have a list of people to look into, but a couple of guys popped. There was one custodial service outsourced to all the apartment buildings. While we looked into them, we dismissed them quickly. When I called them and asked for a list of *all* payroll employees, I reminded them they were impeding a federal investigation if they didn't also include the occasional under-the-table gigs. The list miraculously got a lot longer. Two names have priors that make these guys look good for it."

So I might have been right?

"We'll meet up in two hours and make a trip out to Boston. Bring all the names on that list, and we'll go through them on the flight over."

And that's all the time we have.

I can see by the look in his eyes that he hates this too.

He covers the mouth of the phone as the girl curses him for being too good at his job.

"If I get him, we'll have more time together for a little while," he says, frowning as he studies my face.

Apparently I'm wearing some disappointment, so I mask my expressions and curl into him, kissing his jaw.

"Go catch more bad guys."

The girl on the other end goes silent.

Logan presses his lips to my forehead, and I soak in his scent one last time before he's gone. Last time was a brief trip. Maybe I'll get lucky and things will go that smoothly again.

"You with your profiling girlfriend who helped bring up this lead?" the girl on the line asks.

I really hope she isn't secretly in love with him, because I detect an edge to her tone that I hope I'm overanalyzing.

"Yeah. I'll see you guys in a couple of hours. Don't forget to keep that between us."

"You know it, boss man. I just hope it helps us get this bastard before another woman is hurt."

I breathe out in relief, because that edge is gone. Apparently I was definitely reading into it.

He hangs up, and his arms come around me in one of those awesome hugs I love so much.

"As *soon* as I get back, I swear to take you on that damn date I promised so long ago. You're better than a sex-a-thon with whatever food I burn."

He totally burns pizza. But it was sweet for him to attempt to cook. It might have gone better if we hadn't forgotten it was in the oven and ended up in the bedroom.

"I'll eat burned food every single day that I get to have you to myself. I'd rather not waste time having to go out in public and lose all our privacy."

He chuckles, but I'm not kidding.

I'm greedy. I want him all to myself.

He hurries through the motions of getting ready, and I kiss him much longer than necessary before he leaves.

Since he's going to be gone, there's no time like the present to get back to work and skip the second day of the break.

As I climb into my car, I pull out my phone and call Jake.

"You still with him?"

"I'm on my way to grab Lawrence. You can handle Tyler."

He's cursing as I hang up, and I smirk as I start the long drive to New York. I haven't studied him in his daily life. But fuck it. I'm stronger than all of them.

Chapter 13

We cannot despair of humanity, since we ourselves are human beings.
—Albert Einstein

Lana

New York isn't prepared for me when I arrive. It's dark when I finally set about the task of planning my ambush. My sweatshirt is on, my head is covered, and I prop up in an alleyway.

This place gets dangerous in dark alleyways, but after slamming a guy's face into the brick wall hard enough to knock him out, most of the regular thugs give me a wide berth for the rest of the time that I wait.

"Hey, sweetheart," says another stupid thug who is holding a knife at me as he grins a rotten-tooth grin.

I say nothing.

I guess he missed my earlier demonstrations, unfortunately for him.

He takes a step closer, and that's when I smirk at him. He looks confused for a split second before my hand darts out, colliding with his throat. A pained wheeze escapes him, and he swings the knife.

Midair, I catch his wrist, spin under his arm, and listen with pleasure as a satisfying cry pierces the night. The knife falls to the ground, and I slam my foot into his spine, still wrenching his arm behind him so tightly that I feel it when the bone crunches in my hand.

A shudder of pleasure ripples through me, listening to the way he screams and begs for mercy. It's not as satisfying as it is to hear the ones I want dead, but it's still a high to punish someone like him who preys on the weak—or who he thinks is weak.

With a hard thrust, the knife slices through his back, the skin tearing, and his screams grow louder. People scatter by us, pretending they don't see anything in typical city-alley fashion.

As he starts gurgling on blood, I release the knife with my gloved hand, and let him sink to the ground with a hard *thud*. Right beside the dumpster, all that's visible from the streets are his feet. The city is too loud for the sidewalk dwellers to overhear him.

Even if they did hear, they'd keep walking. That's what people do. They tell themselves they'll just die too. They tell themselves their life is more precious than the person dying close to their feet.

They just don't give a fuck, in short.

A dark smile curves my lips as he stares up at me in surprised horror.

He came into this alley as the predator.

He'll die as the prey.

I tug the sweatshirt over my head, careful not to disturb my blonde wig from its careful placement on my head. I toss it into the dumpster, then shrug out of my sweatpants, revealing the dress I had concealed, and tug on my heels.

It's time to do what I came to do and quit fucking with the scum in the dark that people try to run from. The monsters in here can't compare to the monster I am.

A few eyes swing toward me, but I'm not concerned as I strut by them.

No one will talk about the blonde hooker that just killed a man with very little effort. They'll pretend they never saw a thing.

Even the groups of guys scatter away, stumbling over their feet in their haste. A gun is tucked into the backs of most of their jeans,

The Risk

but they just saw me gut a guy with his own knife. I'm sure they're not feeling too confident the same won't happen to them.

True story: Most people are more terrified when they see a knife than when they see a gun. It's a psychological thing, but it works out in my favor at the moment.

I turn the corner, emerging from the long alleyway onto the busy sidewalk. No one even bats an eye or notices me through the hustle and bustle as I toss the bloody gloves into my purse.

The darkness helps.

I smirk as I see Lawrence stepping out of the building, and I cross the street and slow my pace, letting him get behind me.

Lawrence is predictable.

He's also a pervert.

A sick feeling and the taste of bile rises in my throat when the predictable happens. A warm hand is suddenly on my ass, and I whip my head around, trying to act surprised.

"You," he says, grinning. "Thought that was you. No *blind* date tonight?" He grins like his joke is hilarious.

I bat my lashes at him, and start tugging on his tie, even though my stomach is ready to explode with disgust.

"No date tonight. You trying to pick me up, pretty boy?" I ask with that fake southern drawl I used the last time I was dressed like this.

"I think you must have wanted me to pick you up. New York is too big to run into each other by chance twice," he says smugly, smirking down at me.

"Maybe it's just fate."

His smirk bleeds into a leering grin.

"Your place or mine?"

"Well, that was easy enough." I arch an eyebrow, leading him by his tie as I start guiding him to a parking garage.

"Where are we going?"

"My car is just around the block," I say sweetly.

Parked in a parking garage with no cameras. I leave that juicy morsel out of the conversation.

"You're the kind of girl that makes a guy do something dangerous like get into a car with a stranger," he says, though there's a hint of teasing in his tone, as though he finds me too weak to be of any danger to him.

"You can back out," I say, moving to the right. I release his tie, but he speeds up his steps, still following me into the parking garage.

"I'm not worried. I think I can handle you."

I hold back the snort of derision.

"Baby, I can promise you that you won't survive a girl like me."

Chapter 14

I do not believe in the immorality of the individual, and I consider ethics to be an exclusively human concern without any superhuman authority behind it.
—Albert Einstein

Lana

"Hush little baby, don't say a word. Momma's gonna buy you a mocking bird. And if that mocking bird don't sing, Momma's gonna buy you a diamond ring."

The song flows through the underground cellar, and I walk toward the side as Lawrence slowly rouses from his unconscious state. I watch with rapt fascination from the shadows as a myriad of emotions flicker across his face in sequence.

Confusion. Surprise. Recognition. And my favorite—panic.

He struggles against the chains that are holding his hands and arms out wide, keeping him bound and suspended midair. It's a lovely position to die in. It also leaves you feeling weak and defenseless to be spread out and immobile.

I should know.

The song changes, and "Ring Around the Rosy" starts playing in that creepy kid voice it's in. I love fucking with their heads.

"Who the fuck are you!?" he shouts, struggling as I remain tucked in the dark corner. The light overhead casts a circular glow beneath it, illuminating him and the chains dangling loosely in front of him as I await our second prisoner's arrival.

As soon as I got him to my car, I slammed his head into the side door twice, making sure he was out cold before tossing his heavy ass into my car. He's solid muscle, and I didn't plan on him being quite so heavy as dead weight.

The struggle was worth it.

The bruises are forming nicely around his eyes and forehead. I'm sure the concussion kept him out longer than a usual cold-cock.

"Where are you? Where the fuck am I?" he barks, struggling in vain, making the chains rattle their unrelenting warning.

He jerks his head from side to side, trying to see something other than the light above him. It's just four stone walls in a semi-large square of a cellar. It's every creepy nightmare there is.

I should have started finding creepier places to kill them long ago, because I love the way his body is seizing in terror just from the surroundings.

I'm dressed in all black now. The red lipstick is gone, along with the blonde wig I was donning. The heels have been traded in for boots—the men's boots I wear with the special toe-piece Jake designed for me to leave behind heel-to-toe impressions.

My backpack isn't on, but it's not necessary for this part, since there's no dirt around. The stone floor under my feet will soon be painted with two shades of red. Then I'll paint all four walls.

"Someone fucking answer me! Help!" he roars, only to be met with silence. Tyler's old home is in the middle of nowhere. These are the easy kills. Lawrence would have been difficult to kill in his apartment that he shares with a roommate.

Tyler's wife is out of town right now, after having a fight over the text messages I helped her stumble upon—anonymously of course. Tyler thinks Denise got jealous and sabotaged him. His wife thinks he's a dick weasel—her words—and left in a fit of rage.

I'm currently tracking her cell phone with the clone phone I had made of Tyler's.

Lawrence continues to scream and shout as "The Wheels on the

The Risk

Bus" plays now, drowning out most of his pleads.

His voice is almost hoarse a few hours later when he finally pisses on himself, losing his bladder. It's step one of humiliation. It's step one of stripping their dignity. They always piss and shit themselves.

A smile curves my lips.

He curses as the first tear falls from his eye. He's trussed up and strung out, unable to wipe it away. I want all his tears. I want all his misery and terror.

I want him degraded to the point he has nothing but indignation and humiliation left. Then I want his screams.

Just an hour after that, he breaks, sobbing fiercely as he loses control of his bladder again. His jeans darken, and the smell wafts over me. It's the smell of revenge. Well, it's the smell of piss, but you get the idea.

He's shirtless, and I can see the goosebumps that have pebbled on his skin from the cold. The colder the room, the worse the pain is when the strikes are received.

"The bitch is crying," Morgan says, laughing under his breath as one solitary tear rolls down my cheek.

I'm restrained, unable to wipe it away, as I try to retreat into my mind and block out all the pain.

"Those tears won't save you, whore," Lawrence says close to my ear. "Beg me to stop."

"Please...please stop," I hear my brother crying.

"We have one begging!" I hear Tyler announce, laughing like a hyena.

My arms wiggle free from Tyler's loosened grip, and I scream out as I slam my fist into the side of Lawrence's face.

"You fucking cunt!"

He continues to straddle me as he shoves my hands back down into place.

"Hold this fucking bitch down, or I'll let her claw your eyes out when it's your turn!"

Tyler spits out a curse, and slams my hands back into the pavement. I cry out as my hands find the unforgiving surface, and feel the blood trickling. I focus on it and not on what Lawrence is doing to the rest of me.

"Those tears won't save you, whore," I say, causing Lawrence to jerk his head over to my corner as he squints into the darkness, trying to find me.

"Who the fuck are you?"

I take three steps, slowly letting the light filter across me until his brow pinches in confusion. Fury sweeps across his face, but the chains hold him steady.

"What the fucking hell do you want, bitch?"

"Beg me to stop."

He starts to speak, but the door above us opens, and Tyler comes rolling down the stairs, crying out in agony as Jake takes the steps one at a time. Jake moves with grace, enjoying the fact revenge is finally finding these sons of bitches after the conversation we witnessed.

Tyler already looks half beaten to death. Did I forget to mention that Jake has been taking all the same classes I have? Our mixed martial arts list only grows, as does our black belt count.

Obviously we took the classes in another town with another name, but that part isn't important right now.

"You!" Lawrence shouts, glaring at Jake.

Jake taps his legs. "They work just fine, by the way."

Tyler is a tangle of limbs, still lying on the ground. "Did you leave anything for me?" I ask Jake as he grabs Tyler's wrist, dragging him to the chains.

The Risk

"Who the fuck are you?" Lawrence demands again, as though he has any control.

"There's plenty left. It'll just hurt worse when you extract the debt."

Smirking as Lawrence continues to berate us from his vulnerable position, I help Jake lock Tyler into place. We spread him out like Lawrence, suspending him with the chains. They're right across from each other now.

"You want to know who I am?" I ask Lawrence as Tyler shakes with fear, his eyes wide and his body trembling.

Tears are feverishly pouring from Tyler's eyes, causing me to give a quick appraisal to the state of his body.

His legs are definitely broken. Jake must have gotten out a lot of aggression. Good for him. He needed it.

"You're a crazy bitch!" Lawrence shouts.

I grin, facing him now.

"No. I'm a pissed off crazy bitch. You knew me when I was younger. You knew my brother too."

A smirk graces my lips as the color starts draining from his eyes. "Those tears won't save you, whore," I repeat, though this time I can see him realizing why I'm saying those words. "Beg me to stop."

He turns as white as the ghost he thinks I am, and I face Tyler again as he tries to piece it all together.

"Play nice, Victoria. It'll hurt a lot less if you just play nice."

Don't cry, Victoria. Don't let them see they've broken you.

But I do break. I break hard. I break to the sounds of my brother's screams from behind me as he begs and begs and begs... And they just laugh.

As though the sounds are music to their ears.

I want those ears to bleed.

109

"Play nice, Tyler. It'll hurt a lot less if you just play nice," I taunt, watching as the same wave of realization washes over him.

His eyes widen to the point of being painful, and Jake grins as he takes it all in. He always has to miss this part. I may have a new kind of partner if he can stomach the rest. I'd like for him to be a part of it. It's just as much his revenge as it is mine. We both loved Marcus.

And they took him away.

I move in front of Lawrence, and Jake hands me my favorite knife. It's dull. It's brutal. And it hurts like hell when I finally get the skin to tear apart.

"You're dead," the prick wheezes, watching me in disbelief. "You're supposed to be dead."

I stare up at him, moving the blade over his thigh, feeling his tremble.

"You should have killed me deader," I say just as the blade digs into the yielding flesh.

He cries out in pain when the flesh finally splits, and I take my time. "I'll need a sharp one for his ears," I tell Jake as Tyler vomits to the sounds of Lawrence's screams.

Then I continue, shifting to Tyler, letting them watch each other slowly be killed.

"Hope you boys aren't sleepy. I changed my mind about your debt days. It's going to be a long week."

Chapter 15

You cannot simultaneously prevent and prepare for war.
—Albert Einstein

Logan

I glance down at my phone, reading the latest text from Lana.

LANA: I'll call you tonight if you're free. Sorry I missed your call earlier. It's been a crazy few days. <3

"Oh, heart emoji! Shit's getting real," Craig says over my shoulder, earning an elbow to his gut.
Rolling my eyes as he grunts and coughs, I text her back.

ME: Tonight should work, as long as no one calls in with any leads. We know who the killer is, and we've been blasting his face all over the news. You were right. It's definitely one of the paid-under-the-table custodial workers. He managed to escape though, so there's a city-wide manhunt underway.

LANA: Be careful. He's always been overlooked, and with the new bout of attention, he's likely to enjoy the thrill of notoriety. He may crave more attention and come after you if the buzz wears off too soon. Killing the lead FBI agent who ran the hunt against him would give him even more attention.

I've never wanted to date a profiler, simply because work and sex don't mix well together in my experience. Lisa, for example, is a thorn in my side since things ended years ago, and now she's under my command.

It's awkward. It's frustrating. And she uses our past against me every chance she gets.

Lana, however, is the perfect woman. Someone who understands what I do without being right at my side while I'm doing it. It's literally the best of both worlds.

Which is why I'm still worried she's too good to be true.

ME: It's a slim chance he'll come after me. And if he does, it'll save me the trouble of trying to track him down.

LANA: I'm serious, Logan. Guys like him could fixate on someone like you.

ME: He's a rapist. A serial rapist. He needs a female to relieve his urges. He's more than just a serial killer, which makes the likelihood of him coming after me very slim.

LANA: Anyone who has always lived in the shadows and suddenly gets brought into the light is going to get the high. Especially someone like him. Sexual sadists thrive on the power. It gets them off. Power over you could become an easy surrogate for the power he holds over his female victims.

ME: I like that you care so much.

LANA: I like my orgasms. I want more.

That has me laughing, and I put my phone away as Craig comes up, filling me in on the latest information.

It was supposed to be an easy bust, but someone tipped him off. Had to. Or else he has tabs on the police station somehow. But the guy reads like an open book of our profile.

Now finding him is getting harder. He got paid in cash and never had a checking account. His apartment was a cash-weekly sort of arrangement. His entire life is paperless, tied to no electronics or trails. Even his power bill was included in his rent, furthermore concealing any trails he might have.

He left his phone behind.

He took his clothes.

He's in the wind, and it could be months before he resurfaces if we don't find him now.

***

Four days later, there are still no leads, and I groan as I load up with my team to come back home. Gerald Plemmons. That's the name of the Boogeyman. Putting a face on him has helped alleviate the fears of some of the city, but he's still out there.

One day, he'll kill again. Unfortunately, until he does, we may not be able to find him.

As soon as I step off the jet, I haul ass to my SUV and drive like hell to Lana's house. She's not expecting me, and I can't reach her on her phone. It keeps going straight to voicemail, so I hope I don't piss her off by just showing up.

It seems to take forever to get there, but when I finally do, I pound on the door with purpose.

The sound of hurried footsteps puts me at ease. I don't see her Mustang here, so I'm happy to hear her talking through the door. I'm not so happy to hear what she's saying.

"You have a key! Use it, Jake! Stop making me walk all through the house—"

Her words die when she swings open the door.

In a towel.

Still mostly wet.

"Logan!" she says, shocked as her eyes widen.

I don't give her time to think before I'm kissing her, pushing the door shut behind me with my foot. Her hands go to my hair, and I lift her, groaning when I feel her bare ass against my hands.

The towel falls loose and gets stuck between our bodies as I continue to kiss her and carry her back to her room. She kisses me just as fiercely, letting me know she doesn't mind the fact I've shown up unannounced.

It's been a week. A solid week since I've seen her.

My hand slides down the curve of her ass, moving until I find what I really want. My fingers skate across her slick pussy, feeling her wet and ready for me. As much as I love foreplay, it'll be skipped tonight. Maybe after I get a little bit of this addiction tempered, we can slow things down, and I can give her body the attention it truly deserves.

"I take it you missed me?" she asks against my lips, tightening her legs on my waist as I finally make it to her room.

"Very much."

I don't even give her time to think before I drop her to the bed, and start undressing. She watches me, scooting her naked body up on the bed as she tosses the towel away.

When she bites down on that bottom lip, I finish stripping and grab her ankles, jerking her down the bed. A small squeal of surprise escapes her, but I roll on the condom, adjusting myself between her legs on her very high bed.

As soon as I'm lined up, I thrust in, feeling her walls squeeze against the abrupt intrusion. She moans and arches her back, looking like every fantasy I've ever had.

Gripping her hips, I set a harsh rhythm, fucking her with abandon, letting her moans and gasps fuel me and guide me. When she goes stiff and her pussy clamps down on me, heat spreads through my spine, and an electric current rolls over me in the form of pleasure.

Her mouth parts as she grips the sheet beneath her, her fists twisting in the soft fabric on the messy bed.

My pumps grow lazy until my hips still completely, and she pants while grinning up at me.

"Hi," she says, laughing lightly.

I laugh too before dropping to her.

"Hi."

Rolling over, I toss the condom into the trashcan beside the bed, then face her again, running my finger along her cheek.

She forces me to move up more comfortably on the bed when she moves, making sure she can lie down.

"Who's Jake? And why does he have a key?"

Her smile spreads like she's enjoying a private joke.

"Jealous much?"

I narrow my eyes, and she snickers while tossing a leg over my hip and pillowing her head on my bicep.

"He's my business partner. He just left a few minutes ago, and I thought he might have forgotten something. He thinks it's funny to make me jog through the house instead of using his key. He acts like I'm going to confuse him for a robber and accidentally stab him or something."

I don't like Jake having a key to her house, especially since I don't know him.

"What's his last name?" I ask, fully prepared to do a complete background check on this guy—and see what he looks like.

I really am jealous.

Fuck.

"He's a silent partner, and it's in our agreement that I don't give out his surname. Sorry, but that's how it is. Our latest business thing took a few days longer than expected, but we decided to be thorough. Besides, we've known each other forever. He's like a brother to me. Don't worry. I can assure you nothing sexual is going on."

"Is he gay?" I ask hopefully.

She grins broadly. "He's bisexual, but he tends to lean toward men more than women."

"It'd be better if he was gay."

When she laughs, it's a cute sound, so carefree again. I swear she seems lighter and happier every time I see her.

I frown when my fingers come back red from the side of her head.

"Are you bleeding?" I ask, worried as I try to inspect her hair. How fucking rough was I?

Her eyes widen as she stares at my fingers. "Um…no. That's from some painting I was doing with Jake. I guess I missed some."

I rub the red substance between my fingers. It's definitely blood.

"Don't lie to me," I say, trying to look, but she angles her head away and jumps out of bed.

"Fine. It's blood," she groans. "Jake's blood. Not mine. He cut his finger, and I guess it got on me. I thought I got it all out in the shower."

She goes to the bathroom, and I follow her in, watching as she starts washing out her hair.

A little stream of red flows out, but to my relief, it stops, which means she's really not bleeding.

"Why wouldn't you just say that?"

She shrugs, not looking at me. "You're all freaked out about Jake. I thought not mentioning him anymore would be a good idea."

I blow out a breath, and her eyes meet mine in the mirror.

"Sorry. I don't mean to sound like a jealous ass."

She gives me a tight smile.

"I have no right to lie to you and make you feel guilty about it.

The Risk

Sorry," she says, sighing as she looks down at the ground.

Tilting her face up, I bend down, brushing my lips over hers.

"Looks like we're both still figuring out how to do this thing. It's a learning experience," I tell her, smiling when she groans and presses her head into my chest.

"You're so good," she says quietly. "I'm afraid I'm going to ruin all the best parts about you."

"Not possible. You're good too, Lana."

She tenses against me, and I get worried when her grip tightens around my waist. I'm not sure what happened in the past five minutes, and she's become impossible to read.

Instead of probing her with questions, I just hold her until she finally sighs against my chest.

"I've missed you too," she finally says after a long spell of silence.

"Then let me take you out on that date."

She peers up, arching an eyebrow. "Lobster and wine?"

I nod.

She grins. "Then orgasms."

I laugh as she skips out of the bathroom, her good mood back. She's an enigma, and I think that's half of her appeal.

Chapter 16

Great spirits have always encountered violent opposition from mediocre minds.
—Albert Einstein

Lana

Dinner? Perfect. Lobster? Loved it. Wine? Amazing. Logan? Too good for me.

I lied to him. Then I lied to recover from my lie because I couldn't tell him I was wearing my latest two victims' blood in my hair. The guilt he had on his face made me hate myself.

He apologized.

I realized in that moment how wrong this all is.

Logan is incredible. He's everything I never even hoped to dream about, because someone so good couldn't exist.

Yet he's here.

Well, not at this exact moment. He's currently at his house getting more clothes. He's taking a few days off, since their cases have gone cold. Which means they haven't found my latest bodies yet. Or it could mean that he's not on that case…

Yesterday was a damn close call. Ten minutes earlier and he'd have found me covered in blood as I tossed all my clothes into the burn pile behind my house. I burned those clothes as soon as he left earlier. My floors are so dark that he didn't notice the drips of blood on them. I could have lied my way out of that too, but I couldn't have lied my way around my murder shoes or murder bag.

The Risk

Fortunately all that was upstairs.

I'll never let my phone die again. He tried calling me numerous times, but I was finally at the end game with Tyler and Lawrence, and didn't pause to put my phone on the charger.

The smart thing to do would have been to charge it on my way home, but it was tucked inside my murder bag...that I threw into the closet...and couldn't find until it finally dawned on me.

Jake spent forever puking in a bucket inside his car during the really gory stuff. It's not like he could risk puking inside the cellar and leaving behind all that yummy DNA.

Being a monster doesn't agree with his stomach.

As I sift through the next file on my next victim, looking through the notes of his life, my phone rings. I answer immediately when I see it's Jake.

"You find him?"

"His name is Gerald Plemmons, at least according to the news. The manhunt is still coming up short. And by the way...Boogeyman? Really?"

I snort out a laugh.

"I hope they come up with something cleverer for you."

I shudder just thinking about the names they may don me with. Then Logan will only know me by that name if he ever discovers the truth.

He'll hate the woman he cares for because he'll see the monster lurking within.

"Have you found him, though? I already knew his name," I go on, refusing to go down that road just yet.

"He's in DC."

My heart thumps in my chest.

"You're sure?"

"Dropped a body a few minutes ago," he answers. "He's off

grid as far as any paper trails go. However, he made one hell of a statement announcing his current whereabouts. This time, instead of finding the body in an apartment, he hung her out a window for all to see. And instead of it being a low profile girl, he killed a judge's wife. Raped her brutally, and there was a lot of overkill."

"Normally overkill means rage," I say quietly, trying to process it all.

"I think the overkill was more of a statement than rage. I think he wanted to make a fuck-you statement to the FBI. You're right about him enjoying the attention. He's going to want more of it, since he's becoming an exhibitionist."

"And he's going to go after Logan."

"Yes and no."

"What does that mean?" I ask, moving toward the back of my kitchen to look out the window, paranoid that I've just heard a car.

"There's more. The body he hung out the window was naked. She also had Boogeyman carved into her chest. And one other name…Logan Bennett."

My chest tries to collapse, and I sink to my chair. I knew he'd do this. I knew he'd target Logan.

"They're sure it's him? Not a copycat?"

"Some of the things not released to the public have been verified. This time he even left his DNA behind just to let them know for sure it was him, and now he's laying claim to his work."

"And now he's targeting Logan. We have to find him before he can."

"That's the part I'm getting to. He'll go after your agent, but he'll use a proxy to do it. He'll want to taunt and torment Logan. A few more bodies will drop with that calling card before he makes his big move. What would a sexual sadist go after to really hurt a man?"

It takes me a second to catch up to his train of thought, but when

The Risk

I do, a dark smile plays with my lips.

"His girlfriend."

"Exactly. You sure you can handle a guy like this? He's not like the guys you've been going after, Lana. This guy is the real deal with zero mercy. If he—"

"The guys I kill weren't angels—*aren't* angels, Jake. You know that. They'd kill me if they knew I was still alive, or if they got half a chance when I'm there for them. And yeah. I can handle the Boogeyman. Even a monster has nightmares. I'll be his."

He exhales heavily, weighing the gravity of the situation.

"His MO is breaking into a home. He immediately attacks the woman, using brute force to establish dominance. He'll hit them, then he chokes them until they're on the verge of passing out."

"I'm aware," I tell him.

"He blindsides them, Lana. Your guard will need to be up at all times."

"I want him to get a couple of hits in," I say as I pour some fruits into my juicer. "Gotta make it believable."

"This is too fucking risky. I think I should probably set up surveillance on your house."

"No. Don't you dare. If anyone ever tapped into that—"

"Right. Fuck! Then let me come stay with you?"

"And how would I explain you if Logan shows up unexpectedly again? You know what's eventually coming, right? There's a reason you've been riding in a wheelchair for three years—riding it in and out of your home and in your town."

He groans, and I turn on the juicer, peering out my window again. As if Logan hears me talking about him, a text comes through as Jake speaks.

"Right. Then I'll come up with something else."

LOGAN: Boogeyman problem. I'll call later.

ME: Okay. Please be careful.

LOGAN: Always, pretty girl.

"Are you texting while I'm on the phone?" Jake asks, annoyed.

"Maybe a little."

I look out the window again, and this time I catch sight of a car and a flicker of red before I lose sight of whoever is here.

"Gotta go," I whisper to Jake, hanging up before he can say anything.

I cut my phone off and toss it to the counter before pulling out one of my guns, clicking the safety off as I slowly make my way to the door.

Someone knocks, and I blow out a breath. I doubt the Boogeyman would politely knock before barging in to slit my throat.

I check the peephole, confused when I see a pretty redhead on my steps. Tossing on a pair of jeans that I grab from the back of my couch, I check the mirror. Then I tuck the gun into the back of my jeans and open the door, leaning against it to impede any thoughts of her coming in.

"If you're here to witness, then you have your work cut out for you. If you're here to sell me something, go ahead and leave. I shop online. If you're here to—"

"I'm Hadley Grace," she says, interrupting me. Her name sounds vaguely familiar, though I'm not sure why.

"Okay." I shrug, letting her know that name holds no importance.

"Logan Bennett is my boss."

That's...surprising. "Shouldn't you be in DC? Heard the Boogeyman dropped another body."

The Risk

Her eyes light up in surprise, and she jerks her phone out from her pocket, cursing when she reads something.

"I'll make this quick," she tells me, holding up a file.

She thrusts it at me, and my blood pumps quickly through my veins as I flip it open to see my worst fears starting to come to life.

"Actually, you make this quick," she says flatly. "Tell me why the hell you stole the identity of a dead girl."

End of Book 1

Continue reading for book 2.

sidetracked

Book 2

~~Tim Hoover~~

~~Chuck Cosby~~

~~Nathan Malone~~

~~Jeremy Hoyt~~

~~Ben Harris~~

~~Tyler Shane~~

~~Lawrence Martin~~

~~Random alley guy~~

Getting closer…

Chapter 1

Real knowledge is to know the extent of one's ignorance.

—Confucius

Lana

My mother was a Confucius woman when she needed some motivational words. My father was an Einstein man when everything was crashing down on him.

Neither of the dead wise men are helping me out right now. Neither are my parents and all their words of wisdom.

To be fair, they probably never would have condoned me stealing another girl's identity, taking her inheritance, and using it to get some very disturbing revenge on all the men who scarred me for life.

Five minutes ago, my world was just fine—well, for me it was fine.

Then Hadley showed up at my front door. I never should have opened the door.

"I'm Hadley Grace."

Her name sounds vaguely familiar, though I'm not sure why.

"Okay." I shrug, letting her know that name holds no importance.

"Logan Bennett is my boss."

That's...surprising. "Shouldn't you be in DC? Heard the Boogeyman dropped another body."

Sidetracked

Her eyes light up in surprise, and she jerks her phone out from her pocket, cursing when she reads something.

"I'll make this quick," she tells me, holding up a file.

She thrusts it at me, and my blood pumps quickly through my veins as I flip it open to see my worst fears starting to come to life.

"Actually, you make this quick," she says flatly. "Tell me why the hell you stole the identity of a dead girl."

My mind races through a thousand scenarios, wondering how much she knows. I know without a doubt my inner panic isn't showing on the surface. I'm the picture of composure. I've prepared for this, just not to this extent and with someone close to Logan.

"You always so thoroughly invasive with a friend's girlfriend, or am I just special?" I ask the girl in front of me, keeping my tone cool and aloof.

"You really want to play this off? Fine. I'll just call Logan. Tell him some lying bitch has been playing him like a fiddle."

"Feel free to call him. As for stealing a dead girl's identity, that's a false accusation. But by all means, go ahead and make yourself look like a crazy jealous girl."

I start to shut the door, but she slams her foot in the crack and stops it from shutting.

Got her.

Slowly, I open it back up, arching an eyebrow.

"Ten years ago, Kennedy Carlyle was in a car accident because she was high as a kite. Her wounds were ruled as fatal, but she miraculously survived. Now how'd she manage that?"

She's purposely referring to Kennedy as a separate person from me. She's trying to make me slip up.

"Ten years ago, *I* was a different person. My name was legally changed, and I got sober, made some real life decisions. I was a sixteen-year-old kid back then, angry without a cause. New name, new life, new choices, and a healthier mentality. It *was* a miracle I survived, and I didn't take it for granted."

That's the shit I've been rehearsing, preparing for the day when someone called me out.

She snorts derisively. "You don't even resemble her. And I've run facial recognition software; not even close."

Okay, so when I was rehearsing all this, never did I plan to face down the FBI.

"Did you happen upon my medical charts while you were invading my privacy and breaking the law to do so?"

"I broke no laws, including hacking your medical files."

"Yet knew my injuries from the car accident were so fatal that I should have died." I turn the tables, calling her out on her lies now.

Her eyes narrow to slits, and I tug my shirt up, surprising her.

Her eyes land on the jagged scars. She hasn't even seen the ones on my back. Logan hasn't even mentioned them since I froze up about the two long and nasty ones on my torso.

"You're right. I barely survived." It works that Kennedy was sliced and diced almost like me. "I have the proof. I can always remove my makeup and show you some of the faint scars on my face. I was lucky there. Ten facial reconstruction surgeries by one hell of a plastic surgeon saved my face from looking as horrendous as these two scars."

She backs down a little, her lips tensing. The eyes never lie in facial recognition. Unless you have your face so smashed in that it's ninety percent metal plates in there. But it should match now. Jake fixed all that a long time ago, so she may just be bluffing.

"My face was the worst of the damage. You'll see that on my medical reports. It was so smashed in that it was practically rebuilt. So yeah, it's miraculous I survived. Feel free to dig into my plastic surgeon's file on me. His name is Dr. Calvin Morose. I'm sure you'll offer your apology to Logan when you're finished."

I start to slam the door again, but her foot catches it one more

Sidetracked

time. This time when I open it back up, I'm glaring daggers at her, trying to seem offended more than sick at my stomach.

"Kennedy Carlyle was barely a D student. Yet suddenly she turns her life around after the accident, finishes school with a nice GPA, and manages to go to college as well? Also, she now profiles serials as well as a FBI trained profiler?"

Ah, so this is all because of that damn Boogeyman. I really want to kill that fucker.

"I pointed out the fact he cleaned like someone in the custodial line of work. That's hardly profiling. Rich kids spend more time with maids than they do their parents."

"You told Logan your father was friends with a janitor," she says, smirking like she's catching me in another lie.

Just how fucking close are they? Why is she so hell-bent on finding dirt on me?

Do I need to kill her?

No. No. I can't kill her. Not unless she's a rapist.

Any chance she's a rapist?

I look over her slim body, her puny stature, and wonder. After all, looks are deceiving where I'm concerned. Same could be true for her.

I've officially lost my damn mind.

"My father was friends with numerous janitors. He called them butlers. Sorry I didn't want to tell my boyfriend that I was a rich brat from a privileged household who concentrated too much on bad things before I almost died. I had a wakeup call. As for withholding all this from him... Logan and I have only recently started dating. Vomiting my past into his lap is never a good way to start a relationship. And going psycho crazy jealous and invasively tearing into his girlfriend's past is no way to steal him away. Now kindly fuck off."

"And if I show this to Logan?" she threatens.

"Then I guess I'll show him all the plastic surgeon reports and things done. Then I'll end things with him if he makes me feel as violated as you have."

I slam the door in her face, ignoring the trembling in my hand as I lean against the door. Fuckity fuck.

My past is solid. Jake has made sure of it. Kennedy Carlyle's records have all been adjusted to match me. Her scars. Her injuries. Her blood type. Her fucking DNA. He's covered every single trail there is.

I *am* Kennedy Carlyle.

Well, actually I'm Lana Myers.

Victoria Evans and Kennedy both died, and Lana was born.

It's a wonder I don't have an identity crisis.

As soon as I grab my phone, I turn it back on and dial Jake back.

"What the hell?" he barks. "Why'd you hang up and turn your phone off?!"

"Find out every dark detail on a girl named Hadley Grace."

"What? Why?"

I take a deep breath, steeling myself for his inevitable rant. "Because she just became a problem."

Chapter 2

The superior man is aware of righteousness; the inferior man is aware of advantage.
—Confucius

Logan

"Where the fuck is Hadley? She should already be leading the forensics investigation by now," I snap, looking over at Elise.

"I've called her several times. She just sent a text saying she's on her way."

I run a weary hand through my hair as they finally get the poor woman's body pulled back inside.

That bastard is here.

He's taunting me.

He's calling me out.

He put my name on a dead woman's body, as if stating it was all my fault he was here.

"I want every surveillance camera footage for a five-block radius. I want to know where he came from and where he went!" I bark at Elise, and she nods before running off to do as ordered.

I've never been so pissed. In the seven years I've been working for the FBI, I've never been called out. I've never had a serial killer go so far as to carve a personalized message on the chest of a woman.

My stomach churns with fury as I stalk through the throngs of people. I will find him.

Lana was right. He wants more attention. He's shifted his fixation onto taunting me with his kills now.

I need to stay away from Lana until this is all over with. Until that bastard is behind bars, she's not safe. A sexual sadist won't come after me personally; he'll go after the woman I care about. Not that I pointed that out to her. Then again, I never thought he'd crave this attention.

She saw this coming before I did. Until now, he's shown no signs of needing this sort of attention.

I blasted his face and name all over the news, and instead of lying low, he kills a woman near my front door.

Donny looks as furious as I feel as he comes toward me. The weight of this is bearing down on us, and everyone is ready to point fingers in our direction, as though we created the monster.

"He's developing a narcissistic personality that will clash with his sexual sadist—"

"We just got a lead," Lisa says, interrupting Donny. "Gerald Plemmons was spotted downtown half an hour ago."

I'm already loading into my SUV. Lisa and Donny join me, and we peal out toward the newest lead.

"Director called. We have the shoot-to-kill order," I tell both of them.

It's one time that I don't mind that order.

"You think?" Lisa snips from the passenger seat. "This guy went and made it personal. He's a sexual sadist displaying narcissistic tendencies, and I'm your ex. I think it'd be wise for me to stay with someone."

"He won't focus on you," Donny chimes in from the backseat. "He'll be more focused on Lana."

My grip tightens on the steering wheel as Donny echoes my own worries from earlier.

"Who is Lana?" Lisa asks, confused.

Sidetracked

"I'm going to send two black-and-whites to her house until this is over. Let's not assume he's just fixating on me though. He could be fixating on the whole team."

"I haven't had a relationship with anyone but my hand in over a few years," Donny goes on.

"Who's Lana?" Lisa asks again.

"Elise, Lisa, and Hadley are the only females on the team. We should set up patrol for them as well," I tell him, still ignoring Lisa as she huffs out an annoyed breath of air.

I don't even hesitate to call in the protective detail as I drive toward the lead. That probably won't help. This guy is too smart to stay put for too long.

He knows I'm coming for him.

Chapter 3

Life is really simple, but we insist on making it complicated.
—Confucius

Lana

Two cops are sitting outside my house, guarding me, keeping me safe from the Boogeyman. Yes, I hear how ridiculous that sounds as well.

I have an entire hidden room with tons of information and surveillance shots of all my next victims. That hidden room is where I am now, as two guys hang out in their cruiser, being all kinds of conspicuous.

Do they not know how to keep a low profile?

And their windows are down. Have they never seen a horror movie? Windows down equal throats slashed.

I'm watching through my own surveillance cameras from my murder room, since this room has no windows. The cameras are only on the outside, and I put them up today for the purpose of keeping an eye on the cops.

Logan is pissing me off, not listening to reason. I don't want cops here. Cops hinder my plan. Not that I can tell him that. He's determined to keep me safe. I'm determined to slice and dice a serial killer who may or may not get spooked by the blues outside.

I also check out the monitor that is watching Anthony. My next victim. I've only been able to get two of my cameras installed so far. I'm going closer to home for him. It's getting close to sprint time. I'll have to get creative to continue torturing once I reach that sick, twisted town. The FBI will be all over me.

And my boyfriend has the cops watching my house. The house where I have all my murder supplies that I have to use. Cops that follow me to the store when I get milk. Obviously they can't follow me and guard my kill zone for days on end while I torture people.

Stupid Boogeyman.

I wish I could castrate him. I wish I could dole out the true justice deserved by the ones he's hurt. But I have to make it look like a stroke of luck.

Sighing, I head out of the secret room, move the empty bookcase back where it belongs to cover the hidden door. Then I lock the door to the actual room, concealing the room inside a room.

It's all cloak and dagger right now. That's what happens when you're a serial killer dating a FBI profiler who hunts serial killers.

Somehow, my simple life got very complicated.

After about thirty minutes, I see a familiar SUV pull up, and I grin when Logan steps out, talking to the policeman nearest to the house. What I don't like is the fact he has a guy and a girl with him. Because that means he's not staying.

Walking out the front door, I measure the two unknowns, regarding them. The guy smiles genuinely at me, even offering me a small wave so much less awkward than the wave I gave Logan once upon a time.

The girl, however, doesn't look too happy with what she sees. At least I'm wearing pants. I decided until the Boogeyman is gone, pants are a good idea.

Apparently all the girls on his team seem to have an issue with me, especially since this is the second one I've met and she's regarding me with a scowl. Don't these women know that it's dangerous to piss off a highly trained killer?

Turning my gaze away from her, I refocus my attention on Logan as he walks toward me, his expression grim. His hair looks blonder in contrast to the standard black suit he wears on duty.

As soon as he reaches me, his hands are in my hair, surprising me as his lips come down on mine. I forget about the audience in my yard as I kiss him back, leaning against him as he slides a hand down my back, pulling me closer.

It's not until a loud whistle sounds out that he breaks the kiss. The man he came with chuckles before whistling again and heads toward us as Logan sighs.

"Can we come in?" he asks.

I just nod, and he laces his fingers with mine as the whistler and the staring bitch come into my house and shut the door behind them. The girl looks around, as though she's trying to get a read on me based on my minimum decorations.

"I'm so fucking sorry about this," Logan says against my forehead as he places another kiss there.

"I think I'll be fine, Logan. The cops are overkill, and very annoying. They park in plain sight, so it's not like they're doing much good."

"He'll avoid law enforcement," the unknown guy chirps. "He wants to be free and able to taunt right now. He can't risk being caught. He doesn't know if there's another cop inside or not."

"Which is why I'm here," Logan adds, looking down at me with a grimace.

"No," I say adamantly. "I don't want anyone in the house. Unless you're volunteering."

"Show some gratitude," the girl chimes in, earning a glower from Logan. "These cops are here for your protection. Having someone in bed down the hall would be safer, and they're going out of their way to provide that."

I really don't like her. Can I cut her? Just a little?

"Lisa, go sit in the car if you can't shut your mouth," Logan tells her, a bite to his tone that I haven't heard before.

She glares at him, and I slowly put the pieces together.

Sidetracked

Bitterness. Lots of bitterness in her look.

It's not hard to recognize a woman scorned.

Logan talks to her like he would an ex he was frustrated with, not a normal co-worker.

I really don't like this situation right now.

And I might actually cut her. More than a little.

She drops to a chair instead of leaving, much to my disappointment, and Logan takes my hand, pulling me down the hallway to my bedroom. As soon as he shuts the door, I turn to face him, trying not to go all jealous crazy girl on him.

"You never mentioned you dated someone from your team," I say calmly, like a total rational girl and not a cutting psycho.

"It was over a year ago, and completely unimportant."

"She's jealous."

His eyes spark with humor.

"So are you. Glad to see I'm not the only one losing my mind in this relationship."

His lips twitch, and I stifle my own stupid grin that tries to form in response. He can do that; dissolve my anger with barely any effort at all.

No one else has ever been able to accomplish that.

I toss my arms around the back of his neck, and he wraps his arms around my waist.

"Let someone sleep inside the house. I'd feel better knowing I had every angle covered. I'm going to be sleeping in my office for a few hours at a time at most. This case is priority above all else right now to my department, but you're *my* priority."

"No," I say simply. No way am I risking a cop getting nosy in my house. "I don't feel comfortable with a random stranger sleeping in my house. A badge doesn't make him noble."

His smile falters, and he cocks his head, confused.

"What?" I prompt.

"Nothing. It's just…one time I made a mental note that you seemed trusting of me because I had a badge. I profiled you as not having an issue with law enforcement, meaning you'd never had any bad experiences with them."

"And now I'm throwing you off?" I muse, then smile, trying to mask the flurry of emotions I don't want him to accidentally see. "One day, I'll tell you all there is about me. But no. I don't trust men because they have a badge. Where I grew up, badges just meant people got away with more. It was a corrupt town."

He brushes his hand over my cheek, and I lean into it, hating that I've said too much about my life as Victoria instead of Lana or Kennedy.

"Sorry. I'll try to get some free time to come sleep here for an hour or two with you. Maybe you can tell me some of those past experiences soon."

I shake my head, gripping his wrists. "Do your job. I'm a big girl. I stopped being scared of the Boogeyman by age five." I smile to lighten the morbid joke, but he frowns.

"This is serious, Lana. If he got his hands on you—"

"I've had self-defense training. I have two guns. I also plan to run out the back door instead of up the stairs. We're good. I can handle this."

"If he gets his hands on you, there's nothing you'll be able to do."

I can tell he's getting nauseated just thinking of such an outcome. Little does he know…

"Okay," I say, just to appease him. "Someone can stay inside. Someone you trust. I'm sure you're friends with the local PD."

The relief that washes over his face makes it worth all the million and one things that can go wrong. He genuinely cares about me. He's terrified *for me* right now because a merciless killer might be after me.

Sidetracked

The irony isn't lost on me.

"Not friends, but I know several reputable guys who are definitely trustworthy," he says on a quiet breath. "I'd never leave anyone inside I didn't feel I could trust."

I don't tell him I'd just castrate them and nail their dicks to the wall if they tried anything. Instead, I let him feel as though I'm weak and need protection. Because right now, that's how he needs to feel.

The truth is just too dark to overcome.

And I wonder what will happen if the truth ever comes to light.

He kisses me, tugging me to his body as he melts away all the concerns lingering in the back of my mind. For now, this is worth losing it all. It's almost worth losing my revenge.

But the revenge isn't just for me. Souls beyond the grave beg for a reckoning as well. Those souls need their peace.

It's too soon when Logan pulls away, and I hold back the frustrated groan. "Be safe. I'll be in and out as I can. I'll need to see you with my own eyes to believe you're really safe."

"I won't object to seeing you, but do your job. Don't let him hurt someone else because you're so focused on me. That's what he wants."

He thumbs my lower lip, staring at it for a moment. "Have I told you today that you're perfect?"

I smile against his touch, even though it feels weighted. Perfection. He thinks I'm perfect. It's so far from the truth, but I've told him that before.

"That girl?" I ask, deciding to get some answers before he leaves.

His grin only grows. "We dated a few months. She wanted a commitment. I was married to the job. She transferred to my department, and I broke things off with her because it's against the rules to date within the department."

That has me stiffening. Sheesh. When did I turn into a girl?

"But you'd still be together if she hadn't transferred?"

Even I hear how pathetically clingy I sound.

But Logan, the bastard, grins broader. "No. It was just the easiest way to get the point across that it was over. You're the first woman to make me wish I could skip work, Lana. You make me question my priorities and if it's all really worth it."

My stomach flutters with excitement.

"You know it's worth it. You stop killers. You're a hero."

His smile slips, and he clears his throat. "I don't always stop them in time. It seems like two spring up every time we take one down. And now this is happening. I put you at risk because of my job. Your life is sure as hell not worth it."

I pull him down and kiss him again, and he grips me tightly, tugging me even closer. He lifts me with two hands on my ass, and I land on top of my dresser as he steps between my legs, still devouring my mouth.

When I moan, he swallows the sound, and then someone bangs on the door.

"We need to roll if we're going to meet Elise and Leonard to deliver the adjustments to the profile!" the girl harps.

Definitely cutting her.

Logan doesn't break the kiss. If anything, he kisses me harder, as though he's assuring me she doesn't matter as much as I do. As though nothing matters as much as I do.

It's me who finally breaks the kiss, and his forehead rests against mine as we both take steadying breaths.

"Be careful," I tell him softly. "Don't worry about me. And you do make a difference."

He groans before brushing his lips against mine again, and he tugs me off the dresser, threading our fingers together. The profiler ex is waiting in my living room when we rejoin them.

"Call Chief Harris and tell him to send one of the guys off my

Sidetracked

list," Logan says to the guy profiler, as though he was just waiting for my permission.

The chick just watches us before finally turning and walking out. Logan runs his fingers along my cheek one more time before kissing me quickly and following them out.

The girl gets in the back of the SUV, and the guy gets in the front seat next to Logan, who takes the driver's side. Not surprising. I've noticed he's sort of a control freak. Not that I mind.

As he backs out, he honks the horn twice, and a stupid grin lights up my face. I remember my neighbor always honking as he pulled out, as though it was one last temporary goodbye to his wife.

Annnnd I'm back to being two steps away from that name tattoo on my ass.

After shutting the door, I groan, realizing I never asked him about his relationship with Hadley. Damn women. How many of them should I have to deal with?

I jog upstairs, head into my secret room, and touch the apple on my desk. It's a wax apple, brilliantly red, and there are seven nails sticking out of it. Still many more to go.

Glancing around, I question how stupid it is to leave a murder room inside a house with a cop. Logan respects my privacy and would never snoop. But this guy? I don't know anything about the guy coming to stay in here.

I really hope that hidden door stays hidden. I also hope the metal door with a combination lock is enough to keep a nosy cop out if the door doesn't stay hidden.

Chapter 4

Without feelings of respect, what is there to distinguish men from beasts?
—Confucius

Logan

"He's been quiet for two days," Elise says, still studying the latest reports from the forensics found.

"He's being cautious. He wants attention, but he doesn't want me to win, and especially not before he reaches his endgame."

"What's his endgame?"

"Lana," I say, gripping my pen tightly.

"We don't know that," Lisa argues.

I ignore her. She's acting like a jealous girlfriend, after having not acted that way in over a year. I'm not sure what her issue is all of the sudden, but it's petty and pointless, especially now of all times.

"We have a problem," Donny says, taking brisk steps on his way to my desk.

"We have a board full of problems," I remind him, gesturing to all the unsolved cases.

"Two guys from Delaney Grove are missing."

My skin prickles, and I sit up straighter. "Is it just a coincidence? The unsub has been killing them in their homes."

Sidetracked

"He's also been targeting single males who live in seclusion. Lawrence Martin lives with a roommate, and is a twenty-nine-year-old ad executive from New York. He went missing sometime in the past ten or eleven days."

"Holy shit," Elise says. "All of them have been found no later than four days. It has to be a coincidence, especially since he doesn't fit all of the victimology."

"Too coincidental," I tell her, then focus on Donny. "Why didn't the roommate report him missing sooner?"

"He wasn't sure if Lawrence had hooked up with a girl, or if he was staying at the office. I also got the impression he didn't really care, but rent is due, and he said Lawrence is always there to hand over his half. He never showed up yesterday, he's been missing at work, and no one has seen him."

"And the other?" Elise prompts.

"Tyler Shane," Donny answers. "Twenty-seven-year-old tech analyst from West Virginia. Moved there from Delaney Grove straight out of high school. His girlfriend just reported him missing today."

"So he has a girlfriend?" I ask, confused. "Our unsub has been targeting single males only."

"He also has a wife," Donny says, his eyebrows raising. "Apparently she got pictures and screenshots of messages between Tyler and a Denise Watkins—the girlfriend—from an anonymous tipster. She left that day and hasn't been back. She didn't even know he was missing, and I don't think she cares."

"Any chance she's responsible for him missing?" Lisa asks, glaring daggers through me. "After all, crimes of passion are more likely than a serial kill."

Everyone looks between us, as though they're asking questions, but I have no clue what her problem is.

"She's been in L.A. since she left," Donny says, clearing his throat as he gets back on point. "Her work requires a lot of travel,

143

and she just decided to stay gone this last time and take a couple of days to herself. Across the country is a damn good alibi."

"Check it out," I tell him. "Make sure she's legit. Check into Lawrence Martin's financials too. See if he made any large withdrawals. Same for Tyler Shane. Also check into the roommate and girlfriend. Our guy hasn't been taking them from their homes, and has only been targeting single, solitary men."

"And if it is our guy?" Leonard asks, joining us.

"Then we'll need to revisit the profile and finally deliver the story to the media. A sexual sadist was a stretch to begin with. If these two are linked to our unsub, then he's not a sexual sadist. He's just a sadist. Look into anyone who might have tortured animals."

I grab my notebook, scratching down some notes. "There were never any hesitation marks," I say quietly, studying photos of the first victim. "This guy is comfortable around death and killing. No patterns of rage have been found. He's only targeting people who have left town."

"Which means he could have killed before," Lisa adds.

"Hence the tortured animals bit," I say, shifting the photos around on my desk. "He may be bitter these people left that town and have successful lives. We'll deliver the profile to the media if we find the bodies."

They all nod, and I pick up my phone, dialing Lana. She answers almost immediately.

"Hey, you, how's the hunt?" she asks, sounding breathy and happy.

"Quiet right now. Hadley is running some of the forensics in an effort to see if we can get ahead of him. Why do you sound out of breath?"

"I'm on the phone. I'll be right back," she calls out to someone. "Sorry," she says into the phone. "I was working out with Duke. He's showing me some moves."

My eyebrows hit my hairline as I stand up.

Sidetracked

"Duke?"

"Detective John Duke. He just showed up today to start bunking with me. He said everyone just calls him Duke. He's the guy you assigned to my house, remember?"

No. No I don't remember. It was supposed to be Marley St. James, an older guy who is on the verge of a promotion. He's been there since the day I had to leave. Why did they pull him?

John Duke...I've never heard of him.

"What happened to Marley?" I ask distractedly.

"He had something come up, I guess. I didn't pry for details. We never really spoke. He mostly kept to himself while he was here."

I quickly lean over my chair, remaining standing, and type the new name into the computer as Lana continues. John Duke's picture flashes across my screen, and I almost drop my phone.

Motherfucker.

Twenty-eight. Fit. Single. Ambitious. Newly promoted to homicide detective—a coveted spot. Definitely not ugly—can't believe I'm admitting that.

And he's in my girlfriend's house. Sleeping there. Staying with her while I'm here. Alone together.

I'm going to kill someone for fucking this all up.

"Logan?" Lana prompts, sounding worried. "You okay?"

"Just curious how a homicide detective has time to come babysit," I say casually, grabbing my bag from the floor and heading toward the door. I'm due a few hours of sleep, and I know where I want to take those few hours.

"Um...he said his boss dude told him to come here. The department is taking this threat seriously. Duke is who they thought would be best to surprise Plemmons if or when he shows up."

Throwing a tantrum is not on my agenda. The local PD want to make the arrest, and are using this as a way to get a leg up on us, since we're outsourcing her protective detail to them. Since *I'm* outsourcing her protective detail to them.

I'll deal with Duke when I get there.

"I don't know him, Lana. They apparently sent in someone they want to take credit for any arrests."

"Kind of figured as much," she says quietly, but there's a mocking lilt to her tone.

"Why's that?" I ask, getting into my SUV.

"Because there's no way you'd send *that* guy to come stay in my house while you're gone."

I snort derisively, then relax when she laughs.

"Don't worry, Agent Bennett. I normally don't play with boys who wear badges. You're my only exception."

Then there's that. I'm still confused about that. No criminal record means no run-ins with police. Unless there's a sealed juvie record, but nothing popped when Hadley ran her name through the system.

"Keep me awake while I drive," I tell her, not commenting on any of the other.

"You want me to tell you about how I broke my vibrator this morning?"

I swerve the car, cursing as a horn blares.

"Logan? You okay?" she asks, sounding genuinely concerned.

"Yeah," I grumble. "Fine. How'd you break your vibrator?"

This girl... I swear she gets off on surprising me. Every time I think I have her figured out, she throws me another curve ball.

She laughs lightly. "Well, I pulled it out of my drawer, peeled my panties off on my bed, and when I slid it down my body, building up the anticipation as it buzzed...it slipped out of my hand, hit a crease in the bed, and crashed against the floor. The fun part broke off."

Laughter escapes me before I can stop it, and I feel her smile.

"What if I told you your vibrator could retire for the night?"

"I'd say *duh*. Because it's worthless now."

"I meant, I'm coming there," I say, still partially laughing under my breath.

"Really? You can get away?" The excitement in her tone has me driving a little faster.

"On my way right now," I tell her, smiling when I hear her sigh like she's content.

"Well, good, then you can—"

My phone beeps with an incoming call, and I groan, cutting her off mid-sentence.

"You need to let me go, don't you?" she muses.

"Yes. Unfortunately. I'll see you in about twenty though."

"Be safe."

I hang up and answer my call without looking to see who it is.

"Bennett."

"I found a few things that could give us a lead. Where are you?" Hadley asks.

"Just left a few minutes ago. Take what you found to Donny. I'm going to crash for a couple of hours and get some sleep in an actual bed."

"Your bed?" she asks, an edge to her tone.

"No. Not that it's any of your business."

"Logan, we need to talk about something," she says hesitantly.

"Which is?"

After several long seconds, she finally exhales a loud, frustrated breath. "Nothing. At least nothing for now. I'll let you know if I find something."

Weird.

"Right. So get with Donny on what you've found, and—"

"You seriously don't want to look over this yourself?" she interrupts.

"Is it going to break the case? Will it lead us to him?"

"Well, no, but—"

"Then give it to Donny. I need sleep, Hadley. I'll be back in as soon as my eyes aren't trying to close on their own."

A loud yawn sneaks out, as if cued, and she sighs harshly.

"Okay. See you later."

Hanging up, I run the case over in my head and resist the urge to call Lana back just because I hate the idea of her being there alone with a single guy. A single guy who might be touching her because of their 'workout.' A single guy who is apparently trying to connect with her.

My grip tightens against the steering wheel.

I have to get ahold of this jealousy thing.

Chapter 5

To see and listen to the wicked is already the beginning of wickedness.
—Confucius

Lana

I dodge a slow punch from Duke, smirking at how easy he's taking it on me. He wants me to have some skillset in case things get out of hand. He walked in and demanded we spar so he can see what I need to work on.

He's weak on his left side, constantly leaving himself open to attack. His form is sloppy, amateur boxing style at best. Most likely he was raised in a militant household where the father showed him a few techniques—archaic and outdated techniques.

In a real fight, I'd have him pinned and begging for mercy in under two minutes.

But I'm supposed to be a normal girl. I eat an excess of calories daily to stay a little soft, hiding the skill behind femininity so that I don't tone up too much and cast a sheet of transparency over my façade.

Duke is grinning when I throw a weak, pathetic little punch at his left. He easily bats it down, and I bite back the smirk I want to reveal. I love little secrets.

There's a certain high you get from fooling the world into thinking you're the lamb instead of the rabid wolf.

"Alright. Let's train on the wall. Plemmons always chokes the women to the brink of unconsciousness. I'm going to show you how to break the hold, and you're going to replicate it."

I nod, following along as he wipes sweat off his brow. It's good he's not as apt at profiling as Logan. He'd notice I'm not sweating, meaning I'm in better physical shape than he is. You can't fake sweat.

He stands against the wall and gestures for me.

"Hands on my throat."

I do as instructed, overlapping my thumbs as I form a choking hold with my hands. It's a terribly inefficient way to choke someone. A little bit of wire does the trick much better.

He grins down at me as I tighten my hold, and his arms dart up between mine, shoving them open in a blink. He spins me, and I let him, fighting really damn hard against my reflexes as he slams me against the wall. His hands go around my neck, and he arches an eyebrow as he squeezes just tight enough to piss me off.

"Do what I just did. Okay?" he asks, squeezing a hair tighter.

I feign imitation, acting as though I'm struggling to mirror his earlier movements, when I hear the door shut and something drop.

"What the fucking hell?" Logan's voice has me grinning, but when I try to move, Duke holds me steady, gripping tighter to my neck.

"She needs to be prepared," Duke says, tightening even more.

When breathing actually becomes difficult, my mind shuts down the little fuse that holds back my reflexes, and my hand shoots up between the stupid gap he's left between our bodies.

A pained yelp leaves him as the heel of my palm connects with the soft tissue of his throat, and he falls backwards, choking on air as my senses slam back into me.

Ah, shit.

Logan smirks then recovers, banishing the reaction as Duke heaves for air. I don't think I hit him hard enough to collapse his

Sidetracked

windpipe.

I hope.

"Sorry," I say with forced contrition. "I panicked."

Duke coughs and then a loud sound of an inhale resonates in my ears as he slowly stands. Thank goodness he's breathing.

He rubs his throat, his cheeks flaming with a blushing hue.

"Good instincts," he says, swallowing hard. "Just do that if he comes at you."

Plemmons won't leave that large space between our bodies. He's an experienced choke-artist. Detective Duke is not. If you're going to choke someone face to face, you give them zero room between your bodies.

But I obviously don't point that out. A good, sane, non-stabby girl wouldn't know that.

I move to Logan, wondering if he suspects anything, but he looks like he's more amused than anything as he tugs me to his body, wrapping an arm possessively around my middle.

"You must be SSA Bennett," I hear Duke say from close behind me, but I don't turn around as Logan keeps me pressed to him.

With one arm still around my waist, Logan reaches over with his free hand, and I look over my shoulder as Duke shakes it.

Logan's hand that's on me slides down to my spandex-clad ass, and he rests it there, as though he's proving a point. He's cute when he's jealous.

"I wasn't aware homicide could spare someone to help watch after my girl," Logan says, though I hear the edge he tries to hide.

A slow, calculated grin curves over Duke's mouth.

"We're taking the possible threat very seriously, SSA Bennett."

"I'm sure it'd be a dream come true to get an arrest this high profile, especially in a field that is always overshadowed by the FBI, since we're just down the road and all."

Logan is taunting. Duke is arrogant. And I'm worried there's about to be a sword fight in my living room. And not with actual swords.

"You mean arresting a man you brought to DC? A man who is killing high class residents because the *FBI* slipped up and let him get away, even after figuring out his name?"

Logan's jaw tics, and I internally curse Detective Dipshit.

"Logan, I'm sure you're exhausted. I'd rather not waste what little time I have with you so you can throw down the gauntlet in a pissing match."

Duke snorts, and I turn and glare at him. "You shut up."

He grins and walks down the hall, heading to his guestroom.

"Remove him from my house, and that will solve the problem," I tell Logan, but he shakes his head and runs a hand through his hair.

"I have Donny running a thorough check on him, but if he's as clean and decorated as his file suggests, then he's the best option for keeping you safe."

I'm the best option for keeping me safe. I think it's adorable that he believes Duke to be more capable than me though.

I start tugging at his arm, pulling him toward my bedroom. "You look exhausted. Stop worrying about me and get some sleep."

His eyes are heavy, and I can tell he's tired. The sun set a few hours ago, but it's likely he hasn't slept in over twenty-four hours.

He follows me without argument, and I can tell he's already close to being asleep when he drops to the bed, fully clothed. Grinning, I start undoing his tie, and he smirks as I do.

"Don't get any ideas," I say, pulling away the black fabric and tossing it to the ground. "Sleep first. More later."

"Only if you sleep with me."

I help him shed his jacket, shoes, shirt, socks, and pants, getting

Sidetracked

him down to just his boxers. It's very tempting to run my mouth over all the lines of lean muscle, but I refrain. The exhaustion shining from his eyes curbs all of my other urges.

In my tank and tiny shorts, I snuggle in next to him, and his arms come around me, holding me close. "Wear pants around that guy. No more of this," he murmurs against my forehead, squeezing my ass through the little spandex shorts.

Grinning like an idiot, I roll my eyes. "You're a total caveman."

"Not normally," he says around a yawn.

He doesn't even know how saying things like that does weird things to my soul, adding back the lost pieces I thought were forever gone. I feel more human with each passing day. Less like a soulless monster with a thirst for blood.

Not that I want to stop killing; I just want to feel more like the carefree, happy girl I was before they stole it all. Before they ruined me.

"You should stay in a hotel with more security than this," he says, half asleep already as his body slowly relaxes.

"I'm fine here. You need to stop worrying about me."

I run my fingers through his hair, and he groans as he leans into the touch, getting even more comfortable as he fights sleep.

"Hadley said you're loaded. You can afford something with higher security than any law enforcement can offer. I just want you safe, Lana. I'd never forgive myself if something happened to you."

My entire body goes rigid.

"Hadley? What else did she tell you?"

"Mm?" His eyes are closed, and I hate prying right now. "She said you were loaded, and I told her to stop prying."

Obviously she didn't stop prying.

"Were…um…you two also involved?"

He releases a lazy rumble of laughter as his arms tighten around me. He keeps his eyes closed as he answers.

"We're a pair, aren't we?" he asks in a soft, sleepy tone. "How long before we trust each other?"

Trust…

Yeah, that's a whole other issue for another day.

I'm not talking about trust. I'm talking about a crazy girl who showed up with more information than she should have pieced together. I should have anticipated him asking me those questions, but I thought all was clear after the first few weeks.

I never saw her coming.

I hate surprises.

"Well?" I prompt.

He grins, still keeping his eyes shut.

"She's like a kid sister. I took her under my wing when she first started in our department. Hadley doesn't date, and when she does date, she doesn't date men."

She's into women? Women only?

A sense of calm washes over me. He's making me ridiculous. I have a kill list a mile long that could put me on death row—since some of the states still have death row. I'm playing a constant game of life and death.

He snuggles in closer, content to just hold me. Instinctively, I continue running my fingers through his hair, and he moans as he slowly drifts off. When he starts breathing evenly, I know he's down for the count.

I don't stop running my fingers through his hair. Something inside of me seems to fuse together, and my heart beats to a steadier rhythm than it has in years.

His arms stay around me, and for once in ten years, I feel safe. I feel treasured.

I feel something other than empty.

Sidetracked

I don't even realize how much time has passed until his phone is going off with an alarm. My eyes dart over to the dresser to see it's close to midnight.

He groans as his arms leave me, and a chill settles onto every spot his touch has abandoned. He cuts off the alarm, and he rolls back over, wrapping me into his arms again, and kisses the side of my neck.

"I bet you didn't have this in mind when you signed on to date me," he says in his sexy, sleep-gruff voice.

"You warned me your schedule was crazy. I don't mind."

"I meant all the extra craziness," he says, running his lips up higher, nipping my ear enough to elicit a small shudder from me.

His hand starts working down my shorts, and I lift my hips, eager to give him access.

Then that damn phone rings.

He curses.

I mutter a few words.

"Everything okay in there?" Duke asks from outside my bedroom door, reminding me he's in my house.

A serial killer sharing a house with a homicide detective and a FBI agent.

Life doesn't get more complicated than this.

I just hope it takes Logan forever to find Tyler and Lawrence, that way I have him to myself a little more. He works too much, and I can tell he's exhausted.

It's sad that I want to hide my bodies now so that my boyfriend gets a break and can spend more time with me.

How twisted can one person possibly get?

"It's fine," Logan calls out, glaring at the door.

He grabs his phone, answering it with his last name only, and I sit up to kiss his shoulder as he talks.

"No, I'm at Lana's house, why?"

He grows stiff, and I remove my lips from his shoulder. When he blows out a harsh breath, I run my hand up his back.

"Yeah. Come get me. It's on the way. I'll grab a shower and something to eat before you get here."

He hangs up before turning to me, brushing his lips over mine just barely.

"Care if I use your shower."

I roll my eyes. "You don't even have to ask."

"I'd ask you to shower with me, but we have another body. I need to be ready before Craig gets here."

I gesture toward the bathroom, and he groans as he stands.

Following him in, I hop up on the sink, admiring the view as he strips out of his boxers and climbs into the shower, turning the spray on. I grimace. That has to be cold.

He doesn't so much as flinch.

"I feel like you're getting screwed out of all the good stuff and skipping right to the worst case scenarios," he says over the sound of the water.

"I'm currently not getting screwed. Did he leave more messages?"

He grunts, and I watch as he tips his head back, running his hands through his hair to wet it. I think shower times should get watched from now on. This is hot. I want to video it so I can perv more later — after I buy a replacement vibrator.

"Just his media name and the words 'You can't' were carved. Two bodies in two days is a rapid devolution. He's getting too bold."

I dropped two bodies in one day, but I hardly feel like now is the time to brag about my awesome efficiency.

"How's he choosing his victims?"

Sidetracked

We shouldn't be talking about an active case. It's against the rules. But this one actually concerns me, considering I'm probably a target. So that makes it…okay?

"He's choosing mostly brunettes in their mid-twenties. All were low risk victims, but none were put on display until he came here. This latest one was found tied to the top of her car, and the car was moved to the middle of the street. That's all I know so far."

I think that over before responding.

"He's feeling the high. There's a certain feeling of invincibility when the killer finds it impossible to get caught. It probably turns him on more than the torture to see everyone quivering in fear. He's also approving of his media name, adopting the persona. Everyone fears the Boogeyman growing up. Now he's reigniting that fear in adults."

He blows out a breath of agreement, and I try to think of something to say.

"*You can't?* That's an odd message."

"Yeah. I'm sure it's a taunt. Maybe he got interrupted before he could finish."

Maybe…

When it grows quiet, I think of something else to say, just to make it look like I'm asking more questions than about the killer.

"Does it bother you that I didn't tell you I was rich?"

"No," he says immediately. "I like the fact you're humble. My stepdad always said that those who strive to be humble detest the ways of the arrogant."

I like that.

"And for the record, I can tell your past is a sore subject, so I don't want to press for any information there either. I enjoy just getting to know who you are now," he adds, causing me to smile and grimace at the same time.

He's bringing back parts of me that I thought were dead,

resurrecting my soul from ashes. But all the shadows that lurk inside me, hiding the monster within... Those are parts he can never see.

He shuts off the shower and steps out just as quickly, grabbing a towel from the rack. I'd be lying if I said I wasn't distracted by the way the water seems to follow all the lines of his abs to the towel as he conceals my happy place with the fluffy fabric.

An audible sigh escapes me in dreamy fashion, and Logan smirks, arching an eyebrow at me. I'm not even ashamed that I'm ogling him.

It feels good to crave someone and *want* them. I won't take it for granted or be embarrassed.

He grabs a toothbrush from his bag—when did that get in here?—and sidles up next to me to start brushing his teeth.

We look like a Sunday morning special right now—instead of killer and hero.

As soon as he's finished brushing his teeth, he slides my legs apart and settles in between them. I don't protest at all when he kisses me, tasting minty and ultra fresh.

My fingers tangle in his hair as I pull him closer, savoring this while I can. There's no telling when he'll be back.

He laughs when he tries to break the kiss, only to be pulled back down by me. Unfortunately, his phone rings again, and I'm forced to let go.

This time it's a text, and he reads whatever it says. He puts it away, his face expressionless as he looks up at me.

"I'll take you on another date soon. And another. And another. I'll make all this worth it. I'll also be back here tomorrow. And the next day. And the next. It's not much, but right now—"

"Stop acting like you're not enough," I tell him, kissing him again.

I want to tell him he's too good for me.

I want to beg him to save my soul from damnation.

Sidetracked

I want to plead with some powers above to take away the pain that drives me…

To let karma step in and handle the rest.

But I'm the only reckoning there will be.

"Scream for me, little Victoria. Scream loud."

"Always knew you were a little whore."

"Hold her down!" Kyle says, laughing as I struggle in vain, holding back the sob on the tip of my tongue, refusing to let them see me break.

"Leave her alone!" Marcus cries from behind me, and my heart clenches as excruciating pain slices through my body.

"Open your eyes, sweetheart. You don't want to miss this."

"Do it, Marcus. Do it or we'll make it so you never do it again."

Hours and hours and hours of taunts. The night I should have died is forever seared into my memory. Their sins stained my soul with so much darkness that their deaths are needed to cleanse me.

To make me feel whole again.

I need to replace their taunts and evil laughter with the sounds of their screams.

I sleep better with each new scream I get to add. The screams override the scent of their breath, the strikes of their hands, and their dirty, disgusting fingers.

They'll never hurt anyone else. Even if they rise from the dead, they lost their tools of pain.

The rest will join them soon enough.

I can't stop now.

Not even for Logan.

Chapter 6

The superior man is modest in his speech, but exceeds in his actions.
—Confucius

Logan

"All is quiet since that last kill two days ago," Craig says, stating the obvious.

I nod, my mind buzzing a thousand miles a minute.

I've kept my promise, going back to see Lana, even though I spend all the time sleeping. She stays cuddled against my side, strumming her fingers through my hair, as though she has nothing better to do.

"He's smart. Police presence has increased," I say numbly.

I've never felt so personal about a case.

"What does 'you can't' supposed to mean?" he asks, pensive as he studies the close-up of the writing on the body.

"I don't know. You can't stop me? I think he got interrupted."

"Then there could be a witness. I have that press conference coming up in three hours. I'll see if I can get anyone to come forward."

I nod absently, running my finger over my lips. The director has put all our other cases on hold. This is currently our only priority, and we're to treat it as though it's our only case.

"Forensics came back on those fibers we found on the last

Sidetracked

victim's body," Hadley says, dropping a file to my desk. "I looked into it, and you can only find that type of thing in an old factory that was closed down four years ago. Homeless people shack up in it fairly regularly. He could be there and blending in. It's about two hours from here. I'll send the address to your phone."

I'm out of my chair and grabbing my gun in the next breath, and Donny races to catch up with me as I head out the door. Hadley stays behind, but Lisa and Elise join us as we burst through the doors, practically jogging.

Donny makes the calls for backup, and I pull up my phone to see the address Hadley has already sent. He'd need a vehicle to get from there to here, so I call Hadley.

"What's up?"

"You and Alan start sifting through any car thefts between here and there. He's got wheels. I doubt he's taking the bus after soaking in a blood bath."

"On it."

She ends the call, and I pocket my phone, rushing my steps. We better catch the son of a bitch.

Lisa and Elise take the lead in their SUVs, and I follow behind them with Donny at my side, both of us turning on our lights. "Fuck," I hiss, whipping into a gas station when my low fuel light pops on.

I call Elise as Donny hops out to hurriedly push some gas into the tank.

"You'll get there before us, but don't go in until we're on the scene. Got it?" I say the second Elise answers.

"Got it. We'll have to wait for local PD to back us up anyway."

I hang up, tapping my fingers impatiently on the steering wheel as I wait for Donny. Deciding I need to do something, I text Lana.

ME: You okay?

LANA: Bored to death, but fine. Playing cards with Duke and taking all his money. You okay?

Have I mentioned I really hate Duke being there alone inside the house with her? If she didn't need a protective detail, I'd be kicking his ass for seeing her more than I get to.

ME: I'll be fine once this guy is in cuffs.

I don't mention the shoot-to-kill order.

LANA: Stop worrying about me. I promise I'll be fine. You don't know this about me, but I'm a survivor. <3

I don't know a lot of things about her. But a past doesn't make a person, and that's all she's holding back. I trust that she'll share that when she's ready.

Donny hops into the car, and I pocket my phone before cranking it back up and squealing out of the parking lot.

Donny handles organizing the swat team, telling them to pull back until we arrive on scene.

A loud truck passes us, blowing its horn, and Donny flips off the driver as I keep my tunnel vision, never slowing down.

We're about twenty miles from our destination, when I slam on my brakes, my stomach roiling as I stare at the SUV off the side of the otherwise deserted road. The backend is crushed, the glass busted out.

It's turned on its side, and Donny curses before leaping out of the passenger side, racing to Elise and Lisa who may or may not still be in there.

I dive out as well, juggling my phone free, and calling for an ambulance. Cursing my low battery, I quickly give them our location and tell them to hurry. Putting away my almost dead phone, I slide to the front, trying to see through the window.

From this angle, I can tell they were T-boned from the road

Sidetracked

connecting to this one. Elise and Lisa are both unconscious, and Elise is bleeding from her forehead. Her side took the brunt of the impact, but I can't tell how much damage she's sustained from here.

"Logan!" Donny yells.

I rush around, seeing Lisa's door jammed into the ground as Donny breaks the front glass, trying to peel it back now that he has something to pry open. Using the crowbar, he pries the top down, and I toss off my jacket, wrapping it around my hands to help him peel the windshield all the way back.

Lisa is breathing heavily, and her eyes are dazed as she blinks them open. She cries out, and lifts her right arm—the one closest to her door.

My eyes widen in disbelief when I see the blood flowing from the shallow cuts.

"It was him," she says, sucking in a pained breath. "It was him. It was him."

Her panicked breaths quicken, and Donny tries to calm her down as I look at Elise.

"Elise!" She doesn't answer, but she finally groans.

Relief washes through me that she's still alive.

"He did this," Lisa is saying, still panicking as she points to her bloody arm. "He took our guns. He thought he got all of them. He...He had a gun. He hit us...then he pointed the gun at us. We...we were still upright when he came to my side, telling us to keep our hands where he could see them."

She cries out, trying to undo the seatbelt.

"Then...then he broke my window, and he used the glass... He used the glass to write this," she says, sobbing as she holds her arm up again.

"He was going to kill us, but I grabbed my spare gun when he dropped my arm to retrieve his gun. I shot at him. I shot twice. I grazed him. But...That bastard. He had someone with him. A girl.

163

He had a girl. He knew we were coming. But he carved this."

Her sentences are all over the place, barely making any sense.

All I can see on her arm are blood smears, but she wipes it off on her shirt and holds it up again. Donny's breath leaves as he pales. Carved in her skin is the word "KEEP."

"He knows us," Donny whispers as Lisa breaks down into sobs again. "He chose Lisa instead of Elise. There's a reason he targeted your ex."

His tone is hushed, so as not to agitate Lisa, and my body tenses at the insight. Why "KEEP?" Why that word?

"He's bleeding," Lisa chokes out. "I shot him enough to make him bleed. He'll need stitches at least."

I look around, finding a light blood trail. It's not enough for him to die from though. Fuck!

"The truck that fucking passed us," I say through clenched teeth. "It was him. He even blew his motherfucking horn!"

I slam my fist down on the car, and Donny goes as stiff as I do.

"I hope that shoot-to-kill order remains," Donny growls.

"Someone tipped him off. He knew we were coming."

"Is the girl his accomplice?"

I shake my head, hating what's going on inside it right now. "Nothing in the profile indicates a partner. Nothing in his profile indicates a relationship with police either. No. He's smart. Calculated, even. He had a fail-safe plan. If he was hiding in this town, there was a reason he felt safe. Look into their local PD. Find out if any of the officers who were aware of this raid has a daughter or a wife. Then go door to door. Find out if someone is missing. It wouldn't be reported."

His eyes widen. "You think he took a hostage?"

"Yeah. And now that his location has been burned, he no longer needs her alive."

Sidetracked

And we let him drive right by us. That sick, narcissistic son of a bitch honked at us, taunted us, knowing we were on our way to him. And I never even looked up.

I'm supposed to be observant of my surroundings at all time. My personal involvement in this case is fucking with my head, making me have tunnel-vision, and knocking me off my game.

He's winning.

Chapter 7

Death and life have their determined appointments.
—Confucius

Logan

"Lisa is okay. She's in a little shock, but otherwise okay," Donny says as he hands me a cup of coffee. Our entire team is in a hospital waiting room right now.

The security detail makes me nervous, because someone from the police force sold us out.

"Only cops with no kids or family at Lana's from now on," I say to Donny, who nods. "We've only been out in public once. It's possible he doesn't even know she exists. It's been her house mostly we've stayed at when I see her, and I'd know if I'd been followed."

I take a sip of the coffee as he types out a text, probably relaying my request.

"Elise?" I ask him.

"She's coming around. Her left shoulder was dislocated, and she has two breaks in her left leg where it got pinned on impact. She's not in shock, but she is fucking pissed."

He smirks, and I laugh under my breath. Elise will take this as personally as I am now. Then again, everyone has a personal investment now. He came after two of ours, and called me out by name. It's our mission—our only focus—to bring him down.

Hadley is typing furiously on her laptop. She hasn't been a techie for years, ever since she became the best in the field on

Sidetracked

forensics. But now she's dusting off her old skills, trying to find any footage of which girl Plemmons might have had with him.

Donny and I described the truck — old Ford, beat up, jacked up, and big brush guard on the front. You couldn't tell it'd been the tool to crash them, because it sure as hell didn't look like it'd been in a wreck.

"Anything?" I ask Hadley.

Her eyes narrow to slits.

"Not yet. But I will find this son of a bitch."

"He could be somewhere in the hospital. He'll want to see this show. Or, if he has any computer skills, he may be hacked into the feed," I tell her.

She nods. "On it. I already informed the cops of something like that when we got here," she explains. "They've been canvassing the hallways and such."

"Lisa shooting at him probably pissed him off. He hit them from the rear, sent them sliding around, and then slammed them again. It dazed them enough to give him an edge," Leonard says as he sits down. "Then after Lisa shot him, he got in the truck, got a good run-and-go from that side road, and T-boned them, probably trying to kill them."

"He's a sexual sadist looking for an easy kill? Just to piss us off?" Donny asks, shaking his head.

"He wants us investing all our attention into him. He's winding us up," I say through clenched teeth.

"It's working," Leonard growls.

A woman pokes her head in. "Ms. Clifton is asking for you," she says, looking at us all instead of being specific.

Donny, Leonard, and I stand up, and Craig comes jogging down the hall, joining us as we walk toward the room where they're holding Elise.

Before we make it, my eyes land on a familiar brunette who is racing toward me with wide, terrified green eyes. Her entire body visibly relaxes when she sees me, and she launches herself into my arms.

I grab Lana, holding her to me, as she shakes and trembles. Detective Duke is right on her heels, panting heavily as he doubles over, resting his hands on his knees.

"Fucking marathon runner or something?" he asks between labored breaths.

Lana doesn't speak. She just clings to me, her arms wrapped tightly around my neck.

"I was so worried," she finally says.

"They said your team was hit," Duke explains, running a hand through his hair. "She drove. I couldn't talk her out of coming. They wouldn't tell us who was hit."

I hold her for a second longer. Three of my team members are staring at us with raised eyebrows, before I finally snap back to reality.

Fuck!

I drop her to the ground and push her away, ignoring the way she blanches.

"You can't fucking be here!" I yell, then cut my eyes to Duke. "Why the fucking hell would you bring her?"

His eyes narrow to slits. "Did you miss the part where I said she was coming with our without me. I came to keep her safe."

I gesture to Lana, all 5'4 of her. "She weighs 120 at most. You're at least 200 with law enforcement training, yet you can't restrain her?"

Lana backs away, saying nothing, but my eyes are on Duke, furiously glaring at him. He glares back, just as furious.

"She's not a prisoner or a criminal. I can't legally confine her to her damn house, you arrogant asswipe."

Sidetracked

Donny takes a step between us, as though he's preparing for things to go bad.

"He's possibly here or watching, and you bring her here? I'm not fucking stupid. You *want* him to find her. Especially now. You want a new promotion from a shiny little arrest for the highest profile killer in the nation right now."

He takes a threatening step toward me, and Donny wedges between us more when I take a step too.

"I couldn't give a shit about that. I came because I was trying to keep her safe. I don't have any authority to confine an innocent civilian to her home, and neither do you."

I open my mouth to yell at him some more, when Lana calmly inserts herself into the conversation, her haunted eyes icy and detached, something I haven't seen in a while.

"You told me to have a protective detail, and I agreed," she says quietly. I swallow down my words as she continues. "You told me to let a stranger stay in my house; I agreed, even though I didn't want to. I take someone with me when I leave. I've put my business deals on hold to appease you, not traveling and risking myself. I've sat in a protective bubble, answering all your calls and texts promptly so you don't worry about me."

Her eyes glisten, but I can tell they're nothing more than angry tears. And I realize I've seriously fucked up.

Chapter 8

When anger rises, think of the consequences.
—Confucius

Lana

Harsh. Oblivious. Arrogant.

Three words I never thought I'd use to describe the man before me.

Unfairly confining me to my house, while not giving me the same option of knowing he's safe… I can't even put into words how pissed off I am.

"You don't even take the time to fire off a text that you're okay," I go on, keeping my tone even, refusing to show too much emotion.

I don't bleed for the world anymore.

He saw more than anyone else, and he didn't bother to care when it mattered the most.

"Lana, I get that you're pissed, but you can't be here," he says, his voice softening.

"I see that," I retort tightly, taking a step back. "Sorry I cared. It won't happen again."

Tacky and juvenile as that sounds, it's a bitter girl's prerogative right now.

I turn and start walking away, but he follows, grabbing my arm. I rip it free from his grip.

"You don't understand," he whispers, looking over at a camera.

Sidetracked

"He could be watching. We don't know what he's capable of right now, and his past is mostly a mystery."

"You put me in a bubble, and I gave you peace of mind. You cared. I'd do anything to ease your mind so that you didn't worry." I swallow down the knot in my throat, refusing to get emotional, disallowing my weakness or vulnerability to shine. "I worry too, Logan. Duke got the call your team was hit, and you were all at the hospital. You wouldn't even answer your phone. Or send a text. Or respond to my hundreds of texts. I can handle a lot of things, but I won't let you walk all over me, then refuse to offer me the same peace of mind. And then get pissed at me? Talk down to me? Who the hell do you think I am?"

I turn and walk away, and he lets me, because he can't follow. He can't make a scene.

The Boogeyman could be watching.

Let the sick bastard come.

I need something to stab.

"Stay with her. I'll be there as soon as I can get free," I hear Logan saying, probably to Duke as I keep walking. "And someone find me a fucking phone charger!"

The first tear falls as I step into the open elevator and stab the Lobby button fiercely. I ran up three flights of stairs, worried out of my mind that Logan was hurt when I couldn't get him to answer my million and one calls or texts.

Turns out, I'm just someone he didn't bother to think of when I was going out of my mind with all the worst case scenarios.

Dead phone is not a good excuse. Not when everyone on the team is here with their phones he could have used.

Duke slides into the elevators just before the doors close, and he leans against the wall.

He doesn't say a word, and I toss him the keys the second we hit the lobby. Silently, we make it to the car, and make the long drive home. I don't speak. The radio is silent. The only noise is the sound of my V8 Mustang vrooming down the street.

My phone lights up with a text from Logan—guess he got that charger—but I don't bother reading it. Just like he didn't bother with me.

When we finally reach my house, I take the keys from Duke, but I cross over to the driver's seat.

"What are you doing?" he asks.

"Giving you time to get out of my house. I don't want to be around people right now. All of you better be off my property before I return."

His eyes widen. "Look, Lana, I get that you're pissed right now. He's an overbearing douchebag who just acted like a thoughtless prick, but don't risk your own safety to punish him. Let us stay and protect you."

I hold the door open, one foot inside the car. Duke's a good guy, but it's hard not to take this out on him, since he's the only one around right now.

"You have no legal right to be here. Just as you said. I can't stop you from loitering on the street, but you're officially trespassing if you stay on my property. Be gone before I get back, or, ironically enough, I'll call the cops."

He groans and curses, running a hand through his already disheveled hair. "Where are you going?"

"Wherever the fuck I want to," I say, flipping him off as I get into the car. "If Logan has a problem with that, remind him it's a free country," I add before shutting the door.

Without giving him more time to argue, I crank the car and slam it into first gear, spinning on a dime in my driveway, feeling my rear swing around as I start barreling out. I don't glance back as I drive to the warehouse in town that Jake rented out. I also drive with my knees as I turn off my phone and pull the battery out.

When I get there, I leave my car in the warehouse before grabbing the keys to the Altima. We have several cars I use when I

Sidetracked

go to collect the debts. No cameras are out this way, meaning no one ever sees me do this.

The warehouse has the best security, and even if someone breaks in, they won't know who it belongs to. Well, unless my pretty little Mustang is in here when they hit.

Not likely enough to be concerned.

The cars are disposed of after they serve their purpose.

I leave the warehouse, turning on a burner phone in the car, and call Jake.

"Hello?"

"It's me. Find anything on the Boogeyman?"

"No. This guy is pissing me off," he grumbles. "How's Logan?"

"He's in one piece and untouched. He's also recently single."

He grows quiet, and I ignore the tear that rolls down my cheek.

"I can't believe I'm saying this, since I'd feel so much better if you weren't dating a federal agent or living with cops, but are you sure you're not overreacting?"

"He didn't bother to care that I was going out of my mind with worry, even though I've jumped through hoops to keep him updated on my safe-and-sound state."

"Sounds…petty. Sure you're not just looking for an excuse to get out before you get too attached?"

I'm already too fucking attached. I don't cry.

I haven't cried since the day the tears stopped falling.

Yet tears are breaching my eyes with a renewed vigor as I drive toward Jake's house.

"Petty is getting pissed that he doesn't call when he says he will. Petty is not being livid that he didn't bother to tell me he was alive. I can't do this, Jake. I can't live with cops in my house. Those badges…I want to rip them off and flush them down the toilet. They wear them with pride."

"They're not from Delaney Grove, babe. You can't confuse the two."

"I'm not. They'd be dead if there was any confusion. I just feel…dirty. I don't want them there. I don't want him there anymore—not because he makes me feel dirty. I'm giving up too much by playing by his rules. I haven't even started Anthony's house yet besides the two cameras."

"I've jumped a leg on that one for you, since I knew it'd be hard to go put more cameras in a house if a cop was trailing you to keep you safe. Pretty sure aiding a murderer isn't what they had in mind."

He's trying to be light and funny, but I don't have the headspace for it right now.

"Good. I need something to focus on."

"Feeling stabby?" he muses, still trying to lighten my mood.

"Very."

"Where are you?"

"Heading toward your house. Plotting a murder at mine isn't going to be easy for a while."

"Why the burner phone? And why don't I hear your Mustang?"

"I'm in the new Altima we picked up. I've had a cop in my house for however long it's been—feels like years. I don't trust him not to call friends and put a whatever out on my ride. Also, the FBI have the ability to turn a phone on if the battery is in it, so I don't trust the GPS to not give them my location."

"Paranoid much? They can't do that unless you're a suspect."

"You're acting like they play by the rules. Don't forget Agent Hadley Grace hacked my hospital records. Well, Kennedy's hospital records."

He blows out a long breath. "I take it back. I'm very glad this relationship is over, even though I hate that you're losing the first thing that seemed to make you smile in over ten years."

Sidetracked

Bitterness rises, but I swallow it down as I angrily bat away the fresh tears. I don't have time to cry and wallow over a breakup. It was stupid to think I could ever be in a relationship.

I survive to avenge the wrongs of the past.

Falling in love? It's the end of a girl like me.

"Speaking of Agent Hadley Grace," Jake says, breaking me out of my concentration. "I dug up that dirt you need."

"And?" I prompt, wondering if it even matters now.

"She was recruited by the FBI at sixteen after hacking a secure file in their network. It was jail time or FBI time. It's a pretty common thing, especially amongst juvenile hacking offenders. She apparently became some sort of forensics prodigy though, and moved up to Logan's team."

"That's not dirt," I point out.

"No, but she was a hacker at sixteen because she was a runaway. Her dad died in Iraq shortly after she was born. Her mother remarried Kenneth Ferguson when Hadley was about ten. Hadley was sent to therapy about two years after he came into the picture. Her mother was a major bank president, which means she was barely even at home. And the therapist diagnosed Hadley as a pathological liar within three weeks."

I slow down, processing the facts, waiting on him to go on.

"She claimed Kenneth was touching her. Said he came for her on the nights her mother worked. They found no evidence of sexual trauma, and no evidence in his past that suggested he was a pedophile."

"So was he?"

"She was wetting the bed nightly. I'd say there was some merit."

"Pathological liars believe their lies," I remind him.

"Pathological liars don't get recruited by the FBI. They also never really get better. She's never had any demerits against her.

175

Her file is pristine. And her stepdad is now a social worker with unlimited access to children, Lana. He took a job in that field after she ran away at thirteen. It makes it seem like he needed access to other little girls."

"What about before her?"

"He was married to a woman in Texas. A woman who had a ten-year-old daughter. A daughter who frequently wet the bed and had nightmares, according to this sealed file I just opened. No accusations were ever made there."

A knot buds in my throat. For all the bad shit that has happened to me, that's one thing I never had to suffer.

"I know what you're thinking, and the answer is hell no," Jake says after a spell of silence.

"How far away is he?"

"Damn it, Lana! I just said no. We have a list—a specific one. We have a system. First we get all the sick sons of bitches who wronged you and Marcus. Then we take out the ones who wronged your dad. That's it. We're not some avenging angels who can go after every pervert out there."

"He's a social worker with unlimited access to children— dejected kids who are far more likely to keep their pain silent so as not to feel more dejected. You said it yourself. Can you sit there and tell me you're okay with letting him continue on with what he's doing? Can you say that you're no different than that dirty town who knew what was happening to us and did nothing?"

He grows quiet for so long that I know I have him.

"He's not too far away. I'll text you the address. Don't use your MO. This can't be connected to the Scarlet Slayer."

"The what?" I ask, amused.

"It's the name I'm going to let the media give you."

"You're going to let the media give me a name?"

"Yes. Yes I am. Don't get seen, and then ditch the car in the

Sidetracked

usual place. I'll have that guy pick it up, and I'll come pick you up — same thing as always. No mistakes. Have you got any kill supplies with you?"

"A knife in my boot. It'll do. I'll stick to rocks and sidewalks so as not to leave any tracks. As much as I'd like to cut his dick off, I'll refrain."

"If he's innocent, you can't kill him."

"Don't worry," I tell my overly concerned friend. "They always confess their sins to me."

Chapter 9

The cautious seldom err.
—Confucius

Logan

Frustrated, I try to keep my head here and not on Lana, who hasn't answered my calls since she walked out of the hospital five hours ago. Duke isn't answering his phone either.

Which will have serious fucking consequences.

My eyes settle on the swat team commander who is inside the interrogation room. The glass between us is a one-way glass, not that he doesn't know that.

His hands are shaking. He keeps standing and sitting, acting as though he's jittery and ready to get out.

"His twenty-year-old daughter hasn't shown up for her college classes in four days," Donny says, watching him with me. "The roommate says she had to go home because of a family loss. We're tracking phone calls to see if Plemmons contacted her that way, maybe lied with the ruse of someone passing? The mother seemed genuinely oblivious, had no idea what we were asking so many questions about."

"Brunette?" I ask him, still studying Lee Norris as he paces the room, then sits down, then stands again.

He's definitely agitated.

He's our leak.

"Yes," Donny answers. "Plemmons taking her shows a level of organization that doesn't fit with his background, or what little we know of it. He felt like he was fooling us all this time, but when we found him out, he took it as a personal challenge to one-up us."

I nod, agreeing.

"I'll go in. See if you can get ahold of Detective Duke. What did the patrols say?"

He tightens his lips, and I study him.

"What?" I prompt.

"The guys said Lana kicked them off her property. I didn't want to tell you with so much else going on. She drove off and basically told everyone to fuck themselves. You included."

I slam my fist against the wall, the sheetrock crumbling around it.

"I've never seen you lose your cool like you're losing it now, Logan. Maybe you should take—"

"*Don't* finish that sentence," I bite out, rubbing my bloody knuckles on my pants, ignoring the burn. "Everyone is emotionally invested in this. Not just me. Send Leonard in with us. Norris will want to attack me within the first few minutes."

"You sure you got the head for this?"

"He'll spill immediately. He'll blame us for getting his daughter killed. But he may also be the lead to catching this sick son of a bitch. My head is working just fucking fine. Find Lana. Call me if you do."

I turn and walk out of the room, and head straight into the interrogation room, where Norris jumps up from his seat, glaring at me the second I step inside.

"What the hell do you think you're doing locking me in here?! Do you have any idea what kind of sub-committee reports I could—"

"Erica Norris is your daughter, and she's been missing from her college classes for four days due to a death in your family. There's been no death in your family," I say, shutting him up.

He turns a scary shade of white, and his entire body goes lax as he falls into the chair, losing the ability to stand.

"You just got her killed," he says in a rasp whisper. Then his eyes turn lethal as he slams his fist against the table, fury rushing in to renew his energy. "You son of a bitch! You got her killed!"

He lunges, but Leonard shows up just in time, grabbing him by the collar, as I continue to lean against the wall, keeping my expression blank.

"You leaked the raid to him," I go on. "What phone did you use? Did he give you one?"

"You bastard!" he spits out, choking back a sob as Leonard restrains him. "You knew he had her and still brought me in?! You cold murderer!"

I push off from the wall, moving to the table separating us, and prop my hands on it, leaning over until his eyes connect with mine.

"We had him. You tipped him off. What did you think he'd do with her once she was no longer of any use to him?"

He sobs, breaking in front of me. "He swore he wouldn't hurt her if I alerted him to any threat. He swore I'd get her back. As long as I kept my mouth shut...he swore. Now you've pulled me in here and there's no chance of that!"

"You're the reason he's out there. You're the reason we don't have him in custody right now," I remind him, an icy edge to my tone as I shut off all emotions for what he's going through as a father.

"He wouldn't even be here if it wasn't for you and your fucking team! You set a killer loose in our state, and now he has my daughter!"

"He'd be in Boston," Leonard says calmly, "killing someone else's wife, daughter, sister... We didn't make the killer, Commander. We're trying to stop him. You took our best chance away. We finally had him."

Sidetracked

Norris loses it, sobbing so hard he becomes incoherent. His head drops to his arms, and he cries into the crook of his elbow.

It's possible his daughter is still alive, but unlikely. I have to detach myself from the guilt that tries to wiggle its way in. Casualties are *never* easy to accept. But in this line of work, they're always there. If you don't desensitize yourself from it, you don't make it two months in this field.

What he doesn't know, is that the best chance of his daughter surviving would have been for us to raid that warehouse. He'd have run. He'd have tried to get away. Bringing her along would have been too risky then.

She'd most likely still be breathing, and we'd more than likely have him in custody.

I don't tell him that. It's better for him to blame us than bear the responsibility of his own daughter's death. I can at least offer him that much mercy.

Weakly, he tosses a phone out of his pocket, and Leonard picks it up. "He sent that," Norris whispers hoarsely. "Said he'd let me hear her voice twice a day."

"Did he?" Leonard asks.

Norris wipes his eyes, nodding grimly. "Five seconds at a time. Just long enough for her to beg me to save her."

He breaks again, and Leonard walks out with the phone. By now, Erica Norris is either dead or wishing she was. She may have been wishing it for the past four days.

Sometimes, the homeless turn a blind eye to anything going on around them. It's their survival mechanism kicking in, not their inhumanity. It's street-survival. They've suffered for so long, that suffering more would be too much. But with enough incentive, they'll spill every word you need.

Right now, the ones living in that warehouse are telling what they know in exchange for cash—unethical, but not illegal. But the info isn't much.

Plemmons claimed a backroom and kept the girl chained there. He locked it with a padlock when he was gone. Took her with him at other times.

Blood was found in that room. He's already had his way with her, possibly even sliced her a few times to get what he needed, but not enough to kill her. A couple of suture kits were found in there, meaning he most likely repaired the damage he did with crude methods, just to keep her from bleeding too much.

For four days, she's endured him. For four days, she's likely prayed for death.

For four days, her father kept his mouth shut and played a dangerous game he had no right playing.

He should have come to us immediately, and Plemmons would already be in custody. His daughter would be in her own bed instead of wherever she is right now.

I walk out as he continues to sob, leaving him to cry in peace.

"See if you can get more out of him when the first wave of emotion is over," I tell Donny as he meets me in the hallway. "Anything on Lana?"

He shakes his head slowly. "No. I asked Hadley to see if she could get a beat on her, since Alan is covered up in searching footage for this guy."

I head straight toward Hadley's cubicle and find her pounding away on the keyboard. But it's not Lana she's looking for. She's searching the same footage Alan is.

"What the hell? Donny said you're trying to get a beat on Lana."

"Lana isn't my priority right now, Logan. An innocent girl is in the hands of a serial killer, and I'm trying to help save her life."

I love how she makes it sound like I'm a controlling prick instead of trying to keep someone else from landing in his hands.

"We *know* she'll be a target, especially now. If she wasn't on his radar before, she is since the hospital incident."

Sidetracked

Hadley ignores me, still typing.

"Damn it, Hadley!"

She spins, leveling me with a cold glower. "I'm looking for the girl we know is in trouble. You deal with your girlfriend — who you barely even know — on your own. He's more than likely not skilled enough to hack the hospital feed. It's even more unlikely that he'd be stupid enough to have been there, given how organized and smart he apparently is, given our new predicament. Leave. Me. Alone."

She spins back around, and I blow out a long breath. "Fine. Find Erica Norris. Find him."

"I plan to. Thanks so much for your approval," she says snidely.

I hate to admit it, but she's right. I have no business asking her to stop looking for a girl we know is in trouble to find my girlfriend. She'd be safe and tucked into her house with police protection if I hadn't lost my temper in the hospital. I should have texted her. My phone was dead, and I had no idea someone would notify Duke of what happened.

I didn't want to worry her, so I was just going to tell her about it later. When she could put her hands on me and know I was okay, see it with her own eyes. Who the fuck is notifying Duke about anything?

"Why would anyone from our department let Detective Duke in on that attack?" I ask Craig as I join him at the board, where he's staring endlessly at pictures.

Even he's trying to stop Plemmons before he strikes again.

"I wondered the same thing," he says absently. "His chief called him. The chief is being looped in on the case progression, considering we're sharing this case with local law enforcement to join manpower. He called Duke as a courtesy to your girl, but said he didn't have specifics to share." Craig turns to face me. "He had specifics. He just neglected to share, and our guys wouldn't give her any information or forward her calls to any of our phones. She's not on your call list."

A chill washes over me.

"He knew she'd go there," I say tightly.

"The chief is playing us because he wants this arrest," Craig agrees. "His department gets the least attention because we're their neighbors. All the high profile stuff from DC goes straight to us, along with all the outlying cities too. It's more common here than any other place that we usually wait for an invitation for."

"So he lets her in on it through Duke, knowing she'd rush to the hospital."

"After we'd already told him we had local law enforcement guarding the hospital, checking anyone and everyone who resembled Plemmons. We told him we thought he'd want to find a way to observe our pain and see the fear or panic he'd caused."

"And he wanted him to see Lana," I bite out.

"And possibly even follow her home," Craig says, his jaw ticking. "Fucking son of a bitch. I called patrol. They told me what happened. But I'm sending one of our guys to help watch too. We have some we can spare, even though they're wet behind the ears still."

At least one person understands that Lana is also a target, and where we know he'll eventually strike if he's even aware of her.

I don't feel as paranoid or crazy now.

"Thanks," I tell him.

He shrugs. "People will see me as rational on the matter, but find it an abuse of power if you do it. It made sense for me to step in. But I'm stepping in because I see what you're seeing. Everyone else just sees Erica Norris." His expression turns grim. "She's been dead since the day he took her, even if her heart is still beating right now."

I know this, but I don't want to say it aloud to everyone else. In the backs of their minds, they know it too.

"Our only chance of saving her was stripped away when her

father played a sexual sadist's game," Craig adds on a long sigh. "I don't have to be a profiler to know that much. Our only advantage is knowing Lana is most likely on his list. We should be concentrating all our efforts there."

"But we can't," I say, the frustration welling inside me.

"Because they want us looking for this girl," Craig agrees. "And Lana is pissed at you. Her car's GPS was disabled shortly after she bought it. Found that out, unfortunately. And either her phone is dead, or she removed the battery to keep us from locating her that way. Clever if it's the latter. Any reason your girl would work so hard to cover her trail like that?"

Even I admit that's weirdly suspicious. "Lana is extremely private. She's also not as trusting of law enforcement as I originally thought."

He nods slowly. "Makes sense. Most people don't trust the government in general right now. If she's big on privacy and civil rights, it'd make sense. Does she even have wifi? Because I can't seem to find that either."

"I don't exactly take the time to sync up to wifi when I'm there, so I have no clue."

"Well, anyway, I can't find her. I had Sarah from white collar crimes helping me out. She said the girl knew how to keep from being found. She saw this a lot when she worked sex crimes. Women who were abused repeatedly dropped off grid and became isolated and private. I doubt that's the case with your girl, since she seems comfortable in her own skin and unafraid, but I did find a lot of similarities in her privacy extremes to what Sarah was telling me. It's always the first conclusion she draws."

My stomach plummets. Nothing about her has labeled her as a victim, but I think back to when I first met her. She was more detached, readily defensive, but didn't flinch away from my touch.

No. No. My head is too crowded right now, and I'm not thinking clearly. She's not running from anyone. If anything, she's too brave, not understanding the severity of her situation.

"Anyone who'd ever been physically assaulted in that way wouldn't be turning away cops, when she knows she's a potential victim for a sexual sadist. I want her in protective custody. The protective detail is no longer good enough. They'll take it seriously if you back me."

"Already tried that," he says, grim again. "The director said you couldn't control your girlfriend using FBI resources. He doesn't see a threat to her that can't be handled with extra patrol. He doesn't see him going after her at all, since he wasn't even aware that you were involved with someone."

"As though he's the most observant person in the world," I growl.

"We focus on what we have for now," Craig says. "They're increasing patrol, but there's very little they can do if she's banned them from her property. But due to what just happened with the swat commander, we're strapped as far as extra hands go. No one with any living family members will be allowed to know what's happening before it actually happens. That's a lot of background checks, and then locating him on top of that—"

"I get it. The director wants all our attention focused on the now instead of the possible future. It's as smart as it is stupid. But I'm worried I'm biased."

He claps my shoulder. "I may be biased too, but only because you're one of the few who knows I'm prettier than you."

I huff out a small laugh, and he grins before heading off. I need to focus. Hopefully Lana left to find a very secure hotel, and removed her phone battery because I suggested he might be skilled with a computer.

"How did this guy know the swat commander's name or his daughter's?" I ask aloud to no one in particular.

"Because he does have computer skills," Craig says immediately, as though it just dawned on him too.

"We need to get our heads cleared and start thinking like we would with any other case," I tell the room as I turn around. "Right now, he's in our heads, rushing our thought processes, and turning our emotions against us, me especially."

"Turning us on each other too," Donny says as he steps out, eyeing me. "The commander officially hates the very thing he's always stood for. Plemmons may have a genius IQ that never got detected. There's a reason he suddenly craved the attention. A man who's never had something may be content in going on without it."

"But a man who's had a taste of something he didn't know he wanted, will work harder to taste more," Elise says, shocking us all as she hobbles into the room on crutches, looking battered and beaten, one arm in a sling.

"Damn it," Craig hisses, going to grab the emergency wheelchair from the corner.

"You try to put me in that thing, and you'll be wearing it when I'm done with you," she snarls, stopping him cold.

Her eyes turn to me.

"I want to find this son of a bitch. He's messed up somewhere. He's too comfortable with this city. Too comfortable with this entire situation. He didn't show an ounce of panic until Lisa shot him. Even then he seemed more annoyed than panicked. And if we can't find anything on his past, it's because he found a way to erase himself."

"Let's get to work then," I tell her as she hobbles to her desk. "I get first dibbs on shooting the bastard when that time comes," she adds under her breath, causing my lips to twitch.

As much as I fucking hate it, I have to stop concentrating on Lana. There's a slim chance Erica Norris will survive this, but I owe it to her to give all my effort to that slim chance.

Chapter 10

Only the wisest and stupidest of men never change.
—Confucius

Lana

Kenneth Ferguson weighs more than I expected. These details are usually sorted way ahead of time. This guy is an obese beast, and rolling him to the water's edge proves difficult, especially since I've had to walk in the dirt and will now need to cover my tracks.

At least he lives near the water though—bright side.

Monsters can come in many forms.

A pretty girl who loves the color red, for example—the color her victims bleed when they are begging to be spared.

They can also look like balding, fat slobs who hang out in their briefs and wife-beater tanks. Yeah. Talk about stereotypes. I've seen more ass crack than I care to remember.

I wade out into the water, dragging the dead body with me under the cloak of darkness. I can remember a time that I was afraid of the dark. Now even the snakes fear me.

He confessed. His sins were wrung out, and he confessed it all.

Okay, I might have needed him to get to the nitty gritty that had me swallowing back my own vomit, so I tortured him. Just a little. He broke quickly.

He deserved so much more death. He deserved to die for days. But I can't do that right now. It's risky to be doing this at all.

I swim under the cold water, washing all the blood off me,

Sidetracked

ignoring the way my tired muscles protest the chill. Pushing that beast uphill was a struggle. Not to mention those effin' stairs.

When I emerge, I watch him waver on top of the water. It holds him up with too much ease, despite his size.

The more body fat, the easier they float.

As soon as the current grabs him, I head back, picking up the hoe near the water's edge, and start digging up my tracks with it. I take my route in reverse as I hold the small but bright flashlight in my mouth to see.

It's two in the morning, but I had to wait until now to dump his body. The bastard has neighbors within earshot, so torturing him was a pain in the ass. Fortunately, he had a basement.

Hence the damn stairs I was referring to.

I also had to hose said basement down with bleach and water to get rid of the blood. Counter forensic measures were needed for once.

Killing is so much easier when it's on my list. Less cleanup.

I want them found when they're on the list.

Kenneth has too much trace evidence that has to be destroyed, so the large body of salt water will do the trick. Not to mention all the little critters in the sea will get a nibble before or *if* he's found.

The pictures I found in his nightstand told the story before he could. Seventy small children were in those pictures, mostly naked. Polaroids are a terrible creation, and pedophiles love their pictures.

There was one picture out of all of those that I took. I'm not sure why I took it. But it was Hadley at age eleven. He labeled them. Marked their ages too.

For some reason I know she won't enjoy her coworkers seeing her face on their board if his body is ever found and those pictures are discovered. She's strong and prideful, and most likely felt like it really was in her head all this time.

They convinced her she was crazy. Her own mother convinced

her she was making it up. Paid a professional to aide in this, simply because the woman couldn't come to grips with the possibility she was married to a pervert who was molesting her daughter.

Hadley ran away.

She ran because she thought *she* was dirty and wrong.

So many good people in this world, and it took a monster to end the suffering of so many innocent children.

I have no reason to feel indebted to a girl who wants to take me down, but there's something forcing me to feel as though we're kindred. I'd have gone crazy or killed myself without Jake.

She never had a Jake.

Maybe Logan is the closest thing to Jake she has, which is why she came after someone she thought was playing him.

I'd kill a bitch for Jake.

Hadley doesn't deserve to be broken, so she'll never see that picture.

I change out of my clothes on the gravel driveway, carefully watching anything that falls off me. My hair is bound tightly to my head and covered with a plastic wrap under a beanie.

My clothes are nothing special—generic brand things bought at any local store. I'm careful to buy all things that are found everywhere, so as to have nothing special isolating me.

The nail falls from my pocket, and I lean over, picking it up. I'm not sure why I'm taking a nail from his house. He's not on the list. Maybe it's a habit. Or maybe I really have adopted the serial method of trophy collecting.

Where they die, a nail gets taken.

His nail will go beside the others, finding a home with other perverted sons of bitches.

Warm and toasty in my clean, dry clothes, I drive back to the drop spot, making one detour.

Sidetracked

An old woodshed is twenty miles down the road, resting on private hunting ground. I open the door, and hear a scurrying of motion.

Scared eyes meet mine from the kid huddled in the corner. She's dirty, scared, and all alone.

"I'm here to save you from the monster," I say softly into the dark shed.

The shaking slowly stops as she peers at me, her eyes wide and hopeful.

"Are you an angel?" she asks, her throat raw and raspy, as though she's dehydrated.

"Compared to him, yes," I say honestly.

She slowly stands, warily looking at me. She can't be older than eight.

"Do you know if he has anyone else?" I ask her, knowing he swore it was just her, but it could be more.

She shakes her head. "The other girl didn't come back."

My heart clenches. "Come on. I'm going to take you somewhere you'll be safe."

She nods, and even though she's terrified, she comes to me, ready to face anything terrible I could do versus anything he could come back and do more of.

When she stumbles, I grab her, and she doesn't flinch away. Brave girl.

She lets me help her to my car, and she slides in on the passenger side, tears already leaking from her eyes. Her hope was gone until this moment.

I jog around to the driver's side, a risky plan forming. There's one place she can go to be safe.

"You don't have a family, do you?"

She shakes her head.

"I have a friend—a woman—I knew in another life. She'd be a good momma. She'd take care of you."

She pushes her dirty hair out of her eyes. "Really? She'll keep me safe from him?"

"I'll keep you safe from him. I can promise he'll never return. Okay?"

She studies me for a long time, more tears building in her eyes. I've scared the shit out of her now. Damn it.

"You really are an angel," she says at last, causing my heart to flip.

I don't say anything else as I drive toward Lindy May's house. She's one person who can see a ghost but not flinch.

"What's your name?" I ask the girl who is relaxing more by the minute.

"He called me Pup. But my name is Laurel," she says around a yawn, leaning against the window.

My grip tightens on the steering wheel, wishing I'd cut that dick off and sewn it into his mouth.

Lindy May's house comes into view, and I debate this for a few minutes. She's a good woman. Just like Diana. Both of whom tried to seek justice for me. Lindy suffered a terrible fate because of that. She was five years older than me the night they robbed me of everything.

"I'll call the FBI!" Lindy shouts.

"Go ahead, cunt. The FBI didn't give a damn about their father, did they?" Kyle taunts, smirking.

Dev holds her back, his face grim as she struggles to get to me.

"I'll teach that bitch a lesson later," Kyle mutters under his breath.

Dev starts pushing Lindy away, practically carrying her as she screams for me. She screams for Marcus. She screams for help that doesn't

Sidetracked

come.

Music grows louder, the sounds permeating the air with no concern for the screams they're trying to drown out.

"Now, where were we?" Kyle drawls. "Whose turn is it?"

Kyle did silence her. He didn't just silence her; he ruined her. Lindy suffered a loss trying to save me, but puts flowers on my grave every year. She talks to that grave, saying she's sorry she failed me.

She goes back to that hell to speak to a dead girl who she thinks she let down.

She's a true angel.

It's fate that she's so close by. Fate tells me Laurel would forever be loved and cared for by Lindy. And I'm sure no one would take a homeless child away from a loving home after what this kid has suffered.

Leaving Laurel here though? Knowing this will tie Kenneth to the killer I am? It's a huge mistake. But I can't leave this kid just anywhere.

I pull into the driveway, and I see a set of eyes immediately peer through a crack in the blinds. All these years later, she still feels jumpy. She likely has a gun in her hand right now.

I know the feeling.

She suffered one monster. I suffered a town full of them.

As I get out, the crack in the blinds disappears, and I gently open the door, stirring Laurel awake.

"Are we here?" she asks, her voice still scratchy.

Shit. I should have at least gotten her some water.

This is why I can't take care of her myself. Well, that and I'm sure it's not wise for a monster to raise a child.

Lindy will make her loving. I'll turn her into a knife-throwing killer.

"Yes," I tell her gently, reaching down and taking her frail, light body into my arms.

She wraps her arms around me without hesitation, adorning me with trust she shouldn't give so freely after what she's suffered.

She'll survive.

She'll overcome this.

I know that now more than ever, because only the strong could handle touch after what she's suffered.

Lindy opens the door, peering out as I carry the child toward her.

"Who are you? What do you want?"

"It's me, Lindy. And I'm here to see if you're still as good as I remember."

Just the sound of my voice has her stumbling through the door, her eyes widening in shock. She clutches the doorframe, trying to keep from sinking to the ground as her body shakes.

"You're—"

"I know. I know. I'm dead," I say, tired of hearing that line.

"You really are an angel," Laurel says weakly, her head against my chest.

Lindy's eyes swing to the child as she flips a light on, and the color drains from her face as she sees the torn clothing, the dirty skin, and the matted hair.

"This little girl has suffered too much. I told her she'd be safe here," I say to Lindy, watching as her eyes slowly come back up to mine. "Don't make me a liar."

She gestures us in, and I let her take Laurel from my arms. Laurel flinches ever so slightly, but she recovers just as fast. Lindy rushes her to the couch, putting her there, and covering her with a blanket.

Sidetracked

I watch as the maternal instincts I lacked kick in for my old friend. She runs to the fridge, grabbing a bottle of water, and she rushes back. Laurel practically rips the bottle from her hand, so thirsty that she drinks it too fast.

"Slow down. It'll make you sick to drink too much," Lindy says with a soothing voice, running her hand down Laurel's cheek.

Laurel leans into the affectionate touch, already growing trusting of Lindy. This girl is making me want to cry. I'm too emotional. This is too risky. But she deserves a chance at being safe, loved, and happy.

"I bet you're hungry."

Laurel nods emphatically, and even though it's closing in on three in the morning, Lindy rushes to the kitchen, grabbing the bread and peanut butter.

"You like PB&J?" Lindy asks.

Laurel nods, still drinking the water.

I watch patiently, a little in awe, as Lindy makes a sandwich and grabs another bottle of water.

As she hands the too small girl her food, Lindy looks up to me.

"What happened to her?"

Before I can answer, Laurel answers for me. "The angel saved me from the monster. He won't ever hurt me again. The angel will keep me safe."

I nod toward Lindy as she covers her own mouth. Tears spring to her eyes. That's all she needs to know.

Laurel digs into the sandwich, and I gesture for Lindy to join me in the kitchen.

As soon as we're in there, I check to make sure Laurel hasn't followed us.

With barely a whisper, I tell Lindy, "When this breaks the news, you come forward. Tell them a little girl showed up at your door, but you don't know who brought her to you. The man's name was Kenneth Ferguson. I'm sorry to ask this, but it's the only way they may find the bodies he has buried without me giving them the information myself."

I hand her a piece of paper, and she swallows thickly, as though she's going to be sick.

"Is he still alive?"

I shake my head slowly.

"Good," she says quietly, looking over at the little girl. She stares at her, and I remain silent, studying her, trying to figure out what's in her head.

"You're really here. Alive. Looking so different."

"It's really me."

She nods, her eyes still lost and not on me.

"You're going after them, aren't you?" she asks in a hushed tone, her eyes coming back to meet mine.

I nod once.

"I've heard whispers and rumors that some of them had died, but I haven't found it on the news. I was hoping it was true. I was wishing it was me who had the strength to do it."

My lips twitch. "You're strength comes from somewhere different. Somewhere more pure. Mine? Mine is hollowed out and filled with darkness, Lindy. I'm taking a huge risk by coming here."

"But you needed that little girl to be safe," she says, filling in the blanks. "And you trusted me."

"You lost a lot trying to get me and my brother justice."

Her face changes, a coldness washing over her. "That's not your fault. I tried to tell everyone, but no one wanted to listen. Kyle tried to shut me up. He…He…"

Her voice breaks, and my lips tighten. "I know. He'll have his day, Lindy. He'll suffer the worst."

Sidetracked

She nods, her strength renewing as she angrily bats her tears away.

"Antonio left me when he believed Kyle. Kyle said I had sex with him. I told my husband I was…raped. He believed my rapist over me. Just left me."

I nod, already knowing this. Antonio is on my list, but not for death. He's marked for penance. Should be fun.

Jake has already started the process of ruining him, starting with bankruptcy. With any luck, the bastard will kill himself within the year when he's homeless, penniless, and pointless.

"No one cared. No one wanted to listen. No one wanted to be bothered with something so horribly, inconceivably evil. They wanted to pretend it just didn't exist."

A dark smile takes over my lips. "They'll never keep their silence again. They'll quake in fear every time the lights go off. They'll be the ones scared for a change. The town will burn, Lindy. It'll burn to the ground. Trust me. I have a plan. And no one innocent will get caught in the crosshairs."

She blows out a shaky breath. "I can't believe you're alive."

She bats away fresh tears, looking over at the little girl, who is eating gratefully, oblivious to our conversation. "I'll do whatever you need me to."

"Make Laurel understand she can't tell the cops I'm a woman. Make her understand she can't tell them anything, or else I can't stop other monsters."

"I won't tell them a thing," Laurel says from the living room, proving she's not as oblivious as I thought. She swivels her head, steely determination in her eyes. "I want you to catch all the monsters."

Maybe she's more like me than I thought.

As she turns back around, returning her attention to the sandwich, Lindy whispers to me, "I want you to catch all the monsters too. Your secret is safe with me, Victoria."

A chill runs up my spine. "It's Lana now. They killed Victoria that night," I tell her quietly.

She nods, understanding. "What about Diana? She tried to—"

"I know. They threatened her son," I interrupt, waving off her concern. "She's going to play a different part. My ducks are in a row. I've been patient. I've thought it all through. Now I just wait on the chips to fall in place, and while they play poker, I'll be playing dominoes."

She smirks, leaning back to grab me a bottle of water. As she hands it to me, I take one last look at Laurel.

"She's strong. Make sure she turns out like you and not me," I say to Lindy, whose eyes turn a little duller.

"I'm weak. I quit fighting and ran away."

"You survived. You fought against a war alone. You're stronger than you realize, and you're exactly what she needs." I sigh as I look into her teary eyes. I wish I could stay longer. "I have to go."

I start to turn away, but suddenly she launches herself at me, and I wrap my arms around her, feeling a hug connect to so many dormant emotions. It's the first time I've faced my past with a face I didn't want to cut off.

It hurts as much as it heals.

She hugs me tightly, and I return the affection, though I'm not sure how long we stay that way.

As she pulls away, I hand her a piece of paper. She studies it, reading the directions, and nods at me, proving she's ready to play her new role.

Just as I'm about to leave, Laurel stands on shaky legs and makes her way to me. I kneel just as she tosses her arms around my neck, catching me off guard.

Slowly, carefully, I hug her back.

"Kill all the monsters," she whispers. "That way they don't hurt anyone else."

Sidetracked

Lindy's breath catches, and I frown. I hope her influence outshines mine in the long run.

"I'll kill them all so you never have to," I whisper back, even though it's highly unlikely that it's the right thing to say.

"Good."

"You want a shower?" Lindy asks her.

She nods, tears coming to her eyes, as though she's never wanted anything more.

Lindy swallows again, trying not to cry in front of the heartbreaking little girl.

"I'll turn it on for you and give you privacy. I'll even let you lock the door so you feel safe."

She speaks from experience.

I used to lock my bathroom door too.

You feel vulnerable when naked and distracted by the shower. You feel like you're too easily a target.

"I know the angel won't let me be hurt. I don't like locked doors," Laurel says quietly.

My heart flutters, and Lindy swallows again. "I'll start the shower."

She moves down the hall, and I nod toward Laurel, letting her know she's right; I won't ever let anything happen to her.

She was locked up. Her scars are different from ours. She was held captive. She needs air like we need confined security.

Lindy's scars don't run as deep or painful as mine. One man ruined her.

So many more took a piece of me.

But the pain is just the same. Just as scary. Just as unrelenting.

She returns, and I see the bathroom door open. Apparently Laurel requested that.

"She has different scars," I say quietly.

"I'll learn to be what she needs. Thank you for trusting me with her. I've felt so pointless all these years, but if I can reconcile what happened to me by being what she needs…maybe it won't all seem like it was pointless."

I know the feeling.

"What do I say if they ask about Delaney Grove?" she asks quietly as the shower hums in the distance.

"Say nothing."

Her brow furrows. "Why?"

A dark smile curves my lips. "Because there are so many more to kill. I'm not ready for everyone to know why."

A cold look crosses her eyes.

"Then they won't hear it from me. I'll do whatever you need. Just make sure those sons of bitches never hurt anyone ever again."

I hold up six fingers, and she cocks her head, confused.

"That many are already gone."

Surprise flits across her eyes.

"Then you have a long list ahead of you."

Chapter 11

Never contract friendship with a man who is not better than thyself.
—Confucius

Lana

When I reach the drop spot, I leave the car and keys in the parking lot, along with a couple thousand dollars under the seat. The drop spot changes all the time, and they only get a five minute warning before I'm gone.

I grab my bag of wet clothes, and the black bag from the trunk that has minimal supplies, just as all the warehouse cars have.

I toss the clothes into a trashcan, and start hiking down the road, ignoring the cars that pull over to ask if I need a ride. It isn't until a motorcycle rolls up that I smile and roll my eyes.

"Really? How'd you make it out of your house on a motorcycle?" I groan, hopping on the back as Jake gives me a helmet.

"I didn't," he says with a shrug. "I picked it up from the warehouse when I went to make sure your car didn't have any trackers or anything on it."

I put my arms around his waist, and he pats my hand.

"Did he confess?"

"More than you know. I don't want to talk about it right now. In fact, I never want to tell you the things he confessed to. I want to scrub it from my mind so that I'm not tempted to run down the list of every pedophile out there and repeat the same ending for them. However, there is something I need to tell you, but I'll wait until I have the energy to deal with your rant."

He sighs harshly while revving the bike, and he drives me all the way to the warehouse.

"I'll send the link to the new cameras to you so you can watch Anthony in your free time," he says as I head toward my car.

"I'll be waiting."

With that, I drive straight home, not even acknowledging the patrol cars at the end of my driveway.

I can't stop them from hanging out on the street, unfortunately.

My house is unnaturally quiet, something I find peaceful instead of eerie like most people. I hurry through the motions of stepping into the shower, feeling the warm spray of the water against my back.

The sounds of footsteps have me turning off the water and stepping out of the shower. With silent movements, I wrap up in a towel and open the shower door, watching with a wary eye.

Just as silently, I open the drawer, and pull out the gun I have hidden there. Why is there a gun hidden in my bathroom? Have you ever seen a horror film? The girl always gets stabbed in the shower. Or she runs into the bathroom and locks the door, but has no way to defend herself when the psycho killer breaks in.

I could defend myself and have no plans of hiding in the bathroom, but a backup plan never hurts.

Clutching my towel with one hand and holding the gun in the other, I carefully open the bathroom door. Movement has my hand jerking to the right, but a strong hand clamps around my wrist, and my eyes swing up to meet a devastatingly familiar pair of blues.

Logan arches an eyebrow at me, and my entire body relaxes when I realize it's not the Boogeyman in my room.

"You really do have a gun," he says as though he's surprised.

Sidetracked

"Why are you in my house?" I ask, still holding the gun while he holds my wrist, keeping the barrel aimed away from him.

"Care if I take this?" He gestures to the gun, and I release my hold on it as he takes it away slowly, warily.

He gingerly places it on top of my nightstand, turning the safety on. Then he turns to face me again.

"I'm sorry. I really am, Lana. You have every right to be pissed."

I exhale heavily as he takes a seat on my bed, and I clutch the towel a little tighter with both hands now.

He looks down at his hands as he rubs them together, leaning forward on my bed with his elbows resting on his knees. "I didn't know you knew about the attack. But you're right; I should've called you right away. I didn't want to worry you, but I should've been prepared for somebody else tell you before I could. It won't happen again."

Most of my anger is gone now that I've stabbed a man to death, which allows me to slowly digest what he's saying without too many emotions clogging up my logic.

But to be honest, I have no idea what to say.

Instead of speaking I continue to hold my towel, watching him as he lifts his eyes to meet my gaze.

"I'm not leaving here until this is resolved. I'm not leaving here until I know this is okay."

I believe him.

Twice he's shown up after I've returned fresh from a kill. What happens when he shows up too early? What happens when I have to explain the real reason there's blood in my hair or on my clothes? What happens when he catches me?

Staring into his eyes, I remember why it's so hard to walk away. Without the anger I had earlier driving me farther from his arms, I remember what it's like to feel.

He looks tired, always tired. His tie has been loosened, hanging down below the top two buttons he's undone. The firm, tan flesh is visible through those undone buttons.

His shirt is untucked, and his jacket is strewn across my bed, developing wrinkles as we speak.

"I mean it, Lana," he says, drawing my attention back to his face. His blond hair is disheveled, and those firm, full lips are curved down. "I'm not leaving until we're good, and you're in my arms, and you let the police go back to protecting you when I'm not here."

My lips thin as I think over my options. Leaving here without him seems to create a massive hole in my chest. I've been avoiding feeling the loss since I left the hospital.

The tears earlier overwhelmed me and caught me off guard. If there hadn't been someone to take the brunt of my overflowing emotions, I'd be a sobbing mess in Jake's house right now.

Over this man in my room.

A man who has the power to destroy me.

A man I can't let go.

"Okay." My mind is screaming at me how stupid this is, as the solitary word of damnation weakly leaves my mouth. Never has *okay* held so much power.

"Okay?" he asks, as the tears start to reform on my eyelids.

I nod, not trusting my voice not to crack if I try to say more. I thought I'd rid myself of the emotions earlier, but they're back with a renewed vigor now.

He springs to his feet, and my breath leaves in a rush as he grabs me at the waist with more speed than I was prepared for. He tugs me to him, pulling me flush against him before lifting me, clinging to me with a possessive, desperate hold.

His lips find mine as I wind my arms around his neck, turning off the part of my mind that is still begging me to see reason.

As my fingers thread through his hair, he drops me to the bed, jarring me as the kissing and touching ends abruptly. I look up, feeling flushed as my towel falls open, and he hungrily rakes his eyes over my body.

A breath hisses out of me when his hands cover my knees and force them apart.

"I've been doing everything wrong," he says on a reverent breath, his eyes trained between my legs as he licks his lips. "I've been skipping all the important stuff, giving you the middle instead of the beginning in every way."

Before I can ask what that means, his head dips, and his blond hair tickles against my legs seconds before his mouth fastens around my clit. My hips buck, but he holds me still, gripping my thighs to hold me in place, and to anchor his face right where he wants it.

He's sucking and flicking his tongue at the same time, ratcheting up the pleasure with each passing second. It's almost too intense. It's almost too much.

I've never let anyone touch me this way, and he wouldn't have had the chance either if he hadn't caught me off guard.

My fingers grip his hair, possibly tugging too hard, but he merely growls his approval, the vibrations of his voice driving me that much closer to that powerful edge. It feels perfect and incredible and awesome…and all the other damn good words too.

I cry out when something explosive crackles over me, the force of the orgasm taking me by surprise. I'm practically panting when he continues to suck, bite, and lick in perfect unison against the oversensitive flesh.

He finally shows me mercy by letting go, and my whole body shudders as he starts kissing his way up my damp skin, sliding the towel out from under me with a hard tug. He tosses it away as my body turns limp under his lips that are still kissing their way up my body.

"At least you're good at apologies," I tell him, albeit I'm still all breathy when the words come out.

A rumble of laughter slips between his lips and plays against my skin that he's still teasing, now moving between the valley of my breasts on his ascent.

When his lips finally reach mine, the kiss is hungry, and I forget why we were ever fighting to begin with. His hips settle between my legs as he kisses me harder, holding me under him in a way I never thought I'd be able to stand.

But with Logan, it's as though I've never been hurt. I trust him. It's insane to trust someone so freely after being hurt so irrevocably in the past, but I do. I trust him completely, and there's no doubt in my mind that he'd never intentionally hurt me.

I can feel it in the way he kisses me. I can see it in his eyes when he bares his soul. I can taste it in the way he breathes. And I sense his honesty like a predator can sense its prey's fear.

"You're only with me?" he asks, breaking the kiss as I start stripping his shirt over his head, tugging his tie off too. "It's not something we've discussed, but I think I've made it clear where I stand, and you've made it clear you don't want me with anyone else."

I never even considered that being an option once we had sex.

"You know I don't want you with anyone else," I tell him, confused as to why he feels this is the best time to bring it up.

He grins as he nips at my lips and pulls back, reaching between us to undo his pants.

"How long since you were with anyone before me?"

"Seven months," I say without needing to think about it.

His eyebrows go up. Yeah, I keep track of sex. Sort of happens as an accidental quirk after you've been through what I have and can finally enjoy intimacy again.

"Good," he says, kissing his way across my cheek. "Birth control?"

My heart clenches in my chest, and I swallow down the knot in my throat.

Sidetracked

"I can't have children," I whisper hoarsely.

His head rears back, and his forehead creases in confusion. I could have just lied. I could have glossed over it and promised I couldn't get pregnant.

I'm just sick of lying when I don't have to.

"Why?"

Instead of telling him another lie outright, I point the scars on my side. "I lost a lot that night," I say quietly.

I push at his chest, and he lifts off me enough for me to roll over, giving him my back. I point the scars on my side, the ones closest to my right hip.

"And a kidney," I add.

His fingers trace over the scar tissue, but for once I don't tense away. Instead of it feeling like acid, it feels like a healing balm touching me for the first time ever.

His lips brush my shoulder.

"What else?" he whispers softly, running his hands along the curve of my ass where another long scar is.

I close my eyes. "My face. There's more metal in there than bone right now. There were a lot of very complicated, somewhat experimental surgeries to restore a semblance of bone structure. The man who worked a miracle is quite frankly a genius. He lives in Russia, but came to the states just for my surgery. Money can change the outcome of someone's life."

Just a face. It's just a face. But it could have been disfigured. I could have looked like a monster. Then I'd have been just as ugly on the outside as I am on the inside.

I turn my face around, looking over my shoulder at him running his hand along my hip, tracing the jagged scar there.

"What's this from?"

I don't have to completely lie. "Glass. It cut into me that night, dug so deep that they couldn't remove it right away for fear of me losing even more blood—too much blood. My blood painted the streets that night."

Telling him the truth without telling him the whole truth is oddly therapeutic. I'm sick of constantly lying. Even a little truth makes this feel more real.

I just don't mention that Kyle slammed a broken piece of a mirror there. The same mirror they broke after they used it to taunt my brother.

I have a mirror for Kyle too. Several mirrors. He'll get to watch everything I do.

"I'm sorry," he says softly, sounding so heartbreakingly genuine that tears threaten to return to my eyes again.

"It's not your fault. I didn't want to ruin the moment, but I didn't want to lie either."

"You don't have to lie," he says, the words making me bite back more truth than he could ever handle. "It's amazing you survived."

He has no idea.

"I flat-lined twice. Technically I died twice. Then I was reborn. At least that's how I like to think of it."

His eyes meet mine, and he slides his hand up my side as he leans forward. His lips capture mine, and his weight comes down from behind me. It's another position I never thought I'd be comfortable in, but it's so naturally effortless with him.

The kiss is reverent, soulful, and it actually means more than anything he could say right now. I don't stop kissing him, even though the angle is awkward.

His hand slides around the front of my body, lifting my hips just enough. I moan into his mouth when I feel him pushing inside me, skin-to-skin. He slides in so easily, despite how tight the fit is. His hips rock, slowly pushing in and out, taking me as though he could fuck me all day.

Sidetracked

And I'd let him.

His phone rings and rings, but he doesn't stop. His lips never move from mine, and his hands grip my hips, moving a little faster. I'm the one to finally break the kiss so I can suck in a sharp breath as one of his hands slides around, finding my clit.

I rock against him as his pace quickens. He slides his knees under my hips, giving himself better leverage to push in harder, faster.

The phone doesn't shut up, but we're too lost in each other to stop. His hips stagger, losing the rhythm, and I know he's close. Just as I think I'm not going to follow him over the edge, the orgasm comes out of nowhere, and I'm crying out his name before I can stop myself.

He jerks against me, squeezing my hip tightly with one hand, while his other hand continues to rule me, driving my orgasm on and on.

I collapse, and his hand finally stills, pinned between my body and the bed. He comes down on top of me, his body shuddering in the aftermath as he drags his lips over my shoulder.

"Your phone," I say, panting once again.

I can run up five flights of stairs without my breathing changing at all, yet sex with Logan turns me into a sweaty, breathless mess.

"Let it ring. I have three hours before I'm back on duty."

He kisses my shoulder again, and I grin against the pillow, feeling my eyes grow heavy.

"You're perfect," he says against my cheek as his lips brush a kiss there too.

"I wish," I say softly, lifting his phone from the nightstand where it is. "Answer. It could be important, and I know you're only not answering because of me. I won't get mad."

He groans, still inside me as he takes his phone. "That's not the only reason I'm not answering. I'll never answer my phone if I'm inside you. Not even I'm that much of a company man."

I snort indignantly, then laugh into the pillow, feeling him smile against my cheek as he kisses it again.

He pulls out of me, and I clench my thighs together, already feeling the loss. And the mess. The mess I haven't felt since…

I wait for the wave of nausea to wash over me.

I wait for the panic to seize me.

I wait for the buried memories to resurface and steal this moment away.

But it doesn't happen.

Another grin curls my lips. He's just healed another small piece of me.

If only he could make me think like a normal girl again, I could be the perfect person he wants me to be.

But for now, I'll take the illusion he's offering. I'll savor it like there's no tomorrow.

"What the hell are you talking about?" I hear him saying as he comes out of the bathroom, picking up his boxers from the floor.

When did he get fully naked? I swear I lose all thought process when he's pressed against me.

I head into the bathroom, giving him privacy since he's sitting down—still naked—on the edge of my bed. But even as I shut the door and start cleaning up, I can hear him.

"Hadley has been with the team and has been sleeping in the office. They can check the security footage if they need it."

Oh shit.

"Then get clearance for them to see the time stamps of the window he was killed. She's been with us. There's no way she drove all the way out there and killed her stepfather."

That fat bastard has already been found? Damn him. I should have stabbed him even more for ruining this moment.

Sidetracked

"No. No. No. They can't haul one of ours in for questioning. If they want to talk to her, they can do it on our turf with our rules. They don't get to fuck with her reputation for any reason. Understood?"

A harsh breath escapes him, and I lean against the door, listening.

"What kind of pictures?" I hear him ask quietly, but there's a dark edge to his tone.

"I'll be right in."

Definitely should have stabbed that motherfucker more. And weighed him down with stones. And chummed the water for sharks or something. Are there sharks here?

There would have needed to be a lot of sharks for that douchebag.

But sheesh. I'm only so strong. Not even I'm able to break the laws of science, and it was all I could do to push him out to the water.

"No," I hear him saying. "We won't help them find whoever did this. They want to question her—fine. But fuck him and fuck them for trying to get our help on it after trying to haul Hadley in. Keep an eye on her. Don't let them near her until I get there. Understood?"

I open the door, seeing him stab his legs into his pants, keeping the phone wedged between his shoulder and his ear. The sun has been high in the sky for a while now, though I've barely noticed it through my dark curtains.

Logan never asked where I was all night. Or maybe he didn't know I was gone.

No. No. The cops at my driveway saw me come in. Yet Logan never questioned where I've been.

"Yeah, I'm at her house now. And I'm going to kick someone's ass for interrupting it. Then I'm coming back and getting a solid five hours of sleep. None of us are going to catch him if we're all running on empty. As for this Kenneth guy, I'm glad he's fucking dead."

A small grin spreads on my lips. I don't know why it sounds like he's condoning what I just did. Or why I feel a sense of pride.

I banish the smile, removing the crazy thoughts before I say something stupid aloud. Normal people aren't proud of removing a life from the earth and sending them to hell and all that.

"You're not kidding. I may bring her in with me, if she'll come."

His eyes dart up, meeting mine as I stand in the doorway.

"Yeah," he says, still talking into the phone. "I won't be staying long. I just want to make sure they aren't trying to pin this on Hadley. Then I'm coming back."

He stands, coming to me, fully dressed now. He's probably a pro at talking on the phone and getting dressed.

"I'm still working on that part, but hopefully," he goes on, smirking at me. "Be there as soon as I can."

He looks down the length of my naked body, leisurely raking his eyes over me as I lean against the wall. "As much as I want to keep you naked, I need to go in. I want you to come with me, because we'll be coming right back. I'm not ready to leave you alone just yet."

I roll my eyes. "The cops can sit outside again. Duke can have his room back."

It's a horribly stupid concession.

"Duke got called away on this homicide they just called me about. Hadley's stepfather was killed. He's requesting to interrogate her."

He meets my gaze again, and I try to remain a stone wall as I think over the real reason Duke is probably there. I doubt it's to question Hadley about the monster I killed. If anything, he wants to know the rest of the monster's secrets…the darkest ones he confessed to me. The ones I wasn't expecting. The ones Lindy will have to share.

Sidetracked

Then I realize an expression would be a good idea.

"Were they close?" I blurt out, trying to recover from my cold-as-ice routine slip.

"No," he tells me, grabbing a dress from my closet and handing it to me.

I arch an eyebrow and move past the proffered dress to grab some yoga pants and a T-shirt. As I pull on some underwear and a bra, he drops the dress to the bed, blushing a little. I'll wear a dress on a night when I have on makeup and can do more than pull my hair in a ponytail.

"Is she okay?" I ask, imitating normal questions.

All of my normalcies are usually an imitation.

"She's...I don't know. He's a sick bastard, apparently. Hadley just told me she was a confused kid back when she ran away. Now I wonder if—" He cuts his words off and runs a frustrated hand through his hair.

"Let's go," I say, pulling my hair up as soon as I finish putting on my clothes.

As if my life wasn't complicated enough, I'm about to head into FBI headquarters. Lovely.

Chapter 12

Virtue is not left to stand alone. He who practices it will have neighbors.
—Confucius

Logan

"Just stay here," I tell Lana, gesturing to a large breakroom. "I'd let you into my office to wait, but it's restricted access."

She squeezes my hand, giving me a small, reassuring smile. "I'm fine. Go do your thing."

I head out of the breakroom, leaving the door open, and walk straight toward Craig's office where he's waiting with Hadley and Duke. Hadley's red-rimmed eyes meet mine the second I step through the door, and she jerks her gaze away.

My eyes shift to Duke, who glares at me.

"Why is it necessary to have you guys in here for me to ask her a few simple questions?" Duke asks, annoyed.

"Call it an observation, but your chief put my girl in danger just to have a better chance of catching a serial killer. Then you show up, targeting one of my people for a crime she couldn't have possibly committed."

His eyebrows go up, and a lazy smile curves his lips. "Really? Agent Grace has so many alibies that it'd be a fool's quest to try and pin Kenneth Ferguson's death on her."

"Then why are you here?" I ask, suspiciously.

Sidetracked

His smile dies, and he tosses out several bagged pictures. Hadley's breath catches in her throat when she sees them, and she clutches the chair.

"These aren't all the pictures he had, but these children? They're missing. Some of them have been missing for years."

Hadley doubles over, vomiting into the trashcan. Duke actually looks sympathetic as he watches her.

"I need air," Hadley says, wiping the back of her mouth as she stands.

I nod toward Craig, who takes her out, leaving me alone with Duke in the office.

"You wanted to see her reaction," I tell him as I sit down too.

"She ran away from home for a reason," Duke answers. "She accused him of molesting her as a child."

"So you are trying to—"

"I'm trying to get answers about what 'special' places he took her, as terrible as that sounds. We need to find these kids, even if we're just recovering bodies. Someone killed this guy, but I'm looking for the dozens of kids who are missing more than I'm looking for his killer."

He pulls out his phone, and I glance at the pictures that are on the desk. Most are naked little girls, spread wide on a bed. My stomach roils and I look away. Hadley never told me this part of her past.

"Ferguson left Hadley's mother shortly after Hadley ran away. That means the mother was no longer valuable after the child was gone. How can a mother ignore something like that?" he asks.

"It's often easier for someone to believe evil can't exist inside someone they love, than to admit they've failed someone who should be more important. We see it too often. The blind eye effect is what we call it," I say absently.

Just as I'm about to ask questions, he thrusts his phone at me, and my eyes widen in disbelief. "Someone knew what this guy was doing," he goes on, gesturing to the picture.

Kenneth Ferguson has been tortured. There's no doubt about that. His skin has been flayed off in numerous areas. There are black spots on the flayed portions, as though someone burned him.

"They used a knife. They used a blowtorch—possibly even the one he had downstairs for welding. And they hammered nails into his feet and testicles—seventy nails, to be exact… We found sixty-nine pictures and seventy nails. They did all this before dumping his dead body into the water."

I grimace, wondering why so many killers have to focus on the genitals.

The water has bloated the body, turning the flesh a paler color and showing the blue veins. The eyes are white and glossed over.

"Was he dead before he hit the water?"

He nods.

"So the water was a countermeasure. We're dealing with an organized killer who has the stomach for torture. Could have been a hitman. Where were these kids' parents? One of them could know where these other kids are buried or kept if they're still alive."

"All of them were in the system, homeless, and hadn't been placed with a foster family. They were labeled as runaways. Ferguson was a social worker with unlimited access to files and folders with countless children he could take at his own leisure. The ages range from eight to fifteen."

"Pedophiles have a selective age range from two to three years that they prey on. Never a gap as big as that. Unless…"

"Unless what?" he prompts.

"Unless he's a groomer. It's rare, but some pedophiles select children they can groom and have long-term relationships with, that way, when their bodies are old enough, he can take more than just some touching from them."

Sidetracked

He chokes back a sound, possibly swallowing bile. "Sick fucker. Why kill them?"

"If he killed them, it's because they didn't play their part in the fantasy anymore. Possibly became too distant or detached. Maybe even cried too much. He wants their tears as children. As women, he wants their submission. Most groomed children either break psychologically, or kill themselves. Some of these could be suicides."

"I want to find them. I want to at least give them a damn voice," Duke says angrily. "No one cared. No one looked for them. And no one stopped this demon from carrying on all these years."

"Someone did," I remind him, curious. "Maybe one escaped somewhere along the line and came back for vengeance."

"I released the information to the media, asking any prior victims to come forth. Is it wrong that I don't want to catch his killer? I just want to find the missing children—dead or alive."

He looks truly torn.

"I can't answer questions of moral dilemma. When did you alert the media?"

"His body was found three hours ago. So far no one has called in or stepped forward. He was killed in his basement, but the scene was compromised with bleach. The unknown suspect doused the room in bleach and then hosed it down. Seems like this isn't the first time he's killed."

"You said *he*," I tell him, frowning.

"The guy weighed a ton. There's no way a girl carried him to the water alone. There was signs of him being rolled to the water, but even still, that's a lot of strength. It was uphill for a piece. Then they used a hoe to dig up all the dirt where the footprints were. The tire treads we found weren't enough to get a make or model of a car. They were careful to stay out of the dirt or sand."

Definitely organized. Too organized to have had just one kill under their belt.

"No hesitation marks," I say quietly, gesturing to the picture. "We may be dealing with a serial."

He tenses, his eyes narrowing. "I'm not trying to take your case away, detective," I add, watching as he relaxes. "I'm just saying you may have some avenger seeking justice where the cops haven't. You may want to look into—"

The door opens, and Craig steps in. "We have a little girl here. She's bruised and malnourished, and the woman who brought her in claims that she was left on her doorstep during the night. The little girl is a victim of Ferguson's."

My eyes dart to Duke's as his widen, and we both launch ourselves toward the door, moving briskly.

The little girl is whispering something in Hadley's ear as we walk into the room where they're seated, and Hadley frowns, studying the little girl.

"What?" Duke asks.

The little girl shudders when she hears his voice, harsh and demanding. Duke tenses, realizing his error.

"Sorry," he says softly as the woman puts her arm around the little girl.

She was just found last night? Yet the traumatized kid is clinging to this woman?

"Sorry," Duke says again, his voice barely above a whisper as he takes a seat.

"I'm going to head home," Hadley says as she nears me, clutching my arm on her way toward the door. "Let that girl stay with Lindy. Do *not* let them take her away. I need...I need a moment."

I follow her out, letting Duke speak with who I assume is Lindy. Craig joins him, sitting down with his iPad as he listens intently.

"I don't know. The doorbell rang, and Laurel was there when I answered it. I brought her in, fed her, gave her water, and then let her shower for as long as she wanted. That's when I saw the news, and Laurel gave me her story, along with information you need. I'll tell you everything she told me, but only if you promise she can stay with me. No taking her away."

"Yes," Laurel agrees adamantly.

A bond that deep can't be forged so quickly unless Laurel and Lindy know more than I think they do.

I'm distracted by Hadley as I shut the door on the room, focusing my attention on my friend.

"Are you okay?"

Hadley turns to me with tears in her eyes. No one is around right now, they're scrambling everywhere to find Plemmons.

"No, I'm not okay. I let them convince me it was all in my head. I thought I was sick and crazy, Logan. Now…that little girl is in there. Those kids…all of this is my fault."

She swallows harshly as she sobs, wiping her eyes.

"This isn't your fault, Hadley."

"I should have tried harder. I should have looked into it better when I started working here. No other reports were ever filed…I had it set to ping me. I honestly believed it was all in my head. Now…I just need to go home. I'll call you later."

She walks away, never turning back around, and I blow out a long breath. She needs space, and I get that. I just hope this doesn't break her.

I see her pause, eyeing the breakroom where Lana is. I tilt my head, confused as the emotion flees her eyes, turning into something more concentrated, but I can't see Lana.

Finally, Hadley walks away, and I make a mental note to question that more later.

Just as I start to step back into the room, Craig steps out, his face flushed and his eyes wide.

"Your office. Now," he says, heading straight by me.

Confused, I follow, and I see him gesture for Donny and Leonard to follow. Elise and Lisa are taking a sleep break, like I was supposed to be doing.

As soon as we're all in my office, Craig shuts the door and he lays out his iPad.

"Lindy May Wheeler is the woman Ferguson's killer decided to leave the child with."

Her name doesn't ring any bells.

"And?" Donny prompts.

"Lindy May Wheeler is from Delaney Grove."

The blood chills in my veins, turning to ice as goosebumps pebble my skin. Slowly, I make my way to the chair, dropping to it as the weight of the revelation settles on to me.

"She left nine and a half years ago, started a new life, even dropped her last name," he goes on. "She just goes by Lindy May now."

"What the fuck is going on in that town?" Donny asks in a hushed whisper.

"I was there. It was like the Andy Griffith show. Everyone was smiling and happy, waving at us as we passed. No signs of something wrong. If anything, they live like it's the nineties, refusing to move forward with the rest of the world."

"Someone gets tortured and killed, and an innocent child ends up with a Delaney Grove resident. That's not a coincidence," Donny says.

"No castration," Craig says. "That's his one constant. Why would he deviate if it was him? If anything, this guy deserved castration more than any of the prior victims."

"As far as we know," I say under my breath, looking up as all eyes swing to me. "He didn't want this tied to him. This was an impulsive kill. He wasn't prepared. The footsteps were dug up, meaning he may not have been wearing his boots. He may even be tricking us with his weight. He poured bleach all over the scene of the crime, washing away evidence. That's not in his MO, which means he's normally more prepared. What triggered this?"

"We need to adjust the profile," Donny says.

"Why?" Craig asks him.

"Because a sadist would never take the time to deviate from his list and go kill a pedophile. This was motivated. There was something that triggered the unsub's need to kill this man," I explain. "A sadist wouldn't take the time to find a child and see them off into the hands of someone they felt would care for the child. He wouldn't give a damn."

"There was no rage," Donny says, knowing where I'm going with this. "The kills were brutal, but each slice of the knife was controlled and calculated. No rage means no revenge."

"What if this unsub has been preparing for this for a lot longer than we expected? What if he's numbed himself to his emotions? Rage wouldn't be found in a kill. This would all be about inflicting as much pain as possible, hence the days and days of torture." As the words leave my mouth, and audible breath escapes them all.

"We need to dig deeper into that town. Something seriously fucked up has gone on there."

"What about Plemmons? We're supposed to be working solely on that case right now," Leonard reminds me.

"I'm technically just supposed to be the middle man for the media. I can look into this without getting us in trouble," Craig volunteers. "Maybe Lindy May can shed some light on that town."

"I'll go see what I can find out," Donny says, standing and leaving us behind.

"I'm going to go listen in," I say to them. "Stay on Plemmons. Keep working that. This changes nothing as far as the priority goes," I tell Leonard.

"Revenge would have this guy contacting the media," Leonard

says, lost in thought. "He's killed six. He'd want his story known. He'd want the world to know why he was doing this. It doesn't make sense."

"And targeting Hadley's stepfather? That can't be a coincidence," I point out. "He's watching us. Studying us, possibly. He doesn't want the media knowing yet, because he doesn't want the world to know his motives until he's ready for his endgame. We have no idea how long that list is, which is why we need to know what happened that was so bad that a seemingly normal person who cares enough about a child to deliver them to a safe doorstep, would become a brutal torturer and killer."

"Definitely not a sadist," Leonard sighs. "That's for damn sure."

He stands, running his hand over his stomach as it growls.

"That town was too shiny for something this dark to be in its recent past. I'll see how far back I can go. I won't stop until I find something."

"Work on Plemmons for now. After we catch that bastard, we'll dig into Delaney Grove."

He nods, though it seems like reluctant compliance.

Craig gets up, bringing his iPad with him. "I'll go see if I can dig anything up. You deal with this." He pauses, studying me for a moment. "What does it mean if a serial killer goes after someone who hurt a member of our team?"

I purse my lips as Leonard paces nearby. "When he goes after a pedophile, it means he suffered something similarly traumatic…may even feel a kinship with Hadley. I don't feel like he's targeting us. I feel like he wants us to understand him."

"But he didn't want this linked to him," I counter. "That was forced because he wanted the little girl safe. He's cut himself off from all new relationships, forced to return to the ones from his past that aren't tainted with whatever happened."

I look over at Craig. "You said Lindy May moved nine and a half years ago?"

Sidetracked

He nods. "Look around that time frame. See what you come up with."

He immediately starts pulling something up on his iPad, and I glance over at Leonard.

"Call Hadley. Tell her what we've learned. It's better to err on the side of caution."

"The cautious seldom err," he quips, quoting Confucius as he exits the room.

"We'll revisit the entire profile, examine the evidence from a whole new perspective after we deal with Plemmons," I tell him, following him out.

"This changes everything," he agrees.

I walk into the small conference room where Duke is still speaking to Lindy. Donny shakes his head, letting me know he hasn't asked anything yet.

"She already told you she never saw the person who took her there," Lindy says, glaring at Duke as Laurel rests against her, not seeming the least bit timid.

She knows something. She knows Ferguson is dead, but not even that would put a scared child so at ease. She's already bonded with Lindy May. Something like that has a reason, and more to it than simply feeling safe. And why does she feel so safe?

"She was too exhausted to even open her eyes," Lindy goes on.

She has a protective arm around the child, showing instant maternal instincts. She's bonded with Laurel as fiercely as Laurel has bonded with her. In less than twenty-four hours.

"So she has no idea how she ended up on your porch? And you never saw anything?"

Her eyes narrow to slits. "I came in freely, willing to give you information. You still haven't agreed to my terms, yet I've told you all I could except for what you really want to know. Yet you're interrogating me. I should have stayed home."

Duke opens his mouth to speak, but I put a hand on his shoulder, drawing his attention.

"You said you wanted to know where the other kids were, so why are you grilling her about who brought the kid?"

His lips clap shut, and I cock my head to the side. Finally, he blows out a long breath.

"It doesn't add up. Even you know this sounds wrong."

"What information do you have?" I ask Lindy.

She glares at me now. "I'm not telling you anything until you promise me that Laurel can remain in my house with me. You have to promise no one will take her away."

Laurel clutches Lindy's hand, still leaning on her.

"Donny, make some calls," I say, titling my head. "Make sure Laurel doesn't get removed from Ms. Wheeler's home."

"May," Lindy immediately corrects. "My last name is now May. I don't use Wheeler anymore."

"Why is that, Ms. May?" I ask, acting as though this is news to me.

"Sometimes you just need a fresh start. Same as I'm trying to offer Laurel. Why are we being treated like criminals when we just came to help?"

Duke slumps in his seat, a look of regret crossing his face. He's trained to ask about the suspicious answers. She's definitely hiding something, but I'm not sure what.

Donny walks out, his phone to his ear, making the calls we need.

"Why'd you leave Delaney Grove?" I ask her.

No surprise flickers in her eyes, but her back stiffens. Laurel's hand clutches hers tighter.

She definitely knows something, and I'll bet Laurel knows a piece of the puzzle too.

Sidetracked

"I got a divorce, decided to change my world for the better. Delaney Grove isn't as grand as it seems."

Craig gave me all the info on her, and I'm looking at it on my phone now.

"You were married to Antonio Gonzalez, correct?"

She nods curtly, a coldness washing over her eyes.

"He still lives in Delaney Grove," I go on.

Duke is watching me, a confused expression on his face.

"Why'd you come here instead of the police station?" I ask her. "The local PD is who broadcasted that they needed the information on Ferguson."

"You should call him the monster," Laurel interjects, surprising me as her eyes darken.

There's a fury there. A dark, deeply laced fury. There's not an ounce of fear in her eyes, just determined hatred so out of character for an abused child. The bruises on her arms and face and neck suggest he wasn't gentle about his ways with her.

Has she even been examined yet?

Lindy ignores my question, but I already know the answer. He sent her here.

"Has she seen a doctor?" I ask Lindy, changing my line of questioning.

"We're going to see one today."

She doesn't say more.

"How severe was she injured?"

"Bad enough to leave scars on her soul, but not to the extent it could have been. If you know what I mean, Agent."

He hasn't raped her. She's too young. But he's forced her to do other things, and that's bad enough.

Lindy speaks like a victim herself, as though she understand the trauma on a different level. The unsub knew this, because that couldn't be a coincidence.

She knows him. And she's apparently for whatever crusade he's on. I won't get an ounce of information out of her that tells me who he is. Whatever happened affected more than just the unsub.

But why not tell me what happened?

What the fucking hell is going on in Delaney Grove?

"Ms. May, I know this is difficult, but can you at least tell me what led to you leaving Delaney Grove? Maybe something that affected more than just you?"

Her eyes shift, and a calmness comes over her.

"I left to start anew, Agent. If you want to know about Delaney Grove, maybe you should visit it."

So he asked her not to tell. She spoke with him. There's no doubt about that.

He saved the child. The child feels safe because he's the dark knight that slayed the monster who has haunted her for months, ever since her disappearance. Our unsub handed her over to this woman, who he swore would keep her safe. She trusted him. She was cared for by Lindy, and the bond formed instantly.

That much makes sense.

They both owe him their silence for a reason. They'll never talk. And I'm not in the business of bullying victims who've suffered enough. I'll find out another way.

Donny walks back in, and I look over at him as he nods.

"Laurel is yours," I say to Lindy.

"Paperwork. I want it in writing."

He coached her on this. Told her to make sure she got custody by leveraging information.

Unreal.

We had him all wrong.

Sidetracked

There won't be animal cruelty in his past. He'll have been someone gentle, possibly naïve and trusting — too trusting. Trusting enough to have been someone's victim.

Instead of it shattering him; he came back for cold vengeance. But why target so many? What did they fucking do?

Donny walks out again, going to get something in writing. Duke taps his pen impatiently, his knee bouncing under the table. Across from him, Laurel whispers something into Lindy's ear. Lindy presses a kiss to the child's forehead.

I watch, fascinated by the fact Laurel doesn't seem appalled by the affection. An instant maternal bond has been brought forth by two victims bonding with a killer. A killer they feel slays the monsters of their nightmares.

A killer who won't stop.

They don't realize how dangerous this guy will become. Revenge killers have no limitations on who dies. The smallest of infractions is a death sentence. They take justice into their hands, become judge, jury, and executioner, becoming too immortal in their own minds.

Donny returns, a paper in his hand. He hands it to Lindy, and she reads it carefully, searching for any sort of a trick.

I take the paper and sign it. "This is me calling this the truth," I explain, watching her gauge me.

She must trust whatever she sees in my eyes, because she pulls a piece of paper from her purse and hands it to me. Duke stands and comes to read it over my shoulder.

It's a map to the burial ground, written in blood with a calligraphy penmanship, with most likely a calligraphy pen to disguise the unsub's handwriting. He knows calligraphy?

So organized it's eerie.

How long has he been preparing for every possible outcome?

Signed in blood is one name — Kenneth Ferguson. Only it's not in calligraphy. It's still signed in blood, written with most likely his finger. The strokes are shaky, as though he was trembling when the unsub made him sign this with his own blood.

That's a level of cold that had us profiling him as a sadist.

There's an *x* marking so many graves, the names of each child written in calligraphy. The only structure on the map appears to be a shed of some sort. The graves are all around it. The map goes from his home, the road names marking each turn to take. He went and visited them. The sick fuck knew exactly where he'd buried each and every child.

Sixty-nine photos. Seventy nails.

Those words come back to me, reminding me they were spoken.

I dart out of the room, leaving Duke behind to deal with the murders that have him sagging to a chair in disbelief.

I grab the page Duke left in the office, one listing all the children's names. Our people must have run facial recognition against all the kids in the system. After being runaways, their names and photos are reported.

There's a list of names for each photo. Sixty-nine names.

The same names and ages are written on the photos themselves.

Only one is not listed.

Hadley's.

He spared her the indignity of our team seeing her photos next to these. He sent Lindy here instead of to the police. He knew we'd take it more personally, knew there was a stronger chance of Lindy getting custody of Laurel.

He definitely feels a kinship with Hadley, and could possibly want to see her reaction. Hadley doesn't answer, so I tell all that to her voicemail, hoping she hears it soon.

Then I head into the breakroom where Lana is drinking a coke, kicked back with her feet crossed at the ankles as she stares at the TV. I lean against the doorjamb, studying her easy grin.

Sidetracked

She has no idea at how sick the world is. I hate that I can't take her home right now. Hate that this got more complicated and now I need to stay. She's the only thing keeping me sane right now.

So much for spending some time in bed apologizing even more.

Chapter 13

Be not ashamed of mistakes and thus make them crimes.
—Confucius

Lana

Logan is gone for a little while when I suddenly see Lindy walk in front of the breakroom with Laurel. I guess she was watching the news closely, ready to follow through with what I told her to do.

Lindy's eyes widen in shock when she sees me, and I wink, holding my finger over my lips as the universal *shhhh* sign, while using my other hand to gesture to my visitor's badge.

She masks her surprise immediately, and Laurel grins at me, giving me a small wave. I get a little worried when I see Hadley suddenly approach them, looking in at me.

Laurel diverts her attention to Hadley, as Hadley narrows her eyes at me. "Can I help you?" she asks.

A guy walks up, and he gestures to Laurel and Lindy. "They have information on the Ferguson case. I escorted them up, but I can't find SSA Bennett."

My stomach flips just hearing his name. I hope he doesn't let me down. My instructions were for Lindy to seek out his team, but not by name. He'll get her custody of Laurel if he's the man I think he is, without treating her like a criminal for being linked to me—the monster I hide from him.

"I'll take them to conference three," Hadley tells him, eyeing me suspiciously again. Laurel glances at me one last time, but Lindy remains a face of stone, carrying out her part perfectly.

Sidetracked

Laurel thinks I'm an angel. She probably thinks no one else can see me. In her eyes, I'm keeping a close watch on her, making sure she stays safe, just as I promised.

She's clean now. She's also wearing new clothes that Lindy must have picked up for her on the way here.

"Hey, what's going on?" I hear a familiar voice ask. Craig? Is his name Craig?

I think so.

I don't hear anything after that, because they get too far away. Instead, I feign interest in the TV, drinking the soda I bought from the vending machine in here.

Lindy probably thinks I'm ballsy as fuck for being here right now. She has no clue how tangled up I've gotten myself.

But they're looking for a monster.

Not a girl who loves red.

Not a girl who is falling in love.

Not a girl who died ten years ago.

More time passes before I feel eyes on me, and I dart a glance to the doorway to see Hadley just staring at me. Her eyes are definitely suspicious as she appraises me without any discretion.

Surely Laurel didn't tell her. And certainly not Lindy.

Then again, I'd be in an interrogation room if they had. She's been suspicious of me from the start, so she's obviously still beating that dead horse.

To be certain, I arch an eyebrow at her, as though I'm daring her to say something. She doesn't speak.

Her eyes are rimmed red, as though she's been crying. Surely she didn't care about Ferguson. So why cry?

Finally, she breaks the stare down and walks away, never saying a word. I return my attention to the 'roast' that's going on. It's actually pretty damn funny.

Besides, no one expects a laughing girl in the breakroom to have recently tortured a guy and dug up dark secrets no one even knew existed.

After some more time passes, I feel eyes on me again, and I jerk my head to the doorway to see Logan watching me with a small smile on his lips.

"What?" I ask, relieved he's smiling.

"You. You're just so…I guess you're sick of hearing perfect. But it's true."

I slowly stand, smiling at him. I'm damn glad I'm not a suspect. I worried Lindy wouldn't have the backbone she needed for this, but she must have proven herself.

Laurel has a home.

I'm sure of it.

"You okay? You've been gone a while."

His smile slips. "Sorry about that. Had a lot to do. The only good thing besides seeing you right now, is that a traumatized homeless kid has a safe place to live."

I breathe out silently, feeling a calm wash over me. He didn't fail me. I knew he was perfect for this.

"Are you ready to go now?" I ask, moving toward him.

He grabs me at the waist, pulling me flush against his body, and he bends as I get up on my toes, meeting him as far as I can as his lips find mine.

"No," he says, a sigh following as his lips stay on mine. "I have to stay."

He pulls back reluctantly, regret shading his eyes. "I'll give you my keys. You go home. This could take a while."

Shit. They've definitely linked this kill to me—well, the me they can't name, rather. I knew they would.

Now I have to let him do his job, trying to find me.

Sidetracked

"Okay."

I see Lindy and Laurel walk by, Craig escorting them out. Laurel waves at me again, and I wink at her, while Logan is distracted with running his lips over my forehead.

Craig fortunately doesn't notice the wave goodbye either.

"I had to run a background check on a woman tonight just to make sure a killer chose wisely," the guy who was at my house says as he walks into the breakroom, not noticing me on his way by. "This day is so fucked up."

They know I chose her. But apparently she never talked.

Good girl, Lindy. Thank you.

"Donny, you remember my girlfriend, right?" Logan asks, and my heart does little cartwheels for reasons unbeknownst to me.

I'm his girlfriend.

I have a boyfriend.

This isn't news, but it's still making me gush like a thirteen-year-old who is hovering over the phone.

I don't even think about the fact he's the guy trying to catch the killer I moonlight as.

Donny whirls around, surprised to see me.

"Sorry," he says, then nods in acknowledgment as he pours a cup of coffee. "I didn't even see you."

I just smile, looking all sweet and shit. *No ruthless killer here, boys. Just a harmless woman falling in love. That's all.*

"Here are the keys," Logan tells me, placing said keys into my palm. "I'd walk you down, but I have a shitload to do. I'm so sorry."

I shrug, and some random guy walks over, apparently ready to escort me out.

"I'll see you later?"

Logan's lips find mine, answering that question without words.

A throat-clearing comes from behind me—Donny. But Logan doesn't stop putting on a show, his tongue toying with mine as he pulls me as close as possible.

I melt against him, uncaring if the world sees how head-over-heels I am. When he finally breaks the kiss, I'm dizzy, and maybe a little high.

He cups my cheek, staring at me for a long moment. "Later," he says, then turns and leaves me behind as Craig meets him halfway.

I don't look back at Donny as I let the other guy lead me out. He never says a word, and I don't speak to him. He's blushing fiercely, as though a little PDA shocked him and embarrassed the hell out of him.

Awww. Such a sweet little guy.

He escorts me all the way to Logan's SUV, and I drive away, heading home to get some much-needed sleep. I'm glad I no longer have to hide my exhaustion.

The patrol cars at the end of my driveway are gone, apparently called away to deal with the latest homicide case that involves several missing children.

It's a terrible pun, but I nailed that bastard's balls to the wall.

Well, I actually nailed them to a chair while he cried for hours on end. Thank fuck for gloves. No way was I touching them ugly, wrinkly, hairy things with my hands otherwise.

My phone rings, and I see Jake's name on it. I told him not to call me on this phone anymore.

"What's wrong?"

"That girl, Erica Norris? The Boogeyman let her go."

"What? When?"

"Don't know. She's demanding to speak with your boy. Says she won't talk to anyone but Logan Bennett. She's about an hour and a half away from you."

"How do you know this?"

"Hacked the FBI cameras. Don't worry. They won't know it was me. They'll think it was a Russian guy who has been dead for two

Sidetracked

years."

"Why would he let her go?"

"Beats the hell out of me. I'll let you know when I know. This badass is still on the case."

I grin, rolling my eyes. Only Jake.

Hanging up, I walk up the steps to my house.

Weirdly, I hear music playing when I walk in. I must have left it on.

I shut the door, locking it.

Just as I turn the corner, something collides with my face like a hammer, and I'm thrown against the wall as a cry of pain escapes me. My keys and phone are knocked out of my hands and crash to the ground, but the sound is nothing more than a distant echo.

Before my eyes can adjust to the darkness, an arm bears down on my throat, strangling me, while my dazed head tries to catch up, still reeling from the explosive pain.

My hand shoots up, trying to connect with something, but a strong, vice-grip encases my wrist, twisting it painfully.

"Feisty. I like that. And so pretty. Agent Bennett picks them well," a deep, sinister voice says from the darkness, chilling my blood to the core. Just a glimmer of light highlights malicious eyes too close to mine. "He left you all alone finally. Tell me, princess, are you afraid of the Boogeyman?"

End of Book 2

Continue reading for book 3.

Scarlet Angel
Book 3

~~Tim Hoover~~

~~Chuck Cosby~~

~~Nathan Malone~~

~~Jeremy Hoyt~~

~~Ben Harris~~

~~Tyler Shane~~

~~Lawrence Martin~~

~~Random alley guy~~

~~Kenneth Ferguson~~

To defeat a monster, you have to be twice as monstrous. To love a monster, you have to share your soul.

— Lana Myers

Chapter 1

Better three hours too soon than a minute too late.
—William Shakespeare

Logan

"I don't understand why he let her go. It clashes severely with his profile," I tell Craig as we pull up to the police station. "A sexual sadist who has been on a killing spree doesn't just release a victim."

"I don't know either. The girl is so traumatized that she wouldn't let them bring her to us. She said we had to come here, and she'd only talk to you. Her father hasn't even been allowed in yet. She said she couldn't speak to him until she spoke to you."

Confused, I walk quickly into the police station, leaving the introductions to Craig. Why leave her in this town? Why let her go at all?

A thousand questions are flitting through my mind as I walk into the room they're holding her in. She's shaking, her eyes wide and panicked, and a blanket is draped around her.

Three men and one woman are in there, all of them giving her a wide berth. She's terrified, understandably so, and has most likely already had several panic attacks if someone got too close.

"I'm Supervisory Special Agent Bennett," I say softly, trying to keep my tone warm and non-imposing.

Her eyes dart to mine, and immediately she starts sobbing. Everyone looks as confused as me.

"He…told…me…to contact you…just you," she says through

Scarlet Angel

her sobs. "He said I couldn't show anyone until…you…No one but you."

I'm at a loss, carefully taking a step forward.

"Show me what, Erica?" I ask her, gingerly crouching in front of her, making myself appear smaller, less threatening.

"This," she says, moving the blanket and tugging up her skirt to reveal her inner thigh that is bandaged. Blood has seeped through the bandage, and I look at the female officer closest to me.

"She wouldn't let us check her. She refused until you arrived," she says, answering my silent question.

Erica tears at the bandage, pulling it off, and I see the words he's carved into her skin.

HER SAFE.

There's even a period.

It makes no sense at all.

"Did he tell you where he was going?" I ask her.

She's a sobbing mess, shaking her head. "He said he'd kill me if I didn't follow his orders. Said he'd come back for me. He took me once; he could take me again. Told me to follow his orders precisely, and he'd let me live."

"And he ordered you to show me this?" I ask, still trying to follow her.

"Yes. To get you here and show you this. That's all I had to do, and he'd let me live."

She's crying so hard that it's hard to understand her words, but I think I understand her well enough to spare her more questions. She's not fit to be interviewed right now.

He's shattered her.

"Can I see my father now?" she sobs. "I did what I was told to do. I did it right," she cries.

"Of course, Erica," I tell her.

We still haven't figured out how to charge her father for what he did. He's been temporarily released just for this.

I gesture with my head to let him in, and they open the door. Seconds later, the broken shell of man runs in, and he grabs his daughter who cries out. I turn and let them have a moment as she sobs into his chest.

"Her safe," I tell Craig as I walk out.

"The rest of the message maybe? You can't," he says, pulling up a picture on his iPad of the judge's wife he strung from a building. "Keep," he goes on, pulling up the photo of Lisa's arm. "Her safe," he says, looking at me.

Donny is standing with him, and he shakes his head. "But Erica is with us. Is he saying we can't keep her safe now that we have her? Maybe notching up his game?"

An icy wave washes over me.

"Logan Bennett, you can't keep her safe. He carved my name into that body with the first part of the message."

Their eyes all widen, and I panic, juggling my phone free. Lana's phone goes straight to voicemail, and I curse, calling the patrol car assigned to her house tonight.

"SSA Bennett, how can I—"

"Where's Lana? Do you have eyes on her house right now?"

"No…um…sorry, sir. I thought someone told you. We were pulled off to go help find the kids that other sicko buried."

My stomach twists like a knife in me, and I hang up, frantically dialing Duke.

"Detective Du—"

"Tell me you're with Lana right now," I snap.

"No…I thought she was with you. Didn't I see her back at your headquarters?"

"You fucking left her alone?"

Scarlet Angel

"I thought she was with you! You took her from the house, according to my officers, then I saw her with you!"

"Fuck!"

I hang up, and I start sprinting to the SUV we took here. Craig and Donny are on my heels.

"I'll stay here and see what I can find!" Donny calls out.

Craig hops in the passenger seat, buckling up quickly as I tear out of the parking lot. I toss him my phone.

"Keep calling her."

He does, but curses each time, hanging back up. "Her phone is either off or dead. It's not ringing through."

I push the pedal all the way to the floor, turning the lights on.

"Get someone over there, now!"

"Already on it," he tells me, the phone at his ear. He's shouting orders at someone, telling them Lana's address, and I weave in and out of traffic, never hitting the brakes.

"They said they're twenty minutes out," he tells me, hanging up. "How long has she been home?"

My stomach flips and turns inside out. She left an hour before I did. It would have taken her thirty minutes to get home. It took me almost two hours to get out here. That's at least two and a half hours he's had her to himself.

With no one to save her.

In the middle of nowhere.

Her closest neighbor would never hear a thing.

"Too long," I whisper hoarsely, dreading the worst as I gas the car harder, hearing Craig hiss out a breath as I narrowly dodge a car. "Too fucking long."

Chapter 2

Hell is empty, and all the devils are here.
—William Shakespeare (The Tempest)

HADLEY

Earlier...

They say children see the magic in everything. The eyes peering up at me as I sit down beside her tell a different story. At such a young age, she's seen some of the worst of the world's depravity. There's no magic in that. Only evil.

Lindy May seems to have jaded eyes as well, but I'm too emotional to think practically right now.

This man kept doing things because I let them convince me it was all in my head. The therapist. Him. My mother...

Because of me, this child is hurting right now. Because of me, so many other children are dead. So many other children suffered what I went through.

Because I was weak. So weak I let them manipulate me.

It's a guilt I can't bear, and I'm barely able to breathe as I force myself to sit by her. To distract myself from my own misgivings, I focus on the fact she knew Lana. There's no doubt in my mind that the child who hasn't waved at another soul waved at Lana because she knew her.

"You know Lana Myers?" I ask her.

Her eyes widen, and Lindy clears her throat. "No. We don't."

It's an obvious lie, but I refrain from calling her out on it. She's fidgeting, uncomfortable since the mention of Lana. Craig has already bailed to go tell the others, so I don't have long to get answers.

Laurel frowns, glancing over at Lindy.

"This man that hurt you...he hurt me too," I say, establishing a rapport with her, giving her something to bond with me about. It's hard to detach myself...to not be emotional. But I manage it, because I've had years of training.

Laurel reaches over, tugging on my sleeve, and I lean down to let her whisper into my ear. I feel her cup her hands around her mouth, as though she's ensuring none of her words escape the tunnel from her lips to my ear.

"My angel made sure he'll never hurt us again," she says, and a sickly coldness washes over me. "My angel saved me. She'll always watch over me. She is right now."

I lean up, letting her words process as Duke barges in. I'm not even sure what's being said when I finally leave. Logan follows me out, caring too much.

Words fly from my mouth before I can stop them, and I'm sobbing, taking in the weight of my responsibility in all this.

I could have prevented anyone else from getting hurt.

The words spill from my lips like vomit, pouring out everything I've had trapped in me since the day I ran away. I'm not even sure what we're saying to each other; it's all a blur.

My mind is on auto-pilot, ruled by guilt and self-loathing.

He doesn't stop me when I finally walk away, but my feet hesitate in front of the breakroom. Lana is casually propped up, watching TV as though she's the most relaxed person on the face of the earth.

She looks over at me, her body attuned to someone's attention being trained on her. That's not an innocent person's response.

She watches me, a small smirk on her lips, as though she's daring me to say something here and now.

My angel made sure he'll never hurt us again. My angel saved me. She'll always watch over me. She is right now.

Laurel's words slap me, and I slowly piece things together that don't really fit. *She.* Laurel said *she.*

And she waved at Lana.

There's no way I'm right.

There's no way Lana killed and tortured him…I mean…right?

She arches an eyebrow at me, as if challenging me to speak first. If she killed a man and waltzed into this place…she's a fucking psychopath.

No. I'm just too emotional.

I walk away, ending the staring contest, deciding to get some answers. She came with Logan, so she'll be here for a while. No way is he leaving until he has answers.

But I plan to get some different answers.

I practically sprint to my car, and I'm on the road when my phone rings with an incoming call from Leonard. I start to not answer, but decide to. I'm sure it's about the sick son of a bitch I let terrorize innocent children by never looking deeper than the surface once I became an FBI agent.

"What's going on?" I ask seriously, clearing my throat from the sob that's on the tip of my tongue.

"Our castrating mutilator killed Ferguson," he says so calmly.

I almost drop the phone.

"What?" I ask in disbelief.

"He didn't want us linking it to him, but he left the kid with Lindy May Wheeler, who, surprise surprise, once lived in Delaney Grove."

"That doesn't make sense. You guys profiled him to be a sadist, and a sadist wouldn't—"

"We're revisiting the profile. He's a revenge killer. Not a sadist.

Scarlet Angel

Everything we thought we knew is about to change. We think he feels a kinship with you. He somehow knew about Ferguson and…your past," he says, the last part spoken with regretful hesitance.

I squeeze the phone tighter, driving faster.

"Okay. Keep me updated," I say stoically, my voice not betraying the whirlwind of emotions stirring within me.

As I hang up, I count the ways I'm losing my mind. I suspected Lana to be the one who killed that son of a bitch, but that's insane. I'm too close to this case, not thinking rationally.

But he said the killer knew about my past, focused on it. I gave Lana a reason to focus on me when I stupidly alerted her to my suspicions. She was too calm. Too underwhelmed by my accusations.

It's like she was prepared for those questions.

If it was Lana who killed Kenneth, then Lana would be our serial killer who has been killing men twice her size with psychical domination. There's no possible way I'm right.

So why am I still driving to her house? Why am I still not convinced that she's not the angel Laurel spoke of?

Logan will hate me forever if he learns I've gone crazy enough to accuse his girlfriend—that he finds perfect—of something so bizarrely impossible, not to mention grossly heinous.

The police are gone as I drive into her driveway, trying not to dwell on how insane this all is. It's currently all-hands-on-deck for this case. The PD are looking for dozens and dozens of bodies left behind by a devil I should have killed.

The house is dark, and I carefully twist the knob, surprised to find it unlocked. I leave it unlocked as I head inside. Logan has been in her room, so I skip it, knowing she'd be smart enough to hide all her dirty little secrets.

I ignore the nagging part of my mind that is calling me crazy for suspecting her. She's not even close to being capable of these things physically. Killing Kenneth would have been a hell of a job. First she'd have had to lug him out of the basement. Then push him up the hill that leads to the beach. There's just no way.

But I continue on, letting my gut override my mind.

There's something about her...something eerily composed that Logan doesn't see. Something dark in her eyes when she looks into your soul.

But how dark can a person be if they save a child?

I'm so confused.

I find a door that's locked, and instinct has me immediately picking it. My skills make it easy, and the door pops open in seconds. But it's empty.

Why lock an empty room?

Only four bookcases are against the walls, and all four are empty.

Confused, I turn around, but a scream tears from my throat as a large body suddenly rushes me.

I grab for my gun, but it's too late. The beast collides with me, slamming me into the wall, dazing me as an agonized scream leaves me again.

My gun is stripped from me, tossed to the ground, and another pained sound escapes me as I'm shoved against the wall, feeling my hands wrenched behind my back as a warm breath floats over my skin with a minty smell.

"Well, isn't this a nice surprise, Agent Grace?" a man's voice asks, eliciting a chill that runs up my spine.

"Two for the price of one," he goes on, still keeping me pinned. "Too bad I'm waiting for another. You'll have to wait your turn. I'll even overlook your red hair."

My breath seizes in my lungs as realization hits me hard and fast. With all the chaos, Logan probably didn't even think about the cops being pulled off babysitting detail. There's only one person who would be here right now.

"Tell me, Agent Grace," he says, binding my hands tightly with my own handcuffs as I remain immobile, pinned as I struggle in vain, "are you afraid of the Boogeyman?"

My stomach lurches, and I try to scream again just as he throws me to the ground. He comes down on top of me, laughing as I scream for help. He laughs louder.

"Scream! Scream all you want!" he taunts. "This is the best place in the world to scream, because no one can hear you, Agent."

My feet jerk up, and I realize he's tying them to my hands, forcing my back to arch as he lifts off me to finish the process.

"But you can't scream when my guest arrives," he goes on, smirking in the darkness. My eyes have adjusted, and I see his bald head as he shoves something into my mouth.

I try to fight, but he digs his fingers into my jaw, wrenching it open. He ties the gag, securing it, then I hear the telltale rip of duct tape seconds before it covers my mouth.

I struggle again, fighting, but with my hands and feet bound together. He laughs again as he lifts me, carrying me effortlessly down the stairs, intentionally dragging my head against the wall.

I cry out, only hearing a barely-there, muffled sound through the layers of gagging he's secured. My head slams against the side of the wall when he turns sharply.

"Oops," he says, snickering.

He drops me to the ground, and I whimper, the sound not escaping at all as my elbow hits too hard, along with my hip. The creaking of two folding closet doors becomes noticeable as I see the doors swing open, and he slams his foot into my stomach hard enough to crack some ribs and kick me into the small space.

He kneels as he slides me in the rest of the way, and I twist my head away when he tries to brush the hair from my eyes.

"Enjoy the show, Agent Grace. At least you'll know what's

coming next."

With that, he slams the doors shut, and the small, blind-like centers let me see through the slats as his feet move away.

Music filters through the house, a soft, classical song. I can see the front door from here, and I watch, wishing I had never suspected her of anything.

A tear rolls from my eye, feeling like fire licking against my skin.

Logan will be with her. He'll die right in front of me. And I can't even warn him.

I can feel my phone in my front pocket, taunting me—so close, yet so far away. No matter how I twist, I can't reach it.

It seems like hours later the door is finally opening, and I try to scream. Try to warn her. But the small sound I'm able to make is drowned out by the music in the house.

It's just her as she shuts the door; no Logan. No hope of being saved.

It happens fast.

Plemmons blindsides her, punching her right in the side of the face. She drops the keys and phone she's holding and slams into the wall from the impact, dazed and confused.

He throws his body against hers, and she cries out as he twists her hand that she tries to hit him with, while simultaneously choking her with his arm. Despite the music, I can hear every word he says.

"Feisty. I like that. And so pretty. Agent Bennett picks them well," he taunts. "He left you all alone finally. Tell me, princess, are you afraid of the Boogeyman?"

He lifts off her and throws her into the wall across from him. She hits hard before bouncing to the ground.

What has my ears perking up is the sound of her laughter as she slowly lifts herself from the ground.

"Boogeyman," she says, looking up at him. "Took you long enough."

His footsteps pause as confusion mixed with anger crosses his face. He gets off on fear. On pain.

Yet she's acting immune.

Did Logan coach her on how to act?

Or is she really that fucking stupidly unafraid?

He charges her, kicking her in the stomach, before grabbing her by the hair of the head, jerking her up to her feet.

A strangled sound of pain escapes her, and he pushes her into the wall with enough force to crack something. Her face is to the side, and she's smiling as he comes in behind her.

"Not laughing now, are you?" he asks, reaching down with one hand to start pulling down her pants. "You won't be laughing anymore tonight."

"I think that's enough damage to make this convincing," she says before he can finish.

The weird comment has him pausing, while my heartbeat thrums in my ears.

She throws her elbow around, connecting with his face at such an impossible angle. I suck in air through my nose, shocked as he stumbles backwards.

She wipes her mouth, looking down at her fingers as she flips on a light with her other hand, revealing the bloody fingertips.

Her nose and bottom lip are bleeding, and her face is already bruising where he hit her. Yet she seems unaffected by the pain.

His eyes narrow.

"The Boogeyman isn't so scary in the light," she says, a dark smile turning up at the corners of her lips.

His nose is bleeding from the shot her elbow took, and he releases some sound of fury before charging her. She spins and ducks his fist, and her knee comes up, slamming hard into his ribs.

As he doubles over, she spins again, bringing up her foot, connecting with his back. He slams into the wall, and she grins broader as he whirls around, confused. Furious. Ready to kill.

"I can't leave too many bruises. Don't want them suspicious now, do I?"

My blood freezes inside my body, and I shake my head in disbelief.

He pulls a knife out, the same knife he's killed so many others with. She eyes it carelessly.

"Oh, how I wish I could sit you down and take from you like you took from all those women. Make you feel the same pain and terror they felt," she says, eyeing him with a smirk. "But I can't. I can, however, strip you of all that pride you hold so dearly. All that *power* you think you have. Then I can kill you."

He charges her with the knife, his feet rushing, but she dodges two swipes, almost too easily, as though she's playing with him.

She grabs his wrist on the third strike, and she twists quickly, causing his hand to roll awkwardly as he cries out. The knife drops to the ground, and she spins, kicking his feet out from under him.

When he falls, she kicks the knife to the side, knocking it out of reach. He darts to his feet, rushing toward a table, but she drops and grabs the knife, throwing it into the drawer so hard that it sticks halfway through.

The drawer doesn't budge as he jerks on it, and she laughs as she charges him this time. He tries to grab her, but she's too fast, and her knee collides with his groin so hard that he topples backwards, sobbing as he most likely swallows his balls back down.

"They'll believe a good knee shot to the jewels," she says, jerking the knife out of the drawer before opening it and pulling out the gun. "Nice try, by the way. Too bad I know where I hide my own guns, huh?"

She's the cat and he's the mouse.

Scarlet Angel

The man who has terrorized Boston for so long, and now DC, is just a toy on her strings.

Who the fucking hell is Lana Myers.

I don't make a sound, scared for a whole new reason. I walked in and threatened a girl who has a sexual sadist sobbing on the ground.

"The big bad Boogeyman," she sighs, circling him while holding the knife. "I've always hated the horror movies. You know why?" she asks as he cups his crotch, still rocking on the ground in pain.

"I'll tell you why," she goes on, turning her back on him as she walks toward the living room again. "Because they always portray the women as pathetic little screamers who can't save themselves. The bad guy is always walking. The girl is always running. Yet somehow the big bad *Boogeyman* catches up to them regardless."

I watch as Plemmons manages to get to his feet, and her back is still turned. My eyes are wide, and I don't know who would be worse to face.

Two devils in one room.

How did this happen to me?

"I also hate how they paint them as the idiots with a stroke of luck," she goes on, oblivious to his stealthy approach. "How the girls grab a knife at the last second, and the killer runs into the blade. So anticlimactic. He usually ends up disappearing when they finally run to call for help too. Then he makes one final attempt to kill them."

He quietly creeps up behind her, then charges at the last second.

She grins, and my heart hits my throat as she drops to her hands, kicking her feet up so fast, and her ankles grab his throat before she flips him, all of it happening in one smooth motion.

Holy fucking ninja assassin.

He slams to the ground, and she chokes him, her legs now

binding his throat.

"I like choking men the same way you like choking women," she hisses, her tone so dark and sinister that it makes me sick, confirming my worst fears. "But I don't prey on those weaker than me. I don't prey on the innocent."

She releases him and flips back to her feet with the same ridiculous, almost unnatural speed. Her words slowly sink in, and confusion rattles through me at their meaning.

Revenge killer. Leonard said it was a revenge killer.

Kinship.

All the little pieces try to add up.

Plemmons coughs, strangling on the air that enters his lungs. "Who…are…you?" he asks through labored breaths.

Her smile deepens. "I'm the girl who takes on the darkest of men. Men who've done things dark and twisted to the weak. Men who preyed on the innocent. Men who thought they killed me when I was weak. Just like the women you've killed."

She crouches near his head, as he flops around on his back, still clutching his neck. It's an act. He's a horrible actor. Damn it! He's faking it!

I try to warn her, finally choosing a side, but the words are drowned by the layers of the gag and the steady stream of music.

She brings the knife to his cheek, running the back of the blade against it. He stops struggling, going perfectly still.

"You're like me," he says, more surprise in his tone than fear or malice.

"No," she says quietly. "I'm so much worse and better than you. I'm the thing the monsters in the dark fear. And now I'm even the Boogeyman's nightmare."

She steps away, and he rolls to his feet. When he's facing her, she winks—fucking winks—at him. She's enjoying every second of this.

Scarlet Angel

She's doing what she promised; she's stripping away his pride and power, shattering the immortal feeling of being untouchable he had.

He grabs a lamp, chunking it at her head. As she ducks it, laughing, he picks up the end table, and throws it at her.

She dodges it, using that speed she has to her advantage. It's like she wanted this to happen.

"You can't even get it up like a real man," she goads, grinning when his nostrils flare and fury creases all his features. "You need to cut women up, watch them bleed, just to get a good boner. You're weak," she says, walking across the room. "I shouldn't even bother with you. The men I kill are strong, powerful men who can fuck a woman without forcing her. They only rape when they feel a woman needs to be put in her place."

She's saying all the right things to provoke him, to tear away the façade he's built, and emasculate him. She's so good at profiling because she's studied it. She's learned how to demean and debase all her victims.

The way they debased her.

She's a victim. Or, at least, she was.

Her words add up, telling the story she's yet to lay bare.

"You know what I take from them?" she asks, letting her eyes drop to his lap before looking back up to his face. My stomach roils. I know what she takes. "I take everything," she says at last. "They have more to give."

She turns, putting her back to him, acting as though he has no power over her, showing him he's no threat. The gun is lying in front of the closet doors, but he hasn't gone for it again.

It'd be too weak to go for the gun.

She's playing him too well.

She's playing a man who has played the world.

And she's winning.

He lunges for her, ready to prove himself, and she spins, the knife at her waist as she faces him. He runs right into it, and I hold back the sounds, now worried about being heard.

She rolls her eyes as his eyes widen in shock, his features paling as he stumbles back, the knife sliding out as she jerks it away.

"And now I've gotten lucky," she mocks. "Just like the horror movies. They'll never suspect a thing."

He drops to his knees, the wound in his abdomen bleeding profusely. There's too much blood for him to survive if help doesn't come right away.

I'd have been his next victim. Now I wonder what happens when she finds out I know it all.

She could have already killed me, though. No one would have suspected her.

Instead, she tracked down my stepfather, killed him, and then saved a child's life. A child I let down by not being the hero a devil was.

Lana Myers, or whoever she really is, survived something so dark that she needs revenge.

But Logan is sleeping with her.

He's falling in love.

And she's a fucking psychopath.

My own guilt for my failures has me wondering what happens if I stop her. I don't know enough about her victims to know if they're hurting others the way I let Kenneth get away with.

I failed so many others by trusting the lies.

She brought his evil deeds to an end.

What happens if others are hurt because I stopped her before she finished? I'm barely living with the guilt I've yet to face.

I have no idea what to do.

As I agonize over the options, Lana sits down, watching him bleed out, holding onto the knife as casually as if it's the TV remote and she's watching her favorite show. He chokes and gurgles up blood, staring at her in disbelief.

He came to kill a weak woman, only to find he was really the prey who ran into the lion's den.

"This is my favorite part," she tells him softly. "The look of resignation. The moment the hope slips away and you know you won't be saved. I've been there. It's terrifying, so I know exactly how panicked you are right now. How helpless you feel. The difference is, you won't get up and live to kill them all one day."

Live to kill them all one day.

I file away each bit of information, deciding to make a list of reasons why I should or shouldn't tell the world who she is.

"They took too much. Left too little. I had nothing to lose," she whispers, the words barely making it to me. "Until him."

My heart thumps faster. Logan. She's talking about Logan.

"Then you wanted to kill *him*. He's too good to die. He's everything opposite of us. His light still shines. I hope they have fun with you in hell. You sentenced yourself there the day you targeted the only thing that makes me feel as though there's still a soul inside me left to be saved. The only thing I love more than revenge."

Just like that, I have my answer. And I watch with her as the Boogeyman dies by his own knife. At the hands of a woman.

The hands of a victim.

In a way, it's poetic justice.

Chapter 3

The course of true love never did run smooth.
—William Shakespeare

Lana

My brother was a Shakespeare lover. He lived and breathed the words of a man his generation took for granted. The people of that time didn't respect or appreciate the anguish and torment tied into each tragedy he produced under the guise of true romance.

Marcus was a romantic to the core, with nothing but light and beauty shining from him.

The world around us snuffed out that light.

They stole his grace.

Shamed his name.

Killed him.

Destroyed us.

With great amusement, I watch as the Boogeyman exhales his last breath. No longer will he steal lights as bright as my brother's.

The Boogeyman will no longer be seen as the immortal that taunts the police or FBI. He'll no longer be the nightmare who terrorizes women, haunting their lives. He'll be revered as a mortal who died at the hands of a weak woman he failed to kill.

A woman who got *lucky* enough to kill him first.

Curious, I pull on a glove and check his pockets, finding a remote. Hmmm...

Scarlet Angel

I look around, and spot what the remote goes to. There's an out-of-place little contraption next to my fireplace. I'm fairly positive it's a cell phone jammer. My phone was working before I came in, so he shut it on at some other time.

Putting the remote back in his pocket, I stand to go to my cell phone. It was dropped within the first five seconds that he blindsided me. Sure enough, there's nothing going on when I try to dial out. No signal.

Good. That gives me an excuse as to why I watched him bleed out for over thirty minutes—the same way he let his victims die.

I glance over my shoulder, a horror movie flashback hitting me, but he's still dead. No disappearing act for the mortal who has drawn his last breath.

I return my gaze to my phone and carry it toward the couch. A normal girl wouldn't notice a cell phone jammer—or even know what one was—so quickly after the traumatizing experience of killing a man.

I turn off the music, removing my iPod from the dock. Asshole.

I hate my things being touched by people. Now he's gone and bled all over my floor too. It'll take me forever to clean all that up.

I'd call him inconsiderate, but since I'm the one that sort of stabbed him, then I guess it's my own fault. I should have let him run into the knife on the tile floor instead of the carpet.

Oh well. I can finally get that hardwood I've been considering. I usually don't update my homes, but with Logan living somewhat close by, I've had more reasons to stay than go.

I wonder how long it'll be before someone checks in on me. Or should I run and scream down the street? How does a normal person act after being attacked by a homicidal maniac and miraculously killing him by fluke?

Do they rock in a corner? Do they cry? I hope not. I can't fake tears, and I don't like rocking. Makes me nauseated.

Do I scream and pretend to be inconsolable or terrified? I don't like screaming. Hurts my throat. And acting terrified will be hard to pull off, because…I can't remember how to be afraid.

Obviously he wanted to rape me. I do remember how to feel after that. Numb. Broken. Suicidal. But that was much more than one man that brought me to that point.

It was much more than the rape that left me so broken.

So really, I guess I don't know, which it doesn't matter. He sure as hell never made it that far.

Do I act stunned or shocked? Do I show remorse even though he deserved to die? I'll start laughing if I try to fake remorse for that sadistic piece of shit.

I might be able to pull off stunned or shocked. Maybe play it off like I haven't been able to really wrap my head around the fact I just killed a guy?

Normal girls are hard to understand, because I can't remember the last time I was normal. Normal girls spend too much time reacting to their actions. They take for granted the air they get to breathe, because they've never been deprived of those painless breaths.

Me? I've already walked through hell, so I'm desensitized to all else.

I decide to go with shocked. It's the easiest to fake.

So, while I wait on someone to show up—and they will eventually when Logan realizes I'm unprotected—I practice my blank stare. I keep holding the knife, giving it a white-knuckle grip, certain a girl in shock would do just the same.

Yep.

Got this down.

And I wait.

And wait.

And wait.

Scarlet Angel

Sheesh.

Finally, I hear the telltale *whoops and blares* of sirens, brakes squealing on my driveway. Jeez. I'm glad I didn't need to be saved. An entry that loud would have gotten me killed immediately, giving the fucknut bleeding all over my floor time to escape.

Jackasses.

I am curious when they burst through the doors, using my peripheral to see them training their guns on the air in front of them. How do they know he's here?

I proceed with my blank stare act, waiting.

"Holy shit," someone says, but I remain in *shock*, staring ahead.

How long do I have to do this?

My eyes are burning from how wide I'm holding them open. "Plemmons is in the living room," a loud voice booms.

I don't move my head, but I see him kneel as another man keeps a gun pointed on the Boogeyman.

"Clear."

"Clear."

"Clear."

The voices continue chirping the same word from all around my house. I remain a statue.

"Dead," the guy kneeling says, then grabs the radio hooked to his shoulder. "Dispatch, Plemmons is dead. The house is clear."

He clicks the radio, speaking into it again, repeating his words.

"What the hell?" he asks.

Apparently that jammer does more than just disable cell phone signals.

"I don't know. Mine isn't working either. Neither is my phone. Don't disturb the scene. This is a fed case. Clear the house until they get here. They're already chewing our asses for taking thirty

259

minutes longer than we were supposed to. How was I supposed to know the guy isn't just overly paranoid? They had us knee deep in an unmarked graveyard, all hands available."

"Miss?" the guy prompts, coming closer, not responding to the sulking douchebag whilst I pretend to be a sad little girl in shock.

He carefully touches my wrist, and I jerk.

"Shhh," he soothes, prying the knife from my hand and handing it back to another guy who wraps it and puts it in an evidence bag. "You're safe, Ms. Myers."

His voice is so gentle, and I have to keep a straight face to keep from smiling at him in appreciation for his genuine concern.

Something rattles from behind us, a loud *thump thump thump*, and I turn around without thinking as they draw their weapons, aiming it at the coat closet in the room.

My heart is in my ears as they jerk the doors open, and all the color drains from my face as Hadley struggles on the ground, likely thumping the door with her head.

Her muffled sounds reach my ears as my eyes land on the duct tape on her mouth.

I take it back. I remember now what it's like to be afraid, because the fear is etching up my spine, rising steadily higher and higher. They'll load me full of bullets before I can get away. There are at least fifteen cops in my house right now.

I also don't have to fake being frozen in shock either. Nothing on my body is working, so even if I wanted to run, I couldn't.

Her eyes fix on mine, but she looks away when they start unbinding her feet and freeing her hands from the cuffs. As soon as her hands are free, she starts peeling the tape off.

And I get stiffer by the second, praying against all odds that she's been unconscious this entire time. I mean, it's possible. She hasn't made a sound until now.

As soon as her mouth is free, she starts rubbing her wrists as they help her to her feet. She wobbles, and one offers her support, clutching her under the arms.

"I'm Agent Hadley Grace," she tells them firmly when they open their mouths, probably to get her identity.

All mouths close at once, and the guns lower.

"I came to check on Ms. Myers after learning patrol had been pulled away," she lies, the fib rolling off her tongue effortlessly.

She came to find something on me.

She just did.

Like every stupid fucking idiot in the movies, I showed my hand of cards, let the words roll out of my mouth to a man I knew would never be able to tell a soul. I totally did an evil monologue, for fuck's sake!

I did it to taunt him.

I did it to strip him of power.

I didn't know I was being watched.

She gauges me long and hard.

"What happened?" an officer asks.

She directs her attention to him.

"I was upstairs, clearing the house after I realized the door was unlocked. He hit me from behind, and he tied me up so he could wait on Ms. Myers to get home. He wanted me to watch. He wanted me to see what would happen to me when he was done with her."

Her eyes turn back to mine, and something silently passes from her to me, though I'm not sure what.

"Ms. Myers fought back. She got lucky. Even threw some things at him," she says, causing that shock inside me to expand. She gestures to the shattered remnants of the lamp and the broken disarray of the small end table that *he* threw at me. "She caught him off guard enough for him to drop the knife. Somehow she managed to get it before him, and she turned just in time. He ran right into it."

She continues to study me, as I try to figure out what the actual fuck she's doing right now. Why is she covering for me? Is it just so she can save the truth for her team instead of giving the arrest to the cops?

"Pure. Dumb. Luck," she says, practically quoting my words from my earlier taunt.

Unsure of her motives, I remain frozen.

"Definitely lucky," one guy agrees.

Hadley's lips twitch as she looks away. "I'll call my guys."

My stomach tilts, growing more nauseated by the second. She lifts her phone, then frowns. But then looks at his body. "There's a remote in his pocket. I…saw it earlier."

Sicker and sicker.

I hate this game she's playing right now.

"We can't touch anything on the scene until the feds get here," one guy says, and she arches an eyebrow.

"I am a fed."

"Until your—"

"Where the fuck is everyone? Why isn't anyone answering their damn phones?" Logan's voice has me snapping my head to the door.

"Lana!" he shouts, the clear sense of panic in his tone.

"Here!" I call out, my voice cracking sincerely. I'm not sure what Hadley's about to do, and the tears that are in my eyes are real.

It may be the last time he ever looks at me with anything but horror and disgust if she tells him who I really am.

His wild eyes find me, and his entire body visibly relaxes as he charges across the room, not even noticing the bloody body before he grabs me, crushing me to him.

Scarlet Angel

My eyes dart over to Hadley to see her watching us with an unreadable expression. She looks away, telling the cops something about the attack—another lie.

Logan holds me to him, his entire body rigid as I lean against him, absorbing his feel. He pulls back, his eyes scanning my face as he grimaces, taking in the damage.

There's nothing physically wrong with me that I didn't allow. Well, other than the first hit. He got in one lucky shot that I didn't see coming.

"What the fucking hell?" I hear him say, looking down now as he sees the Boogeyman for the first time.

He draws me back to him, almost as though he's shielding me from the sight.

"She got lucky," Hadley says, regaining my attention.

He looks over at her. "What are you doing here?"

"I came by to check on her after I heard they pulled patrols," she says, lying again.

"I'll let them brief you on the specifics, but let's just say I'm going to have a hell of a headache." She points to her bruised temple. Her eyes flick to mine before returning to his. "She saved our lives tonight."

With that, she walks out, but I still worry what her angle is.

She wanted dirt, and I gave her far more than she ever expected. Why leave? Why not spill it all?

Logan cups my face, and I wince when he squeezes it too tight, thanks to the bruise that's causing my face to swell.

"Shit," he hisses. "Let's get you out of here."

Craig walks in, his eyes landing on the dead man in my living room.

"Well, that's one way to close a case," he says, his eyes wide in disbelief.

"Let the media know the case is closed," Logan tells him before scooping me up, cradling me to him as though I'm fragile.

I let him. When he's around, I don't feel like I have to be so invincible. When he's with me, I feel like I can just be cared for without being weak.

Like it's okay to be vulnerable, because he'd never use it against me.

He carries me through the throngs of cops that are showing up more and more, everyone coming to see the Boogeyman dead with their own eyes.

"Lana!" The familiar voice has me looking over as Duke comes jogging toward us, so much regret coursing through his eyes. "I came as soon as you called," he says, looking at Logan in shock. "How'd you beat me here?"

"He drove so fast that my asshole is still clenched. I don't think he tapped the brakes until we got here," Craig tells him dryly. I didn't know he followed us.

"Get your guys out of the house. We need to clear the scene," Logan says.

"What happened?" Duke asks, looking by us. "He really attacked?"

"Yeah. And Lana got lucky," Hadley says as she walks by us, moving toward Craig, tugging his elbow. "Give me a ride home in case I have a concussion."

My stomach tenses, and Logan gingerly brushes his lips over my forehead, not asking any questions about how I killed the man in my house. All he cares about is that he's dead and I'm alive. All the details seem unimportant, as though I'm priority above all else.

He looks down, his eyes tortured with guilt.

"This isn't your fault," I say, knowing the bruises on my face are the reason for that look shading his usually bright eyes.

My wounds are nothing more than superficial. I've survived

much, *much* worse.

"It's all my fault. But no one will ever touch you again, Lana."

His lips find mine, and I kiss him, deciding to deal with Hadley later.

When he breaks the kiss, he looks over at a man and woman as they drive up, not getting out of the SUV.

"Give us a ride to town. I'm getting a room for the night," he tells them.

"My purse is—"

"I can manage a hotel room," he interrupts, not bothering to look at me.

My lips try to twist into a smile, but I deny it, knowing a girl who just endured what I did shouldn't be smiling about him being so alpha right now. I'm supposed to be meek and timid.

"Hop in," the woman tells him.

"Someone should probably work the scene," the guy says.

They seem completely unaffected or unnaturally guarded about their curiosity.

"He's dead. There's no scene."

"Dead?" the woman asks in surprise, then narrows her eyes. "I wanted to be the one to take him out."

"I'm taking a week off," Logan announces randomly. "This case is closed. Hadley was attacked. Lana was—"

"Hadley?" the man and woman ask in unison.

"He gave her a shiner," Logan explains. "I didn't get all the details. But right now, I don't know if I can handle hearing them. Let Donny deal with it for now. You two can come back after you drop us off."

He keeps me in his lap as he loads us into the backseat. I don't resist the seating arrangement, feeling my eyes grow heavy. With all the adrenaline pumping through me, I almost forgot it's been over twenty-four hours since I slept.

Now I feel beaten and defeated by the clock that displays the hour. It may be closing in on forty-eight hours instead of twenty-four. We spent a while at Logan's office. It was already closing in on midday then. It'd just gotten dark when I got home.

Now it's... Fuck, my eyes are so blurry with sleep deprivation that I can't see the clock. Can't count the hours.

And I don't care.

They talk as the dude drives. At some point I hear Logan refer to them as Leonard and Elise.

"Hadley got a hotel room too," someone says, and that has me jarring back awake. Elise. It was Elise. "She says she's too exhausted to go home, and too creeped out too."

"Which one?" Logan asks.

"The new one closest to us," Elise tells him. "It has a massage place. I'm sure that's why she chose it."

"Take us to that one. I'll check in on her later."

She still hasn't said anything. If she was going to spill the pile of beans, she'd have done it by now, right? She's been in contact with them, apparently.

"That other case was jurisdiction hell," Leonard states, waking me up again. I didn't even realize my eyes had closed.

"The cops were all pissing on their territory. Duke said it was his since the murderer was in his jurisdiction. That place said it was theirs since the burial grounds were in their jurisdiction."

"Yeah, and they called off her patrol because of a pissing contest," Logan growls. "Tonight could have gone severely different."

He holds me tighter, but I pretend I'm still asleep.

"It's a miracle she got that knife away from him. Hadley told me what happened. Sent it all in a long text," Elise says quietly.

Logan stiffens. "I still don't think I'm ready to hear it just yet."

My heartbeat is in my ears.

"She fought, Logan. She fought for her life, and it paid off. She caught him off guard enough that he made a mistake, and he died by his own knife. Ran right into it. I thought that only ever happened in the movies."

My lips twitch, but I say nothing. Hadley is keeping my secret if she's spreading the lie to her friends.

But why?

Chapter 4

Death is a fearful thing.
—William Shakespeare.

Logan

I almost feel like even a week won't be enough. Not that I'll actually be able to take a week. I'll be lucky to get a few days, regardless of the fact my girlfriend was almost killed tonight.

My stomach is in knots just thinking of everything that could have gone wrong.

We're inside the hotel room before I put Lana down for the first time. Checking in was a pain in the ass, but Lana just took my wallet from my pocket, and handed the very curious woman behind the counter whatever she asked for in sequence.

I can tell she hasn't let the gravity of the situation sink in yet. She's too calm. I want to be here for her when it does catch up.

She killed a man tonight. A man almost killed her.

And it's all my fault.

She curls up on the bed, exhaustion weighing heavily in her eyes.

As soon as I'm down to my boxers, I join her, thankful she's letting me touch her. If he'd…

I can't keep thinking of everything that could have gone wrong. Hadley is a trained agent and still couldn't go home alone. She came to a hotel where someone would hear her if she screamed for help.

Lana has to be on the verge of breaking down. She's just a civilian with no training.

"I'm so sorry," I say against her hair.

She hums, scooting back into me.

"Not your fault," she mumbles.

"I knew my job was toxic for relationships, but I naively never thought it'd put you in danger," I say softly, wondering if she's already asleep when she doesn't respond.

She rolls over, facing me, her eyes fighting to stay open.

"If you're trying to break up with me after I just survived the Boogeyman, I may kick your ass."

She says the words with dry humor, but I can see the vulnerable look in her eyes.

"I probably should, to be honest. But I'm too selfish to let you go," I tell her honestly.

She brushes her lips against mine, and she sighs as she snuggles in closer. "I feel the exact same way. I can't let you go, no matter how much better I feel you deserve."

I deserve better? She was targeted by a sexual sadist because *of me*. She was attacked because *I* didn't call the patrol one night to make sure they were in place. She was almost hurt because *I* failed her.

No. She was hurt. Not *almost*.

The bruises on her face and split lip tell that story plain and clear.

My phone chimes as Lana's breathing evens out, and I listen to her sleep, holding her to me like I'm worried it's all an illusion. Worried I'll wake up tomorrow to realize I've had a psychotic break and am now living in my head—in a world where Lana survived.

I read the text from Craig.

CRAIG: Your girl fought back hard enough to leave some bruises on him too. Coroner said it couldn't have been easy, since he was solid muscle. She's tougher than you think. Stop beating yourself up.

ME: When your girlfriend almost dies because of a serial killer targeting you, then talk to me.

CRAIG: Touché. How is she?

ME: I don't think it's sunk in yet. She's sleeping right now.

CRAIG: BTW, I know you want time off, but…I sort of found something major.

ME: Fuck. What?

My phone rings, but Lana doesn't even stir. I answer reluctantly.

"So, this little town is covering up the fact there was a serial killer ten years ago. Sexual sadist much like our dearly departed Boogeyman."

"Too soon," I state dryly.

"Right. Sorry. But there's literally not one mention of this ever in their papers."

"What does the serial killer have to do with anything?"

"That's the thing, it doesn't look like they put away the right guy."

I slowly sit up, careful not to disturb Lana. I'd normally go to another room, but not right now.

"What?"

"The Godfather profiled him to be in his mid-thirties to early forties, and a blue collared worker. But Leonard—yes, I called him first—said that it didn't make sense. The guy was well organized, and displayed psychopathic tendencies when he killed. The women were brutally assaulted perimortem, antemortem, and postmortem. This guy was seriously into annihilating the body."

"What'd he do?"

"In short, he carved them up, with a serrated knife, then drilled nails into their foreheads. It started off being mostly after they died. Then it started happening before they were dead. He developed into a true heartless bastard."

"He's a psychopath with sadistic tendencies. Not a sexual sadist. Sounds like sex was an afterthought. What does this have to do with our killer? I admit it sounds crazy to have another serial killer from that town, but this is obviously not a copycat situation. Our unsub's motivation is revenge."

"That's what I was saying. I think the Godfather locked up the wrong guy. Serial killers rarely have kids. Psychopaths rarely have kids. Hell, ninety percent of all unsubs are childless because they can't form healthy relationships long enough to have children. The guy they locked away was a doting father of two kids. Single parent too. His wife died five years earlier in a car accident. His kids were never late to school or neglected in anyway. They argued how impossible it was that he was the killer, claiming he was home with them every night and helping make supper as a family."

"Why did he get pinned with it then?"

"DNA. They found his jizz at the crime scenes."

"Way to be professional. But that is pretty incriminating."

"Or brilliant. Who gets off on controlling a situation?"

"Narcissists. You think the killer was a narcissist?"

"Maybe it's because of the Boogeyman thing still being so fresh, but yes. I think there was a whatever you said with some narcissism tossed in there. I think the true killer framed our guy. Why else would someone so organized blatantly leave behind DNA? And get this, they found two types of spermicide on each victim."

"But spermicide is from condoms. If he left behind sperm, then why wear a condom?"

"Sounds like questions that should have been asked ten years ago. Anyway, he had two kids, but they're no longer in Delaney Grove. There was an accident that happened shortly after their father was found dead in the county holding cell."

"What?" I ask, confused. "What happened in the holding cell?"

"Yeah. Robert Evans died the day he was convicted. The coroner's report had three words: He hung himself. Legit, that's all it says. Then the kids went missing two nights later."

"Fuuuuck. What happened?"

"I had to dig deep to find the report, because they went to a hospital five towns over. Long way to drive for a doctor when one is right in town. Supposedly there was a car accident, but the boy — seventeen — had severe signs of sexual trauma, and get this…he was castrated."

I swallow the bile in my throat. "That's our unsub."

"You'd think. But unless he's killing as a zombie, it's not possible. He died that night in the hospital after somehow managing to drive him and his sister there, despite his injuries. If he drove from Delaney Grove… Hell, I don't know how he didn't die from the blood loss alone. The sister was beat to hell and back, stabbed multiple times, face caved in, a huge piece of glass sticking out of her. She had severe signs of sexual trauma too, but she claimed it was a car accident, just like he did. It's noted they were too scared to speak, and the girl died later that night from complications. That's all I could charm out of a helpful nurse without a warrant."

My hand runs over the scar on Lana's side, even though it's covered by her clothing. Lana is sleeping hard, not noticing the way I touch her. The glass part strikes a nerve, reminding how she's actually come close to dying twice now.

I'm going to put her in a bubble.

"That's fucked up. All of it is fucked up. Get those case files. Why have I never heard of this before?"

Scarlet Angel

"It never made headline news because of some terrorist threat that was going on at the same time. If they locked up the wrong guy—"

"Then that means there's another serial killer who has had ten more years to pile up a body count. And it also could have set the dominoes in motion for this revenge killing spree. Small town justice is always an issue. We usually have to transport prisoners ourselves, but….why the kids? How sick is that town?"

"The girl was just sixteen at the time. The boy had a scholarship to a drama program in New York. They were leaving town eventually. I know that town put them in that hospital. That's why they drove far away from it to die. The guy might have survived if he'd stopped sooner. But he didn't. He just drove as far as he could to get them away from Delaney Grove. I can't prove it, but my gut is telling me that's what happened."

"Talk to the town. See what you can figure out."

He grows quiet. For a long time.

"Any chance he won't take innocent bystanders down?"

"The unsub?" I ask.

"Yeah."

"Revenge killers always take it too far, killing too many people for the smallest infractions. Don't try to make him a hero. He may kill some monsters, but he'll take out some good people too. And no one has the right to decide who lives or dies."

I'm not entirely sure I'm convinced of that even as the words leave my mouth. If Lana had died at the hands of Plemmons, I would have stalked the world until I found him and put him in the grave.

I don't say that aloud though.

"Right. You're right. I just… These cases are always the hardest."

"You empathize with the killers when you understand their motives. I get it. Just don't forget we're the law. If everyone goes around killing people who've wronged them, then we're suddenly an extinct species. It's obviously someone close to them. Dig into their pasts. Dig into Lindy's past too. She was friends with the unsub."

"On it. Leonard is working it too now. Elise is at the hotel you guys are at. Apparently everyone is creeped out by their houses right now since Plemmons broke into Lana's and locked Hadley in a closet."

My hand instinctively tightens on Lana's hip, and she stirs in her sleep.

"I'm getting some sleep. I'm taking at least a few days, and I mean it. I need several days of straight sleep."

"And straight sex," he quips.

Rolling my eyes, I hang up, curl up behind Lana, and she shifts in closer subconsciously, still very much asleep. She's not screaming or tossing around. There's a small smile on her lips like all is right with the world.

Thank fuck for that small miracle.

She's so damn strong. I was waiting on her to break, but she's impressing me more by the second.

"I love you," she says, though it's the confession of a sleeping girl.

My core still tightens, and my body feels like electric wires are coursing over the top of my skin.

Leaning down, I kiss her cheek, smiling as she sighs. And even though I'd rather stay awake and keep my eyes on her all night, the long days finally catch up to me, and I fall asleep with her in my arms.

Chapter 5

Suspicion always haunts the guilty mind.
—William Shakespeare

Lana

"You're serious," I say to Logan, grinning as he nods, not the least bit unsure of himself.

"Alright then," I say on a sigh, matching his bet, pushing in all my Tootsie Rolls. "Show me what you got."

He grins before putting down his cards. "Read em' and weep. Flush, baby."

It's when he waggles his eyebrows that I start laughing, because he's pretty cute when he's competitive.

"Before you get too excited…"

I put my cards down, and his face falls instantly, causing me to laugh harder as he stares in disbelief at my royal flush.

"But…but…but…"

I pull the Tootsie rolls toward me, and he suddenly launches himself at me, tackling me to the bed as I laugh. His lips find the curve of my neck, and I grin as he kisses a small spot there.

"Somehow, you're cheating," he says against my neck.

"I just have an awesome poker face," I say, winding my legs around his waist.

For three days, I've had him all to myself. I've heard that time heals all wounds, but that's not true. Falling in love? That's what makes you forget your anger. If it wasn't for my brother and father, my quest for vengeance would be over.

The media is all over my lawn, which is concerning. Jake had to sneak in and check my secret kill room, making sure no one had tampered with it. Fortunately, no one realizes there's a room inside a room.

Craig went to my house and retrieved my purse and some clothes for me. He had to take them to work—which Logan got bitched at endlessly for requesting, since people are still giving Mr. Pretty Boy hell for carrying a purse into the building. They even checked it at the search point, while he waited in the purse line, apparently seething.

I find this hilarious, of course.

Then, he passed it onto Elise, who put it inside her duffel bag— Craig was pissed that idea never occurred to him—and she brought it and my clothes to us, so that the media wouldn't learn where we were.

Also, there were some paparazzi shots of Craig carrying my purse. I really love the things that interest the news some times.

I also hate them. Because that makes moving down my kill list harder.

I'm going to have to speed up the timeline once things settle down. My bruised face was splashed all over the newspaper and such, but everyone wants an interview with the girl who killed a man that managed to elude all types of law enforcement.

So, yeah. I didn't think this all the way through. Being a woman who took down a woman's nightmare has made me an accidental celebrity. Celebrity status is not fun when you're a serial killer who needs a low profile.

Logan has gone Peter Pan, essentially sewing himself to me like an errant shadow these past few days. Not that I'm complaining. I could get used to having him to myself so much.

Logan's phone rings, and he groans, still on top of me, as he reaches over and grabs it. My legs stay wound around his waist, keeping him where he is as he answers.

"Bennett."

His brow furrows, and he lifts off me, frowning. I release my legs from his waist as he stands up completely.

"When?" When he closes his eyes, his lips tensing in a tight line, I know he has to leave. "Yeah. Tell them not to touch anything. I'll see if Hadley is up to it and be there as soon as possible."

He gets off his phone, and he blows out a long breath while studying me. "I need to go speak to Hadley and see if she's able to work. We just got two bodies from another one of our killers."

Ice slithers over me. Lawrence and Tyler. They've finally been found. By now they're steaming piles of rot.

"I'll go talk to her for you," I tell him, sliding back on the bed. "We sort of bonded with the whole Boogeyman thing."

He studies me for a long minute. "You sure *you're* okay? We haven't really talked about what went down."

I nod grimly. "It's not something I'm ready to move on from just yet, but I'm handling it better than I thought I would."

It's misleading, but it's not a lie. Well, not in the conventional sense. I'm handling the 'aftermath' better than I thought I would, considering I expected him to be more suspicious. He just seems relieved that I'm not an inconsolable mess.

"You're amazing," he says, thumbing my chin before brushing his lips over mine.

"I'd like to talk to Hadley for a second too," I say, making sure I have time to clear the air with her before she's alone in a car with him.

"Okay. Yeah. Sure. Just let me know if she's ready to work, and let me know when you're finished if so."

I stand and throw my arms around his neck, dragging him down for a kiss. He holds me to him, his touch so demanding and strong. I love being in his arms, feeling that security that exists within a simple embrace.

"I'll hurry," I tell him against his lips.

He grabs my ass, totally groping me, then winks before heading toward the bathroom.

My smile disappears the second he shuts the door.

I've been delaying this, worrying about her game. Wondering why she's not told anyone.

After tugging on some clothes, I check the hallway, always worried about someone finding out where we're staying. When I see it's empty, I take quick steps to the end of the hallway, suck in a breath, and knock on her door.

It opens immediately, and I swallow thickly when I realize I'm staring down the barrel of a gun.

"Been expecting you," Hadley says, peering around me.

She steps back, but her gun stays trained on me as I step inside, closing the door behind me. I keep two feet of distance between me and the gun, ready to react if I see her trigger finger get itchy.

"I actually expected you a lot sooner than this," she says, her eyes watching me, as though she's waiting on an excuse.

Remaining calm, I stare at her with my coldest expression.

"Logan wants to know if you're up for a case. He's waiting for your answer."

"Don't pretend that's why you're here right now," she says, an edge to her tone.

"Why haven't you told Logan who I am?"

She slowly backs up, and she gestures for me to sit on the bed closest to the door. I do as the gun-wielding girl silently beckons, sitting down, and she steps back, sitting across from me on the other bed, never lowering her weapon.

"I'm not here to hurt you," I tell her, and she snorts out a laugh.

Scarlet Angel

"I'll be the judge of that. And to your other question, it's because you told the Boogeyman you were killing him to keep Logan safe. You had no idea I was there, obviously, so that wasn't a show. I believe you actually think you're in love."

"I am in love," I immediately blurt out, then grimace. Didn't mean to tell her before I told him.

Her eyebrows go up. "Psychopaths can't love. They can only imitate."

"You think I'm a psychopath? I mean, I joke that I'm psycho, but I'm not the true definition of the word."

"Really? I saw a different story."

I lean forward, and she wraps another hand around the gun handle.

"Easy," I tell her, holding a hand up. "Just getting comfortable. You're calling me names without knowing anything about me. A good profiler digs into the past."

"I'm not a profiler. I'm a forensics expert and a tech genius. I saw what I saw. And I'm telling Logan. I just wanted you to know that first, since you killed my own nightmare and saved me from Plemmons. Call it a courtesy."

Tears bubble up in my eyes, and the first one spills down my cheek. The air is sucked from my lungs, and my entire body feels like it's dipped in a vat of ice.

She cocks her head, studying me, and I bat away a tear.

"Then give me a five minute head start," I say quietly.

I start to stand, and she moves with me, keeping her gun trained at my head.

"This gun is the only thing keeping you from killing me right now," she says randomly.

I spin so fast that I hear her hiss out a breath, and I snatch the gun from her hand, then completely disassemble it, all in less than two seconds. I toss the pieces to the bed, feeling broken and defeated.

"No. I'm not killing you because you don't deserve to die," I tell her as she stumbles backwards. "Guns don't scare me."

"But losing Logan does," she says quietly, her throat bobbing.

"There are only two people in my life that I love. One is like a brother. The other is the first person I've ever been in love with. So yes, losing Logan terrifies me."

"Revenge killers have had a psychotic break. They lose sight of their intended goals and their morals get skewed. Revenge becomes their sole focus, and anything or anyone that gets in the way becomes collateral damage in the name of revenge."

"You're profiling me, yet claim not to profile. You should stick to your day job, because you know nothing about me or what I'm capable of."

I turn to leave, and she calls out, "Wait! It was a test."

Confused, I turn around as she stands up, her body shaking a little bit.

"Care if I put my gun back together? Obviously you're quick enough to disarm me, but it still makes me feel better to have it after what I saw you do to Plemmons."

"Just use the one you have under your pillow," I tell her, watching as she pales.

"How'd you—"

"You've gone through a lot in the past week. It'd make sense to sleep with one under your pillow if you need it to feel safe right now. You'd have more than just your service gun. I need at least two guns to feel safe when I'm at my most vulnerable."

She sighs harshly before grabbing the gun out from under her pillow, and I sit back down, facing her, staying at the exact right distance I need to disarm her again if the need arises.

She doesn't point the gun at me this time.

Scarlet Angel

"Start at the beginning. Explain what could have turned you into this," she says, gesturing toward me with her hand.

"They turned me into this," I tell her softly. "They stripped away my soul and left me devoid of any empathy toward the monsters in the world. I'm not a psychopath. I know the truth from the lies. I know the reality from the delusions. In fact, there are no delusions."

"We've found nothing in that town to point to this level of violence."

I lean forward, but this time she doesn't react. "Dig deeper."

"Just tell me. I'm not deciding what to do until you tell me what could turn someone into a killer so cold that you didn't flinch when you killed Plemmons. You wanted to torture him."

"Just like he tortured those women. Don't you think death was simply too easy?"

She stares at me with the eyes of an unscarred soul, despite the scars I know she bears.

"Fine. You want the story; I'll tell you. But you can't tell your team. They have to learn for themselves," I bite out.

"Why?" she asks. "Why don't you want them knowing?"

"Because I want the town to confess to the sins they covered up," I say bitterly.

"Prove to me you're not going to hurt someone innocent, and I'll make that deal. Tell me the story."

"I could have killed you several times, Hadley. From the day you walked into my house and called me out for stealing Kennedy's identity."

"Why did you steal her identity?"

"To survive," I say quietly.

Her lips tighten, but she gestures at me, meaning she wants to hear what I have to say. Needs to know I'm not suffering a psychotic break. Needs to know that despite the brutal way I kill, that I'm in control of my mind.

So I tell her. I start at the beginning, telling her about my father. Tell her about how he died. Tell her about how small town justice works. I tell her every sick, twisted, demented detail until she's pale and grabs the garbage can, heaving into it as her stomach loses the battle of control.

The vomit doesn't bother me, so I keep talking as she retches. I tell her about Marcus, about his beauty, and how they stole it all away. About how they destroyed him in the last few hours of his life.

About how he was so desperate to save my life that he sacrificed his own by driving so far away from Delaney Grove while trying to keep pressure on his wound.

I tell her about Jake, and how his father was my father's lawyer and best friend. We proved over and over that Dad couldn't be the serial killer they charged him to be. I tell her about how they ran Christopher Denver out of town for trying to save an innocent man's life.

I tell her about how Jake left before the town could turn against him, because he needed to be innocent for my sake. For the sake of justice—not just revenge.

I tell her about Lindy, and what Kyle did to her. About how even her husband believed a rapist over his own, terrified wife. I tell her about Diana, and the threats they made toward her son to keep her quiet. I tell her every dark detail that town covered up. Every dirty secret finally gets aired.

And though I feel free, knowing another person now knows the truth, Hadley looks like she may never recover.

At least I spared her one detail.

The name of the man who will die the most painfully.

The man who started the dominoes back then.

We sit silently for several long minutes, and I check my phone, knowing Logan is showing patience, even though he's in a hurry. No texts.

"How did you survive?" she asks in a rasp whisper, tears streaming from her eyes when I look back at her. I have no tears left for this. I've cried them all already.

"No one knows," I say honestly. "But my mother always believed in avenging angels. Marcus's last words to me were that we'd come back as avenging angels, and we'd make them pay. We'd do it together. But he didn't come back."

My voice breaks on that last bit, but I force the emotion back. "Jake took his place. He loved my brother as more than just a friend, but was always too worried what the town would say or do if they came out about their relationship. It's his deepest regret."

She wipes away more tears, and she runs a hand through her hair.

"I won't tell the team," she finally says. "Unless someone innocent gets caught in the crosshairs, I owe you my silence. You saved the lives of countless children by ending a monster I let go free. You saved women all over, possibly even Logan, and saved me from Plemmons. Until you have that psychotic break, I'll hold my tongue."

That's more than I expected. My entire chest feels like an anvil is being lifted off it.

"I've trained against the psychotic break. They turned me into a shell of a person. Now I use it against them. But my mind? My mind is whole, even if my soul is not."

"How?" she asks, confused. "How do you train against the break?"

"Every form of martial arts I could squeeze in. From Brazilian Jiu-Jitsu, to American Karate, to Colombian Grima, to Taekwando, to Bokator, to Krav Maga... You get the idea. I've gotten various black belts in an array of martial arts. Not to mention the weapons' training I've mastered—knife throwing being one. You learn discipline over your mind with each new form of fighting or training. You learn control. It made me stronger mentally, physically, and emotionally."

She wipes away another tear, then sucks in a sharp breath.

"Then let's hope it keeps you sane enough to finish without hurting anyone who doesn't deserve to be hurt. I don't know if I can handle more guilt."

I start to leave, then turn back to face her. "You tried to tell people when you were a child. Those people failed you. *They* failed those kids, and they warped your young, impressionable mind into believing you made it all up. Everything that has happened since then is not your fault. It's on them. They may not deserve to die for their failures the way he deserved worse than death, but they do deserve to bear that guilt. Call your mother. Give her the burden to bear. Call that therapist, give her all the nasty details of his sins. Call the police station that ignored the cries of a child in pain. Only they deserve the weight of that failure. Not you."

She sucks in a breath as I turn to leave.

"How'd you get that big bastard out of the basement and up that big-ass hill?"

The question is so random that it makes me smile. "I'm stronger than I look," I say, looking over my shoulder. "But it wasn't fucking easy."

Her brittle smile toward the morbid humor is almost like a peace treaty. We're not going to be besties or anything, but we have an understanding.

"Tell Logan I'll be there in five," she says as I walk out.

As soon as I'm out the door, I text Jake.

ME: Calling in twenty. We need to adjust our timeframes. I have some catching up to do.

Chapter 6

To do a great right, do a little wrong.
—William Shakespeare

Logan

We can barely stay in the cellar, because the air is perfumed with the scent of two rotting corpses.

"He's getting bolder by killing them two at a time," Elise says, gagging even as she soaks in the clean air from above. "Escalating his torture by making them watch each other."

The bodies are already gone, since they cut them down from the chains once we arrived and saw the scene. But it's still toxic down there. Hadley is with the coroner, possibly carrying around a garbage can to puke in.

The stench is overwhelming.

"All the other's he's left in their homes to be discovered quickly. Why the shift? It's a risk to kidnap one and drive them all the way from New York to West Virginia," Leonard says, battling his own nausea.

It's hard to take in the scene down there, considering it needs to air out for several days before it's tolerable.

"He's chasing his endgame, but it's obvious these two really pissed him off. Yet there were still no signs of rage," I say absently.

Hadley's name flashes on my screen, and I answer the phone, putting it on speaker.

"What do you have?" I ask her.

"Well, their mouths were sewed shut, as you know, but when we opened them, we found the missing penises."

Leonard gags and turns away, and my stomach roils as well.

"That's...definitely an escalation," Elise says, her leg in a brace and her arm in a sling as she struggles with the crutches, still refusing a wheelchair.

"That's not the worst part," Hadley goes on. "I took blood samples from their mouths, and...Tyler was O positive. Lawrence was AB positive. I found O positive blood in Lawrence's mouth, and AB positive blood in Tyler's."

"Wait, hold up, are you telling me he sewed Tyler's dick into Lawrence's mouth, and vice versa?" Donny asks, turning an alarming shade of pale.

"Yes. That's exactly what I'm saying."

"I can't tell if he's evolving or devolving," Elise gripes.

"He's definitely suffering a psychotic break if he's getting more stuck on the torture," Leonard says with a grimace.

"No," I say thoughtfully. "These two did something together that pissed the unsub off recently. We couldn't find any footage of the unsub, but Tyler's credit card showed a trip to New York recently. Maybe they met to discuss the deaths of the others, even though it hadn't made the news. If the unsub followed them, maybe heard their conversation, it could have led to this double kill and extra layer of torture."

"That's still a psychotic break," Donny argues.

"No, it's not. There has yet to be any rage found with the overkill. The torture is punishment. It's to prolong the deaths. This unsub is targeting the ones who wronged him, and he's punishing them accordingly, at least in his mind. If they crossed a line, he'd punish them more severely than he's been punishing the others."

I pause, letting them soak that in as I get lost in my own

thoughts.

"We need more info on that serial killer—Robert Evans," I tell Donny.

Hadley makes a strangled sound, reminding me she's still on the phone.

"You okay, Had?"

"Yep. Yep. Fine," she says quickly.

"See what else you can get from the bodies. Email me the final report, but call me immediately if something else stands out."

"Will do."

She hangs up, and Donny frowns. "She's acting weird."

"Her stepfather abused her as a child, she was convinced it was all in her head, and other kids died after she ran away. Couple that with the fact she was almost a victim of Plemmons, and she has every right to be weird," I remind him.

"How's Lana holding up?" Craig asks me as I start typing a message into my phone.

"Much better than I could have hoped. She's a hell of a lot tougher than I gave her credit for being."

"That's good. I was actually worried. I remember the first time I had to shoot someone. It's the reason I went into this field—less need for violence."

I nod, understanding. It was hard on me the first two times, even though I saved many by taking down those two monsters. Didn't alleviate the nightmares. Fortunately, Lana's dreams don't seem to be haunted by those memories. She's fucking incredibly strong.

And it makes me love her even more.

"Plan a trip to Delaney Grove. This unsub would be remembered if we painted a picture of the two Evans kids who were killed."

"There was nothing about that ever mentioned in their police reports," Craig says quietly. "This town is trying to act like the Evans family never even existed. The coroner who wrote that bullshit report on Robert Evans is either dead or playing dead. No phone calls have been returned."

"All the more reason to pay a visit in person."

He nods.

"And deliver the profile to the media. Mention there was something traumatic that might have happened to the Evans kids that didn't sit well with a close friend or family member."

"No family left. It was just the three of them. And the only friends were the lawyer dad and his son," Donny points out.

"We'll pay them a visit, but keep looking. Lindy May was a friend. I'm sure there were others we just don't know about."

He nods, and I walk toward my car, texting Lana as I go.

ME: May be late before I get back tonight.

LANA: I may have to take a business trip today. I've been putting it off and piling it all on my partner. Boogeyman is gone, and now so is the threat to my life.

ME: What about the reporters?

LANA: They don't know about the hotel, and my business is in Kentucky. I'm driving there in a rental car just to be safe.

ME: Then I'll miss you. :(

LANA: I'll be back first thing tomorrow. <3

I put my phone away, hating how possessive I feel. I want to keep her locked away and under me every chance I get. It's selfish. It's ridiculous. It's also a little criminal.

"Just got another body from our night stalking killer," Donny says, sighing harshly. "I think these guys get together to kill at the same time just to stretch our resources thin."

He hands me the iPad with the photos, and something catches my eye. It's not the picture, but the notes. Traces of Siberian tiger fur. "I know who the killer is," I tell him, grabbing my phone. "Call the local PD and tell them to pick up the brother of the first victim. I profiled it to be him, but they ruled him out. Now I know it's him. He's a taxidermist for exotic animals."

"Holy shit," Donny hisses, grabbing his phone as I jog to my SUV.

I love it when they make it easy, and I'm one step closer to catching my Delaney Grove killer too.

Hadley calls back just as I reach the SUV, and I answer, wedging the phone between my shoulder and cheek as I crank the car and let Donny get in the passenger seat.

"You found something?"

"Sort of. The coroner found a nail in Lawrence's stomach. I'm not sure what that's about, but I thought it was worth mentioning," she says.

"Yeah, though I don't understand the significance yet, either. We just figured out the night stalking killer, and we're on our way to Pennsylvania right now."

"You remember how you said you met Lana at a coffee shop you don't normally visit?" she asks randomly.

Weird shift in conversation. "Yeah. Why?"

"Tell me again how all that went down."

I snort derisively. "Okay... Craig went to hit on her and she shot him down. I paid for her food and coffee without her knowledge, and then gave her my card when she acted all pissed off that I was doing something nice for no reason other than the fact she amused me. I wasn't looking for more than that, but I still told her to call me, because after spending those five minutes with her, I wanted to know more. When she finally called, she was...everything I didn't realize I wanted."

"So you approached her, and you sort of chased her."

"It was all me," I tell her, confused where she's going with this.

"And the case…You told her Boogeyman details. Do you always share case details?"

"The first share was an accident, but she helped us identify him. I kept her in the loop later because she was a target, same as we'd do for any target. She doesn't want me sharing details of cases because she doesn't like me breaking the rules for her. She respects my position, and doesn't want me getting in trouble."

"So she never asks for any other case details?" she asks, still dragging me on a confusing trail.

"No. What's this about?"

"Nothing," she says on a heavy sigh. "You know I'm suspicious of every girl you date and their motives. Lisa used your name to get a promotion. I still don't like her."

That's hard not to laugh about.

"Look, Lana is great, Hadley. She's compassionate, understanding, thoughtful, and she really fucking cares. It's more than I ever thought I'd have with this career choice. She's also insanely independent and smart. But if she was using me, I'd be aware of it. She has zero interest in the FBI as a career path, even though I think she'd be one hell of a profiler."

"Right. You're right. Sorry. I need to go over some more lab stuff. Talk later?"

"Yeah. Let me know if you find anything else weird like a nail in the stomach contents."

"Nail in the stomach?" Donny asks from beside me.

"Lawrence Martin had one. Why?" I ask him.

He shakes his head. "Sounds familiar is all. Just can't remember where I've heard it."

Scarlet Angel

Donny, like me, was recruited straight out of college. He's only been in our unit for six years, but he's been with the FBI for eleven total years.

"I'll talk to you later," I tell Hadley.

"Peace out."

Rolling my eyes, I hang up my phone. At least she's starting to sound more like herself. Meddling and quirky.

Donny looks lost in thought, and keeps drawing a nail over and over, confusing me. But it's his thought process when he's trying to resurrect a memory.

"You think he's killed before?" I ask him.

"No," he says immediately. "I think I've heard that before though. Nails in the stomach. It's actually a brutal torture technique. It tears you up as you swallow them, then punctures your stomach lining. Not to mention what happens if you manage to pass them. But just one nail? It means something."

"Lawrence was the son of a cop in Delaney Grove. But he left that place right around our ten year time frame. Several of them did. They went on to be successful. They never showed any signs of violence in their lives, and all had a healthy conscience, it seems. Never the self-destructive spiral of guilt-wrenched minds."

"So you think they are being targeted, but didn't play a part in what happened that night?" he muses.

"I don't know. I'm just profiling them. It's what I do."

He looks down, drawing the nail again, tracing the lines over and over.

We'll figure him out, and we'll stop him. It's what we do.

Eventually, good conquers evil, because evil works alone.

Chapter 7

The devil can cite Scripture for his own purpose.
—William Shakespeare

Lana

In one week, I've marked off two names from my list. We're getting closer. Jake is sweating bullets.

I've sped up the timeline and started hiding the bodies. I've changed my MO. I've also started adding the nails, something I hadn't planned to do until later in the game.

My wax apple also has a lot more nails to mark the new debts I've collected, but we've moved my murder room to Jake's house.

The media are no longer interested in me since Craig delivered the profile of the Scarlet Slayer. Yes, the media named me. Somehow, Jake got me the name he wanted.

It's ironic the media lost interest in the hero side of me in favor of the dark side of me. Just goes to show how twisted and ugly this world can be.

"I hate how fast you're cruising through the names," Jake grumbles as I mark off the latest victim's name.

"Two in a week isn't too fast. I wanted to drag it out, but I'm sick of this. I'm ready for it to be over."

"Because of Logan?" he asks, studying me from his seat.

"Yes and no. I'm tired of being tied to the past and unable to let it go. Aren't you?"

He leans up, perching his elbows on the rails of the chair. "Tell me something, Lana, what do you think happens when this is all over—if we even survive it. Do you think he doesn't find out? Do you ride off into the sunset—the agent and the killer? I want to know what you think for real. I'm good with ending this where we are, and moving on the best we can. I think that's the only way you're going to be able to keep him, if that's your true endgame."

My lip trembles, and I clear my throat. "Stopping now would be wrong. Marcus and Dad…they're still dead and haunted by the way they died."

He leans back, his eyes on me. "Sometimes I think I feel Marcus. I think he's right here beside us, keeping us from being discovered. Other times I realize it's ridiculous, and that our luck will eventually run out."

"Do you want to stop?" I ask quietly, sitting down on the edge of his desk.

"Honestly? No. I want to kill them all for what they did. I want them to suffer. But it's not fair for me to expect that from you when you seem to finally be healing. And it's because of Logan you're healing. He gave you back something you lost."

"What?" I ask as he moves to the other side of the room, grabbing a drink from the mini-fridge.

"Your heart," he tells me, looking at me with sadness in his eyes.

"You could move on," I tell him, shrugging. "Marcus would want that."

"I'll stick to my torrid affairs with no emotional connection for now," he answers with a brittle grin.

"Every time I think I can walk away…that's the only time I close my eyes and see it happening all over again," I say to him, sighing long and hard. "Sometimes I think I really did die, and that I'm truly the avenging angel my brother said we'd be together."

I feel as though I only have one purpose in life.

"Maybe you are," he agrees. "But maybe you're allowed to give up vengeance for hope."

"Then why do I see the nightmares when I consider stopping?"

His lips tense.

"Exactly," I tell him, motioning around the room. "If my life was spared to right the wrongs of that time, then I won't be at peace until they're all dead. Others in that town are suffering. You know it. People just like Lindy who speak out against the 'justice' they dole. Women like Diana who has spent the last ten years worried one day her son would turn up dead or missing. People like my father who was killed for crimes he didn't commit."

He nods dully, knowing I'm right.

"It's your choice, Lana. I'm just saying I'm with you regardless of what you choose."

Tears. I hate tears. But they keep reappearing in my eyes at random.

I go to plop down in his lap, and he wraps his arms around me, pulling to me to him as I hug him. "You know you're my second favorite brother, right?" I ask him, a joke I've said since we were kids.

He laughs against the side of my face. "Yeah. I know. Just like you're my favorite sister, but only because you're the only one I have."

As we both laugh at the small bit of the past we've held onto, my mind turns over the past events of the last few days. The newest additions to my string of kills.

"Scream for me," I tell Anthony, smiling while he bleeds, his cries of agony like sweet music to my ears. But the melody is off key, not hitting the same notes as it usually does.

This normally feels so much better.

"You fucking cunt! I knew you were evil. Just like your father."

"No. I was sweet," I tell him, meaning it, as I slowly slide the blade

across his chest, leaving a shallow cut there. He gives me nothing more than a wince. "I was naïve. I wasn't a virgin, but I wasn't the whore you labeled me. My body was my temple and all that, until you all held me down, took your turns, and left me for dead. You killed Marcus. And he gave his life so that I could come back and pick you off one at a time."

He screams when the knife slides down, and I taunt him again with the words he once used against me.

"Scream for me, Anthony. Scream loud. No one can hear you. No one cares."

He does scream. He screams into the vast nothingness of the basement that is completely underground. Really, they make it too easy sometimes.

But I won't leave him here. No one will ever know I was here at all.

"You'll burn in hell. What we did was try to destroy the evil in the world. Evil is hard to kill," he spits out.

"You seriously want to justify what you did as an act of justice? You claim righteousness even after your acts of violence and sin?"

He grins, his mouth a bloody mess. "You can't sin against the devil. You're straight from his loins, just like your father. They'll stop you. Good always triumphs over evil. I'll be avenged."

My lips twitch, amused at how delusional he truly is. "This is good triumphing over evil," I say quietly, watching as his eyes narrow to slits. He hates me considering myself the avenging angel, and I use it to my advantage. "This is your punishment. The act of good prevailing."

"You and your faggot brother were already going to hell. We just sped things along."

"If you're the one in the right, why isn't there some divine intervention saving you?" I ask him, standing slowly. "I was resurrected from the ashes, surviving against all odds. Yet you're down here, suffering for the crimes of your past. Not me."

He opens his mouth, but closes it. "See?" I muse, smirking. "Even the devil can quote Scripture for his own purpose. William Shakespeare, in case you're wondering. But I'm not the devil, Anthony. I'm the angel who has come to take you all to hell."

He finally screams louder than he has before when I take away that last bit of power he had, slicing it off at the base, kicking it away like the trash it is.

"You'll never hurt anyone else," I whisper darkly, drinking in the sounds of his pain, and ignoring the hollowness I feel for the first time ever.

I won't stop.

I can't.

Now to go back to Kentucky.

"I'll tell the next one you said hello," I go on, talking over the sounds of his sobs. "Your bestie is next."

I'm jarred out of the memory by the sound of someone pounding on Jake's door.

"Shit," he hisses, glancing at the monitor beside us.

I scramble off his lap, my heart thumping painfully in my chest as I see Logan knock on the door again. This *cannot* be happening.

"Mr. Denver," Logan says, looking up at the camera Jake never bothered to hide on his front porch. "If you're in there, we'd like to speak to you."

Donny is beside him, looking all MIB with his glasses on. Logan opens his thingy and flashes his credentials to the camera.

"We knew this would happen," Jake says as I shake with panic.

One man has the power to undo me, and he's about to link me to everything if he finds me here.

"I'm SSA Logan Bennett," Logan goes on, his voice for once not having a calming effect on me. Not even a little bit. I'm full blown crazy panicking now.

"Calm down," Jake says, amused. Freaking amused. This is *not* amusing at all. "Just stay in here and lock the door. They won't have a warrant. And it's all about to be pointless to question me. We're prepared for this. Remember that."

I nod, then swallow hard, trying to lasso my logic back to me and swallow a massive chill pill. We're always careful for me not to be seen when I come over. I park in town, using a rental car, and he picks me up somewhere with no cameras. I ride back in his van—that I call a kidnapper's van—and he parks inside his garage. No one ever sees me.

They won't know I'm here.

So why am I panicking?

Calm and collected, Jake puts several of the kill-list things under the false panel of the floor, then moves the lamp back over it, hiding it from sight. He flips a button, and five of the monitors on the walls sink into the walls as the false panel comes down, concealing them from sight as well.

"Stay here," he repeats, moving out of the room quickly.

Immediately I go and lock the door, and then I listen through the walls like a total creeper. All I need is a glass stuck to my ear.

Nope. I don't look guilty at all.

Chapter 8

The attempt and not the deed confounds us.
—William Shakespeare

Logan

"Think he's just not home?" Donny asks as I pound on the door again.

My eyes rake over the empty driveway, but there's a sealed garage. His vehicle could be in there.

"The neighbor said he rarely goes anywhere and never has visitors. She said he left this morning, but came back and has been inside ever since."

Before I can knock again, the door swings open, and I look down, seeing something I really wasn't expecting.

Jacob Denver is in a wheelchair.

"Sorry," he tells us, looking at us with confused eyes. "It sometimes takes me a minute to transfer to my chair. How can I help you guys?"

The blinds are all drawn, but surely someone should have mentioned him in a wheelchair. I hate surprises, and I rarely have to deal with them.

Donny's eyebrows are at his hairline, just as surprised by this turn of events as I am.

"Um…care if we ask you some questions?" I finally manage to get out.

It's a whole new line of questioning now.

"Sure. Want to come in? The place is a mess, but it's not as easy to clean as it used to be."

Shit.

Shit.

Shit.

"Thanks," I say, moving by him as he backs his chair out of the way.

My profiling mind gets to work as Donny types something into his phone. I glance toward the kitchen that is off to the right. All the countertops are lower than standard, making it more handicap accessible. I didn't notice the ramp by the porch as suspicious, but now I realize I should have. His floors are all level and seamless, not even threshold plates over the connections to rooms.

The cabinets on top in the kitchen have no doors, but all that's there are decorative things. Nothing someone would need to work in a kitchen.

My eyes scan the living room, finding the chair off the side that is at an angle, a remote dangling, as though he had to get help lifting out of it to slide into his wheelchair.

"It's cheating," he says, drawing my attention to him as he gestures to the recliner I was just eyeing. "But it makes life easier."

He's tone and somewhat fit, but I can't see his legs too well in the sweatpants. Hate it is as I do, I discreetly kneel, pretending to adjust my shoe, and my eyes scan the bottoms of his shoes to see perfectly clean soles. They never touch the ground.

Well, fuck. He's really handicapped.

I rise up, and he wheels into the living room.

"What the fuck?" I hiss to Donny.

"Hell if I know. I just texted Alan to find out."

We break apart when Jake turns to look at us, eyeing us like we're idiots. We are idiots, apparently. Someone better tell me why we didn't know this before coming.

"Mind if I asked what happened?" I ask, wondering if this is in any way related to the mystery that is Delaney Grove.

He shrugs. "Motorcycle accident a few years ago. Paralyzed me from the waist down. It's taken some adjusting, but I've managed to move on with my life."

Definitely not our unsub. And his father has had court cases going on during several of the kill times, alibiing out that way. They were our only hopes, and it seemed so easy. Apparently too easy.

There's no way a man in a wheelchair managed to overpower these guys, and do all the things that have been done.

"So why is the FBI knocking on my door and asking questions about my old wreck?" he asks, seeming genuinely confused.

"Any chance you watch the news?" Donny asks him, pocketing his phone.

"Not really," Jacob tells us, shrugging. "It's pretty fucking depressing, and I've had more of that than I care to reflect on."

He crosses his hands in his lap. Not once has either of his legs twitched.

It's a habit, when one is faking something like paralysis, to get twitchy, giving one's self away. He hasn't scratched his legs or *anything*.

I know Donny is watching for the same signs I am.

He's too calm, too disinterested in us.

"So, you came by to ask me if I watch the news?" Jacob asks, looking between us.

He seems to enjoy the off-balance stance we have.

"No," Donny mumbles.

"Actually, I was wondering if you could shed some light on the Evans family."

Scarlet Angel

A coldness crosses his gaze, and he looks away.

"You're welcome to leave at any time."

I look at Donny, and he looks at me. We stare, both of us confused.

"Mr. Denver, you were friends with them, and we think a serial killer is out trying to avenge their deaths. Even though the reports indicate they died because of a car accident."

He looks back at us. "Does a car accident usually castrate a man?" he asks incredulously. "Does it leave a girl and boy so broken they drive for towns and towns to seek medical attention?"

"So you do know something?" I ask, leaning closer.

"I know that if someone is out avenging their deaths, I'd like to shake their hand. Marcus was my boyfriend, though I never had the balls to admit it back then. And Victoria was like my little sister. I was seventeen, like Marcus, when they died."

My lips tense. He's holding something back.

"Can you give us anything to help us follow up on how they were really killed?" Donny asks.

"Now you want to know? Because back then, when I went to the FBI dude who had wrongly profiled Robert Evans as a serial killer and told him my friends—the two sweetest fucking humans ever—had been killed by the town, he told me it wasn't his case. To let the cops do their jobs, and if it was more than a car accident, they'd handle it."

The bitterness in his tone is real, and he definitely doesn't seem to be hiding his anger over it. Which makes him less suspect. Still...my gut is telling me he's somehow involved.

"Who was that?" Donny asks.

"His last name was Bag, and his first name was Douche. Sometimes he went by SSA Johnson."

Donny chokes back a laugh, but I'm not laughing. Johnson was a terrible profiler, tarnished the reputation of the unit so badly that he was promoted. Gotta love fucking politics. As shitty as he was, he was invaluable because of the knowledge he had, so they "promoted" him to a bullshit position and gave him bullshit tasks to keep him under their thumbs.

He's also the Godfather of the department, because he pretty much took profiling in the direction it has grown to be today, made it an actual thing with actual results, no matter how flawed those preliminary results turned out to be.

"You're saying he ignored two dead kids?" Donny asks, no longer laughing as the words catch up to him.

"I'm saying he didn't give a shit. And now I'm putting one foot in front of the other — metaphorically speaking, obviously — to stay out of the past. Now, unless you have something pressing to speak to me about, please leave. I have things to do."

My phone rings as Donny tries to pry more out of him, just something to figure out what really happened.

I see it's Alan calling, and I stand up, walking down the hall a little to answer.

"What the hell?" I hiss.

"Sorry. Sorry. Sooooo sorry. I don't know how I missed it, but I got Donny's text, and yes, Jacob Denver is definitely paralyzed from the waist down. Happened four years ago, to be exact. A drunk driver side-swiped him — hit and run. He was on a motorcycle. He's been in a wheelchair ever since."

Why does this still feel off?

"Thanks. Don't miss anything this big again. We thought we had our unsub."

"I know. I'm sorry. It's just a small mention in his records. It's not like I can open hospital files, and I wouldn't have seen it at all if I hadn't been looking for it."

"Right. Okay. See if you can dig up any other friends from the past he might have shared with the Evans family. Something is definitely off with him. He never asked who was killed."

Scarlet Angel

Something topples to the ground from the room I'm standing in front of, and I try to open the locked door, curious as to why it's locked.

"Can I help you?" Jacob asks, wheeling over to where I'm jiggling the doorknob.

"Why is this locked?" I ask, putting my phone away.

"Um…because it's my house, and I don't like people walking into my office. What's your deal?"

He seems genuinely private, but why lock a door when you live alone unless you're hiding something?

"Do you care if we look around?" Donny asks him, trying to sound non-imposing.

He studies us critically before finally blowing out a breath and rolling his eyes.

"Fine. Fine. But then you leave and leave me alone. I don't need you barging into my life and dredging up memories better left forgotten."

He wheels back to the living room, picks up a set of keys, taking his time to do so, and he comes back, unlocking the door. He backs away, and I open it, looking around. I see the computer screen is blank, and my eyes land on the cracked window in front of where there's a thing of tacks scattered around on the floor.

"Damn it. Not again," he groans, wheeling by me to the mess of tacks. "You can go now. I need to clean this up."

I nod to Donny, and we walk out, leaving him to his task. As soon as we're outside and the door shuts behind us, I glance over, seeing the cracked window.

"Someone is in there with him," I say quietly when we reach the street.

"Looks like the wind caught the curtain, and the curtain knocked over the tacks to me."

"That window was closed, along with the blinds, when we

303

came up. There's a closet in there. Someone was there."

"Why didn't you open the closet?"

"Because whoever it is may be our unsub."

I pretend as though we're taking our time to get in the car as Jacob shuts the window and closes the blinds once again. We loiter on the street, while I call Lisa.

"How close are you to Jacob Denver's address?"

"Elise and I are about five minutes out. Why?"

"Swing by and sit on the house. As soon as we see you in position, we'll drive off. If he leaves, I want you to call me. If he stays, I want you to watch him. Someone is inside, and it may be our unsub. Use extreme caution."

"Shit. Got it. You be careful too."

I start to hang up, when she adds, "And by the way, thank you for the roses. They were beautiful."

My brow creases in confusion.

"I never sent roses."

"I mean from the hospital. I got them, and realized I never thanked you for them."

"Lisa, I never sent roses. At all."

She grows deadly silent. "So it was him? Plemmons?"

I don't have time to ask questions about a dead man's motives. "It may have been. Call the flower company and find out."

"Yeah. Okay. I'll see if Hadley can look into it," she says, distant now.

As I hang up, Donny is smirking. "What?"

"Nothing," he lies, smirking more.

I glare at him.

"Just wondering what Lisa would do to Lana if she got her

Scarlet Angel

hands on her. She's a typical scorned ex — perfectly okay with the breakup until you finally get a new girlfriend that you seem to be pretty head-over-heels for. Lisa is a bitch. Keep her away from your new girlfriend or she may scratch Lana's eyes out."

"Lana's already been subjected to her, in case you've forgotten. Lisa didn't rattle her." I sound dismissive, but I'm masking how uncomfortable this conversation is.

"We all know what a bitch Lisa can be, and right now, she's feeling that jealousy most exes do when their ex finally moves on and exhibits signs of true happiness. She's got a nasty mouth on her, and she may eventually seek Lana out in an effort to ruin things between you two. Just profiling. It's what I do."

Fuck.

"I'll keep them apart. Lisa will eventually forget it."

"When she finds someone who makes her happy," he agrees with a mocking grin. "Should only take a few lifetimes."

I flip him off as he chuckles, and I glance back toward the closed window. Lisa and Elise appear just down the street, parking at the curb.

Donny and I load into the SUV, and we drive away. It's no time before Elise texts us, telling us Jacob is on the move, heading in our direction in a white van. She sends the plates too, just so we know we're tailing the right one.

As soon as the white van passes us, I arch an eyebrow. It looks like any good kidnapper's van.

The driver's side and passenger side have windows, but the rest of the van looks like a work van. He does do some tech work, according to his file, so it could possibly be his work van.

Donny and I follow discreetly, while Elise and Lisa watch the house.

"See if you can get a look inside," I say as Donny puts Lisa on speaker.

"Trying to get a warrant to go in, but the judge says we don't have enough."

"Just get a look around," I say vaguely, hinting for her to break some rules. It's a fucking serial killer we're after. Sometimes rules need to be broken.

"Got it."

"Just don't be obvious," Donny says to the phone.

"I'm not an idiot," Lisa snips.

He hangs up, and I keep a safe tail distance on Jacob. We pull up to the curb as he pulls into a parking spot. It takes a few minutes before his side van door slides open, and I watch as he is lowered down with the wheelchair on the motorized platform.

"That explains the van. It's handicap accessible," Donny points out.

Frowning, I watch as he sits with a basketball on his lap, and then we watch as he locks up his van and starts wheeling down the sidewalk.

When he reaches a basketball court full of kids, Donny hisses out a breath. Most of the kids are suffering some sort of disability. A few are amputees, some are in wheelchairs, and some seem to be struggling with other physical issues.

"We're going to hell," Donny groans as the kids cheer, and Jacob blows a whistle, tossing the ball at them.

They start playing basketball, and he plays with them, laughing right alongside them, making a difference in their day.

Elise calls me, and I answer. "Nothing is in this house. The office closet is empty too. I'm sealing it back up so he doesn't know we were ever here."

"So it's empty, and this guy is a paraplegic coach helping disabled kids. He survived losing his mother at a young age, his best friend and boyfriend as a teenager, and he's paralyzed now. Yet he's the male version of Mother Theresa," Donny states dryly. "And we're accusing him of helping a murderer. I repeat: We're going to hell."

"Check his van," I tell him, frustrated. My gut tells me something is up. There was someone in that house, and if he's not there now, then he's in the van.

Donny curses before getting out, drawing his weapon as he goes to the back of the van. He reaches out with one hand, testing the door, as I shift my gaze between him and Jacob.

He opens the unlocked door, and I frown. I could have sworn Jacob locked the van.

All that's in the back of the van is a box marked MEDIA. The entire back is empty other than that.

Donny arches an eyebrow at me, and I wave him back, rolling my eyes. He shuts the doors and gets back in, and we drive away.

"Forget him. Even if he does know who the killer is, there's no way he's involved," Donny says on a sigh.

I drive away, irked. My gut has always been the driving force, and rarely ever do I feel so strongly about something and end up wrong.

Jacob doesn't even notice us as we pass him. He tosses the ball into the air, getting it to a one-armed little boy on the other end who scores.

By the time I make it back to the office, Hadley is ready to pounce, but I ignore her in favor of moving toward Leonard. "Hey, I need you to pull everything you can find on the Robert Evans case. Let's see if we can start there, and find out what that damn town is hiding. Somehow, it's all linked to that. It's the first domino that set all the others in place."

He nods, gesturing to his laptop.

"Already working on that. There are so many inconsistencies in that file that it's ridiculous. Essentially the only thing that convicted him was the DNA at the crime scenes, and even that seems compromised, due to the poor chain of custody the evidence went through. I'm not sure how he got convicted, other than the fact the judge pretty much ignored all the laws set in place to keep things fair and honest."

"And we know how the Godfather worked things," I add. "See what you can dig up. Find out why the killings stopped, or even if they stopped. If the unsub successfully framed Evans, he may have just moved towns and changed his MO enough to frame someone else."

"On it," Leonard says, going back to work.

I almost run over Hadley when I turn back around.

"Why that look? What'd you find out on Jacob Denver?" she asks me.

She's wringing her hands, anxious for info. I guess we're all in knots.

"Nothing. My gut told me there was more to him, but I was apparently wrong."

"That gut thing gets tricky," she says, frowning. "What happened?"

"Nothing. Hey, Lisa said she was going to have you look in on someone sending her roses from me?"

"They weren't from you," she says immediately.

"I'm aware," I tell her, confused by how odd she's acting.

"I mean, there was never anything to state it was from you. Just a dozen roses sent with no card. I guess she just assumed it was you."

Shaking my head, I look down at the file in front of me.

"Can I go? I'm exhausted and no new leads have come in. I also sent all the forensics I've been able to sift through. Some of the rest of it will need a few days to run through the lab."

I nod, waving her off, and she practically sprints out.

Can't say I blame her. I don't enjoy spending so much time here either. Lana has been away on business most of the week, but I finally get at least a little time to myself with her tonight.

As for this case, Delaney Grove people are going to be the end of me.

Chapter 9

If it be a sin to covet honor, I am the most offending soul.
—William Shakespeare

Lana

I hid in a closet from my boyfriend after stupidly spilling a bowl of tacks. I then crawled into a tiny media box in Jake's van, and hid there for an hour while he did his weekly basketball excursion with his kids that I help fund a special program for. I was stuck there because the box wouldn't open from the inside.

The prick did that on purpose to teach me a lesson, and I'll kick his ass later for that.

I'm exhausted and just ready to curl up on the bed until Logan can break away, when I round the hotel hallway and see Hadley glaring daggers at me, waiting by my door.

I wish she'd leave this hotel.

"You!" she hisses.

"What'd I do?" I ask, confused.

"Roses ring a bell?"

I smirk as I push open the door, and she barges by me, ramming her shoulder into mine on the way.

"Want to come in?" I ask dryly.

The door shuts and she whirls around, pointing an accusatory finger at me.

"Don't get cute, Lana. You sent roses to Lisa. I know it was you.

You let her think Logan did it, and now that she knows he didn't do it, she's nauseated, certain it was Plemmons."

I guess Hadley's humor is on the fritz, because that shit's funny.

"The Boogeyman is dead, and what makes you think it was me or that those were ever my intentions?" I muse, hiding my smile.

"I know it was you. The roses were paid for with a prepaid Visa. Plemmons was done with Lisa, but she's Logan's ex, and you chose a poor way to fuck with her."

"She actually fucked with me first. I just sent her some roses," I say with a coy grin.

Her face gets redder. "Don't fuck with my team, Lana. You have too much too lose to play games with us."

"Us? I'm not playing games with anyone but her, and she started it. She did everything but piss on Logan. And the roses were ages ago. It's not even a good joke if she doesn't get it when the guy is still alive. In case you've forgotten, I sort of killed him, so she has no reason to be afraid…unless she's scared of serial killer ghosts."

I grab a flashlight and shine it under my chin, and Hadley's eyes narrow to slits. She seriously needs a sense of humor.

"This is crazy stuff. You know that, right?" she snaps.

I roll my eyes, cutting the flashlight off. "No, crazy is being his ex and getting all bitchy toward me. And you said I couldn't kill anyone who didn't truly deserve to die. You never said I couldn't send roses to a girl who was an utter bitch to me."

"Don't downplay this," she hisses. "You sent those roses to terrorize her. Mind fuck her even. The guy carved an actual word into her arm while she was conscious, and he damn near killed her and Elise before Lisa managed to get a few shots off."

"And missed him," I remind her. Who can't shoot a guy that size?

"Grazed him," she corrects.

"Missed him," I say again, smirking at the funny little shade of red she continues to turn. "I didn't miss him. And, again, the guy is dead. The joke isn't funny now. How ungrateful is she to just now be thanking Logan for the flowers she arrogantly assumed he sent?"

Her mouth opens and closes, and I half wonder if her skull is going to blow off like it does in the cartoons.

"It's not funny at all! It's cruel. And wicked. And—"

"Lisa your bestie?"

"No," she says, frowning.

"Saved your life or something?"

She shakes her head.

"Do you even like her?"

Her eyes narrow, but she doesn't respond to that question.

"I'll take that as a no. So why the self-righteous, indignant act over me poking a little fun at a bully bitch? I couldn't outright put her in her place, so yes, I fucked with her head a little. And it wasn't even a good head-fucking because she caught onto the joke too late. No harm. No foul."

"It's the fact you targeted one of our team members, and you don't even realize how sick and twisted your *joke* was."

My smile vanishes. "I could have sent her a pig's heart or something, if you want sick and twisted. I could have sent a bouquet that spelled *KEEP*. I could have sent her the twisted Russian song of the Boogeyman. I sent her roses, Hadley. A tiny little mind fuck, as you like to call it. That's all. I spared her, if you really think about it. We both know I could be a lot colder."

Her look pales a little.

"No," I groan, rolling my eyes. "That was not me threatening to kill her."

She drops to the bed, running a hand through her hair. "This is too much. *You're* too much."

"You're overreacting to some roses. Calm down, Hadley. If you didn't want the truth, you shouldn't have searched for answers."

She looks up, and genuine exhaustion shines in her eyes.

"Logan's morals aren't as skewed as mine, Lana. If you really love him, you'll stop this quest for revenge. Let us try to figure out a way to take the others down. We can—"

"Take down an entire police force? Take down rapists whose word will be against mine? The daughter of a convicted serial killer who was wrongly profiled by one of your own?" I deadpan.

"Logan knows the profile was wrong," she says, shocking me.

She studies my face.

"This is the first you've heard of it, isn't it?"

I nod, slowly lowering myself to the seat.

"You really don't ask him any questions about your case, do you?"

I glare at her this time. "If I wanted to know what you all knew, I'd have Jake hack the cameras. I don't need to use my boyfriend or betray him like that. I hate lying to him as it is."

"No more games on my team members," she says, frustrated.

"Only if she leaves me alone," I tell her, watching her as she thinks that over.

"Nothing so morbid."

I shrug, grinning. "I have a morbid sense of humor. And I'm territorial. At least I didn't piss in the roses before sending them."

She studies me; I grin at her.

"You're so confusing, and I stupidly think you really do love him."

"I do love him," I tell her on a long sigh.

"Nice to know." Logan's voice has us both screeching, and Hadley actually drops to the floor.

Logan grins at her as she bounces back up to her feet. If he's grinning, then he missed all the important bits about me being a killing psycho, right?

"How long have you been standing there?!" Hadley demands, looking every bit as guilty as a killer herself.

"Long enough to hear a confession I don't think I was meant to hear," he says, his smile turning into a smirk as he looks at me with heat in his eyes.

Yeah, he totally missed the part where I'm a killer. I need to be more cautious.

"Confession?" Hadley asks, all the color draining from her face.

This girl could never be a killer.

"Yeah," Logan says, his attention focused on me as he stalks forward.

"Logan, this isn't what it looks like. She—"

Her words thankfully die when Logan grabs me at the waist and pulls me to him, crushing his lips to mine. I almost climb up him, making it easier to kiss him without so many tiptoes and bending getting involved. Hadley makes a strangled sound, and I kiss Logan harder to distract him from the leaky sink she is.

No wonder the Boogeyman duct taped her mouth shut.

"Right," Hadley says as Logan continues kissing me. "I'll just go now."

He doesn't even acknowledge her as he kisses me harder, pushing me back against the window that overlooks the city. My mouth stays fused to his, needing this so much after the week of little face-to-face time.

"I've fucking missed you," he says against my lips, still kissing me stupid.

I can't even respond, because he doesn't let me break my mouth apart to reciprocate. Instead, he starts tugging my pants down, pushing me harder against the glass.

Scarlet Angel

My fingers find their happy place, digging into his hair, and I shudder in anticipation when he shoves my pants to the floor. Roughly, he breaks the kiss to tear my shirt over my head, as though he's in a hurry to get me as naked as possible.

"I missed you too," I say while I have the chance, but he's all serious, and that heated gaze could scorch a lesser prepared woman.

He strips out of his clothes as I toss away my bra and shimmy out of my underwear. In the time it takes me to do that, he's fully naked and lifting me so fast my breath catches.

My back hits the glass, and my legs go around his shoulders. My eyes screw shut when he puts his face right where I want it, and he latches on to that bundle of nerves he knows how to manipulate too well.

He's more aggressive than usual, almost as though he's punishing me, taking no mercy on me when I whimper and squirm and try to make him bald with my hold on his hair.

My head falls back against the glass as I cry out, already lost in sensation from the masterful mouth he owns. He drops me to the ground in a smooth motion, and spins me to face the glass.

My palms shoot up, catching me before I slam into it, and he lifts my lower half, lining it up so he can thrust in forcefully.

It feels too good, and he bends, kissing my neck with just as much roughness as he's taking my body. "You should have told me first," he says, giving me insight as to why this feels like an incredible punishment fuck.

If these are the repercussions of disappointing him, I'll never be good again.

It'd be nice if this is how he punishes me when or if he ever finds out who I really am.

I hope that day never comes. I'd rather not know what he chooses.

I push my hands harder against the window, and he keeps me lifted from behind so he can control every second of being inside me. He doesn't stop until I'm crying out, and his hips thrust in hard one last time before he rocks in a slow circle, his breaths labored as he bends over, resting his forehead on my shoulder. He's still holding me in place, and I grin against the window.

"I didn't mean to tell Hadley," I say, breathless and grinning. "She figured it out on her own."

He leans forward, kissing my shoulder.

But he doesn't say it back.

I'm not sure why that makes me feel a little self-conscious, but I try to ignore the seed of doubt that's been planted.

"You can't stay gone that long again. You've only been in town one day this week," he says, kissing the column of my throat, running his hands over my body.

"If this is the reward I get, I may not be able to help myself," I quip, smiling when he releases a rumble of laughter.

He pulls out of me and slaps my ass, and I turn just as he winks. "Get on something nice. I'm taking you out on a real date tonight."

Grinning like a girl, I rush into the shower. But as soon as I step under the spray, Logan is climbing in with me, his lips finding mine as he pushes me against the wall.

"We can go out tomorrow," I murmur against his lips, feeling him grin as he slides inside me again.

Just as he starts a steady rhythm, his lips break apart from mine, and he starts kissing his way to my ear.

"I love you too, Lana Myers," he says so softly.

And in that moment, I'm completely his. There's no revenge; there are no deaths staining my hands. I'm just a girl in love with a man who's destined to hate me when he learns the truth.

And it's devastatingly tragic; more so than any Shakespearian play ever was.

Chapter 10

Expectation is the root of all heartache.
—William Shakespeare

Logan

Lana is wrapped around me, sleeping peacefully, when my phone chimes with a series of rapid-fire texts.

Groaning, I turn over and grab my phone. Lana turns with me, sighing in her sleep as she curls into my side.

I kiss her head before I start reading the texts.

AD COLLINS: We have a situation. Contact me immediately.

CRAIG: The fucking Associate Deputy Director just told me to find you and bring you in. Shit has hit the fan.

HADLEY: I just got to work, and the Godfather is here. You better get in here fast.

Cursing, I bail out of bed, leaving Lana to sleep without me. I'm getting sick of this. My schedule has always been hectic, but it seems to be getting worse with so many high profile killers deciding to go on sprees.

Quickly, I get dressed, wondering what in the fuck Johnson is doing on our unit's floor. I scribble a note for Lana, promising her I'll be back as soon as I can, and bail out the door at four in the morning to deal with the shit that has supposedly hit the fan.

By the time I arrive, Johnson is sitting in my fucking office at my motherfucking desk.

"What the hell do you think you're doing? No one is allowed in here unless I grant them access," I snap.

"Lower your tone to your superiors," he growls, glaring at me.

We've never liked each other, in case that isn't apparent.

"Get out of my office, and you're not my superior, SSA Johnson. In case you haven't noticed, I have the same title. And as for your position in the Bureau, it holds no authority over mine."

He slowly stands, straightening his jacket as he does.

"I was just getting caught up on my case."

"Your case?" I ask, gauging him.

He's more arrogant than usual, and he's definitely selling some shade to go with that menacing gleam in his eyes.

"Yes. My case. It seems as though you're digging into case files that are mine, and apparently the director decided I should come investigate this new case you think is linked to my old one."

"You mean the director caved and let you do whatever you want because you two are golf buddies by day, and swing buddies by night," I restate, saying what he should have.

His jaw tics. He hates that a room full of profilers never let your secrets die.

"It's my case."

"This is my department. In case you've forgotten."

"Well, take it up with the director if you have an issue."

I point my finger at him. "Get out of my office. I won't tell you again."

He smirks, but he strolls by me, acting as though he's won something. I immediately stalk toward the elevator, when Associate Deputy Director Collins steps out.

"I told you to call me," he says quietly, his eyes flicking to Johnson as he moves in on one of the vacant offices.

"What's going on?" I ask again.

He sighs long and hard. "I don't know. Johnson got a call from someone, and he called me, wanting to know why you were working on one of his old, solved cases. I told him that it overlapped with one of your present cases. Next thing I know, the director is waking me up with a call saying Johnson will be running point on the Scarlet Slayer case."

"What the actual fuck?" I hiss.

He gestures to my office, and I pass by Hadley who looks furious as she glares at Johnson. She's never met him before, but he rubs everyone wrong within a matter of moments.

As soon as we're inside, Collins closes the door.

"Something is going on with all this. First the coroner's report was pointless on the dead 'supposed' serial killer that Johnson profiled. The profile is full of holes and inconsistencies, just like the case against Evans was. Then there's a revenge killer who is out there doling out death sentences for men who used to live in this town. The oldest victim would have been nineteen—as far as we know so far—and the youngest would have been fifteen," I tell him, furious right now.

He drops to a chair, his face as white as his shirt. But I'm not finished.

"Then Johnson shows up, bullying his way into impeding this investigation. What's really going on here, Collins? Did he have something to do with an innocent man being killed? Did he intentionally fuck up the profile to make it fit Robert Evans? I can't find much on that case here. We've been scraping together what we can."

He shakes his head. "I remember the Evans case. It got the least publicity because of terrorist threats going on at the same time, or something like that. I remember the case because I went to that town when several of the unit members said they were done; hell, half of them quit, retired, or transferred, which is why so many slots opened up at once. Johnson was left behind on his own to finish the case. Then he came home. That trial happened so fast. I've never seen a trial come and go faster than that one."

He pauses, sucking in a sharp breath as he stares at nothing. Finally, he continues.

"Next thing I know, what little bit of the unit that remained just up and quit. Johnson was on the market to be replaced after that, even though I don't know why. They hired a bunch in, but you were the one they eyed the longest. You came three years after that mess. They finally had the right replacement, and they got rid of him as soon as you were ready."

"Yet now the director sends him back?"

"He's sending him back to clean up a mess, is what it sounds like."

"He's awfully smug for someone trying to cover his ass," I bite out.

"He's not covering his ass. He's covering the director's. Director McEvoy has been on the verge of being replaced for six months now. I've already been approached several times about it by very high ranking officials. They want me in that chair and him gone."

I drop back to my desk, leaning against it as he sits in one of the two chairs by the door.

"So what do we do?"

"You're the profiler. Tell me what gets us out of this situation but offers the best possible resolution to a very dangerous serial killer."

I think it over, weighing the facts and probable outcomes.

"Johnson will profile this guy as a sadist, regardless of all the new information we've discovered. He'll change the game, rewrite the evidence to fit his profile. Then he'll single out someone who doesn't fit the true profile at all. Half of his cases were overturned because of that."

"I'm well aware of his shortcomings," Collins states dryly.

"If he falsified DNA evidence…" I let the words trail off.

"Then he'll be locked away," Collins promises.

I trust him. Always have. He's not involved in the politics. He's old school FBI — the kind who joined the Bureau in the quest for the truth and justice.

"So I work the case on the side, running it through my team. I'm still their boss. Any backlash will fall on me, understood? I don't want their careers jeopardized over any of this."

"While you're doing that, I'll assemble a committee meeting to see if I can overturn this ludicrous ruling. It might take me a week or more, but I'll get him out of your hair if there's any way possible," he offers.

"Tell me it's on me and not my team," I repeat, staring him down.

"As you wish," he says on a sigh. "Hopefully it'll never come down to that."

"He's going to demand we go to Delaney Grove in the next day or so," I go on. "He'll want to get ahead of the endgame regardless of the fact the kills seem to be surrounding us right now instead of the town in question. It might work out in our favor though, because we might finally get some answers about what happened there."

I look up, seeing through my window as Johnson walks toward the center of the room, touching my motherfucking board and erasing crucial profiling information.

"I hate that son of a bitch," I say under my breath.

Collins turns, blowing out a frustrated breath. "Don't we all."

I walk out, listening to what Johnson is instructing half my team to do. Elise and Lisa aren't here yet, but Donny's eyes meet mine, as though he's catching on to how fucked up this is.

"We'll be going to Delaney Grove in two days. Pack a bag. I've called the sheriff, and he's invited us in to help him with this,"

Johnson says.

"Funny," Craig drawls. "He wanted to act like nothing was going wrong when we spoke to him."

Johnson eyes Craig. "You just worry about smiling for the cameras and leave the real work to us."

Craig's jaw tics, and he glares over at me. I smirk, letting him know I'm up to no good, and he restrains his own smirk in return.

"You have a sadist," Johnson says predictably. "This sadist is targeting alpha males."

Donny turns away, probably choking on how inaccurate that profile is. No one argues. Everyone has heard of Johnson's reputation. He's not a team player who listens or even adjusts. He's a domineering prick who thinks his word is gospel.

A true narcissist.

"Kyle Davenport has been put into protective custody by the local PD," he goes on, finally saying something that surprises me.

"Who is that?" Donny asks.

Hadley lowers to her seat, seeming too quiet for her.

"He's the sheriff's son. I've narrowed down the victimology, and he, along with a couple others, fit the profile. But he's more alpha than the others, so we believe he's the next target."

Donny comes to my side as Johnson begins spewing his own praises about how many sadists he's caught and how easy it is to catch them when they have a specific victim type.

"This is bullshit," he growls. "There's no way he narrowed down the victimology to one fucking possibility with as little as we've had to go on."

I rub my chin, staring ahead. "Unless he knows what happened ten years ago."

He jerks his head to me. "Then he'd know this is a revenge killer and not a sadist."

I nod. "But if you fucked something up so bad that you had the director himself insert you into the current investigation, the last thing you'd want to do is profile a revenge killer."

His eyes widen, then narrow to slits in the next second. "That motherfucker really does know what happened. He could be fired and possibly even serve time for impeding an investigation like this."

"I'm aware," I tell him. "Which is why I'm listening to everything he's saying. I'm building my own subcommittee case. For now, work our case. I'm your boss. He's not. Follow my orders. Not his. And when it comes down to it, it'll fall back on me if this goes south."

"I couldn't care less if they fire me over this prick, Logan. Don't take him on alone. He has too many high-ranking friends."

"Yeah, but I prefer to deal with evidence," I tell him, clapping his shoulder on my way back to my office.

I'm seated for a matter of moments before Hadley walks in.

"You should bring Lana to Delaney Grove with us," she says with no emotion.

My eyebrows hit my hairline. "What? Why the hell would I do that?"

"Well, for one, we'll be gone for a while, if this guy isn't any closer to his endgame. And for two, Lana is still struggling to be alone at night. She told me," she says, shrugging.

I tense. Lana hasn't said anything like that to me.

"Why wouldn't she tell me that?"

She shrugs, taking a seat. "She's tough. She doesn't want you to know she's struggling, because you've been proud of how tough she is."

I groan, running a hand through my hair. Of course she's struggling. A man broke into her house and tried to kill her. We've been staying in a hotel since it happened.

"She should stay with a friend. It's too dangerous to take her to Delaney Grove. Not to mention, against the rules."

"I'd agree with all of that, but we're looking for a revenge killer, even though that dickhead out there says otherwise. You know a revenge killer doesn't target someone unless they get in the way. She'll be safe. As for the rules, the Bureau doesn't have any say over where civilians do or don't go. It's a free country, after all."

Her lips twitch with amusement.

"And it'd piss that fucknut off if you brought her and used that line," she adds.

Knowingly taking Lana into a town where a serial killer plans to eventually show up…it's insanely irresponsible and dangerous.

"Please, Logan. She could definitely stand to be around people, and you're really all she has."

Cursing, I run a hand through my hair.

"If the unsub thinks we're getting too close, he could target her to get to me. It's too risky."

"You know that's bullshit," she fires off immediately. "If this guy wants to come after you, he'll come after *you*. He's not afraid or a coward like Plemmons who preyed on the weak. He's not a sexual sadist with an interest in pretty brunettes. You're not thinking logically."

I look at her like she's lost her damn mind. "I'm not thinking logically?" I ask incredulously. "You're asking me to bring an untrained civilian into the field after she was recently attacked once already because of my job."

She leans forward, determination in her eyes. "Lana saved herself from Plemmons. She saved me. You're not bringing her into the field; she'll be locked away nice and safe in whatever place we're going to be in. There aren't any hotels in Delaney Grove, so I'm about to talk to Craig to find out where exactly we'll be tucked in."

As if cued, there's a knock at the door, and Craig walks in before I can invite him.

"Hey, so, care to explain to me what the fucking hell is going on?" Craig asks as he steps inside and closes the door.

"I'm currently telling him to bring Lana along because she doesn't feel safe being by herself. She even hates traveling right now because she feels exposed. Talked to her about it myself," Hadley quickly inserts.

His eyebrows go up. "That's completely understandable after what she suffered. She should come."

Hadley beams at me like a kid who just won the argument over who gets the candy. "You too? You realize how dangerous that could be."

He bats his hand. "A revenge killer who has been targeting strong, fit males is not going after a helpless woman. If he wants someone on our team, he'll come directly after us. He's not afraid."

"Exactly what I said," Hadley gloats.

"Neither of you are profilers," I point out.

"Which is why we shouldn't be so much better at this than you," Hadley says on a long, breathy sigh, mocking me with her eyes.

"Why is this so important to you? First you don't trust her, and now you want her with us?"

Her lips tense. "Things change. Pictures happen. Then things change real fast when shit hits the fan and suddenly SSA Prick Meister walks in and takes over like he's trying to hide something."

"What does that even mean?" I groan.

"Lana will be safer with us than on her own right now," Craig tells me, the two of them doubling up.

Donny walks in, and I glare at him as he shuts the door.

"I'm not sure what's going on, but we need to figure out our next step and soon. He's on the phone with the sheriff now, but instead of delivering the profile out in the open, he shut the door and said it was a private matter."

He looks between the three of us.

"What?" he asks, confused at the tension.

"They think Lana should come with us, because she doesn't feel safe alone right now."

"That's very understandable. You should bring her. It's not like she'll be in any danger, considering he'd just come after one of us directly if he thought we were in the way," Donny says, causing Craig *and* Hadley to smirk victoriously at me.

"Un-fucking-believable."

"Besides," Donny goes on, ignoring my comment, "it'll piss off Captain Douchewad something fierce."

Chapter 11

If you prick us, do we not bleed? If you tickle us, do we not laugh? If you poison us, do we not die? And if you wrong us, shall we not revenge?
—William Shakespeare

Lana

Shakespeare was one of the few philosophers who believed in revenge. Then again, he was a romantic. Romantics always believe in revenge, because romantics love harder, suffer loss more painfully, and hold onto a grudge that has shattered their hearts. Their hearts are of the greatest importance, above all else—body, soul, or mind.

My body grew stronger and my mind turned calculated when I lost my soul to avenge my heart.

I guess that makes me a romantic.

I'm in the middle of texting Jake, who is also a romantic, when there's a knock at the door, interrupting me.

Logan wouldn't knock.

Warily, I go to the peephole, and I spot a very distinguishable redhead with her back turned.

I open the door, wondering what she's come to say this time. But when she turns, there are tears in her eyes.

She walks by me, shouldering her way in.

The burden of my secret is apparently weighing on her too

much. Fuck.

I'm so close now.

Silently, I shut the door, and she takes a seat on the bed, while I lean against the door.

"Sixty-nine pictures and seventy nails," she says, confusing me for a brief second. "Something tells me you're not one to miscount."

Realizing her meaning, I take a seat in the corner.

"This is about Ferguson?"

"I finally had the courage to look at the file today. I got up early to go in and look at it, then some things happened afterwards that we need to talk about. The point is, there were seventy nails and sixty-nine pictures. What'd you do with the other picture, Lana?"

My lips tense. She knows it was her picture I took. I don't know how she's going to react now.

"I burned it."

"Why?" she asks without a flicker of emotion.

"Because the mind is a fragile thing. Your friends would have seen it; you'd have seen it too. It would have been the thing that broke you. Hearing it existed isn't as critical as *seeing* yourself as that child who was exposed and vulnerable, then knowing proof existed all along. Hearing it is processed differently than seeing it. The mind is more delicate to sight than it is to sound. I didn't want you broken. I didn't want him winning from the grave. So I burned it."

She wipes away the few tears that have managed to trickle down her face.

"I'm with you," she says quietly. "Whatever you need, I'm with you."

That...confuses me even more.

"Why?"

"Because a psychopath wouldn't care about someone, who by my own admission, has made your plans so much more difficult.

Scarlet Angel

You show genuine compassion. It's an obvious confliction with a psychopathic personality."

"I have psychopathic tendencies, but I'm not a psychopath," I say on a sigh. "I've told you this."

"Yeah, but I didn't believe it until I saw sixty-nine pictures and seventy nails. Now you have my trust that you're really just someone who is avenging only the wrongs. And if anyone can relate to needing to kill the demons in the world that won't die otherwise, I can."

I blow out a weary breath, not realizing until this moment how much her indecision has been bearing down on me.

The string has been glued into place now, no longer threatening to be the unravelling of this entire thing.

"Then SSA Miller Johnson shows up today, as if more of a sign was needed."

Just his name has my back stiffening, and she notices it.

"He covered this up, didn't he?" she asks, ciphering my reaction too well.

"He did more than cover it up."

"What else did you not tell me?"

"I told you everything that happened before. I didn't tell you anything that happened after. You'll need to learn it with the rest of your team."

"Why? Why not just tell the story to them in a note or something?"

I lean forward. "The mind is a fragile and delicate thing," I repeat. "Hearing it from a letter or from a killer has less of an impact than hearing it from someone who has been dying on the inside from holding in the secret. Several people know the story, Hadley. Find one to tell it. Not to mention, I need that town to feel haunted. The longer it takes for the story to be told, the more questions you and your team will ask. And the more people will start to tremble in fear."

"You want that fear," she states, studying me.

"I can't kill them all," I say with a shrug. "But terrorizing them will remind them to never hold their silence again when the innocent are screaming for help."

She nods once, trying not to show how uneasy that thought makes her. She'll change her mind when they finally get to Delaney Grove.

"I convinced Logan to ask you to come to Delaney Grove with us," she says, shocking me.

"What?"

"You can't just walk around a town and not be noticed by our team. Your face was all over the news after the brush with the Boogeyman. People will know you, and it'll be suspicious if you're in town and you're not with him."

I had thought of that, but was just going to show up and surprise Logan.

"He'll be out a lot, working on the case. We're apparently staying in cabins the sheriff rents out."

My stomach twists. "Those cabins are at the edge of the town, right against the woods. If he thinks you're getting too close to uncovering all they did, he'll come after one of you and try to pin it on me. Well, on the other me," I tell her.

"We're smarter than that. We'll know if it's the Scarlet Slayer. And no one from our team will die. I'll make sure of it somehow, even if I have to hack all the feeds from the town cameras and watch continuously, living on coffee to stay awake."

"There aren't any cameras."

She shakes her head. "There has to be some."

"You're right. There are some. They all face parking lots and the insides of stores. There are no cameras anywhere else. The streets have zero visibility from those few camera angles. Trust me. I've

Scarlet Angel

studied this town since I decided what I had to do."

She slinks back.

"Why no cameras?"

"Because the mind is a fragile thing," I say once again. "It's easier to pretend the words you hear are just rumors or lies. It's not so easy to ignore something you can see. And the sheriff has plenty he doesn't want anyone to see."

She releases a shaky breath.

"Was the sheriff the man who killed those women? The ones your father was framed for?" she asks me, and my stomach clenches.

Before I can answer, Logan steps in, pausing when he sees us. "You already told her?" he asks, narrowing his eyes at Hadley.

Unlike the last time we were in this situation, Hadley doesn't turn into a babbling fool. She flashes him a taunting grin. "Maybe."

Logan rolls his eyes, then he faces me, and a look softens his gaze.

"I'm on my way to deal with a few things, but you're okay with going? You'd have to stay in at night. You'll feel more like a prisoner, but I'll be able to come see you more."

Why does he look like he's so worried about me?

I flash a look to Hadley, but she blinks innocently at me. My gaze returns to Logan.

"I'd rather be with you than be here without you. You could be gone a while, or so Hadley says."

He nods grimly, and I stand as he starts walking toward me. As soon as he reaches me, he wraps his arms around me, holding me as though he feels I need comfort. I hug him back, glancing past his bicep to see Hadley smirking at me.

What's going on?

"You should have told me you didn't like being alone right

now. You're still going to be alone there too, though. I don't really know what to do," he says, sounding truly guilt-ridden and exhausted.

I glare at Hadley, who merely beams at me.

"I'll be okay," I assure him, hugging him tighter, plotting the ways I'm going to hurt Hadley. "Promise."

He pulls back, lifting my chin so he can see into my eyes. I feel like I'm playing him, and I hate that.

"Get packed. We're leaving tomorrow."

"Tomorrow?" Hadley asks as my eyes widen. "I thought we had a few days."

"SSA Johnson decided we should leave sooner after he got off the phone with the sheriff. Maybe we'll get some answers when we get there," Logan tells her. "Go pack. Give us a minute."

Hadley climbs off the bed, and I try not to curse the day she played this part. How am I going to slip away and kill two more people before returning to town?

They still haven't found Kevin or Anthony.

I guess I'll have to pick one and save the other for another day. Morgan was worse than Jason. Jason will die when the time comes. Just not in the order I planned.

"If we're leaving tomorrow, I should go get some things from my house that I need. I also need to speak with my partner and get some business things in order. I should be back tonight," I say, letting him hold me closer.

"You really should have told me you were struggling. And I should have noticed. I'm a profiler, for fuck's sake. It's my job to see things like that."

I'm killing Hadley. No, not literally. Well, maybe a little.

I hug him closer, kissing his chest through his shirt. He smells so damn good.

Scarlet Angel

His blond hair is always tousled these days, mostly from the way he'll run his hand through it when he's frustrated. It's a tell I've noticed about him.

"Logan, I'm fine. I really am," I say, soothing his guilt. Regardless of her intentions, Hadley had no right to make him feel guilty, and it really pisses me off.

He runs his lips over my forehead, and I lean against him, soaking in that warmth he seems to radiate. It always feels like he's sharing his soul with mine, helping it be restored, whenever he holds me like this.

He did what no one else has been able to do in ten years—he made me start healing.

I'll die before I let anything happen to him, and I won't leave him alone in that town, unguarded against dangers he doesn't know exist. He hasn't yet seen the depravity, and won't believe it. Not yet. Not until he's reached the point of being desperate for answers.

That's when it'll register the most. That's when it'll hit home with a knockout swing instead of a simple jab to the stomach.

"I really do have to get back, but get packed. I'll probably be back late, but call me if you need me, and I'll be here as fast as I can," he says softly.

I kiss him to shut him up, letting him feel how good he makes me feel. I kiss him for so many reasons, all of them tangled around one simple, innocuous little four-letter-word that holds more power than I ever imagined.

I now know why my father could never move on after my mother's death.

He was a romantic.

And a true romantic would never recover from losing his love.

Logan's hands slide down to my ass, but before we can get things going, his phone rings. Groaning, he looks down at the screen and rolls his eyes.

"One more reason to hate this son of a bitch," he says, confusing me before he brings his phone up and answers. "SSA Johnson, miss me already?"

I force my body not to tense upon hearing that name. I force myself to keep my face hidden to hide any micro-expressions that might give me away. I continue to kiss his chest, and his free hand strokes my back affectionately, a gesture absent of thought and packed full of feeling.

It's become natural to him to touch me and hold me, to comfort me even when I don't need it. I never thought I'd have that easiness with anyone. I never thought anyone like him even existed.

"What I do doesn't concern you, SSA Johnson," Logan says curtly, a smirk etching his lips. "Don't forget you're no longer my boss."

My stomach tilts, but then I remember he's only been with the FBI for seven years. He wasn't involved.

I relax again.

"I'll let you know when I'm back in. I'm about two inches taller than you with dirty-blond hair. I'm hard to miss."

I grin into his chest, not letting him see it. I love that he's not a sheep like the others were.

Even though I still hear someone talking, he hangs up his phone, and I continue to hide my smile. Logan's arms go back to embracing me, and he holds me for a moment longer.

"Can I ask you something?" he says quietly.

"Yeah."

"Why don't you ever speak of your past? I keep waiting on you to open up, but I'm worried you're going to keep shutting me out if I just let it go."

My blood chills in my veins. "Not now. Not today. Not like this," I say hoarsely. "But one day, I can promise you'll know everything."

Scarlet Angel

And I hope against razor sharp odds that he'll still love me when he does.

He squeezes me tighter, and I ignore the pang in my chest.

"I need to get back. One of the guys may kill Johnson if I don't come to run interference."

I realize I may need to ask questions, to appear as though I don't know anything and seem suspicious and all that.

"Johnson?" I muse, playing coy as he sighs and pulls away.

He kisses me swiftly, careful not to linger, knowing it will escalate quickly if he does. As he walks back toward the door, he says, "Long fucking story. I may get to finally have more time to spend with you when this case is over."

"What does that mean?" I ask, genuinely confused.

He turns and gives me a grim smile. "Going against Johnson to keep him from covering something up will probably cost me my career."

With that, he disappears out the door, leaving that cliffhanger behind like it's okay to do.

I have someone to kill much quicker than I intended, so I hurry up and get changed, pulling on some tennis shoes I'll replace with my big boots soon—if I have to.

I charge down to Hadley's room and bang on the door, and she swings it open, smiling at me.

"What did you tell Logan?" I hiss, stepping into her room.

"That you were struggling with the whole Boogeyman trauma. It was the easiest way to get him to ask you to come along."

I glare at her. "I'm not struggling."

"Yeah, and a normal girl would be. Hell, I'm still scared to go home and sleep in my house, and it wasn't even my house he broke into. I still feel violated."

"He feels guilty now. I haven't faked struggling because I don't want him feeling guilty. I'd rather endure suspicion than hurt him by making him carry an unnecessary burden."

Her smile falls. "I didn't mean to do that," she says seriously. "Shit."

Rolling my shoulders back, I check the time on my phone. "I have something to do, and when I get back, you're going to explain why Logan's career may be in jeopardy."

Her lips turn into a thin line, meaning she does know.

I decide killing Morgan can wait a few more minutes.

"What?"

"Miller Johnson is the Godfather of the unit. That sort of infamy has granted him some extra juice with some higher-ups. They wouldn't fire him when he fucked up so much, but they did move him to another department. The director is bypassing tons of protocols to blatantly have him continue to cover up whatever happened in your town. But if Logan doesn't play ball, he's going against a lot of very high-ranking officials who will destroy his career with the FBI."

I've always hated corruption. It's why I started this journey. No one would do anything.

No one but me.

"You can't go killing off every member of the FBI who would go against him," Hadley immediately points out after studying my face.

I don't see why not.

"Sure I can't," I say patronizingly.

I start to leave, but she grabs my elbow. My eyes drop to the contact, and she releases me immediately, some of her fear of me still present.

My eyes meet hers. "What happens when this is all over?" she asks timidly.

Scarlet Angel

"In a perfect world, Logan never knows this side of me. In a more perfect world, Logan learns the truth but understands all of this, despite the fact his moral compass isn't skewed like mine. But in reality, he may be the one to put me away, because I'd never hurt him, Hadley."

Her eyes continue searching mine, like she's actually looking for something in particular.

"The research shows that almost all revenge serials die at the end of their crusade, Lana. Usually suicide by cop, or taken down by cops to save lives, because the revenge is all they focus on."

"I'm aware of the statistics," I tell her, keeping my tone and expression devoid of all emotion.

"Don't you dare make him the one to have to do it if that's your endgame. Do you hear me? I'll do it myself before I make him have to live with that," she warns, reminding me which side of the law she's used to standing on.

"I'd kill myself before I made him do it," I say in a rasp tone I can't mask.

She clears her throat.

"But that's not your goal? To die and immortalize your message?"

I shake my head slowly, unsure of what I should say.

She visibly relaxes.

"You should know something before going into the pits of hell," I say, regarding her, watching as her loyalties truly shift to me.

"What?"

"The sheriff? He owns *everything* in the entire county. You want cable? You can only get it from the local provider — his business. You want internet? He owns the only local provider, and no 'outsiders' are allowed to do business there. It gets nasty when they try. You want water? It's *his* reservoir that provides it; not the city's. Not the county's either. You want food? He owns every grocery store in the county. You want gas? Well, you get the idea. He also owns the hospitals in the county. Hence the reason my brother got us the fuck out of that county, knowing we'd die if it took too long, or die if we stayed in Delaney County. The county is named *after* Delaney Grove. He had it changed the day he took office, went through all the proper channels to make it official."

"So you're saying he holds a monopoly on basically everything but the air, and no one has stopped it?" she asks incredulously.

"I'm saying he has friends up high too, and he makes those friends a lot of money. It's not just Delaney, Hadley. I just know this one personally. He has his hands in every little pot there is. He's their boss and their sheriff. To them, he's untouchable. You won't find many to turn against him because of that. Especially since he boasts righteousness to cover his sins."

"Why Delaney?" she asks, confused.

"His ancestors were the original settlers there. His last name might be Cannon, but he came from the most influential originals there were. And he uses that to his advantage, wants to remind everyone how deep his roots are when they stand against him. And Kyle? Kyle's the monster he created in his image."

She looks thoughtful for a moment. "Why is Kyle's last name Davenport instead of Cannon?"

I cock my head. "Because the sheriff *wouldn't* ever give Kyle his name. Even his son wasn't good enough. Only one person ever was."

"Who?" she asks as I turn, heading toward the door.

"A girl," I say, looking back as my feet pause. "His daughter. She's the reason my father was convicted."

"Why?"

"You'll just have to see, Agent Hadley."

I turn again, finally leaving as she huffs out a frustrated breath.

"Where are you going?" she asks as I jerk open the door.

"To buy some lube."

"Too much information," she grumbles as I walk out.

Chapter 12

Though she may be little, she is fierce.
—William Shakespeare

Lana

I stare at my future, knowing how bleak it is. And I worry. I worry for my children. What happens to them? They've already lost their mother, and now the sins of another have landed in my lap, destroying what's left of our family with all the dark lies and insinuations.

They'll become outcasts. My name will bring them harm, I fear. My daughter is fierce, constantly fighting for me. My son is fragile right now, barely holding it together.

I worry the most about Victoria. My son will grieve me, but he will recover. My daughter will never stop fighting for me. That could put her in danger. It's obvious I'm supposed to take the fall for this; I just don't understand why.

Why is any of this happening? Why is this happening to us? Haven't we suffered enough?

If I could end my life and spare them the rest of this trial, I would.

But if I do that, then I'm teaching them to give up. I'm setting a precedent my wife would never approve of.

So I'll fight. I'll pray. And I'll hope against all hope that the truth prevails.

For the sake of my children, I'll fight.

I put the journal away, sliding it into my bag just as the sun sets.

Any time I need a reminder of why it's important to always fight, I read the journal of a man who had no choice but to fight. To fight for his kids.

To fight for us.

"Lana, you there?" Jake asks, annoyed as I wedge the phone between my shoulder and cheek.

"Still here," I tell him.

"I don't like this. I haven't even installed any cameras in Morgan's house, and he teaches a MMA class for fuck's sake. You'll be going in blind with a guy who knows how to fight."

"They all know how to fight," I say carelessly.

"Not like him. You know it. You're rushing this, getting too brave. You've reached the point where you think you're indestructible. We talked about this. We agreed you'd let me pull you back a little if you started to develop that complex."

He's frustrated, and I understand. The second I fell for Logan, all our plans became five times more complicated and seven times more fucked up. Not to mention rushed and sloppy.

"I have to be there tomorrow. Morgan has to die tonight. I'm not leaving behind two to run off once they hear what I've done to that town. It'll be hard to kill them afterwards. Well, hard to kill both and not have immediate FBI attention."

"Damn it, Lana. Let me handle it."

"No," I say immediately. "The Scarlet Slayer—as you named her—can't be in two places at once, or they'll know I have a partner. It'll ruin the whole thing. That town once called me the devil's spawn—and they meant it, Jake. They truly believe that. They'll believe in spirits and demons coming back to reap their souls when I'm done. I can't scare the hell out of them without your compliance."

He curses, groaning. "Fine. Fuck. Fine. I'll be there in twenty minutes. Leave your phone on. If you get in trouble, I'll hear it and come in, armed."

"I can take him," I promise.

"You've gotten too cocky."

"You've lost too much faith in me," I say with a smile.

"Never. I just don't want to lose my sister to one of them because she got careless," he retorts.

"At least we don't have to risk spending time in the house to remove the cameras this way."

"Still can't believe they haven't figured out you've been watching them. The FBI, I mean."

"Two tiny holes in the walls at random isn't enough for them to suspect your mini cams being installed, considering the NSA is the only ones who is supposed to have that technology."

"They shouldn't be so easy to hack if they wanted to keep that technology a secret."

I roll my eyes, grinning. "Now who's cocky?"

He mutters a very unflattering word to describe me, and I grin broader.

"You know the worst thing that could happen isn't just death here, Lana. If he overpowers you...You've studied his past just like I have. You're not the only girl he's hurt."

My smile disappears as icy fury washes over me. "I'm aware. Just like I know his father is friends with the governor, and all the accusations disappear when the women turn into lying whores. Right?"

"Just be careful," he says on a sigh. "And get him trapped first. Then have some fun with him."

That has my smile returning.

"I'm going in."

"Leave the phone on."

"Yes, sir!" I say with a mock militant tone.

"It's sir, yes, sir. But whatever."

Slowly, I push the phone into my pocket and head inside to kill one last time before going home to massacre so many more.

I'll paint the town red. Just like they painted the streets with our blood.

Grabbing my purse, I step outside, jogging down the street.

"Don't forget you need to drive to Delaney Grove to start phase one," I say into the Bluetooth earpiece.

"Yeah. I will. As soon as I make sure you don't get yourself killed by being reckless," Jake says too loudly in my ear.

I cut the volume down, and slow my pace, approaching Morgan's house. I watch through the window, seeing him walk through the house in just his boxers without an ounce of shame.

Fortunately, he lives about a mile from anyone, so as long as no one rolls up on us, I should be able to finish this quickly. I hate rushing the kill. I planned for days and days of torture with him.

Now I have to improvise and cram days of torture into one method. Only one way to do that.

"Going in," I whisper before slipping in through the front door.

I twist the knob, not surprised to find it unlocked. Morgan thinks he's a badass who can't be hurt. Talk about feeling invincible…

I push through the door, grimacing when it creaks. I pause, listening for him, but don't hear anything to alert me that he's coming this way.

The house is mostly quiet, so I push the door shut, leaving it a little ajar so as not to allow it to squeak again.

Jake stays silent in my ear, and I bring my hair down to cover the gaudy ear piece. I've considered everything that could happen, and have different plans for each scenario.

Just as I turn the corner, my heart kicks my chest, and my eyes widen on the barrel of a gun that I *wasn't* expecting.

"Shit!" Morgan shouts, dropping the gun to his side, still holding it though, as he looks at me in confusion. "Damn, girl. What the hell are you thinking just walking into a man's house?"

I swallow down my surprise, realizing just how right Jake might have been, as Morgan looks at me with utter confusion. That gun will be blowing my brains out if he finds out who I am right now.

"Sorry," I say, squeaking the word intentionally.

Morgan won't fear a woman, after all. I'm harmless, at least in his mind. It's his mentality. Women are easily overpowered when he has them under him.

"My car broke down, and this is the first house I saw," I go on, clutching my heart as though it's beating too fast.

He eyes my cleavage, and a slow smile spreads across his lips. *Yeah, I did that just for you, big guy. I know what you like. I'm sexy, not dangerous. Keep thinking that way and put the damn gun down.*

"Oh?" he asks, slowly clicking the safety back into place on his gun.

"Yeah. I saw a light on." I pull my hair back, and point to the Bluetooth ear piece. "My phone died, so I was hoping to borrow one. Unless you know something about cars."

He licks his lips, his eyes still on my cleavage.

A fist slams into my face, and I cry out in pain, unable to hold back the tears this time. Warmth spills down the front of my face, and I know it's blood. Know he just broke something.

"Damn, Morgan, don't fuck up her face yet!" Kyle hisses. "I still want another piece, and I can't stare at blood to get off. I'm not like her sick fuck of a dad. And it's not your turn again, anyway."

More tears pour from my eyes as Morgan comes down on top of me. "Just worry about her brother's ass some more. That's where your dick should be."

"What did you say?" Kyle growls.

"You heard me. Maybe they like getting their dicks rubbed by anything with a squeeze, but you don't get to tell me where to put mine. I choose pussy over ass any day. Especially a dude's ass, faggot."

Kyle steps closer, but Morgan flashes him a daring grin. Kyle may be running the show, but Morgan is the only one who isn't suffering from pack mentality. Kyle knows it, and though he might want to kill the sicko on top of me for not knowing his place, he lets it go.

Morgan is only here to fuck me. He's not here to punish me like the others.

He's been waiting for a day when he could do this.

His hands knead my breasts, and he releases an appreciative groan. "I've always wanted a taste of these," he says, bringing his lips down on them.

I'm too numb to feel it. At least that is what my mind is telling me. I'm sick of feeling. I want to be numb forever.

Strong hands are grappling my weaker ones, holding me down, but I've stopped fighting, so there's no need to restrain me anymore. The blow to my face has killed most of my fight, dazing me.

"At least I brought lube," Morgan says against my ear, thrusting in and out, as I try to pretend I'm anywhere else. "I made this feel good, and you fucking bit me?" he hisses acidly against my ear. "I want this to feel good for you, baby. I didn't have to hit you if you'd just kissed me instead of trying to bite me," he says, his thrusts building speed. "I want you to come. I want you to know it was me who made you come. I want you to close your eyes for the rest of the night and see me thrusting in and out of you even when it's not my turn."

My stomach roils, and I swallow back the vomit.

"You're going to love every second I'm inside you." He moves my hair to the side. "Just remember I could have stopped all this if you'd stopped fighting me a long time ago."

He stills inside me, shuddering his release. I stare blankly at the side as he runs his lips along my neck. I'm drenched from the lube, and the pain is more bearable, but to keep from crying, I picture someone riding in to save us. They'll start by chopping his head off while he's inside me.

That way I'll see him die every time I close my eyes, and I'll sleep better at night.

"Who's tapping in?" Morgan asks, laughing as he cups my breasts one last time.

I don't even fight when I'm flipped over on the concrete so the next one doesn't have to see my bloody face. I'm tired of seeing. I'm tired of breathing.

I just want it to stop.

"So you're here alone?" Morgan asks, leisurely raking his eyes over my body, making a tsking sound when I nod. "Must be fate that brought us together then."

He takes a step toward me, not releasing the gun the way I'd hoped. Disarming him will be tricky. He's not as untrained as Hadley.

I let him grab me by the throat. I fake shock when he shoves me against the wall. And I cry out, feigning pain when he shoves a knee between my legs. But I don't make my move until I hear the gun hit the floor.

Then a smile curves my lips, and I make the same tsking sound he just made. His brow creases in confusion seconds before my arms shoot up between us, and the heel of my palm catches his nose, sending blood spraying everywhere as he stumbles backwards.

"Been waiting a long time to repay that favor," I tell him, tossing the ear piece to the side.

He looks at me, and I see it when rage takes hold. Pissed off people are all lunging and no finesse.

As expected, he lunges, and I slam my knee into his torso before bringing my elbow down hard across the back of his neck. He slams into the wall, getting dazed, and staggers a step before falling.

Scarlet Angel

Before he can recover, I grab the wire from my purse, and I wrap it around his throat, choking him from behind. He struggles, standing up with me still behind him, forcing me to ride his back like a monkey as I hang on, choking him harder.

He slams me into the wall, but my grip never loosens, and the pain never comes. My tolerance is so much higher than his.

"You made me this way," I whisper.

I see it in the mirror across from us — the confusion in his eyes.

He has no idea who I am.

I release him when he drops to the ground, not fully unconscious, but not awake enough to fight back.

With quick movements, I cuff his hands and drag the cable connected to the cuffs to tie off at a beam in his living room. I then tie his feet together, and pull out the electric nail gun from my oversized purse.

A bloodcurdling scream erupts from his throat when I use the small — yet powerful — nail gun on his feet, securing them to the ground with rapid succession. Then I pull out the lube while he continues sobbing.

"Who the fuck are you?" he cries out.

An agonized sob rips from his throat when he tries to move his feet. Those nails are too long for him to pull out of the floor without ripping his feet to shreds.

"Don't worry, Morgan," I tell him, grinning as I smear the lube on his bare chest. "I brought lube. I want you to enjoy this. It'll feel good when I'm inside you."

With one hard thrust, I plant the knife in his side, and another bloodcurdling scream erupts, but I see it the second he realizes who I am.

"Doesn't that feel good?" I mock.

"No," he says, shaking his head. "No way. It's not you."

I lean down, getting right against his ear. "You should have saved me all those years ago. Then I could have saved you."

With that last taunt, I tug his boxers down, and I pull on the gloves before lubing his dick. The sicko is actually hard. That's a first.

He watches me, probably thinking I'm going somewhere else with this. The side injury isn't lethal. I know where to stab to inflict pain but spare life.

He's in a lot of pain, but he's such a sexual deviant that he doesn't seem to even care. At least not until I pull out the other knife and slowly slide it down his lubed up torso, nicking the flesh but not slicing into it.

His breathing stops when I reach his most prized possession.

"Don't," he whispers, panic paling his features when he sees what I'm going to do. "I had nothing to do with what they did to Marcus. I swear that wasn't me."

"You held the mirror. You laughed as Kyle took the slice. You're the one who encouraged Kyle to redeem himself in your eyes. You're the reason it happened. Why should you keep this?" I ask, hearing his fearful cry when I nick just the side.

"Don't! Please! I fucking beg you."

A deliciously dark smile curves my lips. "I remember your response when we begged. *Fuck them. Kill them both.*"

With that, I take the slice, struggling to cut through the harder appendage than I've worked with in the past.

His screams pierce the air, and his pleads fall on deaf ears. Just as ours did.

The blood starts running, and I squeeze out three bottles of lube, letting it clump on him as he continues to wail, losing his color as quickly as he loses blood. They bleed more and faster when they're hard. Interesting.

Just to be a total sick freak, I throw a knife to the floor, stabbing it through the severed appendage I've dropped beside his face. He screams and screams, and I laugh as I walk outside.

Two gasoline cans are already waiting. Jake has done as he promised he would. Now that he's heard what I'm doing, he's probably on his way to Delaney Grove to execute the first part of our plan.

Singing while Morgan cries and chokes on his own vomit, I spray the gasoline around, then douse his body.

"They say the most painful way to die is by fire. I wonder who volunteered to find out that information," I chirp cheerfully.

Morgan shakes his head, trying to form words, but he's in too much pain, overwhelmed by agony and shock.

I strike the match, and his eyes widen one last time.

"I didn't even need to hear you confess your sins," I say quietly.

I watch the flame slowly eat away at the matchstick, almost reaching my fingers, before I drop it to his body. The flames start to soar, rapidly licking up the trails of gasoline. I slowly start walking out, hearing the roar of the fire as it spreads, chasing each strip of gas.

"Pretty soon, they'll all burn," I say as I walk out the door.

Chapter 13

Lawless are they that make their wills their law.
—William Shakespeare

Logan

"What's beyond these woods?" I ask the sheriff as he tries to blatantly ignore me.

He's at least 6'3, almost even with me in height. He looks like he spends more time in the gym than any county sheriff I've ever seen. His active deputies are more plentiful than small town sheriff departments I've been around in the past.

One town hall/sheriff's department is large enough to host all the deputies also, and it appears Delaney Grove is their central headquarters, so to speak. The police department has five officers on its own, but the county? So many more.

Twenty-three deputies? Who needs that many in a county this small.

"I asked a question," I say with authority, eyeing down the man with salt-and-pepper hair and dead eyes.

I should have come sooner. I'd have seen more than I expected. Already I see too much Leonard and Elise missed on their visit here.

"Four or five hunters' cabins, and a whole lot of wild life you city boys don't want to tangle with," he says shortly, his tone thick with condescension.

He turns back to Johnson before glancing to one deputy. "You show these folks around. I'm going to go with SSA Johnson back to the fort."

"The fort?" Elise asks.

"It's what he calls our town hall," one of the deputies says, grinning at her like she's his type.

She casts a glare at Craig when he snickers.

I'm happy to get the sheriff and Johnson out of our hair, so I don't object to them leaving us behind.

"Okay," Elise mumbles to the deputy who is still beaming at her. The kid practically has hearts in his eyes. "They seriously don't have women here, do they?" she adds.

"Not in uniform, ma'am," the guy tells her, following us as we go to peer into the woods.

A hunter's cabin would be ideal for our killer. He could come and go without being in plain sight. "The women who work in uniform are only in dispatch. Just two. Tonya and Tasha. They have a different office though."

At least Elise can get some information from her new admirer.

Hadley is supposed to be bringing Lana with her when she drives in. Hadley couldn't leave first thing this morning because there was a Delaney Grove related killing last night. Two towns over, in fact. Though no one here has wanted to talk about the death of Morgan Jones.

In fact, no one wants to talk about any of the deaths or the people who died.

We need to dig into his past and interview his family, just as we have all the victims, but SSA dipshit is making that difficult, since he refused to change the plans of coming here today. Why the rush?

And why did the unsub kill him quickly, compared to the others. It was definitely torture to be set on fire, and he was most likely castrated—they're still trying to determine when the penis was removed, due to the scorched remains.

Words I never thought I'd say.

"These are your cabins," the deputy tells us, resting his hands on his gun belt like he's Barney Fyffe. Grinning like him too.

"Okay," Elise says, eyeing him. "We've already seen the cabins."

"I'm supposed to escort you in while they hold the town meeting, and escort you anywhere you need to go in case you need something."

"We're going to walk around and question the townspeople some," Elise tells the lurker.

His eyes widen, and he shakes his head emphatically.

"You can't do that. Sherriff Cannon said to keep you guys here, and take you wherever you needed to go. But he doesn't want our people spooked by this dark issue."

Dark issue? That's seriously how he's wording it?

"There's a serial killer targeting your people. I held a nationwide press conference. How could they possibly not know?" Craig asks.

"Better yet, why wouldn't you want them to know?" Elise inserts.

The deputy takes a step back, feeling ganged up on. He's a nervous little guy.

"The sheriff controls the news stations we get. We have our own broadcasting network if we need the people to know something immediately. It'll interrupt their regular service for the emergency broadcast."

I turn away, looking at Craig. "This guy is dominating every aspect of their lives. It's almost like a cult here."

"And would be a damn good fit for a psychopath with narcissistic tendencies," Donny says quietly, while Elise keeps Barney — or whatever his name is — distracted.

The original killer used this town's faults to his advantage.

"The sheriff is trying to dominate us by acting as though we have no authority in his town," I go on.

"What do we do?" Craig asks.

"Prove we're the ones in charge. Print up flyers with the information of our profile, and start handing them out to everyone in town. We'll divide into teams to ask questions."

Craig nods, going into his cabin where we've set up our temporary headquarters—since the sheriff assured us his place didn't have the room we'd need.

How generous of him.

"He owns the only spot in town you can rent out too," Donny tells me.

"It's one more step of total domination. He *needs* to be in control."

"Sounds more like an extreme case of alpha personality than a psychopath, though."

"On the surface," I say absently, then turn to face the deputy. "Deputy…"

I let the word trail off, making it clear I have no idea what his unimportant name is. However, the guy grins a dopey, innocent grin, and I grow curious.

"It's Deputy Charles Howser," he says proudly, rocking back on his heels, completely oblivious and unoffended by the subtle barb.

"How long have you lived here or worked for the sheriff?"

"Been here six months, and been on the force for three weeks."

I look at Donny, who narrows his eyes. "He puts us with his newest officer. Coincidence? I think not."

"Likely his most innocent one, judging by the overwhelming stench of corruption everyone else was giving off. Where's Leonard?"

Leonard walks around like he just heard his name, eyeing us. He joins us immediately as Elise resumes her role, distracting the deputy. But I interrupt.

"Why is the sheriff holding a town meeting if he's hiding the fact a serial killer is targeting the town?"

"Oh, because we had some weird stuff happen last night. A lot of random doors were found open this morning to houses—at least fifty or so. Some mirrors were found missing, but that's about it. Weird, huh?" he asks, but doesn't give us time to respond. "The sheriff is holding a meeting to find out who did it."

That makes no sense at all.

"It's way worse now than it was," Leonard tells us quietly. "The sheriff put on a show when we came to town. He's been hiding a lot. And now he feels in control for some reason, acting as though he can also control us."

"Because of the Godfather," Donny states, reading my mind.

I turn back, interrupting Elise and the deputy again. "We're going to go make those rounds now," I tell him, timing it perfectly with Craig's emergence from the cabin.

He's holding a large stack of flyers, and Howser's eyes widen in fear

"But the sheriff said—"

"When the sheriff is my boss, I'll listen to him. But he has no authority over us or this investigation. At this point, his inclusion is merely a courtesy from my people. We outrank him. Do you understand?"

He doesn't understand. I can tell it in his pitifully torn look.

Instead of explaining, Craig and I walk off, and Elise hobbles to the cabin to set up shop. Donny and Leonard take half the flyers, and they set off as well.

"When is Lana coming in?" Craig asks as we ignore Howser calling for us to 'please stop walking.'

Scarlet Angel

"In two days, at most. Possibly sooner. She didn't want Hadley to have to ride alone. Lisa should be here any minute."

"Hadley's seal of approval? Never thought I'd see the day."

"It's surprisingly abrupt, but they seem to have bonded after what they both suffered."

"Nothing forges a quicker bond than a sexual sadist nearly killing you both, then escaping on a stroke of luck."

My stomach tilts, and I glare at him.

"Too soon?"

Muttering a few names for him under my breath, I snatch the staple gun from his hand and post the flyer on a pole.

We spot a woman coming out of the grocery store, tugging her child's hand, and I tilt my head as several others start running out, getting out quickly. A few are even panicked as they race away.

Craig and I both dart across the street, hands on guns, when I see the wall in the back.

The water will run red. Just like your sins. The truth won't be painted over anymore.

What the fuck?

It's painted in large letters on the back wall, and the guy behind the counter is calling it in.

"What happened?" I ask, moving toward him.

"I don't know. It just suddenly appeared. Like, it wasn't there, and then it was. Everyone saw it!" he shouts.

The fuck?

The words are dry, and I go to take a sample, pulling out an evidence bag to scrape some flakes in. I fucking need Hadley here already.

Whispers of spirits hiss around us from the few who are brave enough to stick around.

"It's dry but just appeared? Know any type of paint that does that?"

"I'm sure there's something out there, or something someone smart enough could make," I tell him, watching the people panic over some words. "It's him."

"What? He came to paint magically appearing words?" Craig asks incredulously.

"We profiled this town as religious, but with a cult mentality. Look around. They're all terrified over something this small. In DC, this would have people snapping pictures and rolling their eyes — and that's if they even noticed it to begin with. But here? It's already terrifying them."

He appraises the situation, processing the same thing I am, even though he's not a profiler.

"He's fucking with their heads."

"His endgame isn't just murder. He wants to terrorize the town," I say, only elaborating on his theory.

He follows me out, and I head down the street, looking around for anyone who stands out. But I see no one. Until this paint is analyzed, we won't know how he pulled that off.

We pause, talking to people, watching fear wash over their faces when we tell them about the serial killer the sheriff never warned them about. Most everyone hurries by us, not wanting to hear something like that exists.

One man clutches his heart. "It's true then," he whispers. "There's a dark spirit among us?"

Craig's eyebrows go up.

"No. There's a flesh and blood person who wants revenge for something that happened ten years ago to Victoria and Marcus Evans."

The color drains from his face.

"You speak of the devil's children," he hisses, then turns and darts away, hobbling down the sidewalk like we just invited in evil.

"I don't know about you, but this is the most fucked up case ever," Craig says with exasperation.

His phone beeps, and he looks down. "I sent Leonard a picture of that message, and he sends me this…" He frowns, holding his phone up for me to see.

LEONARD: People are finding that message in the houses with open doors. It's popping up all over town now. We've seen it literally appear from thin air as if it's being written.

"So he's a master of science as well as an organized killer. Lovely. He'll have the whole town believing in ghosts before the end of the day," Craig states dryly.

"But why a ghost?" I ask.

Screams erupt from all around before we can think about it for too long, and we look as people rush out of the park, hands in the air as they shriek.

Again we're running straight ahead, right into the thick of people fleeing as they scream for someone to save them.

The fountain in the middle of the park is running red water. So are the sprinklers that pop up from the ground. I whirl around as more screams erupt, seeing a woman drop a garden hose that is gushing red.

One girl is slapping the red water off her that is running down her face like thin blood. People are covered in it. It's like a bad massacre horror film from the seventies when the blood was portrayed too red and thin.

"Fuck," Craig hisses. "How the hell did he do this?"

"I don't know, but whatever he wanted to achieve seems to be working. This town is crumbling within one day of his mind games."

S.T. Abby

Chapter 14

Fishes live in the sea, as men do a-land; the great ones eat up the little ones.
—William Shakespeare

Lana

The screams sound like music, and Hadley shudders beside me. "How'd he do that with the paint?"

"I can't answer that. They'll be asking you to solve that mystery. Wouldn't want you figuring it out too soon." I grin over at her as she rolls her eyes.

Jake, like me, has had many years to plan this. He's mastered several crafts, and the mind-fuckery is just getting started.

Three years ago we committed to it and started planning it all out. But we'd been fantasizing it and creating hypothetical revenge plans. It was easy enough for me to string together one massive plan, and when I took it to Jake, he just made it that much better by infusing all his ideas.

"I guess you won't tell me about the cameras or the red fountains either, will you?" she asks as she drives.

"I already helped you with your forensics on Morgan so we could leave sooner. I'm not leaving Logan alone for that long. But I'm not helping you more than you need help."

She groans.

"Lube is what you told me the reason was for the lesser scorched places on his body. You didn't give me much else to go on.

Why burn him?"

"Figured he needed to get an early dose of what hell would be like," I say absently.

"Why turn the fountain red? Can you tell me that?"

"It's not just the fountain. It's the entire town's water supply. Don't worry. It's not toxic. I wouldn't risk the children and Logan to that."

She groans, and I grin, knowing she has a love/hate relationship with me right now. Weirdly, she's the only female sorta-friend I've ever had, other than Lindy. We weren't ever too close, since Lindy was much older. But she was my sitter when I was growing up and we talked.

Never mind. I've never had a real female friend.

"Want to tell me what you learned from Morgan's crime scene that I didn't tell you?" I muse.

"I learned you didn't walk on the soft ground to leave a boot impression."

"Always a bonus when I get to skip those heavy boots. Love a good sidewalk."

"There was nothing to implicate you," she says on a sigh.

"I'm too good for that. I was just curious what you learned."

"Can we talk about something normal?" she asks, exasperated.

I turn to face her a little better. "Like girl talk? Girls talk about penises, right?"

She grimaces. "Considering you dismember them from bodies, I'd rather not discuss penises with you."

"Logan's penis is safe, just so you know."

"Forget I said anything," she grumbles.

"Oh, never mind. Logan mentioned you were into girls, so I guess penises don't really appeal to you."

Scarlet Angel

She grows quiet for a minute before finally saying, "Logan has a big mouth."

I shrug, settling back into my seat as I watch the people scream and run, just as I knew they would. I love technology. Delaney's terror is conveniently wired to my phone.

The Boogeyman doesn't have shit on me.

"You shouldn't be ashamed of who are," I tell her quietly.

"I'm not. I just don't like people telling my business. Besides, I don't really put myself in a box. I'm not one hundred percent sure of my sexuality. It's just…men are attractive but harder to trust than women," she confesses softly.

I flip through the screens, checking out all the pretty camera placements Jake has found. He was a busy boy last night while I was finishing off Morgan.

"My brother was gay. Jake is bisexual. Jake was too scared to tell anyone he and my brother were in love. People made my brother feel like he was a walking sin or abomination when he came out a few months before they killed him." I try to say it with no emotion, but it's a lot of effort.

She sucks in a breath, and I rub my chest where the pain, that always accompanies my brother's memory, starts to form.

"Jake always says his biggest regret was being too scared to show Marcus how much he meant to him. Marcus knew he wasn't ashamed of him. He knew how toxic that town was. He didn't confess his sexuality to prove his love for Jake. He did it to be honest with himself. He never once doubted that Jake loved him."

"But Jake is doing this to prove his love?" she asks sadly.

"No. He's doing it because he's a romantic."

The confusion on her face doesn't surprise me, but she doesn't press for me to elaborate. We drive in relative silence after that, until we're nearing Delaney Grove. Then the conversation mostly veers toward a few other cases the team is working on.

Jake sends a text while we're talking, and I read it.

JAKE: Olivia called and said Dad is giving her a hard time about his medicine. I'm going to go take care of that, but I'll be back soon. Step one of our plan is already in action.

ME: Call me if you need help.

JAKE: Don't worry about me. Should only take a couple of hours. Just watch the fun stuff. I'm about to send you some pictures you'll appreciate.

Hadley asks for my opinion on some of those cases, drawing me away from Jake's texts, and I give it. Then she makes voice memo notes.

"Logan will think I'm twice as genius as he already thinks I am if I go spouting off these facts," she says, laughing.

But I don't laugh, because I get distracted. Jake sends me a picture of a street. Of *the* street. Of the words written in red.

The angels shall come forth, and sever the wicked from among the just, and shall cast them into the furnace of fire. There shall be wailing and gnashing of teeth.

"What?" Hadley asks.

Jake also sends me a picture of Logan studying the message, and I pull up the video footage, watching the man I love as he observes the people around him. Most are pale and terrified.

They know what happened on that spot. They painted over it. Made it black again. Pretended as though the red stains aren't there just because you can't see them.

Logan doesn't seem disturbed or terrorized, just as I knew he wouldn't. He's a logical man, after all. He doesn't believe in ghosts.

But Delaney Grove…they'll fall to their knees soon.

"I don't understand why they're all falling for that," Hadley states.

"It's called conditioning. They've been conditioned to be sheep. Sheep follow sheep," I tell her.

"I don't get it," she argues.

"You have someone you look to for inspiration?" I ask her.

"Queen Latifah. Why?"

I smile to myself. "My father was an Einstein man. My mother loved Confucius. My brother, the hopeless romantic who was too easily emotional, lived and breathed Shakespeare."

"What does that have to do with sheep?"

Smiling, I face her. "Personally, I was always in love with the words of Voltaire."

"All that sounds a little pretentious to me. But your family liked dead people who had something to say that people felt the need to recite. Proceed."

Still smiling, I say, "Voltaire said, 'Those who can make you believe absurdities, can make you commit atrocities.' For too long, Sheriff Cannon has ruled the county, and very few ever break away from the corruption he instills. Women are beneath men. And his word is gospel."

I gesture to the flock who are crying, panicking, and already on the verge of an all-out mutiny against the sheriff by now. After one single day of mind-fuckery.

"Sheep," I repeat quietly. "Fucking baa."

She blows out a shaky breath as we drive the rest of the way into town, and she texts someone. I look around, seeing the place that has jaded so many and broken many more.

"I'm back, motherfuckers," I say quietly as we pass the town hall. "And I'm going to make your life hell before I paint your town red."

I try to find Logan on the cameras, using the app Jake installed for me before the first kill, but can't. He's apparently in some blind spots.

I don't even notice we're parked until Hadley turns off the engine.

"I'm letting Logan know you're here, in case—"

Her words end on a shrill scream when my door is ripped open, and Logan reaches in, heaving me out of the car with one pull. I grin against his lips the second he kisses me, and I wind my arms around his neck, enjoying the feel of his body pressing against mine.

"Sheesh! We're in the middle of Fucking Madhouse Hollow, on the edge of the woods, and you give a girl a heart attack?! Not cool, Bennett. Not fucking cool," says the redheaded girl who knowingly drove the killer into town.

Logan smiles against my lips despite the crazy he's had to endure since he arrived early this morning. I'm trying not to laugh at the irony of Hadley screaming and freaking out like he was the killer coming to get us…when…yeah…

As he lifts me, my legs wrap around his waist, knowing their place. He holds me to him as he carries me inside what I assume must be our cabin. I don't look around, worried it'll be the cabin where Kyle used to take me.

Back before I knew the monster he was.

Back when I unknowingly trusted someone so dark.

Back when I was a sheep stuck in the same flock I intend to tear apart.

He bends, and a sense of weightlessness hits when I'm momentarily falling, before a bed hits my back. I grin up at him as he tugs his shirt off.

"You act like you missed me," I say, committing every moment with him to memory.

I'll need it to hold onto. I'll need it to remember. I'll need it to get me through the rest of this. Hopefully alive.

Then I'll need it when it's just me and Jake looking back on the chaos we created; the justice two killers achieved under the guise of avenging angels.

"I'm seriously considering seeing a shrink about this mindless obsession I have with you," he mumbles, but his lips twitch with a smile before he pushes down his pants.

The timing of our arrival is perfect. Halloween is just around the corner.

There's a reason I picked *Myers* as a surname.

But I don't think of any of that right now. Nothing else exists when it's just us, because my time is limited. I know that. He doesn't.

He still loves me like it's the last day when he comes down on top of me, pushing my dress up on my hips.

"You wore a red dress just to drive me insane, didn't you?" he asks.

Before I can answer, we hear Hadley through the door. "I put your bags in here, you horny fuckers. You're welcome."

Logan laughs against my neck, and I run my fingers through his hair, getting high on heaven. That's what he is to me.

"Sometimes I think you're an illusion, and that none of this is really happening. That I really died ten years ago after the accident," I tell him softly as he starts tearing my underwear down.

"I'm real, Lana," he murmurs against my neck as he finally peels off the last of my clothes.

Just the feel of his body sliding against mine as he undressed me has gotten me ready for him.

"And I'm yours," he says before he kisses me, swallowing the words I try to return.

Mine.

Just like I'm his.

For as long as he'll keep me.

"I love you," I say as he slides inside me, shuddering as though the feel of me was exactly what he needed.

I know the feeling.

The words mean more to me than he knows, because they're words I thought I'd never utter in that context. Thought I'd never heal enough to feel that connection.

"I love you," he says, opening his eyes to stare into mine, watching me as he rocks in and out.

It's everything I need and more.

He's everything I wish I could be.

A hero.

A hero loved by a monster.

Chapter 15

If you have tears, prepare to shed them now.
—William Shakespeare

Logan

"One place. Anywhere you could go. Where would it be?" Lana asks me.

"Hmmm," I say, humming against her skin. "Greece."

"Why Greece?" she asks, a tangled mess of naked limbs.

I wish I could just spend my days lying on a beach in Greece with her wrapped around me just like this. This job is starting to take too much and give back too little.

Then again, after this case, I may not have a career at all. But I won't just bow down and let them cover up whatever went on here ten years ago.

"Because my stepdad always said if he had a choice, he'd be drunk in Greece and in love. But he wasted all his sexy years on my mother."

She laughs, and I grin down at her as she wipes a few tears from her eyes from the surprise outburst.

"He sounds like he was great."

"He was," I tell her.

"My father was great too. He did everything he could to make sure my brother and I had what we needed. He was our world, and we were his."

"What about your mother?" I ask, deciding to pounce while she's speaking of the past.

"Amazing," she says wistfully. "She baked. I loved it when she baked. My father always said if she was a witch, children would willfully jump into the oven just because of how good it always smelled." She looks up as I arch an eyebrow. "He was a bit of a morbid sense of humor type of guy. But my mother loved it. Loved him. I never understood how rare that love was when I was younger. Like most things you see daily, I took it for granted."

A sadness touches her eyes, and I slide in closer, brushing my lips over her eyelids, kissing each.

"Where would you go?" I ask her, deciding I don't want to see her sad.

"Anywhere in the world?" she asks.

"Anywhere."

"I'd go to Greece with you."

And this is why I'm so fucking obsessed with her.

My lips find hers again, and I kiss her like it might be the last time. It's the way I'll always kiss her, because she's lost love once — the love of her parents. I never want any lingering insecurities to dwell in her about us.

I want her to know exactly how I feel every time she's in my arms.

When she breaks the kiss, I try not to slide on top of her and take her again. I was way too damn eager to be inside her when I saw her in a dress. I was just going to scare her, but Hadley screamed; Lana smiled. She always surprises me.

And just like that, I had to have her.

"I want you in Greece with me too," I tell her, kissing her cheek.

"We'll get drunk and have entirely too much sex," she agrees. "And of course eat. There's always something amazing to eat in Greece. Unless that's just a false stereotype."

Scarlet Angel

Grinning, I press my lips to her cheek. "We'll find out one day."

Her breath catches, and I pull back, looking into those haunted eyes that pulled me under her spell so long ago.

"What?" I ask, running my finger down her cheek, worried about that look.

She turns toward me a little more. "If you found out I wasn't this perfect girl you want me to be, would you still love me?"

The way she asks it is like a punch to the gut. "Lana, I don't expect you to be perfect. I think *you are* perfect. At least perfect for me."

Her lip quivers, and she forces a smile. What'd I say wrong?

"But what if I wasn't perfect?" she asks again, genuinely distressed over this.

"Then I'd love you anyway. I don't use that word liberally. Well, at least not since high school. But everyone uses it in high school without knowing what it really means to love someone."

That look in her eyes chills just a little. I'm trying to read her, but she's always a mystery. Constantly doing one thing when I expect another.

"But yes," I say again. "I'd love you regardless. In case you haven't noticed, I go a little crazy when it's been too long since I've seen you, and you give me a reason to want to live instead of just exist. You accepted every piece of me, and dealt with the scraps I could offer. And never complained."

She starts to speak, but I go on.

"Those eyes find me when you walk into a room, like I'm the only person you're looking for. You hold your head up when others would cower. You stand tall when others would fold in on themselves. Your strength is beyond amazing. And you always keep me guessing, which is my favorite part about you, as much as it is infuriating."

She laughs under her breath, and I kiss the corner of her mouth before continuing.

"And you smile for me like you smile for no one else. That makes a man feel powerful. And when I'm with you, I smile like I never have before. It's a sense of equality, a partnership even. It's rare to find someone who matches you step for step, and you do. I love that about you. I love *you*."

She kisses me before I can ramble on, assuring her in every possible way there's nothing that could change the way I feel. Just when I decide I have time to prove it a little more thoroughly, there's a loud knock at the door.

"Logan! We have a break!" Donny shouts.

"He has horrible timing," Lana says on a sigh.

"They always do. One day, I'll just throw away the phone and hide from them."

"When we disappear to Greece," she says, her smile not touching her eyes.

I feel like there's more wrong than she's telling me. I can see it in the way her gaze grows increasingly distant. I'll fix that. Just as soon as I figure out what's causing it.

"Yes," I tell her, smirking and pretending as though I don't notice the hint of sadness in her eyes.

I get dressed quickly and meet Donny outside. Then I walk back in just as Lana stands, the sheet strapped around her, and I pull her to me, kissing her long and hard.

She moans against my lips, and Donny loudly clears his throat.

"I'll be back soon," I tell her, then walk out, ignoring the laugh Donny lets go as I step out.

"Gotta say, never thought you'd fall so hard," he quips. "Company men like you usually end up a ride-and-die bachelor type."

"Things change," I tell him as I take the driver's seat. "Where're we going?"

Scarlet Angel

"Craig called and said a guy came up to him and told him we needed to speak to Diana Barnes. He wouldn't say anything else, but Johnson is on a rampage. Says we're inciting terror by posting those flyers, and demanded we tear them all down. Elise and Lisa are putting up more, while the deputies are tearing them down."

"Unreal," I say on a long breath. "He's not even trying to be discreet about this."

"Just makes me wonder what we're going to find."

"The cryptic messages the unsub is leaving us to terrorize the town isn't helping matters. They're all sure a spirit has risen, but no one will speak a name aloud," I point out.

"The Evans kids? Or Evans himself? They definitely aren't speaking about it," Donny says in his own unique way of agreeing.

"It's what he wants. He wants to incite terror. He wants them huddled in a corner. The question is why? We know they were raped, but the hospital couldn't give us anything more than that. The kids were too scared to speak." I'm mostly just speaking aloud, hoping that hearing the words will offer something more than just knowing them.

"The whole town is too scared to speak," Donny says, watching as people read the message on the street and walk away, their steps hurrying like they're going to carry home a piece of the devil if they dawdle too long.

Donny gestures to the road we need to turn on, and stops me when we're in front of a small, white house. It even has a fucking white picket fence.

"Cross your fingers this one doesn't slam the door on our faces too," Donny says as he climbs out.

I hop out as well, straightening my tie, and we walk up the cracked sidewalk to the house. The blinds by the front window crack open, and all I get is a glimpse of an eye before they seal shut again.

Donny raises his hand to knock, but the woman opens the door, staring at us like she's been expecting us all day.

"You the FBI?"

"Yes, ma'am. We're here to—"

"I know what you're here for. You work for that Johnson guy?"

My lips twitch. "We have different agendas. Mine includes getting the truth about what happened here ten years ago. We may be able to save lives if we know more."

Her lips tense. "Ain't a life you can save that needs saving," she says bitterly. "This whole town needs to burn. Only reason I'm still here is because I knew this day would eventually come. One day, someone would want to hear them babies' story, and finally give them justice."

Donny swallows hard as the woman wipes her tears away.

"Come on," she says, gesturing us in.

Donny shuts the door behind him, and Diana points to the couch where she apparently wants us to sit.

"I can't tell you everything. You'll need to learn about Robert from someone who knows all those details. But I can tell you about my babies. They were good to my son. Always good."

She takes a seat in her chair, and she pulls out her phone.

"Any information you could give us at all would be helpful," I tell her, my gut tensing at the prospect of finally having answers and wondering just how fucked up things are about to get.

We wait patiently while she calls someone.

"Hey, baby. Nah, I'm fine," she says to…her boyfriend? Her kid? No wedding ring or men's belongings around, so not a husband.

"You still dating that pretty lawyer lady? The one with all the security at her apartment building?"

She eyes us, as she listens to the person on the other line.

"Good. Go stay with her until I tell you otherwise. Momma's

about to tell a story that's been burning a hole for over ten years."

End of Book 3

Continue reading for book 4.

All The Lies

Book 4

~~Tim Hoover~~

~~Chuck Cosby~~

~~Nathan Malone~~

~~Jeremy Hoyt~~

~~Ben Harris~~

~~Tyler Shane~~

~~Lawrence Martin~~

~~Kenneth Ferguson~~

~~Boogeyman (Gerald Plemmons)~~

~~Anthony Smith~~

~~Kevin Taylor~~

~~Morgan Jones~~

Governments need to have both shepherds and butchers.
— Voltaire

If Logan and I ruled the world together, Voltaire would consider us the perfect blend.

My list might have grown, but the names are coming down quickly. It's almost time to sprint to the finish line. It's time they die at the hands of a dead girl who forgot how to be weak.

I can't wait to watch them burn.

Chapter 1

To the living, we owe respect, but to the dead, we owe only the truth.
—Voltaire

Logan

"Marcus Evans...that boy was a handful when he was a child, but such a sweetheart. And Victoria...she was always his shadow. Wherever Marcus and Jacob went, she followed. They let her. Just a year separated Victoria in age from the boys. And Robert, well, he did all he could to make sure those kids were loved. Jacob spent more time at his house than he did his own, because the man was made of a sort of strength and compassion you can't just find anywhere."

Diana Barnes clears her throat, and I watch as she stands to get a glass of water.

"You boys want anything to drink?"

"No ma'am," we both say in unison.

Her chocolate skin is a stark contrast to her ivory dress that hangs to her knees. She's a regal, timeless sort of woman, with haunted eyes. Haunted eyes like my Lana.

Only there's a sense of guilt there as well, unlike Lana's. There's a jaded harshness to the way she carries herself, as though she's forcing herself to make it through each day.

"You have kids?" she asks us as she returns, sitting down with her water, drawing out the suspense.

All The Lies

"No, ma'am," we both say again.

"I'll bet you both enjoy being bachelors and thinking time will never catch up with you."

Donny shifts in his seat uncomfortably, but I just smile.

"I'm not married, but I'm not a bachelor."

She studies me intently for a moment. "Victoria would have liked you. She was mostly raised by her father after her mother died when she was ten. She shared a house with two men, so she was more comfortable making friends with boys than girls. She was selective with her friends more than her boyfriends. Not that anyone could have known."

I inch forward. "Known what?"

"Nah. I'm getting ahead of myself. You need to know first that Robert died in lockup the night he was convicted of crimes he *couldn't* commit. They threw every shoe and the kitchen sink at him to make him the murderer, as though that would somehow make the killings just disappear and everyone could go on with their lives."

She sips her water again, and I refrain from demanding she get to the point.

"Robert was with his kids every night. My boy was even over there a lot of those nights. Jacob, of course, was there most nights as well. Robert cooked, he cleaned, he cared for his children, and he usually had others come over and hang out as well. Such a good soul and a good home, people couldn't stay away. My boy's daddy left when he was a tiny little thing. Robert always talked to my boy as if he was his own, and as a single working mother, I appreciated all the help I could get. I returned the favor when I could."

She pauses, swallowing down emotion that I didn't detect in her voice. Her eyes grow dimmer.

"He never could have raped and killed those women. He couldn't even raise his hand to his own kids. My boy saw him. Jacob saw him. Several of those nights, he was home with his kids and two extra. Didn't matter. They wouldn't allow the eye witness testimonies or admit them as alibies in the courtroom."

"What? Why?" Donny asks, confused.

"Because then they couldn't convict him of murders he didn't commit," she says as though it's obvious and he's stupid for even asking.

Donny leans back, annoyed. Not at her, but at the situation. He knows how Johnson is. He'll make something stick, and he'll cut all the corners to lock *his* suspect away.

"And the court backed this?"

"The court. The sheriff. Everyone. They held him in interrogation for five straight days. Locked him in that box with no right. Wouldn't let his lawyer in. Then lied and said he never evoked council. It was a witch hunt from the get-go. It was easier to pin it on the school janitor with no other family than his kids in this town. That Johnson fellow pegged it to be him, and from then on, they made it happen. The sheriff was right beside him."

The original profile was a sexual sadist. They don't have kids too often, and if they do, they're distant from those kids. Not loving and doting. He profiled the unsub as a loner, but he wouldn't have been.

No signs of forced entry means he was charming and approachable, likely someone they trusted. Hence the reason it was someone in the town who did it. His ability to frame a man makes him a narcissist, and this town played right into his hand, giving him the power that really got him off.

And fooling the world was the ultimate high.

"Did anyone have any grudges against Evans before that night?"

"No," she says, laughing under her breath. "That man was a saint. If a kid had an accident at school, he cleaned it up and told them to run along before someone saw it. He didn't want them to be embarrassed, and knew kids could be cruel. His own kids were mercilessly mocked for being the janitor's kids."

I lean back, trying to find out what in the hell made Johnson so insistent on pegging this guy as the unsub. Even he has a heart.

"What about the sheriff? Did he have any issues with him?"

Her lips tense. "The sheriff was too emotionally invested in finding someone—anyone—to make pay. His daughter was one of the first victims. The true sick, evil man who killed her…he put her in the middle of the street for everyone to find the next morning. She was naked and raped raw. Her skin was sliced to pieces, and she'd bled out overnight."

Donny swallows thickly, and I sit back, wondering how in the fuck that never made it into the case reports. The sheriff would have been required to step away from the investigation. It also makes him less likely to be the primary suspect, which was the direction I was leaning.

"She was eighteen," Diana goes on, choking back a sob. "The sheriff wasn't right in the head after that. After seeing that. It was the hardest thing this town had ever gone through at that time. And from there, they just got worse. A body was even on the church steps one Sunday morning before church started. One was on the school steps, right there for the children to see. It was Ilene Darvis. She was a kindergarten teacher. Just twenty-three."

She has to stop and blow her nose, her tears falling freely now.

"Anyway, the night Robert was convicted, they were supposed to take him to the prison. Escorts were here and everything. He was found hanging in his cell the next morning after they delayed the transfer. Ain't no fool gonna believe that man really hanged himself when he was desperate to get an appeal. He was gonna seek out true justice. Not go down like that. I never could find out what really happened. I hope you do."

Donny's fists tighten. It's always painful to hear about the wrong man's life getting shattered because of another man's ego. Johnson shattered many lives.

"Couple days later, them babies were walking home, and

Victoria stopped by here. I was beside her when her phone rang. Kyle called Victoria, telling her he could get her in to see her father's body, since they said they couldn't release it. The sheriff said they weren't eighteen, and since there was no one of age to claim the body, the city had the right to dispose of it. I got that taken care of later—too much later."

She blows out a shaky breath, as though she's steeling herself for the rest.

"Victoria had dated Kyle, gave that boy more of herself than she should have. He wasn't too happy when they broke up, but he didn't show his demon right away. He was manipulative and calculated like that. She'd only dated him for a few months, one of the few boyfriends she'd ever had. Her daddy talked sense into her when he heard how Kyle talked down to her. She never said why she broke up with Kyle. But Kyle had never given her a reason not to trust him. Not until that night."

Donny's phone beeps, but he ignores it. When my phone starts ringing, I silence it. Neither of us are stepping away until we have our answers. It's just Johnson trying to find out what we're up to.

"Victoria went to meet him, and Marcus caught up with her, wanting to see his father as well. They needed answers. No note was left. No goodbye was given. He just died, and they slapped suicide on there. Jacob was not with them for once, and thankfully, neither was my boy."

She breaks, becoming a sobbing mess. "I shouldn't have been thankful when those babies suffered, but I was so glad they didn't get my boy too."

She's almost incoherent now, her tears falling too fast and her sobs wracking her body. Donny looks at me, dread in his eyes.

We knew there was assault. We knew it was sexual.

But I'm starting to piece together all the kills now.

Diana calms herself by some miracle, hiccupping around a sob.

"And Kyle, oh that boy was pure evil," she says, her tone

turning angry now. "They met him at the end of Belker Street, and he wasn't alone. He brought several volunteers with him to help him *punish* the 'killer' through his kids."

Belker Street is where the message about angels was written to sound like an omen of things to come.

"They jumped them. Got them down on the ground. Stripped them bare on the middle of the streets. After that, they took turns on both of them."

She has to stop when she gags, and she turns her head.

Donny is white, and his fists are tighter. My entire body is rigid right now.

"How many?" Donny asks quietly.

"Thirteen in all," she says, still sobbing. "Only…Dev didn't…couldn't go through with it. He stood there, though. And he told me the story after it was over. The boy was so twisted up in the head he was sent to therapy for over a year. Then he joined a church ministry group that travels over the country spreading the word of God. He's how I know."

"So twelve of them took turns raping them," Donny states, his calm tone betraying the simmering rage that matches mine.

"Over. And over. And over," she growls, her tears falling angrily. "They didn't stop. Those babies laid on that street for hours, bleeding and screaming for help. And no one came. But that's not even the worst of it."

I don't know how much worse it can get.

"Lawrence, Morgan, and Kyle were the worst offenders; the darkest souls around. After they'd grown bored with raping them, Kyle walked inside someone's house and borrowed a full length mirror. The Whisenants just handed the mirror over like they didn't know what was going on right in front of their home. Kyle returned, handed the mirror to Morgan, and Lawrence jerked Marcus up to his feet."

My phone rings again, but I silence it once more, not even

glancing at the screen.

"Kyle pulled out a knife, and had Morgan hold the mirror behind Victoria. He wanted Marcus to be able to see what was coming next. Then Kyle told Marcus to 'fuck' his sister. To rape his own flesh and blood. Or he'd cut off his dick so he could never use it again."

My stomach roils, and Donny chokes back a strangled sound.

"Marcus refused, told them all to burn in hell and take whatever. Kyle slid the knife over Marcus's waist, cutting him, and told him it was his last chance. Said if he was pervert enough to like it in the ass, then he was pervert enough to fuck his sister. Marcus spit in his face. And Kyle made true to his threat. Castrated him there in the middle of the street."

It's all I can do not to walk out. I don't want to hear anymore. Hell, I'm not sure if I can ever look at anyone in this town without hating them for helping hide this.

Why did Diana not come forward sooner?

When Diana recovers again, she goes on. "The mirror fell and shattered. Victoria had already been beaten to a pulp, her face unrecognizable. They'd pounded her face into the ground, hit her with their fists, and so much more. When the glass shattered, they dragged her through it, then Kyle sliced her at the waist with the knife. After that, he grabbed a piece of the mirror, showed her what she looked like, and he slammed the piece of mirror into her. His parting words to her were that she'd die a monster and a whore. They left them to bleed out in the streets."

"Then Marcus drove them out of the county to give them a chance to survive," I say on a quiet breath. "Because the sheriff owns everything in Delaney County."

She nods slowly, then shakes her head. "Marcus never once thought he'd survive. He just wanted to save his sister's life. Neither one of them made it out of the hospital. And this town lost its soul. We all became hollow shells of who we were, because fear ruled us."

All The Lies

"Why not tell someone sooner?" Donny asks, trying not to sound accusatory.

She gives us a grim, solemn look. "The ones who tried ended up missing or dead. Lindy May Wheeler tried to stop them that night. She ran up, but Dev hauled her back off, tossing her into a car and locking her in it until they were done. She was married. Next thing I know, Kyle is telling her husband he slept with his wife…that she seduced him. Antonio left her, and no one believed her when she said she'd been raped repeatedly by Kyle. Her daddy had to get her out of town because he worried she'd be killed."

My blood freezes, and Donny's eyes meet mine. Lindy May Wheeler. The woman our unsub chose to care for a broken child he took the time to save from a true monster.

Diana doesn't notice our look.

"They threatened my boy. He was on his way to college in less than a year. They told me he'd never even graduate high school if I stirred up problems. I believed them. Still do. That's why I sent him to his girlfriend's place. That girl makes a lot of money, and she has the best security in New York."

"Most of these unsubs left town," Donny tells me.

"They had to," Diana interjects. "The only way the sheriff could keep people afraid, but still living here, was to banish everyone but his boy from this town. His boy is the worst of all of them, but he ain't getting banished. But don't you worry. He paid them boys off real nice."

"Kyle Davenport is the sheriff's son. It's no wonder he covered this up," Donny says on a pained breath.

"Covered this up?" she asks in disbelief. "He orchestrated it. He had his deputies go to each and every house and said if they heard something, to stay inside. If they failed to comply, there'd be consequences. He even sent out a broadcast to our TVs telling us there was an immediate curfew—no one out past sunset until told otherwise. He helped his son plan this out, then let him do what he couldn't stomach to do himself."

"Why?" Donny asks.

But I know why without hearing the answer.

"His daughter was raped, tortured, debased, and shamed even after her death. As far as the sheriff was concerned, Robert Evans was the man who did it. Killing the man wasn't enough for him. He had to go and shatter his kids before killing them too. Said the world needed to be cleansed of the devils it bore. Yet he never sees the evil in his own son's eyes. Even that boy's momma knew he was no good."

Again my phone goes off, but I'm not finished here, so I ignore it once more.

"Kyle was a monster just waiting to be unleashed. Once that sort of evil escapes from a box, it doesn't go back in."

I agree with her whole-heartedly on that. He's raped at least three people that we know of, and one of them was even a male.

"You boys want to stop a killer from hurting this town. But I just want those babies to finally have a voice. People are dying from holding in these secrets for so long."

"Who is Dev?"

"Devin Thomas. He's the judge's son," she says on autopilot.

As I stand, I look at her and recite the names we know, two of which are an uncertainty. "Tim Hoover. Chuck Cosby. Nathan Malone. Jeremy Hoyt. Ben Harris. Tyler Shane. Lawrence Martin. Anthony Smith. Kevin Taylor. Morgan Jones. Kyle Davenport."

She meets my gaze. "Jason Martin. He's Lawrence's cousin. He lives in South Carolina these days. Works as a real estate developer there. He was the twelfth."

"Thank you for sharing this."

"Just tell me you'll do more than hear it."

"I plan to," I tell her honestly.

Donny follows me to the door, and I turn around to face her one

All The Lies

last time. "How'd Victoria and Marcus's mother die?"

"Car crash," she says on a sigh. "A rich couple from a few towns over collided with her after they got drunk at a party. Their last name was Carlyle, I believe. They orphaned their own daughter with that wreck, and killed a damn good woman who was just trying to get home to her kids after a long day at the hospital."

It's like this family couldn't catch a break.

"Nurse?" I ask, though I don't know why I want to know.

"No. She was actually a coroner for the same hospital where the kids died. I figured that's one reason they also chose that one. Their mom was a loved woman with a lot of friends from there."

I nod in understanding, and we turn to leave.

"They worked in a pack mentality that night," Donny whispers as we step outside and shut the door.

"With Kyle as their most dominant alpha. It was more prison pack mentality, joining together so as not to be the odd one out."

"As young as fifteen, some of them," Donny growls.

"Adolescents are easier to manipulate and control. They looked up to the three—Lawrence, Morgan, and Kyle. But Kyle mostly called the shots. Someone that night would have butted heads, with their being so many alphas."

"Not that we'll know. Morgan and Lawrence are already dead."

"Devin. We need to find him."

"He left part of the way through it to lock up Lindy May. What if he came back and watched? How else would Diana have known the rest of the story?"

I purse my lips. I noted that too. But Diana never explained.

"Were we ever able to interview the ones on duty in the hospital the night the kids came in?" I ask Donny.

"No. It's been over ten years ago. We were lucky they were able to give us what they had."

"Why not tell someone there they were hurt?" I ask him.

He shrugs, every ounce of energy suddenly gone from him. I feel like I've been through the same emotional vacuum.

"I don't know, but I do know Johnson knew about this. Kyle was put into protective custody."

"We need more than one woman's word this all happened. She wasn't even an eye witness. And if we're taking on Johnson, then we're also taking on Director McEvoy. We're going to need solid evidence. In the meantime, we need to find out who else is a target and what really killed Robert Evans."

"I've never once in my career wondered if I was on the right side of the law. Until today," he says quietly.

Revenge killings always make us question our standing. "He won't stop just at the ones who killed the kids," I remind him.

"He opened some doors, but didn't touch anyone. He stole some mirrors, put some ink in some water and played with some paint. He could have already killed numerous people. But he hasn't."

"He's terrorizing them. It's his form of revenge against the whole town. He knows how their minds work. They've been drenched in ten years of guilt for knowing this and doing nothing. They believe something supernatural is really going on right now."

"Why do I feel like he's just getting started?" Donny asks as we get in the SUV.

"Why doesn't Kyle Davenport have the same surname as his father?" I ask.

He pulls up his iPad, reading something on it. "Says Jane Davenport was the mother. The sheriff didn't know Kyle even existed until Jane showed up in town one day with Kyle in tow, and she handed over custody."

My eyebrows go up. "What?"

He shakes his head, whistling low. "Hadley dug all this up

All The Lies

somehow. Kyle is one sick fuck. Started torturing and killing animals at the ripe age of five. By seven, his mother decided she couldn't handle him. He had a tantrum and cut her with a knife. She took him to the sheriff, who was all too happy to take away all her custodial rights, and she stayed in town, watching her son grow up from a distance. I bet her life was a living hell."

"Where is she now?"

His brow furrows. "Dead. She died ten years ago, shortly after the trial for Robert Evans started."

"Why do I feel like that's not a coincidence?" I groan.

"Because everything in this godforsaken town is tied to that nightmare somehow."

Just as I crank the car, I look up, seeing a flash of red. Quickly, I get back out, and I climb onto the hood of the SUV, reading the tops of the buildings in the distance. It's the town hall I see from here.

Written in red on the side of the roof is one message: *It is difficult to free fools from the chains they revere.*

Donny climbs up beside me, and he sucks in a long breath.

"First he quotes the bible and now Voltaire? What's the purpose?"

"No clue," I tell him as I hop down. "Even though I think it's pretty clear what the messages separate mean."

Just then, my head snaps to the speaker on the pole, because music starts filtering through it. *"Hush little baby, don't say a word. Momma's gonna buy you a mocking bird. And if that mocking bird don't sing, Momma's gonna buy you a diamond ring…"*

"That's not creepy at all," Donny says with a shudder as the nursery song plays on in a woman's voice.

Everyone in the street turns to stare at the speaker closest to them, all of them paling.

"You think he's going to cleanse the town?"

I tighten my lips. "He's showing a lot of control. I don't think he wants to cleanse, but I think he wants them to confess. He's here because we are. Otherwise, he'd have killed the last name on the list that isn't in this town. He came when we did."

"But why?"

"When I find out, I'll let you know," I tell him, driving away from the house that dropped a bomb on us I wasn't prepared for.

Chapter 2

To the wicked, everything serves as a pretext.
—Voltaire

Lana

"How's your dad?" I ask Jake as he walks around the room, hooking up a final monitor.

"He's taking the meds again. You know as well as I do how hurt his ego is that he's sick. But it's handled. Now we can focus on this."

I watch the look on Logan's face as he steps out of Diana's house, and I know she told him all she knew.

"I'll watch Diana's house, in case they make their move," Jake tells me, brushing my shoulder with his as he sits down beside me, his eyes flicking to the numerous monitors he has spread out on the walls of the old hunter's cabin.

The FBI came through, did a sweep of all these, and *then* Jake set up our temporary headquarters in his father's cabin that has been empty for years.

I nod appreciatively, but I can't take my eyes off Logan, seeing the pain in his eyes. Pain for a girl he never knew. Pain for a boy he'll never know. Pain for a past that has haunted me for ten years.

And he's not even finished getting all his details just yet. There's still more to learn.

"He'll find the evidence he needs, Lana. You're right about him. He's the real deal."

Too good of a man to be sullied by the dark thing I've become.

"I know he will. Then my father's name will be cleared — at least to the people in this town who condemned him."

"And Marcus will have his vengeance from the grave," he adds quietly, cueing the music that has everyone in town pausing almost immediately.

Only the ones too young to remember the sound of my mother's voice singing that song on the church stage are able to shrug it off. But everyone else is growing increasingly terrified.

Terrified of the dead coming back to haunt them.

"You ever wonder what we might have become if my father had never been convicted of those murders?" I ask him softly.

"No. Because if I start wondering, I'll never stop," he says without hesitation.

The musty smell of the cabin will have to be washed off me before I leave.

"I'm putting him in danger by letting him go on this egg hunt," I tell Jake as I turn up the volume on the monitor with the sheriff speaking.

"You have his back," Jake says, his lips twitching as we see the sheriff turning a precarious shade of white, hearing the music play through the speakers.

He remembers that night. The night my mother sung that song on the church stage for a very important play. Almost the entire town was there.

"It'd better be enough, Jake. If he gets hurt because of me, I'll fall over that edge, forget what this is all about, and kill without prejudice."

My hands shake just thinking of the monster I'd become if I lost my entire soul.

Jake's hand covers my trembling one, and he leans toward me. "I'll reel you back in."

I stare at him grimly. "If Logan is hurt because of me — or for any reason—you won't be enough."

I feel it when the tear escapes, and Jake tenses, seeing the single bit of wet proof of how vulnerable I am because of one man. His lips tighten.

"Then we'll both make sure he stays safe."

I wipe away the tear, and I return my attention to the panicking sheriff as he shuts and locks the door of the town hall, turning to face SSA Johnson.

"That's Jasmine Evans singing on that speaker," Sheriff Cannon hisses. "Unless a ghost has come back from the dead, you're missing something."

Then the sheriff turns to one of his deputies. "Kill that damned music! Find out how he got into our town speakers!"

Jake smirks. "Good luck with that, Sheriff. I dare you to out hack me," Jake says smugly.

This is the part he's been waiting for. The part where we show them what sheep they all really are. The part where we show them how weak their minds are.

The part where we fuck the whole town up.

"I told you this was not going to be easy," Johnson growls as the sheriff turns back to face him.

"Oh? Because I remember you saying you could control this team. So far, they've asked too many fucking questions, and they're hanging flyers all over my town. It's just a matter of time before someone gets the courage to talk."

Gotcha, you stupid bastard.

"Logan Bennett is your problem. The rest of the team, I can handle."

My gut clenches as dread unfolds in me. I'll fucking kill him before time if he goes after Logan. And I'll make an example out of anyone he sends.

"You sure you can get to Kyle without anyone figuring it out?" Jake asks me, his eyes trained on the screen too.

I don't answer, because I'm busy listening to what's being said.

"If he takes me down, you're coming with me. Remember that, Johnson," the sheriff snarls as he shuts the door to his office, giving them privacy.

Johnson narrows his eyes. "I never told you to go after those kids. This psychopath is targeting you because of them. He's not targeting you because of Evans. That sick fuck of a son you have needed a leash, and instead, you turned him loose, told him to do his worst. That team is here because you gave that monster free reign."

The sheriff's face twists in anguish, and Jake mutes all the other screens, focusing on this one with me. We knew the sheriff wasn't the original killer, but we never expected to see any remorse, because we profiled him as a sociopath.

"He's not sick. He was hurting. He saw his sister all spread out like that, brutally raped and murdered."

Johnson points a finger in his face. "I went along with Evans, because that cunt lawyer from New York got wind of his case and was already well on the road to proving the case was beyond biased. The trial was never supposed to be here, and too many jury members were affiliated with you. He would have gotten free, and my career would have been ended for all the strings I pulled. You have no idea what I had to do just to get on this case so I could clean up this mess. I gave you the real profile. Find the fucker who is killing your people before Bennett finds out what we buried."

I look to Jake, and he glares at the screen as I speak. "They're on edge."

"Right where we wanted them," Jake says quietly.

The Wheels on the Bus starts playing on the speakers, and one woman trips, falling to the ground as my mother's voice continues to echo through the town. The voices of so many children accompany her voice, making it a hair creepier. The music dies suddenly, and Jake's lips twitch as he studies something on his laptop.

"They unplugged it from the server."

"Just like we knew they would," I agree.

"When they plug them back in, it'll alert me. I'll start it over."

"Until they have no choice but to leave them unplugged, and no way of telling the town what's going on when the haunted house opens."

He nods slowly. "You ready for that?"

A dark grin etches the corners of my lips. "Very much."

Someone entering the sheriff's office has my attention. Chad Briggs steps in, wearing his deputy's uniform, and seals the door behind him. His eyes flick to Johnson, then he addresses the sheriff.

"Some information has come to light."

"Then spill it," Sheriff Cannon growls.

His eyes flick to Johnson again. "Some sensitive information."

He waves dismissively toward Johnson. "He's not the one from that group to worry about. What information?"

I can tell Briggs is hesitant, but he finally answers. "SSA Bennett and another agent were spotted leaving Diana Barnes's home. They were there a while, Sheriff, and I just got word that her son is untouchable right now. Staying with some lawyer in New York. I think she told them everything."

Sheriff Canon curses, running a hand through his hair as he tosses his hat across the room.

"Calm down," Johnson says, regaining his own composure. "That's just the ramblings of an old woman. He'd need proof. There is none. And most of the suspects involved are dead already, so it's not like they can confirm or deny. We need to focus more on making sure there's nothing left that could show what we did to Evans."

"There's nothing," Sheriff Cannon says, but my lips twitch.

"There's plenty," Jake says, grinning broadly. "You're just too stupid to know it, Sheriff."

And we have so much to share. When the time comes.

"Diana Barnes could become a problem if she gets someone to collaborate the story," I hear the Sheriff telling Johnson, then his gaze shifts to Chad Briggs. "See to it that isn't the case."

"They're going after Diana," Jake says as Chad nods and heads out of the room.

"Not until nightfall."

My eyes flick back to the screen where Logan is. I turn up the volume, though he's almost too far away from the camera for me to hear.

"The coroner died two years ago, so that's a bust," Donny is telling him.

"We need to visit the hospital where the kids went," Logan says, and my stomach sinks.

"Fuck," Jake hisses. "He shouldn't be focusing on you. He should be focusing on the corruption."

"If he goes there and pieces things together the way Hadley did, then we're screwed," I say quietly.

"It was fate that Kennedy was dying the same night you needed to survive," Jake says quietly. "And Kennedy Carlyle? The same girl who was the daughter of the drunk drivers who wrecked into your mom? There's no way that was all for nothing. There's no way that wasn't a sign. We're meant to do this. Not meant to get caught midway."

"We need someone to speak up and talk about my father," I murmur absently, watching Logan as he tears off his red tie, frustrated.

Jake stands and goes to the edge of the room, pulling out his wonderful creation of time releasing paint. They're all labeled differently, each one having a different timeframe for when the paint will appear.

"Then let's give them some incentive to talk," Jake says before tugging on his hood and walking toward the door. "Call me if you see anyone slip up on me. I'm going to the school. I'll disable the school cameras when I get there."

"Got you covered," I tell him.

The monitors surrounding us cover the entire town. It's like staring at hell all day.

"Lana needs to go back home." Logan's announcement has me shifting my gaze to his screen.

"Good luck telling Hadley that," Donny says with a grin.

"This isn't amusing. She could be in real danger. I knew better than to bring her."

He looks as though he's agonizing over this.

"No offense, but you're just too emotionally invested in her safety to see she's actually safe. Not one woman has been targeted. Only men. If anything, she's safer than you are."

"I don't trust the sheriff or Johnson right now. This has nothing to do with the Scarlet Slayer."

Donny's eyes widen, and so do mine.

"I sound so fucked up. I'm more concerned over two law officials than I am a fucking serial killer. This town is pure toxic," Logan says on a sigh.

"Johnson is twisted, but he's not an idiot. He knows he can't lay a hand on you and get away with it. We need to find some solid evidence to give to Collins so he can give it to the subcommittee."

"There's someone obvious we haven't spoken to since we acquired new evidence," Logan says thoughtfully. "He only lives about an hour from here."

"Christopher Denver," Donny says on an exhale. "Of course."

Jake's father. My father's lawyer. My father's only friend in a town of traitors.

We knew they'd get around to talking to him sometime.

My eyes pop over to the school screen, seeing Jake with his hood on as he takes quick strokes, hurrying the paintjob. Everyone is inside the school, and the windows are above his head, making it impossible to look out and see him.

I can't believe he's doing it in daylight right out front though. Fortunately, the streets are mostly quiet, and when he hears a car, he ducks behind the holly bushes.

Finally, I see Jake jogging around the side, heading into the woods that will spit him out right back here. My attention returns to Logan, and I focus solely on him.

"Who keeps calling?" Donny asks him as Logan silences his phone again.

"Johnson. I'm sure he's trying to find a way to throw us off this investigation. By now he's probably already heard we talked to Diana Barnes in private. He may be wanting to find out what we know."

"Let's go talk to Denver before he finds out what we're doing."

Logan glances at the time on his phone. "Okay, but I want to be back before it gets too late and make sure Lana is good."

"Call her from the road, lover boy," Donny says, rolling his eyes as Logan takes the driver's seat of the car. Logan seems to be laughing about it.

I can't hear what they're saying when they shut the doors, but I mute everything when my phone rings.

"Hey," I say, smiling like a little girl with a crush.

"I need to run out of town to work on a lead. Any chance you'd go back home? I don't like you being here."

I smile, loving the way he cares. My eyes flick to the screen where people are passing by the school, slowly gathering as the paint appears.

"I think Delaney Grove is growing on me."

He groans at the terrible joke.

"Logan, stop worrying. I'd rather be with you, or at least close to you, than sitting around wondering about you and if you're safe."

"It's not me I'm worried about, babe. I can take care of myself."

I can take care of you better.

My eyes move up as Elise and Leonard arrive on scene, taking pictures of the new message.

"Stop worrying about me. I doubt this guy even cares who I am."

He grows quiet for a long minute.

"Logan?"

"Sorry. Was just thinking about how you completely ruin psychology."

"How so?"

"Because you were attacked by a known serial killer because of my job, yet you stubbornly want to stay, acting as though the thought of another coming after you doesn't faze you."

I swallow hard. Never once has he sounded suspicious. Even now he sounds more confused than suspicious.

"I have a gun," I tell him softly. "And I don't want to be in my house."

I close my eyes, hating the fact the lie will make him feel guilt.

"Go back to the hotel."

"No," I say on a sigh.

"Shit. We'll resume this conversation later. Elise is beeping me."

"Love you," I say without hesitation, finding the words rolling off my tongue with natural ease.

"Love you." I can hear the smile in his voice even as someone makes gagging sounds in the background.

Just as I hang up with him, Jake walks in, eyeing me as I try to wipe the dopey look off my face.

"As soon as this is over, I'm going to find my own goofy grin," he grumbles, but the smile in his eyes betrays his Grinch-stole-Christmas tone. "Did I miss it?"

"Just getting started," I tell him, motioning to the wall of the school.

The lies we tell influences them. The present is pregnant with the future.

The message is getting a lot of pale faces as it finishes appearing like *magic*.

"Logan is leaving town, and the sun isn't too far from setting. I'm going to Diana's."

As I stand, Jake tosses up my knife, and I catch it by the handle as he takes my seat in front of the monitors.

"Stick to the sidewalks. The boots won't lie," he says, eyeing my girly combat boots that are fully equipped with blood red shoestrings.

Walking around with my weighted bags and my men's boots might be a little suspicious.

The cold has washed in, which is perfect. It makes wearing a hoodie less conspicuous. I nearly froze to death in my dress.

But I wanted to return home in style—wearing the color red.

"Lay out pillows in case she faints," he says as I walk out, and I smirk while taking the brisk walk, maneuvering the shortcuts through the buildings. The town is built like a circular maze, the roads getting wider as they circle the city. Town hall is directly in the center.

From the sky, it's amazingly beautiful.

All The Lies

It's only ugly when you're in the middle of it and can see the truth.

I walk around back to keep anyone from seeing me at the front, and I knock twice, checking over my shoulder to make sure no one is watching.

When Diana opens the door, my heart unexpectedly sputters. I thought I'd steeled myself against any emotion I might feel when I came here.

I blame Logan. He's tearing away the ice I put in place.

"Can I help you, hun?" she asks sweetly.

I push the hood back. "You could let me in."

Her eyes narrow, and her smile slips.

I feel like an ass for scaring her.

"Diana, I need to talk to you, and I know what you told them today."

"I'm sorry, dear. I think you should go," she says, closing the door.

My hand shoots out, and I shoulder my way in, feeling worse when she gasps and stumbles back, trembling.

She's on edge because she told the story no one else has had the balls to.

"Diana, I need you to sit down. I don't want you to get hurt, and I'm only here to keep you safe."

"Keep me safe?" she asks, confused as she looks over me, obviously convinced I'm not a match for anyone.

My hoodie hides my knife, but I decide not to show her the blade. She might actually faint.

"Once upon a time you loved a little girl. You betrayed her to save your son. Today, you finally stood up for her and gave her a chance to be heard."

Tears waver in her eyes as she takes another step back.

"Who are you?" she whispers, emotion riddling her voice.

Adjusting the knife under the hoodie to go to the back of my pants, I pull up the front of my shirt, revealing the scars I've hidden for too long.

Her eyes drop to my stomach, and she takes another step back.

"I'm that little girl."

When she hits the ground, I catch her head just in time. Jake was right. I should have put down pillows.

"Well, shit," I say to the woman who has fainted.

I can practically hear Jake saying, "I told you so," in my head.

Chapter 3

Every man is guilty of all the good he did not do.
—Voltaire

Logan

"Thanks for meeting with us, Mr. Denver," I say to the man who hands us both a cup of coffee.

"I'm here to help in any way I can." He studies us like he expects us to be on the wrong side of the law, as though he's waiting for us to trick him.

It makes me hate Johnson even more.

"We're hoping you can shed some light on what happened to Robert Evans."

He grimaces. "It should all be on record. I'm sure the FBI has access to all that."

"All murder trials are usually taped, but this one wasn't."

"It was," he argues. He stands and goes to his bookcase, and he pulls out a book. When he opens the book and grabs a DVD, Donny raises his eyebrows at me.

Christopher Denver brings us the DVD, and he hands it to me.

"You can keep that. I have others."

"The file stated it wasn't filmed."

"It was," he states simply.

I blow out a long breath. "I realize the FBI are probably not on your list of people to trust, but I can assure you that the two of us are looking for real answers."

"Because of the Scarlet Slayer," he says simply.

I cock my head, studying him. He has alibis, so he can't be our guy.

"That's part of what led us there, yes. But also because we feel as though the case might have been mishandled."

He snorts derisively, and I arch an eyebrow at him.

"Sorry. I'm just not used to such understatements being made with true sincerity."

Donny leans back, and I sip my coffee, looking around the house. His walls are mostly bare, other than several achievements from his son and from him.

"We spoke with Jacob as well. He wouldn't give us any information," I say, watching his face.

He remains impassive, years of courtroom training teaching him to school his features.

"My son was broken that night. The boy he loved was killed, and the girl he adored as his own sister died as well. And it was reported as a car accident. He completely withdrew from the world after that night. I struggle to even get him to come here for the holidays now. Although he came to visit recently due to a personal matter."

I want to pry, but doubt he'd tell us why Jacob came to visit.

"Why didn't you tell us about Victoria and Marcus if you knew?" I ask instead.

"Because you would have went after my son, of course. He was the closest to them, other than the Barnes boy. But a NFL football star is less likely to be a suspect."

Just telling us his son was paralyzed would have been good enough. But it's like he almost doesn't want to say that.

"You don't even mind giving us that information, do you?"

Donny asks him.

"That I wanted to keep my son safe from corrupt bureaucrats cleaning up a mess they helped make? Not at all. There was no obstruction of justice, considering this story was squashed by one of your own when my son tried to tell it. My silence in no way interfered with your investigation of this Scarlet Slayer."

"Only it did," I tell him.

He looks just like Jacob, only an older version of him. Dark hair barely dusted by time, and fine wrinkles that almost look intentional.

"How is that, SSA Bennett?"

"The unsub we're looking for is working off a list of the rapists involved that night."

I see the surprise in his eyes. He's genuinely caught off guard by that admission.

"What can you tell us about Robert Evans? And this time, hold nothing back."

He clears his throat, probably not used to being surprised.

"Robert Evans was a brilliant man with no ambition to be more than a janitor. The pay was good enough, and he enjoyed the hours because it gave him more time with his kids."

He sighs long and hard.

"I worked too much. Jacob spent more time there than he did at home. I never even knew he was in love with Marcus until years after the boy's death. He told me everything one night, broke down right there on that couch, told me how much he hated the whole town. Then he felt like he was being punished when he was put in a wheelchair."

He's telling us about Jacob and not Robert, speaking of his shortcomings. That's the tell of a regretful father I've heard too often in cases where they've lost a child. Never a case where the son is still alive.

"Robert was a simple man, who never caused problems. But he painted himself an easy target for the sheriff who just wanted someone to pay for his daughter's death. Didn't matter if he was innocent. Didn't matter if he had an alibi. Nothing mattered except one man's revenge. Robert Evans was the most unlucky soul I ever knew."

"Why do you say that?" Donny asks, though it should be obvious.

"He lost the love of his life to two rich drunks. Both her parents and his parents had passed already, leaving him with no help to care for his kids. He lost his life because of being in the wrong place at the wrong time. And his kids were murdered for crimes he never committed. Don't see how you can get unluckier than that."

Donny clears his throat and loosens his tie. Every time we hear more about the Evans family, we become a little more invested. It's probably the most heartbreaking shit I've heard.

"What happened after the trial?"

"The trial that shouldn't have happened in a town as small as Delaney Grove?" he asks bitterly. "A trial that shouldn't have happened with a biased judge ruling? Do you realize he could have gotten an appeal with little effort?"

We both nod, deciding to hold our silence as he reins in his temper.

"I don't know what they did to him. All I know is he sure as hell didn't hang himself. He'd already had Hannah Monroe contact him, offering to take his case on appeal and wave her fee. She was going to ruin Delaney Grove."

"What happened to her?" I ask.

"She's still a hotshot in Manhattan. After he was dead, she moved on, as the sharks in that city tend to do."

I pick my phone up, and I press play on the recording I made.

"Hush little baby," are the first words that play aloud. It's the same recording from the speakers that took forever to shut up.

His breath catches, and he stares at the phone with an almost unreadable look. Finally, he peers back up, his lips tense.

"That's Jasmine."

"Jasmine?" Donny asks.

"Jasmine Evans."

He stands and grabs another DVD, this one lying in plain sight. He has several that look to be burned at home, all labeled.

When he returns, he hands it to me.

"It's from that play the year before she died. Everyone in the town was there. Both Evans kids were in it as well. Robert too. It was a big deal to the town, because it was the Founder's Day play. It was the last year the town celebrated it."

"Why?"

"The sheriff cancelled it the next year because of something that happened with some of his deputies. The year after that, he didn't reinstate it. Same for the next. Soon it was a forgotten tradition."

"What happened?" I ask, even though I shouldn't have to.

He leans forward, looking me right in the eye. "The same thing that always happens when you have a bunch of men too close to power. They think the sheriff is invincible, and by proxy, so are they. I could give you a list of indiscretions a mile long, but on that particular day, it was a fire that was set. The deputies burned a house down with two people in it because they wouldn't sell their property for the new town restaurant—a restaurant the sheriff put in after their untimely deaths."

"What happened to the deputies?" Donny asks.

"Chad Briggs and his brother still work there. Founder's day was cancelled. Deputies were not reprimanded. The fire was ruled as an accident. It was the catalyst into the corruption that only got worse. The people realized they had to do as ordered, or suffer the consequences. Soon, people just learned to pretend as though Delaney Grove was the sweet little hometown the rest of the world thought it was."

"That's why our unsub is using that music," I say quietly to Donny.

"I'm sorry, what was that?" Christopher Denver asks, expecting me to say it again a little louder.

"What did they do to Robert Evans?" I ask instead of answering him.

"You want those answers, you need to talk to someone who knows. That town wasn't exactly sharing dirty secrets with the one man who tried to defend him."

He leans back in his chair, studying us.

"Can you at least point us in the right direction?" Donny asks. "Tell us the name of someone who will talk?"

"I could tell you someone who would break easily if you leaned on him. But what good will it do to know?"

"Excuse me?" I ask.

He leans back up, his eyes narrowing. "You can hear all the stories you want. Eye witness testimonies mean dick against an entire police force and a judge. They mean even less when those witnesses disappear or decide to recant their statements."

"We'll find evidence," I say, determined to put an end to this.

I called Collins. He told me the words of an old lady who didn't even see all the corruption first hand won't be enough to put the director or Johnson off this case. Then again, I already knew that.

My eyes flick to the console table near the window. There's a tray of medicines there, and I look back to Denver. "Are you okay?"

His lips tense, and he darts a glance to the tray. "I've been sick for several months. Some days are better than others. You're catching me on a good day," he says, then grimaces. "I always hoped I'd have the chance to get my best friend some justice. The doctors aren't even sure what exactly is wrong with me. Sometimes I think it's my punishment for not getting Robert's story out there where it could be heard better."

"Then help us now, Mr. Denver," I say softly, hating that I'm using a sick man's guilty conscious against him, but desperate enough to do it all the same.

He studies me for a long moment before I see the concession in his eyes, deciding he has no choice but to trust me and hope for the best.

"Carl Burrows. He used to work at the coroner's office."

"Thank you for your time, Mr. Denver," I say as Donny and I stand, then hand him my card, which he takes. "Call us if you think of anything else."

Just as we reach the door, he says, "They say the Scarlet Slayer paints a wall in red."

I turn, looking back at him as he slowly faces us.

"That's not something we've shared with the public," I tell him, narrowing my eyes.

"You don't have to share it. I'm from Delaney Grove. Those rumors of these deaths were spreading like fire before you ever announced the killer's existence."

I take a step toward him.

"You know what it means?"

He nods slowly. "Before Victoria died, she spoke to my son. Told him they'd painted the streets with their blood. Marcus wanted to paint the world with theirs."

"Who else did your son tell that to?"

He shrugs. "Anyone who would listen, SSA Bennett. If Victoria had lived, she would have come back. She'd be this Scarlet Slayer you're looking for. That girl's fire always burned hotter and fiercer than anyone else's."

"But Victoria Evans died," I tell him, pursing my lips. "And this killer is most definitely a man."

He nods. "I'm aware. Not even Victoria would be able to have physically taken these men down."

Then why even mention it?

He doesn't stop us as we walk out, and Donny sidles up next to me.

"Besides Kyle, Victoria never really dated, and no one even knew Jacob ever dated Marcus," Donny tells me, reading a text from Elise.

"Jacob wasn't out about being bisexual when he lived in Delaney Grove, so that last part isn't surprising," I say absently.

"Are we going to see Carl Burrows?"

"Yeah. I just want to stop in by the cabins and check on Lana first."

Chapter 4

History is only the register of crimes and misfortune.
—Voltaire

Lana

For the past hour and a half since she woke up, Diana has been staring blankly, looking into my eyes to see if I still have a soul. I wonder what she sees in there besides a dark abyss.

"I can't believe it's really you," she whispers hoarsely, though it's about all she's said since I explained the morbid reality surrounding us.

"They're going to come for you," I tell her, watching the cameras from my phone, flipping between different ones nearest to us.

I expected them to come as soon as it was nightfall. Their specialty is suffocating or strangling. Then they lie and say it was a heart attack when someone is Diana's age. They call it a seizure or something when they're younger.

"And you're going to just kill them?" she asks in disbelief, her voice breaking. "Oh, baby. You shouldn't be scarring your soul with their blood. You should be living the life you almost didn't have."

Coldly, I lift my gaze to meet her teary eyes. "They took *everything*, Diana. My brother and father still need peace. Do you remember Marcus? Do you remember the kind, bright soul that always sought to bring forth a smile from a stranger just to put more good vibes out into the universe? Do you remember what they did to him? Because I can't ever forget it."

She bats away her tears. "I remember." Her voice is barely a rasp by now, but I feel no emotion clogging my throat. I've trained against it. The one moment of unexpected emotion when I saw her has passed, and I'm back in control.

I'm cold.

I'm detached.

I'm the killer right now.

"Confucius said something about digging two graves if you seek revenge. I know your momma always quoted that man."

"Confucius was never brutally raped, stabbed, and forced to watch his brother suffer even worse. I'm sure his viewpoints might have changed. Besides, he wasn't a romantic."

She makes a strangled sound, and I glance back to see her choking back her sobs, as though the image I painted was just too much. She knows the details, but seeing me…*hearing* me confirm the tale… It's hurting her.

However, her morals are still intact.

For now.

"They tried to force Marcus to fuck me," I say with a deadly edge. "And when he refused, they cut off his—"

A beep sounds from my phone, cutting off my words as the silent alert that someone is near our cabins goes off. It could be one of the team members again, but I still check it.

My eyes catch Justin Hollis—a deputy on my list—walking briskly toward the basketball court near the back. It's close to our cabin.

When he steps into the shadows, I cock my head.

I call Jake, putting him on speaker so I can still work the app, and start rewinding the screen, flipping to the next when he's out of view, following his path through several cameras.

"What's up?" Jake asks. "Diana faint?"

All The Lies

Diana's eyes widen when she hears his voice. "Yeah, but she's okay. Justin Hollis is squatting near my cabin. What's up with that?"

He grows quiet for a minute. "I don't know. I had to silence everything earlier. They came to check the cabins again, but didn't come in this time. I just hid, and kept the windows covered. They peered through the one window that shows the kitchen but gives no visibility to everything else."

"I'm trying to track his steps back, but it's taking too long from my phone."

"On it," I hear him saying, and I wait impatiently, my eyes lifting to Diana's again.

She looks as though her world has been turned upside down, and she clutches the bible in her hand. In her mind, there's time to save me, to stop me from tarnishing the rest of my soul with the blood on my hands.

"Found it," he says, then I hear the volume crank up in the background.

The phone is still on speaker, so Diana hears it as well.

"Sheriff said Diana, not them," Justin is growling.

Chad Briggs has a smirk in his tone. "Killing Diana is like killing an ant. More ants are going to come into your house. But if you kill the queen…"

Justin doesn't sound thrilled. "Kill the queen, and the ants disappear."

Who the fuck is the queen?

My eyes flick up to see Diana's wide, horrified gaze. Hearing they want her dead from my lips seems less impactful than hearing it straight from the jaws of the devils themselves.

"Sheriff ain't gonna be happy about this," Justin grumbles.

"Sheriff ain't the only one at stake here. We all need to worry about these guys figuring out the truth. You think you're ready for prison."

"Sheriff can handle this. He's handled all the other things," Justin argues.

I wish I could see the video, examine their expressions, but I don't want Jake to face-time me right now, because he'd have to pause all this.

"He ain't ever handled someone who isn't afraid of him. But if we take out their leader, the others will fall in line. They always do. You cut a head off a snake to end it. You don't just cut off one rat from its food supply."

My stomach plummets like a rocket as I slowly stand to my feet.

"How do we do this?" Justin asks, his voice more determined now that Chad has convinced him this is the answer to all their problems.

"Simple. Block off the road to the cabins. Wait at the courts. It'll give you the element of surprise, and it's just far enough away that the others will never hear or see you if they come back before you finish it."

My heartbeat slams into my throat, and I grab my hood, jerking it over my head as I head toward the backdoor, taking long, quick strides. "They're going after Logan," I tell Jake, panic inching up my spine with paralyzing force.

"Look at camera thirteen," he says quietly.

I pull up the app, and my feet lock into place as I see Logan being detoured by the roadblocks.

Almost immediately, I break into a sprint, tossing my phone into my back pocket, as I use every burst of speed inside me, my adrenaline making me run even faster.

The whole town will bleed if I'm too late.

The whole fucking town will scream for me.

Chapter 5

It is the flash that appears; the thunderbolt will follow.
—Voltaire

Logan

"I'll run in and see if Craig has anything while you're checking on—"

Donny's words end on a grunt, and I turn around, confused as to why he just stopped talking. When I see him on the hard court, a little blood running from his mouth as he lies there unconscious, I grab for my gun too late.

Something hard slams into my head, and I fall forward, disoriented and dizzy, as I crash into the unforgiving pavement below me. My stomach pitches, and my head gains thirty pounds as I try to black out, fighting hard to stay conscious.

A blur of a man's silhouette steps into my vision, the moonlight not favoring me enough to show me his face. At least not until he kneels down and smiles at me.

Deputy Justin Hollis.

"You boys just can't learn to leave well enough alone, now can you?" he taunts, grabbing my gun from my hip.

Weakly, I try to fight for it, but my hands aren't cooperating, and the world is still spinning around me. It feels like gravity has waged a war against my body, pinning me down.

As I struggle up to my hands and knees, Hollis laughs, kicking me in the stomach, sending me spiraling down on my back as my stomach heaves.

I shake my head as his laughter echoes back and forth in my mind, sounding like it's coming from everywhere at once.

"Big bad Supervisory Special Agent Bennett. You don't look so threatening to me. Even the sheriff was worried about you."

The distinct sound of my gun being cocked registers, echoing from all over like his laughter. But before the gunshot can come, I hear a sharp intake of air and a pained yelp escape from him.

The gun falls, rattling somewhere in the distance, and my blurry eyes look up to see Hollis's head snapping back as a figure clad in all black becomes a blurring fury of motion.

My head is too groggy, making the scene nothing but a distorted movie in front of me. The black-clad figure spins, shooting a foot out to the deputy's chest. Hollis cries out, crashing to the ground. And the figure comes down on top of him, raining punches on his face.

Even the hands are clad in all black, so I can barely see what he's doing.

Until he pulls out a knife, holding it at his side.

He leans forward, and I watch as his head comes down next to Hollis's. Hollis cries out as the knife plunges into his side. And I see as the figure leans back up, staring down at him as he thrusts the knife inside Hollis's chest while straddling him.

He twists the knife as Hollis screams, and I hear almost a delicate, feminine laughter floating through the air.

The knife stays in Hollis's chest as the figure stands, and Hollis gurgles on blood, trying to speak. I sway on my side, trying to push back up before he can come for me.

But I see him bent over. He's small. Very small. And as my vision clears just barely, I notice the small set of shoulders and very small frame.

Small. Small. Small.

All The Lies

That word just keeps replaying as the figure leans down and dips its finger into Hollis's blood that is rushing from his chest. I can't see what the figure is doing in its crouched position, but when it stands, it grabs the knife from Hollis's chest, and then it throws it right into his groin.

One last pained sound escapes Hollis, and the unsub grabs the knife before walking away, disappearing from my sight.

I limply grab for my phone, struggling to form a grip around it when I finally find it. It falls to the ground, tumbling from my uncooperative fingers. My eyes close and open for who knows how long, before suddenly there's a familiar face in front of me.

"Logan! He's over here!" I hear her calling out, cupping my face.

"Run," I whisper. "Run."

Her face is barely visible through the blur, but I can smell her, feel her, and know it's her by the way she touches me.

"I'm not going anywhere," Lana says, checking something on my head.

"Here!" she shouts again to some echo in the distance.

"Logan!" Craig's voice is barely recognizable through the veil of white noise surrounding me. "Get an ambulance out here now."

"Donny!" someone shouts, but Lana never leaves my side.

My head is in her lap, and she's barking out orders, asking me questions too fast for me to answer them.

My eyes finally close as she shouts my name one last time.

Too many thoughts are going through my mind as I play the scene on repeat, trying to piece it all together.

It's not a man who just saved my life.

It wasn't a beast at all.

It was a woman.

Chapter 6

Doubt is not a pleasant condition, but certainty is absurd.
—Voltaire

Logan

"It couldn't have been a woman," Donny argues as I wince, sitting up from the ER bed.

He's sitting down, holding an icepack to his own jaw. He was hit across the side of the face with the bat Hollis used to attack us.

"I agree with him," Elise says on a sigh. "A woman would have gone for the gun. Not used the knife. And by the way, the sheriff is playing this like Hollis was acting on his own accord, and Johnson is backing him, saying they'd already discussed his possible discord with you being here. The director, of course, is saying it sounds like this is one man's actions, and that we're safe. He's still trying to cover this up, even at the cost of our lives."

She's furious, and should be.

Lisa clutches my arm from my bedside, easing closer as she brushes her fingers over my cheek. "We're going to find out if that's the truth," she promises.

I jerk away from her touch, and look to the doorway where Lana is standing with Craig. Lisa's hand falls away completely as Lana glares icy daggers at her, then her gaze softens as she meets my eyes.

She stays on the other side of the room, and my stomach tightens. She had to see all that. She's probably been scared out of her mind.

Craig gauges our silence, and decides to break it. "Our Scarlet Slayer is who saved you," Craig announces, freezing the blood in my veins.

Hadley stands, going to Lana as my girl's gaze returns to Lisa. My still groggy head is struggling to keep up with everything going on.

As Hadley whispers into Lana's ear, Craig's words register.

"What?"

He nods. "It's confirmed. He even left a message."

He hands me his phone, zooming in on the image for me.

Touch him again, and I'll burn the town to the ground with everyone still in it.

"He used the blood of Justin Hollis to write it," Leonard says from the corner, studying me, his eyes flicking over to Lana, then back to me again.

"The fucking hell?" I ask, confused.

"He's protective of us," Craig says on a sigh. "First Hadley, now you and Donny."

"In short, one of the deputies attacked you, and you were saved by a ruthless serial killer who gets off on being stabby," Elise quips.

I look back at Lana, motioning for her to come to me. She looks hesitant at first, but she finally makes her way to me with slow, measured steps. As soon as she's close enough, my arms go around her waist, and she shakes in my grip, her body trembling as she buries her face in my neck.

"You have to go home," I say softly, squeezing her tighter. "If the sheriff is bold enough to come after me, he'll come after you too."

"Unlikely," Leonard says, watching us with a curious expression. "She's actually probably safer here than at home, where Johnson could use her against you. He's not brilliant, but he's smart enough by now to have figured out your attachment is deep."

And again, my job is putting her at risk.

Lana keeps her arms around me and her face in my neck, her grip tightly digging into my back.

She'd have been so much better off if I'd never come into her life.

It's like we've been cursed from the very beginning.

"I need to go check on something," Leonard says, walking out of the room.

"Could the rest of you give us a minute?" I ask, looking around at everyone.

"No," Hadley says with a shrug. "It's too dangerous. Deputy Director Collins may not see how things have escalated, but we do. We're taking turns watching you."

"Leonard just walked out alone," I point out. "I doubt I'm the only target."

"You're the primary," Hadley says immediately. "You're the one with the power to stand up to Johnson. He outranks us all, but he's even with you. Collins had to make a damn good case just to send you along and not let the director bulldoze this case completely."

Hadley's pissed. Lana is shaking. Everyone in here is on edge and uneasy.

A serial killer had to save me from a sheriff's deputy. The world is officially upside down.

Lana kisses the side of my neck, a chaste show of affection as she blows out a long breath.

"And we're in the sheriff's hospital," Lana says quietly.

"I've checked everything they've done before they've done it, just to make sure no nurse or doctor tries to do anything really fucking stupid," Hadley says with a twisted smirk.

My head hurts.

All The Lies

A lot.

Lana pulls back, wiping her eyes quickly before I can see if there's a tear there. She didn't even cry the day after her attack by the Boogeyman.

She clears her throat as Leonard walks back in, and his eyes zero in on her face that is definitely blotchy with tears. I need out of here and time alone with her.

I stand, still feeling a little unsteady. Lana and Donny crash to my side, and they help keep me upright as Leonard walks out and comes back in with a wheelchair.

"Just until you get to the car," Leonard says with a smile when I glare at him.

Not feeling quite up to arguing or leaning on my girlfriend all the way down, I reluctantly accept the chair. Leonard wheels me to the elevator. As soon as we emerge into the lobby, a SUV pulls up with Hadley behind the wheel.

I'm so loopy, that I don't know how long it took her to get here or how she got by us.

We ride in relative silence back to the cabins, and Leonard deals with the calls from the hospital about us leaving too soon. No one argued leaving, considering it might have just been a matter of time before they took me out and made it look like an accident.

"Two per cabin. Take shifts staying awake," Donny says, taking charge while I'm in and out of it, as we arrive at the cabin and start unloading from the SUV.

"I'll stay with Lana and Logan," Leonard inserts.

"I'll stay with them," Hadley argues.

Leonard points his finger at Hadley. "You stay with Elise. I'll stay with them. Logan, sober, wouldn't want you risking yourself, and as you pointed out, he's the primary target."

She starts to argue, but I cut her off. "Go with Elise," I tell her.

She claps her lips shut, then looks to Lana. Something silent passes between them, and Hadley walks away, glaring at Leonard on her way by.

Leonard helps me inside, and Lana tries to help him. I force most of my weight onto Leonard.

"If he gets sick or starts talking funny, come find me immediately," Leonard tells Lana as they put me to bed like a fucking baby.

"I will," she says softly, her eyes distant as she runs her hand over my face.

"I'll stay up until sunrise, then I'll get some sleep. You stay in here with him, and yell if you need help." He points at the windows in the room. "Two entry points from outside. Pay attention to them in case they get too bold. Don't be afraid to use Logan's gun."

He puts my gun down on the nightstand, and Lana studies it.

She nods absently, her hand still on me, as though she needs reassurance I haven't disappeared.

"Keep me updated if any new information comes to light," I tell Leonard before he walks out.

Lana curls up against me, putting her arm around my waist. Leonard's eyes drop to her as she slides her leg around me too. I have no idea why he finds her so fascinating tonight.

"I will. Tomorrow, anyway. Not tonight. Your head needs some rest."

As soon as he shuts the door, Lana exhales heavily, and I pounce.

"I'm sorry you had to get entangled in all this again. I want you to go somewhere safe," I tell her, kissing the top of her head as she snuggles in even closer.

"No," she states simply. "I'm not leaving you."

"You have to. If you—"

"Either I stay here with you, or I find somewhere else to stay in town. Your choice," she says firmly, a hint of anger in her tone.

"Lana, I just want to keep—"

"There's no such thing as safe, Logan," she says on a soft breath. "No such thing."

I'm too out of it to continue arguing, and my eyes shut without my permission. I'll argue tomorrow.

Chapter 7

My life is a struggle.
—Voltaire

Lana

Leonard's eyes are on me, just as they have been since last night. He watches me make two cups of coffee, and he watches me fix the cups with cream.

"You want a cup?" I ask the watcher.

"I've already made some, but thanks for the offer."

At first I thought he was suspicious, then he left me alone in the room with Logan and also left me with a gun. Then I thought he was a perv, but he turned away abruptly when he walked in the room this morning to check on Logan and saw me in my panties.

So I don't know why he's watching.

Unless I'm just that fucking interesting.

"So you and Logan are pretty serious, yeah?" he asks, lifting the cup of coffee he's drinking. I'm not sure why he's not crashing. The sun has just peeked out, and he's been up all night.

"I think so. At least, I'm serious."

"You don't think he is?"

I need to learn when to shut up.

"I think he is," I say with a tight smile as I turn to face Mr. Watch Me.

He runs a finger over his lips in a pensive manner. "Any family in the DC area?"

I shake my head and return to my task, stirring both coffees.

"Any family at all?"

I shake my head again.

"This is making you uncomfortable, isn't it?"

"No. As an extremely private person, I love talking to a stranger about my past first thing in the morning after my boyfriend was attacked in a town full of weak and evil people," I state dryly, holding his gaze.

His eyes widen marginally. "Sorry. Just making conversation. None of us have great conversational skills. Occupational hazard."

I shrug it off. "Logan was the same when we first met."

"He stopped pressing for your past? As I said, it's an occupational hazard."

Have I mentioned I hate nosy people?

"I told him the important parts. Not everyone enjoys talking about the past," I say with a shrug. "I've told him more than anyone in years. But he doesn't push for more than I give. It's one of the things I love about him."

We stare each other for several uncomfortable minutes. I'm not sure what he's trying to see.

"Hey." Logan's voice has us both jerking our heads to the bedroom doorway where he's shirtless and moving toward me. His eyes flick to Leonard. "Anything happen while we were out?"

Leonard shakes his head. "All was ghost-town quiet. The sheriff is standing by his promise that Hollis was a bad seed who acted alone, and that he has no idea what set him off. Johnson says he's already vetted the rest of the guys, ensuring us none of them are hostile toward our team." Leonard rolls his eyes.

"Amazing. He managed to vet over twenty other deputies since last night, not to mention an extra five police officers," Logan says with no emotion, but a definite suspicious lilt.

"This is the most fucked up shit I've been involved in," Leonard says, his jaw ticking.

"Leave Donny with Lisa today. You ride with me. I'm going to go find Carl Burrows today and get some answers about Robert Evans."

The glass in my hand almost slips, and I curse as coffee sloshes over, scalding my fingers.

Logan grabs some paper towels, and he brings my wounded hand to his face, inspecting it. I feel Leonard's eyes on us, but I ignore it. I don't know or care what his defect is.

My heart almost thudded out of my chest as I raced through the town last night, running faster than I ever have. When I saw Hollis training Logan's own gun on him, something inside me snapped. The killer came out and reveled in spilling his blood even more than I enjoyed killing Lawrence and Tyler.

If Logan hadn't been hurt, I would have dragged the kill out for days.

"Haunted House is tonight in town," Leonard says randomly as Logan kisses my fingers where the coffee burn has already ebbed.

"And?" Logan asks, looking over.

"And Kyle Davenport will be there. Says he 'ain't missing the only good thing in this fucking town because of some cowardly piece of shit killer.' His words."

Leonard shrugs, his eyes now not on me for a change.

I knew Kyle wouldn't miss the Haunted House. He always takes a girl in there—whether she wants to be there or not—and fucks her in a corner to the sound of screams that get him off.

He's sick like that. It's one of the things that should have given him away long ago, but I didn't see it until it was too late and I was a victim. People just walk by, thinking it's all part of the 'adult' show of the Haunted House. It's the 'Sin House' after all. It's set up to show all the sins in the dark, demented world just outside the lines of Delaney Grove.

They condition kids to be afraid of leaving early on. The adult house is for sixteen and older, terrifying the impressionable minds from early on isn't enough. They need to get the rebellious teens submitting to the terror tenfold, upping the Haunted House to be over-the-top. Rape scenes are even played out. Sometimes they were real.

Lindy was raped in the Haunted House.

Speaking of Lindy, Antonio is already bankrupt, which was faster than promised. She'll be happy to know he's currently losing all his possessions. His car was taken away just yesterday. I got to watch it live on my phone.

The man who called his wife a whore, even though he knew all Kyle was saying was a lie, is finally getting his piece of justice pie. He just wanted to continue to be a 'highly respected' patron of this town, and he cast his wife aside to suffer alone.

Now it's just a waiting game of making his life miserable enough to kill himself.

"He's a stupid fuck," Logan mumbles, running his lips over my forehead. It takes me a second to realize he's talking about Kyle.

"I agree. But the sheriff is sending four deputies with him. Just letting you know," Leonard says, but his eyes shift to me for an eerily long second.

I ignore his eyes like I have all morning.

Four deputies? Only two will go in with him. Those can be easily dispatched — well, as long as those two are on my kill list. So far, there's only one deputy who is innocent of the crimes committed ten years ago, and then the two dispatch officers.

The other two deputies will be outside, watching for any suspicious *man*. They'll never know.

"Grab some sleep. We'll go see Carl when you've had some rest," Logan tells Leonard, snapping me out of my thoughts.

"I'll only need about three hours," Leonard grunts as he stands.

While he's leaving us, I study Logan's temple where he has four stitches.

Logan doesn't say anything else before his lips come down on mine, surprising me with an intense, deep, bone-crumbling kiss. I lean into him as he lifts me up, putting me on the counter. When he steps in between my legs, I spread them wider in invitation.

Someone knocks on the door, and our kiss is broken, leaving both of us panting as I put my forehead on his chest.

"Yeah?" Logan calls out, staying put where he is.

"Just making sure you're okay," Lisa says through the door. "I have coffee if you want to unlock the door."

She really wants to be cut.

"I've got coffee, and I'm fine. Thanks," Logan says shortly before kissing me again, pulling me to him by my hips.

I break the kiss as Lisa knocks again, but I ignore her calling his name.

"Are you really okay?" I ask him, ignoring the pang of panic for how close I was to being too late.

"Yes," he says softly, brushing his lips over mine. "Go away, Lisa," he adds louder.

She huffs loud enough to be heard, but Logan lifts me, carrying me to the bedroom again. Our room is right beside where Leonard is trying to sleep, so I aim for quiet when Logan puts me down on the bed.

I hiss out a breath when he starts tugging my shorts off me.

"Leonard is—"

"Already snoring by now. He sleeps like the dead, and won't hear a thing."

I grin against his lips when he kisses me again, and my shorts fall off my legs. I keep kissing him even as he basically tears my panties away. And our lips remain fused together when he finally thrusts in, taking me slowly, longingly, and reminding me how much I love him.

"I love you," I whisper into the air so quietly that I don't think he hears it.

I just hope our love is truly strong enough to conquer all.

Sweaty and breathless, he thrusts in over and over, and I claw his skin, holding onto him, needing every second of closeness I can drag out. Our lips clash, unable to find a rhythm for a smooth kiss, and he pumps his hips harder, hitting that spot inside me that sends me spiraling and has me calling out his name.

When his hips still, he nuzzles the side of my face, shuddering as he finds his own release.

"I love everything about you," he says softly, brushing his lips over my jaw.

Grinning, I hurry to the bathroom to clean up, and he slaps my ass on my way. I'm slowly calming down now that he seems okay.

As I exit the bathroom, the faint music of a familiar song and the distinct voice of a too familiar woman hits me like a ton of bricks.

Hush little baby, don't say a word. Momma's gonna buy you a mocking bird.

I turn the corner, looking in on the living room as Logan studies the TV, and tears fill my eyes as my heart plummets to my toes. My mother's smiling face is on the screen. She's happy, oblivious to the harsh future ahead.

I remember this night so clearly. She died before she could see how bad this town got.

And if that mocking bird don't sing, Momma's gonna buy you a diamond ring.

She pulls out a gaudy piece of costume jewelry that resembles a diamond ring, and hands it to the young girl at her side. The young girl with bright green eyes and a little tremor in her hand, because she's on stage and scared. But the girl's mother soothes her, cupping her chin, making the child focus only on her and not the audience.

And if that diamond ring don't shine —

The video pauses, and my heart stutters in my chest as Logan swings his gaze to me.

"You okay?" he asks, studying me with a frown.

Clearing my throat, I nod. "Yeah," I say hoarsely, hearing the strain in my tone. "Who's that?"

I point to the frozen screen with my mother's smiling face.

"Jasmine Evans. I'm trying to see anyone in the audience who might have been more enamored than anyone else, since the unsub is using this night to terrorize the town."

He looks back at the screen, presses play, and I watch my mother sing to the young, innocent child I used to be. I'm smiling up at her on the screen now, no longer aware of all the eyes from the audience. She could do that—soothe me with just her eyes.

A tear trickles down my cheek when she bends, kissing my forehead in the old film. She was the best at this role. It was the same play every year, and my mother spent three of those years on that stage because people were entranced by her voice and emotion.

She should have been an actress and spread the same love and joy throughout the world with just her smile.

I used to want to be just like her.

Until them.

Until they ruined me and turned me into this.

The mirror still shows the same eyes, but all else is different. It's like seeing a different person. A person who has devoted her life to real justice.

"The film just stays focused on her. I can't seem to get a view of the audience," Logan says, interrupting my thoughts as he fast-forwards through the footage of my better memories.

All The Lies

"No one could look away from her," I say to myself, wiping a tear from my eye.

He doesn't hear me, and I hold back the inner plea for him to watch the entire thing, to see how incredible my mother was. To get a glimpse of who I might have been.

But I simply bite my tongue when he ejects the DVD and puts in a new one. My stomach roils when I see the footage of my father's trial replacing the sweet memories of my mother on the screen.

As he watches, I return to the bedroom. It's like I told Hadley — the mind is just too fragile for some visual stimulants, and I know my limits.

Chapter 8

The secret to being a bore... is to tell everything.
—Voltaire

Logan

"Where's Craig?" Leonard asks, breaking the silence in the car.

"Conveniently, the director called him over to aide in a media thing upstate. Johnson is currently handling all media for this case."

He mutters something under his breath before adding, "It's pissing me off how obvious it is what they're doing, yet no one is helping us stop it."

"We just need evidence. We also need the entire story."

"It'd be a lot easier to piece together this puzzle if our killer would just spell it all out for us. It's obvious he wants us to know the truth," Leonard grumbles.

He's been lost in thought for most of this trip.

"He wants us to figure out the truth for ourselves. He thinks we'll be on his side, considering he's been saving us."

Leonard turns to face me. "Are you conflicted?"

I shake my head. "No. I understand what happened ten years ago was beyond fucked up, and I have no sympathy to the victims we've found so far, but playing judge, jury, and executioner is not excusable. I also know how these cases go. It starts off as revenge, individuals getting targeted. But it turns into a massacre when the unsub devolves rapidly, and anything at all that's perceived as a threat is killed as collateral damage."

He looks back out the window. He's seen these cases too.

"What if this one was different?"

"What?" I ask, confused.

He faces me again. "There were rare cases where the revenge killers actually killed just those who had wronged them. No one else was caught in the crosshairs."

"Very few," I remind him. "And almost all end with a shootout between law enforcement and the unsub."

"Most all revenge seekers are seeking revenge for themselves. It's what causes the psychotic break—being too close to the triggers when the emotions finally take over," he goes on. "We profiled this unsub as being one to avenge for someone else. He could have separation and even be able to form attachments, unlike other revenge killers, since I doubt it's a proxy killer who is suffering a delusional paradigm."

I heave out a long, weary breath. "I get the confliction you're dealing with. Especially in this case, given what we've already learned and now seen. But innocent people will die if we don't stop him. No one has the right to take the law into their own hands," I say calmly, even though a silent argument in my mind contests my own words.

He cuts his gaze away before replying, "They tried to get help. They tried to seek justice. They were denied."

"They?" I ask curiously.

"The unsub," he states flatly. "I don't know if I should keep referring to the unsub as *him*, since you said you feel it was a woman."

"You believe me?" No one else has.

"You saw Hollis. You saw Lana. What made you believe the unsub was a woman when you never saw a face? Men can be small as well, and I strongly believe in counter forensics in all cases with an unsub this organized. He or she could have easily masked their true size and weight with the right counter measures."

I grow quiet, letting a chill creep in over me. No one at all has even considered believing me.

"Men can be small," I say in agreement.

"How small are we talking?"

"Someone as short as Lana."

He clears his throat. "That's specific," he says under his breath. "Still doesn't explain why you think it's a woman."

My mind goes back to the blurry images of the small frame taking down Hollis, landing on top of him.

"I swear I heard a feminine laugh. It was cold and taunting, and almost enjoying the killing part."

He shifts beside me, turning a little pale.

"Really?"

"This unsub may be somehow projecting obsessively onto Victoria or Marcus Evans, creating the illusion of either being them or being involved with them. It would make the most sense, considering we've ruled out the few friends they had in this town. So don't rule out a proxy."

"An unsub who can fight, kill, and meticulously plan murders with counter forensics is too organized to be killing as a proxy. Killing as a proxy would indicate a psychotic break," Leonard argues. "And obviously he or she is still rational enough to show patience and control, which would immediately rule out any sort of psychotic break."

I grow quiet, thinking of all the contradictions this unsub has left us with. It all fits, and none of it fits at the same time.

It's as though he or she needs their own profile. Even considering it to be a woman is a direct confliction with a female serial killer profile because of the torture.

All The Lies

"Remember the case we worked in San Antonio six years ago?" Leonard finally asks, his tone thoughtful as he stares out the window.

I don't even have to ask for details to refresh my mind. "The father who killed the five guys who raped his daughter at a frat party."

He nods, still lost inside his own mind.

"He also went on to the campus police," I remind him. "He killed two of them before we caught him."

"The campus police never filed a report. When we interviewed them, they said poor girls get drunk and call rape all the time at frat parties, trying to get a settlement out of the rich guys," Leonard says, his hands turning to fists. "I have a sister. Anytime something like this happens, I think of her."

"Caroline can take care of herself," I remind him. "She'd obliterate any guy who tried to touch her."

"Which is why it was stupid to rule out a female killer based on the fact these were all fit men who were taken down physically. My sister has been in twenty different competitions and has won several of them. She could easily overpower any of these guys," he says thoughtfully. "If a woman knew what she was going up against and had the forethought to prepare counter forensics, she'd know our profile would be sexist enough to rule out a female."

My lips purse. I'd argue this if it wasn't for the fact I saw our small unsub. I heard her feminine laughter.

"Lindy May Wheeler was in her kindergarten classes during some of the kill times," he goes on. "I checked last night."

Lindy May was too timid to be a calculated killer. I never even considered her.

"If someone had ever hurt Caroline like this, and she never saw justice, I don't know that I'd be any better than the killer we're trying to catch," he says quietly. "Albert Rawlings let himself be killed when he'd finished. His gun was empty when he pointed it at the police who'd cornered him. He was done. He never planned on killing anyone else. And he forced the police to kill him because he had nothing left to do or live for."

Blowing out a weary breath, I think back to that case. It was a rare instance where there was no massacre.

"Caroline learned how to use her smaller frame and weight to her advantage against a larger opponent, as well as all the weaknesses on a body she could exploit. She also learned a lot of control when learning various forms of martial arts," Leonard goes on. "It's not just a strengthening of the body; it's also a strengthening of the mind. This unsub could have been training her body for the fight, but she might have also been training her mind against the impending psychotic break. It's obvious she did all her research, so it makes sense."

If that's the case, this unsub is ten times more organized than we assumed.

"The two people missing right now are probably already dead if the unsub is here with us," he continues. "She started sprinting through the kills so she could be here with us when the time came."

"Even left one alive to return to," I add.

"So she has enough control to put a pin in her agenda just to join us in this town, possibly even watch over us."

Watch over us...

"Which is another confliction with the profile," I say on a long sigh.

"Exactly. Revenge is more important and the primary focus for revenge killers, yet our girl comes to make sure we don't get caught unawares by a town she knew was corrupt enough to try and kill an agent of the FBI."

"So the truth is more important than the revenge," I say aloud as we bounce theories off each other.

"Or the unsub is firmly grounded in reality and doesn't want to let anyone else innocent die by the hands of this town."

All The Lies

His words speak to a mentality the unsub would be incapable of if this is revenge. Again, nothing but conflictions no matter how we profile.

"Let's focus on what we have. The unsub has been in town for as long as we have, yet has only killed once," Leonard says as I drive. "And that was to save you."

"And Donny," I remind him.

He clears his throat. "The unsub has enough control to let us find out what we need to know, and hold off on killing more," he adds.

"Only because Kyle is possibly next, and he has around-the-clock protection. He hasn't even left his home since this started."

He nods slowly.

"Our unsub is leaving messages to taunt the town, and using the voice of Jasmine Evans to remind them of how the corruption started."

I take a turn, and he continues.

"I spoke to Lindy May last night," he says, surprising me. "When I told her what we'd learned about the past, she told me that I only knew about three of Kyle Davenport's victims. That he was a serial rapist and possibly a sociopath."

I pull up at the curb and shut off the engine as I turn to face him.

"He's the sheriff's son, and they've kept us from getting an interview."

He cocks an eyebrow. "We're profilers who could see through him. If he's someone who gets off on raping women…"

He lets the words trail off.

"Then he could be the original killer," I groan, then curse before punching the steering wheel.

"May be why our unsub has held off on killing him."

My eyes flit to the innocuous blue house that sets idly between two white ones. This town is outside of the sheriff's jurisdiction. Something tells me Carl Burrows moved here for a reason.

"Let's deal with this before we go digging into Kyle," I tell Leonard.

"Sheriff Cannon and Johnson are going to block us from speaking to Kyle. I don't get why Johnson would cover up a true killer. Even at his worst, he's still a fucking agent."

"Because he fucked up. His ego is more important than justice could ever be," I say as I get out.

Kyle would have been nineteen at the time. Nineteen seems too disorganized to be the killer from back then, but he fits the profile in every other way.

Unless Lindy May is right and he's a sociopath. We're looking for a psychopath. Sociopaths can't imitate empathy. Psychopaths can.

As we walk up the sidewalk, I notice someone peering out of the window, watching us as we approach the door. The curtains pop closed and sway from the disturbance, and the door swings open before we even make it to the stoop.

He's short, has a touch of oriental in his bloodline, given the shape of his eyes and cheeks. His hair is dark and long, tied back in a ponytail. He looks like he doesn't get out too much either, given the disarray of his wrinkled clothing and smell of body odor I get a whiff of from here.

"Are you SSA Logan Bennett and Agent Stan Leonard?" he asks as we step onto his small stoop.

Creasing my lips to hide my surprise, I hold up my ID, as does Leonard.

Burrows adjusts his glasses on his nose as he reads our names, then he looks up and then gestures for us to hurry inside. I resist the urge to cover my nose when we walk in. Old food is lying haphazardly around, covered in flies and sealed in aquariums. Various other aquariums have other things inside them, though my stomach is reeling too much for me to focus on it.

Leonard coughs and covers his nose.

"Your sense of smell is the weakest sense. Give it a few minutes, and you won't smell it anymore," Burrows assures us as he leads us through his house.

"What is all this?" Leonard asks, coughing back a gag.

"I study the decaying process and the insect activity that follows. It's part of the forensics program I run to help identify time of death in hard to date cases."

"In your home?" Leonard asks, gagging again.

"My lab has several other experiments going on, and I can monitor things better from home anyway."

"How did you know we were coming?" I ask him as we move through his kitchen, where several more 'experiments' are underway.

It smells like death met a rotten asshole and had five puke babies.

He shudders, popping a piece of nicotine gum and chewing it frantically.

"Do you believe in ghosts?" he asks us seriously, looking around nervously.

Leonard tilts his head. "No, why?"

"Because I do. I'm a man of science, but I believe there are too many unexplained variables in the course of a lifetime to believe things are as cut and dry as science implies. A psychic actually solved one case I was involved in one time."

Confused, I lean against the wall, letting him ramble.

"He said the killer had one eye. He saw the killer through the eyes of the dead victim, and he described him down to the eye and snake tattoo on his neck. Police found the guy, and they also found his next victim in the trunk of the car. She was still alive. And no, the psychic was in no way linked to him. He actually helped solve many cases. He called himself a medium, but I still refer to him as a psychic. Because psychics see shit the normal person can't, right?"

I look over to Leonard, and he looks back at me.

As one, our gaze swings back to the looney toon doctor who has apparently spent too much time in solitude with rotting food. I'm not sure what an extended period of time in an environment like this would do to one's psyche. But I bet we're looking at the product of that answer.

"Why are we talking about psychics?" I ask him warily, trying and failing to follow his thought process.

"I tried calling him today. He said he'd need a victim to touch or something involved with the killer. I had him over, and he touched my wall. He told me nothing about the killer. Instead, he told me SSA Logan Bennett and Agent Stan Leonard would be on their way. Said you'd be here within ten minutes. He said to tell you everything I knew about Robert Evans."

Leonard immediately pulls out his phone. "What's his name?" he demands.

"Neil Mullins. He's clean. He's not your guy. He's a true medium, and he helps solve cases that can't otherwise be solved. But he said he refused to be involved with this one, because the killer is after souls too dark for him to save. He said there are souls begging him to help the killer, and the darker souls were trapped by the lighter ones, being held down. He's only had that on a very rare occasion."

Leonard lowers the phone, eyeing Burrows like he's lost his mind.

"You can check him out. He's been helping the FBI for a really long time," Burrows adds.

Leonard walks away, probably going to do just that and find out if this guy has any ties to Delaney Grove or our victims.

We told no one we were coming here, other than our team.

All The Lies

"Why your wall?" I ask Burrows.

He points above my head, and I turn, stepping back to see the red words that were behind me.

"It started appearing one letter at a time this morning right in front of my eyes," he says on a shaky whisper.

The time for secrets is over. Tell my story. Save your soul.

"I never wanted to keep Robert Evans's death details a secret. That was all the sheriff and Doc Barrontine. Not me. Not me," he says rapidly, his fear, caffeine and nicotine causing his words to rush together.

"What details?" I ask, turning to face him.

"I don't have any proof. I remember the case. I was doing my residency there. That case derailed my ambitions to be a coroner and turned me into a forensics scientist. Science isn't politics. It's organically dirty, not sullied by people. It's simple math and truth, and all I have to do is deliver the facts. I never wanted to lie, SSA Bennett. I swear to you that's the truth."

"He checks out," Leonard says, sounding confused as he walks back in. "Hell, he's been in Mexico helping solve a string of murders near the border for the past two months."

A medium. I've worked with them before, and they're always crooks or attention seekers who do more harm than good by filing away unfounded facts that derail or sidetrack the investigation.

Yet this guy knew us by name? Hell, Elise doesn't even know Leonard's first name. He keeps a lid on that, because the name came from his father, and there's a lot of beef there.

"We'll look into him more later," I say, gesturing at the message above us.

Leonard's breath catches.

Our killer knew we'd come here. He might not have named us, but he knew we'd come today.

He's watching us.

That's how he knew Donny and I were being attacked.

That's how he's leaving these messages without being seen.

"I know it was the ghost of Evans," Burrows rambles on. "He left these," he says, picking up a pack of small nails.

I hiss out a breath. "He left these? You're a forensics scientist! You should know not to touch evidence," I growl, grabbing a glove and an evidence bag.

He tosses them to the top of the microwave carelessly, scratching nervously at his arms. "Ghosts don't leave prints," he says, chewing endlessly on that gum.

"Tell us what you know about Robert Evans," I say to the fidgeting scientist who is popping yet another piece of nicotine gum into his mouth.

I label the bag, and Leonard snaps a picture of it and the words over the doorway.

"Those are the exact same nails they used on him."

A piece of the puzzle falls into place. "What?" I ask, confused.

I realize there are a mixture of nails in the bag, and not just the small ones. Longer ones like we found in the stomach of one victim are also in here.

"They fed him nails. Made him swallow them," Burrows says, swallowing hard like he can taste the nails. "Sheriff Cannon shoved the nails into Robert's mouth himself. Robert was crying, begging them to stop, still pleading his innocence. I tried," he says quickly, looking me in the eyes. "I tried to stop them. One of his deputies pistol whipped me and left me bleeding in the corner."

He swallows the gum, and he pops in two more pieces, chewing just as vigorously as Leonard slowly lowers himself to a chair.

"The nails sliced through his esophagus. He was spitting up blood and screaming in pain. They took out their batons and did terrible things to his backside then. They used the batons to rape him repeatedly, held his face against the table as he bled out from

All The Lies

both ends. The sheriff then beat him the rest of the way to death once everyone had their turn at depravity."

He chokes on his gum, and he spits it out into his hand, leaving a slobbery, sticky mess until he dumps it into the trash.

"I told the leading agent back then. Johnson was his name. Miller Johnson. He said it was small town justice, and he had real killers to track down."

Leonard and I exchange a look, and fury creases his expression. *This* is what Miller has been covering.

"He knew," Burrows goes on, biting his nails now as he shifts his weight from one foot to another and back again. "He knew before it happened. There was no surprise on his face when I told him. They came to me later that night, and they told me if I wanted to tell what I saw again, they'd repeat the performance on me. I left town, finished out my residency elsewhere, and moved into the field of forensics. Bugs are safer than people."

Leonard blows out a long breath, and I suppress my urge to find Johnson and beat the actual fuck out of him.

"He was innocent, you know?" Burrows says, peering over at me again. "Evans, I mean. He didn't kill those women. Couldn't have. The serial killer was left handed, and Evans was right handed. His left hand was broken after a kid slammed his hand in a locker as a joke. Kyle Davenport, to be more specific."

My blood chills more.

"Victoria Evans broke up with Kyle because of that. She yelled at him in front of the school. Three months later, Robert Evans was convicted of those murders. Quickest hearing process in the history of murder cases. And two kills occurred the very week after his left hand was broken. He couldn't have been the murderer. But that didn't matter. They wouldn't listen to the science. They only listened to that pompous prick Agent Johnson. Sheriff Cannon just wanted someone to persecute."

He pops in a fresh piece of gum and wipes his hands on his wrinkly, somewhat smelly shirt.

"Who else would know about what happened to Evans?" I ask him.

"No one who would talk. Most of the deputies were involved. And Kyle Davenport, of course. He was there. I heard rumors he did basically the same thing to the kids, only he didn't bring the nails for that night."

Kyle Davenport seems to be at the root of every problem.

"Any chance he was left handed?"

"Kyle?" Burrows asks, his face paling. When I nod, he barely whispers, "Yes."

Nineteen. Nineteen is just too young of an age to be so methodical as the original killer. Each kill was filled with rage, according to the reports. A temper tantrum could send a sociopath into a homicidal rage, if Lindy was right and not just abusing the word she used to describe him.

If he'd been ten to twenty years older, he'd fit the profile perfectly.

"We need to find a way to speak with Kyle Davenport," Leonard says grimly.

"Right now," I add.

"I'll call that medium on the way back to Delaney Grove," he says as we head toward the door. "And I'll send Hadley over here to see if she can pull anything from the house," I say on a sigh, closing the door to Burrows's home behind me.

"Doubtful. Our unsub never leaves any trace."

"Is that all?" Burrow shouts from behind us, and I turn to see his head poking through the door.

"For now."

"Can I get a hotel room? I don't feel safe right now."

Since I don't feel like making a scientist see a ghost story as ridiculous, I just nod.

All The Lies

Leonard seems distant, thoughtful even.

"What?" I ask him as we get into the car.

I don't crank it, because I lift my iPad, bringing up pictures from the previous crime scenes.

He turns to face me. "We decided last night we were coming to Carl's house this morning. Our unsub would have had to hit sometime between our decision after we returned from the hospital and our arrival at the home today."

I nod slowly. "I thought I had something figured out, but apparently that was wrong, because now it's impossible," he sighs.

"What?" I ask, curious, my fingers hovering over the screen.

"Nothing that sounds sane anymore. Guess it was all just in my head. What are you looking for?" He gestures toward my iPad.

"The unsub knew Donny and I were being attacked. The unsub knew we were coming today. The unsub has known every move of his or her victims. This unsub is a watcher. There are eyes on us somewhere, and—"

My words cut out when I notice the small holes. I barely remembered them because they seemed so unimportant.

"Each house has these in almost every room," I tell Leonard. "Except for some of the later kills the unsub sprinted through." I gesture toward the small holes the size of a nail head.

"Too small to be a camera," he says.

"We've already suspected the unsub of a much higher intelligence. What if she has this sort of technology? It'd explain how she managed to save me in time last night."

"You're just saying *she* now," he notes.

"Everything in me is saying it was a woman."

"I believe you," he says absently.

"You lack the conviction in your tone that you had on the way down here."

I put the car in drive and push my iPad away. Knowing the unsub is watching us is actually a good thing. Hadley can tap into the video stream if she can find the signal, and possibly even back-hack the unsub to find him.

"Like I said," Leonard mumbles under his breath, "thought I knew something else."

Chapter 9

There are truths which are not for all men, nor for all times.
—Voltaire

Logan

Two deputies block us the second we step up on the front porch of Kyle Davenport's home.

"Sorry, Agents, but no one is going in without the sheriff's permission," the one in front of me says.

Chad Briggs. I remember him.

I just smirk.

"Unless you guys want me calling more of my guys in because you're impeding a federal investigation, I suggest you step out of the way."

Briggs takes a step toward me, a dark challenge in his eyes. "SSA Johnson is the lead on your end. If he wants to come chat with Kyle, I'll step down. But we're taking the threat on his life seriously, and you're not stepping—"

His words end on a grunt when I grab his wrist and twist, sending him face first into the side of the house. Leonard pulls his gun when the other deputy stupidly tries to make a grab for his own weapon.

"Let me be very clear here," I say to Briggs, wrenching his arm tighter behind him and making him cry out. "I'll speak to whoever the fuck I want to speak to, considering your guys tried to take me out last night. And if you're smart, you'll keep your mouth shut until I'm gone. Or I'll call in every fucking favor I'm owed inside the FBI to get an entire army of agents in this town, telling them about how the corrupt little fuckwad county deputies are trying to take down a federal agent. Now, do you want to back down, or should I start making all those phone calls."

He stops struggling, and I feel him go rigid.

"Yeah. Think about what you'd do if one of your guys was targeted by an outsider. I have friends like that too, Deputy."

He curses, and the other guy turns and heads inside, calling for Kyle as Leonard holsters his weapon.

Briggs rubs his newly injured wrist, and I nudge him, forcing him inside in front of us. I'd rather talk to Kyle alone, but I don't want them calling the sheriff in like an attack dog before I get a few words in.

"Kyle!" the other deputy shouts again.

"Yeah. Yeah. Coming," says a voice from down the hall.

Kyle Davenport emerges, wearing nothing but a towel, and an arched eyebrow. "The fuck are you?"

He's leaner than the other victims, but still solid, as though he works out but doesn't want bulk. His hair is dark and hanging almost over his dark eyes. He's tall, a lot like me.

"How about I ask you some questions," I say with a smirk.

"These are some of the FBI guys," the other deputy grumbles.

"Thought Dad said to keep those fuck sticks away from me," Kyle drawls, completely unaffected by our presence.

He drops to a chair, still just wearing a towel.

"What you want with me?" he asks indifferently.

"We actually know quite a bit about you. Just wanted to get a read on the man who raped and murdered two kids when he was only nineteen. A man who also participated in a brutal assault a few nights before," I toss out there.

All The Lies

Kyle's lips twitch, but both deputies gasp.

"Hell no! You said you just wanted to talk. Not come in here and accuse him of murder," Briggs shouts, lifting his phone.

Kyle just eyes me, his head tilting carelessly. He thinks he's untouchable. Not even a flicker of emotion is on his face. He's a sociopath. Not a psychopath.

He's not our guy.

"I have all I need, Deputy," I say as I stand.

They immediately start calling the cops, but Kyle speaks just as I get to the door.

"That sweet little brunette in town... That your girl, *Agent?*" Kyle asks, smirking at me when I turn around.

"Yeah." The word is said with ease, not letting him see the rage simmering close to the surface.

He licks his lips, still smirking. "Better keep her close. Girl like that might get snatched up in a town full of bachelors."

He expects me to lash out, probably wants me to. The veiled threat is meant to rattle me for his pleasure. It takes every ounce of effort I have not to let him win.

"Funny. I was just thinking how Lana would probably make you wish you'd never been born," I say carelessly.

Leonard relaxes at my side, following my lead as he forces his posture to exhibit a calmness.

"Women love me," Kyle goads. "They love everything I do to them. I bet she'd like it too."

Leonard steps in before I can lose my cool.

"I guess you don't watch the news, do you?" Leonard asks him, holding the door open for our exit.

"Not much time for the news," Kyle drawls.

"Figured," Leonard goes on. "Or you'd know that Lana is the one who killed the Boston serial killer known as the Boogeyman."

Kyle's smirk vanishes, and he studies us, probably searching for a lie.

"With his own knife," I add, holding a smile that relays a darkness I'm not used to feeling.

"After he attacked her," Leonard goes on. "He was twice her size and had raped and murdered several women. She beat the shit out of him and stabbed him, ended his life when he came for her."

With that, Leonard walks out, and I force myself to do the same. Yeah, he exaggerated the story, but Kyle wasn't smirking when I turned back around.

"He won't touch her now," Leonard says quietly.

"I should get her the fuck out of this town," I say in a tone just barely above a whisper as we get into the vehicle, not looking back.

With all the driving, it's already getting late now. The sun isn't far from setting, and all I want to do is hold Lana against me and feel her safe.

"Kyle Davenport may or may not have been our serial killer back then, but I guarantee you he's going to be one soon, if he's not already," Leonard says as we drive back toward the cabins.

"And he just threatened my girlfriend."

"Like I said, he won't do anything. Telling him she's not some weak girl he can dominate didn't settle well with him."

"And if he perceives it as a challenge?" I point out.

"He's not interested in a challenge. He wants easy," he says on a sigh. "Lana is safer with us than alone somewhere else right now."

I shift in my seat, driving faster through the town. "My job keeps putting her at risk."

"Occupational hazard," he says grimly. "She can handle it, Logan. She may be one of the few who can."

"But how selfish is it of me to ask her to handle it?"

He doesn't get to answer, because we're pulling up at the cabin where the sheriff and Johnson are standing outside and waiting on me. Lana is guarding the door, her hip cocked as she smirks at them when we get out.

"Sheriff, you can say all you want, but you're not getting by me without putting your hands on me. If you do that, I'll press charges for assault. I don't care if it's your cabin. There's a little thing called the law that you can't search this place when it's occupied by guests, unless said guests give you permission. I can pull it up on my phone for you, if you'd like."

She's poised, staring them down, and Johnson's jaw is tight.

"You have no right to—"

"What the hell is going on here?" I demand, stepping up on the porch.

Lana wags her finger at the sheriff when he tries to barge by her. Somehow, she manages to block his path, despite his size.

"Don't want to touch me sheriff. My phone is recording every bit of this, and I'll make it go live."

He looks around, and she smiles. "I'm not stupid enough to leave it in plain sight."

"I said what the hell is going on!"

I step in front of the sheriff, shielding Lana. "You crossed a line today," the sheriff growls. "And I got a call that you were seen buying drugs off Lenny Tolls, the local dealer. So I'm here to search your room. When I find something, I'll be shipping your ass back to your superiors to deal with."

"You're fucking kidding me with this, right?" Leonard snaps.

Unbelievable. They're getting desperate and overreaching now that I've talked to his son.

"I already told them that if they let Elise and them search their guys, they could come in and look," Lana states with a sweet smile but daring eyes.

The sheriff glares at her, and my hand goes to her hip, trying to tug her back. I don't want him viewing her as a target, damn it.

"Why would I let you fucking search me?" the sheriff barks.

"Because if you have something you plan on planting in here, then it'd be smart to have you searched. If you have nothing to hide, then why not let them search you?" Lana goes on, refusing to just shut up as she shoulders her way to my side again.

"You need a leash on her, Bennett. Now step aside if you have nothing to hide," Johnson barks.

Lana starts to open her mouth, and I slide my hand over it, tugging her closer. She doesn't fight me, but she does lick my fucking hand like an errant child.

"Let them search you, and I will," I say with a shrug.

Lana relaxes at my side. She's fucking brilliant and seriously observant.

Leonard restrains a grin.

"I'm not letting you search me," the sheriff growls.

"Then I'm not letting you in here."

"It's my motherfucking cabin."

"That the bureau has paid for and leased it until this case is solved. It's listed under my name. To gain access, you need my permission, or a search warrant, that will have to go through several channels, considering I'm on an active case that involves corruption in this town. You'd be surprised how many people would come pay a visit when accusations like this so conveniently pop up."

The sheriff takes a step back, his eyes narrowing to slits. He points a finger at me. "Stay the fuck away from my son. This ain't over. I'll get you out of my town, boy."

"It's SSA Bennett to you, Sheriff. Good luck with that. I'll be busy proving you're a corrupt, murdering, lying son of a bitch while you work on getting me out."

He pales a little, and Lana smirks against my hand; I can feel it.

All The Lies

Apparently she's proud.

She should be.

He could have caused a shit-ton of problems with false bullshit getting planted in here and 'found' by him.

Johnson glares daggers at me.

"This is *my* fucking case! You're only here as a courtesy!" Johnson snarls.

"This is *my* fucking team. You're only here because you're covering your ass. The director can only do so much for you, Johnson. It's only a matter of time before people take notice of the attention he's paying you and this case. Don't push your luck."

He curses, and I watch as he and the sheriff turn and walk away. Leonard visibly relaxes, then looks over at Lana.

"How'd you know what he was going to do?" he asks her.

She shrugs as I release her mouth completely, and wipe my wet hand on the leg of my jeans.

"Saw it on some crime episode one time. The bad cop got rid of the good one by framing him with drugs. Figured it was a good possibility in a town like this, and I didn't want to risk it."

Elise steps onto the porch. "Hadley's inside with a camera. She recorded the entire thing. Since Lana is staying here as well, she had the right to block their entry. She did good."

Elise says this as though she's surprised.

I cup Lana's chin and tilt her head up before staring down at her eyes. "Don't fuck with either of them. The last thing I need is a target painted on your back."

"I wasn't fucking with them. I was simply stating my rights as a citizen of the United States," she says innocently. She even bats her fucking eyelashes, and Leonard snorts, turning away as his body shakes with silent laughter.

"I'm serious," I tell her sternly.

She continues to bat those eyelashes over faux innocent eyes. "I'll never just bend over and take it, SSA Bennett. Unless I'm bending over for you, of course."

Leonard does lose it now, laughing as he walks away. I groan as her lips etch up in a smile. Lisa mutters something, surprising me with her presence as she steps away from the side of the cabin.

Lana battles a smile unsuccessfully, and I roll my eyes.

"Hadley, you're staying here tonight. The rest of us have somewhere else to be. Keep your eyes open," I tell her while tugging Lana against me.

"Always got my eyes open, Bennett," Hadley quips as she stands and walks toward the door.

As she steps out, I push Lana against the wall and crush my lips to hers, shutting her up before she can talk more. She moans into my mouth, gripping my shirt to pull me closer.

And I decide my plans can wait.

Chapter 10

Chance is a word void of sense; nothing can exist without a cause.
—Voltaire

Lana

"Do you believe in coincidence?" I ask Jake as I prop my feet up on the dash of his car.

We're lurking in the car, parked in the shadows, and watching the long line form for the one-night-only Sin House. You'd think people would realize this little one-night show gets more action than anything in town all year long. It should attest to the fact the sick people around here are dark and demented from years of oppression.

"Coincidence? Yes."

"Coincidences as big as ours?"

He sighs hard. "What's this about, Lana? You're seriously starting to worry me."

I toy with the ends of my hair, staring down at it while we wait.

"Marcus always believed that nothing happened by chance. That everything was interweaved in fate's plan, and that there was a purpose for everything."

"What purpose is there in what happened ten years ago to your entire family and the only man I've ever loved?" He asks the question calmly, but he's good at hiding his anger.

"I didn't say it was a good purpose," I tell him softly, reaching over to lace our fingers together.

He squeezes my hand and inhales deeply.

"If it hadn't been our family, it would have been another," I go on.

He lays his head back, staring down the end of his nose at the ever-growing line to the Sin House.

"What would Marcus say the reason was?" he asks, though his voice is rasp.

"You knew him just as well as I did. If not better. You tell me," I go on, squeezing his hand this time.

His lips tense for a moment, then finally he speaks. "If he'd survived, you and I wouldn't have had the anger to dig into the darkness and do what it took to reap revenge. If your father hadn't been targeted, another man and his family would have been."

"And not everyone has the ability to go dark enough to slice men's cocks off several times and torture them for days without losing all sense of humanity," I add with a shrug.

He laughs under his breath, shaking his head.

"Yes. He'd definitely point that out, and he'd say it almost just like that. He'd also say that no one would have the determination to see it through like you and me. He'd point out that I learned code for this very reason. That I learned tech for this very reason."

My eyes settle on Logan as he walks by, looking around the line like he's searching for someone or something. We're perfectly hidden here amongst the other cars, and there's a sensor to alert us if someone gets too close.

My bestie is awesomely paranoid like that.

"He'd tell us that Kyle Davenport might be the worst fucking person in the world and get away with it if I hadn't been the one to survive and come back to collect his debt," I say more seriously.

"And he'd say that the sheriff would get away with just as much, and no one would ever stand up to him," he adds, the same serious tone.

"What would he say about Logan?" I ask as Logan lifts his phone, probably trying to find a teammate.

They're waiting for Kyle, probably planning to watch him and see if anyone pays him any attention. I've already laid eyes on him. He's right in the middle of the line, waiting his turn.

My stomach roils every time I see his face, so I refuse to keep looking. This will be the hardest one to find control. I'll want to slice the flesh from his body over and over and over... Rage will be evident.

Unless I completely skin the fucker.

The haunted house is not really a house at all. It's four large trailers that have holes cut in the fronts and backs, and they're wedged together on the street, supported by blocks underneath. They'll be wheeled back tomorrow, stored away until next year.

I doubt there will be a next year.

Kyle runs a hand through his dark hair, squeezing the ass of the girl with him who doesn't look happy to be with him. He was too rough all those years ago when I stupidly dated him. I can only imagine he's worse now, given the shiner on her eye.

Forcing my eyes away, I turn to Jake, waiting for him to answer. He looks lost in thought, and I start to think he never heard me.

"He'd say it was too coincidental not to mean something," he finally answers, the words sounding almost reverent.

"What do you mean?"

"I mean, what are the odds of you running into the lead FBI agent on your case? And falling for him? And him falling for you? Your paths were meant to cross, but he wasn't meant to stop you, or he already would have. Even I, a man of pure science, cannot belittle what you have by labeling it with mere coincidence. Maybe he was meant to drag out your humanity the most right when you needed it."

His eyes soften as he looks over at me.

"I'm sorry. I know each kill dulls you more. You got the worst end of this job. Just helping what little bit I have has seared pieces of my soul that I can't get back."

My lips purse as I resume watching Logan. "He makes me feel," I say, though it's something I've said many times before. "My soul actually feels restored with the kills as long as I have him afterwards."

"He keeps you grounded and firmly attached to reality so you don't end up like the profile." He reaches over and squeezes my knee before kissing my cheek.

I give him a brittle smile as he presses his forehead against mine.

"He gives you a reason to want a future," he adds quietly. "And through him, you found a piece of yourself you thought you'd lost. That's given me hope for a future one day too, Lana. So maybe Marcus was right. Fate is a fucking cold-hearted bitch, but everything has a purpose."

I snort and wipe away a tear, while he smirks and looks straight forward, leaning away from me. The lost, pained look in his gaze lets me know he's thinking of all he and Marcus might have been, even though he says he never thinks of that.

Too many tears have fallen after I swore I'd never let another tear fall. I guess Jake is right about Logan bringing back out my humanity.

He can't stop me from being a monster though.

If he was meant to stop me, he already would have, just like Jake said.

Kyle steps closer to the front of the line, and Chad Briggs moves with him. His second deputy accompanying him is Trevor Byron. Two more are stationed near the front, where the Sin House ends.

Those two will survive.

For tonight, anyway.

All The Lies

They're on my kill list, but I think it'd be a little overly ambitious to try and take out five in one night. After all, I'm just one little girl.

Smirking, I watch as they get closer.

"Show time," Jake tells me, handing me the wig/mask.

I'm already dressed in my jumpsuit. The padding will disguise my build and my weight. I pat my pocket, checking for the syringe. It's still there.

Jake and I will have to tag team Kyle, to ensure Logan doesn't catch me elbow-deep in his blood.

"Think you can get your car around there without anyone seeing?" I ask him.

"I think no one will say a word," he taunts, arching an eyebrow.

"Let the sheep change shepherds," I say as I get out of the car, tugging the mask on.

Everyone is dressed in so many costumes, that only a few even notice me as I pass by. I can't hide my height, but after saving Logan last night, that doesn't really matter anymore.

He saw me.

Well, he saw most of me. I worried he saw more, but he was so concussed he didn't get a good look. I risked it all to make sure I saved him.

It's hard to fight and keep your face hidden, but obviously I managed.

I still wonder what he would have said or done if he'd seen me and knew the killer of one's nightmares was the one to save him because she loves him.

I take the side door, and no one even questions me, considering my costume. No one ever asks questions in this town. They just go with the flow, as their conditioning tells them to do.

The throngs of people divide for me, screaming as I split through them. Everyone loves a good scream, and as I pop out of the shadows, more of those screams find my ears.

It takes me a moment to find the corner Jake has set up, and I nudge a girl out of it, letting her think I'm taking over as part of the plan. Gotta love disorganization. Popular as it is, it's still just put on by the high school, and has no organization extending beyond the original setup.

She leaves, carrying her fake axe with her, and I plug in my power saw.

Trevor is the first one I see, and I rev the saw, listening to some of the ones in front of him scream in terror, even though they think it's all fake.

The dingy room is lit by a strobe light that flickers amongst the fog machines and red lights in the background. Trevor steps aside, waiting for Kyle and the others to catch up. I smirk behind the mask before grabbing him.

"Let go, fuckstick!" he snaps. "You're not supposed to put your hands on people."

Oh, how I wish he could see me smile.

Screams erupt from all around as I slam a knife into his chest and toss him into the corner. People burst out laughing as he gurgles on blood.

"That's so fake!" one teenager shouts. "Nice try, Deputy Byron. Stick to your day job."

As the deputy continues to bleed out, I catch a glimpse of Kyle in the back, unsurprisingly lingering by the 'whore house' stand that's off to the side. My current box is labeled the 'liar' box.

We picked it on purpose.

I toss a sheet over Trevor as blood continues to plume and spread across his chest. He stares up in shock as I cover his head, tucking him in for a long sleep.

He'll bleed out in front of everyone.

But that's not my main event.

All The Lies

Chad Briggs comes into view just as I rev my power saw, and more screams erupt all around me as I pretend like I'm getting too close to the line of people. I cock my head from side to side, going with creepy overload.

Just as Briggs nears, leaving Kyle to dawdle at the whore house box a little longer—watching two girls make out while fake blood drips from their nipples through their white shirts—I rev the saw again.

Briggs eyes me, confused as to why this particular costume is in play. I walk up to him, and he smugly holds his ground while more people rush by, screaming like I'm an insane serial killer.

Well…

With one fast, unexpected yank, I toss Chad to the ground, and everyone around us erupts into frenzied screams. Chad's eyes widen, and a curse spills from his lips when realization sets in seconds too late.

"You can't see me," I tell him as I dig the saw into him, turning it on full power.

A bloodcurdling scream erupts from his lips as the saw powers across his chest, slicing through flesh and spraying out blood that splatters against people in the line.

"Holy shit! That looks so fucking real!" one guy hoots.

I smirk, digging the saw in deeper, slicing it across his abdomen, spilling his intestines for all to see.

Everyone starts rushing by us, screaming as they point and take pictures. It's sad that the world thinks visual effects are this good. Little do they know they're witnessing a murder.

As Chad chokes on his blood, Kyle nears, and I lean down to whisper my favorite part.

"I'm Victoria Evans. The daughter of the man you killed. The sister to the boy you let die. The victim you turned into a monster. And I'm going to fucking kill you all."

He tries to form words, but I stand, watching with sick fascination as he makes a pathetic attempt to hold his intestines inside his body. Kyle pales, the girl on his arm stumbles back, and I walk right toward him.

He's seen the real stuff. He knows this isn't fake.

He tries to turn and run, but I sling out the saw, catching him right in the back of the head.

Pity it's not on.

It hits him hard enough to knock him to the ground, and his girlfriend screams and sprints through the massacre.

I grab a bottle of lye as I drag Kyle by the foot toward the door.

"Best. Liar Box. Ever! Holy shit! We'll never top this next year!" one teen shouts in complete awe as Chad continues to silently mouth for help.

I toss the lye I brought onto the sheet by the door, drenching Trevor in it.

More screams erupt from under that sheet as the scent of rotting flesh and lye collide and permeate the air.

My eyes start burning, but the mask I'm wearing under the mask—yes, a mask under a mask—prevents most of the fumes from getting inhaled.

Others, however, start rushing out, screaming in real fear when they feel the burn.

With all the commotion, no one notices me dragging the unconscious Kyle to the box, where there's a hole cut into the floor. No one sees me push him down in it as the screams continue from Trevor.

No one notices who it is the person in the mask is dragging down under the traveling house of horrors.

I drop down into the hole, seeing no one's feet rushing away. Yet. Wheels roll up from behind, and I check my phone, watching the cameras as Logan speaks to Leonard.

All The Lies

The two deputies at the end are suddenly rushing into the house when the girlfriend runs out alone. It's now or never.

I quickly roll out from under the trailer, and I drag Kyle with me. He's out cold when I see the backdoor of a car opening. A few eyes swing toward us, and I hold my finger over my lips, the universal hush sign.

A woman pales and turns away, her entire body freezing. She doesn't make a move or say a word.

Jake's mask is on, and he turns around in his seat, grabbing Kyle's arm and helping me shove him into the vehicle. I shove the syringe into his hip, making sure he stays out.

We don't speak, and I let him go as I turn and walk away like I didn't just help kidnap the sheriff's son. I can't wait to have five minutes alone with him.

As sirens wail and the craziness gets crazier, I hear Logan shouting for someone, and I know they've figured it out.

Now the fun begins.

Like the killers do in the movies, I disappear calmly into the woods, and no one follows me.

Something tells me Delaney Grove will never view a Haunted House the same again.

Chapter 11

Common sense is not so common.
—Voltaire

Logan

"How the fucking hell does a killer walk by us, come inside, and kill two officers, before stealing the sheriff's son, yet no one sees a damn thing?" Donny hisses, covering his nose.

If our unsub wanted to ruin the crime scene, she did a damn good job by dumping out a tub of lye.

I'm not sure what was here before Kyle Davenport stupidly went in, and what the killer brought with her.

"You sons of bitches go see my son today, and now he's missing!" the sheriff bellows as I try to piece together the gruesome attack.

Chad Briggs. I spoke to him earlier. Trevor Byron is—*was*—familiar as well.

Chad was sawed open right in front of a crowd who watched with rapt attention, assuming he was just part of the show. Trevor was stabbed then doused in lye.

"He's now targeting anyone in the way," Lisa says as she pulls off her glove, staring in disgust at the parts of the body of Chad Briggs we were able to retrieve. Trevor's body can't be touched until the hazmat suits arrive.

Chad Briggs has been hollowed out, all of his insides spilling when we had to lift him to carry him outside for proper examination. We don't have a M.E. here, but they have their own coroner—who I don't trust.

The sheriff has already called in a canine unit, and most of his deputies are in the woods, trying to follow the blood trail the unsub left behind.

"I think this was planned," Leonard interjects. "Chad Briggs was an officer ten years ago. So was Trevor Byron. They were a part of what happened to Robert Evans."

"Just a coincidence," Lisa says dismissively.

"She could have hurt the girl with Kyle, who alerted the other two what was going on. She didn't. So she's in control of the kills," Leonard argues.

"She? Now *you* think it's a girl too?" Lisa groans. "We can't do this to our profile, or what's the point in profiling."

"Not adjusting the profile makes it just as pointless, and you start thinking like Johnson," I point out.

She glares at me, and I shift my attention to Elise. "Anything?"

She shakes her head. "Nothing of any use. People saw a guy in a Michael Myers mask in the 'liar' section, and thought Trevor Byron was part of the show. Same for Chad Briggs. Some even thought Trevor was a terrible actor, not even realizing he was dying. Others thought the 'special effects' with Briggs was amazing."

"Michael Myers?" Leonard says, stepping closer.

She nods.

"How'd they know it was a guy if the unsub was masked? And what about height and weight?" I ask her.

"The guy was dressed in full-on Michael Myers gear. Mask, hair, clothes...everything. I guess they assumed it was a guy. And no one was paying attention enough to get a height estimation. I got everything from five feet to six and a half feet. Some said it was a big guy. Some said he was skinny."

"Balls of stone is what it takes to devise a plan as brazen as this,"

Leonard says quietly.

"It fucking took you long enough!" I hear the sheriff snapping.

I look over as the canine units arrive, and he starts directing them. If they find Kyle, it'll be a small miracle. By now, the unsub is possibly already at play.

I glance over, studying the faces of everyone standing behind the caution tape. The girlfriend looks a little bruised, but those bruises were there before the unsub came in.

It took her longer than it should have to get help. The unsub had time to drag Kyle out of this place. She most likely used the hole cut into the floor.

This was all thought out, and somehow the unsub overlooked the girlfriend? Doubtful.

Leonard follows me as I make my way toward the girl who is chewing her nails, a blanket over her shoulders as she sways from side to side.

"Ms. Blanks?" At her name, she pops her head up, looking directly into my eyes. "Do you care to come talk with us?"

She nods dully and moves under the tape, coming closer to us. She's not in shock, despite what she saw.

"Ms. Blanks, I know the sheriff already talked to you, but if you could tell us anything you saw, it'd be greatly appreciated," I say softly, trying to sound calm and approachable, unlike the madman who shouldn't be directing this manhunt.

"It was dark. I just saw blood, and guts, and that crazy guy threw his saw at Kyle. It cocked him in the head. I thought he was going to get me next."

"But that didn't happen," Leonard says soothingly. "What happened next?"

She nibbles her lip. "I ran out, but turned around and saw him dragging Kyle. People were stepping over him and stuff, laughing or screaming. No one knew it was real, but I did. Some people panicked when they saw Chad, because it was gross. They started to question it, but still didn't say anything aloud. I finally got out when I saw him continuing to pull Kyle, and told the other two deputies where they were inside."

"You didn't see the escape hole? It wasn't covered or anything," I point out.

"I was too scared to focus," she says, not meeting my eyes.

I exchange a look with Leonard. Her not telling them about the hole would lead to them coming all the way through the setup backwards, fighting against hordes of people who would slow them down. She saw the hole. She elected not to mention it, but still told what was going on to clear herself of any wrongdoings as far as the sheriff was concerned.

"Thank you for your time, Ms. Blanks," I say as Leonard walks away with me.

"I almost think the girlfriend wanted Kyle gone," Leonard says under his breath.

I look around, surveying all the faces that don't seem the least bit upset.

"Someone here saw something," I say to him, looking back at all the people whispering amongst themselves, but not saying anything to us or the sheriff's men.

"Loyalties are shifting," Leonard says quietly.

"What?" I ask with the same hushed tone.

He gestures around. "These people have been conditioned from speaking out for years and years, finding punishment instead of reward. Finding terror instead of pride. Now this masked crusader comes in and is calling them out on their lies, killing the corrupt ones who've oppressed them for this long. They're loyalties are shifting to our killer instead of their oppressors. Before long, they'll develop a hero worshiping complex and consider the killer to be a vigilante speaking out against injustice."

"Our killer is doing much more than speaking out against

injustice," I say on a sigh.

He nods. "Killing was the only option for our girl. Because speaking only ever got these people killed or worse," he states flatly before walking away.

I'm starting to question *his* loyalties. Out of everyone, Leonard is the last one I thought would feel too much empathy for our killer.

And we need to stop calling her *our* anything.

Enacting possession or ownership makes the empathy ties stronger, and he's been referring to her as *our* girl or *our* killer all day. Knowing she's a female fighting against rapists also demands more sympathy and empathy. It's fucking with our heads, more so him than me.

But even I'm struggling to give a damn about finding Kyle before it's too late. I haven't even called Hadley out yet to run the forensics.

Deciding to force the issue, I text her, asking her to join us, and get a message back immediately that she's on the way. I also text Lana.

ME: You okay? Hadley has to come here, so I can send someone else.

LANA: All good. No need. I have to go home, deal with something tonight, and then I'll be back. My house was broken into and Duke called to ask me to come see if anything was taken.

The fuck?

ME: A homicide detective is calling you about a possible burglary?

LANA: The cops couldn't reach me on my phone, because my house number was the number the security company had. Duke had my cell, and he knew I was out of town. It'll be a quick trip. Promise. Love you. <3

All The Lies

I want to tell her to stay gone, but the sheriff might really do something stupid like stage a break-in and go after her. Hell, for all I know this is part of his retaliation for his son coming up missing four hours ago.

His deranged mind believes I'm somehow involved. What if this is all a trap?

ME: Stay. Don't go. I have a bad feeling.

LANA: Already on the road. Stow your bad feeling. Duke will be there, and I'll deal with all the insurance stuff. Don't focus on me. Worry about your case.

"Everything okay?" Leonard asks me.

"No. Lana is too fucking stubborn," I groan, putting my phone away. I'll call Duke later.

"Just curious, how much do you know about Lana?"

I arch an eyebrow. "Why do you ask?"

He shrugs. "No reason." His face changes as he looks at something in the dirt, and he kneels.

"Were there any cars parked over here tonight?" he asks.

"We taped this side up, not allowing cars to pass."

His eyes dart up to the path between the trees. It's big enough for a small car, but...

"The blood trail led into the woods," Elise says, interrupting my thought. "All of it was blood from the two victims he killed, but that's what happens when you saw a guy to pieces and stab another."

"Kyle Davenport didn't go into the woods. There'd be drag marks," I say, finally getting my head on right.

"The killer went into the woods, but not Kyle," Elise says, confused. "How?"

Leonard pales as he and I look at each other.

"Because our unsub has a partner."

Chapter 12

Clever tyrants are never punished.
—Voltaire

Lana

"You sure you'll be able to sit in on this?" I ask Jake as I walk in, pulling my sweatshirt off.

"Waited too long, and I'm pissed off enough to handle the gore tonight, Lana. Just looking at him makes me want to kill him. I'll be fine."

"It'll be the worst," I remind him.

He rolls his shoulders back. "I'll let you know if I need a break. But I doubt I will for this one." His jaw tics, and I nod, looking idly at the selection of shiny knives that are just waiting to turn red.

"What vehicle did you drive?" Jake asks me randomly.

"The Lexus you parked at Lindy's old house."

"No one saw you?"

I shake my head to answer his question.

"Logan?" he asks.

"I'll tell him I took the bus until I could call a cab."

My eyes lift to his. "Why the third degree?"

He purses his lips. "They know you have a partner now. It's just a matter of time before they unravel the whole thing, Lana."

He holds up his phone as the cameras catch them all heading

into the thick of the woods. Dogs are going crazy, but they won't find anything. Everything was tossed into the water after I saturated the clothing and mask in bleach.

"We knew we couldn't afford the time to leave behind fresh drag marks. It was inevitable they'd learn of a partnership," I say casually, moving toward the viewing window.

Kyle is banging against the one-way glass that serves as a mirror from his perspective. In fact, the entire box he's screaming inside is full of this glass, other than the ceiling, which is actually a mirror. The walls are bulletproof, practically impossible to break, despite his frantic punching and kicking.

His hand is a bloody mess from trying to punch through it, and I smirk. Maybe I know he hates small spaces and planned this beautiful killing spot two years ago. Maybe I built this underground tomb full of mirrors just for him.

Just for his death.

Jake already stripped him of his clothing, leaving him completely naked and vulnerable. The sight of Kyle's naked body makes my stomach roil.

"Was Duke suspicious?" Jake asks as I flip on the intercom switch, allowing us to hear the endless threats spilling from the lips of my next victim.

He doesn't know how empty those threats are.

"No. The police called him when they couldn't reach me immediately, since he took it personally that the Boogeyman attacked after he let his guard down on his quest to a bigger, better case. His guilt-induced involvement actually helps us, because I had to see him, and he's far more reliable as a witness to my whereabouts than any regular cop. He's watching my house, convinced I'm inside right now."

"And if he decides to knock and check up on you?"

"You're showing signs of the paranoia we promised to discuss if either of us suffered from it," I say, turning to face Jake. "Paranoia

All The Lies

evokes recklessness."

"That's a logical question," Jake says, clearing his face of all emotion, hiding the inner panic I know is there.

I turn down the intercom as Kyle threatens to tear a spine out.

"If he knocks and I don't answer, he'll call." I wag my phone at him. "And I'll answer. If he asks where I am, I'll tell him I went for a run to clear my head. Which I did run right through the trails in the back of the woods. We're two miles from my house. I can easily run right back. I bought that house for this reason, even though I only moved in not too long ago. You know all this already, so why the freak-out?"

He blows out a harsh breath as Kyle starts throwing himself against the glass in a desperate attempt to break it. He simply bounces off, not even making so much as a crack in the resilient surface.

"Sorry," Jake finally says. "It's just, things are starting to go wrong. First, Logan sees you, but doesn't see your face by some miracle. Then you deliberately find him when you shouldn't have been able to, and get him an ambulance. He suspects a woman, Lana. You told me that. And now they know you have a partner. It just feels like everything is going to end before we're ready."

I put a hand on his shoulder, giving him a sympathetic half smile. "I get it. But he could have died if I hadn't saved him, and we ran the risk of the partner thing with no drag marks. It was the only way to get Kyle, though. Breaking into his house would have been twice as hard with all four deputies inside."

He sighs harshly.

"If your life had been at risk, and Marcus was the one reaping revenge for me, he'd have sacrificed it all to save you. Just as you would have for him."

His gaze softens, and he leans forward, kissing the top of my head. A brotherly show of affection. "If it was Marcus doing this, I'd still be at his side," he whispers softly. "I'd be helping him. Can you say the same for Logan?"

My heart squeezes in my chest, and I fight back the emotion that tries to surface as I turn away, watching as Kyle staggers back from another failed attack on the glass.

"I should get in there and get started before he kills himself. That would suck all the fun out of this," I say calmly.

As I turn to head toward the door, Jake calls after me. "I worry that when the time comes, Logan isn't going to choose you the way you keep choosing him, Lana."

I keep my back facing him as I stand in the doorway, trying not to let the words sink in.

"I worry that he'll never understand and only see the fault and not the good. I worry he doesn't truly love you enough to give you what I would give Marcus. And I worry that you'll let him kill you before you fight to stay alive. Every day, I worry more. Because I love you like Marcus loved you. You're my only family, Lana. You're all I have. And Marcus might actually rise from the grave to kill me himself if I see this happening and do nothing about it."

A small smile tries to form as a tear rolls down my cheek.

"Marcus would have chosen you over me," I whisper hoarsely.

"I doubt that, Lana. And I've already failed you once. I failed you worse than I ever could have imagined."

"You didn't fail me, Jake," I say without turning around. "We were failed by everyone else."

I twist my head around so that our eyes meet, and add, "But you? You're the hero in all the fairytales that doesn't expect the heroine to put out."

He bursts out laughing, and I flash a smile before walking away. The smile falls the second I'm not in sight, and I put a hand on my chest, fighting the pain I don't want him to see.

So much we learned. So much we know. So much we have going on at once.

And all I can think about is what Logan will do if he learns the truth.

Once again pulling up a façade of composure, I push through the door, and the killer inside me emerges, turning my heart to ice and my nerves to steel.

Kyle doesn't even notice me until the door shuts and seals with a lock, the sound echoing around us.

His murderous gaze swings to me, but then he falters, his eyebrows raising in confusion.

"The fucking feds? The fucking feds are responsible for this?!" he shouts. "I'll have you all on a fucking platter when my father finds out about this."

A dark grin slithers across my lips like a serpent's ominous smile.

"Oh, the feds have nothing to do with this, Kyle. Don't you remember me?" I ask, my tone light but taunting as I take a step to the right, moving idly through the mirrored room.

He cocks his head to the side.

"You're that fed's girlfriend. Surely he's not stupid enough to piss me off and leave me all alone with someone so fragile."

His eyes drop down my body, the look in his eyes all too familiar as his gaze sweeps over me, leering, contemplative, calculated. "You really don't want to do this, SSA Bennett! You have no idea what I'm capable of!" he calls out. "Playing games with me will end badly," he goes on.

A voice comes over the com, as Jake decides to play a part.

"Actually, the feds are hours away, Davenport. Hope you don't expect Daddy to save you tonight."

Kyle tenses, looking around. He recognizes Jake's voice, yet hasn't placed mine. Well, that's just insulting.

"Jacob Denver?" Kyle asks, confused as he looks around. "The fucking hell do you think you're doing?" he demands, slamming his fist against the glass.

"Helping me reap a debt that's long overdue," I answer, smirking when his dark glare returns to me.

He tilts his head, and he starts coming right at me. "You want to fucking play? Let me show you what a mistake that is," he growls.

"Please try," I mock.

He lunges suddenly, and I dart to the side, bringing my foot up just in time to connect with his stomach. He barely gives himself time to recover before he's grappling for me again, but it's like watching a child fight with a teenage bully — the teenage bully being me.

With quick succession, I deliver one blow after another, my fist colliding with his nose; my knee making contact with his ribs. His cry of pain is like sweet music to my demented ears.

As I spin, my foot comes around, catching him on the side of the face hard enough to cause blood to fly from his mouth. His body spirals around and he collides with the glass, leaving a bloody smear before dropping to the ground.

As he spits up his blood, he glares over at me.

"Who the fuck are you?"

The music starts playing through the com; my mother's voice wafts over us, serenading this moment with past memories that have his eyes widening and his features paling.

That song is what the Scarlet Slayer has been tormenting the town with. He's starting to figure things out slowly.

He scrambles back, crab-walking right into the wall where he has no more room to run.

"I'm the girl you thought you broke," I say quietly, taking a step toward him as his body seizes in delicious fear. "I'm the girl you took too much from." Another step from me, and a pained sound from him as he tries to stand, but falls back down in his haste. "I'm the girl you thought you killed."

He finally gets to his feet, and my fist shoots out, connecting with his face over and over as he weakly tries to shield himself.

I finally grab his hair and slam his face into the glass, knowing Jake is on the other side and enjoying this like I am.

"I'm the girl who finally ends your reign of terror."

"No," he groans, wincing when I slam his face into the wall again. Then I grab his hair, jerking his head back, letting him see the bloody reflection of his face staring back at him.

"I'm going to let you watch every fucking second of it, just like you did for Marcus."

He cries out in pain when I wrench his arm back hard enough to dislocate it from its socket, using just the right angle.

He turns and tries to hit me with his good hand, but it's a pathetic swing that I dodge with too much ease.

"So weak," I taunt. "All those women were hurt by such a weak man."

His eyes darken, and a sick smile spreads over my lips as a knife slides to my feet, accompanied by the sound of the door shutting and sealing again.

"I think I'll join you on this one," Jake says as he nears.

Kyle dives for the knife, but I pick it up and kick him away, ignoring the burning tears trying to breach my eyes. I've envisioned this moment for so long, but he's so much weaker than I remember.

I remember the strength he held us down with. His words coming back to me as Jake wrestles the screaming Kyle to the ground, restraining his arms just the way he held us restrained.

"Oh, you're going to love this, baby. Just like you used to."

I grab the knife, and I slam it down on one finger, listening to the ripe screams that follow. A shudder slithers through me, the high of revenge oozing through my veins with a tangible presence.

It takes a little effort, but the knife finally cracks through the fragile bone, and another bloodcurdling scream is released into the box.

Jake smirks as I hold up the first finger.

"Hold her down! Hold Marcus down too. This is going to be fun."

"This is going to be fun," I say, echoing his words from the past as I shove the finger into his mouth and hold my hand down as I clutch his nose. I straddle his body to hold him steadier, and listen as he gags and chokes on his own finger that I cut off mid-knuckle.

He fights it hard, but the instinct to swallow finally overrides all else, and I release him after his throat works painfully to take the finger down.

As soon as I release him, he vomits, turning his head to the side as tears run down his face.

"Don't get sick, Victoria," Kyle taunts as I retch, spilling my guts on the pavement, then forced to wallow in it as he holds me down for Lawrence to have his turn. *"We're just getting started."*

"Don't get sick, Kyle. We're just getting started," I say, slicing through another finger, taking one more digit that once held me in place.

As he cries out, more memories assault me, and tears of pure hatred skid down my cheeks unexpectedly.

"The daughter of a whore and a fucking pussy. You see, I know your dad never had the balls to kill those women. I just don't care. Now take it, Victoria. Take it and shut the hell up."

"Take it!" I shout, slicing through another finger. "Take it and shut the hell up!"

Jake holds him down harder as I work through all ten fingers, then tie up the damage, preventing him from bleeding too much.

Kyle is a sobbing mess, but I wasn't lying. We're just getting started.

"Your turn, Tyler. Saddle up. It's bareback and fun tonight," Kyle goads, grabbing my naked crotch and then slapping it. *"It's getting a little worn out."*

All The Lies

"This is for me," I hiss, slicing the blade down his torso, scooting back as he screams in agony. The slice is just shallow enough to burn like fire but not deep enough to bleed too much.

Another memory surfaces, one that has my heart being suffocated and squeezed to death.

"I'm sorry, Ms. Carlyle. But it seems like the damage done to your internal organs and the life saving measures they took at the hospital have prevented you from ever being able to have children. They were forced to perform an emergency hysterectomy."

More tears cascade down my cheeks as I slice him to the side, slowly flaying a piece of flesh from his body like the monstrous pro I've become.

"This is for my father," I tell him, carving another section.

"Your father was weak. He cried as my dad's guys took turns. Oh, let me tell you everything they did and how your father cried like a little bitch."

I peel back a square of flesh, removing it from his body. Barely any blood flows because of how perfectly executed it is, but he still screams and cries, because it burns like hell.

He'll be skinned alive before I'm done.

"His ass is tighter than her cunt, if anyone wants a turn on that. He's a fucking faggot, so he's enjoying it," Kyle says while laughing.

"Did you get shit on your dick?" Morgan taunts.

"Nah. Just needed to feel something that worn out whore can't provide. She stopped being tight the first time I shoved my dick in her."

Another piece of flesh is carved away, and Jake continues to restrain Kyle as my tears grow more fervent and feverish, burning my own flesh.

"I took your virginity a long time ago. It's only right that I take this too," Kyle says, flipping me to my stomach as I cry out, forcing the tears back as he pushes me up on my knees and spreads my butt cheeks.

"Please don't!" I scream.

"Beg, whore. Won't do you any good. No one cares."

"Please stop!" Kyle cries out as I wave another square of flesh in front of his eyes.

"Beg, whore. Won't do you any good," I whisper darkly. "No one cares."

His eyes try to shut, but I grab his jaw, forcing them to open and stare at the mirror above our heads.

"We have a long way to go," I tell him calmly. "And you're going to be awake for all of it, even if I have to sew your eyelids open. So you choose if that's necessary or not."

Tears pour from his eyes for a different reason than they fall from mine. Mine fall from ten years of anguish that I've suppressed. Ten years of hatred I've confined. Ten years of pain I've ignored.

This is the monster that led the charge, and he'll die by my hands.

My tears fall for freedom.

They fall because he'll no longer haunt my nightmares. I'll lull myself to sleep with the memories of the screams he shares so freely.

"Don't worry, Victoria. You won't die yet," Kyle says as he slides the small knife over my body, leaving behind a faint trail of blood. "We still have all night."

My knife slides down as I climb off his body, and it nicks the limp flesh between his legs. Unlike Morgan, he's not a sexual deviant. He's just a sick son of a bitch who happens to have sociopathic tendencies.

He freezes, his eyes widening in horror, knowing what's to come.

"Don't worry, Kyle. I'm not ready for the grand finale just yet. We still have all night."

"Now everyone will know you're the whore. The whole town will see what you really are."

"You'll never get away with this!" my brother shouts, but Kyle ignores him, speaking to me as though I'm the one who shared those words.

All The Lies

"It'll be like this never happened, Victoria. Because you don't matter. And my father will still be the one they all fear, while you rot in your grave with your faggot brother and pussy father."

I lower my voice as I stare into his wide, terrified eyes that are still streaming with unrelenting tears.

"But tomorrow? The whole town will see what you really are. A weak, pointless man they once feared. Now I'll be what they fear. And your father's turn is coming. Then the two of you will rot in your graves, while I walk away from all of this, knowing the better monster won the war."

As another scream pierces the air, my tears slow down, the memories ebb, and the coldness only Logan can thaw washes over me with a choking hold.

Kyle Davenport won't last the whole night.

But I'm damn sure going to try and take as long as possible.

Chapter 13

In justice in the end produces independence.
—Voltaire

Logan

I'm half asleep when I feel a body sliding over mine and lips strumming my cheek. At first, I just lie there, feeling the warmth of the other person, but then my eyes fly open and my hand shoots out, ready to slam into—

My eyes widen as Lana catches my wrist with a stronger grip than I thought her capable of, and yanks her head back, her eyes widening in shock as she barely dodges my swing.

"Fuck!" I shout, jerking upright as she straddles me. "I'm so sorry! What the hell? I didn't—"

She starts laughing, confusing the hell out of me.

"I guess that was a stupid way to wake you up when you didn't go to sleep without me," she says, smiling now as she drops my wrist and tosses her arms around my neck.

I'm almost shaking with how close I came to nearly hitting her. Thank fuck she has good reflexes.

"Damn it, Lana, I'm so sorry."

"Don't be," she says, grinning as she brushes her lips over mine. "At least I don't have to worry about some other woman seducing you when I'm away."

I groan, returning her kiss as my body continues to quake.

All The Lies

"You'd never have to worry about that anyway. I told you I don't love easily," I murmur against her lips.

She kisses me harder, her fingers threading through my hair. Just as she starts grinding against me, my door swings open, and a feminine curse is spewed.

"Sorry!" Lisa's voice is like a wet blanket over both our libidos.

"I'll bet," Lana grumbles, looking over her shoulder as I sigh and hold her to me. She doesn't even make a move to get off me, which is fine by me.

"What?" I ask Lisa, who has the grace to look embarrassed.

"Really, I'm sorry. I didn't know Lana was here."

"So it's okay for you to walk into my boyfriend's room without knocking if I'm not here?" Lana asks her with an eerily cold tone.

I frown, looking at Lana's face. It's devoid of all emotion, and it's as though she's hiding the anger she's feeling too easily. What the hell?

Lisa draws my attention when she rolls her shoulders back, a smirk coming over her lips.

Ah, hell.

"I guess old habits die hard, considering I used to walk into his room all the time. Sometimes we forget we're not together anymore."

Fucking immature bullshit.

"*I never* forget," I decide to point out, only to keep Lana from thinking otherwise, because she should honestly know I'd never do anything with Lisa.

Lana doesn't move, her posture never changes, and for some reason, a twisted grin tugs at one corner of her mouth.

"Do you now?" Lana asks quietly. "I suppose I could remind you some time."

Hadley clears her throat, glaring at Lana as she shoulders by

Lisa and walks on into the room. I'm really glad everyone is seeing Lana on my lap while I'm in bed with nothing but a pair of boxers on.

Great professionalism.

"Lisa, you really shouldn't try to piss her off when you don't even have any true interest in Logan," Hadley sighs.

She casts a warning glare at Lana for some reason, then directs her attention to me.

"Sheriff called a town meeting in the park. Said he wants everyone there. They're about to send every single citizen in town out on a search for Kyle, now that there's daylight."

Kyle was taken right after sunset yesterday, and in a vehicle. There's no chance of us finding him in the woods, but the sheriff refuses to believe a car was involved because *nobody* says they saw a vehicle.

I think he underestimates this town's fear.

I also think he overestimates his son's value to this town.

"In that case, do you think you two could get out of here so I can get some clothes on?"

Lisa snorts. "Like I haven't seen you in less."

Lana's smile only grows, but it's actually kind of creepy, as though she's plotting something nefarious for Lisa.

"I'll get her out of here," Hadley says to Lana, then points a finger. "Nothing happens."

Lana shrugs and turns to face me, while Hadley berates Lisa. As their voices fade, Lana gets more comfortable on my lap, and I kiss her before she can say anything.

"I'm sorry," I murmur against her lips as I break the kiss. "Lisa's a bitch."

"She's just used to women *and* men letting her say whatever she wants with no consequences. I've dealt with the mean girl types before. All bark. No bite. But lots of tears."

I tilt my head, studying her. She seems...off. As though she's distanced herself somehow.

"Hey, you okay?" I ask her seriously, searching her eyes.

It's like they're colder. Almost eerie.

"Long night," she says on a sigh, running her finger down my cheek. "But I'm feeling better by the second. It's like you're magical or something, reminding me I'm human."

I have no idea what that means, but it's obvious she's hurting and trying to close herself off right now.

"What happened?" I ask, cupping her face.

Her eyes instantly glisten as they warm, and she blinks rapidly like she's holding back tears.

"Nothing," she says with a brittle smile. "Just not a lot of sleep. I wanted to get back to you as soon as possible."

I kiss her again, feeling her slowly relax in my arms, as though she's shedding whatever wall was weirdly between us for a moment. Her kiss is searching, as though she needs something only I can provide. But before I can deepen it, my phone goes off, reminding me there's a lot of work today, and I've only had about two hours of sleep.

Groaning, I break the kiss, resting my forehead against hers. "As soon as this day is over, we're going to resume that kiss. Hadley has a lot of forensics to go through in the far cabin today. Stay with her."

"I love how protective you are," she says softly.

Her eyes meet mine, and I try again to decipher what's going on in her head. It's like she's waged a war with herself, but she's not telling why. I almost want to ditch this day and just spend it in bed with her, wishing I could offer her the same escape she's so often given me.

"Go," she says on a sigh as she stands, straightening her red shirt. She's worn red almost every day since we've been here. Or maybe it has been every day.

"Why so much red?" I ask her, fingering the hem of her shirt as she stands.

"I just tossed a bunch of clothes in my bag. Apparently I picked stuff from my red section."

She flashes a smile, rolling her eyes.

"You have a red section?"

"I have a massive closet. Has to be organized somehow."

She skips out of the room, and I stand, running a hand through my hair. I don't even have time to take a shower to wake me up, since my phone won't shut the hell up.

As I leave the cabin, I glance down, catching a glimpse of Lana as she disappears inside our temporary headquarters.

Leonard is waiting for me when I get outside.

"Problems?" he asks, his eyes on the far cabin where Lana and Hadley are inside.

"Lisa."

He snorts and gets in, and I start pulling out.

"Lisa looked pleased with herself when she left."

"She's a pain in the ass." Quickly, I also tell him the details of the wonderful fucking morning I've already had.

"What'd Lana do?"

"Smiled at her and made a snide remark, but there was no bite to her tone. It was actually sort of weird. There was no aggression. Almost any other woman would have flown off the handle if my ex stalked in and stirred shit like Lisa did. Then again, Lana always surprises me with her reactions."

"Takes a lot control to not react in the heat of the moment," Leonard says, though it sounds like he's saying it more to himself

All The Lies

than me. "Can I ask you something?"

I shrug.

"How do you really feel about our killer? If you found out her identity today and heard her out, would you really be able to lock her away, knowing there'd never be any justice without her?"

My brow furrows. "Justice isn't torturing and killing a bunch of people, Leonard."

"Pretend you're not FBI for just a minute. Pretend you're a person who has witnessed the worst in humanity, and seen good in the monsters."

"I'm not following," I tell him as we pull up to the street that is blocked off. Cars are everywhere, so we're forced to park at the rear.

"My sister's best friend, Katie, once dated a drug dealer," he says randomly, and I twist in my seat, arching an eyebrow at him.

He stares me in the eye as he continues. "He never sold to kids, always held his distance from the drug life when he was home, and if any of his guys sold to a kid, their bodies would be found floating in the river, minus their heads, hands, and feet."

"Awesome choice in men," I say, confused.

He rolls his eyes. "At first glance, anyone would say that. But not one kid in his city could get their hands on drugs. No outsiders would even sell to a kid from that city for fear of what he'd do to them. But Katie? He never touched her. In fact, he fucking worshiped her, treated her like a queen, and every day he came home to her, swearing she saved him from his demons."

"Where are you going with this?" I ask, still confused.

"Katie was oblivious to what he did for a living, even though most of the city knew. She was always safe. The cops turned their heads, simply because if you get one dealer behind bars, another one pops up, and this guy wouldn't deal to kids. Better the devil you know and all that."

He blows out a heavy breath.

"He eventually got picked up on a misdemeanor, because not all cops believed in the 'devil you know' logic. Two weeks after his lock-up, Katie found out the truth. She felt betrayed. She was furious. She broke things off, and a new dealer moved into town. Within three weeks, ten kids between twelve and fifteen had died of an overdose."

"So you're saying that it's better to let one dealer keep doing illegal shit as long as he's not selling to kids?" I ask, still wondering where any of this is coming from.

"I'm saying, bad shit is in the world. But some of the monsters have morals, where others are pure evil. Katie moved on after a few months, found a guy with a nice normal job and life. He went to work at the accounting firm, but when he came home, he'd beat the hell out of her. She left him twice, and twice he hunted her down and made her pay. She pressed charges, and the cops let it slide, since he had no priors and Katie had been involved with a known drug dealer."

His lips tense, and I bristle.

"I had to step in when my sister called. I threatened the piece of shit, even used my status as leverage. Didn't stop him. And the cops didn't arrest him even after he put her in the hospital with half a dozen broken bones."

"What happened?" I ask, leaning forward.

"The drug dealer ex got out of jail after a year. He found Katie, and the cops found the abusive accountant. Well, they found his body floating with no head, hands, or feet. They also found the new dealer in the city a few weeks after that — same shape, if you know what I mean. Katie is married to him with three kids, and he still treats her like gold, while running a business that makes most furious. Katie learned that what you do for a living doesn't determine if you're a monster. And a killer can sometimes be more gentle than a man who's never killed before. I guess I'm saying I wouldn't fault our killer, because she could be worse, and these people, Logan… These people are fucked up. And how do you arrest an entire law enforcement department?"

All The Lies

I settle back in my seat and stare out my window, letting his words slowly register.

"Why did you tell me all that?"

He pushes his door open. "Katie subdued the real monster by loving the man and accepting all of him. I'm saying I hope our girl has someone doing the same for her, otherwise, she may lose herself to all of this. And it won't be the ending she deserves."

I should kick him off this case for admitting that. He wants her to get away with it.

For some reason, I just get out of the car instead, and keep my mouth shut.

Donny approaches, and Leonard stiffens, possibly worried that I'm about to announce the fact he's compromised and shouldn't be on this case.

"What do you have?" I ask him.

Leonard relaxes as Donny answers. "Kyle Davenport is one twisted son of a bitch," Donny says under his breath.

"I'm well aware. I mean, what is the sheriff speaking about?" I ask dryly.

"Wanting to find his son, and reminding the town he owns everything here, so if someone is helping the killer hide, they're going to regret it. He blatantly threatens the entire town, abusing his authority, and Johnson is letting it go. I can't even process this."

"Kyle Davenport really is sick," Lisa says as she joins us, her eyes finding mine and holding my gaze.

"So are you," I growl. "Ever try that shit on Lana again, and I'll make sure they demote you to some bullshit unit that deals mostly in paperwork and isolation."

Her eyes widen, and everyone around us shifts awkwardly.

"What about Kyle?" I ask Donny, moving my eyes away from Lisa.

Fuck it. I'll have her ass shipped to another unit regardless.

"You mean other than he vanished into thin air? Well, let's see, over five women have already told us this morning what he did to them in the Haunted House over the years. The girlfriend met us in private, saying usually he makes a second girl join them on the nights he gets really drunk. She's broken up with him three times, and has ended up in the ER three times."

Leonard's gaze swings to mine, and my lips tense. Something tells me he already knew that.

"So he's an abusive bastard with a fetish for raping women. We can all agree that he doesn't deserve to keep breathing clean air. Now I'm asking if there's any news about him."

They all shake their heads, and I walk around, wondering if anyone on the team is willing to put this girl behind bars if we manage to find her.

I even question it myself.

But this is a proxy killer. Has to be. No one was personally invested in these people enough to have revenge on a personal level. That makes her twice as dangerous, because she'll find another target to obsess over, and she'll eventually kill innocent people for minor infractions.

It sucks.

It really sucks.

But she can't just walk away from this.

She'll probably end up in an asylum as opposed to prison, but she sure as hell is too dangerous to leave on the streets, no matter what personal quandaries we're all suffering over this.

The entire team is compromised by this point, because the victims make it hard to be compassionate. It's the future I'm most worried about.

"Now get out there and find my damn son, or I swear this town will never sleep again!" the sheriff shouts, his face red as a bloated tomato on the verge of exploding.

"We need to deliver our profile to the psych hospitals in the surrounding areas," I say as the people listen to the sheriff rant for a few more minutes.

"If our unsub was mentally unstable, they wouldn't have the control to pull this off," Leonard argues.

"A partner changes everything. There's always a dominant in the partnership. This time, however, the dominant figure isn't the actual killer."

"Then who is?" Elise asks.

"Send someone back to Jacob Denver's house. Something was off when we paid him a visit," I tell them.

"It can't be him," Leonard sighs. "This partner would have had to be able to aid in painting these messages and all the other crazy shit. Jacob isn't physically capable of any of that. You saw the medical records."

"Our—I mean *the* killer, wouldn't have needed Jacob's help for that. He could have just masterminded all this," I point out.

Leonard gives me a grim look before shaking his head like he's disappointed. Then he walks away.

"What's his deal?" Donny asks, confused.

"He's having a rough day," I lie, unsure why I'm even lying.

Just as the crowd is about to disperse on a fruitless trek through the woods to look for Kyle, the church bells blare their song.

My brow furrows, and I tilt my head, wondering why bells would sound at six-fifteen in the morning. Usually they only chime on the hour.

There's a large, curious looking tarp-like bag hanging from the bell tower of the church.

There's a suspicious looking rope tied to one of the clock hands on the tower, and I watch as it clicks down to six-sixteen, and something suddenly swings out of the bag.

A collective gasp sounds out seconds before screams break across the park. People heave, spin away from the sight, and several start running like fire is on their heels.

The sheriff staggers, his eyes wide, his skin pale, and his legs weak. He crashes against a deputy who helps steady him. The deputies who aren't stunned to their spots are racing toward the church, along with Lisa and Donny.

Even my stomach roils as I stare at the tower in complete horror.

I'm not sure if it's Kyle Davenport I see hanging, considering there's not a piece of flesh to make him identifiable, but everyone here has the same conclusion.

Even if we can't identify him, we all know it's him.

The rope holds his neck, and his naked, fleshless body dangles from the tower as the bells chime on. If she wanted to make a statement that would incite a full-blown panic, she just won that war.

Then again, the mastermind probably planned this.

They knew this park would be crowded down with people at this time, even though the meeting was impromptu. They know the sheriff. They knew what he would do before he even did it.

The castrated corpse sways, crashing against the brick on occasion. And I can't look away.

Who is capable of something this depraved and dark without being psychotic?

"Still think she should have a happy life?" I ask quietly as Leonard swallows audibly.

"I expected him to be found in the worst condition," he says on a breath. "He orchestrated it all."

I shake my head. "This is someone with a psychosis so deep, they feel they have the right to do this, even though they themselves were never wronged personally."

All The Lies

"And if your sister had ever been subjected to Kyle Davenport, would you feel this was too much?" Leonard asks, a hard edge to his voice.

"I don't have a sister," I say before walking toward the chaos.

Elise hobbles up next to me, and I slow down so she doesn't have to struggle to keep up. "You think this was the endgame?" Elise asks, looking over at the gruesome sight before flicking her gaze back to me.

It seems unlikely this was the end, considering the unsub isn't displaying the usual signs of devolvement.

"I honestly don't know."

Lisa comes jogging up to us, her color curiously puce. She looks like she's on the verge of being sick.

"Skinned and castrated?" I ask her.

She nods, swallowing hard. "All ten fingers are missing as well."

That should have been a given.

"There was one new thing besides the complete flaying," she says, grimacing.

"What?"

"The eyes were sewn open."

Chapter 14

It is dangerous to be right when the government is wrong.
—Voltaire

Lana

"You can't hurt Lisa," Hadley tells me as I throw another knife into the picture of the offending bitch she speaks of.

It hits right between her eyes, and I go to pull it out.

"I'm getting out my anger. Not plotting her murder," I say dully.

"You're throwing a knife at her face."

"Her picture," I correct.

I feel her glare, but elect to ignore it.

"Do I want to know how you got so good with knives?"

I line up my next shot and take it, landing the knife in Lisa's throat. Oh, how I wish. Too bad that's not going to happen. After all, I can't kill someone for simply pissing me off.

Unfortunately.

"Come on. Logan doesn't want you left alone, and apparently I have a crime scene to go investigate," Hadley says on a long sigh.

"It's Kyle Davenport, and he was skinned alive before dying. There. Your job just got easier," I state dryly.

She strangles on a sound, and I turn to face her.

"Need me to recite some of those details of all the horrible things he did to wipe that horror off your face?" I ask.

She shakes her head vigorously. "I can't stomach hearing anything else that psycho has done. I just… You skinned him alive?"

I nod. "Yep. I was careful to remove the skin piece by piece and only the top layers, so that he didn't bleed too much during my fun."

I pull my knife free from Lisa's picture, then grab her picture — that I printed off from Hadley's computer — and toss the annihilated photo into the trash, covering it with some other rubbish.

"That's not creepy at all," Hadley mutters.

"I torture and kill men. Being creepy should be a given."

She studies me, and a frown creases her lips.

"You're even colder than usual."

"Usually I have more time with Logan after facing the worst side of me to do what needs to be done. *Lisa* was eager to interrupt that this morning, and it's fortunate I have my killer on a leash. She pushed at all the wrong times. I need cooling down periods after going that dark. It's how I keep my sanity. I've had to raise the timelines, losing a piece of myself with each kill."

I follow her out, and considering the jammed up streets, we elect to walk, moving briskly down the sidewalk.

"I'm worried about you, Lana. You're telling me you're losing yourself and struggling with not murdering Lisa."

I roll my eyes. "If I was going to kill her, I would have already done it while everyone was distracted with Kyle's flayed body."

She gags, and I smirk.

"Seriously. You're normally not this cold and detached," she says as we walk toward the town where the chaos I unleashed is fully at play.

I wanted to see the looks on their faces when they discovered Kyle, but knew it wasn't smart to be present. Jake and I drove like hell to get back in time to hang the body, and I still haven't slept.

"I'm almost done," I say as I ignore the tremor in my hand.

Killing Kyle the way I did… Digging deep enough to give him the true torture he deserved over such a limited amount of time… A lot was taken out of me. I felt rushed, and I made him pay for it.

I don't regret anything but not having more time to draw out his suffering.

"She's a bitch, I know. But she doesn't deserve any of your stabby urges."

I hold my hands up innocently, absently listening to the sobs of the people I may or may not have scarred for life. As of this morning, they no longer fear the sheriff who has *always* protected his son. Now they fear the one person who can break the untouchable.

They belong to me now.

The flock have a new shepherd to fear. *Baa, bitches.*

"I'm not going to stab her. Promise."

My emotions aren't in check the way they normally are. They're all over the place, and the memories I've controlled with each kill ran awry, stirring up all the feelings I iced so long ago. It's killing me not to go for the endgame now. Not to hit the sheriff before the shock of his son wears off.

I want him to marinate in his grief for longer than a few moments though. I want him broken before I arrive for the next phase.

"You got sloppy with counter forensics. You should have dragged him."

"I'd have been caught."

"They know you have a partner."

"I'm aware."

I grin over at her as she rolls her eyes, and I force the composure that normally comes with so much ease. It's fractured right now, and I don't have time to regroup before it's time to bring out the arsenal.

I have to strike soon, just not *too* soon.

I pop a piece of gum into my mouth, and Hadley groans when she sees Lisa talking to Logan and Leonard.

"Please behave. This is a crime scene, and you can't give me another one." Her tone is joking, but also serious.

"I'll be good," I say with a dark smile, my eyes on Lisa as I picture what her screams would be like.

I really need to get my control back before I cut her a little.

That would be bad.

"Witnesses are all around," Hadley says in a singsong voice.

I keep staring at Lisa as she tries to touch Logan. He wisely backs away, not letting her touch connect with his arm. His back is to me, but Lisa spots me, and a devious smile curves her lips.

Oh, I could so teach her a lesson.

Hadley starts getting worried again, stepping in front of me to cut off my vision.

"Don't, Lana. I'm onboard with your crusade, but I'm not cool with petty cattiness."

My eyebrows go up, but before I can speak, Lisa's voice interrupts.

"It's sad that she has to hurt the team by needing a constant babysitter," Lisa says, because she's stupid enough to provoke someone who could kick her ass for hours and never grow tired.

"Go. Away," Hadley snaps, glaring at Lisa.

Lisa snickers as she starts walking by, and I spit my gum out. Because I'm an awesome aim, it lands right in the back of her hair, hitting hard enough to imbed in there *real* good.

Lisa gasps and grabs the back of her hair, whirling around with wide eyes that look ridiculous paired with that gaping mouth.

I grin and wag my fingers at her before walking again, moving toward Logan.

Hadley groans while running to catch up with me.

"Now *that* was petty," I quip, grinning proudly.

Oddly, I don't feel so stabby anymore. I doubt I could spit gum out at all my impending victims and feel free, but with Lisa, it seems to do the trick.

I should buy more gum.

"I can't believe you did that," Hadley hisses, but I can tell she's biting back a smile that matches my immature one.

"Better than sending her roses from a serial killer." I shrug, and Hadley's smile vanishes.

"Too soon?" I ask, playing coy.

She flips me off and walks away just as Logan walks up, eyeing the interaction between us.

"You're not Hadley's friend until she flips you off at least twice," he says, cupping my chin and tilting my head back.

"Then we must be besties because she uses that gesture quite often with me."

He smiles, but I see the heaviness in his eyes and how weighted he feels. Kyle's body was too much for him, and I knew it before I delivered it to the town.

He doesn't understand.

Jake's words try to climb into my head, but I ignore them, forcing myself to focus on the here and now.

"As soon as this case is over, I'm taking a long, overdue vacation and turning my phone off for at least a week. We'll go somewhere they can't find us," he says, running his lips over mine.

I entertain the illusion, distancing myself from reality as I stay the Lana Myers he loves, and not the girl he's chasing.

All The Lies

"I'll take you up on that, SSA Bennett."

He grins against my lips, but a loud shout has us breaking apart.

"My son is dead, and you're making out with your girlfriend after they just cut down his body!" the sheriff shouts, outraged as he charges Logan full speed.

Two deputies charge us as well, but Logan's fist shoots out, connecting with one face before he lands a hit to the sheriff's stomach, halting the attack as the dickheaded man doubles over.

My instincts take over before I can refrain, and my hand flies up, slamming into the throat of the third man before his punch can land on me. He coughs and his eyes bug out, and Leonard tackles him to the ground, while Donny wrangles the other one back.

Leonard's eyes meet mine, and for a brief moment, I panic. My movements were precise, showing far more experience than Lana Myers should have.

"Nice reflexes," he says, giving me a tight smile as he cuffs the man on the ground.

Logan spins the sheriff, shoving him into a tree and cuffing his hands behind his back.

"Get your fucking hands off them!" Johnson shouts, charging toward us. "You can't arrest the sheriff!"

"He attacked a federal agent," Leonard says. "Just as they did."

"I didn't," the one under him groans.

Leonard makes him cry out in pain as he tightens the cuffs more. "No, you tried to attack a *defenseless* woman."

I really don't like being called that. It's rather insulting.

I turn around, walking away before Johnson pisses me off too much. Logan is one hell of a fucking trigger for me, because I want to blow Johnson's head off even as he and Logan argue, their voices raising.

The war has started, and it's not too long before Logan is sent away. We've guessed their every move. We've already hit checkmate, but they still think it's the middle of the game.

I can't blow it all by stabbing Johnson right between the eyes in the middle of the park full of badges and witnesses.

So I walk away. I count to ten. Then to two thousand. I jog. I run. I fucking meditate.

But the urge to kill those sons of bitches is still raw and raging inside me. I'm fighting to hold back my urges until the endgame. Right now it feels almost impossible.

For once, I'm worried about my sanity.

So I call the only person who cares enough to help talk me down.

"Talk me down," I say to Jake, my heart thumping heavily. "Talk me down now."

"Ducks have corkscrew penises," he says as my footsteps pause. "Come on over. I'll show you some pictures. Nasty little fuckers."

I roll my eyes, finding myself smiling for no reason at all. "Do I want to know why you know about this?"

"I have a vast amount of useless, sometimes disturbing knowledge for purposes such as this. The more random, the better to throw you off your game with, my dear."

"I don't want to see corkscrew penises."

"Then I'll pull up a blue waffle for you. Come over. Now. Before you do something stupid."

"What is a blue waffle?"

I can almost hear his mocking grin. "You'll see. Guarantee you won't be thinking about killing for a while. Your mind will need to be bleached."

"The things I do to stay sane," I grumble, changing course as I go to investigate this blue waffle thing.

Chapter 15

It is forbidden to kill; therefore all murderers are punished, unless they kill in large numbers and to the sound of trumpets.
—Voltaire

Logan

"Hey," I say, relaxing when Lana answers the phone.

I don't blame her for bailing on the madness that followed the sheriff's unprovoked attack, but I've been worried since she hasn't answered her phone for the past few hours.

The sheriff and his deputies are cooling down back at their station. Johnson won the war on the arrests, but he's running out of juice. This is one more strike against him in the file Collins is currently preparing.

"Hey," she says softly, her voice like a soothing balm.

"Where are you?"

I look around the cabin, finding no sign that she's been back.

"I went for a run. I was getting...annoyed. I don't like being annoyed," she says sadly. "I hope you're okay. I didn't want to call until I knew for sure you weren't around any of them."

"I'm fine, Lana," I say with a smirk. "Trust me, I can handle a few backwoods cops and an outdated agent with superiority complexes."

"Don't underestimate them."

Her voice comes from behind me, and I toss my phone to the

bed when I see her standing in the doorway, her chest rising and falling rapidly as a small sheen of sweat beads at her forehead.

"A body drops from the tower, and you go for a run," I say on a sigh, not realizing how tense I was until this moment.

"They were attacking you. I knew if I said anything, I'd just make it worse," she says as she pulls off her jacket and steps farther into the room. "And I suck at biting my tongue."

My grin etches up as I move in closer, tugging her to me by her waist.

"I can handle my own battles, so you can use your tongue for better things," I murmur against her ear, feeling her smile even though I can't see it.

I start kissing a trail down her neck, and she presses her body to me.

"I've needed this," she says, her arms tightening around me in an embrace.

As much as I'd love to do something more than hug, I realize it's sort of what I need in this moment too. Mostly because she's fucking ridiculously brave enough to wander around a town where a man was just skinned alive. Why can't she be normal and lock herself inside this cabin?

I'm getting an ulcer over her.

"We're getting away as soon as this case is over. Just you and me and a beach far, far away."

"I know you said a week but…maybe longer than a week?" she asks, leaning her head back. "My treat?"

"I can't take more than a week at a time, given our current work load. But maybe soon. And I'll pay for it."

She rolls her eyes before her head finds my chest, and she continues holding onto me.

"I love you," I say softly.

All The Lies

Her arms squeeze me tighter as the chatter outside the window grows restless, everyone waiting on me.

"I love you too," she says on a long sigh. "I take it you have somewhere to be?"

"Sort of have to find the guy who just skinned a grown man alive."

She nods and steps back, wiping something away from her eye. "Right. Sorry."

"You okay?" I ask, lightly gripping her chin and turning her to face me.

She peers up at me, her eyes hesitant. She never asks for anything, but always gives so much. Yet I see a question in her eyes, and I'm willing to do whatever she wants. Even if it's getting the hell out of here and abandoning this case.

Then again, I still have a lot of justice to find in an extremely unjust town, while pretending to focus only on the current killer. Although, considering Johnson and the sheriff are already plotting my demise, I suppose I could give up pretenses. They know by now I'm doing more than gathering some background that could point to our killer. Hell, I've basically announced it.

I'm building a whole fucking case against them.

It's just really hard to do without any physical evidence.

"What do you need?" I ask her when she grows silent.

"This afternoon, if you get a chance, do you think we could spend a couple of hours together?"

It's the first time she's ever asked that. Usually it's me asking her to bend her life around my crazy schedule, not to mention put up with possible death threats.

"I can take off the entire afternoon," I say, strumming her cheek with my fingertips.

I really can't afford it right now, not with Johnson scheming with the director as I speak. But I won't tell her that.

"Just a couple of hours," she says with a small smile. "I know you have a lot on your plate."

The chatter outside keeps growing louder, and I bend to press a kiss to her lips.

"I'll be back at seven, and then I'm all yours for the rest of the night."

She closes her eyes as I touch her, as though she's absorbing the feel of my hand on her cheek.

"Okay," she says softly, her eyes opening to reveal those haunting green eyes that have forever been seared into my memory.

I kiss her quickly, and head for the door, feeling like I'm doing something wrong. Never once, until now, has she seemed so vulnerable.

When I reach the outside, there are people lined up all around, everyone talking at once. What the hell? How long was I inside? This wasn't going on when I came in.

"What's going on?" I ask Elise.

She turns to me with a stoic expression.

"Apparently the amnesia is gone, and suddenly everyone wants to tell the tale of what happened ten years ago, along with everything that's been going on before and since then. We're going to be taking statements for the rest of the night."

People are lined up all the way down the street, and I run a hand through my hair. I turn to see Lana standing on the porch, her eyes settling on the long line of people who are ready to spill the secrets they've kept for so long.

That coldness is back in her eyes.

It's as though she resents them right now.

Fear is always a good motivator to make people grow honest.

I turn back to Leonard, and he gestures me toward him.

"I'm supposed to ride with Donny to the M.E. to get the report on Davenport," I tell him.

"I'm taking his place. He's going to help with this mess and deal with the deputies who keep showing up and trying to squash the line. Unsurprisingly, no one is backing down. I guess they fear a killer who has the power to skin a monster more than they fear the men who've had them cowering for who knows how long."

I shake my head, leaving behind the mess.

As soon as we're in the car, I crank it and start driving.

"Did you get ahold of Jacob Denver?" I ask.

"He's in California on business, according to his answering machine."

"You don't say," I murmur. "How very convenient. Look into it and see if there's proof."

"Alan confirmed the plane ticket was used and someone checked into a hotel under his name in California. He's pulling security footage, but we both know that a ball cap will obscure most of the visibility for a guy in a wheelchair. I'm guessing he planned this out carefully if he's involved. His alibi will check out, even if it's not really him."

He raps his fingers on the dash like he's nervous, and I give him a sidelong glance.

"What's wrong?" I ask, curious.

"I have a feeling you're not going to like the next part I tell you."

"What part?"

He turns to face me, and I pause at a stop light.

"Alan has been getting watched closely by the director, so I had an old friend do some extra research. I found out that Jacob Denver has another business he's basically a silent partner in."

"Okay..."

"Remember how I told you I had a theory, but thought I was wrong? But then we found out our unsub has a partner?"

"Sure. Why is this making you so nervous?" I ask, confused.

"Does the name Kennedy Carlyle sound familiar for any reason?"

I think on it, trying to mull it over. "The name Carlyle does... Shit. That was the name of the drunk drivers who were behind the wheel of the car that killed Jasmine Evans."

He nods slowly. "They orphaned a daughter who was young. Same age as Victoria, actually. Their birthdays were even close together. Her name was Kennedy."

"What does this have to do with anything?"

He raps his fingers harder, acting more nervous than I've ever seen him before.

"At first I thought it was just serendipitous. I visited the hospital to ask about Victoria Evans, but when I said a sixteen-year-old girl involved in a car crash on that date, they said they'd already spoken to one FBI agent about her. I got confused, until they handed me a file on Kennedy Carlyle instead of Victoria Evans. They couldn't show me much, but they hit the highlights."

"You've lost me, Leonard," I groan.

"Hadley Grace called them about Kennedy. Pretty typical of her."

"Why?"

He suddenly climbs over the middle, his hip smashing into my shoulder on his way to the backseat.

"What the actual hell?" I harp, swerving when he hits my shoulder again.

"Sorry!" he calls out as he settles into the backseat. "Just wanted to make sure I'm out of hitting range."

My eyebrows hit my hairline.

"Look, it sounded absolutely absurd, but I struggle to believe in coincidences," he rambles on.

All The Lies

"Leonard, I swear, I'm this close to losing my fucking patience." I pinch my fingers together to show him exactly how little patience is left.

"Hadley always researches any girl you're involved with," he finally says.

"I realize everyone thinks I get around a lot, but I've never heard of Kennedy Carlyle," I tell him dryly. "And I don't get around nowhere near as much as the rumors like to say I do."

"She was in the hospital the same night as Victoria Evans — the same night she and Marcus Evans died."

"And?"

"And I found that really coincidental, considering her parents were the reason Jasmine Evans died. So I dug into it a little. Kennedy Carlyle changed her name a long time ago. Ten years ago to be exact. She also left the hospital against doctor's orders the next day after her life-saving surgery."

"Damn it, Leonard!" I shout.

"Fine! Fine." He takes a long breath. "Before I tell you this, you should know there is no romantic involvement with any other man going on. I researched that very, *very* thoroughly. In fact, she's had very few romantic involvements over the years."

"Why do I give a damn?" I groan.

His eyes dart around the car as I glare at him through the rearview mirror.

"She left with Jacob Denver. The two of them own a buy, sell, and trade store online. And Kennedy Carlyle now goes by Lana Myers."

My blood seizes in my veins as all the oxygen leaves my lungs painfully. The car skids to an abrupt halt, and Leonard catches himself on the back of the seat in front of him.

"Seatbelt," he mutters, grimacing. "Why didn't I think of a seatbelt?"

But my ears are thumping wildly with the drumming of my over-stimulated heart. My hands grip the steering wheel too tightly as I stare ahead but see nothing.

"She loves you, Logan. I think you should know that before you react at all."

Something ignites loudly, and a hissing of fire drags me out of my head for a brief moment as a fire lights and slithers over a wall at the town hall. People trip and stare—gawk, actually—as the words appear, written in fire this time.

Run. Before the town burns to the ground. Run. Run. Run.

"No," I say quietly, shaking my head. "No. There's no way it's Lana."

"I thought that at first," he says too quietly. "Then I read the reports on Plemmons from the autopsy. Lana had a few bruises. Plemmons was loaded down with them. A man who had easily subdued so many women in the past just ran over a knife after taking a beating? We just never looked into it, because—"

"Hadley," I say on a rasp whisper.

"Yeah. Hadley. And then there was the pedophile who hurt—"

"Hadley," I say again, feeling the binds of betrayal squeezing tighter and tighter, almost as though it's becoming a tangible noose around my neck.

"Yeah," he whispers, so much pity in his voice. "Obviously she believes in whatever Lana has told her about this crusade. After what Hadley went through, it's not surprising. I understand it too, but…I don't understand how she can be a proxy but not be suffering any signs of psychotic breaks. I feel like I'm missing something."

My chest gets heavier and heavier as the truth slowly creeps into my every bone, robbing me of my ability to use any of my motor functions.

"She does love you," he says quietly from the back seat. "I've seen it, Logan. She risked it all to—"

"*Stop* talking," I say on a rasp, unable to say more when my throat knots up.

Cars pass us as we idle in the middle of the street, and I continue to stare aimlessly.

Every morning I woke up and spent the day worried about her safety, dreading every second away. And every night she laid down with her secrets, possibly laughing at me.

"You're a profiler," Leonard says, ignoring my demand for silence. "You know what she feels isn't imitation. Don't do anything stupid, Logan. You may be the only thing grounding her to reality, and if you love her... Just remember the story about Katie."

I snort derisively as my heart kicks my chest.

"Stop. Talking."

Instead of driving to the M.E., I turn around and drive back to the cabins.

"Don't tell anyone else yet. I want a confession," I say with a deadly calm tone.

"I said don't do anything stupid, Logan."

My hands grip the wheel tighter, betrayal continuing its course through my bitter veins.

I've loved a killer who I knew nothing about. I've loved a girl who was obsessed with a dead family to the extent of killing, or manipulated by a man who preyed on her psychosis.

One way or another, I'm finding out tonight.

Chapter 16

Tears are the silent language of grief.
—Voltaire

Lana

I'm just stepping out of the bathroom, adjusting my towel, when Logan steps through the bedroom door, scaring the shit out of me.

"You gave me a heart attack," I groan, gripping my chest. But then my lips turn up in a smile, despite his very serious expression.

"Come back for the circus outside?" I ask, adjusting the towel.

"Everyone is gone. There was a new message in fire this time. I'm sure everyone all over town has said something to someone else. Things get around fast in a small town."

"Small towns everywhere have that nasty little habit," I chirp, swallowing anything else I might want to say on the matter.

He continues staring at me, his serious expression growing foreboding.

"Are you okay?" I ask, getting worried.

"Yeah," he says, stalking toward me.

I don't have the chance to ask more, because he's suddenly on me, his lips crushing mine in a painful kiss. There's no finesse or tenderness the way there usually is.

It's hard, demanding, almost punishing, but I kiss him back, clinging to him. I'm not sure how he already got some free time, but I'm all for it.

All The Lies

"I love you," I say against his lips, which earns me an even harder, just shy of painful kiss as he lifts me and drops me to the bed, coming down on top of me.

He doesn't return the words, possibly because he's too busy tearing his clothes off, frantic to have me. When his lips find mine again, it's no gentler.

He shoves my legs apart with the same rough vigor, and then he thrusts in. I cry out in surprise, thankful that I happen to get wet easily around him. That could have hurt otherwise.

And he thrusts in harder, and harder, and harder… It just goes on and on, his hips thrashing angrily to no rhythm.

"I love you," I say against his ear when he breaks the kiss and drops his head beside mine.

Again he doesn't return the sentiment, and he continues to fuck me wildly, violently, furiously. As good as it feels, a hollowness forms in my chest, a dull ache growing and expanding over me.

I cling to him harder as a tear falls, realization slowly sinking in. He grips my hips, arching me up, taking me like I'm his to own…his to break.

Another tear. And another. Not from any physical pain, because there's only intense pleasure. It's because you don't have angry sex unless you're angry, and Logan is furious.

And he's using me.

One last time.

Punishing me.

Because he knows.

But he still doesn't know the whole truth.

Tears slip free faster, and I take it. I wish it didn't feel so incredible, but the flesh enjoys it even as the heart shatters beneath it.

I cry out, unable to help myself when an orgasm tears through me. Even as I cry from emotional anguish, the physical pleasure still forces my body to shudder with desire.

As he stills inside me, my heart pounds, shattering more and more with each passing beat. I knew it would hurt.

I knew it would devastate me.

I had no idea it would strangle me with a heavier hand with each passing second.

"You know," I whisper softly, the broken sound of my voice nearly scratching my own ears.

He pulls off me as abruptly as this all began, and my hands are jerked above my head. I don't even fight as I stare at him, watching him refuse to look at me as my hands get bound to the wrought iron headboard with his handcuffs.

My tears fall without mercy, embarrassing me, humiliating me, robbing me of any dignity I might find in this moment.

And he leaves me naked as he stands and pulls on his clothes, not saying a word until he's fully dressed.

He still doesn't look at me.

"I shouldn't have done that," he says bitterly. "Then again, I also should have known I was sleeping with a killer for the past several months."

Finally, he levels me with cold blue eyes that lack a single ounce of warmth.

There's pain, and then there's agony.

It's been a long time since I felt the agony I unleash on my victims.

But I feel it now.

It's bone-deep, gut-wrenching, and powerful enough to pulverize you from the inside. Naked and cuffed to a bed as I cry the painfully hot tears, I try to ignore the agony that continues to rip through me with a relentless force.

But it's useless.

I'm still too raw from the wounds I opened up last night.

I'm too in love to pretend I don't care.

All The Lies

And the heartache is too real not to feel it through every cell of my very existence.

I no longer wish to be a romantic. Because it hurts too fucking much.

"Logan, I—"

"You'll shut the hell up right now, Lana," he snaps, his eyes glistening with his own unshed tears. "I loved you. I cared about you. And you? All you fucking did was lie! You used me!"

I start to speak again, but he grabs my mouth, painfully pushing it closed. The worst thing he could do is what he's doing now.

Silencing me.

It was the worst part of it all.

Being silenced, because no one wanted to hear.

Now the one person I've opened myself up enough to love is silencing me.

I grasp for anger; I search for the cold; but I'm greeted with nothing but more misery and tears as they cascade with too much freedom.

But he's cold. He's like ice. Yet says what I felt was a lie.

"You're sick. You need help. And I honestly have no fucking clue what to do with you right now, because… You know what? You figure out why. You made this mess, threw me in it without giving a damn about how it would affect me, and you can stay in here and stew on what's about to happen."

He turns abruptly, and I rein in my words.

"Kennedy Carlyle," he says under his breath. "Un-fucking-believable."

It's on the tip of my tongue to explain everything, but that coldness finally washes over me, stealing some of the pain as I close my eyes and search for it…beg for it.

Jake was right. Logan never would have chosen me.

He just proved it.

He didn't even ask.

He didn't even care.

As he slams the door and storms away, I slowly open my eyes, staring at nothing as I slide my wrists down the pole. My body works on auto-pilot, my foot finding my purse and dragging it up.

I never take my eyes off the wall as more of the coldness creeps in, rushing through my veins with renewed purpose. I want to be numb, but that will take a while. It'll take more kills than I have time for today.

It'll take more of my soul that I just got back.

As I find the lock pick kit and work it up to my hands to find the proper tools, I continue staring ahead, not needing my eyes for anything. I'm not usually too good at picking locks, but apparently having your heart ripped out is some extra incentive to get it right.

As soon as I'm freed, I slowly climb out of bed, dress myself, grab my things, pack my bag, and casually walk out of the cabin like there's no reason to be in a hurry. My mind is almost blank. Even as fresh tears fall, the coldness grows stronger.

As soon as I make it to the newest place Jake has set up since abandoning his father's hunter's cabin, I find my best friend.

His eyes come up, and his features pale as I drop to my knees, my body giving out as it starts to shake with the silent pain I'm working so hard to suppress.

I thought love would rip my heart out.

I thought it would set me on fire.

Instead, it turned me into ice.

End of book 4
Continue reading for final book.

Paint It All Red

Book 5

Love is not supposed to be beautiful. It's supposed to be a raw, gritty struggle that forces you to face the most vulnerable parts of yourself, so that when the good times come, you can savor and enjoy them, fully appreciate what they're worth. Otherwise, you take it all for granted.

— Lana Myers

Fuck the list. It's time for the endgame.

Chapter 1

We are rarely proud when we are alone.
—Voltaire

Logan

Hadley jumps when I sling open the door to her room. She jerks out her earbuds, clutching her chest with her free hand.

"Cheese and rice, you lunatic. Don't scare someone like that when there's a serial killer literally in our backyard."

"Or living just a few cabins down, right?" I ask dryly, though there's an edge to my tone that has her entire body stiffening.

She doesn't even have to say the words, but I want to hear them.

"You knew?" I ask her quietly, my tone full of disbelief and heartbreak.

Everything hurts right now, even as I fight off the onslaught of emotions. In this unit, you train against showing emotion at all costs. I've never found that to be harder to do than today.

Her lips move for several seconds before words actually start coming out.

"Logan, I'm sorry, but—"

"You knew!" I shout with accusation, as my fist slams into the wall, and my entire body heaves for a breath of air that doesn't feel lined with lead.

"Logan!" she yells, but I turn around and face her, slowly

regaining my calm. "Listen. It was complicated, and she—"

"We're done, Hadley. You and me. I'm fucking done with you," I say on a broken promise.

Tears immediately spring from her eyes.

"Are you serious?" She has the nerve to ask that with incredulity in her tone.

"Yeah. I can't be friends with someone who could watch me fall in love with someone like that and *not* tell me the truth."

Her eyes narrow, and her lips tremble. "Someone like *that*? Someone who would kill or die to keep you safe? Someone who loved you so much that she almost gave up her revenge?"

"Her revenge?" I ask bitterly, shaking my head as I turn and stalk away. "It's not *her* fucking revenge!"

I slam the door behind me, and stalk next door to where Leonard almost falls off the chair when I burst in. "Shit! Easy, man. I'm trying to find some more info on Ken—"

His words die when he sees my face. "Oh shit," he says on an exhale.

"Yeah," I say, dropping to a chair and grabbing the bottle of whiskey he has hanging out of his go-bag. "She admitted it."

"She what?" he asks, shocked.

"She basically admitted it. I couldn't stick around for a full confession."

"Where the hell is she?"

I run my sleeve over my eyes, then turn up the bottle.

"Cuffed to my bed," I say when I lower the bottle.

His eyes grow wider.

"I have no idea what to do right this second. She's fucked my head up so much that I can't bear turning her over to anyone in this town or the FBI. But I know I have to do something. Since I don't know what, I cuffed her in place."

Paint It All Red

It's a terrible fucking way to stall, but it's the only solution I currently have.

He scrubs his face before shoving a file at me.

"I can't find anything at all in her history — besides drug use — that would make her willing to do anything like this. She's been clean for years though, and I haven't noticed any track marks. And she's not delusional or suffering a psychotic—"

"Hence the fucking reason I don't know what to do," I growl. "She's lucid, well aware of her surroundings, too fucking smart to be too stupid, and definitely not the type to be easily manipulated by anyone — not even Jacob Denver."

I laugh humorlessly as a memory surfaces. She called him Jake, even fucking told me *Jake* was her bisexual *business* partner. I never pieced the shit together. Because I was too blinded by everything I felt for her to even *consider* such a possibility.

"Here's the file," he says quietly. "Have a look at it. Maybe it'll help you figure it out."

I jerk the file from the tabletop, and I flip it open. I'm immediately grimacing when I see the folder, because of the grizzly pictures. But there's one thing that doesn't make sense.

"What the hell?" I ask quietly.

Blue eyes. In the picture they have on file *before* the accident, Kennedy Carlyle looks nothing like Lana Myers. And her eye color was blue — no contacts.

I flip the pictures, finding the photos taken for the police report of Kennedy's damage. I know Lana's body too well, and the marks in the picture, though somewhat similar, aren't exact.

A chilling sensation creeps up my spine as sickening possibilities start to unfold.

"Any chance you have the file on Victoria Evans?" I ask calmly, keeping my voice steady.

He hands it to me immediately.

"Why?"

I take a quick, steadying breath before I open the file, and a pair of haunted green eyes stare back at me with a face that doesn't match Lana's, but still carries some resemblance.

My heart sinks to my toes as I flip open the pictures, finding the ones they also sent to the police. Nausea almost overwhelms me when I see the marks aligning perfectly with the scars I know by heart.

"Oh shit," I say on a hissed breath.

"What?" Leonard demands.

My eyes pop up as regret wells and explodes inside me, shaking me to the core.

"Lana Myers is not Kennedy Carlyle."

He looks genuinely confused, and I hand him the same folder.

"Lana Myers is Victoria Evans."

He drops the folder like it's on fire as his eyes jerk up to meet mine, wide with shock.

Somehow, probably with some help from Jake, she went in as Victoria Evans, and left as Kennedy Carlyle. Considering I can barely stomach looking at either of their badly crushed faces in those photos, it's not a surprise that he did it with such ease.

"That changes everything," he says on a weary breath.

He breaks out his laptop, and I lean back, my anger slowly fading as my mind starts to work. I stopped at that coffee shop by chance, because our usual spot was too crowded. I pursued her, wanted to earn her trust, even saw something in her I needed for myself.

Every smile before me was probably rare. Every smile with me was given freely with genuineness. Every touch was hungry and full of emotion she struggles to show.

She trusted me.

Paint It All Red

"You may very well be the damn reason she's not suffered a break," Leonard hisses, still typing away on his laptop.

I take another shot of liquid courage and stand, but Leonard catches my wrist.

"These images don't match up on the computer."

"What?"

He points to the files. "I got copies of their paper files. You know I'm old-school. But on the computer, the images are swapped."

I look on the screen, and sure enough, Victoria Evans has the wounds of Kennedy Carlyle and vice versa. Green eyes meet mine from Kennedy's file.

"Jake could change what they had in the computers, but not before they started a physical file," I whisper to myself.

I'd have never known.

"What are you going to do?" Leonard asks me.

"Tell Hadley not to say anything. I can't talk to her right now. And you don't say anything either."

He almost smiles, but stops himself. He's been advocating for her from the sidelines, and I've been on the verge of removing him from this case.

All along, I was in love with the girl who wants this town dead.

I jog back to my cabin, swing open the door, and practically sprint to the bedroom. That's when my heart sinks.

The handcuffs are tossed on the floor, along with the sheet. And everything Lana brought is gone.

I swallow against the knot in my throat, slowly lowering myself to the bed.

She saved my life.

I cast her aside.

It takes me a minute to realize I've been gone for over an hour, even though it feels like only minutes. I gave her too much time to disappear.

I grab my phone and dial Leonard as I walk outside.

"I need to know any ties to this town that they still have."

Typing rattles in the background. I'm tempted to ask Hadley, but after what I just said to her, I doubt she'd be likely to help.

"Christopher Denver owns one of those hunting cabins in the woods. I'll text you the location."

I hang up and immediately change clothes and shoes. You can't run through the woods too well in a suit.

I dart out of the house seconds later, reading the text with the location. More memories flit through my head as I run.

Lisa fucking taunted her, practically tried to provoke Lana. Lana could have destroyed her.

Or Victoria, rather.

She left the argument with Johnson and the sheriff earlier because they were pissing her off, and she was afraid of what'd she'd *do*, not what'd she say.

Seeing the sheriff had to be hard on her, and she asked for two fucking hours, as though she needed me. And I came back, fucked her, then unloaded mayhem, as if I was daring her to show her true colors.

I walked out when she simply cried. The cold-hearted killer who tortured and slaughtered the monsters from her past… I made her cry. She never even got angry.

There are so many unpredictable variables about her, and I have no idea what to do.

As soon as I reach the cabin, I pull my gun from my ankle holster, holding it at my side. After two quick breaths, I kick in the door, but stop moving, my gun still at my side and not aimed at anything.

Paint It All Red

Jacob Denver is sitting on a couch like he's been waiting for me.

I cock my head, my eyes narrowing, and he sits comfortably, completely relaxed.

My eyes dart around, seeing the empty cabin and bare walls. He speaks as I clutch the gun with both hands, ready to aim it at him if he gives me a reason.

"I knew you were coming," he drawls, leaning up. "So put your gun away. If I was a threat, you'd already be dead. Fortunately for you, I happen to enjoy breathing, and I'm not sure Lana would be okay with me retaining oxygen if I laid a hand on you."

I cut my gaze toward him, releasing the gun with one hand, while holding it with the other.

"Where is she?"

He snorts derisively. "You came alone, which means you haven't told your team yet. Well, other than the Leonard guy whose cabin you charged into then ran out a little while later."

"You're watching us. Big surprise. I already knew this. Where *is* Victoria?"

His eyes widen marginally. "Oh, so you've figured out the truth now instead of slamming her with accusations and silencing her. Little late, don't you think?"

There's a harsh bitterness to his tone, like he hates me and has been waiting to be proven right.

"Her name is Lana. Victoria Evans was killed by this town. She *can't* be Victoria Evans. She had to reinvent herself just to find the will to go on. You called her sick, but you have no idea what you're up against. You have no fucking idea what she survived."

His words grow angrier with each new sentence, and he slowly stands.

I grip the gun tighter with one hand, watching him warily.

"Looks like your legs work just fine," I quip, eyeing the man who has played the world.

He taps his legs. "They work better than your mind."

"I thought she was Kennedy Carlyle, and had developed an unhealthy obsession with the Evans family due to the two coincidental times their paths crossed with death. And—"

"Kennedy Carlyle was a self-absorbed drug addict, who, quite frankly, was a motherfucking menace to society. It was only a matter of time before she got as high as her parents got drunk and killed someone. As fate would have it, she only killed a tree the night she also killed herself. Seemed like a waste of a perfectly good identity and funds for someone who needed to survive."

"I assumed it was you," I say calmly. "The one who changed her world."

"Falsifying hospital records is actually easy, as long as you know where to start," he says, once again tapping the sides of his legs that he fooled the world into believing were useless. "She needed a legitimate identity; she needed money; she needed a chance. If they'd found out she survived, they would have come. And back then? They would have killed her with almost no effort."

He blows out a breath, trying to calm his anger. I continue staring, letting him speak, trying to figure all this out as he does.

"When she told me she was screwing around with a FBI agent, I almost had a fucking brain aneurism," he says, looking away while laughing humorlessly. "I'd killed myself trying to make sure no one ever figured out who she was."

His eyes meet mine again.

"Then we talked face-to-face, and she fucking smiled when she said your name. She smiled like there was hope." He swallows a knot. "I forced her to separate the kills by a month, telling her it was more cautious, when really—"

"You worried when this was all over, she'd no longer have a purpose to stay alive."

His eyes glisten, and he clears his throat, nodding stoically.

"I was stalling," he says quietly. "But after she met you? I saw so much fucking hope. As of today, I saw an empty shell. I wanted to be wrong about you, SSA Bennett. I went along with all her changes to our plans. Do you know why she refused to let you hear the story from Lindy?"

I tilt my head before putting my gun in the back of my pants.

"She wanted us to hear the story when we got here. She wanted it to have maximum impact."

He stares me hard in the eyes. "She wanted it to have the maximum impact on *you*. To hell with all the others. She may still want revenge, but everything else has been centered around you. She practically prayed the Boogeyman would come after her, just so she could kill him and end the threat he posed to *your* life. And you treat her like a monster. Why? Because she kills? Do you treat your military like monsters? Do you stare at your own reflection with such disdain? Because I've seen your file. You've shot and killed thirteen serial killers since your career began. Those were real monsters, just like all the men Lana has dispatched."

I stagger on my feet, struggling with that thin line between madness and sanity.

"But she's supposed to what? Just move on and forget it happened?" he goes on. "Because the law says it's wrong to exact revenge on monsters unless you have a badge or a government decree?" He takes a step toward me, holding his finger in my direction. "This is a girl who spent *years* training, learning control to keep her mind sound. Something our military or law enforcement doesn't even require. These men? They destroyed her entire family. They destroyed her. Two fucking kids!" His voice breaks, and he turns around, putting his back to me when his emotions get the better of him.

I don't even know what to say. Anything but agreement would result in a possible violent outburst from him, and for some reason, I can't bring myself to fully agree aloud either.

I've always been on one side of the law, working tirelessly for justice through all the proper channels.

But Lana tried. Jake tried. They were denied.

"I loved him," he says as he turns back around, unshed tears battling to drop from his eyes. "I loved him and treated him like my dirty little secret in public, while loving him with all I had behind closed doors. Marcus accepted the scraps I offered, because he loved me so much he couldn't let me go, even though he deserved better."

Tears fall from his eyes, and he bats them away angrily.

"There wasn't a time in all these years that I questioned what I'd do for him since failing him so terribly when he was still alive. I took him for granted. I took what we had for granted. I never realized how very fucking rare it all was or how quickly it could all be gone."

He slowly drops to the couch again, his knees seeming to give out.

"Lana... I never thought she'd love anyone the way I loved Marcus. I thought they'd broken her. I thought they'd stolen every last shred of her heart. The only thing keeping her alive was the fire inside her that burned with pure, unadulterated hatred."

He looks up, meeting my gaze once again. "She loved you. She had two visions of how this would all go. One ended with you loving her as much as she loves you, and you'd stand by her no matter what, feel her pain as if it was your own. Unfortunately, you chose option number two, proving me right, even though I desperately wanted you to prove me wrong."

I still can't find the right words, and he continues to have tears drop occasionally as he glares at me with nothing less than contempt.

"Real love? The kind Lana gave you? It's the kind of love that looks beyond one's offenses against others and only calls to the soul. Lana saved a child. Lana risked *everything* to save you. Lana saved countless women by killing Plemmons. Yet you still view her as a monster by not meeting your generalized populous version of morality. In your eyes, it's better to forever be the victim than to ever feel peace again, because a real monster might die at the hands of someone who won't show mercy."

"Where's Lana?" I ask softly, trying not to agitate him farther.

"If Lana wants to be found, she'll let you find her. Knowing her identity won't stop her. In his life as a selfless, loving, incredible person, Marcus only ever made one selfish request. I'll go to the grave before I deny him that request, and so will Lana. Revenge, that's all he wanted from her. And revenge he'll have."

"Where is she?" I ask again.

"She let the story fall into place, guiding you to the truth slowly, letting it sink in…all the torture she endured. All the pain her family faced. She changed absolutely everything to accommodate her hopes for you. Way to fuck it all up."

"Where is she, Jacob?" I growl.

He eyes me, and a smirk crosses his lips. "I prefer Jake," he quips. "And you've already lost. Lana and I worked tirelessly for a long time to profile this entire town, deciding each and every possible path the key players would take. We've prepared for every outcome, and we stay ten steps ahead. Knowing our identity won't help you. In fact, tell them it's Victoria back from the grave with my help? The entire town will erupt in panic."

My jaw tics as I stare him down.

"Where. Is. She?"

"That's no longer your concern," he says dismissively. "I only came here to make sure her words were spoken, since you did the worst thing you could possibly do. You silenced her. You refused to listen. Now I have to pray I'm enough of a reason for her to want to live."

I lift my gun, aiming it at him, even though I have no intention of actually pulling the trigger.

"Where is she? I won't ask again."

His eyes grow colder. "As I said, we've prepared for every possible outcome of every situation."

He raises his hands slowly, like he's going to put them behind his head, but instead, he puts something in his ears.

"I should mention, I even estimated the amount of time this conversation would take."

Before I can even question that, a high-pitch, piercing noise attacks my ears, and I drop the gun to clutch my head that seems to be wobbling like a drum under attack. I'm forced to my knees as the sound grows excruciating to my ears, and my eyes screw shut as I fight to stand back up.

Just as suddenly as it began, the noise stops, and even though my hearing might take a few minutes to get right, I feel instant relief. My eyes fly open to see that Jake is already gone, and I look at the box on the wall that just brought me to my knees.

He really has fucking planned everything down to the last detail, just as Lana has. Only she had hoped for a different outcome.

My mind feels like it's gone through a mind-fuck blender. Up is down. Right is left. Good is bad.

Before I can stop myself, I slam my fist into the wall, ignoring the searing pain that shoots up my arm when my knuckles strike the unforgiving wood.

I learned to control all my emotions long before I joined the FBI. I learned to hide the anger. Learned to be stoic. Learned to taper any sort of feeling that was too strong.

But not today.

I fall apart, tossing everything in the cabin as my heart gets yanked out of my chest, and I lash out for the first time in over fifteen years.

Chapter 2

By that sin, fell the angels.
—William Shakespeare

Lana

Alyssa Murdock grimaces as she takes a sip of her drink, unaware that I'm watching her through the trees. Every time her shirt rises up, I see the bruises on her back.

Hearing it and seeing it are two different things.

Very few of my victims have children. Alyssa is the only offspring who isn't an adult.

At eight, she's still a child, with far too many bruises in her history, and too many scars on her heart. Despite the shit-hand life has dealt me, I never once felt the strike of my father's anger. He never hit me. I was doted on and loved. As a child should be.

But Greg Murdock has hit his daughter too many times.

He gets bumped up on the list because of that.

Turning away and leaving her to hide her bruises in front of her friends who are playing on the treehouse with her, I pull my hood back up and leave my lurking shadows.

Hadley's number silently flashes on my screen again, and I ignore her call once more. My eyes flit over her text, and a twinge of guilt hits me, even though no other emotion is infiltrating the barrier I have in place right now.

HADLEY: Logan knows!

I know she's worried, which is why she keeps calling. But right now, in this moment, I don't trust myself to speak to anyone.

Since Jake left earlier, my tears have all dried up, and my heart keeps garnering a new layer of ice with each passing moment.

I'm back in survival mode, shutting off everything to keep from drowning in the pain. If I allow myself to feel right now, I'll never stop crying.

And there is no time for tears.

ME: I know. Look after yourself. Don't worry about me.

ME: And thank you for accepting me and understanding.

My finger hovers over the option to send that last message, but I finally press it and turn my phone off, removing the battery. Then I head back toward the house we've commandeered, courtesy of the Dalia family that only lives here during the Christmas season and summer.

It's secluded, the house hidden from the main road by a veil of thick trees. Only a slender driveway leads to the home, and we have sensors in to alert us if anyone passes over them.

The end is coming.

But I almost don't even care anymore.

My dispassion is just one repercussion of turning numb to survive.

A car rolls by me as I walk down the long driveway, and I glance over, seeing Jake's eyes meet mine through the window. I cut my gaze away, because he's searching me, watching me, worrying about my intentions now that the light is officially gone.

My brother sacrificed his own life to save mine. Even without Logan standing by me, I owe it to my brother to survive, regardless if it is a soulless, empty existence. I just don't have the drive to make that my ultimate goal any longer.

My main priority is to see this through, grant my brother's dying wish, and finally lay to rest all the misery from the past.

Jake drives on, parking at the end of the driveway, and he gets out, heading straight toward me.

"So you disappeared into the woods again?" Jake asks.

"I did some recon. Hitting Murdock tonight."

"Tonight?" he asks, a worried note to his tone.

"I need something to stab, and he needs to be stabbed. Seems like we could help each other out," I tell him dryly.

He grabs my arm, halting me from walking by, and I stare into his concerned eyes.

"Lana, take a minute and regroup. Logan—"

"Logan is a guy who was never meant to be in my life," I answer coldly, ignoring the trickle of pain that slowly starts sparking across my heart.

I suppress the urge to rub my chest, knowing it would give me away, and I walk inside the house with Jake following me. When I turn around, I hate what I see.

So much pity is staring at me right now through my best friend's eyes.

"You should see this," he says, pulling out his phone. "I spoke to Logan."

My eyes widen, and my mouth falls open. "What?! Why would you risk that?"

"I didn't risk anything, and for you, nothing is too big of a risk. He wouldn't hear your words, so I made him listen." He turns and walks away, but I follow on his heels.

I blink back the tears I've barely been staving off all day. "You had no right," I growl.

He spins, facing me as he walks backwards.

"He figured out all the good parts by himself by the time he found me. Don't worry, Lana. I'm playing the game your way."

My feet freeze to their spot, and that coldness reforms, stealing away the tears that almost fell. It's as though Jake sees it, because his face falls.

"I'm not playing a game, and there's no longer a prize."

He groans as I pass him. "Damn it, Lana. That's not what I meant and you know it."

"I do know it. I need to go for another run, and then we'll talk about tonight's murder."

He grabs my wrist, and I react, slinging him around and coming down on top of him as he crashes to the living room floor. He grunts as I pin him, working all my muscles to hold him in place.

"How is it that we both took all those damn classes, but you're the fucking master and I still feel intermediate."

Despite my best efforts, my lips twitch as the shield around me thaws a fragment.

"For the same reason I took all those same tech classes and can barely work my smart phone, whilst you create virtual empires."

He smiles up at me, and I climb off him, helping him to his feet. When his smile starts to slip, I know the seriousness is about to come back.

"There's something you should see."

Curious, I follow him as he grabs his phone from the ground, where it fell during his takedown. As he lifts it and moves his fingers rapidly over the screen, searching for something, I stare idly through the window.

Delaney Grove was once my home. Then it became my hell.

Now I just want out of here because it's nothing to me anymore.

But it was something to Marcus.

To my mother.

Paint It All Red

To my father.

Their bodies are all buried here, just like Kennedy Carlyle is. Although her tombstone actually says Victoria Evans.

What a fucked up mess we wove so delicately.

It was a fool-proof plan. I thought the worst thing I could do was go insane from the dark depths I had to reach. Turns out, falling in love was truly the worst. The darkness is just my twisted little friend.

"Here," Jake says, pressing play on his phone.

He sits down as I study the screen, seeing the time stamp on the video being almost an hour old. It doesn't stop my heart from pounding just seeing Logan.

He slams his fist into the wall, and I grimace, ignoring the heat of my tears as they beckon to fall. From there, he loses it, slinging a chair across the room. One thing after another gets smashed as he yells at nothing and no one.

He grabs a bat from the corner, and he slams it into the window, busting it out. Then he takes the bat to the rest of the room, smashing anything he can break as he loses all control.

I slowly back against the wall, and my body slides down it until my ass touches the floor. And I watch. I watch the man who never loses control have a meltdown.

This is my fault.

I should have walked away.

"He loves you," Jake says, clutching my shoulder, no longer sitting as he crouches beside me.

I move away from his touch as Logan continues to annihilate the room, destroying anything that will break.

"He doesn't love me like I love him," I say hoarsely. "I love him enough to burn the world to the ground in his name."

I touch the screen as Logan's warpath comes to an end, and his chest heaves as he drops his head back, staring up at the ceiling. Finally, he stalks out of the cabin, his mask of composure back in place as he slams the door behind him so hard it simply bounces open again.

"He just loves me enough to feel betrayed," I add on a rasp whisper.

Jake goes stiff beside me, and I hand him his phone as I wipe away a stray tear.

"You didn't give him time, Lana. Maybe now—"

"Now what?" I ask, exasperated. "Don't you think I'd love to ride off into the sunset with him? I'm not being stubborn, Jake. You're constantly worried about my hold on reality because of the dark places I have to go to finish all these kills. But you're the one being irrational right now. Logan found out the truth. He fucked me and left me cuffed to a bed, and when he left…there was nothing but disgust and pain in his eyes."

I choke back a sob, refusing to fall apart again right now.

Jake's eyes are full of tears as my lip trembles, but I go on. "He's so pure. So good. So honest and genuine. So gentle and kind. It's all those qualities that made me fall in love, because he was everything—*everything!*—I'd always wanted in someone. And he loved me. Yet, I wanted to taint the very things about him that made me fall in love, just so I could selfishly take him to the dark with me and keep him. It was wrong."

"It's not selfish, Lana," Jake argues gingerly.

"You haven't found love since Marcus, even though Marcus only ever wanted that for you. His note begged you to move on and find love. His words beseeched me to burn down this fucking town. You haven't done your part to ensure his last request, because you've been too busy helping me with mine. Maybe it's time to break up this partnership so you can finally have that chance."

Anger flashes across his eyes, and he pushes to his feet, coming to get right in my face.

Paint It All Red

"We swore we'd never do this to each other, Lana. Never push the other away no matter how intense the world around us got. You don't get to fucking send me away because you're hurting. Got that? You don't get to use Marcus against me *ever* again. Understood?"

I swallow the knot in my throat as tear after fucking tear escapes my eyes, and I nod weakly, hating myself for doing that. Jake's arms go around me, and I immediately wrap my arms around him in return.

We stand there, fixed in an embrace, and for a brief moment, he feels and smells just like Marcus always did. I close my eyes, pretending for a second that my brother is back, holding me to him, regretting the weight he put on my shoulders.

He wanted happiness for Jake. He wanted wrath from me.

He thought Jake too kind for such a task.

He knew the anger would burn harshly in my broken heart.

He knew I was a monster before I did.

My face is pressed against his chest as the illusion of it being Marcus slowly starts to fade. It's just as comforting knowing it's Jake. He's been my brother for ten years.

Turning my head so that my cheek is cushioned by his chest, I stare at the monitor with Logan on the screen. He's in the town square now, no longer looking like a betrayed man.

He's talking to his team, but the sound is muted, so I don't know what he's saying. It was over an hour ago that he had his meltdown. By now, he could be sending them to find me.

"Sometimes, I wonder what my brother must have thought of me to know I'd be able to do all of this," I say softly.

Jake's arms tighten around me. "He thought you were the strongest person he ever knew, and he raved about your fire all the time, Victoria," he tells me.

I shake my head. "Never call me that again," I whisper.

He kisses the top of my head, sighing harshly. "We can stop this anytime you want. You've more than fulfilled the promise you made."

My eyes lift to another screen where Sheriff Cannon is holding a private meeting with his deputies. My eyes narrow, because I know they're plotting.

"No. I can't. If I don't finish this today, someone else could face the pain we did. They'll never stop, and no one else will ever stop them. If I stop now, it was all for nothing. I need there to be a reason why this happened to us, even if that reason is simply because I'm the only one capable of being sick enough to finish this once and for all."

As I push away from him, Jake grabs my wrist, turning me back to face him. When our eyes collide, I see the steely glint in his gaze.

"*You* are not sick. Marcus was right—you're the strongest fucking person I know. You're not sick, Lana. You're a fucking dark angel that can set the world free from this *sick* town."

I offer him a brittle smile, giving him the illusion that his words have helped me. Doesn't matter what I am. Doesn't matter who I am.

All that matters is that I finish my mission.

Avenge my family.

And burn this town to the ground.

I don't need to feel love in order to be a monster.

I just need to remember.

It's not hard to do with the sun getting close to setting. The dark sky always calls to the memories if I allow it. For once, I let them in.

"No!" I shout, reaching for my father as Deputy Murdock restrains me, almost ripping my left arm out of socket to jerk me back. "He didn't do this! He couldn't!"

"He's always with us at night!" Marcus shouts, battling his own fight with Deputy Briggs as he wrenches Marcus's arm behind his back and slams him into the wall.

Paint It All Red

"It's okay, kids," Dad says, tears pouring from his eyes. "Don't fight them. I'm okay. It'll all be okay. There's no way they can convict me of crimes I didn't commit."

"Good thing we can convict you of crimes you did commit, you evil son of a bitch," Sheriff Cannon growls, slamming his fist into my father's stomach so hard that my father buckles at the waist and collapses to the ground, his hands cuffed behind him.

Marcus and I both scream in vain, begging them to stop the sheriff when he kicks our father in the face while he's down. Dad flips to his back, blood pooling from his mouth after the strike.

He's trying to be strong in front of us, but a small sob escapes him when the sheriff kicks him again, this time right in his side.

"Easy, not here," SSA Johnson says, smirking at us as we continue to try and break free from our holds. "But you should know, there is evidence to your father's crimes."

He bends, crouching beside my father.

"You're never going to see freedom again, and I'll make sure of that, no matter what I have to do," Johnson says acidly, a sinister grin on his face.

Murdock slings me back against the wall when I try to break free again, and I cry out when his weight comes down on top of me. "Maybe I should teach him a lesson and let him watch all the sick things he did to our women..." His words trail off as he brushes my hair to the side, and I go rigid against him. "Using his daughter," he adds, his voice an eerie promise.

"No!" Dad shouts, earning another kick from the sheriff.

"Do that, and I'll arrest you myself," Johnson growls. "We're after Evans. Those are just kids. Now come on. We have our man. We still have a long road ahead of us."

"Or we could just end it now," Briggs says, still holding Marcus.

Murdock continues to restrain me, still pressing his disgusting body against mine.

"We do things my way," Johnson growls. "You'll have your

vengeance. But for now, we do things my way."

My father is beaten and almost incoherent as they jerk him to his feet. His head hangs as I cry, begging once again for them to listen to the truth. To HEAR me. But no one listens.

No one cares.

Johnson and the sheriff drag my father out the door, and I watch my life get ripped apart.

Murdock pulls me back, creating a small separation between me and the wall, then shoves me hard back into it. I get dizzy and taste blood in my mouth.

"This isn't over for you two," he says, a dark gleam in his eyes.

Briggs tosses my brother to the ground, and I rush to his side as he slowly lifts up. Briggs and Murdock laugh on their way out, and I hold Marcus's hand.

"They can't convict him. This will all be a nightmare soon," my brother promises as he sits up, his eyes hard and determined as he looks at me. "I promise, Lana. We'll prove him innocent."

Innocence didn't matter in the end. Not with the DNA evidence.

"Holy shit," Jake says, drawing me out of my own head as he sits down in front of the far monitor.

My eyes widen in disbelief as Dev Thomas steps out of a small Honda, standing to his full height as he looks around at the church in front of him. No doubt he heard about Kyle.

"What's he doing here?" Jake asks.

"Only one way to find out," I say with a smirk.

I spared him, given what I heard from Lawrence and Tyler, and the fact Dev never really participated in the night's festivities. But why would he come to town if not to join in on the manhunt?

"You going to him?" he asks as Dev steps inside the church where we have no cameras.

I don't have to answer that. Murdock will have to wait a few hours to die.

"Be careful. I need to back up the footage to see what Logan has told the others."

"Just call Hadley," I say to him instead, looking over my shoulder.

"You sure we can trust her?" he asks, his lips tensing.

"You don't have to trust her. Just trust that I wouldn't jeopardize your safety."

He sighs while nodding, and he grabs a phone.

"I'll drive to the edge of town, just in case."

I walk out as he carries on with his task, and I hop in the car with the darkly tinted windows. I drive fast out of the forest, and don't slow down until I hit the town limits. It's not like the cops are worried about speeding right now, since the sheriff is on the warpath to avenge his son's death.

It broke him when his daughter was killed. She was put on public display, which is what led to us being raped and beaten in the streets.

I hope it fucking kills him to lose his son. Displaying him to the town was a nice touch to recognize his afore mentioned grief. His daughter was a bitch and a snob, but she didn't deserve to die.

Kyle? Kyle deserved more than he got.

I park near the pharmacy, and I walk the two blocks to the church, carefully gauging my surroundings to ensure I'm not being set up.

When I'm positive no one is focused on the church, I step in through the back and creep inside. I'm happy to report that I don't burst into flames, so maybe I'm not completely consumed by evil just yet, despite the fact I desecrated the church bell tower with Kyle's mostly skinless body.

As I reach the main part of the church, I stop, staying behind the curtain that leads to the stage where my mother once performed for the town plays.

Dev is on his knees, his hands folded in prayer, and his eyes are closed as tears leak from his eyes.

Well…that's unexpected.

"Please forgive me of the sins committed when I was last in this town," Dev says hoarsely. "Even though I don't deserve it. Give me the strength to do what needs to be done now, and keep my sister safe from any harm or retaliation."

I cock my head, studying him. My eyes flit around the room next, still expecting a trap. No such thing looks to be in place.

To be absolutely certain, I text Jake from my burner phone that I've swapped to.

ME: You got eyes on the church?

JAKE: No one is on their way there. The feds are all in the square, and they're talking about going door to door to unearth new evidence about the original killer. Johnson, Cannon, and the deputies are all at town hall talking about who you might be and how to draw you out. Coast is clear.

ME: Original killer? Why?

JAKE: They want to figure out who it really was. For now, their focus has shifted. Looks like Logan kept your secret…as long as Hadley didn't lie to me and they aren't setting up a ruse.

ME: What are they asking?

JAKE: They found out the first killing was on the anniversary of your parents' first date. And they also learned the women had all the same features as your mother.

I clutch the phone tighter in my hand, and I blow out a weary breath, deciding not to question it. I don't need distractions right now.

Paint It All Red

I pull up the mask of a cold-hearted killer, settling into my role with familiar ease. It's easier to be this version of me. The version who doesn't care or flinch.

Dev's eyes stay closed, and I hop down to take my seat on the edge of the stage, sitting right beside the pulpit—*still no flames*—and approximately seven feet in front of Dev.

He continues praying for a minute longer, and when his eyes open, he stumbles back to his ass, shocked to see someone in front of him.

"Hello, Dev. Long time no see."

The color drains from his face. "Victoria," he whispers, surprising me.

I hide my surprise. "You're the first one to recognize me."

He swallows audibly while nodding slowly. "I knew it was you when I heard about the killings," he goes on, slowly shifting back onto his knees, but not attempting to stand. "Marcus swore you'd rise from the dead as an angel that night. He always knew this day would come. And your eyes... Your eyes give you away."

I roll said eyes, and I lean forward, studying him with a careless coldness.

"I spared you, and you come to this town right as Kyle is flayed and hung from the tower of this very church. Why are you here?"

His lip trembles, and his hands begin to shake in fear. I like that fear.

"I came to do the right thing. To tell them—"

"To tell them a dead girl rose from the grave to exact revenge?" I drawl, a dark, taunting smile curving my lips.

"No!" he says, panicking a little. "No," he says again, quieter this time as he looks around.

I glance at my phone, using the app to show me the cameras, flicking from screen to screen as Dev recovers. I give him my attention again when I see no one is near me.

"I came to tell the feds what happened," he goes on. "I heard there was a divide, and that Johnson was getting worked against from the rest of the feds."

My lips twitch. "Ah, I see. Well, they know what happened."

"Diana told me she called them."

My small smile falls. Diana? She's stayed in contact with him?

Ignoring the bitter sting of betrayal, I continue to focus on Dev.

"So you've come to tell them the story they've already heard?"

He slowly shakes his head. "No. I've come to tell them the rest. The parts they don't know. The part about Kyle's mother."

My breath hitches.

"I also plan to tell them who the real killer was, Victoria. I want them to clear your father's name, and give your family the rest it deserves. Then your soul can be at peace."

I laugh humorlessly. "You think I'm really a ghost who has risen from the grave?" I mock.

He shakes his head. "I think you're selling your soul to the devil for revenge, and I'm trying to help you before it's completely gone. I want to save you."

More laughter slips out of me, this time mocking him. "If you wanted to save me, you should have done it ten years ago."

I hop off the stage, and he tenses as I pull out a knife. "I'm already too far gone now, Dev. You had your chance. Instead, you watched from the sidelines as they tore my soul from my body. It was anger or brokenness. Which path do you think I chose?"

His lips purse. "No soul is above saving, Victoria. No—"

I throw the knife, and he screams while diving away as it slams into the wall beside him, nowhere even close to his body, despite his attempt to flee. I find that a little humorous.

The knife is stuck in the picture of Sheriff Cannon and the plaque that praises him for donating so generously to the church.

Paint It All Red

It's right between his eyes, and I never had to look to aim it that well.

Once again, the color drains from Dev's face, because he sees proof I'm no longer the weak little girl they let bleed on the streets.

"I'm stronger. Faster. Smarter. And far more lethal than anyone in this town. If I wanted you dead, you'd already be dead. Kyle had the sheriff's love and his protection. Yet I flayed him and hung him from the tower for the entire town to witness his demise. Don't piss me off, Dev. I'm not the girl you turned your back on ten years ago. This girl will carve out your spine if I find your back to me again."

He gulps as I walk over to pull the knife out of the sheriff's head, and I look over my shoulder at him.

"And never call me Victoria again, or I'll cut out your tongue like I almost decided to do already. I'm still not certain you're in the clear, so don't remind me about you again. Understood?"

He nods, tears falling from his eyes.

I walk by him, and he shudders in my wake as my icy breeze follows me.

"I'm sorry," he says as I pass him. "I'm so sorry."

My footsteps pause, and I clutch the knife tighter, willing myself not to lose control and kill him when it's unnecessary. It's hard to forget his part in that night when he's so close.

"Just remember I can't be stopped," I say without turning around. "Don't make me regret showing you mercy when I've withheld it from all others. Jason's time is coming too. Don't make me return for you as well. And your father is still on my list."

"My mother and sister are innocent," he blurts out immediately.

I stay facing the door. "Your mother's innocence is debatable, but she's not on my list. Your sister was always sheltered from the *rumors* when she went off to college. For her own sake, make her less naïve, Dev. It's a cruel world to those who don't believe such evils exist. I would know."

I walk out without saying another word, and I tuck the knife back into my boot before anyone sees me.

That was not what I needed.

I don't want one of *them* trying to save my soul when they're the reason it's so damaged. I don't want one of *them* trying to preach to me. The hypocrisy is too laughable to even dwell on.

Feeling a chill on my back, I turn, seeing Dev coming after me, and I stop on the sidewalk, cloaked in darkness in this section with no lights.

"I'm going to the feds, but I wanted you to know it was for the right reasons. Can I ask where you're going?" he asks softly, timidly, like a lamb protesting a lion's grip.

"To kill someone," I say flippantly.

He blanches, then looks down at the ground. "You didn't ask who the original killer was when I said I knew."

Turning around again, I start walking quickly into the night before calling over my shoulder, "Because I already know."

Chapter 3

To be wronged is nothing unless you continue to remember it.
—Confucius

Logan

I hate myself. I hate this fucking case. And I hate everything that is standing between me and Lana right now.

"I fucked up," I say quietly to Hadley as I drop to a chair in her cabin.

"I'll say," she mumbles.

"I don't know what to do right now, but I shouldn't have done what I did. I didn't know she was Victoria when..."

I blow out a long breath, letting the words trail off, unable to finish them.

"When what?" Hadley prompts, leaning up.

"I fucked her out of anger, and then cuffed her to the bed, left her naked and exposed, and didn't let her speak."

Hadley goes stiff beside me.

"You didn't," she says in a harsh whisper, her teeth grinding.

I clench my hands together, lacing my fingers with each other tight enough to cause pain. "I thought she was Kennedy and obsessed with Victoria Evans. I had no idea she *was* Victoria Evans. I'd have handled *everything* differently. I'd be no less confused, but I sure as fuck wouldn't have done that to her. I thought she'd been playing me. I was hurt. I felt duped. And—"

"And obsessed proxies are unstable and unable to love without fixation," Hadley points out grimly. "But she's not an obsessed proxy. She's a scarred girl with more shit in her life than any one person should ever have to endure. And you just took your turn shitting on her. Great job, Bennett. Great fucking job."

She stands, and I curse while standing with her. "I realize I fucked up. I'm trying to fix it, Hadley. But I can't find her. That's why I'm here."

"Define your version of fixing it," she says, eyeing me suspiciously.

"I have no idea just yet. It's not like I can simply condone all she's doing. And it's not like I can lie and say I don't understand it either. I feel…fucked up," I groan, putting my head in my hands.

She leans up, her eyes on mine. "I realize I'm not the Boy Scout you are, but—"

"Don't do that, Hadley," I interrupt, my jaw ticking. "Don't act like being conflicted about torture and murder means I have a stick up my ass."

She collapses back against the chair, releasing a tortured breath.

"My stepfather was a monster, and my mother and her shrink convinced me I was a pathological liar for seeing him as such." Her random, yet pained comment has me tensing. "Seventy kids in total that we know about, Logan."

Her eyes tear up, and she clears her throat.

"I was conflicted too. Then I realized there were only sixty-nine pictures."

"Your picture was missing," I say quietly, but I already knew this. I just didn't piece together at the time that it was my girlfriend sparing Hadley the indignity of the others seeing it.

"She didn't want me to see the vulnerable little girl I was because she was afraid it would break me. Lana has lived through more pain than most people can endure. The physical pain alone from the numerous surgeries she needed to rebuild her facial structure was bad enough. Imagine the psychological toll that took on her. She lost her family. She lost her home. She gave up her identity so that it couldn't be taken away. She's stronger than you're giving her credit for, and yeah. Maybe I'm a sick motherfucker, but I'm on her side."

I scrub my face with both hands, staring at nothing as I try to process everything around me.

"It took me a minute to wrap my head around it, which is why I'm not punching you for doing the same. It's also why I let you in here after you said you were done with me," she adds.

Her lips quirk, and I run my hand over the stubble on my jaw, thinking about the way Lana would do that to me when she first woke up. She constantly touched me, as if checking to make sure I was still real.

"You were everything to her," Hadley says quietly. "I've never been loved like that. She saved your life, Logan. This town tried to kill you, and she saved you. Personally, I think it's over-the-top to stab a guy for the man you love, but still perfectly affective."

Usually I appreciate her dry humor. Not so much today.

She rolls her eyes when I don't crack a smile. "You need to pick a side soon, Logan. You can't hang out in limbo. I chose mine, and it's her."

"So you've been falsifying all your forensic reports on—"

"Haven't had to. Lana is too good to leave behind trace evidence." She sighs as she stands. "But I would have. Yes. As far as risks go, you're the only one she's ever taken. You're the one string to unravel all she has worked for since the night they shattered her and her brother. Are you going to take that away?"

"According to Jake, that's not possible, no matter what I choose," I state bitterly, wondering just how close he is to Lana. I don't doubt her words when she said there was nothing sexual going on—for some reason I trust her on that, even though she told me that before I knew he was helping her slaughter ghosts from her pasts.

"He doesn't know you or how good you are," Hadley says as she starts grabbing her laptop.

"Do you know where she is?"

She looks me in the eye. "I have a hunch. I'll share it with you if you pick the right side. Let me know what you decide."

I follow her out, determined not to let her out of my sight, when a guy walks up. He's familiar for some reason, and I watch his hands that are nested in his pockets. With his shoulders hunched forward and trepidation in his eyes, he looks too meek to be a threat.

"Can I help you?"

"I'm looking for SSA Bennett. My sister said you guys were camped out here." He darts a glance around.

"I'm SSA Bennett," I say warily, my hand leisurely hanging out on my gun holster, as my fingers slowly click open the strap that tucks my weapon in.

He pulls his hands out of his pockets, letting them dangle by his sides.

"I'm Devin Thomas."

His name tells me why his face is familiar.

"You really shouldn't be in this town right now," I tell him, my jaw ticking.

Every fiber in me is fighting to restrain the urge to pummel his face into oblivion; a dark, protective side emerging on accident and surprising me. Knowing Lana was Victoria is changing everything about this case, making it personal. I didn't know to what extreme until this moment.

"It's a risk I'm willing to take," he says grimly. "I have information you need."

My eyes narrow. "You're too late. We have tons of statements about what the thirteen of you did that night."

He grimaces before running a hand through his hair. "That night has haunted me every waking and sleeping moment for the past decade. I may not have committed the same sins, but I was just as guilty. And if the Scarlet Slayer decides I need to die, I won't blame her in the least."

"Her?" I muse, my lips twitching when he pales.

Lana has already paid him a visit, it seems.

"I mean, *him*. Her. Whatever. Anyway, I came to tell you about Jane Davenport. I know you already know about that night."

My eyebrows knit together. "Kyle's mother," I state flatly.

"Can we go inside?" he asks, looking around warily at the woods that surround us.

I gesture for him to go inside Hadley's cabin, and I glance around, seeing Leonard. I nod for him to join me, and he jogs up.

"Who's that guy?"

"Devin Thomas."

He sucks in a breath, and we both enter the cabin as Devin takes a seat, rubbing his hands together nervously. "Why haven't you arrested anyone? If you knew what we did, I mean."

"Words mean nothing without any physical evidence. But if you'll sign a confession, I'll gladly take you in."

I smile darkly, and he swallows, nodding.

"I've turned my life around, but if I feel as though that's what God wants me to do, so be it. For now, let me tell you about Jane."

"What about her?" Leonard asks, sitting down.

Devin eyes him, but finally faces me again. "The first several women found in the original killings had no DNA evidence on their bodies. Johnson came during the middle of those, and after he pretty much decided Evans was the killer, DNA evidence suddenly started turning up at all the new scenes."

"You're saying he falsified the evidence?" I ask flatly, not surprised. I've already had my suspicions. "How'd he get Robert's semen inside the bodies?"

"Jane Davenport," he answers immediately. "The sheriff had his claws deep in her. He hated that woman, and as punishment for hiding his son for so many years, he kept her here. Threatened to kill her if she ever left. And she knew for a fact it wasn't a bluff."

"That doesn't explain anything," Leonard points out.

Devin nods. "Jane was the town outcast. The only person who was ever nice to her was Robert Evans. He was nice to everyone. He loved his wife so much that he could never move on after her death. But even a man who loves a ghost still has needs, if you know what I mean."

Leonard leans up, and I lean back.

"You're saying they had a sexual relationship—Robert and Jane," I surmise.

"The whole town knew about it, including Victoria and Marcus. Victoria wanted him to be happy again. Marcus was adamant that his father should stop hiding the relationship. Kyle? Kyle was furious. He already hated Robert because he was one of the few around here who would stand up to him. Victoria soon after humiliated Kyle. He thought he was the guy no girl could turn down, and she broke up with him very publically because of his treatment toward Robert."

He sighs harshly, shaking his head.

"I was so desperate to fit in back then. I thought it was just petty stuff, no one would get hurt. Kyle was always a bully, so it was either be his friend or be his enemy. No one wanted to be his enemy. His father would ruin them and their family if they stood against Kyle. Just look at Lindy Wheeler and Robert Evans. Those are just two examples."

He gives us a rueful smile.

"So what part did Jane play?" Leonard prompts.

Paint It All Red

"Kyle bragged that night," he goes on, not jumping to the point. "I came back after convincing Lindy to run before Kyle got finished with Marcus and Victoria. I heard Kyle telling Victoria that his 'cunt mother' had been the one to bring Robert down in the end. Jane gave Johnson the used condoms with Robert's semen in them, after Sheriff Cannon threatened her life. Victoria was a bloody pulp by then, but she managed to speak. She told Kyle she'd prove it, and her father's name would be cleared. And we'd all burn in hell when she was finished."

He laughs humorlessly.

"I've been living in hell ever since that night, so she held true to her word. At least for my part. Kyle just laughed and told her that his own mother had been silenced by the grave, and found it hilarious that the girl bleeding out on the streets thought she could scare him."

He looks between us.

"Guess he's not laughing now."

Leonard looks to me, and I look at him. Devin has all but said he knows it's Victoria who came back to kill them all.

But why does he suspect a dead girl when no one else in town believes it's possible?

"You guys should look into Kyle," he goes on. "First make sure he's really dead, and—"

"He's definitely dead," Leonard says on a shudder.

"Deep down, I always knew he was the original killer. The Nighttime Slayer, they called him," he goes on.

Again, Leonard and I exchange a look before I return my gaze to Dev.

"You think it was him?"

He nods. "Apparently someone else did too, if what I heard about his death was true."

"He was killed a little more brutally, but because he was the one who orchestrated the night Marcus and Victoria died. Why do you think he was the killer?"

He snorts, rolling his eyes. "Isn't it obvious?" he asks loudly, gesturing around us. "The world was a puppet on strings for Kyle. His father covered up the worst of his indiscretions, never seeing the pure evil in him. Kyle could charm anyone into seeing the best, but when he unleashed his dark side, it was consuming, suffocating, and downright scarring."

A tear leaks from his eye, and he bats it away.

"I stood by and watched a helpless girl and boy be raped and brutally beaten to death. All because of the fear Kyle easily instilled. No one in this entire town had the balls to go after him with someone like Cannon backing his every move."

"But saying he was the killer is saying he raped and killed his own sister. From what I've heard, the sheriff's affections toward his daughter ran deep enough to make him frame an innocent man just to have someone to blame," I point out.

"If you don't think Kyle is capable of raping and murdering his own sister, then you don't know anything. Rebecca Cannon was the daughter of Mary Beth Cannon. Mary died of ovarian cancer when Rebecca was just five. She was only a year older than Kyle, who the sheriff didn't know existed yet."

"Which means the sheriff wasn't faithful," Leonard points out.

"Which made Rebecca hate Kyle when he came into the picture," Dev goes on. "The sheriff favored her, for obvious reasons, and it was the one person in town Kyle wasn't allowed to lay a finger on. If he'd ever so much as threatened Rebecca, the sheriff would have ended him without pause. Yet Rebecca was put on display in a way so tragic and scarring that it drove the sheriff over the edge. Sounds like one sadistic mind came up with all that, and Kyle's IQ will let you know he was capable of orchestrating each piece of the puzzle, knowing they'd eventually frame Robert."

"Why Robert?" I ask, seeing where he's going with this. "And why time the first killing with the anniversary for when Robert and

Paint It All Red

Jasmine had their first date? And why did most of the girls resemble Jasmine?"

"Well, for one, that Johnson guy railroaded the investigation, certain it was Robert, partially because of that day and the victimology. That was just one step into setting Robert up. Secondly, Victoria was always on Kyle and Morgan's radar—constant battle between those two. Victoria looked a lot like Jasmine, so maybe your victimology should center around the daughter more than the mother. Lastly, Rebecca was a typical mean girl, and mean girls tend to pick on the lesser privileged. Rebecca went after Victoria on a regular basis, running her mouth, mocking her family and her janitor father."

He smirks, pausing as though he's remembering something.

"One day she went too far, saying something about Victoria's dead mother. Victoria grabbed Rebecca by the hair of her head and slammed her face into the locker. Rebecca ended up with a busted nose. The sheriff tried to come after Victoria, but Robert had some kind of dirt on him that made him back off. Sheriff Cannon doesn't like being backed into a corner. Then Rebecca, the girl who so often bullied Victoria, is the one disgraced the most? The sheriff got onboard and they went after Evans with everything they had after that."

He grows quiet, and I run over the facts in my head.

"What was the dirt Evans had on the sheriff?" Leonard asks.

"Some financial stuff he'd used to get out of taxes or something. Sheriff shut that down before the trial, so it wasn't heavy enough leverage for that."

It'd be so easy to fall into his line of thought, go with the fact Kyle was the killer. It'd make that case ready to close.

"Kyle wasn't the killer," I finally tell him.

His eyes grow angry. "Then you underestimate him."

I shake my head. "No doubt he was on a fast track to becoming a serial killer, but it wasn't him back then. The killer was armed with the same knowledge and definitely had a hatred strong enough to let them frame Robert, even aided in persuading their profile and suspicions. He holds or held an IQ high enough to mastermind each and every calculated step. But Kyle never went to the trial."

He frowns. "What does that have to do with it?"

Leonard takes on the explanation. "We have footage of the trial, including everyone in the trial room instead of just the immediate trial factions. Kyle was never there because he genuinely didn't give a fuck," Leonard says bluntly. "The killer would have wanted to watch each and every event unfold as he'd planned, and revel in the downfall of Evans in person."

Devin sits back, deflated, as though he's considering it. "So it wasn't Kyle?"

I shake my head.

"Then who was it?" he demands.

"We're still trying to figure that out," I say, motioning toward the stack of DVDs. "We have every face that was there on a daily basis, and we're ruling them out one-by-one based on all the facts and profiling we can possibly do. It's odd how more of these discs are arriving by the minute by anonymous tipsters."

He shakes his head, disgusted. "I still think it was him, and until you can prove otherwise, I think the current killer believes the same thing."

"Doubtful," Leonard says immediately. "The one killing now? They've spent ten years examining all the evidence and know far more details than we do now."

His eyes meet ours. "I hope you never catch this one. I hope this one ends every shred of evil this town has left in it. I believe in avenging angels, Agents. And I think this killer has been granted a dark gift to rid this world of the corruption this town offers. I thought there was a soul left to save, but now I don't think there is. I think the angels' wrath is here."

He stands abruptly.

Paint It All Red

"Where are you going?" Leonard asks.

He turns to face us. "If you're not arresting me, I'm going to go pick up my baby sister and take her far, far away from this place."

I cock my head. "Why?"

He heads to the door and doesn't turn around until it opens. "Because this place is going to burn. I can promise you that."

Chapter 4

Weakness of attitude becomes weakness of character.
—Albert Einstein

Lana

"I thought you were just going after Murdock," Jake hisses into the phone as I finish tying the last knot on Murdock's ropes, binding him to the chair.

He wriggles in the chair, his threats muffled by the gag in his mouth.

"Due to our latest visitor, I'm ensuring that no one escapes the list. Just playing it safe," I chirp, grinning when I back up and see Murdock glaring daggers at my face.

It was almost too easy to beat the hell out of him and tie him up. The hard part was loading him into my trunk and dragging him up the stairs of the courtroom without being seen.

Fortunately, with all the chaos following Kyle's death, no one was guarding the back entrance. I just needed Murdock's key to get us in.

I pick up the gavel, examining it. *Judge Henry Thomas* is engraved on the handle.

"This is too risky."

"Not at all," I promise Jake.

"Shit," he hisses.

Paint It All Red

"What?"

"Some redhead is getting out of a car in our driveway."

My body tenses. "Hadley found us," I groan.

"Shit. Shit. Shit. What the hell do I do with her?"

"Don't hurt her," I warn him.

"So invite her in for tea?" he deadpans.

"If she's there alone, that means she's there to help us. Just see what she wants. And I mean it; don't hurt her."

"Great. I'll just make nice with the FBI while you're killing a deputy and a judge," he says dryly.

"Exactly," I say before hanging up on him.

I put my phone away and study Murdock as he sweats, still glaring at me like he can condemn me to hell with just that scathing look.

"Your daughter and wife will be home tonight, safe and sound, in case you're worried. I'm sure they won't miss you if you don't return." I crouch in front of him, keeping my eyes on his as that anger slowly gets replaced by reluctant fear. "I'm almost positive they'll cry a little, but secretly, when no one is looking at them, they'll treasure that small bit of peace they have now that you can no longer hurt them."

I stand abruptly, and he screams, the sound muffled by the gag.

Casually, I turn on the old vinyl record Judge Thomas has on the player, waiting for him to return to his chambers after a long day of hiding or burning any remaining evidence from my father's case. Too bad he's a decade too late in covering up his trail.

You know what they say about hubris…

For ten years, they got lazy, thinking this case was over and done with, not much cleanup necessary, considering they killed everyone involved and a FBI agent was on their side.

Mozart's Requiem streams through the chambers, a dramatic

composition full of passion and excitement.

I sway with the music, listening to it with my eyes closed. My father was always a Bach man, but Mozart had so much more emotion in all his compositions, in my opinion.

The sound of the door opening has me turning around and a smile dancing on my lips as Judge Thomas shuts the door behind him. I press the button on my remote, and my newly installed lock slides into place. The only way to open it is to get the remote from me.

Good luck with that.

The judge backs away, staring at the door in confusion. It seems to take forever for him to realize music is playing, and he whirls around, staring at the record player as I lurk in the shadows.

Murdock screams over the gag, growing loud enough to draw the judge's attention to him. Judge Thomas almost trips over himself when he spots the restrained deputy.

"Greg!" Judge Thomas gasps as I step out of the shadows.

He struggles to untie the deputy, and Murdock wriggles harder, screaming and trying to get the judge's attention. Murdock blinks and eyes the judge, then darts panicked glances in my direction, doing all he can with eye communication to warn the fool.

It's a valiant effort, but pointless. My favorite part in the horror movies is when the idiot won't turn around while the restrained buddy is doing all they can to alert them of danger.

"Damn it, Greg, hold still. These knots are—"

"Awesome," I say, finishing that sentence for him.

Henry Thomas trips, falling to the ground on his knees, staring up at me with wide, horrified eyes.

How fitting.

"While you're down there, you can say your last words," I tell him, holding up the knife. "And maybe confess your sins while you're at it."

Paint It All Red

He trembles, his lips move, but no words come out. Finally, he gets out three words. "Who are you?"

Pretty sure that's the least important thing he could have asked.

"Isn't it obvious?" I ask as the music plays on and Murdock struggles against his bindings. "I'm the girl whose life you destroyed. I just have a different face, considering the lynch mob you and Sheriff Cannon sent after us crushed the old one."

He swallows hard, his color paling.

"You even cast away your son for not following through with the barbaric show the others put on. Did you think him less of a man for not being able to rape a sixteen-year-old girl or seventeen-year-old boy?" I ask, sounding amused, when really it's all I can do not to slit his throat now.

"No," he says on a rasp whisper. "You're dead—"

"So I've heard. Over and over. Funny thing about death—someone has to do a damn good job at killing a girl like me. So far, everyone has sucked at that task."

He scrambles up to his feet, backing toward his desk where he thinks he has a gun hidden. I smirk when he jerks open the drawer, slinging shit everywhere as he rifles through it, searching aimlessly for a gun I've already taken the liberty of removing.

"You won't find it," I tell him as he jerks the drawer completely out, tossing it at me in a desperate attempt to make time for him to dash to the door again.

I dodge the drawer easily enough, and watch with fascination as he jerks on the handle of the door over and over.

Einstein believed that the definition of insanity was doing the same thing over and over and expecting different results. By that definition, the judge is clearly insane for thinking the door is going to magically swing open.

I turn up the music as he starts screaming for help. I know the halls are empty. It's late, well after hours in our small town courtroom. Only a few people are here, and they're all on the floor below us.

"Tell me how you suppressed evidence, Judge Thomas. Tell me how you overlooked eye-witness testimonies and ruled them inadmissible."

He spins, his back to the door, his chest heaving as the music plays on, creating the perfect ambience for a Judge's murder.

"I had to," he growls. "I had to, or Sheriff Cannon—"

"Let's not lay blame," I drawl. "Tell me your part, Judge. And maybe I won't leave you hanging from the church tower like I did Kyle."

Murdock's fight leaves him as panic freezes him in place. A slow smile curves my lips when the judge staggers forward, his entire body a pasty shade of white now as he gawks at me in disbelief.

They know if I could kill a monster like Kyle so savagely and live to tell about it, then I'm the real thing of nightmares. Love it.

I throw the knife, and he screams, diving to the ground as it sticks into the picture of him on the wall. He's wearing his robes in that picture, looking prominent and pompous. The real man is sobbing on the ground while trembling in fear.

"Tell me!" I shout, smiling on the inside while playing the out-of-control mad-woman on the outside.

He curls in on himself, sobbing harder. "I did it," he says, sobbing harder. "I did it. I suppressed all the evidence that cleared Robert Evans. But at the time, I swear I thought it was him. Johnson promised us it was him."

I crouch, pulling another knife from my boot and toying with the handle for a nice little psychotic show.

"Tell me the rest," I say quietly. "Tell me how you and the sheriff, along with all his deputies, sent a gang of boys to rape the children of the man you wrongfully imprisoned."

He chokes on his sobs, hiccupping out the next words. "I never

Paint It All Red

meant for the rape—"

"Bullshit!" I snap, holding the knife in front of me. "The truth, Judge. I already know it. I just want to hear it."

His breaths grow labored and his cries get harder. It takes effort, but he finally speaks again.

"We just wanted you to feel the same pain as those women because you two wouldn't stop defending him!"

That familiar coldness washes over me, and I slowly stand, moving toward Murdock who is positively quaking in fear now that he knows I'm a fucking crazy bitch with a knife. I'm sure the fact I'm the one who peeled all the flesh from Kyle's body is wreaking havoc on his nerves right now.

The record starts skipping, the song coming to an end, and I let the annoying sound continue as I slice the knife across Murdock's torso with no warning. Blood spills from the wound and red plumes grow bigger and bigger against the tan shirt.

The judge screams, as well as Murdock as I slice again, aiming at Murdock's middle just right, and this time, the gash is deep. Everything on the inside spills out, intestines rolling from his body like an uncurling ball of yarn.

He stops moving, dying almost instantly, and I face the judge again as he spills his own stomach contents in a different sort of way.

As he retches, I come up behind him, finding his lack of fight anti-climatic. These are the men who I feared for so long? One who beats his child and wife, but couldn't land a single punch on me? One who cries on the floor in the fetal position, praying I'll disappear like a bad dream, instead of fighting for his life?

Instead of drawing it out, I slice the knife against his throat, finding no excitement with these kills. The blood sprays across the room, and gurgles of agony are all that escape his lips, as all other sounds struggle to make it past the gash in his throat.

I leave him there in his fancy suit, allowing it to be stained red, along with the carpeted floor of his chambers. After cleaning off my knife, I tuck it back into my boot, but I leave my other one stuck into the picture of the judge.

Then I pull out the paintbrush I brought, and I dip it into the blood. Instead of painting a wall this time, I leave a message.

A message for the man who broke my heart.

A message for the man I never should have loved.

It's completely juvenile, but I can't help myself.

By the time I leave, the blood has mostly drained out of them, and I walk out, stained in their shades of red, but no one notices. At least I put on the horribly huge boots, though I don't know why I bothered.

Eventually Logan will out me.

I drive back to the house, finding myself in desperate need of a shower. There's a silver sedan in our driveway, and my brow furrows. Hadley drives the FBI issued SUV. Maybe she got another car to keep them from looking at her GPS history or something.

Wary, I pull out a knife as I slowly open the door. All the lights are off, and none of the monitors are on.

With silence, I step into the house, stealthily close the door, and gingerly make my way through the eerie quiet. A garbled sound comes from the back room, something sounding like pain as a loud grunt follows.

Without hesitation, I kick open the door to Jake's room, flipping on the light immediately, raise the knife in the air, and…freeze.

Jake curses, Hadley squeals while covering her bare breasts with her hands, and my mouth opens and closes a few times in complete shock.

"What the hell?" Jake asks, as though I'm the one who has lost my fucking mind.

"What the hell?" I shoot back.

Paint It All Red

I rarely get surprised. Usually I hate surprises. This time...I'm not really sure how I feel about this little nugget of unexpectedness.

Hadley groans while dropping her head to Jake's chest, and he grips her hips, rolling her under him. "Close the door," he says over his shoulder.

And holy shit. His hips start moving.

He can't even wait until I pick my jaw up off the floor to finish?

I slam the door, stumbling backwards as I head toward my temporary room. I've dripped blood everywhere now. I have to look like Carrie after the prom, yet neither of them felt compelled to stop fucking on my behalf.

My first thought is to call Logan.

My second thought is how stupid that is, considering I can never speak to him again.

My third thought is...I really need a drink.

I step into the shower, clothes and all, and start stripping under the cold spray. I don't even flinch against the chill, but I melt into the warmth when it finally comes. My clothes lie in a puddle at my feet as I wash away the blood and death, refreshing and cleansing myself of the madness.

I'm almost done when I hear the door to the bathroom opening.

"Any reason you kicked down my door armed and ready to kill?" Jake asks from the other side of the shower curtain.

"I should have killed someone in the shower," I state randomly. "Like in the horror movies when the murderer always sneaks up and slices the knife through the curtain. The water runs red then."

"Nice. And yeah, I've seen all the same movies, Lana. It was something you tortured me and Marcus with, because we hated them, and you refused to watch them alone."

"I was scared," I state quietly. "I can watch them alone now."

He blows out a breath. "Answer my question please. What

happened back there?"

I roll my eyes and stick my head out of the shower to glare at him. "I heard noises that didn't sound like pleasure—which really should say something about your skills—so I barged in to save your life. From a lesbian who had your dick captive in her vagina. What the hell, Jake?"

His lips twitch. "You said to play nice."

"I didn't say those words. And how does 'play nice' translate to fuck her raw?"

He shrugs. "She's cool. Hacker like me, only not as good as me because she got caught."

"I was a kid!" I hear Hadley yell, admitting her eavesdropping.

I try not to smile. "And you're not a lesbian?" I ask.

She walks into the bathroom, her hair a red disarray of wildness. Her clothes are not exactly on right, as though she hurriedly got dressed.

"I told you I wasn't. I like women, but I've been put off by men for a long time. Since you killed Ferguson…some of the unease has lifted. Tonight I met Jake, already knew he was the same as me, and…well, you know what happened in the end."

"Can we discuss this when I'm finished washing off the judge and deputy?" I ask dryly.

Jake grimaces, his eyes flicking warily to Hadley, but she just shrugs. "You've seen what I'm working with. It's only fair I see what you have."

I'd laugh under normal circumstances, but I haven't thawed enough for that yet.

Jake, however, snickers under his breath, seeming to relax at her casual reaction.

"Later. What's up? Why'd you track us down? And more importantly, how'd you find us?"

She flicks her gaze to Jake. "He's not as good as he thinks he is."

Paint It All Red

She smiles sweetly at him, her double entendre clear, and he arches a challenging eyebrow at her.

"Alright then. Jake, make sure no one else can find us the same way she did."

Hadley bats her hand. "I'm way better than Alan, and he's the only one who would be tracking you. No way will he find you the way I did."

Her phone goes off, and she checks it. Her frown forms immediately.

"What?" Jake asks her, peering over at her phone.

I expect her to shield it from him, but she hands it to him instead. "Guess I need to borrow a brush," she says to me. "And some clothes. Thor over there ripped my pants open, and now the zipper is gone. My shirt has something on it too. I'll spare you the guessing game as to what."

I groan while waving my hand in her general direction. "Take what you need. But I hope you look good in red."

She curses before flicking her red hair. "Red is the one color I can't pull off. Every shade clashes with this. I thought you had a black hoodie or something."

"My black hoodies are kill shirts, and probably have traces of blood on them. Not a good idea to wear them."

She spins and walks out, plucking her phone back out of Jake's hand on her way. I look at him questioningly.

"They already found the judge and the deputy."

A smile curves my lips. "Good. Now the real fun begins."

Chapter 5

False face must hide what the false heart doth know.
—William Shakespeare

Logan

"What do we know?" I ask Leonard, peeling the glove off.

"You mean besides the fact the sheriff is trying to get us the hell out of here? Not much."

Johnson eyes me from across the room, pure hatred in his glare. I ignore him.

He knows I'm close to digging up hard evidence against him. It's just a matter of time.

"I think that message was meant for you," Leonard whispers as my eyes lift from the gory remains of Deputy Murdock.

My eyes flit up to the message he's pointing out.

They stole. They lied. They brokered peace with the devil in exchange for the souls of an innocent family. Yet you call me the monster.

Fuck you. <3

The little heart on the end is definitely a signature Lana used to leave for me. Apparently she's going to personalize these kills now, even address them to me without using my name.

"I silenced her, so now she's getting her words in," I say quietly.

Paint It All Red

Leonard looks around, making sure no one is close enough to overhear.

"This is quite literally a 'fuck you' message. It's not rage or even a threat to us. She's just basically sounding like a true ex. People might do the math."

"No one here knows Lana and I broke up. I told the others she went back home because I convinced her it wasn't safe."

"What happens when people see her in town?"

I lean back, surveying the damage to the neck of Judge Thomas. I doubt it's a coincidence his son came back to town today, and Lana decided to kill the father tonight.

"She won't be seen," I say absently. "Dev Thomas was there *that* night, and he seemed certain he'd been spared when he talked to us earlier. I think she paid him a visit when he arrived in town today."

"Why?"

"To see why he was here."

He looks confused, but I don't want to talk in front of everyone.

"I shouldn't be involving you in this and forcing you to—"

"You're not forcing me to do anything," Leonard says on a sigh. "Like I said, I get why she's doing it. This town has been killing and torturing people for years, and no one even cared about it until her."

I start to say something else, but Donny walks up, silencing our private conversation.

"So our unsub goes from quoting Voltaire to leaving a crude 'fuck you' message with a heart? Maybe you were right about it being a female, but why bother with the men's boot prints if you're going to leave a heart signature?"

"That message is about as petty as your girlfriend," Lisa says as she joins us.

Leonard chokes on air, but I remain composed.

"Says the petty girl who keeps trying to make her jealous,"

Hadley announces as she walks in, avoiding eye contact with me as she squats down with her kit to start taking samples.

My eyes rake over her, seeing her wearing different clothes than she left in. What is particularly eye-catching is the fact she's in a red shirt.

Over the years, I've heard her bitch more than once about the fact her red hair limits her wardrobe. She never wears red.

But I know someone who does.

"She spit gum in my hair," Lisa hisses.

"When?" I ask, hopeful this was recently and hopeful it *wasn't* recently at the same time.

"After I accidentally walked in on you two," Lisa mumbles, her cheeks turning pink.

"And provoked her," Hadley says from her crouch, not bothering to look up. "Twice. I would have slapped you. Lana went for a less obvious approach."

Leonard tugs my arm, guiding me out as Hadley and Lisa bicker. As soon as we're outside of the courthouse, he looks around, making sure no one can hear.

"They called Elise to New York to help with a case."

"I know. I'm the one who told you. And Elise volunteered to go because she's still not physically one hundred percent and wanted to make sure no one else was pulled."

"They called Craig back for something else."

I nod.

"It's just a matter of time before they pull us out of here completely, even if it is one by one."

"They'll try," I say with a shrug. "But short of any charges, the director has no weight to pull us completely."

Leonard looks out into the woods behind the courthouse.

"She could have easily killed Lisa."

Paint It All Red

My eyebrows hit my hairline.

"What?"

He looks back at me. "She's fiercely protective of you, even killed to keep you safe. Yet Lisa provokes her over and over and she spits some gum in her hair?" he asks, his lips twitching.

"She still has a firm grip on reality."

He leans back, his look going thoughtful again. "So Dev Thomas coming back prompted the demise of Judge Thomas. Why handle two at once? That's risky. What was so important about Murdock that he needed to die tonight as well?"

Before I can answer that, Hadley walks up, eyeing us. "Here."

She hands us a blood-stained folder, and I tilt my head as I pull on my gloves again.

I open it, looking over the files. It takes me a second to realize what I'm looking at.

"Those are Murdock's eight-year-old daughter's medical charts. Her wrist has been broken twice, and she can't even play sports because of how weak it is now. Other bones have been broken over the years as well, including her ribs on multiple occasions. His wife's chart looks thirty times worse, or at least I'd put money on it. It's not here, but I bet I can hack into it for you," Hadley states flatly.

"Why would his daughter's charts be here?" Leonard asks, looking on with me.

"Because someone wanted you to see this," Hadley says vaguely.

I close the file, blowing out a breath as I hand it to Leonard.

He skims over it quickly as Hadley walks away, a smug smirk on her lips.

"He was beating his kid?" Leonard asks, an edge to his tone.

"How much would you bet all the other deputies and the sheriff knew?" I ask rhetorically.

"We need to speak to Murdock's widow before the sheriff gets to her first," I say quietly as two deputies walk out, eyeing us on their way by.

"What is Collins saying about all this?" Leonard asks me as I fire off a quick text to Hadley, telling her what we're doing and to keep it quiet.

"Collins is saying we still need physical evidence. Johnson backed the sheriff on the matter of one of the deputies trying to kill me as being one rogue cop. As of right now, he's having to play politics, since the subcommittee nor the senate has convened over the actions of Johnson and the director."

He follows me to the SUV, both of us avoiding drawing attention from any of the local law enforcement.

"I joined this unit because I thought there'd never be any politics with serial killers," Leonard says dryly.

"I'm sure you never thought you'd find yourself compromised on a case either," I point out.

He snorts derisively as I start the car.

"I bet you never thought you'd find yourself in love with a serial killer."

I grimace, and he shakes his head. "Right. Sorry. Too soon. I'm still trying to wrap my head around all this, and awkward jokes seem to find their way out of my mouth."

"Let's just go see Murdock's widow," I grumble.

Chapter 6

Memory is deceptive because it is colored by today's events.
—Albert Einstein

Lana

My eyes are on Cheyenne Murdock as she wraps her arms around Alyssa, her daughter. Alyssa cries, but Cheyenne seems to shed ten years of age as she closes her eyes, exhaling relief.

Or maybe I'm just seeing what I want to see in case there's even an ounce of guilt inside me for killing a father. An abusive husband *and* father.

My hair is still damp, considering I didn't take the time to dry it before leaving. I knew what was to come the second they found the bodies.

I watch through the window, waiting on something to happen. Someone will surely try to shut her up, and she has something Logan needs.

Murdock was a sick fuck, but he was also a smart one. He knew it was stupid to burn all the physical evidence as he was tasked to do. He also knew it would be wise to harbor it, keep it safe, in case the sheriff ever decided to turn on him the way he did my father.

The name of my father has become a cautionary tale to not get on Cannon's bad side.

I'm going to turn this town into a cautionary tale of what happens when you destroy a family like mine.

But to instill fear, I have to show mercy as well. Mercy to those who were victims in their own right. Mercy to those who are tired of being weak and silenced.

They'll come for her. No doubt Murdock has run his big mouth about his evidence hoarding at some point. His wife wouldn't know of its existence. But some of the other deputies—if not all of them—would.

As if to prove me right, I see headlights in the distance, the car shutting off and the lights being killed down the street.

I sit on my perch in the tree behind the house, cloaked in the shadows of darkness.

I guess I'll be showering twice tonight.

The two silhouettes move toward the house, and I hop down from my tree and stealthily move inside the backdoor that has been left unlocked.

"Your bath is finished running," I hear Cheyenne saying to her daughter as I stop inside the kitchen, gauging the windows that are concealed by the blinds. Only the back had visibility. The men are coming in from the front, but I need to prepare for one to slip around back.

"Okay," the child says weakly, and I ignore the pang in my heart, reassuring myself that I did the right thing.

As soon as the child heads up the stairs, I step inside the living room, finding a spot I can't be seen from the back, and study the back of Cheyenne as she lifts a picture of her late husband.

A small smile crosses her lips. "Rot in hell, you stupid bastard. Let's see if the devil lets you lay your hands on him, or if he shows you a taste of your own medicine."

A dark grin emerges on my own lips.

"I'm sure the devil will enjoy playtime with Greg," I drawl.

She stumbles, eyes wide and panicked as her head swivels around to see me.

"Who are you?"

Paint It All Red

"Someone who is about to save your life. Two men are coming. One will come from the front, one from the back," I say, keeping my voice quiet. "They know Murdock hid some evidence."

She pales, and I nod. "I've already saved you once tonight; this will be the second time. You'll owe me, Cheyenne."

Her lip trembles, but before she can speak, the door is kicked in from the front, and she screams, drawing the barrel of the gun toward her. The end has a silencer on it, because these guys came to kill—not fuck around.

I dart across the room before the first shot can be fired, and I grab the man's wrist, twisting it back. I don't know this guy. I guess the sheriff outsourced this job to keep his nose clean.

He cries out when I slam the heel of my palm up, connecting with his nose. Blood sprays, and I spin, disarming him in the process. Just as I grab my knife from my side, I hear a *click* from behind me.

"Just who the hell are you?" a man's voice asks.

Everyone wants my name. There's a Rumpelstiltskin joke in there somewhere.

Again, it's someone I don't recognize. I catch a vague image of him through the reflection of the picture glass on the wall.

The guy I was fighting with is staring at me with contempt in his eyes as he cradles his broken nose.

"Who cares? Kill that bitch," the bleeding one growls.

"My name now doesn't really matter. But once upon a time, people called me Victoria Evans."

I may not know them, but judging by the audible breaths and the surprise in the bleeding one's eyes, they know me.

"In case you haven't heard…I don't die too easily."

I spin just as a shot is fired, with the diluted sound sparing my ears. I feel the heat of the bullet as it grazes my cheek, burning just barely. In one swift move, I slam the knife into the man's throat behind me, and grab his gun, firing it twice without even having to look.

I hear a pained cry from behind me, knowing the original man is now in a heap, as the man in front of me gurgles on his own blood, choking on it. The knife is still planted in his throat like a gruesome piece of artwork.

I finally turn my head as I jerk my knife out, and I see the two shots hit directly into the other man's chest.

I'd brush my shoulders off, but that seems a bit cocky.

"You know them?" I ask Cheyenne, who is clawing the corner she's in, shaking fiercely.

"Yes," she rasps, her lips trembling. "The Durham brothers," she says a little stronger, trying to stand on unsteady legs. "They play poker with the sheriff and…sometimes they handle things he doesn't want his deputies involved in."

"I guess they came after my time," I muse, watching them both slowly die.

They did good to escape my interest in the town as well. I really hate surprises.

"Yes," she says, her voice trembling again. "Are you… Are you really Victoria?"

Her tone is reverent, hushed, and somewhat fearful. I look around at the bloody mess and hope Alyssa stays upstairs.

"Is your daughter safe?" I ask instead of answering, looking over at Cheyenne.

She nods timidly. "Alyssa?" she calls out.

When the child doesn't answer, Cheyenne rushes by me, racing up the stairs. I'm covered in blood, looking every bit as scary as Jason Vorhees, so I stay down here, listening, deciding to spare the kid some unnecessary nightmares.

In a few moments, Cheyenne comes back down, her shoulders easing. "She likes to go under the water during her baths. She didn't

Paint It All Red

hear anything." She stares at me, then at the men at my feet. "It's been you, hasn't it? The one who has been killing all those men from…from that time?"

She swallows against the knot in her throat, and I cock my head.

"The one who killed Greg?" she goes on, her voice cutting out.

"The one who killed a child abuser, a murderer, and a violent, sadistic man in general," I amend, studying her curiously.

She runs a hand through her hair, her eyes intentionally not dropping to the gory mess in her living room again.

"I thought it was all a horrible urban legend, something to make the sheriff and Kyle seem all the more untouchable. I came to town after you were gone, and I barely heard whispers about anything. Then one night, Greg got drunk. It was the first time he hit me. I always stepped between him and my daughter, but I couldn't leave. He wouldn't let me—told me the sheriff would help him hunt me down, and he'd kill me and take Alyssa away."

She chokes back a sob, shaking her head. "I wanted him dead. I even went to the sheriff, hoping Greg's threats of Cannon helping that abusive bastard were all a bluff. But they weren't. The sheriff listened to all I had to say, then he called Greg right in front of me. I dealt with a broken jaw as punishment. That's when he told me he had all the evidence he needed to keep the sheriff in line, and that the next time I tried to run or get help, he'd slit my throat in front of our daughter."

I wish I'd come sooner for Greg now.

Surprisingly, his wife does know about the evidence, after all.

"He has a safe. I've never seen what's in it, but I know he keeps the combination in his favorite shoes. He's always had a terrible memory with numbers, so he had to write it down. I'll get it for you."

I step in front of her, and she stumbles back. "Save it for the feds. SSA Bennett, to be more precise. Don't give it to Johnson."

More lights draw my attention, and I peer out the window,

hissing out a breath when I see a SUV stopped beside the abandoned car just down the road. Logan walks in front of the lights, and my stomach somersaults. Shit!

I lift my phone, cursing when I see that I have a text I didn't know came through.

HADLEY: Logan is going to the widow's house. The deputy's widow, that is. Not the judge's.

Obviously Jake gave her my burner phone number.

I put my phone away, and look back to see Cheyenne is pale and shaking.

"Who are they?"

"The good guys. They'll be who you give the evidence to."

"But you look scared. Why are you scared if they're the good guys?" she demands.

I gesture to my bloody appearance, then the dead guys in her floor. She doesn't have a speck of blood on her.

"I'm not the good guy," I remind her, and she exhales like that's a relief to hear.

What a twisted town...

I grab a piece of paper from the table, and I scribble down an address as fast as I can, trying to get out of here before Logan makes it to the house.

"Have him escort you out of town. Tell him you never saw me, only knew I was in here because you heard the commotion. You were in the bathroom with your daughter the entire time, okay?" I ask, careful not to touch her with my bloody hands.

She nods, her throat bobbing with nerves.

I hand her the piece of paper.

"You can't go anywhere there might be family or friends. They'll track you that way. Leave your cell phone. Go to this house.

Paint It All Red

It's my Connecticut home, and a woman named Olivia lives there. She'll give you the funds to replace anything you need."

Her eyes water as she looks over the paper.

"Why would you do this for me?"

I watch her eyes as they lift back up. "I'm doing it for your child more than I'm doing it for you. This town doesn't care if it's a child. They planned to not only kill you, but to kill her tonight as well. Keep that in mind. And the evidence won't be somewhere as obvious as his safe. Think of somewhere he goes daily. He would have been paranoid, always checking to make sure it was still there, but discreet enough not to do it in front of you."

I peer out the window again, and curse, immediately dropping the curtain when I see the SUV moving this way now.

She looks lost in thought, then finally her eyes widen. "I know where it is."

"Good. Have him escort you there, get it, and then leave. Make sure he follows you out of the town, just in case the sheriff gets wind of your retreat. And don't stop driving until you absolutely have to—for gas or whatever."

She nods vigorously, clutching the paper like it's the anecdote to life. The door to the front is still open from it being kicked in earlier, so I don't dawdle with racing to the back when I hear approaching footsteps.

But just as I reach the back, I catch a glint of blonde hair at the door, through the window there. His eyes are down, so he doesn't see my cartoonish slide to a stop. Internally cursing, I spin back and dart into the broom closet, hating myself for being so reckless.

Please don't let there be a blood trail. Please don't let there be a blood trail.

I should have known he wouldn't be alone.

Just as I silently get the door shut, I hear the back door opening without so much as a knock.

I can't see, only listen.

"Logan, we have bodies," Leonard's voice announces.

Logan doesn't respond. My stomach sinks to my toes when his shadow interrupts the stream of light coming under the door. This shallow closet isn't going to hide me if he opens the door.

The door knob starts to turn, and I hold my breath, waiting for the inevitable. I've planned for everything except him, and the waters keep getting murkier. What will he do if he finds me? Shoot me? Arrest me? Hurt me? Hate me more?

I don't have to find out right now, because he apparently changes his mind, leaving the door shut as the sound of footsteps move away from me. I expel the painful breath I've been holding, and I listen as he talks to Cheyenne.

She tells them the story I crafted on the spot, and I hear the little girl's voice calling for her from upstairs. "Stay there, sweetie," Cheyenne says with a broken voice. "We have people down here right now."

"I'll be right back," Cheyenne tells them, as I try to think of a magical way to get myself out of the damn closet without being seen.

"She's right. We have to get her out of this town," Leonard tells Logan.

"We just can't let anyone know that's what we're doing, considering that's against protocol."

They both grow quiet for a moment. "She knew they'd come for her," Logan says quietly.

"Yeah, and if she hadn't been here, there'd be two different bodies lying at our feet right now," Leonard says, sounding as if he's defending me.

So he's compromised?

I touch my cheek, finding that my fingertips burn the exposed flesh the bullet grazed. That's going to leave a scar. Stupid fucker.

Paint It All Red

I should have stabbed him harder, dragged out the pain. I would have if not for the fact a child could have walked in and saw the horrors for herself.

"Find out who these two are. I'm sure they're linked to the sheriff somehow."

"Why come after the widow, though?" Leonard asks.

"Because I have something you need," Cheyenne tells them, apparently surprising them with her reentry. "My daughter is packing a bag and putting on clothes. My husband went to the basement regularly, and I never thought anything of it. He'd go down there for just a few minutes at a time. There's a loose floor plank down there, and I never questioned why he wouldn't fix it until today."

I listen as footsteps disappear into the basement, and very cautiously, I try to hear if anyone stayed here. It'd make sense for one to stay here, considering a child could walk down and into the massacre show I've left on display.

"Get the daughter to the car without letting her see this," I hear Logan saying as he comes up the stairs again. "And take this with you."

It feels like I've been in this closet forever.

"Where are you going?" Leonard asks.

"With you. Come on. There may be more coming if the sheriff doesn't hear back from them."

I blow out a breath, relieved when I hear the rustle of them leaving. When the front door shuts—the best it can, since it's broken—I finally peer out of the crack I make in the door.

When the coast is clear, I dart to the backdoor, and with light footsteps finally leave the damn house behind.

I hear the sound of doors opening and closing as I retreat into the woods, cursing the leaves for crunching under my feet as the chill kisses my bloodstained skin and hair.

My retreat isn't too quiet, but they're so caught up in getting her out of here, that I doubt they notice. Finally, I find the path I beat out earlier, the leaves too damaged and broken to crunch beneath my feet, and I quicken my pace. I'm leaving a bloody trail right to my house if I go directly there.

Searching the area around me, I strip out of the hoodie I'm wearing. Then I kick off the boots, opting to wear socks only. Just as quickly, I peel away the top layer of pants, pulling a bag out of the back pocket. I unfold the bag then toss all the bloody apparel into it. My leggings catch a chill from the night, but there's also a chill that shoots up my spine.

My eyes dart around, but all is silent. Nothing is moving.

Why does it feel like someone is watching me?

I finish closing up the bag, checking to make sure no blood is dripping. After one last wary glance at my surroundings, I turn and start jogging in my socked feet back to the house, ignoring the way the twigs and acorns try to hobble me.

Pain is something I learned to ignore a long time ago.

But ignoring the sensation that someone is watching me is harder to let go of.

Maybe I'm being paranoid, but I doubt it.

I turn again, but hear nothing and see no motion.

Then, like every fucking horror movie I've ever seen, a chill rides up my spine, and I know without a doubt someone is directly behind me.

I drop the bag and spin, bringing my elbow up to collide with a face, but a hand grabs it, and my breath seizes as another hand comes around, grabbing my other arm. In one smooth motion, I'm shoved against a tree, and a hard body bears against mine.

The only thing that halts my lethal reaction, are the familiar blues staring directly into my eyes.

My breaths turn painful as I heave for air that escapes me. It's not because he's hurting me, it's because it hurts just to see him.

His eyes are hard as they level me, and his grip stays tight, even though we both know I could escape him if I wanted to. The problem is doing it without hurting him.

"I won't be arrested," I say softly.

"So you'll do whatever it takes to stay free?" he asks, his voice not as hard as his eyes. He runs his gaze over my face, taking me in.

"No," I whisper hoarsely. "I won't do whatever it takes, but I won't be arrested either."

His gaze lingers on my lips. "You could break away with ease right now, couldn't you?"

His eyes pop back up, holding my stare.

I don't speak. I don't have to.

He doesn't need to hear the words aloud, and I'm not quite prepared to admit all I'm capable of to him.

He doesn't ease his hold, but his grip doesn't tighten either. "Leonard is escorting Cheyenne and Alyssa out of town, but since you were hiding in the closet, I'm sure you heard all that."

I suck in a breath, and his lips twitch.

"You've been the huntress for so long that I'm sure you've forgotten what it felt like to be the hunted. But I've been looking everywhere for you, Lana. And I'm a lot better than you give me credit for."

I start to move, but instead of gripping me harder, he eases his hold and brings his hand up to my face, cupping it as he studies my eyes.

"I had no idea you were Victoria when I fucked up. I never would—"

"Does it really matter?" I ask bitterly, hoping those damn tears don't start falling, even as they crowd my eyes and turn him blurry. "I'm still the twisted monster of the night, while you're the honest hero in the light."

Even through my blurred vision, I see his expression soften. "I wouldn't have fucked you and left you naked on my bed if I'd have known. So yes, it makes a huge difference. I thought you were suffering an obsession disorder that had you killing as Victoria's proxy. It's a lot different than you being Victoria, because a proxy killer is most definitely suffering a psychotic break and is highly unstable. In my mind, you were being manipulated by Jacob Denver, and I was being played as a pawn."

My heart is thumping painfully in my chest, and I almost wonder if he can feel it too.

"Jake can't and wouldn't ever try to manipulate me. And as far as you go, I *never* asked for any case information. *You* came on to me. And—"

Usually, as everyone is aware, I hate surprises. But my heart ends up beating to a new rhythm when Logan surprises me by crushing his lips to mine.

At first I try to weakly push him away, but the tears start falling as he kisses me harder, his hands going from restraining to needy as he pulls me flush against his body. My arms go around his neck as I give in, kissing him back as the tears streak down my face.

He lifts me, his kiss almost consuming me, and every pent-up emotion flows into it, making it powerful and destructive at the same time.

My legs wrap around his waist, and he pushes me against the tree again as he devours me, taking in every taste and flick of my tongue as it battles his. I'm not sure if it's angry or sensual, but I know I can't just let go right now.

Even though I know I should.

Something cracks near us, and we both break the kiss, our eyes darting over to a fox as it runs by. My breath gets shaky as I turn to face Logan again, seeing the softness in his eyes that wasn't there the last time we were this intimately placed.

"I never would have hurt you like that if I'd known," he says softly.

I swallow hard. "You didn't hurt me physically. And as far as the sex goes, I could have stopped it. I knew you knew. I knew what was happening. I just loved you enough to take your anger, knowing I deserved it."

He groans, his forehead pressing against mine.

"You didn't deserve it. For the first time in my life, I have no clue what to do, Lana," he whispers with such tragic honesty that it slices through me.

Part of me wants to corrupt him, to make him see what I'm doing is a twisted version of the right thing, despite the torture and massacre I still have planned. But to do that would be stealing his soul and condemning it to join mine.

Just knowing he hasn't told the others and he's holding me to him right now is more than I ever realistically expected. But to go forward with me would be to irrevocably damn him to my same fate.

"I love you," I say on a broken whisper, because I'm just too weak to turn him away so soon.

"I love you," he says back, thawing my heart completely as the tears start leaking again. "Which is why I'm begging you to end this now and go away with me," he adds, his voice cracking.

He has no idea what an offer like that does to someone like me. Leave? Stop now? Walk away with him as a prize?

It's so tempting, and if not for the fact the sheriff and his deputies still live, still spread dark shadows over everyone's halls…I'd do it. I'd walk away from the revenge. But I can't walk away from all the innocent lives still being scarred.

People just like Cheyenne and her daughter who would have been killed by a man who is supposed to protect them, all to conceal his darkest secrets.

"We have enough evidence to put him away," Logan says, as

though he's reading my mind.

But he believes in the justice system. He doesn't understand a man like Cannon can only be killed *after* he's buried. Only then will anyone care about evidence. He lines the pockets of too many important and powerful men.

Just like Director McEvoy.

Just like SSA Johnson.

Just like the fucking governor.

"Don't decide right now. Right now, just be with me, and for tonight, we can simply forget the rest of the world exists," he goes on, brushing his lips over mine again.

"What about the case?" I ask stupidly.

His case is solved. He has the murderer in his arms.

He grins like he's thinking the very same thing. "They can do without me for tonight. Leonard will cover for me."

I've already killed four people in twenty-four hours. I suppose I can pretend as though the world around us isn't collapsing for just one night.

"This isn't a ploy to find out where you're staying. I could do that just by following Hadley," he adds, kissing my lips again.

Pathetically, I never doubted his intentions.

"I know," I say on a sigh. Because Logan Bennett makes me forget the fact I'm not untouchable.

It's been a dangerous game since the beginning.

Now I have to stop myself from dragging him to the pits of hell with me.

Chapter 7

Better a diamond with a flaw than a pebble without.
—Confucius

Lana

Jake's eyes almost bulge out of his head as I walk in with Logan. Logan slides his arm around my waist like he's ready to protect me, as though Jake is about to do something stupid.

I lace my fingers together with Logan's, as Jake continues to gawk at me.

"Are we under arrest?" Jake asks, so confused that it's almost comical.

Logan grunts out a breath, and I lean against him. "This is neutral ground. No talk of killing people, and no talk of arresting," Logan finally says. "As of right now, there is no talk of this town or what's going on inside it."

Jake looks between us, his eyebrows still raised as he keeps the laptop in his lap. The monitors all around have the town from various angles, and Logan glances at each one.

"That explains a lot," he says on a long breath. "You really have the entire town under surveillance. But yet I haven't spotted a single camera."

"I thought we weren't discussing the case," Jake says warily.

Logan pinches the bridge of his nose, and I stifle a sad smile. He's in love with his job and curious by nature. Right now he's suffering the ultimate battle of right and wrong; a confliction I haven't faced in a long time.

That struggle I see in his eyes is my fault.

"It's NSA tech Jake swiped a few years ago, and he built his own versions," I explain.

Jake looks like he's about to fall off the couch, but I shrug like it's no big deal. "The monitors cover all the most important parts of town, and we stay with the sheriff, watching his every move. We also keep a close eye on the deputies. It's how I knew Hollis was coming after you."

I don't look at him as I say the words as emotionlessly as possible. But my voice unfortunately cracks and betrays me on that last sentence.

Logan's hand tightens on my side, and he pulls me to him, hugging me against him. I take in his scent, closing my eyes, soaking it all in while I can.

He doesn't know what's to come, because he can't see all the conversations the way we can.

"So you're safe here?" Logan asks, the heartwarming concern in his tone coupled with a defeated sigh. He knows which route I'm going to choose, even though his option sounds better.

"It's not just about me," I say, peering up from his chest as he looks down.

He breathes steadily, but I can tell it's with strain.

"Just like it's not just about you," I add, clutching the front of his shirt. "You're good. I won't take that away."

He starts to speak, when suddenly the front door opens, and I turn in time to see Hadley stumble in, her eyes wide and fixed on Logan.

Her mouth opens and closes several times before finally locking shut. Then it pops back open. "What's going on?"

"I'm wondering the same thing," Jake says, not moving from his spot on the couch.

Paint It All Red

Logan groans, and I tug his hand. "We're going to the bedroom to have a night off."

"Four bodies is your idea of a night off?" Hadley asks dryly.

I grimace, but Logan doesn't make an expression as he follows me to the bedroom.

I hear whispers erupt in the living room as Jake and Hadley panic a little, but I shut the door on them and lean back on it, studying the man in my temporary bedroom.

He looks around at the floral patterns lining every surface and quirks an eyebrow at me.

"The owners only come here for summer and Christmas." Just in case he wants to look for their missing bodies or whatever. I don't know if he trusts that I'm not killing innocent people.

He sits down on the bed, clasping his hands together. One glance in the mirror has me cringing. Blood is splattered across my face and matted in my hair.

"I'll shower," I say awkwardly.

I'm pretty sure there should be a sense of horror filling me, considering his white shirt has smears of blood on it as well.

The bloody ex-girlfriend takes on a new meaning.

He doesn't object or say anything as I step out, leaving him overwhelmed with everything going on.

I feel like the devil's advocate who has lured a saint to the edge of a cliff and now beckons him to jump.

With quiet steps, I grab the note from the drawer in the hallway—the note I never knew if I'd use or not. The living room is quiet, but I'm sure Jake and Hadley are in the back bedroom, making use of their kindred ways.

Instead of interrupting them, I tuck the note inside Hadley's bag, right where I know it'll be safe until I want it found. Then I retreat to the bathroom, and start stripping.

My sense of self-loathing left a long time ago, washed away with the tears and pain. Yet it's coming back with a vengeance as I step under the shower with a new flow of tears that refuse to stop falling.

I scrub away the blood, watching the red run down the drain for the second time tonight. I'm barely holding it together when the shower curtain slides open, and I jump, startled.

Logan steps in fully naked, that trademark smirk playing on his lips as he nears me. I half wonder if I'm dreaming, until he kisses me, tangling his hands in my hair as he tilts my face up to devour me better.

I moan into his mouth as he lifts me, sliding his hands under my ass as his naked body gets more slicked by the spray of the shower. Our heights are so different that picking me up always makes it easier for him to kiss me, but it also lines up our bodies in a much better way.

Our kiss turns frantic, hungry, and desperate. We both know that tonight might be the last time we're ever allowed to love each other. The gray area has only a brief window of opportunity before it's closed and we're back on our opposing sides.

But this? This is the right way to say goodbye. Not the way we left things before.

My back slides against the wall as I struggle to find friction, but Logan is strong enough to maneuver my body without my help.

He thrusts in hard, and I cry out, breaking the kiss to keep from accidentally biting him. He buries his face in the crook of my neck as he starts working his hips, driving me crazy from all the right angles.

My fingers dig into his shoulders, clinging to him, as my back slides up and down on the slick wall. Water hits our sides as Logan moves us closer to the back, his face still against my skin as he kisses, licks, and nips a trail up the column of my neck.

That all-consuming, bone-deep sensation of ecstasy starts to unfurl at my core, and I grip him tighter, praying I don't draw blood as I move against him, desperate to tip over that edge.

His hips falter as he nears the same intense feeling, and his lips find mine as I cry out, my entire body shuddering with the force of the orgasm. A guttural noise escapes his lips as he stills inside me, struggling to keep me up as his strength tries to give out, his body going lax.

My legs lazily slide down his sides as he lifts me off him, and I wobble a little when I'm standing on my own again. His lips find mine in a soft, reverent kiss as he backs me under the spray of the shower again.

I lose track of time, and it isn't until the water starts getting cold that we're forced to finally end the shower.

"I can't let you go," he says against my lips as he shuts the water off.

My eyes meet his as my lips fall away, losing the contact that keeps me grounded in reality.

But then I'm on him, kissing him again, passionately, deeply, hungrily…

And I stave off the onslaught of emotions that would surely wreck me if given that sort of power.

I can't let you hold on, I silently tell him, refusing to ruin any more of our night with heartbreaking truths.

Chapter 8

Give every man thy ear, but few thy voice.
—William Shakespeare

Logan

Lana is pressed against me, her head on my chest, as my fingers idly run through her hair. It's after three in the morning, and neither of us have even thought about sleeping.

Instead, we've spent the past several hours just talking about anything and nothing at all. Mostly it's been mundane stuff, when we weren't wrapped around each other and doing less chatty things.

Her cheek has a small graze on it from a bullet that got too damn close, but it's not bleeding. It should be a reminder that she's not invincible, but she seems to think battle scars are better than victim scars.

"So I spent all that time worried about Plemmons targeting you, and you spent all that time annoyed with me for keeping him from you?" I ask, staying on the conversation we've veered to.

I feel her smile against my chest, and she runs her fingers down my stomach, tracing the lines there.

"A little annoyed, but mostly I just felt cared for. If I hadn't wanted him dead so he could never hurt you, then I would have appreciated all your concern a lot more."

She presses a kiss to my chest, and I tug her tighter to my side as I stare up at the ceiling, trying to sort through everything. It's a mess in my head. It's a mess everywhere inside me.

Paint It All Red

I'm questioning everything I've ever stood for.

Judge, jury, and executioner has never been something I've agreed with. I've fought for legality and true justice. My entire world has centered around it since I was offered a position within the FBI.

"How'd you learn to fight like you do?"

"You haven't seen me fight," she sighs. "I'd never fight you."

My lips twitch as I glance down at her. She peers up at the same time.

"Should we test to see who's better?"

She stifles a grin, trying to keep a serious face. "Agent Bennett, I think it'd be emasculating if I kicked your ass. So don't worry, I'll hold back if you ever get brave enough."

I laugh, finding the sound almost sad. Her smile is just as grim amidst the heavy air around us when she lays her head back down and resumes her task of tracing idle circles.

"So now that all your worst secrets are aired, maybe you can share a little about your past," I say quietly, feeling her stiffen next to me as her fingers still on my chest.

"You've already heard everything they did. Do you need more detail than that?" she asks in a harsh whisper.

I tilt her face up, palming her cheek. She meets my eyes with the same fearlessness she faces the rest of the world, but I see the vulnerable girl tucked away inside her; the girl she has to protect after all she's been through.

"I was talking about your past before all that happened. Something that would tell me about the girl you used to be."

She cuts her gaze away, blowing out a breath.

"The girl I used to be is dead. Knowing how naïve and fragile she was won't do anything but break your heart right now. Because you'll picture me as her. You've had the real me the entire time, Logan. Nothing between us or how I was with you was a lie. Only snippets of my past were altered for the sake of keeping my secret."

I can feel her drifting away even as she presses closer to me.

Instead of letting her float off inside her own mind, I shift, turning and coming down on top of her. She tries to kiss me, but I pull back as I settle comfortably between her legs and keep my lips just out of reach of hers.

"Part of the reason you're so fierce today is because of that girl. Pretending as though you were never her is one step closer to detachment from reality. It's a dangerous slope."

She rolls her eyes, but a small smile forms on her lips, surprising me. I'll never get tired of how she never reacts the way I predict. Half of the reason I fell so hard was the constant mystery cloaking her.

Even as pieces of the puzzle continue to fall together, I'm still just as intrigued and mystified by her.

"You sound like Jake," she finally says, running her fingers through my hair as her legs tangle with mine.

"I hope Jake never held this position while having this conversation."

She laughs, rolling her eyes again, and finally she sighs.

"Jake is just a friend," she says quickly.

"So you've said."

She flashes that smile that is real and not weighted like all her other ones have been tonight. For some reason, she likes it when I get jealous.

"My mother and father were peculiar people with varied interests. My brother always said they had 'eclectic' personalities."

It's so out of the blue that I don't know how to respond. Fortunately, she doesn't need me to speak to continue her story.

"They loved classical music, and hated that none of us had an ounce of musical talent. But they also loved their hard rock and jazz

Paint It All Red

too. You're supposed to be able to judge someone based on their taste in music—hence the reason my brother deigned them with the eclectic personality label."

Her smile grows.

"They were this amazing team. Dad worked a thankless job as a janitor—the true reason I pieced together the Boogeyman's cleaning background—and Mom was a coroner. She was such a perky person for someone who dealt with death every day, and I was a little too comfortable around dead people, since she often had to take me to work with her. They took turns cooking, and they cleaned together. No one was ever more important than the other."

Her eyes grow distant, as though she's recalling a memory, and I watch her, unable to tear my own eyes away from her face. I've never seen such a serene look on her.

"They'd dance," she says, her eyes sparking back to life as she meets my gaze again and smiles.

"Dance?"

"Every night after we went to bed, they'd stand in the living room, put on a slow song, and dance." She clears her throat as her eyes water. "Mom would always have her head on Dad's chest, and he'd be holding her to him with his eyes shut as they swayed off-rhythm to the music. Mom could sing so well, and she'd often sing as they danced."

I brush a tear from her cheek with my thumb, and she leans into the touch.

"I would sneak out just to watch them dance. Sometimes Dad would catch me, but instead of scolding me, they'd have me dance with them. Same for Marcus. Even Jake was invited into the dancing ring on the nights he stayed over. It was a time so perfect that it eventually had to end in tragedy. Good things have a lesser reign than the bad."

She exhales heavily, and she offers me a tight, less genuine smile.

"They were really in love. That must have been nice to grow up in," I say, trying to encourage her to continue.

Her spark fades again as a coldness surfaces, confusing me.

"You see something for so long, and you take it for granted. In our minds, Marcus and I believed a love like that was common, easy to find, and effortless. In our minds, falling in love with someone had to be the simplest thing in the world."

She presses her hand to my chest, holding it against my heart, and her eyes stay fixed there.

"We didn't know how messy love could be or how jealous people would lash out."

"Jealous people?"

Her eyes come up, and she releases her hand from my heart. "Everyone was envious of what my parents had. My father was a lowly janitor, but he was handsome. My mother was beautiful, and her smile could save the lives of the almost-dead. She radiated purity and warmth. Everything the opposite of me."

"I'm sure there's a little girl living with Lindy Wheeler who would object to that," I remind her.

Her eyes harden again, and I decide not speaking would be a good idea. I have no idea what to say that won't drive her farther into her own head.

"Lindy suffered. She knows how to offer comfort to another. The little girl is in good hands. I made sure of that. One good deed doesn't make me the angel she accuses me of being. And I'm not even bothered by it. I don't *want* to be an angel. I *was* like my mother, only a little more hotheaded and ready to defend myself. I was just like her other than that. I saw the good in everyone, and I smiled even when someone was trying to break me down. I thought I was so strong and so smart. The problem is, I saw good where no good even existed."

"Like with Kyle?" I ask, an edge to my tone. Just knowing he touched her…

Paint It All Red

"Like with Kyle," she repeats, her tone flat and emotionless. "I trusted him even after he'd proven himself to be a jackass. I never saw the pure evil in him until that night. And my brother was just as naïve. The two of us walked directly into that trap, unprepared and outmatched, with no chance of walking away. And we never saw it coming, because we never thought people could be that cruel."

She blows out a breath, as though she's keeping herself in check. I don't press the issue or say anything, allowing her to tell the story however she wants to.

But if I hear the details from her mouth, I may end up joining her on her killing spree. I just don't think I'm strong enough to hear her break down and tell me what they did without killing everyone else involved in all of it.

"We learned differently, and I shed the coat of naivety once I managed to survive. I made a promise to my brother that I intend to keep. A promise he knew I would be able to make. Now I only see the good when it's there to see. I'm smarter. They made me smarter. They also made me what I am today—lethal and merciless. I have to believe there was a reason for that, and each time I save someone else from the same possible fate I suffered, I feel a bit closer to Marcus."

My mind is fucked. All she has to do is ask me to join her, and I'll be at her side. So I'm grateful that she doesn't, because I'm not even sure what to feel about this.

"When the lights go off and the music is playing, I often think back to my mother dancing with my father. I was so young. My younger self didn't understand how important it was to treasure and soak in all those memories. But the ones I have stay with me. Those memories kept me alive and helped drown out some of the nightmares."

My thumb traces over her lip as I study her.

"Come on," I say, rolling off her and standing up.

She looks at me like I've lost my mind until I flip on my phone and the music starts streaming through. Her eyes glisten almost instantly, and she smiles as I tug her hand, urging her to join me.

Naked in the middle of the bedroom, I pull her to me. Her head falls to my chest, and my lips press against the top of her head as I hold her as close as possible.

And we dance.

We dance for several songs.

Until she's suddenly climbing up me and kissing me hungrily, like she can't hold back any longer, and the night is too close to ending.

And I take her over and over, until the sun is shining down on us and we're both too spent to even attempt another round.

As she gets comfortable on top of me, her eyes lazily drifting shut, I ask, "Why Lana Myers? What made you choose that name?"

She grins as her eyes struggle to remain open.

"My mother said she and my father always argued about my name before I was born. They agreed immediately on Marcus, but my name? It was one of the few arguments they ever held. She wanted Victoria because of my late grandma. My father loved the name Lana, had heard it when he was traveling as a teen with his parents. He said he felt like I was going to be a Lana, and not some regal girl like the name Victoria suggested."

She laughs under her breath, her gaze shifting as she drifts into her memories again.

"Mom said after I was born, she knew she was right. But Dad said he was right, because the definition of Lana suited me perfectly, even though my mother argued I was as hot-tempered as any Victoria there ever was."

I tilt my head, wanting in on the inside joke. "What does Lana mean?"

"Depends on the country. Precious. Little Rock. Sun Ray. But Dad said it was the Hawaiian meaning above all else that suited

Paint It All Red

me — *afloat; calm as still waters.* It took a storm to offer me a calm."

She meets my gaze again, and I smile, thinking of how well it does suit her.

"I needed a name that meant something; I needed something to keep me from fading into a new persona. That was the only one I had," she goes on.

I run my finger along her nose, tapping the end of it. "It fits you perfectly. But why Myers?"

A darker smile lights her lips. "My father was also a horror movie buff. Old school horror movies. He said he didn't have the time or patience for pretty boy douchebags who had mommy issues."

I laugh unexpectedly, and she grins.

"Mom always teased him that he just liked the scary, in-your-face psychopaths with mommy issues. Michael Myers was one of his faves."

I laugh harder, shaking my head, and she lifts her hand, running her fingers through my hair. Our eyes meet and a calm silence washes over us.

"Can I ask a case related question?" I ask hesitantly.

"You know everything that's happened," Lana says warily. "I can't tell you what's left."

"Do you know who the original killer was?"

That's when there's a knock at the door, pausing our conversation.

"Yeah?" Lana calls out, her body sprawled across mine.

"I hate to break up the reunion, but there's an emergency meeting going on right now. Donny says we need to be at the cabins ASAP."

"Shit," I groan, cursing the day already.

Lana rolls off me with effortless grace and grabs a robe, tying it together before I even manage to pry myself from the bed. She leans against the wall and just watches me as I quickly dress.

"You're good, Logan," Lana says quietly, drawing my attention to her as she perches on the edge of a dresser. "It's the thing I love most about you. Do whatever you feel is right. Don't worry about me. I'll be okay."

I knew what her answer was going to be when I asked the question last night, but hearing the finality in her tone is like a sledgehammer to my stomach.

"This isn't goodbye, Lana. I'll be back tonight. We may have to actually sleep, but I will be back."

She smiles at me, but it's weighted once again.

I turn my phone back on, letting it go crazy with messages I don't have time to read. Instead of wasting these last few minutes, I kiss her, letting her know I love her even if she is choosing to finish this.

My head is still spinning with a thousand conflicting arguments as to why this is wrong or right, but I refuse to give her up.

"Later," I say against her lips.

"Later," she whispers back.

Hadley and I leave and head to her vehicle, and I take in her disheveled hair and realize…that house has only two bedrooms.

"I thought you were gay," I say as she works from her laptop in the passenger seat in the silver car she got from who knows where.

"I told you I wasn't. I've always liked guys and girls…but you know what? Let's have this conversation later. Whatever is bugging Donny has me worried."

"I'm sure it's nothing," I say dismissively.

It's not until we're almost back at the cabins that I realize I never got an answer to the question I asked Lana about the original serial killer.

Paint It All Red

But the look in her eyes told me she knows.

Chapter 9

Everything's fine today; that is our illusion.
—Voltaire

Lana

"Showtime?" Jake asks as I walk into the living room. My hair is pulled back, my combat boots are on, and my red shirt is the only pop of color on the otherwise black apparel.

"Final countdown."

I take out the paintbrushes, pull up my hoodie, and grab two cans of paint.

"You take the east, and I'll take the west. I'm assuming you know what that meeting is about?" Jake asks.

"Yeah. It's what we predicted from the start. Johnson and the director are about to railroad the entire investigation. Johnson has his target, which happens to be Diana's son, despite his numerous alibies and the fact he's states away."

"And dating a damn fancy lawyer who will give them hell before they ever even think about arresting him," Jake adds with a smirk.

"It's almost anti-climatic how predictable they all are." I feign a sad sigh, but he doesn't smile the way I expect him to.

"I'm having reservations about the final leg of the plan. I think

Paint It All Red

we should just leave and let the fireworks happen instead of you risking yourself."

I quirk an eyebrow at him, ignoring all the festering emotions that are aching inside my chest. Today, Logan will leave. Tonight, Logan will be free to forget me.

His life will go on, and he'll eventually just see this as a blemish in his otherwise flawless character.

"I'm not risking anything but them surviving if we deviate now, Jake. Have a little faith. I'm better than them. They've not even laid a hand on me."

His lips thin, and his gaze flicks to the bullet graze on my bandaged cheek, but he doesn't argue as we pack our separate vehicles with the paint.

"Quit dawdling. We have an entire town to terrorize," I say when I know he's about to press the issue.

He's worried about me surviving.

I see a life too empty to be concerned with the notion of survival.

Chapter 10

The road to perdition has ever been accompanied by lip service to an ideal.
—Albert Einstein

Logan

"You're fucking kidding me," I snap, glaring at Johnson as he pokes his chest out, posturing like a motherfucking gorilla about to beat the damn thing.

"You have your orders. You and the rest of your *team* are to return to Quantico. The director signed off on it. That's what happens when you stray from the current case to work on a *closed* case from ten years ago, while people continue to die in this town. Four people in one night died, and you didn't even bother to ask any questions. Nor did you bother to show up to where all the officers set up to canvas the surrounding woods in that area."

Donny grips me before I can launch myself at the smug son of a bitch smirking at me.

I brush Donny off, grabbing my phone as I walk out the door, ignoring the stupid fucking deputy who has the audacity to act like he's going to lead me to one of the SUVs.

Collins finally answers, and I immediately start snapping at him.

"You're letting this happen? You're letting them pull us out so they can do what? Launch a new witch hunt like the one they did ten years ago? It's obvious they didn't learn their lesson. You're really going after a pro athlete with a fucking lawyer girlfriend?"

Collins heaves out a breath. "It's out of my hands, and the girlfriend already knew about the intent to arrest before it was ever decided. Obviously they have a leak, and she's pretty much squashed their entire case. It's not going to be like last time."

There's no fucking leak. Lana or Jake knew this was coming and warned them through Diana most likely. Or in a way that didn't give them away. Or maybe they just don't care who knows at this point and are gambling more.

They can't manufacture evidence this time, because Diana's son has airtight alibis. It'd be too obvious.

"Get back," Collins says.

"Fuck that. I'm not going anywhere."

"You have to, Logan," he says, exasperated. "The director has called a meeting to see about having you removed from all your duties, pending an investigation into your actions. He's claiming your entire team is compromised and exhibiting signs of empathy with the killer. He even said you helped a woman and child leave town, despite her husband's murder, along with two other murders in her home, before you even reported the latter two murders. I told you to be discreet when looking into the past case. You ignored me."

"So you're playing politics. I thought you were better than that. And the woman had no hand in those murders. Someone else acted on her behalf in self-defense. Those men were sent to silence Cheyenne Murdock."

He grows quiet for a moment, and I turn to see the rest of my team already packing up, giving in so easily. I can't fucking leave Lana in this town. I'll quit and stay here on my own if they try to make me.

"I'm not playing politics, but I do have to play their game until I can see if that evidence you recovered is enough. If you don't leave and return to us willingly, Johnson will arrest you for obstruction, and I can't save you from anything while you're there. It could be too late before I get there. Don't risk it. It's not worth it. Keep a lid on what you've discovered. Just come back. Don't let them toss you in one of their cells. You know what that town is capable of."

My eyes rake over the men here. No doubt Lana wouldn't trust me to take care of myself if I was locked up here. Too many violent memories from the past would have her risking her life to come after me.

And that's the only reason I won't risk it.

"Fine," I bite out. "But you better have this resolved by the time I return so I can come right back."

"I'm trying, Logan. I really am. Just give me some time to—"

A loud white noise sound comes over the speakers, and my eyes flick to the television in the living room. I vaguely remember the only innocent deputy telling me the sheriff owned the television network service, and he had a special broadcasting ability.

But that's not him broadcasting.

"Logan?" Collins prompts, but I ignore him as I walk into the living room, watching the slideshow unfold on the television. It's just a few pictures of the town at sunset, all of them flicking around at random.

A voice comes on, speaking like the damn creepy voice from SAW.

"Citizens of Delaney Grove. It's time to purge the town. You have until sunset to leave…to save yourself. We're claiming this town now. For your sins, you shall repent. For your past, you shall endure the nightmares you caused. And for your eyes that you closed so willingly, now you shall see."

The slideshow starts to make sense, and my stomach roils as I see a familiar young girl and boy on the street. Someone fucking recorded this?

A younger version of Kyle Davenport appears in front of them, and the screen cuts to Victoria on the ground, and Marcus right behind her. His screams almost make me heave as he begs them to stop, but Victoria fights. She fights with all the limited strength she has.

They hold her down.

Thirteen to two.

Their fingers dig into her arms to restrain her. All ten fingers. Which is why she cuts them off.

"Someone fucking stop this!" the sheriff barks, running out of one of the cabins. "Call Hank and tell him to pull the plug now!"

"He's trying!" a deputy shouts back. "The sick fuck is overriding the system."

The screen cuts away from the horrors, like whoever was filming got too tired to keep on, and the next screen is that of Robert Evans suffering a fate just as sickening.

I turn my head away as the deputies do their worst on the screen.

"Now!" the sheriff shouts. "You have to kill it now!"

He's on the phone, but I barely notice him, because my attention turns back to the TV when the voice comes on again.

"Hear no evil."

The black screen is blank, but several screams of agony are coming out loud and clear.

"See no evil."

The screen lights up with both disturbing movies playing side by side on a split screen.

Then the screen fades to black again, before a cloaked silhouette comes into view. All you can see is the dark hood. The face is nothing more than a shadow as a red-gloved hand comes up. One finger extends, covering the spot where the lips would be if you could see them, making the universal 'shush' sign.

"Speak no evil."

The screen goes blank again, then lights up with images of

different people as they watch their TV. Screams and panic erupt. It's like the jumbo-tron at ballgames flicking to different people, and them noticing it on a delay. Only instead of excitement, there's pure horror when they see their faces.

It continues throughout the town, as though they have cameras in every family room of every home. People practically leap from their seats when their faces flash across the TV screen.

I remember the day when everyone said their doors were found open, but nothing but some mirrors were taken.

The mirrors are still a mystery, but it's clear now why those doors were open. Jake planted cameras while families slept in the next room, completely unaware.

The screen continues to cycle from one home to the next, and the sheriff continues to panic more and more.

"Sundown," the voice says again as the shadowed, hooded figure comes into view once more. "Or the monster comes for you."

Suddenly, the shadow disappears as the figure jerks toward the screen, revealing the face… Well, the mask.

The mask is a mirror, reflecting nothing in particular, but sending a message all the same. In other words, the person you see in the reflection is the mirror.

"The monster who comes is no worse than the monsters who deserve to die. Pick a side. Pick it now."

The screen cuts to Belker Street. The sign is in the background, but the focal point is the large amounts of blood on the asphalt. My eyes narrow on what looks like a set of wings imprinted in the blood, where Marcus was, and my mind goes back to the message written about angels on that first day.

"You let them die. Now save yourselves. While you still can."

The screen goes blank again, and white noise fills the air. A deputy flips several channels, but every one is the exact same.

"Did you hear all that?" I ask Collins, stepping back outside as

Paint It All Red

Leonard and Donny stare at a TV blankly.

"I heard. But you still have to come back. There's nothing I can do. Just hurry back so we can clear this up, and then hopefully this will all backfire on them in time for you to get back and stop this."

I look around at all the furious faces, including the sheriff who is having a temper tantrum, kicking feet and swearing, placing blame on blameless men who obviously didn't help Jake hack into the station.

"Fine. I'm on my way."

I hang up and walk over to Donny and Leonard. "We have to go if we're going to get back before sunset."

"Are they calling anyone in?" Donny asks as he turns to face me.

My eyes flit around. "They won't ask for help if they're intent on sending us away. This investigation is about to turn into a shitstorm. Johnson and Cannon are too busy hiding their crimes of the past to protect their future. Let's go."

Leonard doesn't speak, but I know what he's thinking. I just had to watch my girlfriend getting raped. It's all I can do not to kill every-fucking-body wearing a deputy badge right now. Not to mention the sheriff.

I've never once thought of killing someone as a desire. I've never blurred that line.

That's not the case at the moment.

I hope she fucking kills every last person with a badge who didn't come to save her when she was left to bleed out.

Chapter 11

They say miracles are past.
—William Shakespeare

Lana

Twenty minutes after the broadcast, people were fleeing town. Just as predicted, Logan and his team are already gone. The video will find them soon—the same video we just shared with the entire fucked up town.

Our original plan was to have Jake handle that little fun part, but it'd be easier to have someone inside the FBI to do it.

"At least they're fleeing," Jake says as we watch from the distance, our eyes on the phone screen that has the sheriff all but imploding.

"What the hell are you doing?" Sheriff Cannon barks, slapping his hand on the driver's side window of a car.

The man cracks the window an inch. "I'm getting my family out of this damn town before you drag us all to hell for what you've done."

My lips twitch. They're abandoning their captain.

"Looks like they're more scared of us than the sheriff now," Jake gloats. "Finally standing up to him."

"By comparison, the sheriff now seems insignificant to a monster who sees all, hears all, and knows all."

"It's just one fucking person! Stay and defend this town!" the sheriff snaps to the guy.

We knew they'd abandon him. They've heard it all, but until today, they've never seen it.

Jake nudges me with his elbow, and I look at his phone's screen which is diagonal from the sheriff's location. On the back of the old gym's wall, a message appears as though Jake timed this all too perfectly.

One person cannot change the world. But one person can strike terror into multitudes.

— Robert Evans

The man in the car sees the message, probably thinking something supernatural is going on, giving the timeliness of the message's appearance. He gasses the car, driving away from the sheriff, and almost sideswiping another vehicle in the process.

"Find that fucker now!" the sheriff barks, giving up his endeavor of stopping the rats who are fleeing the sinking ship.

"Heat signatures have a flurry of motion right now, but we still need to up the game if we're going to get everyone out," Jake says as more and more messages start to appear throughout the town.

With everyone distracted with Logan's team and our little special broadcast, we ran around town, hurriedly painting the messages with the faster paint. Jake painted some last night with the slower paint.

I'm still wearing my damn harness from all the drop-downs I did to paint the messages high, making them as visible as possible.

You can do a lot in forty minutes when you have a plan and a goal.

On the church, a massive message appears.

Any demon is capable of cruelty, but only an angel is majestic enough to rain down vengeance for the innocent.

— Marcus Evans

Jake smirks as people running by stumble over their own feet, seeing that message appear like magic. They were actually inside the church when I painted that earlier.

Jake swipes his screen, letting me see the newest one appear on the side of the school.

Little eyes see. Little eyes learn. Be a good example for all the little eyes watching you. They're everywhere.

— Jasmine Evans

Out of context and written in red paint, that message is creepy.

More people panic, more people abandon the town, taking only the essentials before locking their families in the car. I even see some people sprinkling salt in their vehicles as though it'll keep the devil away during their trip ahead.

I flip my screen, letting Jake look on with me as another message appears on the side of the town hall.

The wicked can fake nobility, just as the damned can fake innocence. But only the truth will rise from the ashes when we all start to burn.

— Victoria Evans

More panic. More fleeing.

Jake pops up his app, showing me all the heat signatures still in town.

"Turn on the broadcasting system and cut screens to all the

Paint It All Red

chaos; show the messages too."

He smirks, and he starts doing just that, streaming the footage live through the channel. I love hearing the sheriff demand that station be cut off. We've already taken all precautions to halt that action. Well, Jake has. I'm an idiot with tech stuff.

My role is to slaughter; his role is to do all the geek stuff.

Killer and geek seems like an odd combination, but the screams we've composed from the town make an intoxicating melody.

Several messages appear, all of them sliding up and down the town. People try to read them while running, unable to stop themselves from seeing what we have to say, ironically enough.

A wise man knows when the war is lost, and will understand retreat is the only way to save lives. A foolish man will condemn all his followers to death because of his pride.

— *Robert Evans*

Everyone knows that's geared toward the sheriff, and let's face it, no one but his deputies are willing to die for him. The few strays that will join his side will be the ones he's used on the side to keep people in line without tying it to the department — just like with Cheyenne last night.

I'm not going to discriminate and leave them out of the slaughter if they so choose to join him now.

If hatred didn't exist, love wouldn't either, for one is formed by the other. I love and hate this town.

— *Marcus Evans*

I believe the souls of the wrongfully persecuted often haunt our world, bringing the same grief they feel from beyond the grave.

S.T. Abby

— *Jasmine Evans*

"It's time for the bell drop," Jake says, almost shaking with anticipation.

He's the master of timing, so he should be proud.

He presses a button on his phone, and a mild, contained explosion happens at the top of the church tower. The bell groans and wines before it crashes through the rock. We watch it in real time, not needing a screen to see it plummet to the street.

People screech and dive away, but he timed it to be when no one was too close.

It crashes to the ground so hard that it splits the street on impact right in front of the church. Everyone slowly approaches the mess as the front of the church reveals the last message.

Never mock or harm the passionate, for they are the fiercest with their wrath.

— *Victoria Evans*

More screams. They sound so pretty.

I cock my head, watching the people scatter, everyone rushing into their homes to gather their belongings. Our plan is to break the record for total town evacuation.

We also have a plan for the stragglers. Tranquilizing darts are a last resort, but we have them in spades, along with a dump truck to toss the unconscious ones into.

Nothing will stop us from finishing this.

Today.

My father would love this horror movie, because the bad guy finally wins.

Paint It All Red

"Ready for phase two?" Jake asks me.

"Where are we at on heat signatures?"

He pops up his app, showing me all the dots still in town.

"Broadcast phase two. Let the ones hiding in their homes see the show that will push them over the edge."

"Planned on it," he tells me with a dark grin.

My attention turns to one of the two cemeteries, the one where my parents and brother are buried. This is the part I've been dreading, but it's a necessary evil. Besides, I know my brother and father would want to be involved in any way possible. I'm probably creating the illusion in my head, but I'd like to believe that if my mother had lived to see the horrors that were bestowed on her family, she'd be equally onboard.

For she was a romantic.

"Now," I say quietly.

Though it's in the distance, I still see with perfect clarity as the tombstones start exploding one by one. A fire starts in front of the cemetery, zipping down the line that Jake laid out.

We can hear the screams as the headstones continue to explode, and Jake presses a button on his phone that releases shadows made by light boxes. They look like souls rising.

To a town so full of guilt and religion, it'll be like a mini-apocalypse.

Every headstone there finally explodes, and the lines of the fire finish, spelling out two words.

We're back!

No longer is it one flesh-and-blood killer. Their worst suspicions have just come true. The spirits buried in that cemetery are back to wreak havoc on everyone here.

Jake pulls up his heat signature app, seeing more and more dots leaving their homes, fleeing to their cars to drive the spiral out of town.

One road in. One road out.

He broadcasts the second graveyard, following the same suit, the fire sparking and forming more words as the headstones explode one at a time. I idly watch the deputies running around the town, trying their best to calm everyone and convince them they're safe.

Spirits don't exist, after all. But their eyes tell them another story as they see the shadows emerge from the cemetery, convinced the illusion is the truth.

I love this town right now, because they're so fucking predictable.

Cars zoom by us, getting out of here as fast as they can.

The second string of letters form more words in the fire, and Jake zooms in, broadcasting it flawlessly.

And we're taking everyone with us back to the grave.

"Phase three," I say, backing behind a tree as a deputy races by on foot, trying to stop a fight that has broken out in the street.

The stubborn fools who don't want to leave may change their minds now.

The mirrors Jake stole on night one are suddenly launched from the ground where they've been hiding, the soil blanket being pulled back by another of Jake's genius inventions. After all, he's been planning each detail of this day for years.

People shriek in horror as the mirrors line up, all the varieties of them shining the reflections of the monsters hiding beneath their own flesh. Then the mirrors explode, slinging glass everywhere.

Paint It All Red

The shards get cut down so small that they merely slice a few flesh wounds. Don't worry; no children are harmed in this act. We're more careful than that.

One woman screams as the small cuts on her face starts to bleed, and she touches them with shaking hands, going into shock.

Weak.

Pathetic.

All of them.

But that's what tips the scales. More and more heat signatures start disappearing or moving down the road too fast to be on foot. They're retreating.

"I'll handle phase four in fifteen minutes. That should be enough time for the retreaters to run," Jake says as I unstrap the harness I'm wearing.

"Make sure you completely get everyone out," I tell him distractedly.

"I will, Lana. Trust me."

I smile as I push the harness to his chest. "I do trust you. With my life. Now I need to go get ready for phase five."

He glances over at all the chaos, then he flicks his screen to the sheriff who has his hat off, running a hand over his salt and pepper hair in defeat. "You shouldn't have to wait too long."

Chapter 12

'Tis one thing to be tempted, another thing to fall.
—William Shakespeare

Logan

"They have the evidence. There's a fucking video of what they did to Robert Evans, for fuck's sake! And you're still holding me here? On what grounds?" I snap, glaring at Collins and Director McEvoy.

"On the grounds you aided a possible murder suspect in fleeing a town the same night her husband was killed, along with two men inside her home."

"Cheyenne Murdock feared for her life, and she was not a suspect. She was attacked in her home, and our unsub saved her life."

McEvoy points a finger at me. "And that mentality is why you're here. You don't get to assume she's innocent because she says she is. Especially after you swore to your team the unsub was a female. Your entire profile for this case is all over the map, and it doesn't make a damn bit of sense. Then you just release a woman after two men are slaughtered in her living room with a skill far too advanced to ignore?"

"Two hit men," I growl.

"Speculation," McEvoy growls back.

"Let's all take a step back," Collins says, easing his hands between us and pushing us apart, creating much needed separation.

Paint It All Red

"I've sent the evidence to be examined," he goes on.

McEvoy narrows his eyes at Collins. "A woman digs up her basement floor and happens to hand you the keys to a closed case from years ago? And yet she's nowhere to be found now, as though she magically vanished. It's not like she can corroborate this story if we can find her, which makes it completely inadmissible."

"You hope," I add, glaring at him.

He takes a step forward, and Collins lands a hand on his chest, holding him back.

"All the lies and cover-up schemes in the world won't do you a bit of good once I get my hands on that video evidence and have it authenticated."

He takes a step back, his eyes narrowing. "You have no idea who you're dealing with. I'll bury you, boy. I'll ruin your name so fucking well that nothing out of your mouth will mean a damn thing. All the evidence in the world won't do you a bit of good with a reputation like I plan for you."

"Is that a threat?" Collins asks him, eyeing the director like he just slipped up.

A sinister smile lines the director's lips. "He's being held for charges of obstruction and conspiracy to aide a known serial killer."

"You can't do that," Collins growls.

"Watch me. He doesn't leave this floor until they come with an arrest warrant and escort him out."

He turns and stalks away, and Collins runs a hand through his hair.

"He must have played a really big part in covering all that shit up if he's pushing the limits this far," Collins says, looking over his shoulder. "I need to meet up with some people and get this sorted before he really does try to have you arrested. If you leave here, though, it'll look bad. I won't doubt that he has people blocking your exit. They'll have permission to restrain you by any means necessary. So stay put. Don't do anything stupid."

He turns and walks away, and I grab the first thing I can get my hands on and throw it across the room. People gasp and scatter away as the broken stapler falls to the ground in two pieces.

"They just pulled in Donny," Leonard says near me, looking around like he's wary of everyone's intentions.

"They're going to split us all up and talk to us one-by-one. Just remember this is about me and none of you. Say whatever you need to in order to keep any blame off you."

"I escorted Cheyenne Murdock and her daughter out of town. Not you," he argues.

"Under my orders," I remind him.

He narrows his eyes. "I'm not letting them take you down."

I look around, making sure no one is close enough to overhear. "Their allegations aren't wrong. I'm definitely compromised and you know it. In all honesty, I started obstructing this case the second I learned of Lana's involvement."

"In that case, Hadley and I are both in the same tub of shit you're in. You're not going down for this. Lana's methods may be barbaric and illegal, but after seeing what they had to endure and then contend with in the aftermath, I can't fault her logic."

"Makes you question everything we've ever stood for, doesn't it?" I ask, exhausted as I lean back against someone's deserted desk.

"No. We've always fought to save the innocent from the sick and depraved. Lana had no one to fight for her or her family. She was tasked with the worst case scenario on her own."

I cock my head as Hadley walks by, glancing over her shoulder as though she's checking to see if she's being followed. She holds her laptop closer to her body, clutching it like she's up to something.

"She wasn't on her own," I say distractedly, watching as Hadley ducks into Craig's office and closes the blinds.

His door doesn't have a lock on it though.

He's still out on the bullshit assignment they used to keep him

Paint It All Red

away from Delaney Grove.

"Keep an eye on things and come find me if anything new reaches you. I'm confined to this floor for now."

My eyes lift to where one of the director's men is standing at the doorway, his eyes trained on me. He definitely plans to keep me in place.

"Where are you going?" Leonard asks me, but I don't answer.

I'm sure he watches me as I head through everyone whispering about me, and burst into Craig's office without knocking.

Hadley squeals and slams her laptop shut.

"What are you doing?" I ask, suspicious.

I shut the door behind me, and she blows out a relieved breath before reopening the laptop. Her fingers fly rapidly over the keys as her eyes grow determined.

"They won't give me an office with privacy, so I'm borrowing Craig's, since he's still gone."

"But what are you *doing?*" I ask again, coming up behind her so I can see the screen.

I lean over, putting one hand on the desk beside her, and one on the back of her chair, as I stare at all the nonsensical lines of code on her screen.

"I'm hacking into Jake's video feed." She motions to the three monitors in Craig's office that he uses for work. "It's not quite as elaborate as Jake's twenty monitors, but it'll do."

"I guess that means you lied when you told Leonard you couldn't hack the feed," I grumble.

"I didn't lie. I couldn't hack them at the time. Jake's brilliant, by the way. I never would have found the frequency he uses if he hadn't shown me how to discover it. It runs at the same frequency normal power lines do. I don't even understand how he did that."

She continues to type in random letters, symbols, and numbers that make zero sense to me.

"Why would he tell you?"

"Because he trusts me. It was that instant sort of trust that he doesn't usually feel. We're kindred. He wanted someone to really appreciate the effort and genius that went into all his work, and I'm as much of a tech nerd as he is. You and Lana are both oblivious to the layers and difficulty level that goes into something like this. Me? I had a nerd-gasm that led to a real orgasm later on. I got that turned on."

"More information than I needed," I mumble.

She ignores me. "And he is a fucking genius. I only thought I was good. No wonder he's never been caught."

Suddenly, all the monitors come alive with images of the town. Cars are fleeing by the second, rushing to get away from something. My eyes move from screen to screen as Hadley flips to different views. I'm searching for some explanation.

But all we see is the aftermath of whatever has happened.

"Can you rewind this?"

"Not right now. He has it set to live feed only. We can only view what he's viewing. He's using the feeds to broadcast this live over their TVs. He's so fucking perfect."

I ignore that last part, focusing on the rest of it. I catch glimpses of words, but the screen changes before I can read them. I thought Hadley was flipping screens, but it's Jake. Like she said, we can only observe as he observes.

"I want to find Lana. Is there any chance you can hack into a different—"

"Don't even pretend you know how to speak geek. If I tried to hack anything from this point on, it would mess up what he's doing. Even if I didn't care to do that, he'd immediately back hack me and possibly close out everything, may even lock me out of the system completely. I wouldn't doubt that he'd be able to bring the entire federal network down. Like I said, he's better than me. Much better.

Paint It All Red

But he's also more passionate and has pushed himself to the limits for this very goal."

I try calling Lana's phone, cursing when I realize she must have already switched burners again. This one is no longer an active number.

A different screen pops up, one I know too well. "They're reading heat signatures? Why?" I ask, watching as more and more red dots join into the middle of the street, everyone heading for the exit.

"For whatever their endgame is. That monitor is linked to his phone, bringing up any screens he brings up—"

The monitor shuts down, and Hadley curses. "He apparently didn't want me watching that part."

She waits, staring at the other screens, but none of them shut down.

"So he knows you've hacked him?"

"Like I said, he's brilliant. He probably has a system set up to alert him of any interference. He doesn't seem to mind us watching this, but he wants his phone a secret."

"Because he's running this show from that phone, and he doesn't want us knowing what comes next," I say, worried.

A screen flips to a residence where an older man and an older woman are sitting in their living room. They're right across from where Lana would have been assaulted.

They're talking about the madness going on outside and how they plan to wait it out, when suddenly the TV flicks on, and a masked face comes into view. Instead of the mirror mask Lana was wearing, it's a red mask.

"Get out, Whitmires! Get out now!"

The woman and man both scream, and the man clutches his heart, his eyes wide in horror. That's all the prompting they need.

They don't even bother grabbing a bag before rushing out.

The screens all change again, and I try to focus on the ones that seem the most important.

"How is he viewing all this from one phone?" I ask Hadley.

"He has a system set up to flip between screens, but he can minimize up to five at a time and watch them in thumbnail size. I wonder if he'll go house to house with that tactic."

"What happens if that tactic doesn't work?" I ask more to myself than her, dread creeping up my spine.

There has to be a reason they're focusing on evacuating the town.

My eyes hone in on the monitor with the most activity. The deputies are scattered, all of them looking angry and desperate to keep people in the town. One even punches a civilian, but two men grab the deputy and sling him into a car.

He backs off when one pulls a gun on him, and the civilians help the fallen man back to his feet before backing away into a car.

"They've bound them together to stand up to the sheriff and his men," I surmise.

"No one will fight for the town, and after the show they put on with the broadcast, no one wants to be there when the sheriff goes down either," she says, but then sucks in a breath.

She turns to face me, her eyes wide. "I think I know where Lana is."

"Where?"

She gestures to the screens. "Who's missing?"

Chapter 13

Don't impose on others what you yourself do not desire.
—Confucius

Lana

The door slings open, and I watch through the wooden slats of the closet door as the sheriff stomps in, angrily slamming the door behind him. He grabs an empty glass off the table by his recliner and slings it across the room. It shatters against the wall as he roars like a beast enraged.

For a few long minutes, his head hangs, his chest heaves, and he grips the sides of the chair for support. He always puts up a good front, but he's as mortal as the rest of us.

My smile kicks up as he predictably goes to the bar in the living room, opening the door and pulling out a bottle of whiskey. His hands are shaking when he pours a glass and drinks it down quickly.

Any time the pressure mounts, the sheriff has to have a drink. But he can't let his deputies see him carry a bible and a glass of whiskey. He can sentence innocent people to a gruesome death, but being so weak as to need a drink is simply unforgivable. Not to mention shameful.

I'd roll my eyes, but I'm busy watching as he takes his gun off, putting it by the door.

Finally.

"You'll pay for this," the sheriff hisses, glaring at my brother and me as we get carried out of the courtroom.

"He was with us!" I shout again, staring frantically at the jury as they continue to wrangle me out. "They're hiding the truth! They're suppressing evidence! This is just a fucking witch hunt, and my father is being framed!"

"Just make them show you our statements!" my brother bellows as they finally haul us all the way out.

As soon as the doors seal shut, they reopen, and the sheriff stalks out.

Cuffs are being put on our wrists, but they can't lock us away for long. It's on film. We're in contempt of court and nothing else.

"Put them in a cell until this damn thing is over. I won't deal with them again until I have to," the sheriff barks. Then those cold eyes turn to us. "You're making a deal with the devil by betraying the souls of the innocent. Your father is guilty. And I'll make sure he hangs for his sins."

He starts to walk back inside as we start demanding to be turned loose.

The sheriff turns just as we reach the corner, and he eyes me.

"I'd hoped you see the devil you loved through clearer eyes, but I guess you never did and never will."

I wait patiently, silently stalking him with just my eyes as he finishes off another glass. His eyes dart toward something near the couch, and his head tilts as he studies something I can't see from this angle.

He looks away from whatever it is that no longer holds his interest, and carries his glass around the corner to the kitchen, which is near his master bedroom. Pushing the door open silently, I step out, putting my knife in its sheath on my hip.

As I near the couch, my eyes dart down, curious at what held his attention. And I close my eyes as I refrain from blowing out a frustrated breath. My flashlight is there. I put it down earlier when I was looking for any hidden weapons, and forgot to pick it back up.

Rookie mistake.

Paint It All Red

Opening my eyes back up, I clutch the handle of my knife and walk into the kitchen. But I screech to a halt when my gaze is suddenly locked on the end of a barrel.

"Boo," the sheriff says, drawing my eyes to his as I slowly raise my hands, feigning compliance.

He looks over the pistol to stare down at me, the barrel just inches from my face.

"Any reason why the fed's girlfriend is slinking around my house?" he drawls lazily, hiding that welling frustration he showed just moments ago when he didn't know I was watching.

"Probably because she's not just a fed's girlfriend," I quip, smiling bitterly at him.

He cocks his head, watching me.

"And who exactly are you?"

I smirk as I take a step forward, pressing that barrel right up against my temple with my hands still raised. His eyes widen fractionally, but he masks all other signs of surprise.

"I'm the girl you sent your son to kill. I'd hoped you see the devil you loved through clearer eyes, but I guess you never did and never will."

Confusion only lights his eyes for the barest of moments before recognition slides over his face.

"No," he says in a rasp whisper.

But then his eyes turn to ice, and the resonating sound of a dead *click* rattles around the room that is otherwise cloaked in silence. Fear replaces determination when I smile.

And he pulls the trigger again, and again, and again…all while I take a step back.

"Hope you don't mind, Sheriff. I took the liberty of emptying all the bullets from every other gun in the house, sans your service weapon you left in the other room."

He starts to rush by me, surprising me by not lunging for the helpless looking woman before him. I guess I gave him too much credit for being masculine and all that.

My knee slams into his stomach, halting his retreat, and he hits the ground, collapsing with a pained cry.

"I've always preferred knives," I say as I pull mine out, sliding it under his throat as he goes stiff and still beneath the blade.

I crouch beside him, holding the knife there.

"How are you alive?" he asks almost too quietly.

I grin, waggling my eyebrows. "A lot of pain. A lot of healing. And a hell of a lot of tequila. But mostly, I'm here because of Jake. You remember him, right? Jacob Denver? The boy you overlooked as any sort of threat once you realized he'd been in love with my brother? Because what sort of weak man loves another man, right? No way would such an abomination be awesome enough to help a dead girl slaughter so many of your monsters."

His lips part for a breath of surprise to escape, and the knife presses closer to his throat with the motion.

Casually, I pull out my phone with my free hand, dial Jake, and set it on the ground beside me after putting it on speaker.

"I take it you're still working on phase five?" Jake asks as I stare at the sheriff's face.

"He's still letting it all sink in that all this is his fault. What's the fun in simply killing him if he doesn't go through at least a little mind torture of the reality he's spun from all his lies and corruption?" I ask, grinning down as the sheriff's eyes turn hard.

There's the arrogant son of a bitch I know.

"Phase six worked better than planned. The personalized messages got through to everyone except three. I've just loaded the last one in the car, skipping the dump truck that was unnecessary. I'll drop them at the safe zone as soon as I check for the whereabouts of the deputies, and then I'll move on to phase eight."

Paint It All Red

"Good. I want the sheriff to hear phase seven, which is why I called."

I can almost hear Jake smile as I watch the sheriff watch me.

"Getting out my clone of the sheriff's phone now," Jake says.

The sheriff's eyes shift to my phone, curious. I press the mute button, holding it up for him to see it, while still keeping the knife pressed to his throat with my other hand.

"Deputy Hayes, I need you to assemble all the names I'm about to read out to you. They're the ones I trust. The deputy and uniformed officers not mentioned should go to the outlying borders and start seeing if they can find anything. Understand?"

There's a pause, and I watch the sheriff's face. We can only hear Jake's side of the conversation.

"They'll know it's not me," the sheriff growls, then winces when talking causes the blade to nick his throat just barely. A trickle of blood spills, and I continue to hold him in place.

"You hear Jake's voice. But when it passes through that particular phone, it sounds just like you on the other end," I tell him, grinning as his face pales. "Did I mention Jake is a boy genius?"

Jake starts listing the names of everyone involved with my father's death and the assembly that resulted in the death of my brother and the death of Victoria Evans as everyone knew her.

Even the retired deputies get called in, considering they've already rallied to help 'defend' the town. Saves me an extra trip of paying them individual visits.

"You have one hour," Jake goes on, finishing up the list of names.

I hang up the phone, watching as the hope fades from the sheriff's face. Helpless is a delicious look on him.

"Now stand up," I say, pulling the blade back and slowly standing to my feet.

He watches me warily as he slowly sits up, but doesn't move

past that.

"I've had to be patient for ten long years, Sheriff. Stop stalling, because I'm out of patience."

His eyes narrow in challenge. He's planning something stupid.

His arms open wide.

"If you want me up, then—"

His words end on a scream as I stomp his ankle with the heel of my combat boot. A satisfying crunch follows the stomp, and I grind my heel into his ankle before he lurches to grab at my foot. Then my foot flies up, connecting with his face.

Blood sprays from his mouth as he sails backwards again. He stops his head from pounding the tile, and I calmly walk toward his head.

"I said get up. You decide how much of a beating it takes for you to comply."

"What's the point?" he growls, spitting out blood. "You just plan to kill me. You're a monster. The devil's own spawn."

I kneel beside him, keeping a safe distance between us, and my eyes meet his.

"Your son was a monster, Sheriff. Holding a bible or wearing a badge doesn't offer you absolution from your own inhumanity either." I tilt my head, watching the fury and unprecedented indignation sweep over his eyes.

"You're wrong," he seethes.

"It might have taken you a year, possibly even longer, to realize you'd made a mistake. When there was another rape and kill a year later, maybe? One just outside Delaney Grove? Same victimology as all the others," I say casually, watching his gaze shift again.

"Once your anger and grief calmed and started to ebb, you realized Robert Evans was never the right man, and you'd framed him, punished him brutally for sins he never committed."

Paint It All Red

Every fight in him deflates as those words settle in, and a surprising glisten appears in his eyes.

"You realized too late that a true monster was still killing women and taking from them, and you're the reason he was free to do it. All that blood is on your hands, Sheriff. It wouldn't wash away."

Tears start to form in his eyes as I go on.

"You knew all those claims against Kyle couldn't all be false either, but you'd already lost one child. You forced yourself to live in denial that the other one was rotten to the core. But then again, you killed his mother after forcibly enlisting her help with framing my father. Tell me, Sheriff, did you collect the condoms yourself? Or was that Johnson's job?"

He clears his throat, trying to get rid of all the guilt in his eyes, but struggles to do so. It means I'm spot on.

"Because you'd killed your son's mother in your quest for framing an innocent man, you excused all the disgusting acts of your vile son. Lied to the town. Lied to yourself. That night when you told him to take care of us, you never really expected him to bring all his friends. You never expected they'd reach for the limits of depravity, then cross them even more severely than you crossed them with my father. But you still hid the truth. Covered us up. Acted as though the lives of *two* innocent children never mattered."

The anger in my voice can no longer be masked, and the sheriff's lip trembles as a tear drops from his eye.

"I hated your daughter. But I never wished her dead. My father fixed her car window once. Did you know that?"

He slowly shakes his head.

"She'd slept with another girl's boyfriend from a rival school. The girl wrote 'slut' all over your daughter's car. Then she busted out the driver's window. Your daughter knew she'd have to explain, but she was too afraid to tell you she was sleeping around. My father stepped in and helped her even though that girl was a despicable bitch to me for no reason. Because my father said she was a kid. And he could never be mean to a child, for fear that one day someone might do the same to us."

He sucks in a breath, working damn hard to restrain his emotions.

"She didn't even thank him. She acted like it was his job to replace that window before you got home from your hunting trip. She didn't even pay him for the window, and we were struggling for money. But he never said a word. Because she was *just a kid*. Yet you labeled him a monster. You shattered every ounce of dignity he ever had. And you sent real monsters after all three of us, yourself included. Tell me, Sheriff, do you feel as though all your prayers for forgiveness have worked?"

I slide the blade across the floor, watching his eyes fall to it.

"Or do you think a punishment has finally been sent for all your sins?"

His chin wavers, but he continues to stare me in the eyes.

"Stand up," I say again, a harsh bite to my tone.

This time, he lumbers to his feet, his shoulders not pushed up so high.

He doesn't look at me as I gesture toward the bathroom. "Get in the shower."

"Why?" he snaps.

"Either do what I say, or I'll let the entire town watch the video of Kyle confessing everything."

His eyes dart to mine, wide and horrified. "Yes, Sheriff. They may be gone, but they'll still see the video eventually. All his sins on one long video. He's crying during his confessions, by the way. In between the spouts of begging for his life."

The sheriff gags, staving off a breakdown as he turns away from me, tears now leaking.

"All the other videos have them all confessing. Little by little, I had all I needed. They spilled details of where to find all that

Paint It All Red

precious camera footage from both those *incidents*, as you liked to call them. They told me *everything*. And people *will* see that footage."

"Even Kyle's?" he asks on a rasp. "Regardless if I do what you say?"

I smile to myself. "I guess you've called my bluff. Yes, they'll see it regardless. But I'll make a deal to keep all his torture off the camera if you just go get in the damn shower. Don't make me drag you. I'd have to break your hands to make sure you didn't try anything stupid, and that will take some time and effort to thoroughly break them."

He releases a pained sound, swallowing hard.

"How did you turn into this?"

My eyes widen. "Is that rhetorical, Sheriff? Because I'm pretty sure it'd be obvious."

He lunges suddenly, taking me off guard. But I slam the heel of my palm into his chest, forcing the wind from his lungs, then drop and kick up at the same time, catching him right in the groin.

Always wanted to hit him there.

When he hits the ground, I kick him in the face hard enough to almost knock him out. He stares, dazed, as blood leaks from between his lips.

"Fine. We'll do this the hard way," I chirp.

I kick him over to his stomach, grab his cuffs from his hip, and pin him down with my knee against his spine as I roughly jerk his arms behind his back. He's still too dazed to fight with me, so I hurry before he gets his bearings back.

I have a deadline, after all.

Reaching down, I grab him at the collar of his shirt and start dragging him toward the bathroom, ignoring the groaning fabric. His fight comes back, but it's futile at this point. I grab him by his hair as we reach the bathroom, and force him to his feet.

The idiot tries to head-butt me when he's standing in front of me, but I'm much shorter, and simply dodge it, spin around him, and kick him into the open tub.

A pained grunt escapes him as he lands on his back.

"What are you doing?" he asks, staring up at me while his legs hang over the sides.

"Using you to fulfill a fantasy," I quip as I close the shower curtain. "Two fantasies, actually."

Staring at the white, plain shower curtain, I pull out my knife. A dark smile curves my lips before I start playing the music from my phone, and I stab him through the curtain.

A cry of pain and surprise echoes off the bathroom walls.

But I stab again.

And again.

And again.

Until he's just gurgling sounds.

Then I jerk back the curtain, smirking. "Life goals," I say to myself, still smiling as I leave the dying man in the tub. I walk through the house and back to the living room where his service weapon is still on the table.

It's the only loaded gun in the house, and shooting the sheriff—with his own gun—is just too poetic to pass up.

The song continues to play as I walk back in, and blood is flowing from all the wounds and the sheriff's mouth as I watch him from the doorway.

His eyes are barely staying open as I point the gun at his groin. Words try to form, but he's too injured to make an intelligible sound.

I grab a stack of towels and drop them to his lap, then I press the gun against the towels and fire. The sound is still loud, despite the muffling of it against the towels, but at least my ears aren't ringing.

Paint It All Red

I hate guns.

But again…too poetic.

The sheriff jerks as I pull the gun back, and the white towels get redder and redder as he bleeds out. The tub catches all the blood, taking it down the drain as he continues to spill his shade.

I wipe my knife off as the sheriff slowly dies, and I listen to the song that is playing on repeat.

I shot the sheriff…

Then I take a picture for Jake once the life finally leaves the sheriff's eyes.

Just to be sure, I check for a pulse. It's gone. Then, to be doubly sure, I slice the knife across his throat, leaving his blood to continue to drain.

I wipe the knife off again, place it back in its sheath on my hip, pull my hood up, and walk out with my phone still playing that song.

The town is like an old western ghost town now. I half expect tumbleweeds to start rolling by me as the wind blows. The sun is three hours from setting, but the endgame is moments away from starting.

Everyone expects sundown to be the endgame time, since that's what we told them.

But we have another set of rules we're playing by.

And we're ready.

Jake is already in my old house when I step inside the familiar home. This house is in the perfect location.

My heart thumps a little faster when I see the inside, because it's like stepping into a different vortex. No pictures of us line the walls the way they used to.

The carpet has been replaced with hardwood. The blues have all been replaced with neutral colors. And they knocked out the wall between the living room and kitchen.

Everything is different, yet there's a pang of familiarity in my chest.

He's put in all his monitors, ready to start this process.

"You took longer than you were supposed to," Jake says as I step in and strip out of my hoodie.

"I shot the sheriff," I start singing, and he grins.

"Time to shoot the deputies."

I strip out of the rest of my clothes, and start pulling on my kill clothes. I can't wear a baggy hoody or restricting pants. This is the ultimate kill zone.

"Phase nine complete?" I ask him.

"As soon as you step into the middle of town, all I have to do is press a button. The next button gets pressed when you step inside. Then you're on your own. You know the charges are set; you know the small window you have to get out; and you know to keep your head down. Don't get killed on a part we could skip."

I tug on my leggings, making sure to do the splits and double check their flexibility.

Jake watches me grimly.

"I'm not skipping this part, Jake. They need to feel the same fear. Just dying isn't good enough. And risking someone surviving isn't any good either."

He blows out a breath as I grab my tank top, ready to brave the chilly air while being sleeveless. I'll warm up once I start fighting.

After getting my boots back on, I grab the bulletproof vest that is thinner and less constricting than most—*thank you, Jake.*

Then I start packing all the weapons into my many holsters, and use the action game assembly Jake has laid out.

"I'm having a moment," Jake says, biting down on his knuckle as I finish loading the last of the weapons into their designated spots on my body harness.

"What?" I ask, arching an eyebrow.

"Times like these remind me why I can't give up women. Something about a girl with a gun, and right now, you're every

Paint It All Red

nerd's comic-book-sexy fantasy girl."

I roll my eyes.

"Seriously! The tight pants, all the guns, the sleeveless shirt—"

"All meant for functionality," I state dryly.

"Still doesn't shatter the illusion." He mocks a dreamy sigh, and I laugh despite the impending madness I'm close to stepping into.

"You ready?" he asks more seriously as I finish clipping on the last knife.

"As I'll ever be."

"Then I'll get your theme song ready."

"You're really going to play music?" I muse as I walk to the door.

"Every epic climax needs a good theme song," he quips, forcing a smile.

He crosses the room in a few quick, long strides, and his arms go around me, tugging me to him as he kisses the top of my head. I return the embrace, steeling my nerves and my breaths.

"I love you, little sister," he says softly.

"I love you, big brother," I say back, clutching him tighter.

He pulls back, cupping my chin in his hand as our eyes meet.

"Now go kill them all while I burn the town to the ground."

I nod. "Phase ten."

Chapter 14

The attempt to combine wisdom and power has rarely been successful, and then only for a short while.
—Albert Einstein

Logan

"Why isn't anything happening?" I ask Hadley, watching the monitors that have been flipping at random for the past hour on the completely evacuated town.

A screen pops up; the heat signature screen from earlier that Jake shut down. It has the entire town on the screen, but the only heat signatures are all coming from one building.

"Town hall," Hadley says to herself, echoing my own thoughts. "They cleared out the entire town with the exception of the deputies."

"What are these?" I ask, pointing to the few near the side of the town, and the one right on the border but still inside the town.

"That's probably Jake or Lana, just like this one," Hadley says, motioning to one that is moving through the streets like it's walking.

My stomach clenches as my eyes train on the moving ones.

"These here are probably some officers who were sent to the edge of the town border for some reason," Hadley goes on, gesturing to the three dots off to the side.

A message box pops up before I can ask any more questions.

Paint It All Red

You ready for this? Or do you want to look away? It's going to get messy.

Hadley sucks in a breath, staring at the message box.
"Is that Jake?" I ask, leaning forward.
"Yes," she says as she types back.

Why are there officers outside of town?

Immediately, another message pops up.

Because I sent them there. They're innocent.

Hadley's eyes meet mine, a question in their depths.
"I need to see her, Hadley."
She nods, then types back.

Logan is with me. He wants to see Lana.

The monitors flip to a whirl of dark hair from the back, guns loading her down as she carries a backpack through town. But I can't see her face from this angle.

My heartbeat drums in my throat, and another message box comes through.

He should probably look away. Lana isn't the sweet girl right now.

"I'm not looking away," I say to Hadley.
She blows out a breath and nods.

We're in.

Another message.

Check your email, and I'll give you a front row seat to the show when you're finished.

Hadley flips screens on her laptop immediately, and I see an email to her from a weird address. She opens it, and my stomach churns when I see a video download there. I also see tons of files to be downloaded, a complete gathering of evidence.

The computer dings like it has a new message, and Hadley pulls up the message box.

All you have to do is download it. The files will do the rest.

Hadley doesn't even hesitate. She downloads the files, and within a matter of moments, we hear the commotion outside.

I go to look through the blinds, seeing everyone standing and moving toward the monitors. On the screen, I see the same footage I saw earlier at Delaney Grove, only this time, there's also a lot of footage of the behind the scenes, including all the guys who were tied up and confessing their sins from that night.

I peek out the door, cracking it just a little.

"You're supposed to fight for the truth. Not fight for the corrupt," the Saw voice says from behind the mirrored mask.

Everyone exchanges wide-eyed horror as the video continues playing.

"Be careful of the eyes you never see on you," the voice adds, bringing up a new screen with familiar faces.

Director McEvoy rushes in, his eyes panicking when he sees himself on the screen talking to Johnson ten years ago inside Delaney Grove.

"You helped make this mess, you clean it up!" McEvoy barks, pointing a finger in Johnson's face. *"Get rid of the evidence. Get rid of any reports involving those kids. And destroy anything linking us to this godforsaken town."*

Everyone's eyes snap to the director who scrambles to unplug the overhead monitor. But another one just comes on.

"And what about my team? They're already trying to get this out," Johnson hisses.

Paint It All Red

"I'll handle them," McEvoy growls.

Everyone swings their gaze to a horrified director, and he turns and bolts out of the room, probably running all the way to his office.

"Get this down!" he shouts somewhere in the distance. "Find out who is doing this!"

Hadley smirks as I close the door and open the blinds so I can keep an eye on everyone. Someone will probably come to me now.

"Don't worry," Hadley says, grinning over at me. "I made it look like those files were put into the system by Director McEvoy himself. It'll have his IP address all over it. It can't be traced to us."

The screen inside Craig's office flips from the heat signatures to a wide shot of the town, just as music starts playing.

I glance over, seeing Johnson walking inside town hall from a different camera angle, and my eyes flick back to the girl dressed in black leggings and a red tank top as she stalks through town, armed to the guild.

"Disturbed," Hadley says with a smirk.

"What?" I ask, entranced by the fierceness I can finally see in those haunted green eyes.

"Disturbed. Down with the Sickness," she says. "The song. It's almost perfect."

Lana pulls out a mask, a red one with black lines over it, and she tugs it on.

"Why a mask?" I ask, confused.

"I don't—"

Before she can answer that, the monitors outside the office change over to a news station with a breaking bulletin that has been leaked from an informant inside the FBI—who is probably Hadley pretending to be McEvoy. It's the same video we were just watching, minus all the graphic scenes involving Victoria, Marcus, and Robert Evans.

637

My eyes flick back to the monitor near me that has Lana moving through the empty town streets, heading straight for town hall.

Knots form in my stomach, and my mouth goes dry as I watch her take her time.

On another screen, I see one of the deputies look up at one of the speakers playing the song that's on a loop, and he says something I can't hear as he turns back and heads inside the building.

Another steps out, looking at it too, and I hear him yell for them to call the sheriff.

By now, I think Lana has already killed him, considering his absence and hers for so long.

The last deputy steps back in just as Lana rounds the corner, less than a block away from the building now. She reaches back, grabbing her backpack, and she tosses it to the sidewalk next to the building when she reaches it.

My eyes move to the screen in the main room, watching as the newsroom pulls up live feed from Delaney Grove, and my heart sinks when I see Lana on there, tugging out a shotgun.

I see her pump it once, then back against the wall beside the door. Her chest inflates and deflates rapidly and harshly, then she cracks her neck to the side before kicking open the doors.

The screen on that TV doesn't change, but the one near us does, and I watch as all the deputies swing their surprised gazes toward Lana. She fires without hesitation, and my stomach roils as half a head explodes from a deputy's body before he can even reach for his gun.

Immediately she pumps the shotgun and fires again, this time blowing a hole through another's chest.

It's like the room catches up and their shock wears off, as everyone grabs their guns at once.

Lana dives and slides across the floor, firing with the shotgun again, and nailing a deputy in the waist.

Paint It All Red

"So she's also a great shot," Hadley says with no emotion.

My heart is hammering in my chest, and I flick my gaze to the news, seeing it still just showing the angle from the outside as they report on the craziness that is Lana and Jake's revenge against the world.

Everyone is just staring, watching like we're not supposed to do anything. Everyone is too stunned to even react as they hear the blasts of gunfire in rapid succession, windows crashing and blowing out with the force of the gunfire.

My eyes drop to our private viewing screen, and I see as Lana slides across the floor, tugging her mask off. Apparently the mask was just for the news, and she doesn't care who sees her inside there.

Which means...

"She's planning to live," I say on a tight breath.

"Then why the hell would she walk into a room full of trained officers?" Hadley growls, furious as Lana ducks and rolls across the floor again, tossing her empty shotgun aside and pulling out two glocks.

She fires rapidly, hitting the hordes of men wearing badges. One tries to race the door, but it doesn't budge, as though it's been locked.

Another tries to dive out the broken window, but he stops, his body convulsing as he drops. Somehow they set up an electric field, making their station a prison.

"Shit," Hadley hisses as Lana flips over a desk, landing on top of it as she fires and flips back over to duck behind another desk.

My heart is flipping worse than her agile body. Everything in me demands I go save her, but I'd never make it there in time. It's killing me to have to watch her go at all of them alone.

"Oh damn," Hadley says on a breath as I go to open the door, making it easier to hear everything going on outside us.

"What?" I ask, needing to stop myself from watching Lana

tackle an entire army on her own.

"The town is on fire," Hadley whispers, pointing to another monitor.

A screen flips again to show three unconscious deputies, along with three unconscious people lying on top of each other in the back hatch of a SUV far away from the fire line.

The fire looks to be moving toward the town, spreading around the maze-like structure in a perfect circle, as though an experienced fire burner is controlling the directionality of the flames.

"He knows how to burn shit. Now I'm really turned on," Hadley whispers to herself as I move back behind her.

"They've been planning this for years, him longer than her probably," I say as I force myself to look at Lana again.

She's pinned against a corner, smiling as they fire at her in rapid succession. The bullets can't reach her unless they get another angle, but they can keep her pinned there until they can finally shoot through the steel.

"She looks...happy?" Hadley says, swallowing hard.

It's like she has a death wish, which would mean she might not have been wearing that mask to keep her identity safe from the world because she's going to live in it.

"What if she only wore that mask because she didn't want anyone linking her to me?" I ask on a pained breath.

Hadley's breath catches, but I fight back the emotions, refusing to give up hope that Lana plans to live.

She flips back from the corner, spinning as she fires her guns simultaneously again. By some miracle, not a single bullet connects with her, but her aim is almost dead on as she puts a bullet in four heads before diving behind another desk.

She flips the desk, and she kicks it into a deputy, who falls down in front of her. Then she grabs him, jerking him up to his feet, and using him as a human shield for a brief second as she fires at two others.

She's pushing them back. For some reason, she's advancing, and they keep getting closer and closer to the basement door.

One finally rushes into the basement, and she drops her shield when a bullet goes through the man and cuts into her shoulder. I blow out a breath of relief when I see it's nothing more than a graze. Jake even zooms in on it, as though he's freaking out as much as I am.

He zooms back out as Lana fires over the top of the desk, keeping them corralled toward the back.

"Call in the national guard! Call in every-fucking body you have!" someone is shouting into the phone from outside the office we're in.

The one who ducked into the basement comes running back out, his eyes wide and panicked as he shouts something to the others I can't understand amidst the gunfire.

Something changes. They start advancing, risking their lives in the open instead of staying shielded as they fire on her hard.

She ducks, covering her head as one grabs a MK 47 and fires rapidly.

She slides toward the front, crawling, but suddenly her head throws back and her mouth opens for a scream as blood spatters from her leg.

"No!" I shout, racing out of the room, rushing toward the exit.

I'm shoved at the chest, the man guarding the door who has been eyeing me.

"You're to stay put," he growls.

"Let me by!" I snap, reaching for my weapon, but Leonard crashes into my side, grabbing my hand before I can.

"What the fuck are you doing?" he snaps.

"They're going to fucking kill her!"

He jerks me back, dragging me toward Craig's office again. His face pales when he sees our private monitor.

"They'll lock you up. There's no way you'll even get there in time," he hisses, slamming the door as his eyes turn back to the monitor.

Johnson emerges from the sheriff's office for the first time since Lana showed up. He comes up behind her, firing rapidly as she drags herself in between two desks.

I see the fear in her eyes turn to anger as she loads her guns again. She pulls out a knife, and I watch as she jumps to stand on her one good leg and throws the knife. Johnson's eyes widen seconds before the knife sticks into his forehead, but the gunshots ring out faster, and I watch as her body jerks and drops, the bullets hitting her.

"No!" I shout again, slamming my fist into the wall as my heart caves in on itself.

Then I look at Leonard.

"The chopper. Get me to the fucking chopper now!"

He shakes his head slowly. "Even if we could get to it, it'd be too late, Logan."

My stomach rolls and my heart implodes in my chest as I slide down the wall, gripping my head as everything in me turns to stone, weighing too much to move. Tears burn against my eyes as I watch Lana weakly climb across the floor, firing again at the deputies.

I can't watch.

I can't watch her die.

Chapter 15

I should like to lie at your feet and die in your arms.
—Voltaire

Lana

Pain shoots through my body, and my hearing is nothing more than a constant roar of never-ending gunfire.

I cry out as I tie off my leg to help stop the bleeding. My chest and back ache with the amount of bullets that have pounded into the vest, but they didn't break through. My shoulder burns from the graze, but it's overshadowed by the bullet that passed through my hand earlier.

I wrap my hand next, struggling with shaking hands as I fight through the pain. Jake's voice comes through my earpiece, and I take a breath, firing back at the men behind me.

"You have to get the fuck out of there, Lana! They know about the basement!"

"I can't," I say through strain, shooting around the corner and clipping a guy in the knee. He falls, his MK 47 spraying bullets wildly as he collapses. A stray bullet hits one of the other deputies, but not enough to kill the fucker.

"You have to!" Jake barks. "You didn't come this far to fucking die!"

I refuse to let the tears fall as I jerk my head back in time to avoid a new onslaught of bullets. The desk barrier I've built won't continue to hold back the bullets. The three pushed together will only stop them for a little while longer.

"I need to talk to him," I say quietly, choking back a sob as I try to stand up, only to fall back down again when my leg hurts too much to cooperate.

"No! You're not fucking saying goodbye, Lana. I'm not letting you talk to him. Get out of there! The charge can't be stopped and you know it. It's a fail-safe. You have nine minutes and fifty-four seconds."

I bang the back of my head on the desk, my vision clouded by the tears teeming in my eyes. I stare at the door in dismay. Those twenty feet seem so much farther with the never-ending spray of unrelenting fire.

They're harder to kill than I was expecting. Not as cowardly as we'd predicted.

We've been so right about everything else.

"I love you," I say to Jake, biting back the pain as I twist around to fire more.

"I'll hate you if you die," he says angrily.

I hear the tears in his voice, taste his pain from here.

"The fire is coming, Lana. Nine minutes exactly now. Get. The fuck. Out of there."

"Remember that time when we were kids and we found that stick of dynamite in your father's basement?"

"Don't, Lana. Don't fucking do this!" he begs as the tears start to leak from my eyes.

I fire blindly just to keep them from getting closer, lifting the gun up.

"You told us it was too dangerous to mess with, but I convinced you it'd be fun. Marcus and you tried to stop me, but I refused to listen."

"Damn it, Lana! Get out! Get out now!"

I try to stand again, but I cry out in pain as I drop to the ground one more time. I blink away the tears, blowing out a breath as I continue to stave off the pain that would overwhelm me otherwise.

I wish I hadn't turned my nose up at the grenade suggestion Jake made a few months ago now.

But I still wouldn't be able to get out of here in time. It hurts too bad. My leg refuses to move, and without the speed it prevents, it's pointless.

"You wanted to study it, but I just wanted to blow shit up," I say, laughing humorlessly.

"Don't," he whispers.

"So we blew up that old barn outside of town. I lit the fuse and threw it, and Marcus covered your body with his when it exploded. The explosion never touched me, but the force of it slammed into my back like a solid wall, throwing me across the field. We had no clue it was that powerful."

"Stop," he says again, even as I hear a motor roaring in the background.

He should be on his way far out of town by now.

"You explained it to me later. Explained what happened. I was sore for about two weeks. We laughed. It was a brush with death like we'd never experienced, and the adrenaline stayed with us for days. Every time I ached, a jolt of adrenaline shot through me with the memory."

"Please stop," he says again, his voice barely a broken whisper.

"You were always right. I was always reckless. I should have listened to you," I tell him through strain.

"Get out," he hisses.

"Don't cry for me, Jake. I've survived because of you. You kept me alive," I say through strain, still firing blindly over my head to keep them pushed back.

"You don't get to fucking say goodbye!" he barks before the line goes dead.

645

"Goodbye," I whisper.

With my wrapped hand that is throbbing with pain, I weakly try to dial Logan. It's a struggle, but I finally manage.

He answers immediately.

"Please be you," he says as though he's in agony.

"I love you," I say into the earpiece, still firing in the background.

"No. Don't do this to me. Fight, Lana. Get out of there. You can do it. I know you can. I've seen what you're capable of."

Just hearing the genuine plead in his voice is breaking my heart.

"You showed me what living was like again. I'd forgotten," I say softly, hoping he hears me over the rapid firing squad in the background.

"You're the only reason I'm still breathing right now, Lana. Don't give up. Not now. Not after all you've survived."

Tears start pouring freely from my eyes as I close them, letting the sounds drone on.

"You're a survivor too," I whisper. "And you make the world a better place. Don't ever stop."

"Lana!"

He shouts as I hang up, closing my eyes again, while still firing behind me.

Something loud explodes from somewhere, sounding like a new range of gunfire. I'm too weak to hold my eyes open.

I know Logan is watching.

I know Hadley is too.

I force myself to open my eyes at the nearest camera hole, but it's just a black hole with no reflective spark…no longer watching me. I brought my bag with my entirely new identity; it's lying just outside and waiting for me to retrieve it.

Paint It All Red

There's an ATV waiting for me to zip through the woods where the fire hasn't made it.

I was going to get on a plane and meet Jake where we promised to meet.

I was going to live.

There were so many other ways of doing this, but deep down, we both knew this was me tempting death to reunite me with my family. I thought I was okay with that.

Too late did I realize I still wanted to live.

Too late did I realize I'm not ready to die.

I cry out in pain as I struggle to no avail to get up once again, tears streaming down my face. But I'm stuck here, pinned down. There's no escape.

I'll die with them.

My eyes flick to the camera holes around me, all of them blacked out with no sparkle, meaning they're cut off.

It'll be a tragic, poetic ending that will immortalize all I've done.

At least no one has to watch the end.

Suddenly there's a face in front of me, and more tears leak out as I see my brother.

"Marcus," I whisper, touching his cheek as more tears race down my face.

His face disappears with the touch, and I break, sobbing as I quit firing back. Logan's face is the last thing to cross my mind before I see the blaze of the fire nearing.

Chapter 16

They say miracles are past.
—William Shakespeare

Logan

All the screens go blank at once, and nothing but white noise fills the air around us. I shake a monitor as though it'll force the screen to work again.

"He's shut down the cameras," Hadley says, her fingers flying over the keyboard.

"Get them back on!" I snap.

"I'm trying!"

My face is burning with the tears, and it's all I can do not to collapse to the ground.

Leonard is sitting silently, wringing his hands as he stares at the ground and bounces his knee.

The news is reporting the interruption to the live feed, but I can barely hear the words they're saying.

My heart is hammering against my chest.

"Got it!" Hadley shouts as the screens come back to life.

My eyes go to the fire that is now closing in on the town hall, and suddenly it explodes, a deafening sound roaring through the speakers around us. I stagger back as the building continues to erupt, pieces of it blowing up at different times.

Silence falls on the entire room, the newsfeed also coming back

Paint It All Red

up with Hadley's link reactivating it.

Everyone outside the room is staring at the news with the same shock we're staring at our monitor. But I barely notice anything around me as I break, throwing anything I can get my hands on as I fall apart.

Glass shatters around us. Voices call my name. Everything and nothing happens all at once as I slam my fist into Leonard's face, fighting against the hands grappling me to the ground.

Ice and fire wash over me with no mercy, and I shut down. Everything on me turns to stone as I'm restrained and forced to watch the fire join the building, blanketing the town.

There's no way she got out in time.

Chapter 17

Three months later...

Logan

I run my hand over the stubble on my chin, looking at the case files in front of me.

"Welcome back," Elise says as she passes my desk, looking at me like she's concerned.

Only three of us know why I broke down three months ago. Only three of us know why I'll never be the same again.

Everyone else thinks I broke down because we were pulled out of that town when it needed us.

By the time ambulances and fire trucks arrived on scene, there was nothing left but flames they couldn't put out in time to save anything. The town burned, leaving nothing but charred, empty structures in its wake.

None of the bodies were recognizable. They were too burned to be identified. And the only place with bodies was the town hall and the sheriff's home.

For three months, the news has spoken of nothing else, giving contradictory reports from truthful and falsified sources.

That's why I'm back.

Lana gave her life for the truth.

The last thing I'm going to do is let them cover it all up again.

Elise pauses like she's waiting for me to respond. I just dip my head at her in acknowledgement, and she blows out a breath as I finish typing up the full report.

Hadley has been looking for Jake nonstop, but she'll never find him. If he survived, he's long gone by now, possibly stuck in a drunken stupor after having to watch his best friend die.

There's no doubt that's why he turned off the video footage. He couldn't bear to see it. I wish I hadn't.

I should have never left Delaney Grove. I should have risked my career. Now I don't even want to be anywhere.

I didn't realize until she was gone that nothing else mattered at all.

Nothing I stood for was worth more than her.

Nothing I valued held any true value at all.

Everything I have is pointless without her.

I could have saved her, but I walked away instead. She's dead because of me.

Reading over the report one last time, I print it off and stand up. Leonard eyes me on his way to the copier, watching me as I place the papers in a folder.

"Day one back, and you're already putting together a new case file?"

I shake my head. "No. I'm fixing the old report they refuse to go public with."

He sighs harshly. "Let it go, Logan. They're never going to admit any of the truths to the public. The entire Bureau has been humiliated by everything out there. They've given all the concessions they're going to."

"Yet they still claim the allegations of falsifying DNA evidence is a hoax and a lie. They're claiming the video evidence isn't authentic. And they're also not redeeming the name of Robert Evans."

"And they're not going to," he says softly, putting a hand on my shoulder. "Like I said, they've given all the concessions they're going to. The director is gone now. Johnson is dead. No more corruption from this point on, Logan."

I look at the file in my hands.

"Whatever Collins says today will determine if that's true or not," I say when I look back up.

He blows out a breath, and I place the file back on my desk. I have an appointment with Director Collins very soon. Whatever he says will determine my future course.

For the past three months, I've been on leave. Everyone agreed I needed a break after the breakdown I had. I was also relieved of my duties temporarily until I go through a department psych evaluation.

If anyone knew what I'd lost, no one would question my sanity. They'd know for certain I'm too fucked up to be here without needing a piece of paper to tell them as much.

During my forced leave, the only way I could keep myself together was to look into the original killer case. No one tried to stop me, and Collins gave me all the information I needed or requested. He even had Leonard drop it off by my house.

At first I couldn't figure out the mystery.

At first, it made all the sense in the world for it to be the sheriff, with the exception of his daughter. That threw the entire thing into a tailspin.

But finally, I realized the women were surrogate kills. And once I figured out why they were surrogates and who they were surrogates for...everything made perfect sense.

Especially when I linked the trigger to a specific date—the date of the first kill. It's not surprising that Johnson never linked the two together. He focused on one man and made the evidence fit.

He never took the time to look around, which was my problem, until I finally forced myself to rule out the sheriff.

Paint It All Red

It didn't make sense that Lana would kill so many in such grizzly ways without ever going after the original killer that started all this. It didn't make sense that she wouldn't have figured it out, given how fucking brilliant she and Jake were.

But then I discovered how genius they actually were.

I realized the true depths of their forethought and their planning that went into each and every detail of the masterful plan they put into play.

I just wish I had realized how little the rest of the world meant to me post-Lana before I lost her. I could have been with her right now. The two of us could have survived that firestorm together.

Instead, I let her think my career and morals meant more than she did.

I was wrong.

Nothing else fucking matters but her.

Time passes by slowly as I get the rest of my information, printing off everything in case this thing with Collins doesn't go as I hope it does.

Hadley comes up to my desk, hopping on the top of it.

"Why are you running searches on this Olivia chick?" she asks curiously, holding up a page she brought with her.

"Because I needed some information."

She grunts. "Obviously. But why are you looking into a microbiologist who also happens to be one of the original killer's victim's sister?"

"Because she was getting payments from a dummy account I linked to Jake. All that money in that account transferred directly to Olivia's account the same day as D-day."

She hisses out a breath. "Why?"

"Because they knew who the original killer was. Now I do too. And I know why I couldn't find any evidence of retaliation before now."

"Why?" she asks quietly.

"Because they're fucking brilliant."

My eyes dart to the clock on my computer, and I stand, shuffling together the file I've compiled.

"I'll talk to you about it later," I tell her, smiling tightly. "I have a meeting right now."

She nods, knowing what's to come, both of us hoping we're wrong. I've supported Collins for so long. He's always been a man of integrity. I hope the position hasn't already corrupted him.

Her phone dings, and she cocks her head before darting off to her cubicle. I watch for a moment as her fingers fly over the keys, but then remember I have my own mission right now.

I head up to the director's office, clutching the file in my hand. Every detail is accurate. It's from the original case that needs to be reopened and the true suspect arrested, so he can spend the rest of his days in misery.

Collins answers when I rap my knuckles against his door, and I walk in.

"I've prepared the file to reopen the original case," I tell him.

Immediately, he tenses. "You just got back, Logan. You're not even technically off desk duty yet."

"Good thing I prepared this at the desk," I quip, tossing the file to the top of his desk.

I can tell what he's going to say before he even says it. He steeples his hands in front of his face before blowing out a long breath.

"I realize Robert Evans was the wrong man, but the killer is either dead or already behind bars."

"Actually, he's living not too far from here," I tell him, narrowing my eyes.

Paint It All Red

He doesn't even glance at the file. Instead, he keeps his eyes trained on me.

"You have no idea at the pressure that's on me to clean this all up. And—"

"You mean to cover it all up," I growl.

"Damn it, Logan. I've already explained this to you!" he snaps, slapping a hand on his desk. "If I reopen this investigation and concede that one of ours really did falsify DNA evidence, it'll be the end of your unit, as well as possibly allow numerous other serial killers to reopen their own cases and even get out of prison if their lawyers shine enough light on this as reasonable doubt for their clients."

"So politics," I state flatly. "You're no better than McEvoy."

His lips thin, and his eyes narrow to slits. "I'm cleaning up his mess. But I can promise you no one else will ever go through what that family did as long as I'm in this office."

"No, an innocent man's name will just go on tarnished because you're too scared to stand up for what's right."

He curses and runs a hand through his hair. "He's dead, Logan. Destroying your unit and all the good it has done won't bring that man back to life. The end justifies the means right now."

I stand, knowing he's not going to budge. And I pull off my service weapon and toss my badge on the desk with it.

"Then consider this my resignation," I tell him.

His eyes widen. "Don't be stupid, Logan. Take some more time off. You're too close to this case, and you're not thinking clearly right now."

"I'm thinking very clearly. I joined the FBI with the naïve notion we were going to always do the right thing no matter the personal costs to ourselves. I dedicated my every waking moment to this place, sacrificing any chance at a healthy lifestyle or any actual living. I didn't sign up to be corrupted by the one thing that is supposed to be filled with honor. And I won't be a part of it. Plenty of corruption is just outside those doors, and at least I get to have a life out there."

He looks frustrated, but not as frustrated as I feel.

"You're making a mistake," he says as I start to walk out.

I turn and face him. "No. I'm fixing the mistakes, Director. Just remember that."

I slam the door behind me, and I head back to my office to clear everything out. People glance at me as I walk through, and Leonard reads my face, his eyes dropping to my empty holster at my hip.

I've always hated wearing a tie anyway.

Taking my tie off and tossing it to the corner of my office, I grab a box, and pack up the few things that mean anything to me. Including the picture of Lana and me that I put on my desk a long time ago.

Hadley walks in as I finish up, and she shuts the door behind her.

"Don't bother telling me I'm making a mistake," I say without looking up.

"I'm not," she says, walking toward me quickly.

My brow furrows when I see how wide her eyes are.

"What? If it's a case, then you should take it to Donny."

"Logan, Jason Martin was just found dead and castrated in South Carolina," she says in a hushed tone reserved for blasphemy.

Blood rushes through my veins, and I squeeze the box in my hands as I lower it back to the desk.

"Was it—"

The words break off, because hope like that could destroy me if I'm wrong.

She nods slowly. "They sent me the pictures. I told them it wasn't our Scarlet Slayer because she was dead. But it's her, Logan. The knife is the same type, the wall was painted red, and there were no hesitation marks at all. Also, the shoe was a woman's size. It wasn't Jake. It was her. She's alive, Logan. She's actually alive."

Tears start pouring from her eyes as I sag to my chair, unable to keep standing as my skin prickles all over. I'm almost afraid to believe it, knowing it'd be the final nail in my coffin if Hadley is wrong.

"I've been trying to find Jake since D-day, but haven't found him anywhere. I checked plane logs, and couldn't find any evidence that they came or went. That body was over a month old, but they just uncovered it. They found it in a cellar of a house that's been on the market for a while," she goes on.

"I know where you can search for them, and I think I know how you'll find them," I say quietly as I grab my things.

"What?! How?"

I look her in the eyes. "If you go to him, you can't come back Hadley. If you leave with me right now, it's the end of your life here. Do you understand that? It'd be too dangerous for them if we keep any sort of attachment to this life."

"I'll be packed and ready within the hour," she says without hesitation. "I can't quit, since this is a mandatory position, but I can disappear. I can make us both disappear if you want to give me two hours."

"Do it," I tell her. "I'll meet you out front in ten minutes."

"Where are we going?"

"I'm going to talk to the only person who can give me answers. You're going home to get everything ready, including emptying our accounts."

She grabs her laptop from her cubicle as she passes. I don't glance behind me at anyone who might be looking at us.

"Where are you going?" she whispers.

"To learn the truth."

Chapter 18

They do not love that do not show their love.
—William Shakespeare

Logan

There's a note on the door when I arrive, and I tear it off, shaking my head as I read it. I pocket the note and walk inside without knocking.

I find the man in the back room with deteriorating health. He's on a hospital bed, monitors and IV's hooked into him, probably keeping the pain down just enough to keep him conscious.

His eyes are droopy when he sees me, and I pull up a chair, staring right at him. The tube in his mouth will prevent him from speaking, but there are other ways to get answers. After all, I'm a profiler. Micro-expressions are my specialty.

"It's funny how even now Lana can surprise me," I say quietly.

He looks confused, and I smirk, knowing he doesn't know who Lana is.

"A psychopath with narcissistic tendencies," I say on a sigh. "That should have been the profile. A psychopath can feign empathy. Can imitate regret, remorse or even emotional pain. Can even become a believable actor in his or her well-adjusted life. It makes them the hardest ones to find, to be honest. You don't always know your neighbor is a psychopath."

I gesture around at the seemingly innocent looking house he's living in.

Paint It All Red

"It took me a while to figure it out, but when I did, all the pieces clicked into place. Victoria's mother was beautiful, if the photos have done her any justice," I say, leaning up as I study his eyes.

The machine that is monitoring his heart beeps just a little faster at the mention of Jasmine Evans.

"She was just as beautiful when she died in that car crash as she was in high school. It's funny I never even thought to look into her past. After all, all the women who died looked strikingly similar to her when she was in high school, with the exception of Rebecca Cannon. But she died for a different purpose. Someone needed the sheriff to be blinded by rage and ready to take down anyone to punish."

I lean back, studying his face as his eyes narrow. The monitor beeps a little faster.

"Her high school sweetheart was pictured with her in one of the prom photos. I can't believe I never knew it. But I was distracted by an entirely different killer at the time. Turns out she happened to be the girl I love and a guy known as Jake Denver."

His monitor starts beeping a lot faster as his eyes light up with surprise.

"Victoria Evans didn't die that night. Jake helped save her life."

Again, that monitor starts going wild, beeping with even more speed.

"She was beautiful, like her mother, and it's surprising Jake — someone who appreciated both male and female beauty — never saw her as more than a sister. But he loved her brother. He hated anyone involved who lent a hand in creating the cluster fuck that ended the love of his life."

He continues to study me, unable to speak, and I know it's killing him. A man who loves power is now confined to a bed, living in agonizing pain and never-ending helplessness. Even now, he can't form words with that tube down his throat that is keeping him alive, and all he can do is listen.

"You can't even piss without a catheter right now, can you?" I ask, then notice the sheets are wet.

"I guess Olivia decided to remove it for your final moments."

My eyes pop back up to his, and I see the fury washing around in his gaze.

"You want to write a note?" I ask him, putting a pen in his dominant hand.

His left hand weakly tries to clamp around it, but can't, and it topples to the ground. I grin like the sadistic asshole I feel like right now. His suffering actually pleases me.

"I'd rather do all the talking anyway," I say with a shrug. "Olivia was the final piece of the puzzle. I wondered why Lana—Did I mention Victoria is Lana?—and Jake hadn't bothered to strike out against the man who started the domino effect. But I was looking for a torture-and-kill like all the others."

The monitor beeps grow stronger and stronger.

"But they had figured it out. And they started your torture long before anyone else's. Olivia was sister to Caroline—one of the original victims. Unlike Caroline, Olivia looks nothing like the beautiful Jasmine Evans. Her red hair and lighter complexion did nothing for the killer who wanted to kill the same woman over and over. Olivia spoke out for Robert Evans, said there was no way he was capable of such monstrosities. She knew Robert, and he'd been alone with her sister countless times, always lending a hand to fix anything in their house that was messed up because Olivia was in school, and neither of them could afford a real handyman."

I sigh long and hard, thinking about how life can be so cruel to such a good man.

"Robert never charged them. He was just a damn good guy. Which is probably what made Jasmine fall in love with him and leave behind a man who was only capable of loving himself. And let's face it, that man moved on to another woman, but the only person to ever sting him with rejection was the one who loved a man so beneath him that it was disgusting. You hated Robert Evans, but

Paint It All Red

you hid it well."

I study his eyes as they continue to burn with hatred for me while I unravel his masterful disguise.

"You hated him so much, but you pretended to be his best friend even as you led the investigation in the direction of him — to punish him for taking a woman from *you*. From a man *like* you. How dare he, right? Am I missing anything, Christopher Denver?"

The monitor beeps faster and faster, letting me know his anger continues to rise.

"I should have noticed the way you put all your accolades up higher on the walls than your son's. I should have paid attention to all the videos you had readily available of the trial. And all the numerous videos you had of Jasmine Evans. You knew her voice immediately."

I pull out a copy of the same file I prepared for Collins. "Your wife died after running her car off a bridge. She died when your son was small. No one questioned the suspicious bruising she had. They all chalked it up to the accident. But it wasn't an accident, was it? You punished her regularly for Jasmine choosing Robert over you, and she finally ended the pain the only way she knew how."

I flip the page.

"Your first murder was on the anniversary of your breakup with Jasmine. It was the same day of her first date with Robert, something the profile had suggested to be *his* trigger instead of yours."

I flip the page again, and I start reading off the facts I've gathered since piecing together Olivia's involvement.

"You mentioned your son had to be forced to show up on holidays, but I didn't do the math until later. After all, family squabbles are not uncommon. I just didn't realize his depth of hatred toward you until I finally pieced it all together. Jake stayed with the Evans family more than he stayed at home, because even back then, he hated you. But he didn't know for certain you were a monster until last year. When he finally figured it all out around last

Christmas."

I hold up the file, and his eyes try to read into what I'm saying. He thought he was too brilliant to ever be discovered.

He's clueless. His hubris is his own downfall.

"You see, you thought you were smarter than everyone. After all, you'd gotten away with countless murders. You didn't stop after Evans went to jail for the murders you'd committed. After that, you killed another girl, almost as though you were taunting the sheriff, using your same MO. But then you borrowed from other serial killers across the country after that, stealing their style and linking those kills to their names. Anyone who had a similar victimology to yours. You still wanted to punish Jasmine Evans even after all this time."

I turn the page again, flipping through the countless credit card hits that put Jake in this town for two solid weeks, right about the time the first phone call was made to Olivia from this very house.

"But you never realized your son was smarter than you," I say, taunting the man who grows more furious by the moment. "You never realized he crafted an even more elaborate, masterful plan than yours had ever been."

He still hasn't figured out the best part yet.

"Olivia was a microbiologist for a prestigious lab last year when your son gave her a call. It was right about the time he spent two solid weeks in your home, probably finding every bit of proof he needed to solidify his resolve. I'm sure he called Lana—she hates being called Victoria these days."

His eyes shift as he starts trying to assemble the pieces I'm laying down.

"You suspected Victoria had survived, didn't you? You even hinted as much to us. But you didn't know for certain. Even before Jake found out the truth, he never trusted you with that secret. His loyalty was to her and her alone," I go on, watching the utter fury continue to build.

Paint It All Red

"You assumed Olivia was a sweet girl who loved you for trying to 'save' Robert Evans. After all, you defended him. Very poorly, I might add. A man as smart as you should have worked a little harder to get his best friend out of the murders he didn't commit. But you weren't really his friend, were you? I'm sure Jake learned the same thing when he watched that trial footage all over again with a clear head and from a distance."

I flip the page once more.

"But why would Olivia quit her coveted place at the lab—something she'd worked so damn hard to achieve—to come play nursemaid to you when you got a strange sickness? Weekly deposits started going into her account from your son when she came to help you. Weekly deposits also came from you. Why get paid twice?"

I smirk as I lean forward, watching the realization spread over his paling face.

"Microbiology… It's a fascinating field. You learn all about parasites. The right person could use that knowledge to slowly kill a man. To strip away all his power over a year. To make him gradually sicker in a way the doctors—who aren't specialists in that field—could never understand. Especially if someone used an exotic parasite or something. I'm not saying that's what she did, but she's brilliant enough to have figured out a way to kill you slowly without anyone detecting the cause, all while taking care of you when the doctors gave up and just handed you half the drug store."

I gesture to the tray of drugs near the wall. The number of bottles have multiplied since my last visit.

"But the endgame was coming, so Olivia bumped up her regimen, tipping you over the edge faster, reaping revenge for her sister and all those other women. And your son funded her. Lana conceded her own revenge for someone who needed it more. And here you are: impotent, weak, powerless, utterly helpless and literally pissing yourself."

The tears start gathering in his eyes; angry tears lined with pure, unadulterated hatred.

"She did her part, and left this note for me. Somehow she knew I was coming," I say, lifting the note, and I read it aloud. "It's too late for him. I drew out his agony as long as I could. But you can't save him now. Good luck finding me."

I lower the note and smirk at him.

"She thinks I want to save you and find her so I can lock her up. She doesn't understand why I'm really here."

I pull out my gun, cocking it as I stand and push the note back into my pocket.

"You should know, your son was twice the mastermind you ever were, because he didn't kill just to be powerful. He killed for revenge. And his own father helped aide in the murder of the boy he loved."

I point the gun at his groin, even though I almost grimace at what's to come. But Lana needs to know I'm not going away once I find her. One irredeemable act will mean I can never come back.

"As much as I want you to die slowly, I need to show my girl how serious I am about staying with her. Originally, I was content to watch you die slowly. But something changed today. Something I'm still too scared to fully embrace until I put my eyes on the physical promise of it. For the first time ever, I have hope."

I put the earplugs in, cracking my neck to the side as I finish. He makes a sound, his eyes widening as I put my finger on the trigger.

"Have fun in hell, Christopher."

With that, I fire the gun into his groin until it's empty. The monitors go crazy as he crashes, and his body starts to convulse as blood plumes form across the sheet and blankets.

They played the longest game of torture for the worst offender. As I said, I underestimated the true genius of dark minds.

As I put my gun away, I pull out the earplugs and pick up my phone. I have limited time before this body is discovered. Collins and my team will know it's me the second they find out who it is.

Paint It All Red

I labeled him the original killer.

He ends up shot in the groin over and over.

It's not rocket science to piece it together.

Dialing Hadley, I walk out of the house, leaving behind the last piece of the intricate puzzle.

"You ready?" she asks.

"I'll be there in fifteen. Did you find them?"

"Not yet. But I will."

Chapter 19

Wherever you go, go with all your heart.
—Confucius

Lana

Three months ago, I thought I was going to die.

But once again, I was saved by a brother, though not the same one.

Jake walked in, firing rapidly, and threw in a smoke bomb. I wish I'd thought of a smoke bomb. I was too busy thinking I was invincible.

I'd thought I saw Marcus, but it wasn't him. It was the other brother. The one who had stood by me through hell and high water, and dragged me out of the pit one last time, saving me just barely in time.

And we made it out before the fire caught up. Before the building exploded. Before anyone ever knew he'd saved me.

He'd already paid off a hospital staff who closed off a wing like I was royalty, and they patched me up enough to travel by sea—on the yacht Jake also bought, since flight plans had to be changed to avoid anyone noticing my condition.

From time to time, I check in on Logan—or try to. He's been on leave, but Jake won't hack the FBI data base to find out more than that.

We know we have to let Logan and Hadley go. It's what's safest for them.

Paint It All Red

We can't condemn corruption then drag more souls into our own damnation without facing our own hypocrisy.

I pick up Jake's underwear and groan as I toss them into the laundry basket he can never seem to find. I still have a small limp, but I'm getting stronger with each passing day.

My hand has healed up much quicker than my leg, but the doctor swears I'll make a full recovery with just a scar as a reminder. At least I won't mind my new scars. They tell a better story of survival than the others.

We're both a little lost right now, trying to find a new purpose to channel all our energy into. Jake has gotten good at fishing—weirdly enough. We've both gotten really good at being drunk half the day.

The pain in my leg is barely even there anymore. I'll be glad when it's gone completely.

My wax apple is proudly stationed next to a portrait of the ashy remnants of Delaney Grove, and I smirk at all the nails sticking out of it. The last one was added over a month ago. There's only one more nail to go before the apple art is complete.

Something falls, and I whirl around, a knife in my hand, just in time to see a black blur of fur as it dives behind my couch. I see the coaster that has been knocked off the table, and I curse Bennett.

"Bennett," I hiss at the fur ball.

A small meow follows the scolding as Bennett pokes his head out from behind the couch and peers at me with innocent eyes. Damn cat.

I fill up his food bowl, and he slides across the slick, tile floor when he tries to tackle it. Then I kick on some sandals and head out for my daily walk, making my leg stronger and stronger.

At least I'm good at rehabilitation.

Per the usual, I plug in my earbuds and start playing my music, while also internet searching for any news from the states that might pertain to the FBI finally fessing up to the truth.

I know it's doubtful, despite the mounds of evidence, but I keep hoping they'll eventually exonerate my father's memory.

Delaney Grove has started rebuilding, according to one article. The people are trying to piece their town together, and the dorky but sweet deputy has been named the new county sheriff. It might have helped that we spared his life, along with two others who weren't involved.

The rest of the world may forget us and the legacy we left behind, but Delaney Grove will forever be changed. No one there will forget.

And maybe Jake and I took a long trip back to the states just to kill Jason for the purpose of letting Logan know I was alive.

Jake had to help me subdue him, considering I'm still not as fast, given the leg injury.

But I don't know if Logan ever figured it out. It took them longer to recover the body than I expected. Sheesh. That house must have the lowest interest in the market.

However, it was discovered over two weeks ago, and nothing suspicious has happened. Jake is too busy fishing and still too mad at me to hack anything for me, so I'm stuck with the regular articles everyone sees.

Most of the buzz is still going, and weird conspiracy theories have formed, overshadowing the actual conspiracy theory.

But one article has me almost tripping over myself when I'm right in front of my house. My eyes read over it quickly, trying to understand the words.

The same day Jason's body was discovered, another man died, though his body was just recovered yesterday afternoon.

It's the man's name that has my skin prickling.

Christopher Denver.

Olivia hasn't called to tell us anything. At least Jake hasn't mentioned it. Then again, he's still pissed at me for almost dying, so prying information about following events has been difficult, since that's part of my punishment.

I turn and look at the beach where Jake is lying down, a pole between his legs as he sleeps and fishes at the same time. I trudge through the sand, wincing when I try to run. Then I kick the jerk.

A loud *oomph* leaves his lips as I kneel beside him.

"What the hell?" he snaps, rubbing his side as he glares at me.

"When did Olivia call? And don't tell me she hasn't."

He looks genuinely confused.

"I haven't felt it safe enough to contact her with a new number yet, considering there was some federal activity on her name. I set her phone up for alerts to notify her if anyone got wind of her trail, and had her a new identity ready and waiting. If she has to leave, she'll go to the safe house, and I'll get an alert when she does."

He holds up his phone and I sink to the sand a little more as I hand him my phone to read.

He skims the article at first, then bolts upright to a seated position.

"Olivia wouldn't have shot him," he says, shaking his head. "She was content with drawing it out as long as possible once his organs started failing."

"Apparently something happened. I never pictured her as a crotch shooter, but that's where he bled out from."

"Maybe she spent too much time with you," he quips, still reading it.

I remember the day Jake figured it out. I'd already been suspicious, but couldn't bring myself to fully believe it. Not until Jake walked in and we both confirmed the worst case scenario together.

He had all the copies of his father's DVDs in his hands, and tears were in his eyes. We watched the trial again together, saw the occasional slip up when Christopher would smirk as my father sobbed.

It became overtly obvious during one home video when his father couldn't look away from my mother at a birthday party. And his jaw was grinding when my father came up and kissed her, causing her to giggle in his arms.

It was the most painful realization.

My father's best friend.

My best friend's father.

The same man who had sat at our table for holidays when we were growing up, was the same man who'd sentenced my father to the worst death imaginable.

That's when we called Olivia.

Jake didn't even hesitate. He hated him already, but he said his father was dead to him after that.

He started the regimen Olivia concocted—a new synthetic parasite she'd been working on in her lab—and so it began. The first thing to leave him was his sex drive. Not even a little blue pill could fix that.

The second thing to go was his energy.

From there, things just slowly, agonizingly, started getting worse and worse. She assured us the pain would grow to be unbearable, and she was all too happy to make it happen.

Jake helped her get the synthetic parasite off the lab property and even hacked the files that held the information about it. She also took a few extras for later on—the endgame.

My part was miniscule. All I had to do was be the lookout during the planning of this.

This wasn't just my revenge. It was theirs more so than mine.

Christopher Denver wronged my father in more ways than I can even fathom, even played his best friend and lawyer, but at the end of the day, Jake was his own son. He was wronged the most.

Paint It All Red

Because of his father, Jake lost the love of his life back then.

Because of his father, Olivia's sister was raped and murdered.

My misery was placed on the backburner. I had enough people to kill.

"This is crazy. Olivia should be on the run if they suspect her," Jake says thoughtfully, drawing me out of my own reverie.

"It says they have a male suspect they're looking into," I say, confused. "They don't suspect her."

"Can you find more on it?" he asks as I try scaling down.

"No. It's just a small article that barely even cares to mention this at all. I'll see what I can find, but I know someone far better at all this computer stuff than me."

I shove at his chest, and he grunts while rubbing the spot like I hurt him as he winks at me.

"Not right now. I was in the middle of dreaming up a good threesome. I'd like to return to that dream."

I narrow my eyes at him, and he groans while lying back down.

"I'll look into it later, Lana. I genuinely don't give a shit who killed him. I'm just glad the fucker is finally dead."

He covers his face, his breathing already steadying as he starts drifting back off to sleep. Rolling my eyes, I push back up to my feet and walk back to the house.

For once, Bennett doesn't attack my feet the second I walk in, and I kick off my shoes while looking around and making kissing noises. "Bennett! Come on, Kitty. I need to give you a bath."

He doesn't come, and I frown. Usually he's all over us after we've been gone for a minute.

Deciding to chase him down later, I go to the fridge and grab a bottle of water, but my hand hovers over a bottle as I stare and tilt my head.

It's a habit to count things and take in my surroundings, always aware of any change. And I'm positive there were three beers beside my water this morning. Now there's only one beer.

Slowly, I grab my water as a chill slides down my spine. It's possible Jake has already started drinking, but doubtful, considering there were no beer cans near him.

It feels like someone else is here, but I don't make it obvious by looking around. The living room is just beyond me, and I grab a knife and an apple, acting as though I'm about to peel it.

Abandoning the water bottle, I stab a new nail into my wax apple to represent the man I wanted dead the second most, but I pause, noticing it's been turned. I look at this apple every single day. I know it's not facing the right angle.

I move through the house, seeing nothing obviously out of place, but there is more sand in the dining room than normal. Bennett should be all over my feet right now, but he's not.

Slowly, I start peeling the apple as I move into the living room, and the chill in my spine has it stiffening. There's no doubt that I feel eyes on me right now.

"If you've hurt my cat, you have no idea what that will cost you."

I spin around, the knife in hand as I drop the apple, but my entire body turns to stone when I see someone smirking at me from the corner.

Logan pushes off from the wall, and I'm tempted to pinch myself just to be sure I'm not hallucinating or dreaming.

"Your cat's name is Bennett?" he asks, his lips twitching as the knife tumbles from my hand. "I'm not sure how I feel about that," he goes on, stalking closer.

My bad leg tries to give out, and I stumble, but Logan's arms are immediately around me, his scent engulfing me as those hands grip my waist.

I tilt my head back as unshed tears start clouding my eyes, and he stares expectantly.

Paint It All Red

"You're here," I rasp, which is a ridiculous thing to say after three months.

"You let me think you were dead," he says, his voice strained.

"I didn't want to risk contacting you and getting you in trouble," I quickly explain. "They were monitoring your calls because you were stirring up trouble even on leave and—"

He puts a finger over my mouth, silencing my babble.

"They still don't know it was you. Did you kill Jason as a sign to me that you're still alive, or was he just unfinished business? The torture was mild in comparison to the others, almost as though you were in a hurry."

He pulls his finger down from my lips, dragging it, and I shudder against him while staring into those too-familiar blues.

"It was the safest way to tell you. I didn't think it'd take them so long to find him. And I couldn't do it sooner because I couldn't even walk without crutches until—"

He silences me when his lips come down on mine, and I melt against him, reveling in the feel of his kiss. Tears spring from my eyes as I kiss him harder, clinging to him like I can't let go.

I'm breathless and dizzy when he finally breaks the kiss, but I manage to blink the tears away and speak.

"How'd you find me?"

"You said if you could be anywhere, you'd be in Greece with me. I hoped that meant you came to wait," he says softly, thumbing my chin.

"But your job—"

"I left it," he says, studying my eyes.

"And your life—"

"Is wherever you are. Guess you shouldn't have been so perfect if you didn't want me to love you this much."

I blow out a frustrated breath over that word. Perfect. He knows the truth is so far from that now.

"I didn't want you to sacrifice everything for—"

He kisses me again, most likely to shut me up, but I don't care. Any reason for his lips to be on mine is a perfect reason.

Finally, he breaks the kiss.

"I signed up to ensure justice," he says, brushing his lips over mine. "I didn't sign up to play politics. I'd rather be in Greece with you than sitting in someone's pocket back home. And before you get the clever idea to leave me behind because you think you're ruining anything for me, you should know I can't ever go back."

My brow furrows. "Why?"

"Because I made sure there was no way to leave you with any doubt."

My eyes search his, and it finally dawns on me. "It was you who shot Christopher," I whisper in shock.

"That was my message to you," he goes on. "Didn't realize it'd take them so long to find the body."

I shiver in his arms, realizing how fucked up this token of love would be to the rest of the world. But to me, roses and poems can't compare.

"So you're here to stay?" I ask, still reeling.

"You can't ever leave me again. I'm assuming there aren't any other secrets?"

"No other debts to collect," I assure him.

He stares at my lips like they're fascinating, still cupping my chin as he starts backing me toward my room. I guess he's been getting familiar with the home.

"Where's my cat?" I ask, which sounds stupid.

"I was surprised you had a pet," he says, amused as he dodges my question.

"Did he run out?"

Paint It All Red

"No," he says, smiling broader. "He's probably purring away with—"

"Oh, good. You're here." Hadley's voice has me snapping my head around as she walks out of my room, holding a purring Bennett in her arms. "Your cat has bald spots that are confusing me."

"What are you doing here?" I ask, shocked.

She shrugs, inspecting Bennett's ugly coat that is gradually getting better.

"Where else would I be? Now about your cat... What's wrong with him?"

"He was a stray and had something stuck in his fur. Jake shaved off the glue-like stuff about two weeks ago when we found him."

She rolls her eyes. "Speaking of Jake, where is he?"

"He's the bum with his arm over his face who is sleeping on the beach."

Hadley grins at us and puts Bennett down as she skips toward the door. I hope Jake is prepared to be surprised. I also hope she wasn't just a fling to him, since she's sort of in Greece right now.

"Back to where we were," Logan says, turning my face back to meet his. "I had Hadley do a search of a list of surnames. I knew you wouldn't change your first name. Lana Vorhees was pretty obvious, considering I watched *Friday the Thirteenth* all the time when I was a kid."

I smile like an idiot for no reason at all.

"Me too."

He brushes his lips over mine again, still backing us toward my room.

"Then it was even more obvious when I saw Jake Vlad listed under this address as well. Not sure that Vlad is the best name for him."

"He used to dress up as Vlad the Impaler every Halloween when we were kids," I explain, still smiling.

We're so morbid.

"I picked a little less obvious name," he says with a shrug.

"Oh?"

"White," he says, shrugging while smirking.

"As in Carrie White?"

He nods slowly, still backing me toward the room until my legs finally hit the bed. In one motion, he bends and tosses me to the bed, and I squeal like a little girl.

He comes down on top of me, and I giggle like an idiot, smiling up at him as he kisses the tip of my nose.

"So this is real. You and me. We're actually going to get to be together?"

"Not possible for you to get rid of me," he says, kissing my lips.

"I can't believe you're actually here," I moan as his lips start trailing down my neck.

He leans up on his elbows as I start stripping. He watches me, but finally he decides to shed his clothes too. As soon as we're both bare, he settles between my legs, but he stares into my eyes while pushing a piece of hair away from my face.

"I decided if I could choose anywhere in the world to be, it'd be wherever you were," he says before he kisses me, silencing whatever girly, swoony thing that would have come out of my mouth.

And I kiss him back with everything in me as he thrusts inside me, filling me so completely that every nerve in my body feels electrified.

"I love you," I whisper across his lips.

"I love you, Lana Vorhees," he says, grinning.

It's our own twisted version of perfection.

Paint It All Red

EPILOGUE

Three years later...

Logan

Lana is laughing with Hadley as they read Laurel's latest letter. Lindy May sends all of Laurel's letters to Olivia. And Olivia sends them to a home in Greece that Lana owns, but we don't ever stay there.

Laurel has turned into a fun, witty girl who has managed to put her past behind her and move forward. Lindy has given her all the tools to do that, and she's finally moved on herself in her quest to save Laurel.

Her ex-husband killed himself a little over two years ago. Lana and Jake broke out the champagne to celebrate, since they'd apparently driven him to that.

Olivia also writes, telling them about Cheyenne and Alyssa, who both still live with her. No one ever suspected Olivia after I put a round of bullets in Christopher Denver.

Diana Barnes went to live closer to her son. He bought her a home, and she's finally able to enjoy her life without the past hanging over her like a daunting shadow. She thinks Lana died in that explosion, and Lana says it's best if she believes that.

I check in on my team from time to time, using a burner phone to contact Leonard. He assures me that no one on our team is looking for me. Most everyone thinks I snapped. He's the only one still there who knows the truth.

He said Craig is just happy that he's officially the prettiest face

Paint It All Red

in the unit.

But I know what I did still weighs heavily on all of them, because they're worried it could be them one day. They just don't understand how unlikely that is. And it's not like I can tell them.

Jake walks down the stairs in just a towel. It'd be nice to *not* share a house with him and Hadley, but this home is massive, and I'd never tear Lana away from her best friend after all they've been through.

Besides, I sleep peacefully at night, more so than ever. Our house is the most dangerous place in the world to try and break into because of the four of us.

A guy walks down the stairs, also wearing a towel, and Hadley whistles at him as she stands and struts from the dining room, her hair mussed and her clothes disheveled.

"Glad you two finally finished up. I couldn't go another round," she tells Jake as he tugs her to him, nipping her lips with his teeth as he grins.

"You still have to go another round with just me tonight," he says. "And next week, you get to pick who joins us."

She beams like he just offered her Christmas. Personally, I don't get it. I'd fucking kill someone if they touched Lana, and there's no doubt she'd cut someone to pieces if they touched me.

Literally.

But Jake and Hadley are both bisexual, and though they'd never cheat on each other, they do include select individuals in their bedroom on occasion.

Twice a month to be more precise. Trust me, I know more about Hadley's sex life than I *ever* wanted to.

"I want a girl," she says as the guy they spent the night with goes to the fridge, making himself at home.

"Deal," Jake tells her, and she grins again while I carefully maneuver my way out of the threesome afterglow.

Lana is holding back a laugh when I near her, because she knows I hate hearing all the gritty details Jake and Hadley love to share.

She takes my hand, and I pull her up, my thumb brushing the red ruby on her ring finger.

"You ready, Mrs. White?" I ask her, waggling my eyebrows.

"I've just been waiting on you."

"As of now, I can't wait to get out of this house and out on the boat."

She laughs again as I practically drag her away from the house. Her leg is completely healed now. She walks with no limp, and she's back to taking classes—kickboxing classes to be exact. Though I think it'd be smarter for her to actually teach the classes, since she's a little too good to still be a student.

Her fingers thread with mine, and I drink my beer as we walk down the beach, heading to where the boat awaits us.

This has been our life for the last three years. I had no idea how much I was missing out on. Life is pretty damn good when you take the time to live it.

Most importantly, we dance every night.

Hadley and I took over the online site for Lana and Jake, since they started another internet business that needed their attention. Lana outsourced the appraisal jobs to some trusted people who needed the extra income.

Five years ago, I never pictured myself leaving the Bureau and spending my days with a semi-retired serial killer, while walking the beaches of Greece. I never pictured me sharing a house with another couple. I never pictured anything at all about my life as it is today.

Which is why I love Lana so much. She still continues to surprise me, and I'm fairly positive I'd be the one burning the world down if anyone ever tried to take her from me.

Paint It All Red

She calls me a romantic for that.

It's a life I love.

"What are you thinking about?" Lana asks on a sigh as she leans her head against my arm.

Two months after I showed up in Greece, Lana and I got married. It was just the four of us with one officiate, but it was perfect. Hadley and Jake took two years to follow our lead.

"How crazy life can be, and how good it can turn out," I tell her, lifting her hand so I can kiss her fingers.

She grins as she snuggles in closer to my side, her white dress blowing in the wind.

Today's our anniversary, and we're taking the boat out for a long weekend away from the house.

"Our story is definitely unique," she says, sliding her arms around my one and hugging it.

"I have no idea what you're talking about," I say, balking mockingly.

She laughs while rolling her eyes.

"Yeah. We're just a typical romance," she deadpans, but her lips lift in a small smile.

"Horror romance. That's a genre, right?" I ask, smiling when she laughs.

She spins, turning to walk backwards as she faces me.

"You want me to be honest?" she asks, biting her lip.

I grab her waist, loving the way she laughs when I lift her.

"Yes," I say, nipping her chin before kissing it.

Her legs slide around my waist as she tightens her hold on me, and I continue to carry us in the direction of the boat.

She grins as she says, "It's my favorite horror story of all time."

I grin against her lips as we reach the pier, and she slides down to walk beside me, locking our fingers together. She's getting giddy. I can feel it.

There's something you need to learn about loving a girl like Lana. She had to open something up inside herself to do what it took to end Delaney Grove's reign of terror.

And that something can't just be locked away.

She has special needs. Needs that I tend to once a year, because I love keeping her sane. And she can't live in denial of who she is.

We load up on the yacht, and she takes care of pouring the champagne, while I get us away from the pier and start driving us out into the ocean. We toast the champagne, and I brush my lips over hers as she stays close.

We're floating with no land in sight before I anchor us down and check the monitors to make sure we're completely alone and no one can bother us.

She flashes me a smile, anticipation sparking in her eyes.

"You ready for your present?" I ask her.

She grins.

"Yes."

I tug her hand in mine and guide her to the lower deck. She follows, practically walking on my heels in her excitement. As soon as we reach the downstairs and her eyes fall on her present, she stops walking, her smile growing bigger.

"Where'd you get this?" she asks.

"It was actually a favor called in from a friend. Apparently, this one has raped numerous girls up and down the coast, but his father's diplomatic immunity status has prohibited anyone from being able to touch him. They were in the process of getting that status revoked when his father sent him back to Columbia."

Her eyes flash with excitement, as Juan Alvarez's eyes widen, and he struggles, cursing us through his gag. Lana tilts her head, watching him as he jerks against the chains.

Paint It All Red

"And you trust the source?" she asks, looking Juan over, her fingers itching to take action.

"Leonard's the one who called. The last girl was just fifteen, and he slit her throat. I trust Leonard, and I reviewed the file myself. They have enough physical evidence to prove it, and he hasn't bothered denying it. They just can't touch him."

She gets up on her toes, smiling as she kisses me. Juan continues to struggle in vain.

"Thank you," she murmurs as I hand her the knife.

She clutches it as her body shudders with the impending high. Too much steals her soul. Too little could cause her to lash out from denying what she had to become.

But once a year? That's just right. And Leonard uses that to his advantage, because not all monsters can go to prison.

Lana's unique, and I wouldn't change anything about her. Because now I see the world the way it really is, and I know my only place is right by her side.

I move in behind her as she cuts on the music, and my arms go around her waist as we sway to the rhythm. She's eager to get to work, but savoring the moment, taunting him with the hope he hasn't released just yet.

Her head falls back against my chest as she revels in the moment, drawing it out.

I put my lips against her ear and whisper, "Happy anniversary, baby."

THE END

This is for the ones who lost their voice. This is for the ones who wish they could be Lana Myers. This is for the ones people still whisper about.

This is for the ones who fight every single day to forget.

You're not alone.

Thank you for reading the Mindfuck Series! Hope you take the time to review, as that really helps spread the word about books.
<3

Check out my website for a list of all my books.

www.cmowensbooks.com